VOICES OF THE SOUTH

The Web and the Rock

ALSO BY THOMAS WOLFE

NOVELS
Look Homeward, Angel
Of Time and the River
You Can't Go Home Again

STORY COLLECTIONS
From Death to Morning
The Hills Beyond

NONFICTION
The Story of a Novel

PLAYS
Mannerhouse
Web of Earth (monologue)

Thomas Wolfe

THE WEB

AND

THE ROCK

Louisiana State University Press

Baton Rouge

Copyright © 1937, 1938, 1939 by Maxwell Perkins as Executor
Copyright © renewed 1967 by Paul Gitlin, Administrator, C.T.A. of the Estate of
    Thomas Wolfe
Originally published by Harper & Brothers
LSU Press edition published 1999 by arrangement with the Estate of Thomas Wolfe
All rights reserved
Manufactured in the United States of America

08 07 06 05 04 03 02
5 4 3 2

Library of Congress Cataloging-in-Publication Data

Wolfe, Thomas, 1900–1938.
    The web and the rock / Thomas Wolfe.
        p. cm. — (Voices of the South)
    ISBN 0-8071-2389-7 (pbk. : alk. paper)
        I. Title. II. Series.
    PS3545.O337W4   1999
    813'.52—dc21   98-54651
                                            CIP

The paper in this book meets the guidelines for permanence and durability of the
Committee on Production Guidelines for Book Longevity of the Council on Library
Resources. ∞

AUTHOR'S NOTE

This novel is about one man's discovery of life and of the world—discovery not in a sudden and explosive sense as when "a new planet swims into his ken," but discovery through a process of finding out, and finding out as a man has to find out, through error and through trial, through fantasy and illusion, through falsehood and his own foolishness, through being mistaken and wrong and an idiot and egotistical and aspiring and hopeful and believing and confused, and pretty much what every one of us is, and goes through, and finds out about, and becomes.

I hope that the protagonist will illustrate in his own experience every one of us—not merely the sensitive young fellow in conflict with his town, his family, the little world around him; not merely the sensitive young fellow in love, and so concerned with his little universe of love that he thinks it is the whole universe—but all of these things and much more. These things, while important, are subordinate to the plan of the book; being young and in love and in the city are only a part of the whole adventure of apprenticeship and discovery.

This novel, then, marks not only a turning away from the books I have written in the past, but a genuine spiritual and artistic change. It is the most objective novel that I have written. I have invented characters who are compacted from the whole amalgam and consonance of seeing, feeling, thinking, living, and knowing many people. I have sought, through free creation, a release of my inventive power.

Finally, the novel has in it, from first to last, a strong element of satiric exaggeration: not only because it belongs to the nature of the story—"the innocent man" discovering life—but because satiric exaggeration also belongs to the nature of life, and particularly American life.

THOMAS WOLFE

New York, May 1938

Could I make tongue say more than tongue could utter! Could I make brain grasp more than brain could think! Could I weave into immortal denseness some small brede of words, pluck out of sunken depths the roots of living, some hundred thousand magic words that were as great as all my hunger, and hurl the sum of all my living out upon three hundred pages—then death could take my life, for I had lived it ere he took it: I had slain hunger, beaten death!

Contents

Book I

THE WEB AND THE ROOT

I

The Child Caliban

UP TO THE TIME GEORGE WEBBER'S FATHER DIED, THERE WERE SOME UN-forgiving souls in the town of Libya Hill who spoke of him as a man who not only had deserted his wife and child, but had consummated his iniquity by going off to live with another woman. In the main, those facts are correct. As to the construction that may be placed upon them, I can only say that I should prefer to leave the final judgment to God Almighty, or to those numerous deputies of His whom He has apparently appointed as His spokesmen on this earth. In Libya Hill there are quite a number of them, and I am willing to let them do the talking. For my own part, I can only say that the naked facts of John Webber's desertion are true enough, and that none of his friends ever attempted to deny them. Aside from that, it is worth noting that Mr. Webber had his friends.

John Webber was "a Northern man," of Pennsylvania Dutch extraction, who had come into Old Catawba back in 1881. He was a brick mason and general builder, and he had been brought to Libya Hill to take charge of the work on the new hotel which the Corcorans were putting up on Belmont Hill, in the center of the town. The Corcorans were rich people who had come into that section and bought up tracts of property and laid out plans for large enterprises, of which the hotel was the central one. The railroad was then being built and would soon be finished. And only a year or two before, George Willetts, the great Northern millionaire, had purchased thousands of acres of the mountain wilderness and had come down with his architects to project the creation of a great country estate that would have no equal in America. New people were coming to town all the time, new faces were being seen upon the streets. There was quite a general feeling in the air that great events were just around the corner. and that a bright destiny was in store for Libya Hill.

3

It was the time when they were just hatching from the shell, when the place was changing from a little isolated mountain village, lost to the world, with its few thousand native population, to a briskly-moving modern town, with railway connections to all parts, and with a growing population of wealthy people who had heard about the beauties of the setting and were coming there to live.

That was the time John Webber came to Libya Hill, and he stayed, and in a modest way he prospered. And he left his mark upon it. It was said of him that he found the place a little country village of clapboard houses and left it a thriving town of brick. That was the kind of man he was. He liked what was solid and enduring. When he was consulted for his opinion about some new building that was contemplated and was asked what material would be best to use, he would invariably answer, "Brick."

At first, the idea of using brick was a novel one in Libya Hill, and for a moment, while Mr. Webber waited stolidly, his questioner would be silent; then, rather doubtfully, as if he was not sure he had heard aright, he would say, "Brick?"

"Yes, sir," Mr. Webber would answer inflexibly, "Brick. It's not going to cost you so much more than lumber by the time you're done, and," he would say quietly, but with conviction, "it's the only way to build. You can't rot it out, you can't rattle it or shake it, you can't kick holes in it, it will keep you warm in Winter and cool in Summer, and fifty years from now, or a hundred for that matter, it will still be here. I don't like lumber," Mr. Webber would go on doggedly. "I don't like wooden houses. I come from Pennsylvania where they know how to build. Why," he would say, with one of his rare displays of boastfulness, "we've got stone barns up there that are built better and have lasted longer than any house you've got in this whole section of the country. In my opinion there are only two materials for a house—stone or brick. And if I had my way," he would add a trifle grimly, "that's how I'd build all of them."

But he did not always have his way. As time went on, the necessities of competition forced him to add a lumber yard to his brick yard, but that was only a grudging concession to the time and place. His real, his first, his deep, abiding love was brick.

And indeed, the very appearance of John Webber, in spite of physical peculiarities which struck one at first sight as strange, even a little startling, suggested qualities in him as solid and substantial as the houses that he built. Although he was slightly above the average height, he gave the curious impression of being shorter than he was. This came from a variety of causes, chief of which was a somewhat "bowed" formation of his body. There was something almost simian in his short legs, bowed slightly outward, his large, flat-looking feet, the powerful, barrel-like torso, and the tremendous gorillalike length of his arms, whose huge paws dangled almost even with his knees. He had a thick, short neck that seemed to sink right down into the burly shoulders, and close sandy-reddish hair that grew down almost to the edges of the cheek bones and to just an inch or so above the eyes. He was getting bald even then, and there was a wide and hairless swathe right down the center of his skull. He had extremely thick and bushy eyebrows, and the trick of peering out from under them with the head out-thrust in an attitude of intensely still attentiveness. But one's first impression of a slightly simian likeness in the man was quickly forgotten as one came to know him. For when John Webber walked along the street in his suit of good black broadcloth, heavy and well-cut, the coat half cutaway, a stiff white shirt with starched cuffs, a wing collar with a cravat of black silk tied in a thick knot, and a remarkable-looking derby hat, pearl-grey in color and of a squarish cut, he looked the very symbol of solid, middle-class respectability.

And yet, to the surprised incredulity of the whole town, this man deserted his wife. As for the child, another construction can be put on that. The bare anatomy of the story runs as follows:

About 1885, John Webber met a young woman of Libya Hill named Amelia Joyner. She was the daughter of one Lafayette, or "Fate" Joyner, as he was called, who had come out of the hills of Zebulon County a year or two after the Civil War, bringing his family with him. John Webber married Amelia Joyner in 1885 or 1886. In the next fifteen years they had no children, until, in 1900, their son George was born. And about 1908, after their marriage had lasted more than twenty years, Webber left his wife. He had met, a year or two before, a young woman married to a man named Bartlett: the fact of their relationship had reached the proportions of an open scandal by 1908, when he left his wife, and after that he did not pretend to maintain any secrecy about the affair whatever. He was then a man in his sixties; she was more than twenty years younger, and a woman of great beauty. The two of them lived together until his death in 1916.

It cannot be denied that Webber's marriage was a bad one. It is certainly not my purpose to utter a word of criticism of the woman he married, for, whatever her faults were, they were faults she couldn't help. And her greatest fault, perhaps, was that she was a member of a family that was extremely clannish, provincial, and opinionated—in the most narrow and dogged sense of the word, puritanical—and she not only inherited all these traits and convictions of her early training, they were so rooted into her very life and being that no experience, no process of living and enlargement, could ever temper them.

Her father was a man who could announce solemnly and implacably that he "would rather see a daughter of mine dead and lying in her coffin than married to a man who drank." And John Webber was a man who drank. Moreover, Amelia's father, if anyone had ever dared to put the monstrous suggestion to him, would have been perfectly capable of amplifying the Christian sentiments which have just been quoted by announcing that he would rather see a daughter of his dead and in her grave than married to a man who had been divorced. And John Webber was a man who had been divorced.

That, truly, was calamitous, the cause of untold anguish later—perhaps the chief stumbling block in their whole life together. It also seems to have been the one occasion when he did not deal with her truthfully and honestly in reference to his past life before he came to Libya Hill. He had married a girl in Baltimore in the early Seventies, when he himself had been scarcely more than a stripling old enough to vote. He mentioned it just once to one of his cronies: he said that she was only twenty, "as pretty as a picture," and an incorrigible flirt. The marriage had ended almost as suddenly as it had begun—they lived together less than a year. By that time it was apparent to them both that they had made a ruinous mistake. She went home to her people, and in the course of time divorced him.

In the Eighties, and, for that matter, much later than that, in a community such as Libya Hill, divorce was a disgraceful thing. George Webber later said that, even in his own childhood, this feeling was still so strong that a divorced person was spoken about in lowered voices, and that when one whispered furtively behind his hand that someone was "a grass widow," there was a general feeling that she was not only not all she should be, but that she was perhaps just a cut or two above a common prostitute.

In the Eighties, this feeling was so strong that a divorced person was branded with a social stigma as great as that of one who had been convicted of crime and had served a penal sentence. Murder could have been—and was—far more easily forgiven than divorce. Crimes of violence, in fact, were frequent, and many a man had killed his man and had either escaped scot-free, or, having paid whatever penalty was imposed, had returned to take up a position of respected citizenship in the community.

Such, then, were the family and environment of the woman John Webber married. And after he left her to live with Mrs. Bartlett, he became estranged from all the hard-bitten and puritanical members of the Joyner clan. Not long thereafter, Amelia died. After his wife's death, Webber's liaison with Mrs. Bartlett continued, to the scandal of the public and the thin-lipped outrage of his wife's people.

Mark Joyner, Amelia's older brother, was a man who, after a childhood and youth of bitter poverty, was in the way of accumulating a modest competence in the hardware business. With Mag, his wife, he lived in a bright red brick house with hard, new, cement columns before it—everything about it as hard, new, ugly, bold, and raw as new-got wealth. Mag was a pious Baptist, and her sense of outraged righteousness at the open scandal of John Webber's life went beyond the limits of embittered speech. She worked on Mark, talking to him day and night about his duty to his sister's child, until at last, with a full consciousness of the approval of all good people, they took the boy, George, from his father.

The boy had been devoted to his father, but now the Joyners made him one of them. From this time forth, with the sanction of the courts, they kept him.

George Webber's childhood with his mountain kinsmen was, in spite of his sunny disposition, a dark and melancholy one. His status was really that of a charity boy, the poor relation of the clan. He did not live in the fine new house with his Uncle Mark. Instead, he lived in the little one-story frame house which his grandfather, Lafayette Joyner, had built with his own hands forty years before when he came to town.

This little house was on the same plot of ground as Mark Joyner's new brick house, a little to the right and to the rear, obscured and dwarfed by its more splendid neighbor.

Here John Webber's little boy was growing up, under the guardianship of a rusty crone of fate, Aunt Maw, a spinstress, his mother's oldest sister, old Lafayette's first child. Born thirty years before Amelia, Aunt Maw was in her seventies, but like some weird sister who preaches doom forever but who never dies, it seemed that she was ageless and eternal. From this dark old aunt of doom, and from the drawling voices of his Joyner kin, a dark picture of his mother's world, his mother's time, all the universe of the Joyner lives and blood, was built up darkly, was wrought out slowly, darkly, with an undefined but overwhelming horror, in the memory, mind, and spirit of the boy. On Winter evenings, as Aunt Maw talked in her croaking monotone by the light of a greasy little lamp—they never had electric lights in his grandfather's cottage—George heard lost voices in the mountains long ago, the wind-torn rawness, the desolate bleakness of lost days in March along clay-rutted roads in the bleak hills a hundred years ago:

Someone was dead in a hill cabin long ago. It was night. He heard the howling of the wind about the eaves of March. He was within the cabin. The rude, bare boards creaked to the tread of feet. There was no light except the flickering light of pine, the soft, swift flare of resinous wood, the crumbling ash. Against the wall, upon a bed, lay a sheeted figure of someone who had died. Around the flickering fire flame at the hearth, the drawling voices of the Joyners, one hundred years ago. The quiet, drawling voices of the Joyners who could never die and who attended the death of others like certain doom and prophecy. And in the room again there was a soft and sudden flare of pine flame flickering on the faces of the Joyners, a smell of camphor and of turpentine—a slow, dark horror in the blooded memory of the boy he could not utter.

In these and in a thousand other ways, from every intonation of Aunt Maw's life and memory, he heard lost voices in the hills long, long ago, saw cloud shadows passing in the wilderness, listened to the rude and wintry desolation of March winds that howl through the sere grasses of the mountain meadows in the month before the month when Spring is come. It came to him at night, in Winter from a room before a dying fire, in Summer from the porch of his grandfather's little house, where Aunt Maw sat with other rusty, aged crones of her own blood and kin, with their unceasing chronicle of death and doom and terror and lost people in the hills long, long ago. It came to him in all they said and did, in the whole dark image of the world they came from, and something lost and stricken in the hills long, long ago.

And they were always right, invincibly right, triumphant over death and all the miseries they had seen and known, lived and fed upon. And he was of their blood and bone, and desperately he felt somehow like life's criminal, some pariah, an outcast to their invincible rightness, their infallible goodness, their unsullied integrity. They filled him with a nameless horror of the lost and lonely world of the old-time, forgotten hills from which they came, with a loathing, with a speechless dread.

His father was a bad man. He knew it. He had heard the chronicle of his father's infamy recounted a thousand times. The story of his father's crimes, his father's sinfulness, his father's lecherous, godless, and immoral life was written on his heart. And yet the image of his father's world was pleasant and good, and full of secret warmth and joy to him. All of the parts of town, all of the places, lands, and things his father's life had touched seemed full of happiness and joy to him. He knew that it was wicked. He felt miserably that he was tainted with his father's blood. He sensed wretchedly and tragically that he was not worthy to be a death-triumphant, ever-perfect, doom-prophetic Joyner. They filled him with the utter loneliness of desolation. He knew he was not good enough for them, and he thought forever of his father's life, the sinful warmth and radiance of his father's world.

He would lie upon the grass before his uncle's fine new house in the green-gold somnolence of afternoon and think forever of his father, thinking: "Now he's here. At this time of the day he will be here." Again:

"He will be going now along the cool side of the street—uptown— before the cigar store. Now he's there—inside the cigar store. I can smell the good cigars. He leans upon the counter, looking out into the street and talking to Ed Battle, who runs the store. There is a wooden Indian by the door, and there are the people passing back and forth along the cool and narrow glade of afternoon. Here comes Mack Haggerty, my father's friend, into the cigar store. Here are the other men who smoke cigars and chew strong and fragrant plugs of apple tobacco. . . .

"Here is the barber shop next door, the snip of shears, the smell of tonics, of shoe polish and good leather, the incessant drawling voices of the barbers. Now he'll be going in to get shaved. I can hear the strong, clean scraping of the razor across the harsh stubble of his face. Now I hear people speaking to him. I hear the hearty voices of the men, all raised in greeting. They are all men who come out of my father's world—the sinful, radiant, and seductive world, the bad world that I think about so much. All the men who smoke cigars and chew tobacco and go to Forman's barber shop know my father. The good people like the Joyners go along the other side of the street—the shadeless side of afternoon, that has the bright and light. . . .

"Now he has finished at the barber's. Now he goes around the corner quickly to O'Connell's place. The wicker doors flap back together as he passes in. There is a moment's malty reek of beer, a smell of sawdust, lemon, rye, and Angostura bitters. There is the lazy flapping of a wooden fan, a moment's glimpse of the great, polished bar, huge mirrors, bottles, the shine of polished glasses, the brass foot-rail, dented with the heel-marks of a thousand feet, and Tim O'Connell, thick-jowled, aproned, leaning on the bar. . . .

"Now he is out again. See him go along the street. Now he is at the livery stable. I see the great, raw shape of rusty, corrugated tin, the wooden incline, pulped by many hoofs, as it goes down, the great hoofs clumping on the wooden floors, the hoofs kicked swiftly, casually, against the stalls, the wooden floors bestrewn with oaty droppings, the clean, dry whiskings of coarse tails across great polished rumps of glossy brown, the niggers talking gruffly to the horses in the stalls, the low, dark voices, gruff and tender, hoarse voices full of horseplay, the horse smell, and horse knowingness, men and horses both together, close: 'Get over dar! Whar you goin'!' The rubber tires of carriages and buggies, the smooth rumble of the rubber tires upon the battered wooden floors. . . . The little office to the left where my father likes to sit and talk with the livery-stable men, the battered little safe, the old roll-top desk, the creaking chairs, the little, blistered, cast-iron stove, the dirty windows, never washed, the smell of leather, old, worn ledgers, harness. . . ."

So did he think forever of his father's life, his father's places, movements, the whole enchanted picture of his father's world.

His was, in fact, a savagely divided childhood. Compelled to grow up in an environment and a household which he hated with every instinctive sense of loathing and repulsion of his being, he found himself longing constantly for another universe shaped in the colors of his own desire. And because he was told incessantly that the one he hated was good and admirable, and the one for which he secretly longed was evil and abominable, he came to have a feeling of personal guilt that was to torment him for many years. His sense of *place*, the feeling for specific locality that later became so strong in him, came, he thought, from all these associations of his youth—from his overwhelming conviction, or prejudice, that there were "good" places and "bad" ones. This feeling was developed so intensely in his childhood that there was hardly a street or a house, a hollow or a slope, a backyard or an alleyway in his own small world that did not bear the color of this prejudice. There were certain streets in town that he could scarcely endure to walk along, and there were certain houses that he could not pass without a feeling of bleak repulsion and dislike.

By the time he was twelve years old, he had constructed a kind of geography of his universe, composed of these powerful and instinctive affections and dislikes. The picture of the "good" side of the universe, the one the Joyners said was bad, was almost always one to which his father was in one way or another attached. It was a picture made up of such specific localities as his father's brick and lumber yard; Ed Battle's cigar and tobacco store—this was a place where he met and passed his father every Sunday morning on his way to Sunday School; John Forman's barber shop on the northwest corner of the Square, and the grizzled, inky heads, the well-known faces, of the negro barbers— John Forman was a negro, and George Webber's father went to his shop almost every day in the week; the corrugated tin front and the little dusty office of Miller and Cashman's livery stable, another rendezvous of his father's; the stalls and booths of the City Market, which was in a kind of great, sloping, concrete basement underneath the City Hall; the fire department, with its arched doors, the wooden stomping of great hoofs, and its circle of shirt-sleeved men—firemen, baseball players, and local idlers—sitting in split-bottom chairs of evenings; the look and feel of cellars everywhere—for this, curiously, was one of his strong obsessions—he always had a love of secret and enclosed places; the interiors of theatres, and the old Opera House on nights when a show was in town; McCormack's drug store, over at the southwest corner of the Square opposite his uncle's hardware store, with its onyx fountain, its slanting wooden fans, its cool and dark interior, and its clean and aromatic smells; Sawyer's grocery store, in one of the old brick buildings over on the north side of the Square, with its groaning plenty, its crowded shelves, its great pickle barrels, flour bins, coffee grinders, slabs of bacon, and its aproned clerks with straw cuffs on their sleeves; any kind of carnival or circus grounds; anything that had to do with railway stations, depots, trains, engines, freight cars, station yards. All of these things, and a thousand others, he had connected in a curious but powerful identity with the figure of his father; and because his buried affections and desires drew him so strongly to these things, he felt somehow that they must be bad because he thought them "good," and that he liked them because he was wicked, and his father's son.

His whole picture of his father's world—the world in which his father moved—as he built it in his brain with all the naïve but passionate intensity of childhood, was not unlike a Currier and Ives drawing, except that here the canvas was more crowded and the scale more large. It was a world that was drawn in very bright and very innocent and very thrilling colors—a world where the grass was very, very green, the trees sumptuous and full-bodied, the streams like sapphire, and the skies a crystal blue. It was a rich, compact, precisely executed world, in which there were no rough edges and no bleak vacancies, no desolate and empty gaps.

In later years, George Webber actually discovered such a world as this in two places. One was the small countryside community in southern Pennsylvania from which his father had come, with its pattern of great red barns, prim brick houses, white fences, and swelling fields, some green with the perfection of young wheat, others rolling strips of bronze, with red earth, and with the dead-still bloom of apple orchards on the hills—all of it as exactly rich, precise, unwasteful, and exciting as any of his childhood dreams could have imagined it. The other was in certain sections of Germany and the Austrian Tyrol—places like the Black Forest and the Forest of Thuringia, and towns like Weimar, Eisenach, old Frankfort, Kufstein on the Austrian border, and Innsbruck.

2

Three O'Clock

TWENTY-FIVE YEARS AGO OR THEREABOUTS, ONE AFTERNOON IN MAY, George Webber was lying stretched out in the grass before his uncle's house in Old Catawba.

Isn't Old Catawba a wonderful name? People up North or out West or in other parts of the world don't know much about it, and they don't speak about it often. But really when you know the place and think about it more and more its name is wonderful.

Old Catawba is much better than South Carolina. It is more North, and "North" is a much more wonderful word than "South," as anyone with any ear for words will know. The reason why "South" *seems* such a wonderful word is because we had the word "North" to begin with: if there had been no "North," then the word "South" and all its connotations would not seem so wonderful. Old Catawba is distinguished by its "Northness," and South Carolina by its "Southness." And the "Northness" of Old Catawba is better than the "Southness" of South Carolina. Old Catawba has the slants of evening and the mountain cool. You feel lonely in Old Catawba, but it is not the loneliness of South Carolina. In Old Catawba, the hill boy helps his father building fences and hears a soft Spring howling in the wind, and sees the wind snake through the bending waves of the coarse grasses of the mountain pastures. And far away he hears the whistle's cry wailed back, far-flung and faint along some mountain valley, as a great train rushes towards the cities of the East. And the heart of the hill boy will know joy because he knows, all world-remote, lonely as he is, that some day he will meet the world and know those cities too.

But in South Carolina the loneliness is not like this. They do not have the mountain cool. They have dusty, sand-clay roads, great mournful cotton fields, with pine wood borders and the nigger shacks, and something haunting, soft, and lonely in the air. These people are really

13

lost. They cannot get away from South Carolina, and if they get away they are no good. They drawl beautifully. There is the most wonderful warmth, affection, heartiness in their approach and greeting, but the people are afraid. Their eyes are desperately afraid, filled with a kind of tortured and envenomed terror of the old, stricken, wounded "Southness" of cruelty and lust. Sometimes their women have the honey skins, they are like gold and longing. They are filled with the most luscious and seductive sweetness, tenderness, and gentle mercy. But the men are stricken. They get fat about the bellies, or they have a starved, stricken leanness in the loins. They are soft-voiced and drawling, but their eyes will go about and go again with fear, with terror and suspicion. They drawl softly in front of the drug store, they palaver softly to the girls when the girls drive up, they go up and down the streets of blistered, sun-wide, clay-dust little towns in their shirt-sleeves, and they are full of hearty, red-faced greetings.

They cry: "How are y', Jim? Is it hot enough fer you?"

And Jim will say, with a brisk shake of the head: "Hotter'n what Sherman said war was, ain't it, Ed?"

And the street will roar with hearty, red-faced laughter: "By God! That's a good 'un. Damned if ole Jim didn't have it about right too!"— but the eyes keep going back and forth, and fear, suspicion, hatred, and mistrust, and something stricken in the South long, long ago, is there among them.

And after a day before the drug stores or around the empty fountain in the Courthouse Square, they go out to lynch a nigger. They kill him, and they kill him hard. They get in cars at night and put the nigger in between them, they go down the dusty roads until they find the place that they are going to, and before they get there, they jab little knives into the nigger, not a long way, not the whole way in, but just a little way. And they laugh to see him squirm. When they get out at the place where they are going to, the place the nigger sat in is a pool of blood. Perhaps it makes the boy who is driving the car sick at his stomach, but the older people laugh. Then they take the nigger through the rough field stubble of a piece of land and hang him to a tree. But before they hang him they saw off his thick nose and his fat nigger lips with a rusty knife. And they laugh about it. Then they castrate him. And at the end they hang him.

This is the way things are in South Carolina; it is not the way things are in Old Catawba. Old Catawba is much better. Although such things may happen in Old Catawba, they do not belong to the temper and character of the people there. There is a mountain cool in Old Catawba and the slants of evening. The hill men kill in the mountain meadows—they kill about a fence, a dog, the dispute of a boundary line. They kill in drunkenness or in the red smear of the murder lust. But they do not saw off niggers' noses. There is not the look of fear and cruelty in their eyes that the people in South Carolina have.

Old Catawba is a place inhabited by humble people. There is no Charleston in Old Catawba, and not so many people pretending to be what they are not. Charleston produced nothing, and yet it pretended to so much. Now their pretense is reduced to pretending that they amounted to so much formerly. And they really amounted to very little. This is the curse of South Carolina and its "Southness"—of always pretending you *used to be* so much, even though you are not now. Old Catawba does not have this to contend with. It has no Charleston and it does not have to pretend. They are small, plain people.

So Old Catawba is better because it is more "North." Even as a child, George Webber realized that in a general way it was better to be more North than South. If you get too North, it gets no good. Everything gets frozen and dried up. But if you get too South, it is no good either, and it also gets rotten. If you get too North, it gets rotten, but in a cold, dry way. If you get too South, it gets rotten not in a dry way— which if you're going to get rotten is the best way to get rotten—but in a horrible, stagnant, swampy, stenchlike, humid sort of way that is also filled with obscene whisperings and ropy laughter.

Old Catawba is just right. They are not going to set the world on fire down there, neither do they intend to. They make all the mistakes that people can make. They elect the cheapest sort of scoundrel to the highest offices they are able to confer. They have Rotary Clubs and chain gangs and Babbitts and all the rest of it. But they are not bad.

They are not certain, not sure, in Old Catawba. Nothing is certain or sure down there. The towns don't look like New England towns. They don't have the lovely white houses, the elm green streets, the sure, sweet magic of young May, the certainty and purpose of it all. It is not like that. First there are about two hundred miles of a coastal plain. This is a mournful flat-land, wooded with pine barrens. Then there are two hundred miles or thereabouts of Piedmont. This is rolling, rugged, you can't remember it the way that you remember the lavish, sweet, and wonderful farm lands of the Pennsylvania Dutch with their great red barns which dominate the land. You don't remember Old Catawba in this way. No; field and fold and gulch and hill and hollow, rough meadow land, bunched coarsely with wrench grass, and pine land borderings, clay bank and gulch and cut and all the trees there are, the locusts, chestnuts, maples, oaks, the pines, the willows, and the sycamores, all grown up together, all smashed-down tangles, and across in a sweet wilderness, all choked between with dogwood, laurel, and the rhododendron, dead leaves from last October and the needles of the pine—this is one of the ways that Old Catawba looks in May. And then out of the Piedmont westward you will hit the mountains. You don't hit them squarely, they just come to you. Field and fold and hill and hollow, clay bank and cut and gulch and rough swell and convolution of the earth unutterable, and presently the hills are there.

A certain unknown, unsuspected sharpness thrills you. Is it not there? You do not know, for it cannot be proved. And yet the shifting engines switch along the tracks, you see the weed growth by the track-side, the leak-grey painting of a toolshed hut, the bleak, unforgettable, marvelous yellow of a station of the Southern Railway. The huge black snout of a mountain engine comes shifting down the track to take you up behind, and suddenly you know the hills are there. The heavy coaches ride up past mountain pastures, a rail fence, a clay road, the rock-bright clamors of a mountain water. You feel upon your neck the hot, the thrilling, the immensely intimate, the strange and most familiar breath of the terrific locomotive. And suddenly the hills are there. You go twisting up the grades and snake round curves with grinding screech. How near, how homely, how common and how strange, how utterly familiar—the great bulk of the Blue Ridge bears imminent upon you and compels you. You can put your hand out of the slow, toiling train and touch it. And all life is near, as common as your breath, as strange as time.

The towns aren't much to look at. There is no lovely, certain thing the way there is in New England. There are just plain houses, nigger shacks, front porches, most of the current bungalow and country-club atrocities, a Public Square, some old buildings that say "The Weaver Block, 1882," some new ones for Ford agencies, cars parked around the Square.

Down in the East, in Old Catawba, they have some smack of ancientry. The East got settled first and there are a few old towns down there, the remnants of plantations, a few fine old houses, a lot of niggers, tobacco, turpentine, pine woods, and the mournful flat-lands of the coastal plain. The people in the East used to think they were better than the people in the West because they had been there a little longer. But they were not really better. In the West, where the mountains sweep around them, the people have utterly common, familiar, plain, Scotch-Irish faces, and names like Weaver, Wilson, Gudger, Joyner, Alexander, and Patton. The West is really better than the East. They went to war in the West, and yet they didn't want to go to war. They didn't have anything to go to war about: they were a plain and common people and they had no slaves. And yet they will always go to war if Leaders tell them to—they are made to serve. They think long and earnestly, debatingly; they are conservative; they vote the right way, and they go to war when big people tell them to. The West is really a region of good small people, a Scotch-Irish place, and that, too, is undefined, save that it doesn't drawl so much, works harder, doesn't loaf so much, and shoots a little straighter when it has to. It is really just one of the common places of the earth, a million or two people with nothing very extraordinary about them. If there had been anything extraordinary about them, it would have come out in their houses, as it came out in the lovely white houses of New England; or it would have come out in their barns, as it came out in the great red barns of the Pennsylvania Dutch. They are just common, plain, and homely—but almost everything of America is in them.

George Webber must have known all these things twenty-five years ago as he lay on the grass one afternoon before his uncle's house. He really knew the way things were. People sometimes pretend they don't know the way things are, but they really do. George lay in the grass and pulled some grass blades and looked upon them contentedly and chewed upon them. And he knew the way the grass blades were. He dug bare toes into the grass and thought of it. He knew the way it felt. Among the green grass, he saw patches of old brown, and he knew the way that was too. He put out his hand and felt the maple tree. He saw the way it came out of the earth, the grass grew right around it, he felt the bark and got its rough, coarse feeling. He pressed hard with his fingers, a little rough piece of the bark came off; he knew the way that was too. The wind kept howling faintly the way it does in May. All the young leaves of the maple tree were turned back, straining in the wind. He heard the sound it made, it touched him with some sadness, then the wind went and came again.

He turned and saw his uncle's house, its bright red brick, its hard, new, cement columns, everything about it raw and ugly; and beside it, set farther back, the old house his grandfather had built, the clapboard structure, the porch, the gables, the bay windows, the color of the paint. It was all accidental, like a million other things in America. George Webber saw it, and he knew that this was the way things were. He watched the sunlight come and go, across backyards with all their tangle of familiar things; he saw the hills against the eastern side of town, sweet green, a little mottled, so common, homely, and familiar, and, when remembered later, wonderful, the way things are.

George Webber had good eyes, a sound body, he was twelve years old. He had a wonderful nose, a marvelous sense of smell, nothing fooled him. He lay there in the grass before his uncle's house, thinking: "This is the way things are. Here is the grass, so green and coarse, so sweet and delicate, but with some brown rubble in it. There are the houses all along the street, the concrete blocks of walls, somehow so dreary, ugly, yet familiar, the slate roofs and the shingles, the lawns, the hedges and the gables, the backyards with their accidental structures of so many little and familiar things as hen houses, barns. All common and familiar as my breath, all accidental as the strings of blind chance, yet all somehow fore-ordered as a destiny: the way they are, because they are the way they are!"

There was a certain stitch of afternoon while the boy waited. Bird chirrupings and maple leaves, pervading quietness, boards hammered from afar, and a bumbling hum. The day was drowsed with quietness and defunctive turnip greens at three o'clock, and Carlton Leathergood's tall, pock-marked, yellow nigger was coming up the street. The big dog trotted with him, breathing like a locomotive, the big dog Storm, that knocked you down with friendliness. Tongue rolling, heavy as a man, the great head swaying side to side, puffing with joy continually, the dog came on, and with him came the pock-marked nigger, Simpson Simms. Tall, lean, grinning cheerfully, full of dignity and reverence, the nigger was coming up the street the way he always did at three o'clock. He smiled and raised his hand to George with a courtly greeting. He called him "Mister" Webber as he always did; the greeting was gracious and respectful, and soon forgotten as it is and should be in the good, kind minds of niggers and of idiots, and yet it filled the boy somehow with warmth and joy.

"Good day dar, Mistah Webbah. How's Mistah Webbah today?"

The big dog swayed and panted like an engine, his great tongue lolling out; he came on with great head down and with the great black brisket and his shoulders working.

Something happened suddenly, filling that quiet street with instant menace, injecting terror in the calm pulse of the boy. Around the corner of the Potterham house across the street came Potterham's bulldog. He saw the mastiff, paused; his forelegs widened stockily, his grimjowled face seemed to sink right down between the shoulder blades, his lips bared back along his long-fanged tusks, and from his baleful red-shot eyes fierce lightning shone. A low snarl rattled in the folds of his thick throat, the mastiff swung his ponderous head back and growled, the bull came on, halted, leaning forward on his widened legs, filled with hell-fire, solid with fight.

And Carlton Leathergood's pock-marked yellow negro man winked at the boy and shook his head with cheerful confidence, saying:

"He ain't goin' to mix up wid *my* dawg, Mistah Webbah! . . . No, sah! . . . He knows bettah dan dat! . . . Yes, sah!" cried Leathergood's nigger with unbounded confidence. "He knows too well fo' *dat*!"

The pock-marked nigger was mistaken! Something happened like a flash: there was a sudden snarl, a black thunderbolt shot through the air, the shine of murderous fanged teeth. Before the mastiff knew what had happened to him, the little bull was in and had his fierce teeth buried, sunk, gripped with the lock of death, in the great throat of the larger dog.

What happened after that was hard to follow. For a moment the great dog stood stock still with an eloquence of stunned surprise and bewildered consternation that was more than human; then a savage roar burst out upon the quiet air, filling the street with its gigantic anger. The mastiff swung his great head savagely, the little bull went flying through the air but hung on with imbedded teeth; great drops of the bright arterial blood went flying everywhere across the pavement, and still the bull held on. The end came like a lightning stroke. The great head flashed over through the air and down: the bull, no longer dog now—just a wad of black—smacked to the pavement with a sickening crunch.

From Potterham's house a screen door slammed, and fourteen-year-old Augustus Potterham, with his wild red hair aflame, came out upon the run. Up the street, paunch-bellied, stiff-legged, and slouchyuniformed, bound for town and three o'clock, Mr. Matthews, the policeman, pounded heavily. But Leathergood's nigger was already there, tugging furiously at the leather collar around the mastiff's neck, and uttering imprecations.

But it was all too late. The little dog was dead the moment that he struck the pavement—back broken, most of his bones broken, too; in Mr. Matthews' words, "He never knowed what hit him." And the big dog came away quietly enough, now that the thing was done: beneath the negro's wrenching tug upon his neck, he swung back slowly, panting, throat dripping blood in a slow rain, bedewing the street beneath him with the bright red flakes.

Suddenly, like a miracle, the quiet street was full of people. They came from all directions, from everywhere: they pressed around in an excited circle, all trying to talk at once, each with his own story, everyone debating, explaining, giving his own version. In Potterham's house, the screen door slammed again, and Mr. Potterham came running out at his funny little bandy-legged stride, his little red apple-cheeks aglow with anger, indignation, and excitement, his funny, chirping little voice heard plainly over all the softer, deeper, heavier, more Southern tones. No longer the great gentleman now, no longer the noble descendant of the Dukes of Potterham, no longer the blood-cousin of belted lords and earls, the possible claimant of enormous titles and estates in Gloucestershire when the present reigning head should die—but Cockney Potterham now, little Potterham minus all his aitches, little Potterham the dealer in nigger real estate and the owner of the nigger shacks, indomitable little Potterham forgetting all his grammar in the heat and anger of the moment:

"'Ere now! Wot did I tell you? I always said 'is bloody dog would make trouble! 'Ere! Look at 'im now! The girt bleedin', blinkin' thing! Big as a helefant, 'e is! Wot chance 'ud a dog like mine 'ave against a brute like that! 'E ought to be put out of the way—that's wot! You mark my words—you let that brute run loose, an' there won't be a dog left in town—that's wot!"

And Leathergood's big pock-marked nigger, still clutching to the mastiff's collar as he talks, and pleading with the policeman almost tearfully:

"Fo' de Lawd, Mistah Matthews, my dawg didn't do nuffin! No, sah! He don't bothah nobody—my dawg don't! He wa'nt even noticin' dat othah dawg—you ask anybody!—ask Mistah Webbah heah!"—

suddenly appealing to the boy with pleading entreaty— "Ain't dat right, Mistah Webbah? You saw de whole thing yo'se'f, didn't you? You tell Mistah Matthews how it was! Me an' my dawg was comin' up de street, a-tendin' to ouah business, I jus' tu'ned my haid to say good-day to Mistah Webbah heah, when heah comes dis othah dawg aroun' de house, jus' a-puffin' an' a-snawtin', an' befo' I could say Jack Robinson he jumps all ovah my dawg an' grabs him by de throat—you ask Mistah Webbah if dat ain't de way it happened."

And so it goes, everyone debating, arguing, agreeing, and denying, giving his own version and his own opinion; and Mr. Matthews asking questions and writing things down in a book; and poor Augustus Potterham blubbering like a baby, holding his dead little bulldog in his arms, his homely, freckled face contorted piteously, and dropping scalding tears upon his little dead dog; and the big mastiff panting, dripping blood upon the ground and looking curious, detached from the whole thing, and a little bored; and presently the excitement subsiding, people going away; Mr. Matthews telling the negro to appear in court; Augustus Potterham going away into the house blubbering, with the little bulldog in his arms; Mr. Potterham behind him, still chirping loudly and excitedly; and the dejected, pock-marked nigger and his tremendous dog going away up the street, the big dog dropping big blood flakes on the pavement as he goes. And finally, silence as before, the quiet street again, the rustling of young maple leaves in the light wind, the brooding imminence of three o'clock, a few bright blood-flakes on the pavement, and all else the way that it had always been, and George Webber as before stretched out upon the grass beneath the tree there in his uncle's yard, chin cupped in hands, adrift on time's great dream, and thinking:

"Great God, this is the way things are, I see and know this is the way things are, I understand this is the way things are: and, Great God! Great God! this being just the way things are, how strange, and plain, and savage, sweet and cruel, lovely, terrible, and mysterious, and how unmistakable and familiar all things are!"

Three o'clock!

"Child, child!—Where are you, child?"

So did he always know Aunt Maw was there!

"Son, son!—Where are you son?"

Too far for finding and too near to seek!

"Boy, boy!—Where *is* that boy?"

Where *you*, at any rate, or any other of the apron-skirted kind, can never come.

"You can't take your eye off him a minute. . . ."

Keep eye *on*, then; it will do no good.

"The moment that your back is turned, he's up and gone. . . ."

And out and off and far away from *you*—no matter if your back is turned or not!

"I can never find him when I need him. . . ."

Need me no needs, sweet dame; when I need you, you shall be so informed!

"But he can *eat*, all right. . . . He's Johnny-on-the-spot when it is time to eat. . . ."

And, pray, what is there so remarkable in *that*? Of course he *eats*—more power to his eating, too. Was Hercules a daffodil; did Adam toy with water cress; did Falstaff wax fat eating lettuces; was Dr. Johnson surfeited on shredded wheat; or Chaucer on a handful of parched corn? No! What is more, were campaigns fought and waged on empty bellies; was Kublai Khan a vegetarian; did Washington have prunes for breakfast, radishes for lunch; was John L. Sullivan the slave of Holland Rusk, or President Taft the easy prey of lady fingers? No! More—who drove the traffic of swift-thronging noon, perched high above the hauling rumps of horses; who sat above the pistoned wheels of furious day; who hurled a ribbon of steel rails into the West; who dug, drove through gulches, bored through tunnels; whose old gloved hands were gripped on the throttles; who bore the hammer, and who dealt the stroke?—did such of these grow faint with longing when they thought of the full gluttony of peanut-butter and ginger snaps? And finally, the men who came back from the town at twelve o'clock, their solid liquid tramp of leather on the streets of noon, the men of labor, sweat, and business coming down the street—his uncle, Mr. Potterham, Mr. Shepperton, Mr. Crane—were fence gates opened, screen doors slammed, and was there droning torpor and the full feeding silence of assuagement and repose—if these men had come to take a cup of coffee and a nap?

"He can *eat*, all right! . . . He's always here when it is time to *eat*!"

It was to listen to such stuff as this that great men lived and suffered, and great heroes bled! It was for this that Ajax battled, and Achilles died; it was for this that Homer sang and suffered—and Troy fell! It was for this that Artaxerxes led great armies, it was for this that Caesar took his legions over Gaul; for this that Ulysses had braved strange seas, encompassed perils of remote and magic coasts, survived the Cyclops and Charybdis, and surmounted all the famed enchantments of Circean time—to listen to such damned and dismal stuff as this—the astonishing discovery by a woman that men *eat*!

Peace, woman, to your bicker—hold your prosy tongue! Get back into the world you know, and do the work for which you were intended; you intrude—go back, go back to all your kitchen scourings, your pots and pans, your plates and cups and saucers, your clothes and rags and soaps and sudsy water; go back, go back and leave us; we are fed and we are pleasantly distended, great thoughts possess us; drowsy dreams; we would lie alone and contemplate our navel—it is afternoon!

"Boy, boy!—Where has he got to now! . . . Oh, I could see him lookin' round. . . . I saw him edgin' towards the door! . . . Aha, I thought, he thinks he's very smart . . . but I knew exactly what he planned to do . . . to slip out and to get away before I caught him . . . and just because he was afraid I had a little work for him to do!"

A *little* work! Aye, there's the rub—if only it were not always just a *little* work we had to do! If only in their minds there ever were a moment of *supreme occasion* or *sublime event*! If only it were not always just a *little* thing they have in mind, a *little* work we had to do! If only there were something, just a spark of joy to lift the heart, a spark of magic to fire the spirit, a spark of understanding of the thing we *want* to do, a grain of feeling, or an atom of imagination! But always it is just a *little* work, a *little* thing we have to do!

Is it the little *labor* that she asks that we begrudge? Is it the little *effort* which it would require that we abhor? Is it the little *help* she asks for that we ungenerously withhold, a hate of work, a fear of sweat, a spirit of mean giving? No! It is not this at all. It is that women in the early afternoon are dull, and dully ask dull things of us; it is that women in the afternoon are dull, and ask us always for a *little* thing, and do not understand!

It is that at this hour of day we do not want them near us—we would be alone. They smell of kitchen steam and drabness at this time of day: the depressing moistures of defunctive greens, left-over cabbage, lukewarm boilings, and the dinner scraps. An atmosphere of sudsy water now pervades them; their hands drip rinsings and their lives are grey.

These people do not know it, out of mercy we have never told them; but their lives lack interest at three o'clock—we do not want them, they must let us be.

They have some knowledge for the morning, some for afternoon, more for sunset, much for night; but at three o'clock they bore us, they must leave us be! They do not understand the thousand lights and weathers of the day as we; light is just light to them, and morning morning, and noon noon. They do not know the thing that comes and goes—the way light changes, and the way things shift; they do not know how brightness changes in the sun, and how man's spirit changes like a flick of light. Oh, they do not know, they cannot understand, the life of life, the joy of joy, the grief of grief unutterable, the eternity of living in a moment, the thing that changes as light changes, as swift and passing as a swallow's flight; they do not know the thing that comes and goes and never can be captured, the thorn of Spring, the sharp and tongueless cry!

They do not understand the joy and horror of the day as *we* can feel it; they do not understand the thing we dread at this hour of the afternoon.

To them the light is light, the brief hour passing; their soaps-suds spirits do not contemplate the horror of hot light in afternoon. They do not understand our loathing of hot gardens, the way our spirits dull and sicken at hot light. They do not know how hope forsakes us, how joy flies away, when we look at the mottled torpor of hot light on the hydrangeas, the broad-leaved dullness of hot dock-weeds growing by the barn. They do not know the horror of old rusty cans filled into gaps of rubbish underneath the fence; the loathing of the mottled, hot, and torpid light upon a row of scraggly corn; the hopeless depth of torpid, dull depression which the sight of hot coarse grasses in the sun can rouse to a numb wakefulness of horror in our souls at three o'clock.

It is a kind of torpid stagnancy of life, it is a hopelessness of hope, a dull, numb lifelessness of life! It is like looking at a pool of stagnant water in the dull torpor of the light of three o'clock. It is like being where no green is, where no cool is, where there is no song of unseen birds, where there is no sound of cool and secret waters, no sound of rock-bright, foaming waters; like being where no gold and green and sudden magic is, to be called out to do *little* things at three o'clock.

Ah, Christ, could we make speech say what no speech utters, could we make tongue speak what no tongue says! Could we enlighten their enkitchened lives with a revealing utterance, then they would never send us out to do a *little* thing at three o'clock.

We are a kind that hate clay banks in afternoon, the look of cinders, grimy surfaces, old blistered clapboard houses, the train yards and the coaches broiling on the tracks. We loathe the sight of concrete walls, the fly-speckled windows of the Greek, the strawberry horror of the row of lukewarm soda-pop. At this hour of the day we sicken at the Greek's hot window, at his greasy frying plate that *fries* and oozes with a loathsome sweat in the full torpor of the sun. We hate the row of greasy frankfurters that *sweat* and *ooze* there on the torpid plate, the loathsome pans all oozing with a stew of greasy onions, mashed potatoes, and hamburger steaks. We loathe the Greek's swart features in the light of three o'clock, the yellowed pock-marked pores that sweat in the hot light. We hate the light that shines on motor cars at three o'clock, we hate white plaster surfaces, new stucco houses, and most open places where there are no trees.

We must have coolness, dankness, darkness; we need gladed green and gold and rock-bright running waters at the hour of three o'clock. We must go down into the coolness of a concrete cellar. We like dark shade, and cool, dark smells, and cool, dark, secret places, at the hour of three o'clock. We like cool, strong smells with some cool staleness at that hour. Man smells are good at three o'clock. We like to remember the smells of all things that were in our father's room: the dank, cool pungency of the plug of apple tobacco on the mantelpiece, bit into at one end, and stuck with a bright red flag; the smell of the old mantelpiece, the wooden clock, the old calf bindings of a few old books; the smell of the rocking chair, the rug, the walnut bureau, and the cool, dark smell of clothing in the closet.

At this hour of the day we like the smell of old unopened rooms, old packing cases, tar, and the smell of the grape vines on the cool side of the house. If we go out, we want to go out in green shade and gladed coolnesses, to lie down on our bellies underneath the maple trees and work our toes down into the thick green grass. If we have to go to town we want to go to places like our uncle's hardware store, where we can smell the cool, dark cleanliness of nails, hammers, saws, tools, T-squares, implements of all sorts; or to a saddle shop where we can get the smell of leather; or to our father's brick and lumber yard where we can get the smells of putty, glass, and clean white pine, the smell of the mule-teams, and the lumber sheds. It is also good to go into the cool glade of the drug store at this hour, to hear the cool, swift slatting of the wooden fans, and to smell the citrus pungency of lemons, limes, and oranges, the sharp and clean excitements of unknown medicines.

The smell of a street car at this hour of day is also good—a dynamic smell of motors, wood work, rattan seats, worn brass, and steel-bright flanges. It is a smell of drowsy, warm excitement, and a nameless beating of the heart; it speaks of going somewhere. If we go anywhere at this hour of day, it is good to go to the baseball game and smell the grandstand, the old wooden bleachers, the green turf of the playing field, the horsehide of the ball, the gloves, the mitts, the clean resilience of the ash-wood bats, the smells of men in shirt-sleeves, and the sweating players.

And if there is work to do at three o'clock—if we must rouse ourselves from somnolent repose, and from the green-gold drowsy magic of our meditations—for God's sake give us something *real* to do. Give us great labors, but vouchsafe to us as well the promise of a great accomplishment, the thrill of peril, the hope of high and spirited adventure. For God's sake don't destroy the heart and hope and life and will, the brave and dreaming soul of man, with the common, dull, soul-sickening, mean transactions of these *little* things!

Don't break our heart, our hope, our ecstasy, don't shatter irrevocably some brave adventure of the spirit, or some brooding dream, by sending us on errands which any stupid girl, or nigger wench, or soulless underling of life could just as well accomplish. Don't break man's heart, man's life, man's song, the soaring vision of his dream with—"Here, boy, trot around the corner for a loaf of bread,"—or "Here, boy; the telephone company has just called up—you'll have to trot around there . . ."—Oh, for God's sake, and *my* sake, *please* don't say *'trot* around' —". . . and pay the bill before they cut us off!"

Or, fretful-wise, be-flusteredlike, all of a twitter, scattered and demoralized, fuming and stewing, complaining, whining, railing against the universe because of things undone *you* should have done yourself, because of errors *you* have made yourself, because of debts unpaid *you* should have paid on time, because of things forgotten *you* should have remembered—fretting, complaining, galloping off in all directions, unable to get your thoughts together, unable even to call a child by his proper name—as here:

"Ed, John, Bob—pshaw, boy! *George,* I mean! . . ."

Well, then for God's sake, *mean* it!

"Why, pshaw!—to think that that fool nigger—I could wring her neck when I think of it—well, as I say now. . . ."

Then, in God's name, *say* it!

". . . why, you *know* . . ."

No! I do *not* know!

". . . here I was dependin' on her—here she told me she would come—and all the work to be done—and here she's sneaked out on me after dinner—and I'm left here in the lurch."

Yes, of course you are; because you failed to pay the poor wench on Saturday night the three dollars which is her princely emolument for fourteen hours a day of sweaty drudgery seven days a week; because "it slipped your mind," because you couldn't bear to let it go in one gigantic lump—*could* you?—because you thought you'd hang on to the good green smell of money just a *little* longer, didn't you?—let it sweat away in your stocking and smell good just a *little* longer— didn't you?—break the poor brute's heart on Saturday night just when she had her mind all set on fried fish, gin, and f——g, just because you wanted to hold on to three wadded, soiled, and rumpled greenbacks just a *little* longer—dole it out to her a dollar at a time—tonight a dollar, Wednesday night a dollar, Friday night the same . . . and so are left here strapped and stranded and forlorn, where my father would have *paid* and *paid at once*, and kept his nigger and his nigger's loyalty. And all because you are a woman, with a woman's niggard smallness about money, a woman's niggard dealing towards her servants, a woman's selfishness, her small humanity of feeling for the dumb, the suffering, and afflicted soul of man—and so will fret and fume and fidget now, all flustered and undone, to call me forth with:

"Here, boy!—Pshaw, now!—To think that she would play a trick like this!—Why as I say, now—child! child!—I don't know what I shall do—I'm left here all alone—you'll have to trot right down and see if you can find someone at once."

Aye! to call me forth from coolness, and the gladed sweetness of cool grass to sweat my way through Niggertown in the dreary torpor of the afternoon; to sweat my way up and down that grassless, tree-less horror of baked clay; to draw my breath in stench and sourness, breathe in the funky nigger stench, sour wash-pots and branch-sewage, nigger privies and the sour shambles of the nigger shacks; to scar my sight and soul with little snot-nosed nigger children fouled with dung, and so bowed out with rickets that their little legs look like twin sausages of fat, soft rubber; so to hunt, and knock at shack-door, so to wheedle, persuade, and cajole, in order to find some other sullen wench to come and sweat her fourteen hours a day for seven days a week—and for three dollars!

Or again, perhaps it will be: "Pshaw, boy!—Why to think that he would play me such a trick!—Why, I forgot to put the sign out—but I thought he knew I needed twenty pounds!—If he'd only asked!—but here he drove right by with not so much as by-your-leave, and here there's not a speck of ice in the refrigerator—and ice cream and iced tea to make for supper.—You'll have to trot right down to the ice-house and get me a good ten-cent chunk."

Yes! A good ten-cent chunk tied with a twist of galling twine, that cuts like a razor down into my sweaty palm; that wets my trouser's leg from thigh to buttock; that bangs and rubs and slips and cuts and freezes against my miserable knees until the flesh is worn raw; that trickles freezing drops down my bare and aching legs, that takes all joy from living, that makes me curse my life and all the circumstances of my birth—and all because *you* failed to "put the sign out," all because *you* failed to think of twenty pounds of ice!

Or is it a thimble, or a box of needles, or a spool of thread that *you* need now! Is it for such as *this* that I must "trot around" some place for baking powder, salt or sugar, or a pound of butter, or a package of tea!

For God's sake thimble me no thimbles and spool me no spools! If I must go on errands send me out upon man's work, with man's dis-patch, as my father used to do! Send me out with one of his niggers upon a wagon load of fragrant pine, monarch above the rumps of two grey mules! Send me for a wagon load of sand down by the river, where I can smell the sultry yellow of the stream, and shout and holler to the boys in swimming! Send me to town to my father's brick and lumber yard, the Square, the sparkling traffic of bright afternoon. Send me for something in the City Market, the smell of fish and oysters, the green, cool growth of vegetables; the cold refrigeration of hung beeves, the butchers cleaving and sawing in straw hats and gouted aprons. Send me out to life and business and the glades of afternoon; for God's sake, do not torture me with spools of thread, or with the sunbaked clay and shambling rickets of black Niggertown!

"Son, son! . . . Where has that fool boy got to! . . . Why, as I say now, boy, you'll have to trot right down to. . . ."

With baleful, brooding vision he looked towards the house. Say me no says, sweet dame; trot me no trots. The hour is three o'clock, and I would be alone.

So thinking, feeling, saying, he rolled over on his belly, out of sight, on the "good" side of the tree, dug bare, luxurious toes in cool, green grass, and, chin a-cup in his supporting hands, regarded his small universe of three o'clock.

"A little child, a limber elf"—twelve years of age, and going on for thirteen next October. So, midway in May now, midway to thirteen, with a whole world to think of. Not large or heavy for his age, but strong and heavy in the shoulders, arms absurdly long, big hands, legs thin, bowed out a little, long, flat feet; small face and features quick with life, the eyes deep-set, their look both quick and still; low brow, wide, stick-out ears, a shock of close-cropped hair, a large head that hangs forward and projects almost too heavily for the short, thin neck—not much to look at, someone's ugly duckling, just a boy.

And yet—could climb trees like a monkey, spring like a cat; could jump and catch the maple limb four feet above his head—the bark was already worn smooth and slick by his big hands; could be up the tree like a flash; could go places no one else could go; could climb anything, grab hold of anything, dig his toes in anything; could scale the side of a cliff if he had to, could almost climb a sheet of glass; could pick up things with his toes, and hold them, too; could walk on his hands, bend back and touch the ground, stick his head between his legs, or wrap his legs around his neck; could make a hoop out of his body and roll over like a hoop, do hand-springs and cut flips—jump, climb, and leap as no other boy in town could do. He is a grotesque-looking little creature, yet unformed and unmatured, in his make-up something between a spider and an ape (the boys, of course, call him "Monk")—and yet with an eye that sees and holds, an ear that hears and can remember, a nose that smells out unsuspected pungencies, a spirit swift and mercurial as a flash of light, now soaring like a rocket, wild with ecstasy, outstripping storm and flight itself in the aerial joy of skyey buoyancy; now plunged in nameless, utter, black, unfathomable dejection; now bedded cool in the reposeful grass beneath the maple tree, remote from time and brooding on his world of three o'clock; now catlike on his feet—the soaring rocket of a sudden joy— then catlike spring and catch upon the lowest limb, then like a monkey up the tree, and like a monkey down, now rolling like a furious hoop across the yard—at last, upon his belly in cool grass again, and bedded deep in somnolent repose at three o'clock.

Now, with chin cupped in his hands and broodingly aware, he meditates the little world before him, the world of one small, modest street, the neighbors, and his uncle's house. For the most part, it is the pleasant world of humble people and small, humble houses, most of them worn, shabby, so familiar: the yards, the porches, swings, and railings, and the rocking chairs; the maple trees, the chestnuts and the oaks; the way a gate leans open, half ajar, the way the grass grows, and the way the flowers are planted; the fences, hedges, bushes, and the honeysuckle vines; the alleyways and all the homely and familiar backyard world of chicken houses, stables, barns, and orchards, and each one with its own familiar hobby, the Potterham's neat backgarden, Nebraska Crane's pigeon houses—the whole, small, well-used world of good, small people.

He sees the near line of eastern hills, with light upon it, the sweet familiarity of massed green. His thought soars westward with a vision of far distances and splendid ranges; his heart turns west with thoughts of unknown men and places and of wandering; but ever his heart turns home to this his own world, to what he knows and likes the best. It is—he feels and senses this obscurely—the place of common man, his father's kind of people. Except for his uncle's raw, new house, the sight of which is a desolation to him, it is the place of the homely, simple houses, and the old, ordinary streets, where the bricklayers, plasterers, and masons, the lumber dealers and the stonecutters, the plumbers, hardware merchants, butchers, grocers, and the old, common, native families of the mountains—his mother's people—make their home.

It is the place of the Springtime orchards, the loamy, dew-wet morning gardens, the peach, cherry, apple blossoms, drifting to the ground at morning in the month of April, the pungent, fragrant, maddening savor of the breakfast smells. It is the place of roses, lilies, and nasturtiums, the vine-covered porches of the houses, the strange, delicious smell of the ripening grapes in August, and the voices—near, strange, haunting, lonely, most familiar—of the people sitting on their porches in the Summer darkness, the voices of the lost people in the darkness as they say good-night. Then boys will hear a screen door slam, the earth grow silent with the vast and brooding ululation of the night, and finally the approach, the grinding screech, the brief halt, the receding loneliness and absence of the last street car going around the corner on the hill, and will wait there in the darkness filled with strangeness, thinking, "I was born here, there's my father, this is I!"

It is the world of the sun-warm, time-far clucking of the sensual hens in the forenoon strangeness of the spell of time, and the coarse, sweet coolness of Crane's cow along the alleyway; and it is the place of the ice-tongs ringing in the streets, the ice saw droning through the dripping blocks, the sweating negroes, and the pungent, musty, and exotic odors of the grocery wagons, the grocery box piled high with new provisions. It is the place of the forenoon housewives with their shapeless gingham dresses, bare legs, slippers, turbaned heads, bare, bony, labor-toughened hands and arms and elbows, and the fresh, clean, humid smell of houses airing in the morning. It is the place of the heavy midday dinners, the smells of roasts of beef, corn on the cob, the deep-hued savor of the big string beans, cooking morning long into the sweet amity and unction of the fat-streaked pork; and above it all is the clean, hungry, humid smell and the steaming freshness of the turnip greens at noon.

It is the world of magic April and October; world of the first green and the smell of blossoms; world of the bedded oak leaves and the smell of smoke in Autumn, and men in shirt-sleeves working in their yards in red waning light of old October as boys pass by them going home from school. It is the world of the Summer nights, world of the dream-strange nights of August, the great moons and the tolling bells; world of the Winter nights, the howling winds, and the fire-full chimney throats—world of the ash of time and silence while the piled coals flare and crumble, world of the waiting, waiting, waiting—for the world of joy, the longed-for face, the hoped-for step, the unbelieved-in magic of the Spring again.

It is the world of warmth, nearness, certitude, the walls of home! It is the world of the plain faces, and the sounding belly laughter; world of the people who are not too good or fine or proud or precious for the world's coarse uses; world of the sons who are as their fathers were before them, and are compacted of man's base, common, stinking clay of fury, blood, and sweat and agony—and must rise or fall out of the world from which they came, sink or swim, survive or perish, live, die, conquer, find alone their way, be baffled, beaten, grow furious, drunken, desperate, mad, lie smashed and battered in the stews, find a door, a dwelling place of warmth and love and strong security, or be driven famished, unassuaged, and furious through the world until they die!

Last of all, it is the world of the true friends, the fine, strong boys who can smack a ball and climb a tree, and are always on the lookout for the thrill and menace of adventure. They are the brave, free, joyful, hope-inspiring fellows who are not too nice and dainty and who have no sneers. Their names are such wonderful, open-sounding names as John, Jim, Robert, Joe, and Tom. Their names are William, Henry, George, Ben, Edward, Lee, Hugh, Richard, Arthur, Jack! Their names are the names of the straight eye and the calm and level glance, names of the thrown ball, the crack of the bat, the driven hit; names of wild, jubilant, and secret darkness, brooding, prowling, wild, exultant night, the wailing whistle and the great wheels pounding at the river's edge.

They are the names of hope, the names of love, friendship, confidence, and courage, the names of life that will prevail and will not be beaten by the names of desolation, the hopeless, sneering, death-loving, and life-hating names of old scornmaker's pride—the hateful and accursed names that the boys who live in the western part of town possess.

Finally, they are the rich, unusual names, the strange, yet homely, sturdy names—the names of George Josiah Webber and Nebraska Crane.

Nebraska Crane was walking down the street upon the other side. He was bare-headed, his shock of Indian coarse black hair standing out, his shirt was opened at his strong, lean neck, his square brown face was tanned and flushed with recent effort. From the big pocket of his pants the thick black fingers of a fielder's mitt protruded, and upon his shoulder he was carrying a well-worn ash-wood bat, of which the handle was wound round tight with tape. He came marching along at his strong and even stride, his bat upon his shoulder, as steady and as unperturbed as a soldier, and, as he passed, he turned his fearless face upon the boy across the street—looked at him with his black-eyed Indian look, and, without raising his voice, said quietly in a tone instinct with quiet friendliness:

"Hi, Monk!"

And the boy who lay there in the grass, his face supported in his hands, responded without moving, in the same toneless, friendly way:

"Hello, Bras."

Nebraska Crane marched on down the street, turned into the alley by his house, marched down it, turned the corner of his house, and so was lost from sight.

And the boy who lay on his belly in the grass continued to look out quietly from the supporting prop of his cupped hands. But a feeling of certitude and comfort, of warmth and confidence and quiet joy, had filled his heart, as it always did when Nebraska Crane passed his house at three o'clock.

The boy lay on his belly in the young and tender grass. Jerry Alsop, aged sixteen, fat and priestly, his belly buttoned in blue serge, went down along the other side of the street. He was a grave and quiet little figure, well liked by the other boys, but he was always on the outer fringes of their life, always on the sidelines of their games, always an observer of their universe—a fat and quiet visitant, well-spoken, pleasant-voiced, compactly buttoned in the blue serge that he always wore. . . . There had been one night of awful searching, one hour when all the torment and the anguish in that small, fat life had flared out in desperation. He had run away from home, and they had found him six hours later on the river road, down by the muddy little river, beside the place where all the other boys went to swim, the one hole deep enough to drown. His mother came and took him by the hand; he turned and looked at her, and then the two fell sobbing in each other's arms. . . . For all the rest, he had been a quiet and studious boy, well thought of in the town. Jerry's father was a dry goods merchant, and the family was comfortably off in a modest way. Jerry had a good mind, a prodigious memory for what he read, all things in books came smoothly to him. He would finish high school next year. . . .

Jerry Alsop passed on down the street.

Suddenly, the Webber boy heard voices in the street. He turned his head and looked, but even before he turned his head his ear had told him, a cold, dry tightening of his heart, an acrid dryness on his lips, a cold, dry loathing in his blood, had told him who they were.

Four boys were coming down the street in raffish guise; advancing scattered and disorderly, now scampering sideways, chasing, tussling in lewd horseplay with each other, smacking each other with wet towels across the buttocks (they had just come from swimming in Jim Rheinhardt's cow pond in the Cove), filling the quiet street with the intrusions of their raucous voices, taking the sun and joy and singing from the day.

They slammed yard gates and vaulted fences; they dodged round trees, ducked warily behind telephone poles, chased each other back and forth, gripped briefly, struggling strenuously, showed off to each other, making raucous noises, uttering mirthless gibes. One chased another around a tree, was deftly tripped, fell sprawling to the roar of their derision, rose red and angry in the face, trying mirthlessly to smile, hurled his wet, wadded towel at the one who tripped him—missed and was derided, picked his towel up, and to save his ugly face and turn derision from him cried out—"Pee-e-nuts!"—loudly passing Pennock's house.

The boy surveyed them with cold loathing—this was wit!

They filled that pleasant street with raucous gibes, and they took hope and peace and brightness from the day. They were unwholesome roisterers, they did not move ahead in comradeship, but scampered lewdly, raggedly around, as raucous, hoarse, and mirthless as a gob of phlegm; there was no warmth, no joy or hope or pleasantness in them; they filled the pleasant street with brutal insolence. They came from the west side of town, he knew them instinctively for what they were—the creatures of a joyless insolence, the bearers of the hated names.

Thus Sidney Purtle, a tall, lean fellow, aged fifteen, and everything about him pale—pale eyes, pale features, pale lank hair, pale eyebrows and a long, pale nose, pale lips and mouth carved always in a pale and ugly sneer, pale hands, pale hair upon his face, pale freckles, and a pale, sneering, and envenomed soul:

"Georgeous the Porgeous!" A pale sneer, a palely sneering laugh; and as he spoke the words he smacked outward with his wet and loathsome rag of towel. The boy ducked it and arose.

Carl Hooton stood surveying him—a brutal, stocky figure, brutal legs outspread, red-skinned, red-handed, and red-eyed, red-eyebrowed, and an inch of brutal brow beneath the flaming thatch of coarse red hair:

"Well, as I live and breathe," he sneered (the others smirked appreciation of this flaming wit), "it's little Jocko the Webber, ain't it?"

"Jockus the Cockus," said Sid Purtle softly, horribly—and smacked the wet towel briefly at the boy's bare leg.

"Jockus the Cockus—hell!" said Carl Hooton with a sneer, and for a moment more looked at the boy with brutal and derisory contempt. "Son, you ain't *nothin'*," he went on with heavy emphasis, now turning to address his fellows—"Why that little monk-faced squirrel's—they ain't even dropped yet."

Loud appreciative laughter followed on this sally; the boy stood there flushed, resentful, staring at them, saying nothing. Sid Purtle moved closer to him, his pale eyes narrowed ominously to slits.

"Is that right, Monkus?" he said, with a hateful and confiding quietness. A burble of unwholesome laughter played briefly in his throat, but he summoned sober features, and said quietly, with menacing demand: "Is that right, or not? Have they fallen yet?"

"Sid, Sid," whispered Harry Nast, plucking at his companion's sleeve; a snicker of furtive mirth crossed his rat-sharp features. "Let's find out how well he's hung."

They laughed, and Sidney Purtle said:

"Are you hung well, Monkus?" Turning to his comrades, he said gravely, "Shall we find out how much he's got, boys?"

And suddenly alive with eagerness and mirthful cruelty, they all pressed closer in around the boy, with secret, unclean laughter, saying:

"Yes, yes—come on, let's do it! Let's find out how much he's got!"

"Young Monkus," said Sid Purtle gravely, putting a restraining hand upon his victim's arm, "much as it pains us all, we're goin' to examine you."

"Let go of me!" The boy wrenched free, turned, whirled, backed up against the tree; the pack pressed closer, leering faces thrusting forward, pale, hateful eyes smeared with the slime of all their foul and secret jubilation. His breath was coming hoarsely, and he said: "I told you to let go of me!"

"Young Monkus," said Sid Purtle gravely, in a tone of quiet reproof, wherein the dogs of an obscene and jeering mirth were faintly howling—"Young Monkus, we're surprised at you! We had expected you to behave like a little gentleman—to take your medicine like a little man. . . . Boys!"

He turned, addressing copemates in a tone of solemn admonition, grave surprise: "It seems the little Monkus is trying to get hard with us. Do you think we should take steps?"

"Yes, yes," the others eagerly replied, and pressed still closer round the tree.

And for a moment there was an evil, jubilantly attentive silence as they looked at him, naught but the dry, hard pounding of his heart, his quick, hard breathing, as they looked at him. Then Victor Munson moved forward slowly, his thick, short hand extended, the heavy volutes of his proud, swart nostrils swelling with scorn. And his voice, low-toned and sneering, cajoling with a hateful mockery, came closer to him coaxingly, and said:

"Come, Monkus! Come little Monkus! Lie down and take your medicine, little Monk! . . . Here Jocko! Come Jocko! Here Jocko! Come Jocko!—Come and get your peanuts—Jock, Jock, Jock!"

Then while they joined in hateful laughter, Victor Munson moved forward again, the swart, stub fingers, warted on the back, closed down upon the boy's left arm; and suddenly he drew in his breath in blind, blank horror and in bitter agony, he knew that he must die and never draw his shameful breath in quietude and peace, or have a moment's hope of heartful ease again; something blurred and darkened in blind eyes—he wrenched free from the swart, stub fingers, and he struck.

The blind blow landed in the thick, swart neck and sent it gurgling backwards. Sharp hatred crossed his vision now, and so enlightened it; he licked his lips and tasted bitterness, and, sobbing in his throat, he started towards the hated face. His arms were pinioned from behind. Sid Purtle had him, the hateful voice was saying with a menacing and now really baleful quietude:

"Now, wait a minute! Wait a minute, boys! . . . We were just playin' with him, weren't we, and he started to get hard with us! . . . Ain't that right?"

"That's right, Sid. That's the way it was, all right!"

"We thought he was a man, but he turns out to be just a little sorehead, don't he? We were just kiddin' him along, and he has to go and get sore about it. You couldn't take it like a man, could you?" said Sidney Purtle, quietly and ominously into the ear of his prisoner; at the same time he shook the boy a little— "You're just a little cry-baby, ain't you? You're just a coward, who has to hit a fellow when he ain't lookin'?"

"You turn loose of me," the captive panted, "I'll show you who's the cry-baby! I'll show you if I have to hit him when he isn't looking!"

"Is that so, son?" said Victor Munson, breathing hard.

"Yes, that's so, son!" the other answered bitterly.

"Who says it's so, son?"

"I say it's so, son!"

"Well, you don't need to go gettin' on your head about it!"

"I'm not the one who's getting on his head about it; you are!"

"Is that so?"

"Yes, that's so!"

There was a pause of labored breathing and contorted lips; the acrid taste of loathing and the poisonous constrictions of brute fear, a sense of dizziness about the head, a kind of hollow numbness in the stomach pit, knee sockets gone a trifle watery; all of the gold of just a while ago gone now, all of the singing and the green; no color now, a poisonous whiteness in the very quality of light, a kind of poisonous intensity of focus everywhere; the two antagonists' faces suddenly keen, eyes sharp with eager cruelty, pack-appetites awakened, murder-sharp now, lusts aware.

"You'd better not be gettin' big about it," said Victor Munson slowly, breathing heavily, "or somebody'll smack you down!"

"You know anyone who's going to do it?"

"Maybe I do and maybe I don't, I'm not sayin'. It's none of your business."

"It's none of your business either!"

"Maybe," said Victor Munson, breathing swarthily, and edging forward an inch or so— "Maybe I'll make it some of my business!"

"You're not the only one who can make it your business!"

"You know of anyone who wants to make it anything?"

"Maybe I do and maybe I don't."

"Do you say that you do?"

"Maybe I do and maybe I don't. I don't back down from saying it."

"Boys, boys," said Sidney Purtle, quietly, mockingly. "You're gettin' hard with each other. You're usin' harsh language to each other. The first thing you know you'll be gettin' into trouble with each other—about Christmas time," he jeered quietly.

"If he wants to make anything out of it," said Victor Munson bitterly, "he knows what he can do."

"You know what you can do, too!"

"Boys, boys," jeered Sidney Purtle softly.

"Fight! Fight!" said Harry Nast, and snickered furtively. "When is the big fight gonna begin?"

"Hell!" said Carl Hooton coarsely, "they don't want to fight. They're both so scared already they're ready to —— in their pants. Do you want to fight, Munson?" he said softly, brutally, coming close and menacing behind the other boy.

"If he wants to make something out of it—" the Munson boy began again.

"Well, then, make it!" cried Carl Hooton, with a brutal laugh, and at the same moment gave the Munson boy a violent shove that sent him hurtling forward against the pinioned form of his antagonist. Sid Purtle sent his captive hurtling forward at the Munson boy; in a second more, they were crouching toe to toe, and circling round each other. Sid Purtle's voice could be heard saying quietly:

"If they want to fight it out, leave 'em alone! Stand back and give 'em room!"

"Wait a minute!"

The words were spoken almost tonelessly, but they carried in them such a weight of quiet and inflexible command that instantly all the boys stopped and turned with startled surprise, to see where they came from.

Nebraska Crane, his bat upon his shoulder, was advancing towards them from across the street. He came on steadily, neither quickening nor changing his stride, his face expressionless, his black Indian gaze fixed steadily upon them.

"Wait a minute!" he repeated as he came up.

"What's the matter?" Sidney Purtle answered, with a semblance of surprise.

"You leave Monk alone," Nebraska Crane replied.

"What've we done?" Sid Purtle said, with a fine show of innocence.

"I saw you," said Nebraska with toneless stubbornness, "all four of you ganged up on him; now leave him be."

"Leave him *be*?" Sid Purtle now protested.

"You heard me!"

Carl Hooton, more brutal and courageous and less cautious than Sid Purtle, now broke in truculently:

"What's it to you? What business is it of yours what we do?"

"I make it my business," Nebraska answered calmly. "Monk," he went on, "you come over here with me."

Carl Hooton stepped before the Webber boy and said:

"What right have you to tell us what to do?"

"Get out of the way," Nebraska said.

"Who's gonna make me?" said Carl Hooton, edging forward belligerently.

"Carl, Carl—come on," said Sid Purtle in a low, warning tone. "Don't pay any attention to him. If he wants to get on his head about it, leave him be."

There were low, warning murmurs from the other boys.

"The rest of you can back down if you like," Carl Hooton answered, "but I'm not takin' any backwash from him. Just because his old man is a policeman, he thinks he's hard. Well, I can get hard, too, if he gets hard with me."

"You heard what I told you!" Nebraska said. "Get out of the way!"

"You go to hell!" Carl Hooton answered. "I'll do as I damn please!"

Nebraska Crane swung solidly from the shoulders with his baseball bat and knocked the red-haired fellow sprawling. It was a crushing blow, so toneless, steady, and impassive in its deliberation that the boys turned white with horror, confronted now with a murderous savagery of purpose they had not bargained for. It was obvious to all of them that the blow might have killed Carl Hooton had it landed on his head; it was equally and horribly evident that it would not have mattered to Nebraska Crane if he *had* killed Carl Hooton. His black eyes shone like agate in his head, the Cherokee in him had been awakened, he was set to kill. As it was, the blow had landed with the sickening thud of ash-wood on man's living flesh, upon Carl Hooton's arm; the arm was numb from wrist to shoulder, and three frightened boys were now picking up the fourth, stunned, befuddled, badly frightened, not knowing whether a single bone had been left unbroken in his body, whether he was permanently maimed, or whether he would live to walk again.

"Carl—Carl—are you hurt bad? How's your arm?" said Sidney Purtle.

"I think it's broken," groaned that worthy, clutching the injured member with his other hand.

"You—you—you hit him with your bat," Sid Purtle whispered. "You—you had no right to do that."

"His arm may be broken," Harry Nast said, in an awed tone.

"I meant to break it," Nebraska said calmly. "He's lucky that I didn't break his God-damn head."

They looked at him with horrified astonishment, with a kind of fascinated awe.

"You—you could be arrested for doing that!" Sid Purtle blurted out. "You might have killed him!"

"Wouldn't have cared if I had!" Nebraska said firmly. "He ought to be killed! Meant to kill him!"

Their eyes were fixed on him in a stare wide with horror. He returned their look in Indian-wise, and moved forward a step, still holding his bat firm and ready at his shoulder.

"And I'll tell you this—and you can tell the rest of 'em when you get back to *your* side of town. Tell 'em I'm ready to brain the first West Side —— who comes here looking for trouble. And if any of you ever bother Monk again, I'll come right over there and climb your frame," Nebraska Crane asserted. "I'll come right over there and beat you to death. . . . Now you clear out! We don't want you on our street no longer! You get out of here!"

He advanced upon them slowly, his hard black eyes fixed firmly on them, his hands gripped ready on his bat. The frightened boys fell back, supporting their injured comrade, and, muttering furtively among themselves, limped hastily away down the street. At the corner they turned, and Sid Purtle put his hands up to his mouth and, with a sudden access of defiance, yelled back loudly:

"We'll get even with you yet! Wait till we get you over on our side of town!"

Nebraska Crane did not reply. He continued to stare steadily towards them with his Indian eyes, and in a moment more they turned and limped away around the corner and were lost from sight.

When they had gone, Nebraska took his bat off his shoulder, leaned gracefully on it, and, turning towards the white-faced boy, surveyed him for a moment with a calm and friendly look. His square brown face, splotched large with freckles, opened in a wide and homely smile; he grinned amiably and said:

"What's the trouble, Monkus? Were they about to get you down?"

"You—you—why, Nebraska!" the other boy now whispered—"you might have killed him with that bat."

"Why," Nebraska answered amiably, "what if I had?"

"Wuh—wuh—wouldn't you care?" young Webber whispered, awe-struck, his eyes still with wonder, horror, fascinated disbelief.

"Why, not a bit of it!" Nebraska heartily declared. "Good riddance to bad rubbish if I *had* killed him! Never liked that red-head of his'n, anyway, and don't like none of that crowd he runs with—that whole West Side gang! I've got no use for none of 'em, Monkus—never did have!"

"B-but, Bras," the other stammered, "wouldn't you be *afraid*?"

"Afraid? Afraid of what?"

"Why, why—that you might have killed him."

"Why, that's nothin' to be afraid of!" said Nebraska. "Anyone's likely to get killed, Monk. You're likely to have to kill someone almost *any* time! Why, look at my old man? He's been killin' people all his life—ever since he's been on the police force, anyway! I reckon he's killed more people than he could remember—he counted up to seven-teen one time, an' then he told me that there was one or two others he'd clean lost track of! Yes!" Nebraska continued triumphantly, "and there was one or two *before* he joined the force that no one ever knowed of— I reckon that was way back there when he was just a boy, so long ago he's plumb lost track of it! Why my old man had to kill a nigger here along—oh, just a week or so ago—and he never turned a hair! Came home to supper, an' took off his coat, hung up his gun and cottridge belt, washed his hands and set down at the table, and had got halfway through his supper before he even thought of it. Says to my maw, all of a sudden, says—'Oh, yes! I clean forgot to tell you! I had to shoot a nigger today!' 'That so?' my maw says. 'Is there any other news?' So they went on talkin' about first one thing and then another, and in five minutes' time I'll bet you both of them had forgotten clean about it! . . . Pshaw, Monk!" Nebraska Crane concluded heartily, "you oughtn't even to *bother* about things like that. Anyone's liable to have to kill someone. *That* happens every day!"

"Y-y-y-yes, Bras," Young Webber faltered—"b-b-but what if anything should happen to *you*?"

"Happen?" cried Nebraska, and looked at his young friend with frank surprise. "Why what's goin' to happen to you, Monk?"

"W-w-why—I was thinking that sometimes *you* might be the one who gets killed *yourself.*"

"*Oh!*" Nebraska said, with a nod of understanding, after a moment's puzzled cogitation. "That's what you mean! Why, yes, Monk, that *does* sometimes happen! But," he earnestly continued, "it's got no *right* to happen! You ought not to *let* it happen! If it happens it's your own fault!"

"*L-l-let! Fault!* How do you mean, Bras?"

"Why," Nebraska said patiently, but with just a shade of resignation, "I mean it won't happen to you if you're *careful.*"

"*C-c-careful?* How do you mean careful, Bras?"

"Why, Monk," Nebraska now spoke with a gruff, though kind, impatience, "I mean if you're careful not to *let* yourself be killed! Look at my old man, now!" he proceeded with triumphant logic— "Here he's been killin' people in one way or 'nother goin' on to thirty years now—leastways way before both you an' *me* was born! An' he's never been killed his-self *one* time!" he triumphantly concluded. "And *why?* Why, Monk, because my old man always took good care to kill the other feller before the other feller could kill him. As long as you do *that*, you'll be all right."

"Y-y-yes, Bras. But if you g-g-get yourself in trouble?"

"Trouble?" said Nebraska, staring blankly. "Why what trouble is there to get into? If *you* kill the other feller before he kills you, *he's* the one who gets in trouble. *You're* all right; I thought *anyone* could see that much!"

"Y-y-yes, Bras. I do see that. But I was thinking about getting arrested . . . and being locked up . . . and having to go to jail—that kind of trouble."

"Oh, *that* kind of trouble!" Nebraska said a little blankly, and considered the question for a moment. "Well, Monk, if you get arrested, you get *arrested*—and that's all there is to that! Why, pshaw, boy— *anyone* can get arrested; that's likely to happen to anybody. My old man's been arrestin' people all his life. I reckon he wouldn't have any notion how many people he's arrested and locked up! . . . Why yes, and he's even been arrested and locked up a few times himself, but he never let that bother him a *bit.*"

"F-f-for *what*, Bras? What did he get arrested for?"

"Oh—for killin' people, an' doin' things like that! You know how it is, Monk. Sometimes the relatives or neighbors, or the wives and chil-

dren of people that he killed would raise a rumpus—say he didn't have
no right to kill 'em—some such stuff as that! But it always come out
all right—it always *does!*" cried Nebraska earnestly. "And why? Why
because, like the old man says, this is America, an' we're a *free* country—an' if someone gets in your way an' bothers you, you have to kill
him—an' that's all there is to it! . . . If you have to go to court an'
stand trial, you go to court an' stand trial. Of course, it's a lot of trouble
an' takes up your time—but then the jury lets you off, an' that's all
there is to it! . . . I know my old man always says that this is the only
country in the world where the poor man has a chance! In Europe he
wouldn't have the chance a snowball has in hell! And why? Why because, as my old man says, in Europe the laws are all made for the rich,
a poor man never can get justice *there*—what justice there *is* is all for
the kings an' dukes an' lords an' ladies, an' such people as that. But a
poor man—why, Monk," Nebraska said impressively, "if a poor man in
Europe went an' killed a man, almost anything might happen to him—
that's just how rotten an' corrupt the whole thing is over there. You
ask my old man about it sometime! He'll tell you! . . . But, pshaw,
boy!" he now continued, with a resumption of his former friendly and
good-humored casualness, "you got nothing in the world to worry
about! If any of that West Side gang comes back an' tries to bother you,
you let *me* know, and I'll take care of 'em! If we've got to kill someone, we'll have to kill someone—but you oughtn't even to let it worry
you! . . . And now, so long, Monk! You let *me* know if anything
turns up and I'll take care of it!"

"Th-thanks, Bras! I sure appreciate . . ."

"Pshaw, boy! Forget about it! We got to stick together on *our* side of
town. We're neighbors! You'd do the same for me, I knew *that!*"

"Y-yes, I would, Bras. Well, good-bye."

"Good-bye, Monk. I'll be seein' you 'fore long."

And quiet, steady, unperturbed, moving along at even steps, his
calm, brave face and Indian eyes fixed forward, his baseball bat held
firmly on his shoulder, the Cherokee boy moved off, turned right into
his alley, and was lost from sight.

Nebraska Crane was the best boy in the town, but Sid Purtle was
poor white trash and a mountain grill. If Sid Purtle had been any good,

his people never would have named him Sid. George Webber's uncle had said that they were nothing but mountain grills no matter if they did live out upon Montgomery Avenue on the West Side of town; that's all that they had been to start with, that's what he called them, and that's what they were, all right. Sid! That was a fine name, now! A rotten, dirty, sneering, treacherous, snot-nosed, blear-eyed, bitch of a name! Other rotten sneering names were Guy, Clarence, Roy, Harry, Victor, Carl, and Floyd.

Boys who had these names were never any good—a thin-lipped, sneer-mouthed, freckled, blear-eyed set of hair-faced louts, who had unpleasant knuckly hands, and a dry, evil, juiceless kind of skin. There was always something jeering, ugly, unwholesome, smug, complacent, and triumphant about these people. Without knowing why, he always wanted to smash them in the face, and not only hated everything about them, but he hated the "very ground they walked on," the houses they lived in, the streets on which they lived, the part of town they came from, together with their fathers, mothers, sisters, brothers, cousins, aunts, and close companions.

He felt that they were not only foully different from the people that he liked in all the qualities that make for warmth, joy, happiness, affection, friendship, and the green-gold magic of enchanted weather—he felt there was also in them a physical difference, so foul and hateful that they might be creatures of another species. In blood, bone, brains, white-haired, juiceless-looking flesh, in sinew, joint, and tissue, in the very spittle of their mouths—which would be a vilely ropy, glutinously murky stuff of the very quality of their blear eyes and their sneering lips—as well as in all the delicate combining nerves, veins, jellies, cements, and fibrous webs that go to knit that marvelous tenement, that whole integument of life that is a human body, these people whose very names he hated would be found to be made of a vile, base, incalculably evil stuff. It was a substance that was as different from the glorious stuff of which the people that he liked were made as a foul excrement of fecal matter from the health and relish of sound, wholesome, life-begetting food. It was a substance not only of the mind and spirit but of the very texture of the body, so that it seemed they had been begot from acid and envenomed loins, and nurtured all their lives on nameless and abominable rations. He could not have eaten of the food their mothers cooked for them without choking and retching at each mouthful, feeling that he was swallowing some filth or foulness with every bite he took.

And yet, they seemed to score an evil and unfathomable triumph everywhere he met them. It was a triumph of death over life; of sneering mockery and ridicule over gaiety, warmth, and friendly ease; of wretchedness, pain, and misery over all the powerful music of joy; of the bad, sterile, and envenomed life over the good life of hope, happiness, and the glorious belief and certitude of love.

They were the dwellers in accursed streets, the very bricks of which you hated so you had to fight your way along each grim step of the hated pavement. They were the walkers underneath accursed skies, who evilly rejoiced in the broad, wet, wintry lights of waning March, and in all the cruel, houseless, hopeless, viscous, soul-engulfing lights and weathers of misery, weariness, and desolation.

They were the people that you never met in all the green-gold magic of enchanted weather. They were the accursed race who never came to you in places where strong joy was—in sorceries of gladed green by broken, rock-cold waters starred by the poignant and intolerable enchantments of the dandelions. No! They were the bathers in the humid, shadeless waters where the soul sank down. They came to no encircled pools of greenery; the brave shout was not in them, and they sang no songs.

In a thousand barren and desolate places, a thousand lights and weathers of the soul's grey horror, in the brutal, weary heat of August in raw concrete places, or across rude paths of gluey clay beneath the desolate wintry reds of waning Sunday afternoons in March, they moved forever with the triumphant immunity of their evil lives. They breathed without weariness, agony, or despair of soul an accursed air from which your own life recoiled with a shuddering revulsion; they sneered at you forever while you drowned.

They were the vultures of the world, who swoop forever over stricken fields, and, with an evil and unfailing prescience of woe, they always come upon you at your life's worst hour. If your bowels were wretched, queasy, sick, and diarrheic; if your limbs were feverish, feeble, watery, and sick; your skin, dry, loose, and itchy; your stomach retching with disgusting nausea, your eyes running, your nose leaking snottily, and your guts stuffed full of the thick, grey, viscous misery of a cold—then, certain as death and daylight they would be there, gloating on your wretchedness with the evil and triumphant superiority of their sneering faces.

Similarly, if the grey and humid skies of desolation pressed down upon your spirit; if the broad, wet lights of shame were eating nakedly into your unhoused, unwalled, unprotected flesh; if the nameless and intolerable fear—huge, soft, grey, and shapeless—was pressing at you from the immense and planetary vacancy of timeless skies; if grey horror drowned you, and every sinew, power, exultant strength and soaring music of your life, together with the powerful, delicate, and uncountable fabric of the nerves lay snarled, palsied, and unedged, leaving you stricken, wrecked, impotent, and shuddering in the hideous shipwreck of your energies: then they, *they*—Sid, Carl, Guy, Harry, Floyd, Clarence, Victor, Roy, that damned, vile, sneering horde of evil-loving, pain-devouring, life-destroying names—would be there certain as a curse, to dip their dripping beaks into your heart, to feed triumphant on your sorrow while you strangled like a mad dog in your wretchedness, and died!

And oh! to die so, drown so, choke and strangle, bleed so wretchedly to death—and die! die! die! in horror and in misery, untended and unfriended by these ghouls of death! Oh, death could be triumphant—death in battle, death in love, death in friendship and in peril, could be glorious if it were proud death, gaunt death, lean, lonely, tender, loving, and heroic death, who bent to touch his chosen son with mercy, love, and pity, and put the seal of honor on him when he died!

Yes, death could be triumphant! Death could come sublimely if it came when the great people of the living names were with you. Heroic fellowship of friendship, joy, and love, their names were John, George, William, Oliver, and Jack; their names were Henry, Richard, Thomas, James, and Hugh; their names were Edward, Joseph, Andrew, Emerson, and Mark! Their names were George Josiah Webber and Nebraska Crane!

The proud, plain music of their names itself was anthem for their glorious lives, and spoke triumphantly to him of the warmth, the joy, the certitude and faith of that heroic brotherhood. It spoke to him of great deeds done and mighty works accomplished, of glorious death in battle, and a triumph over death himself if only they were there to see him greet him when he came. Then might he say to them, with an exultant cry: "Oh brothers, friends, and comrades, dear rivals with me in the fellowship of glorious deeds, how dearly I have loved my life with you! How I have been your friendly rival and your equal in all things! How proudly and sublimely have I lived!—Now see how proudly and sublimely I can die!"

To die so, in this fellowship of life, would be glory, joy, and triumphant death for any man! But to die wretchedly and miserably, unfed, famished, unassuaged; to die with queasy guts and running bowels, a dry skin, feeble limbs, a nauseous and constricted heart; to die with rheumy eyes, and reddened, running nostrils; to die defeated, hopeless, unfulfilled, your talents wasted, your powers misused, unstruck, palsied, come to naught—the thought of it was not to be endured, and he swore that death itself would die before he came to it.

To die there like a dull, defeated slave in that ghoulish death-triumphant audience of Sid, Roy, Harry, Victor, Carl, and Guy!—to die defeated with those sneering visages of scornmaker's pride upon you, yielding to that obscene company of death-in-life its foul, final victory—oh, it was intolerable, intolerable! Horror and hatred gripped him when he thought of it, and he swore that he would make his life prevail, beat them with the weapons of certitude, nail their grisly hides upon the wall with the shining and incontrovertible nails of joy and magic, make their sneering mouths eat crow, and put the victorious foot of life upon the proud, bowed neck of scorn and misery forever.

Nebraska Crane was a fellow that he liked. That was a queer name, sure enough, but there was also something good about it. It was a square, thick, muscular, brawny, browned and freckled, wholesome kind of name, plain as an old shoe and afraid of nothing, and yet it had some strangeness in it, too. And that was the kind of boy Nebraska Crane was.

Nebraska's father had been a policeman, was now a captain on the force; he came from back in Zebulon County; he had some Cherokee in him. Mr. Crane knew everything; there was nothing that he could not do. If the sun came out the fourteenth day of March, he could tell you what it meant, and whether the sun would shine in April. If it rained or snowed or hailed or stormed three weeks before Easter, he could prophesy the weather Easter Sunday. He could look at the sky and tell you what was coming; if an early frost was on its way to kill the peach trees, he could tell you it was on its way and when it would arrive; there was no storm, no sudden shift in weather that he could not "feel in his bones" before it came. He had a thousand signs and symptoms for foretelling things like these—the look of the moon or the look of a cloud, the feel of the air or the direction of the wind, the appearance of the earliest bird, the half-appearance of the first blade of grass. He could feel storm coming, and could smell the thunder. It all amounted to a kind of great sixth sense out of nature, an almost supernatural intuition. In addition to—or as a consequence of—all these things, Mr. Crane raised the finest vegetables of anyone in town—the largest, perfectest tomatoes, the biggest potatoes, the finest peas and greens and onions, the most luscious strawberries, the most beautiful flowers.

He was, as may be seen, a figure of some importance in the community, not only as a captain of police, but as a sort of local prophet. The newspaper was constantly interviewing him about all kinds of things—changes in weather, prospects for a cold Winter, a hot Summer, or a killing frost, a state of drought, or an excess of rain. He always had an answer ready, and he rarely failed.

Finally—and this, of course, made his person memorably heroic to the boys—he had at one time in his life been a professional wrestler (a good one too; at one time, it was said, "the champion of the South"), and although he was now approaching fifty, he occasionally consented to appear in local contests, and give an exhibition of his prowess. There had been one thrilling Winter, just a year or two before, when Mr. Crane, during the course of a season, had met a whole series of sinister antagonists—Masked Marvels, Hidden Menaces, Terrible Turks, Mighty Swedes, Demon Dummies, and all the rest of them.

George Webber remembered all of them; Nebraska had always taken him on passes which his father gave him. The thought of the very approach of these evenings was enough to put the younger boy into a fever of anticipation, a frenzy of apprehension, an agonized unrest. He could not understand how Mr. Crane or Nebraska could face one of these occasions, with all of its terrible moments of conflict, victory or defeat, injury or mutilation, broken bones or fractured ligaments, with no more perturbation than they would show when sitting down to eat their evening meal.

And yet it was true! These people—son and father both—seemed to have come straight from the heart of immutable and unperturbed nature. Warmth they had, staunch friendliness, and the capacity for savage passion, ruthless murder. But they had no more terror than a mountain. Nerve they had, steel nerve; but as for the cold anguish of the aching and constricted pulse, the dry, hard ache and tightness of the throat, the hollow numbness of the stomach pit, the dizzy lightness of the head, the feeling of an unreal buoyancy before the moment of attack—they seemed to know no more about these things than if they had been made of oak!

Time after time on days when Mr. Crane was due to wrestle at the City Auditorium, the boy had watched him pass the house. Time after time he had searched the policeman's square-cut face for signs of anguish or tension to see if the strange, hard features showed any sign of strain, if the square, hard jaw was grimly clenched, the hard eyes worried, if there were any signs of fear, disorder, apprehension in his step, his look, his tone, his movement, or his greeting. There was none. The policeman never varied by a jot. A powerful, somewhat shambling figure of a man, a little under six feet tall, with a thick neck, coarsely seamed and weathered with deep scorings, long arms, big hands, gorillalike shoulders, and a kind of shambling walk, a little baggy at the knees—a figure of an immense but rather worn power— he passed by in his somewhat slouchy uniform, seamed down the trouser-legs with stripes of gold, turned in at his house and mounted the front porch steps, with no more excitement than he would show on any other day of the week. And yet the male population of the whole town would be buzzing with excited speculation on the outcome of the match, and the hearts of boys would thud with apprehensive expecta- tion at the very thought of it.

Later on, when dark had come, a half hour or so before the time scheduled for the match, Mr. Crane would leave his house, bearing underneath his arm a bundle wrapped up in a newspaper, which con- tained his old wrestling trunks and shoes; and with the same deliberate, even, bag-kneed stride, turn his steps in the direction of the town and the City Auditorium—and, Great God! his approaching and now ter- ribly imminent encounter with the Bone-Crushing Swede, the Masked Marvel, or the Strangler Turk!

A few minutes later Nebraska would come by Monk's house and whistle piercingly; the Webber boy would rush out of the house and down the steps still gulping scalding coffee down his aching throat— and then the two of them would be off on their way to town!

What nights they were—the nights of smoke-smell, stillness, and the far-off barking of a dog, a fire of oak leaves at the corner, and the leaping fire-dance of the boys around it—great nights of the approaching contest of the wrestlers, the nights of frost and menace, joy and terror—and October!

Oh, how each step of the way to town was pounded out beneath the rhythm of the pounding heart! How tight the throat, how dry the mouth and lips! How could Nebraska walk on so steadily, and look so cool! Arrived before the Auditorium, and the press of people, the calcium glare of hard white lights, the excited babble of the voices. Then the inside, seats down front in the big, draughty, thrilling-looking place, the great curtain with "Asbestos" written on it, horseplay and loud-mouthed banter in the crowd, the shouts of raucous boys, catcalls at length, foot-stamping, imperative hand-clapping, the bare and thrilling anatomy of the roped-in square. At last the handlers, timekeepers, and referees; and last of all—the principals!

Oh, the thrill of it! The anguish and the joy of it—the terror and the threat of it—the dry-skinned, hot-eyed, fever-pounding pulse of it, the nerve-tight, bursting agony of it! In God's name, how could flesh endure it! And yet—there they were, the *fatal, fated,* soon-to-be-at-bitter-arm's-length *two* of them—and Mr. Crane as loose as ashes, as cold as a potato, patient as a dray-horse, and as excited as a bale of hay!

But in the other corner—hah, now! hisses, jeers, and catcalls for the likes of you!—the Masked Marvel sits and waits, in all the menaceful address and threat of villainous disguisement. Over his bullet head and squat gorilla-neck a kind of sinister sack of coarse black cloth has been pulled and laced and tied! It is a horrible black mask with baleful eye-slits through which the beady little eyes seem to glitter as hard and wicked as a rattlesnake's; the imprint of his flat and brutal features shows behind it, and yet all so weirdly, ominously concealed that he looks more like a hangman than anything else. He looks like some black-masked and evil-hooded thing that does the grim and secret bidding of the Inquisition or the Medici; he looks like him who came in darkness to the Tower for the two young princes; he looks like the Klu Klux Klan; he looks like Jack Ketch with a hood on; he looks like the guillotine where Sidney Carton was the twenty-third; he looks like the Red Death, Robespierre, and The Terror!

As he sits there, bent forward brutishly, his thick, short fingers haired upon the back, an old bathrobe thrown round his brutal shoulders, the crowd hoots him, and the small boys jeer! And yet there is alarmed apprehension in their very hoots and jeers, uneasy whisperings and speculations:

"Good God!" one man is saying in an awed and lowered tone, "look at that neck on him—it's like a bull!"

"For God's sake, take a look at those shoulders!" says another, "look at his arms! His wrists are thick as most men's legs! Look at those arms, Dick; they could choke a bear!"

Or, an awed whisper: "Damn! It looks as if John Crane is in for it!"

All eyes now turn uneasily to Mr. Crane. He sits there in his corner quietly, and a kind of old, worn, patient look is on him. He blinks and squints unconcernedly into the hard glare of the light above the ring, he rubs his big hand reflectively over the bald top of his head, scratches the side of his coarse, seamed neck. Someone shouts a greeting to him from the audience: he looks around with an air of slight surprise, surveys the crowd with eyes as calm and hard as agate, locates the person who has called to him, waves in brief greeting, then leans forward patiently on his knees again.

The referee crawls through the ropes upon the mat, converses learnedly across the ropes but too intimately for hearing with Dr. Ned Revere, compares notes with him, looks very wise and serious, at length calls the two gladiators, attended by their handlers, bucket carriers, towel swingers, seconds, and sponge throwers, to the center of the mat, admonishes them most earnestly, sends them to their corners—and the bout begins.

The two men go back to their corners, throw their battered bathrobes off their shoulders, limber up a time or two against the ropes, a bell clangs, they turn and face each other and come out.

They come out slowly, arms bear-wise, half extended, the paws outward, circling, crouching, crafty as two cats. Mr. Crane in wrestler's garb is even looser and more shambling than in uniform; everything about him sags a little, seems to slope downward with a kind of worn, immensely patient, slightly weary power. The big shoulders slope, the great chest muscles sag and slope, the legs sag at the knees, the old full-length wrestler's trunks are wrinkled and also sag a little; there are big, worn knee-pads for the work down on the mat, and they also have a worn and baggy, kangaroolike look.

Mr. Crane shuffles cautiously about, but the Masked Marvel shifts and circles rapidly; he prances back and forth upon his bulging legs that seem to be made of rubber; he crouches and looks deadly, he feints and leaps in for a hold, which Mr. Crane evades with a shuffling ease. The crowd cheers wildly! The Masked Marvel dives and misses, falls sprawling. Mr. Crane falls on him, gets a hammerlock; the Masked Marvel bridges with his stocky body, squirms out of it, locks Mr. Crane's thick neck with vicelike power; the big policeman flings his body backward, gets out of it, is thrown to the corner of the ring. The two men come to grips again—the house is mad!

Oh, the thrill of it! The fear and menace of it, the fierce, pulse-pounding joy and terror of it! The two-hour-long grunting, panting, sweating, wheezing, groaning length of it! The exultant jubilation of it when Mr. Crane came out on top; the dull, dead, hopeless misery when Mr. Crane was on the bottom! And above all the inhuman mystery, secrecy, and the sinister disguisement of it all!

What did it matter that the Terrible Turk was really just a muscular Assyrian from New Bedford, Massachusetts? What did it matter if the Demon Dummy was really a young helper in the roundhouse of the Southern Railway Company? What did it matter if all this sinister array of Bone-Crushing Swedes, Horrible Huns, Desperate Dagoes, and Gorilla Gobs were for the most part derived from the ranks of able-bodied plasterers from Knoxville, Tennessee, robust bakers from Hoboken, ex-house-painters from Hamtramck, Michigan, and retired cow-hands from Wyoming? Finally, what did it matter that this baleful-eyed executioner of a Masked Marvel was really only the young Greek who worked behind the counter at the Bijou Café for Ladies and Gents down by the railway depot? What did it matter that this fact was proved one night when the terrible black hood was torn off? It was a shock, of course, to realize that the Bone-Crushing Menace, the very sight of whom struck stark terror to the heart, was just a rather harmless and good-natured Greek who cooked hamburger sandwiches for railway hands. But when all was said and done, the thrill, the threat, the danger were the same!

To a boy of twelve they *were* mysteries, they were Marvels, they were Menaces and Terrors—and the man who dared to meet them was a hero. The man who met them without a flicker of the eye was a man of steel. The man who shambled out and came to grips with them—and heaved and tugged, escaped their toils, or grunted in their clutches for two hours—that man was a man of oak, afraid of nothing, and as enduring as a mountain. That man did not know what fear was—and his son was like him in all ways, and the best and bravest boy in town!

Nebraska Crane and his family were recent-comers to this part of town. Formerly, he had lived out in "the Doubleday Section"; perhaps this was one reason why he had no fear.

Doubleday was a part of the town where fellows named Reese and Dock and Ira lived. These were ugly names; the fellows carried knives in their pockets, had deadly, skull-smashing fights with rocks, and grew up to be hoboes, pool-room loafers, pimps and bullies living off a whore. They were big, loutish, hulking bruisers with bleared features, a loose, blurred smile, and yellowed fingers in which they constantly held the moist fag-end of a cigarette, putting it to their lips from time to time to draw in on it deeply with a hard, twisted mouth and lidded eyes, a general air of hardened and unclean debauchery as they flipped the cigarette away into the gutter. Then they would let the smoke trickle slowly, moistly from their nostrils—as if the great spongy bellows of the lungs was now stained humidly with its yellow taint—and then speak out of the sides of their mouths in hard, low, knowing tones of bored sophistication to their impressed companions.

These were the fellows who grew up and wore cheap-looking, flashy clothes, bright yellow, box-toed shoes, and loud-striped shirts, suggesting somehow an unwholesome blending of gaudy finery and bodily filth. At night and on Sunday afternoons, they hung around the corners of disreputable back streets, prowled furtively about in the dead hours of the night past all the cheap clothing stores, pawn shops, greasy little white-and-negro lunchrooms (with a partition down the middle), the pool rooms, the dingy little whore-hotels—the adepts of South Main Street, the denizens of the whole, grimy, furtive underworld of a small town's nighttime life.

They were the bruisers, brawlers, cutters, slashers, stabbers, shooters of a small town's life; they were the pool room thugs, the runners of blind tigers, the brothel guardians, the kept and pampered bullies of the whores. They were the tough town drivers with the thick red necks and leather leggins, and on Sunday, after a week of brawls, dives, stews, the stale, foul air of nighttime evil in the furtive places, they could be seen racing along the river road, out for a bawdy picnic with their whore. On Sunday afternoon they would drive along as brazen as you please beside the sensual, warm, and entrail-stirring smell, the fresh, half-rotten taint and slowness of the little river, that got in your bowels, heavy, numb, and secret, with a rending lust each time you smelled it. Then they would stop at length beside the road, get out, and take their woman up the hill into the bushes for an afternoon of dalliance underneath the laurel leaves, embedded in the thick green secrecies of a Southern growth that was itself as spermy, humid, hairy with desire, as the white flesh and heavy carnal nakedness of the whore.

These were the boys from Doubleday—the boys named Reese and Dock and Ira—the worst boys in the school. They were always older than the other boys, stayed in the same class several years, never passed their work, grinned with a loutish, jeering grin whenever the teachers upbraided them for indolence, stayed out for days at a time and were finally brought in by the truant officer, got into fist fights with the principal when he tried to whip them, and sometimes hit him in the eye, and at length were given up in despair, kicked out in disgrace when they were big brutes of sixteen or seventeen years, having never got beyond the fourth grade.

These were the boys who taught the foul words to the little boys, told about going to the whore houses, jeered at those who had not gone and said you could not call yourself a man until you had gone and "got yourself a little." Further, Reese McMurdie, who was sixteen, as big and strong as a man, and the worst boy in the school, said you couldn't call yourself a man until you'd caught a dose. He said he'd had his first one when he was fourteen years old, boasted that he'd had it several times since then, and said it was no worse than a bad cold. Reese McMurdie had a scar that turned your flesh sick when you looked at it; it ran the whole way from the right-hand corner of his mouth to the corner of his ear. He had got it in a knife-fight with another boy.

Ira Dingley was almost as bad as Reese. He was fifteen, not so big and heavy as the other boy, but built as solid as a bullock. He had a red, small, brutal kind of face, packed with energy and evil, and one little red eye that went glowering malignantly and truculently around at the whole world. He was blind in his other eye and wore a black shade over it.

One time, when there had been the great, jubilant shout of "Fight! Fight!" from the playing field at recess, and the boys had come running from all directions, Monk Webber had seen Ira Dingley and Reese McMurdie facing each other in the circle, edging closer truculently with fists clenched, until someone behind Reese had given him a hard shove that sent him hurtling into Ira. Ira was sent flying back into the crowd, but when he came out again, he came out slowly, crouched, his little red eye fixed and mad with hate, and this time he had the knife-blade open, naked, ready in his hand.

Reese, who had been smiling after he was pushed, with a foul, loose smile of jeering innocence, now smiled no more. He edged cautiously away and back as Ira came on, his hard eyes fixed upon his enemy, his thick hand fumbling in his trousers for the knife. And while he fumbled for his knife, he edged back slowly, talking with a sudden, quiet, murderous intensity that froze the heart:

"All right, you son-of-a-bitch!" he said, "Wait till I git my knife out!" Suddenly, the knife was out and open; it was an evil six-inch blade that opened on a spring. "If that's what you want, I'll cut your God-damned head off!"

And now all of the boys in the crowd were stunned, frightened, hypnotized by the murderous fascination of those two shining blades from which they could not take their eyes, and by the sight of the two boys, their faces white, contorted, mad with fear, despair, and hate, as they circled continuously around. The strong terror of their heavy breathing filled the air with menace, and communicated to the hearts of all the boys such a sense of horror, fascination, and frozen disbelief that they were unwilling to continue, afraid to intervene, and yet unable to move or wrench themselves away from the sudden, fatal, and murderous reality of the fight.

Then as the two boys came close together, Nebraska Crane suddenly stepped in, thrust them apart with a powerful movement, and at the same time said with a good-natured laugh, and in a rough, friendly, utterly natural tone of voice that instantly conquered everyone, restored all the boys to their senses and brought breath and strength back to the light of day again:

"You boys cut it out," he said. "If you want to fight, fight fair with your fists."

"What's it to you?" said Reese menacingly, edging in again with his knife held ready in his hand. "What right you got to come buttin' in? Who told you it was any business of yours?" All the time he kept edging closer with his knife held ready.

"No one told me," said Nebraska, in a voice that had lost all of its good nature and that was now as hard and unyielding in its quality as his tar-black eyes, which he held fixed, steady as a rifle, as his foe came on. "Do you want to make anything out of it?" he said.

Reese looked back at him for a moment, then his eyes shifted, and he sidled off and half withdrew, still waiting, unwilling to depart, muttering threats. In a moment the boys broke up in groups, dispersed, the enemies sidled uneasily away, each with his partisans, and the threatened fight was over. Nebraska Crane was the bravest boy in school. He was afraid of nothing.

Ira, Dock, and Reese! These were savage, foul, and bloody names, and yet there was a menaceful wild promise in them, too. World of the "mountain grills," the poor whites, the nameless, buried, hopeless atoms of the wilderness, their lives yet had a lawless, sinful freedom of their own. Their names evoked the wretched, scabrous world of slum-town rickets whence they came; a painful, haunting, anguished memory of the half-familiar, never-to-be-forgotten, white-trash universe of Stumptown, Pigtail Alley, Doubleday, Depot Street, and that foul shamble of a settlement called, for God knows what ironic reason, Strawberry Hill—that sprawled its labyrinthine confusion of unpaved, unnamed, miry streets and alleys and rickety shacks and houses along the scarred, clay-barren flanks of the hills that sloped down towards the railway district in the western part of town.

It was a place that Monk had seen only a few times in his whole life, but that always, then and forever, as long as he lived, would haunt him with the horrible strangeness and familiarity of a nightmare. For although that world of rickets was a part of his home town, it was a part so unfamiliar to all the life he knew the best that when he saw it first, he came upon it with a sense of grotesque discovery, and after he had gone from it he could hardly believe that it was there, and would think of it years later with a sense of pain and anguish, saying:

"Here is the town, and here the streets, and here the people—and all, save *that*, familiar as my father's face; all, save *that*, so near that we could touch it with our hand. All of it was ours in its remotest patterns—all save *that*, save *that*! How could we have lived there with it and beside it, and have known it so little? Was it really there?"

Yes, it was there—strangely, horribly there, never-to-be-forgotten, never wholly to be remembered or believed, haunting the soul forever with the foul naturalness of a loathsome dream. It was there, immutably, unbelievably there, and what was most strange and terrible about it was that he recognized it instantly—that world of Ira, Dock, and Reese—the first time that he saw it as a child; and even as his heart and bowels sickened with their nauseous disbelief of recognition, he knew it, lived it, breathed it utterly to the last remotest degradation of its horror.

And for that reason he hated it. For that reason, nausea, fear, disgust, and horror overwhelmed the natural sense of pity which that wretched life evoked. It haunted him the moment that he saw it with a sense of buried memory, loathsome rediscovery; and it seemed to him that, so far from being different from these people, he was of them, body and brain and blood to the last atom of his life, and had escaped from them only by some unwarranted miracle of chance, some hideous insecurity of fortune that might return him into the brutish filth and misery and ignorance and hopelessness of that lost world with the same crude fickleness by which he had escaped.

No birds sang in that barren world. Beneath its skies of weary desolation the cry of all-exultant joy, the powerful, swelling anthem of youth, certitude, and victory burst from no man's heart, rose with a wild and uncontrollable shout from no man's throat. In Summer the heat beat down upon that baked and barren hill, upon the wretched streets, and on all the dusty, shadeless roads and alleys of the slum, and there was no pity in the merciless revelations of the sun. It shone with a huge and brutal impassivity upon the hard red dirt and dust, on shack and hut and rotting tenement.

It shone with the same impartial cruelty on mangy, scabby, nameless dogs, and on a thousand mangy, scabby nameless little children— hideous little scarecrows with tow hair, their skinny little bodies un recognizably scurfed with filth and scarred with running sores, staring at one forever with gaunt, empty eyes as they grubbed in the baked dusty, beaten, grassless dirt before some dreary shack, or scrabbled wretchedly about, eaten by swarming flies, in the sun-stench of a little lean-to porch, the very planks of which were as dry, hard, baked, and wretched-looking as the beaten earth in which they merged.

And the sun shone also on the slattern women of the district, revealing them in all their foul unloveliness, their loathsome and inexplicable fecundities—the Lonies, Lizzies, Lotties, Lenas of the district, the Sals, the Molls, the Millies and Bernices—as well as on all their wretched little progeny of Iras, Docks, and Reeses, their Asas, Jeters, Greeleys, Zebs, and Roys. They stood there at the edge of a ramshackle porch, tall and gaunt and slatternly, while their grimy little tow-haired brats scrabbled wretchedly around the edges of their filthy, lop-edged skirts. They stood there, those foul, unlovely women, with their gaunt, staring faces, sunken eyes, toothless jaws, and corrupt, discolored mouths, rilled at the edges with a thin brown line of snuff.

They stood there like some hopeless, loveless, wretched drudge of nature, bearing about them constantly the unbroken progressions of their loathsome fertility. In their arms they held their latest, youngest, wretched little child, swaddled in filthy rags, and staring forth at one with its blue, drowned eyes, its peaked and grimy little face, its nostrils and its upper lip gummed thickly with two ropes of snot. And in their pregnant bellies, which they proposed from their gaunt, unlovely figures like some dropsical ripeness foully fructifying in the sun, they carried the last and most revolting evidence of the germinal sequence of maternity, which thus was odiously revealed in every stage of its disgusting continuity—from sagging breast to swollen womb and thence to the grimy litter of their filth-bespattered brats that crawled and scrabbled round their foul skirts on the porch. The idiot proliferations of blind nature which these wretched rakes and hags and harridans of women so nakedly and brutally revealed as they stood there stupidly proposing their foul, swollen bellies in the merciless and shameful light of the hot sun filled Monk with such a feeling of choking and wordless fury, loathing, and disgust that every natural emotion of pity and sorrow was drowned out below the powerful flood tide of revulsion, and his antagonism to the women and their wretched children was scarcely to be distinguished from blind hatred.

For pity, more than any other feeling, is a "learned" emotion; a child will have it least of all. Pity comes from the infinite accumulations of man's memory, from the anguish, pain, and suffering of life, from the full deposit of experience, from the forgotten faces, the lost men, and from the million strange and haunting visages of time. Pity comes upon the nick of time and stabs us like a knife. Its face is thin and dark and burning, and it has come before we know it, gone before we can grasp or capture it; it leaves a shrewd, deep wound, but a bitter, subtle one, and it always comes most keenly from a little thing.

It comes without a herald or a cause we can determine at some moment of our lives when we are far and lost from all the scenes that pity comes from; and how, why, where it comes we cannot say. But suddenly in the city—in the great and million-footed city—pity comes to us at evening when the dust and fury of another city day is over, and we lean upon the sills of evening in an ancient life. Then pity comes to us; we will remember children's voices of long ago, the free, full shout of sudden, gleeful laughter from a child that we once knew, full of exulting innocence, the songs that we sang on Summer porches long ago, a note of pride in our mother's voice and her grave, worn eyes of innocence as she boasted of a little thing, the simple words that a woman we once loved had said in some forgotten moment when she left us for another day.

Then pity is there, is there at once with its dark face and sudden knife, to stab us with an anguish that we cannot utter, to rend us with its agony of intolerable and wordless regret, to haunt us with the briefness of our days, and to tear our hearts with anguish and wild sorrow. And for what? For what? For all we want that never may be captured, for all we thirst for that never may be found. For love that must grow old and be forever dying, for all the bone, brain, passion, marrow, sinew of our lives, our hearts, our youth, that must grow old and bowed and barren, wearied out!

And oh! for beauty, that wild, strange song of magic, aching beauty, the intolerable, unutterable, ungraspable glory, power, and beauty of this world, this earth, this life, that is, and is everywhere around us, that we have seen and known at ten thousand moments of our lives, that has broken our hearts, maddened our brains, and torn the sinews of our lives asunder as we have lashed and driven savagely down the kaleidoscopic fury of the years in quest of it, unresting in our frenzied hope that some day we shall find it, hold it, fix it, make it ours forever— and that now haunts us strangely, sorrowfully, with its wild song and aching ecstasy as we lean upon the sills of evening in the city. We feel the sorrow and the hush of evening in the city, the voices, quiet, casual, lonely, of the people, far cries and broken sounds, and smell the sea, the harbor, and the huge, slow breathing of deserted docks, and know that there are ships there! And beauty swells like a wild song in our heart, beauty bursting like a great grape in our throat, beauty aching, rending, wordless, and unutterable, beauty in us, all around us, never to be captured—and we know that we are dying as the river flows!

Oh, then will pity come, strange, sudden pity with its shrewd knife and the asp of time to stab us with a thousand wordless, lost, forgotten, little things!

And how, where, why it came we cannot say, but we feel pity now for all men who have ever lived upon the earth, and it is night, now, night, and the great stars are flashing in the lilac dark, the great stars are flashing on a hundred million men across America, and it is night, now, night, and we are living, hoping, fearing, loving, dying in the darkness, while the great stars shine upon us as they have shone on all men dead and living on this earth, on all men yet unborn, and yet to live who will come after us!

Yet, when Monk looked at these foul, pregnant hags in slum-town's gulch and hill and hollow, he could feel no pity, but only loathing, sickness of the flesh, disgust and nameless fear and dread and horror, so overwhelming in their tidal flood that he looked upon the filth and misery of these people with a shuddering revulsion and hated them because of it. For joy, faith, hope, every swelling certitude of glory, love, and triumph youth can know went dead and sick and rotten in that foul place. In the casual, filthy, and incessant littering of these ever-pregnant hags was evident not a love for life, but a contempt and carelessness for it so vile and criminal that it spawned its brood of rickety, scabby, mangy, foredoomed brats as indifferently as a bitch might drop its litter, and with a murderous nonchalance and bestial passivity that made man less than dung and instantly destroyed every proud illusion of the priceless value, dignity, and sanctity of his individual life.

How had man been begotten? Why, they had got him between brutish snores at some random waking of their lust in the midwatches of the night! They had got him in a dirty corner back behind a door in the hideous unprivacy of these rickety wooden houses, begotten him standing in a fearful secrecy between apprehensive whisperings to make haste, lest some of the children hear! They had got him in some bestial sudden wakening of lust and hunger while turnip greens boiled with their humid fragrance on the stove! He had been begotten in some casual and forgotten moment which they had snatched out of their lives of filth, poverty, weariness, and labor, even as a beast will tear at chunks of meat; begotten in the crude, sudden, straddling gripe of a half-rape on the impulsion of a casual opportunity of lust; begotten instantly as they were flung back rudely on the edge of an untidy bed in the red waning light of some forgotten Saturday when work was done, the week's wages given, the week's brief breathing space of rest, repose, and brutal dalliance come! He had been begotten without love, without beauty, tenderness, magic, or any nobleness of spirit, by the idiot, blind hunger of a lust so vile that it knew no loathing for filth, stench, foulness, haggish ugliness, and asked for nothing better than a bag of guts in which to empty out the accumulations of its brutish energies.

The thought of it was not to be endured, and suddenly the boy cranes his neck, he grips his throat hard with his fingers, he squirms like something caught in a steel trap, a bestial grimace contracts his features—it is like drowning, drowning, not to be endured. The congress of their foul and bloody names—the loathsome company of these Iras, Docks and Reeses, the Jeters, Zebs and Greeleys of these poor-white slums—return to torment memory now with the white sear of horrible and instant recognition. Why? Because these people are the mountain people. These people are the poor-white litter of the hills. These people—Oh! it is intolerable, but true—these people came out of his mother's world, her life! He hears lost voices in the mountains long ago! They return to him from depths of sourceless memory, from places he has never viewed, from scenes that he has never visited—the whole deposit of inheritance, the lives and voices of lost people in the hills a hundred years ago.

They were a sharp-distinguished and strong-fibered people of his mother's stock, a race eccentric, powerful, thoughtful, honest, energetic—much better than this brutish and degraded kind. They were a race that lived upon the mountain slopes and river bottoms of old wild and rugged Zebulon; a kind that mined for mica in the hills, and hewed for tan-bark on the mountains; a kind that lived along a brawling mountain stream, and tilled the good land of the bottoms. It was a kind apart from these, hard-bitten in its pride, and hard-assured in its complacence, scornful in its own superiority, conceited, individual, strongly marked—but kinsman of this kind, as well.

He hears lost voices of his kinsmen in the mountains one hundred years before—and all as sad, faint, and remote as far-faint voices in a valley, all passing sad as a cloud shadow passing in the wilderness, all lonely, lost, and sad as strange, lost time. All hill-remote and lonely they come to him—the complacent, drawling voices of the death-triumphant Joyners long ago!

The vision changes, and again he sees the scar and squalor of the white-trash slum, the hill-man's rickets come to town—and it is night; there is a shrew's cry from the inner depth and darkness of some nameless house, lit only by the greasy, murky, and uneven light of a single lamp. It comes from scream and shout and curse, from drunken cry and stamping boot, from rancid flesh, fat pork, and rotting cabbage, and from his memory of a foul, sallow slut, gap-toothed, gaunt and shapeless as a pole—who stands there at the border of the rotting porch, her wisp of lank, unwashed hair screwed to a knot upon her head, proposing her pregnant belly for the fourteenth time.

Drowning! Drowning! Not to be endured! The abominable memory shrivels, shrinks, and withers up his heart in the cold constriction of its fear and loathing. The boy clutches at his throat, cranes with a livid face at the edges of his collar, draws one hand sharply up, and lifts his foot as if he has received a sudden, agonizing blow upon the kidneys. Less than his mother's stock he knows, far less in sense, mind, will, energy, and character—they yet have come from the same wilderness, the same darkness, the same nature from which his mother's people came—and their mark is on him, never to be changed—their taint is in him, never to be drawn out. Bone of their bone, blood of their blood, flesh of their flesh, by however various and remote a web, he is of them, they are in him, he is theirs—has seen, known, felt, and has distilled into his blood every wild passion, criminal desire, and rending lust they have known. And the blood of the murdered men, the rivers of blood of the murdered men which has soaked down quietly in the wilderness, which has soaked quietly away with all its million mute and secret tongues into the stern, the beautiful, the unyielding substance of the everlasting earth, is his, has stained his life, his flesh, his spirit, and is on his head as well as theirs!

And suddenly, like a man who is drowning and feels a rock beneath his feet; like a man lost, dying, freezing, famished, almost spent in the dark and howling desolation of the strange wilderness, who sees a light, comes suddenly upon a place of shelter, warmth, salvation, the boy's spirit turns and seizes on the image of his father. The image of his father's life, that image of decent order, gaunt cleanliness and dispatch, the image of warmth, abundance, passionate energy and joy, returns to the boy now with all that is beautiful and right in it, to save him, to heal him instantly, to restore him from the horror and abomination of that memory in which his spirit for a moment drowned.

And at the moment that he sees the huge salvation of his father's figure, he also sees his father's house, his life, the whole world that, he has made and shaped with his own single power, his unique color, his one soul. And instantly he sees as well his father's country, the land from which his father came, the beautiful, rich country which the boy has never seen with his own eyes, but which he has visited ten tousand times with his heart, his mind, his spirit, and man's ancient, buried, and inherited memory, until that country is as much a part of him as if he had been born there. It is the unknown land which all of us have known and have longed to find in youth. It is the undiscovered complement of all that we have seen and known, the lost half of our dark heart, the secret hunger, need, and magic working in our blood; and though we have not seen it, we recognize it instantly as the land we know the minute that we come to it.

And now, like an image of certitude, peace, joy, security, and abundance to restore his life out of the filth and shambles of that other vision, he sees his father's land. He sees the great red barns, the tidy houses, the thrift, the comfort, and the loveliness, the velvet pastures, meadows, fields, and orchards, the red-bronze soil, the nobly-swelling earth of southern Pennsylvania. And at the moment that he sees it, his spirit comes out of the brutal wilderness, his heart is whole and sound and full of hope again. There are new lands.

And at the same moment he sees the image of the brave companionship of Nebraska Crane. What is there to fear? What is there to fear on earth if Nebraska Crane is there? Nebraska stands there in his life like the image of that heroic integrity in life which cannot be touched or conquered, which is outside a man, and to which his own life must be united if he will be saved. So what is there to fear as long as Nebraska Crane—the free, the frank, the friendly, the fierce, the secret, and the unafraid—is there to show him with his life where he can go? What boys who live out on the West Side, for all their manners, customs, looks, and ways, for all their names and cunning stratagems, can he fear, as long as Nebraska Crane is there with him?

No—though they stood there massed against him in the whole concert of their hateful qualities, all the Sidneys, Roys, Carls, Victors, Guys, and Harrys of the earth—though he had to meet them on their own earth of red waning March and Sunday afternoons, what nameless and accursed horror can quench utterly the fearless light, the dark integrity of that fierce and lonely flame? He could breathe in their poisonous and lifeless air, stand houseless, naked, unprepared beneath their desolate skies—he could yet endure, meet them, beat them, carry the victorious power of his own world in his own life, and make exultant joy, all-conquering certitude, triumphant sense, and lusty love prevail forever above the wretchedness and scornful doubt of their own life-denying lives—if only Nebraska Crane were there to see him do it!

So the old wild joy of three o'clock has risen in his heart again—wordless, tongueless as a savage cry, with all its passion, pain, and ecstasy—and he sees the world, the East, the West, the lands and cities of the earth in triumph, for Nebraska Crane is there!

George Webber and Nebraska Crane! The splendid names flash in the sun, soar to the westward, wing together over the roof of the whole world, together back again, are there!

George Webber! George Josiah and Josiah George! Josiah George Nebraska Webber and Crane George!

"My name is George Josiah Webber!" cried the boy, and sprang erect.

"GEORGE JOSIAH WEBBER!"

The great name flashed then through the shining air; flashed, too, the great name to the flashing of the leaves; all of the maple leaves a-spangle with the proud flash of the great, proud name!

"GEORGE JOSIAH WEBBER!"

cried the boy again; and all the gold-proud afternoon was ringing with the sound; flashed, too, the aspen leaves, and flashed the honeysuckle hedge a-tremble; flashed, too, and bent each blade of velvet grass.

"My name is George Josiah Webber!"

Flashed the proud name to the brazen pounding of the courthouse bell; flashed, too, and rose and struck upon the ponderous, solemn strokes of three!

"ONE! . . . TWO! . . . THREE!"

And then upon the stroke the black boys came:

"Hi, Paul! . . . Hey, Paul! . . . How are you, Paul?" the black boys cried and flashed before him.

"My name is George Josiah Webber!" cried the boy.

Solemnly, in perfect line, the black boys wheeled, swept round platoon-wise, faultless in formation, and with spin-humming wheels rode slowly back in lines of eight, squads-righted perfectly, and, halting on their wheels in perfect order, with grave inquiry greeted him:

"How's ole Paul today?"

"My name," the boy said firmly, "is not Paul! My name is George!"

"Oh, no, it's not, Paul!" cried the black boys, grinning amiably. "Yo' name is *Paul*!"

It was a harmless mockery, some unknown and unknowledgeable jest, some secret, playful banter of their nigger soul. God knows what they meant by it. They could not have said themselves what made them call him by this name, but Paul he was to them, and every day at three o'clock, before the markets opened up again, the black boys came and flashed before him—called him *"Paul."*

And he contended stubbornly, would not give in, always insisted that his name was George, and somehow—God knows how!—the unyielding argument filled his heart with warmth, and delighted the black boys, too.

Each day at three o'clock he knew that they would come and call him "Paul," each day at three o'clock he waited for them, with warmth, with joy, with longing and affection, with a strange sense of ecstasy and magic, with fear they might not come. But each day at three o'clock, hard on the market's opening and the booming of the courthouse bell, the black boys came and flashed before him.

He knew that they would come. He knew they could not fail him. He knew that he delighted them, that they adored the look of him— the long-armed, big-handed, and flat-footed look of him. He knew that all his words and movements—his leaps and springs, his argument and stern insistence on his proper name—gave them an innocent and enormous pleasure. He knew, in short, that there was nothing but warm liking in their banter when they called him "Paul."

Each day, therefore, he waited on their coming—and they always came! They could not have failed him, they would have come if all hell had divided them. A little before three o'clock, each day of the week except Sundays, the black boys roused themselves from their siesta in the warm sun round the walls of the City Market, saying:

"It's time to go and see ole Paul!"

They roused themselves out of the pleasant reek of cod-heads rotting in the sun, decaying cabbage leaves and rotten oranges; they roused themselves from drowsy places in the sun, delicious apathy, from the depth and dark of all their African somnolence—and said:

"We got to go now! Ole Paul is waitin' for us! Stay with us, footses; we is on ouah way!"

And what a way it was! Oh, what a splendid, soaring, flashing, wing-like way! They came like streaks of ebon lightning; they came like ravens with a swallow-swoop; they came like shot out of a gun, and like a thunderbolt; they came like demons—but they came!

He heard them coming from afar, he heard them racing down the street, he heard the furious thrum of all their flashing wheels, and then they flashed before him, they were there! They shot past, eight abreast, bent over, pedaling like black demons; they shot past on their flashing wheels, the fibrous market baskets rattling lightly; and as they flashed before him, they cried "Paul!"

Then, wheeling solemnly in squadrons, they rode slowly, gravely back, and wheeled and faced him, steady and moveless on their wheels, and said, "Hi, Paul! . . . How's ole Paul today!"

Then the parade began. They did amazing things, performed astounding evolutions on their wheels; they flashed by in fours, and then by twos; they did squads-right, retreated or advanced in echelon, swooped past in single file like soaring birds, rode like demons soaring in the wind.

Then madness seized them, and desire for individual excellence, a lust for championship, wild inventiveness, whimsical caprice. They shouted with rich nigger laughter, howled derisory comments at their fellows, strove to outdo one another—to win applause and approbation—all for Paul! They swooped down the street with lightlike swiftness and a bullet speed; they swooped down in terrific spirals, snaking from one side to the other, missing curbs by hair-line fractions of an inch; they shot past, stooping like a cowboy from the saddle, and snatching up their ragged caps as they shot past. They shouted out to one another things like these:

"Outa my way, ole Liver Lips! I got somethin' dat I got to show to Paul!"

"Hey, Paul—look at ole Slewfoot ride dat wheel!"

"Move ovah deh, M'lasses! Let ole Paul look at someone who *can* ride!"

"Get outa my way, Big Niggah, 'fo' I rides all ovah you! I'm goin' to show Paul somethin' dat he nevah saw befo'!—How's dis one, Paul?"

And so they soared and swooped and flashed, their rich black voices calling back to him, their warm good voices bubbling with black laughter, crying, "Paul!"

And then they were off like furies riding for town and the reopening of the markets, and their rich, warm voices howled back to him with affectionate farewell:

"Good-bye, Paul!"

"So long, Paul."

"We'll be seein' you, Paul!"

"My name," he shouted after them, "is George Josiah Webber!"

Flashed and rose the splendid name as proud and shining as the day. And answered faintly, warm with pleasant mockery, upon the wind:

"Yo' name is Paul! Paul! Paul!"

And coming faintly, sadly, haunting as a dream:

"—is Paul! Paul! Paul!"

3

Two Worlds Discrete

WHEN AUNT MAW SPOKE, AT TIMES THE AIR WOULD BE FILLED WITH unseen voices, and the boy knew that he was listening to the voices of hundreds of people he had never seen, and knew instantly what those people were like and what their lives had been. Only a word, a phrase, an intonation of that fathomless Joyner voice falling quietly at night with an immense and tranquil loneliness before a dying fire, and the unknown dead were moving all around him, and it seemed to him that now he was about to track the stranger in him down to his last dark dwelling in his blood, explore him to his final secrecy, and make all the thousand strange, unknown lives in him awake and come to life again.

And yet Aunt Maw's life, her time, her world, the fathomless intonations of that Joyner voice, spoken quietly, interminably at night, in the room where the coal-fire flared and crumbled, and where slow time was feeding like a vulture at the boy's heart, could overwhelm his spirit in tides of drowning horror. Just as his father's life spoke to him of all things wild and new, of exultant prophecies of escape and victory, of triumph, flight, new lands, the golden cities—of all that was magic, strange, and glorious on earth—so did the life of his mother's people return him instantly to some dark, unfathomed place in nature, to all that was tainted by the slow-smouldering fires of madness in his blood, some ineradicable poison of the blood and soul, brown, thick, and brooding, never to be cured or driven out of him, in which at length he must drown darkly, horribly, unassuaged, unsavable, and mad.

Aunt Maw's world came from some lonely sea-depth, some huge abyss and maw of drowning time, which consumed all things it fed upon except itself—consumed them with horror, death, the sense of drowning in a sea of blind, dateless Joyner time. Aunt Maw fed on sorrow with a kind of tranquil joy. In that huge chronicle of the past which her terrific memory wove forever, there were all the lights and weathers of the soul—sunlight, Summer, singing—but there was always sorrow, death and sorrow, the lost, lonely lives of men there in the wilderness. And yet she was not sorrowful herself. She fed on all the loneliness and death of the huge, dark past with a kind of ruminant and invincible relish, which said that all men must die save only these triumphant censors of man's destiny, these never-dying, all-consuming Joyner witnesses of sorrow, who lived, and lived forever.

This fatal quality of that weblike memory drowned the boy's soul in desolation. And in that web was everything on earth—except wild joy.

Her life went back into the wilderness of Zebulon County before the Civil War.

"Remember!" Aunt Maw would say in a half-amused and half-impatient voice, as she raised the needle to the light and threaded it. "Why, you fool boy, you!" she would exclaim in scornful tones, "What are you thinkin' of! Of course I can remember! Wasn't I right there, out in Zebulon with all the rest of them, the day they came back from the war? . . . Yes, sir, I saw it all." She paused, reflecting. "So here they came," she continued tranquilly, "along about ten o'clock in the morning—you could hear them, you know, long before they got there—around that bend in the road—you could hear the people cheerin' all along the road—and, of course, I began to shout and holler along with all the rest of them," she said, "I wasn't goin' to be left out, you know," she went on with tranquil humor, "—and there we were, you know, all lined up at the fence there—father and mother and your great-uncle Sam. Of course, you never got to know him, boy, but he was there, for he'd come home sick on leave at Christmas time. He was still limpin' around from that wound he got—and of course it was all over or everyone knew it *would* be before he got well enough to go on back again. Hm," she laughed shortly, knowingly, as she squinted at her needle, "At least that's what he said——"

"What, Aunt Maw?"

"Why, that he was waitin' for his wound to heal, but, pshaw!"—she spoke quietly, shaking her head—"Sam was *lazy*—oh, the laziest feller I ever saw in all my life!" she cried. "Now if the truth were told, *that* was all that was wrong with him—and let me tell you something; it didn't take long for him to get well when he saw the war was comin' to an end and he wouldn't have to go on back and join the rest of them. He was limpin' around there one day leanin' on a cane as if every step would be his last, and the next day he was walkin' around as if he didn't have an ache or a pain in the world. . . .

" 'That's the quickest recovery *I* ever heard of, Sam,' father said to him. 'Now if you've got some more medicine out of that same bottle, I just wish you'd let me have a little of it.'—Well, then, so Sam was there." She went on in a moment, "And of course Bill Joyner was there —old Bill Joyner, your great-grandfather, boy—as hale and hearty an old man as you'll ever see!" she cried.

"Bill Joyner . . . why he must have been all of eighty-five right then, but you'd never have known it to look at him! Do anything! Go anywhere! Ready for anything!" she declared. "And he was that way, sir, right up to the hour of his death—lived over here in Libya Hill then, mind you, fifty miles away, but if he took a notion that he'd like to talk to one of his childern, why he'd stand right out and come, without waitin' to get his hat or anything. Why yes! didn't he turn up one day just as we were all settin' down to dinner, without a hat or coat or anything!" she said. " 'Why, what on earth!' said mother. 'Where did you come from, Uncle Bill?'—she called him Uncle Bill, you know. 'Oh, I came from Libya Hill,' says he. 'Yes, but how did you get here?' she says—asks him, you know. 'Oh, I walked it,' he says. 'Why, you know you didn't!' mother says, 'And where's your hat and coat?' she says. 'Oh, I reckon I came without 'em,' he says, 'I was out workin' in my garden and I just took a notion that I'd come to see you all, so I didn't stop to get my hat or coat,' he said, 'I just came on!' And that's just exactly what he'd done, sir," she said with a deliberate emphasis. "He just took the notion that he'd like to see us all, and he lit right out, without stoppin' to say hello or howdy-do to anybody!"

She paused for a moment, reflecting. Then, nodding her head slightly, in confirmation, she concluded:

"But that was Bill Joyner for you! That's just the kind of feller that he was."

"So he was there that day?" said George.

"Yes, sir. He was right there standin' next to father. Father was a Major, you know," she said, with a strong note of pride in her voice, "but he was home on leave at the time the war ended. Why yes! he came home every now and then all through the war. Bein' a Major, I guess he could get off more than the common soldiers," she said proudly. "So he was there, with old Bill Joyner standin' right beside him. Bill, of course—he'd come because he wanted to see Rance, and he knew he'd be comin' back with all the rest of them. Of course, child," she said, shaking her head slightly, "none of us had seen your great-uncle Rance since the beginning of the war. He had enlisted at the very start, you know, when war was declared, and he'd been away the whole four years. And oh! they told it, you know, they told it!" she half-muttered, shaking her head slightly with a boding kind of deprecation, "what he'd been through—the things he'd had to do— whew-w!" she said suddenly with an expostulation of disgust—"Why, the time they took him prisoner, you know, and he escaped, and had to do his travelin' by night, sleepin' in barns or hidin' away somewheres in the woods all day, I reckon—and that was the time—whew-w!— 'Go away,' I said, 'it makes me shudder when I think of it!'—why that he found that old dead mule they'd left there in the road—and cut him off a steak and eaten it—'And the best meat,' says, 'I ever tasted!'— Now that will give you some idea of how hungry he must have been!

"Well, of course, we'd heard these stories, and none of us had seen him since he went away, so we were all curious to know. Well, here they came, you know, marchin' along on that old river road, and you could hear all the people cheerin', and the men a-shoutin' and the women folks a-cryin', and here comes Bob Patten. Well then, of course we all began to ask him about Rance, said, 'Where is he? Is he here?'

" 'Oh, yes, he's here, all right,' said Bob, 'He'll be along in a minute now. You'll see him—and if you don't see him' "—suddenly she began to laugh—" 'if you don't see him,' says Bob, *why, by God, you'll smell him!*' That's just the way he put it, you know, came right out with it, and of course, they had to laugh. . . . But, child, child!" with strong distaste she shook her head slightly—"That awful—oh! that *awful, awful,* odor! Poor feller! I don't reckon he could help it! But he always had it. . . . Now he was clean enough!" she cried out with a strong emphasis, "Rance always kept himself as clean as anyone you ever saw. And a good, clean-livin' man, as well," she said. "Never touched a drop of licker in *all* his life," she said decisively, "No, sir— neither him nor father.—Oh father! father!" she cried proudly, "Why father wouldn't let anyone come near him with the smell of licker on his breath! And let me tell you something!" she said solemnly, "If he had known that your papa drank, he'd never have let your mother marry him!—Oh! he wouldn't have let him enter his house, you know —he would have considered it a disgrace for any member of his family to associate with anyone who drank!" she proudly said. "And Rance was the same—he couldn't endure the sight or taste of it—but *oh!*" she gasped, "that awful, awful odor—that old, rank body-smell that nothing could take out!—awful, awful," she whispered. Then for a moment she stitched silently. "And of course," she said, "that's what they say about him—that's what they called him——"

"What, Aunt Maw?"

"Why," she said—and here she paused again, shaking her head in a movement of strong deprecation, "to think of it!—to think, they'd have no more decency or reverence than to give a man a name like that! But, then, you know what soldiers are—I reckon they're a pretty rough, coarse-talkin' lot, and of course they told it on him—that was the name they gave him, the one they called him by."

"What?"

She looked at him quietly for a moment with a serious face, then laughed.

"Stinkin' Jesus," she said shyly. "Whew-w!" she gently shrieked. "'Oh, you know they wouldn't say a thing like that!' I cried—but that was it, all right. To think of it! . . . And of course, poor fellow, he knew it, he recognized it, says, 'I'd do anything in the world if I could only get rid of it,' says, 'I reckon it's a cross the Lord has given me to bear.' . . . But there it was—that—old—rank—thing!—Oh, awful, *awful!*" she whispered, peering downward at the needle. "And say! yes! Didn't he tell us all that day when he came back that the Day of Judgment was already here upon us?—Oh! said Appomattox Court-house marked the comin' of the Lord and Armageddon—and for us all to get ready for great changes! And, yes! don't I remember that old linen chart—or map, I reckon you might call it—that he kept strung around his neck, all rolled up in a ball, and hangin' from a string? It proved, you know, by all the facts and figures in the Bible that the world was due to end in 1865. . . . And there he was, you know, marchin' along the road with all the rest of them, with that old thing a-hangin' round his neck, the day they all came back from the war."

She stitched quietly with deft, strong fingers for a moment, and then, shaking her head, said sadly:

"Poor Rance! But I tell you what! He was *certainly* a good man," she said.

Rance Joyner had been the youngest of all old Bill Joyner's children. Rance was a good twelve years the junior of Lafayette, George Webber's grandfather. Between them had been born two other brothers—John, killed at the battle of Shiloh, and Sam. The record of Rance Joyner's boyhood, as it had survived by tongue, by hearsay, which was the only record these men had, was bare enough in its anatomy, but probably fully accurate.

"Well, now I tell you how it was," Aunt Maw said. "The rest of them used to tease him and make fun of him. Of course, he was a simple-minded sort of feller, and I reckon he'd believe anything they told him. Why, yes! Didn't father tell me how they told him Martha Alexander was in love with him, and got him to believin' it, and all!—And here Martha, you know, was the belle of the neighborhood, and could pick and choose from anyone she liked! But didn't they write him all sorts of fool love letters then, pretendin' to come from Martha, and tellin' him to meet her at all sorts of places—up on the Indian Mound, and down in the holler, or at some old stump, or tree, or crossroads—oh! anywheres!" she cried, "just to see if he'd be fool enough to go! And then, when she didn't turn up, wouldn't they write him another letter, sayin' her father was suspicious and watchin' her like a hawk! And didn't they tell him then that Martha had said she'd like him better if he grew a beard! And then they told him, you know, they had a special preparation all fixed up that would make his beard grow faster if he washed his face in it, and then didn't they persuade him to wash his face in old blue indigo water that was used to dye wool in, and didn't he go around there for weeks as blue in the face as a monkey! . . .

"And didn't he come creepin' up behind her after church one day, and whisper in her ear: 'I'll be there. Just swing the light three times and slip out easy when you're ready, and I'll be there waitin' for you!'—Why, he almost frightened the poor girl out of her wits. 'Oh!' she screamed, you know, and hollered for them to come and get him, 'Oh! Take him! Take him away!'—thinkin' he'd gone crazy—and of course that let the cat out of the bag. They had to tell it then, the joke they'd played on him." She smiled quietly, shaking her head slightly, with the sad and faintly troubled mirth of things far and lost.

"But, I want to tell you," she said gravely in a moment, "they can say all they like about your great-uncle Rance, but he was always an upright and honest man. He had a good heart," she said quietly, and in these words there was an accolade. "He was always willin' to do anything he could to help people when they needed it. And he wouldn't wait to be asked, neither! Why, didn't they tell it how he practically carried Dave Ingram on his back as they retreated from Antietam, rather than let him lay there and be taken!—Of course, he was strong— why, strong as a mule!" she cried. "He could stand anything.—They told it how he could march all day long, and then stay up all night nursin' the sick and tendin' to the wounded."

She paused and shook her head. "I guess he'd seen some awful things," she said. "I reckon he'd been with many a poor feller when he breathed his last—they had to admit it, sir, when they came back! Now, they can laugh at him all they please, but they had to give him his due! Jim Alexander said, you know, he admitted it, 'Well, Rance has preached the comin' of the Lord and a better day upon the earth, and I reckon we've all laughed at him at times for doin' it—but let me tell you, now,' he says, 'he always practiced what he preached. If everybody had as good a heart as he's got, we'd have that better day he talks about right now!' "

She sewed quietly for a moment, thrusting the needle through with her thimbled finger, drawing the thread through with a strong, pulling movement of her arm.

"Now, child, I'm goin' to tell you something," she said quietly. "There are a whole lot of people in this world who think they're pretty smart—but they never find out anything. Now I suppose that there are lots of smarter people in the world than Rance—I guess they looked on him as sort of simple-minded—but let me tell you something! It's not always the smartest people who know the most—and there are things I could tell you—things I know about!" she whispered with an omened tone, then fell to shaking her head slightly again, her face contracted in a portentous movement—"Child! Child! . . . I don't know what you'd call it . . . what explanation you could give for it—but it's mighty strange when you come to think about it, isn't it?"

"But what? What is it, Aunt Maw?" he demanded feverishly.

She turned and looked him full in the face for a moment. Then she whispered:

"He's been—*Seen!* . . . I *Saw* him once myself! . . . He's been *Seen* all through his life," she whispered again. "I know a dozen people who have *Seen* him," she added quietly. She stitched in silence for a time.

"Well, I tell you," she presently said, "the first time that they *Saw* him he was a boy—oh! I reckon along about eight or nine years old at the time. I've heard father tell the story many's the time," she said, "and mother was there and knew about it, too. That was the very year that they were married, sir, that's exactly when it was," she declared triumphantly. "Well, mother and father were still livin' there in Zebulon, and old Bill Joyner was there, too. He hadn't yet moved into town, you know. Oh, it was several years after this before Bill came to Libya Hill to live, and father didn't follow him till after the war was over. . . . Well, anyway," she said, "Bill was still out in Zebulon, as I was sayin', and the story goes that it was Sunday morning. So after breakfast the whole crowd of them start out for church—all of them except old Bill, you know, and I reckon he had something else to do, or felt that it was all right for *him* to stay at home so long as all the others went. . . . Well, anyhow," she smiled, "Bill didn't go to church, but he saw them go, you know! He *saw* them go!" she cried. "He stood there in the door and watched them as they went down the road—father and Sam and mother, and your great-uncle Rance. Well, anyway, when they had gone—I reckon it was some time later—Bill went out into the kitchen. And when he got there he saw the lid of the wool-box was open. Of course father was a hatter, and he kept the wool from which he made the felt out in the kitchen in this big box.—Why, it was big enough for a grown man to stretch out full length in, with some to spare, and of course it was as good a bed as anyone could want. I know that when father wanted to take a nap on Sunday afternoons, or get off somewheres by himself to study something over, he'd go back and stretch out on the wool.

" 'Well,' thinks Bill, 'now who could ever have gone and done such a trick as that? Fate told them'—that's what he called my father,

Lafayette, you know—'Fate told them to keep that box closed,' and he walks over, you know, to put the lid down—and there he *was*, sir!" she cried strongly—"There he *was*, if you please, stretched out on the wool and fast asleep—why, Rance, you know! Rance! There he *was*! . . . 'Aha!' thinks Bill, 'I caught you that time, didn't I? Now he's just sneaked off from all the others when he thought my back was turned, and he's crawled back here to have a snooze when he's supposed to be in church.' That's what Bill thought, you know. 'Now if he thinks he's goin' to play any such trick as that on me, he's very much mistaken. But we'll see,' thinks Bill, 'We'll just wait and see. Now, I'm not goin' to wake him up,' says Bill, 'I'll go away and let him sleep—but when the others all get back from church I'm goin' to ask him where he's been. And if he tells the truth—if he confesses that he crawled into the wool-box for a nap, I won't punish him. But if he tries to lie out of it,' says Bill, 'I'll give him such a thrashin' as he's never had in all his life before!'

"So he goes away then and leaves Rance there to sleep. Well, he waited then, and pretty soon they all came back from church, and, sure enough, here comes Rance, trailin' along with all the rest of them. 'Rance,' says Bill, 'How'd you like the sermon?' 'Oh,' says Rance, smilin' an' grinnin' all over, you know, 'it was fine, father, fine,' he says. 'Fine, was it?' Bill says, 'You enjoyed it, did you?' 'Oh, why, yes!' he says, 'I enjoyed it fine!' 'Well, now, that's good,' says Bill, 'I'm glad to hear that,' says he. 'What did the preacher talk about?' he says.

"Well, then, you know, Rance started in to tell him—he went through the preacher's sermon from beginnin' to end, he told him everything that was in it, even to describin' how the preacher talked and all.

"And Bill listened. He didn't say a word. He waited till Rance got through talkin'. Then he looked at him, and shook his head. 'Rance,' he says, 'I want you to look me in the eye.' And Rance looked at him, you know, real startled-like; says, 'Why, yes, father, what is it? What's wrong?' he says. Then Bill looked at him, and shook his head. Says, 'Rance, Rance, I'd have let you go if you had told the truth about it, but,' says, 'Rance—you have *lied* to me.' 'Why, no, father,' says Rance, 'No, I haven't. What do you mean?' he says. And Bill looked at him; says, 'Rance—you have not been to church,' says, 'I found you in the wool-box fast asleep, and that is where you've been all morning. Now' says Bill, 'you come with me,' and took him by the shoulder. 'Oh, father, I haven't done anything'—begins to cry, you know, says, 'Don't whip me, don't whip me—I haven't lied to you—I'll swear to you I haven't.' 'You come with me,' says Bill—begins to pull and drag him along, you know, 'and when I'm through with you you'll never lie to me again.'

"And that," she said, "that was where *father*—my father, your grandfather—stepped into the picture. He stepped between them and stopped Bill Joyner from going any further. Of course, father was a grown man at the time. 'No,' says father, 'you mustn't do that,' he says, 'You're makin' a mistake. You can't punish him for not attendin' church today.' 'Why, what's the reason I can't?' Bill Joyner said. 'Because,' said father, 'he was *there*. He's been with us every minute of the time since we left home this morning. And he heard the sermon,' father said, 'He's tellin' you the truth—I'll swear to that—because he was sittin' next to me all the time.'

"And then, of course, the others all chimed in, mother and Sam, said, 'Yes, he's tellin' you the truth, all right. He was right there with us all the time, and we'd have known if he left us.' Then Bill was bitter against them all, of course, thinkin' they had all joined against him in an effort to shield Rance in a lie. 'To think,' he said, 'that childern of mine would turn against me in this way! To think that you'd all join together in a lie in order to shield him. Why, you're worse than he is,' he said, 'for you're abettin' him and leadin' him on, and you—' he said to father—'*you* are certainly old enough to know better,' says, 'Fate, I didn't think it of you, I didn't think you'd help him to lie like this.' And father said, 'No.' He looked him in the eye, said, 'No, father, no one is helpin' him to lie. He's not tellin' you a lie. We're all tellin' the truth—and I can prove it.'—Why yes, didn't it turn out then that the preacher and all the folks at church had seen him and were willin' to testify that he was there?—'Now I don't know what it is you saw,' said father, 'but whatever it was, it wasn't Rance. At least, it wasn't the Rance you see here, for he's been with us every moment.' And then Bill looked at him and saw that he was tellin' him the truth, and they say Bill Joyner's face was a study.

" 'Well,' he said, 'this is a strange thing! God only knows what will come out of it! Rance has been *Seen*!' "

She paused; then turned to look straight and silent at George. In a moment she shook her head slightly, with boding premonition.

"And let me tell you something," she whispered. "That wasn't the only time, either!"

There were, in fact, from this time on, an increasing number of such apparitions. The news of the first one had spread like wildfire through the whole community: the uncanny story of the boy's discovery in the wool-box when his corporeal body was two miles distant at the church became instantly common property, and inflamed the wonder and imagination of all who heard it.

And, as seems to be almost the invariable practice in these cases, the public did not question at all the evidence which was dubious; they questioned only that which was indubitable, and, finding it to be confirmed beyond the shadow of a doubt, swallowed the whole, hook, line, and sinker! They took it instantly for granted that Bill Joyner had seen the boy, or "at least, seen something, now—that's one thing sure." But was Rance really present at the church that day? Had he been with the other members of his family from first to last? Had there been any opportunity for him to "slip away" and leave them without their knowing it? To all this there was only one answer—testified to by a hundred people. He *had* been present at the church from first to last; he had been seen, greeted, and remembered by minister, sexton, deacons, choir, and congregation, not only before, but also after services. Therefore, the fact was now established in their minds with an unshakable conviction. There was no longer any possible doubt about it— Rance had been *Seen*.

Then, about eight months after this, when the story of this ghostly apparition was still fresh in people's minds, and made matter for awed conversation when they gathered, another extraordinary incident occurred!

One evening, towards the end of a harsh and ragged day in March, a neighbor of the Joyner's was driving hard into the backwoods village of Blankenship, which stood about two miles distant from his home. Night was coming on fast; it was just the few minutes of brief, fading grey that end a Winter's day, and the man, whose name was Roberts, was driving along the hard, clay-rutted road as fast as the rickety rig in which he sat, and the old grey horse he drove, could carry him. His wife had been seized suddenly by a cramp or colic, or so they called it, and now lay at home in bed in mortal pain until Roberts should reach town and fetch help back to her.

Just outside of town as the troubled man was urging on his nag to greater speed, he encountered Rance Joyner. The boy was trudging steadily along the road in the grey light, coming from town and going towards home, and, according to the story Roberts told, Rance was carrying a heavy sack of meal which he had plumped over his right shoulder and supported with his hand. As the man in the buggy passed him, the boy half turned, paused, looked up at him, and spoke. In this circumstance there was nothing unusual. Roberts had passed the boy a hundred times coming or going to the town on some errand.

On this occasion, Roberts said he returned the boy's greeting somewhat absently and curtly, weighted down as his spirit was with haste and apprehension, and drove on without stopping. But before he had gone a dozen yards the man recalled himself and pulled up quickly, intending to shout back to the boy the reason for his haste, and to ask him to stop at his house on the way home, do what he could to aid the stricken woman, and wait there till the man returned with help. Accordingly, Roberts pulled up, turned in his seat, and began to shout his message down the road. To his stupefaction, the road was absolutely bare. Within a dozen yards the boy had vanished from his sight, "as if," said Roberts, "the earth had opened up and swallered him." But even as the man sat staring, gape-mouthed with astonishment, the explanation occurred to him:

"Thar were some trees thar down the road a little piece, a-settin' at the side of the road, and I jest figgered," he said delicately, "that Rance had stepped in behind one of 'em fer a moment, so I didn't stop no more. Hit was gettin' dark an' I was in a hurry, so I jest drove on as hard as I could."

Roberts drove in to town, got the woman's sister whom he had come to fetch, and then returned with her as hard as he could go. But even as he reached home and drove up the rutted lane, a premonition of calamity touched him. The house was absolutely dark and silent: there was neither smoke nor sound nor any light whatever, and, filled with a boding apprehension, he entered. He called his wife's name in the dark house, but no one answered him. Then, he raised the smoky lantern which he carried, walked to the bed where his wife lay, and looked at her, seeing instantly that she was dead.

That night the people from the neighborhood swarmed into the house. The women washed the dead woman's body, dressed her, "laid her out," and the men sat round the fire, whittled with knives, and told a thousand drawling stories of the strangeness of death and destiny. As Roberts was recounting for the hundredth time all of the circumstances of the death, he turned to Lafayette Joyner, who had come straightway when he heard the news, with his wife and several of his brothers:

". . . and I was jest goin' to tell Rance to stop and wait here till I got back, but I reckon it was just as well I didn't—she would have been dead a-fore he got here, and I reckon it might have frightened him to find her."

Fate Joyner looked at him slowly with a puzzled face.

"Rance?" he said.

"Why, yes," said Roberts, "I passed him comin' home just as I got to town—and I reckon if I hadn't been in such a hurry I'd a-told him to stop off and wait till I got back."

The Joyners had suddenly stopped their whittling. They looked upward from their places round the fire with their faces fixed on Roberts' face in a single, silent, feeding, fascinated stare, and he paused suddenly, and all the other neighbors paused, feeling the dark, premonitory boding of some new phantasmal marvel in their look.

"You say you passed Rance as you were goin' in to town?" Fate Joyner asked.

"Why, yes," said Roberts, and described again all of the circum- stances of the meeting.

And, still looking at him, Fate Joyner slowly shook his head.

"No," said he, "you never saw Rance. It wasn't Rance that you saw."

The man's flesh turned cold.

"What do you mean?" he said.

"Rance wasn't there," said Fate Joyner. "He went to visit Rufus Alexander's people a week ago, and he's fifty miles away from here right now. That's where he is tonight," said Fate quietly.

Roberts' face had turned grey in the firelight. For several moments he said nothing. Then he muttered:

"Yes. Yes, I see it now. By God, that's it, all right."

Then he told them how the boy had seemed to vanish right before his eyes a moment after he had passed him—"as if—as if," he said, "the earth had opened up to swaller him."

"And that was it?" he whispered.

"Yes," Fate Joyner answered quietly, "that was it."

He paused, and for a moment all the feeding, horror-hungry eyes turned with slow fascination to the figure of the dead woman on the bed, who lay, hands folded, in composed and rigid posture, the fire-flames casting the long flicker of their light upon her cold, dead face.

"Yes, that was it," Fate Joyner said. "She was dead then, at that moment—but you—you didn't know it," he added, and quietly there was feeding a deep triumph in his voice.

Thus, this good-hearted and simple-minded boy became, without his having willed or comprehended it, a supernatural portent of man's fate and destiny. Rance Joyner, or rather, his spiritual substance, was seen by dusk and darkness on deserted roads, was observed crossing fields and coming out of woods, was seen to toil up a hill along a narrow path at evening—and then to vanish suddenly. Often, these apparitions had no discernible relation to any human happening; more often, they were precedent, coincident, or subsequent to some fatal circumstance. And this ghostly power was not limited to the period of his boyhood. It continued, with increasing force and frequency, into the years of his manhood and maturity.

Thus, one evening early in the month of April, 1862, the wife of Lafayette Joyner, coming to the door of her house—which was built on the summit of a hill, or ledge, above a little river—suddenly espied Rance toiling up the steep path that led up to the house. In his soiled and ragged uniform, he looked footsore, unkempt, dusty, and unutterably weary—"as if," she said, "he had come a long, long ways"—as indeed, he must have done, since at that moment he was a private soldier in one of Jackson's regiments in Virginia.

But Lafayette Joyner's wife could see him plainly as he paused for a moment to push open a long gate that gave upon the road below her, halfway down the hill. She turned, she said, in her excitement for a moment, to shout the news of his approach to others in the house, and in that instant he had vanished from her sight. When she looked again, no one was there; the scene was fading into night and stillness, and the woman wrung her hands in her despair, saying:

"Oh, Lord! Oh, Lord! What's to become of us? What's happened now?"

Such was her story. And, as always, it confirmed a fatal event. On that day in April, more than two hundred miles to the westward, the bloody battle of Shiloh had been fought in Tennessee, and at that moment, although the news did not get back to them for several weeks, one of the brothers, John, was lying on the field, his shattered face turned upward, dead.

Such, then, were some of the stories Aunt Maw told to George. And always, when she spoke so in the night, as the coal-fire flared and crumbled in the grate, and the huge demented winds of darkness howled around them and the terror of strong silence fed forever at his heart—he could hear the thousand death-devouring voices of the Joyners speaking triumphantly from the darkness of a hundred years, the lost and lonely sorrow of the hills, and somehow smell incredibly—always and forever!—the soft, fragrant ash of the pine blaze, the pungent sharpness of the whittled wood, the winy warmth and fullness of mellow apples. And horribly, somehow, to these odors were always added the death-evoking smells of turpentine and camphor—which were a lost memory of infancy, when his mother had taken him, a child of two, to such a room—warmth, apples, Joyner room, and all—to see his grandfather the night before he died.

Upon a thousand lost and lonely roads in the ever-lost and ever-lonely hills he heard the unctuous, drawling voices of the Joyners. He saw them toiling up a wooded hill in sad, hushed, evening light to vanish like a wraith into thin air; and the terrible prophecies of old wars and battles, and of all the men who had that day been buried in the earth, were in that instant apparition and farewell! He saw them in a thousand little houses of the wilderness, in years more far and lonely than the years of Vercingetorix, coming in at darkness always to watch the night away beside the dead, to sit in semi-darkness in some neighbor's ill-starred house, to sit around the piny fire-flame's dance of death, and with triumphant lust to drawl and whittle night away while the pine logs flamed and crumbled to soft ash and their voices spoke forever their fated and invincible auguries of sorrow.

What was it Aunt Maw thus evoked by the terrific weavings of her memory? In the boy's vision of that world, the Joyners were a race as lawless as the earth, as criminal as nature. They hurled their prodigal seed into the raw earth of a mountain woman's body, bringing to life a swarming progeny which lived or died, was extinguished in its infancy or fought its way triumphantly to maturity against the savage enemies of poverty, ignorance, and squalor which menaced it at every step. They bloomed or perished as things live or die in nature—but the triumphant Joyners, superior to all loss or waste, lived forever as a river lives. Other tribes of men came up out of the earth, flourished for a space, and then, engulfed and falling, went back into the earth from which they came. Only the Joyners—these horror-hungry, time-devouring Joyners—lived, and would not die.

And *he* belonged to that fatal, mad, devouring world from whose prison there was no escape. He belonged to it, even as three hundred of his blood and bone had belonged to it, and must unweave it from his brain, distill it from his blood, unspin it from his entrails, and escape with demonic and exultant joy into his father's world, new lands and mornings and the shining city—or drown like a mad dog, die!

From the first years of coherent memory, George had the sense of the overpowering immanence of the golden life. It seemed to him that he was always on the verge of finding it. In his childhood it was all around him, impending numbly, softly, filling him with an intolerable excultancy of wordless joy. It wrenched his heart with its wild pain of ecstasy and tore the sinews of his life asunder, but yet it filled his soul with the triumphant sense of instant release, impending discovery— as if a great wall in the air would suddenly be revealed and sundered, as if an enormous door would open slowly, awfully, with the tremendous majesty of an utter and invisible silence. He never found a word for it, but he had a thousand spells and prayers and images that would give it coherence, shape, and meanings that no words could do.

He thought that he could twist his hand a certain way, or turn his wrist, or make a certain simple movement of rotation into space (as boys will learn the movement to unsolve a puzzle of linked chains, or as an expert in the mysteries of locks can feel the bearings faintly, softly, rolling through his finger tips, and know the instant that he finds the combination to unlock the safe)—and that by making this rotation with his hand, he would find the lost dimension of that secret world, and instantly step through the door that he had opened.

And he had other chants and incantations that would make that world reveal itself to him. Thus, for a period of ten years or more, he had a spell for almost everything he did. He would hold his breath along a certain block, or take four breaths in pounding down the hill from school, or touch each cement block upon a wall as he went past, and touch each of the end-blocks where the steps went up two times, and if he failed to touch them twice, go back and touch the whole wall over from the start.

And on Sunday he would always do the second thing: he would never do the first on Sunday. All through the day, from midnight Saturday until midnight Monday morning, he would always do the second thing he thought about and not the first. If he woke up on Sunday morning and swung over to the left side to get out of bed, he would swing back and get out on the right. If he started with the right sock, he would take it off and pull the left one on instead. And if he wanted first to use one tie, he would discard it and put on another.

And so it went the whole day through on Sunday. In every act and moment of his life that day he would always do the second thing he thought about instead of the first. But then when midnight came again, he would, with the same fanatic superstition, do the first thing that he thought about; and if he failed in any detail of this ritual, he would be as gloomy, restless, and full of uneasy boding doubts as if all the devils of mischance were already out in force against him, and posting on their way to do him harm.

These spells, chants, incantations, and compulsions grew, interwove, and constantly increased in the complexity and denseness of their web until at times they governed everything he did—not only the way he touched a wall, or held his breath while pounding down a hill from school, or measured out a block in punctual distances of breathing, or spanned the cement blocks of sidewalks in strides of four, but even in the way he went along a street, the side he took, the place he had to stop and look, the place he strode by sternly even when he wanted bitterly to stay and look, the trees out in his uncle's orchard that he climbed until he had to climb a certain tree four times a day and use four movements to get up the trunk.

And this tyrannic mystery of four would also get into the way he threw a ball, or chanted over Latin when preparing it, or muttered παιδεύσω four times in the Subjunctive of the First Aorist, or ἔθηκα in the Indicative Active of the First. And it was also in the way he washed his neck and ears, or sat down at a table, split up kindling (using four strokes of the axe to make a stick), or brought up coal (using four scoops of the shovel to fill the scuttle).

Then there were also days of stern compulsion when he could look at only a single feature of people's faces. On Monday he would look upon men's noses, on Tuesday he would stare into their teeth, on Wednesday he would peer into their eyes, save Thursday for their hands, and Friday for their feet, and sternly meditate the conformation of their brows on Saturday, saving Sunday always for the second feature that occurred to him—eyes when feet were thought of, teeth for eyes, and foreheads when his fine first rapture had been noses. And he would go about this duty of observing with such a stern, fanatical devotion, peering savagely at people's teeth or hands or brows, that sometimes they looked at him uneasily, resentfully, wondering what he saw amiss in their appearance, or shaking their heads and muttering angrily as they passed each other by.

At night, he said his prayers in rhymes of four—for four, eight, sixteen, thirty-two were somehow the key numbers in his arithmetic of sorcery. He would say his one set prayer in chants of four times four, until all the words and meanings of the prayer (which he had composed himself with four times four in mind) were lost, and all that he would follow would be the rhythm and the number of the chant, muttered so rapidly that the prayer was just a rapid blur— but muttered always sixteen times. And if he failed to do this, or doubted he had got the proper count, then he could not sleep or rest after he got into bed, and would get up instantly and go down upon his knees again, no matter how cold or raw the weather was, no matter how he felt, and would not pause until he did the full count to his satisfaction, with another sixteen thrown in as penalty. It was not piety he felt, it was not thought of God or reverence or religion: it was just superstitious mystery, a belief in the wizard-charm of certain numbers, and the conviction that he had to do it in this way in order to have luck.

Thus, each night he paid his punctual duty to "their" dark authorities, in order to keep himself in "their" good graces, to assure himself that "they" would not forsake him, that "they" would still be for him, not against him, that "they"—immortal, secret. "they" that will not give us rest!--would keep him, guard him, make his life prevail, frustrate his evil enemies, and guide him on to all the glory, love, and triumph, and to that great door, the huge, hinged, secret wall of life—that immanent and unutterable world of joy which was so near, so strangely, magically, and intolerably near, which he would find at any moment, and for which his life was panting.

One day a circus came to town, and as the boy stood looking at it there came to him two images which were to haunt all the rest of his childhood, but which were now for the first time seen together with an instant and a magic congruence. And these were the images of the circus and his father's earth.

He thought he had joined a circus and started on the great tour of the nation with it. It was Spring: the circus had started in New England, and worked westward and then southward as the Summer and Autumn came on. His nominal duties—for in his vision every incident, each face and voice and circumstance, was blazing real as life itself— were those of ticket seller. But in this tiny show everyone did several things, so he also posted bills, and bartered with the tradesmen and farmers in new places for fresh food. He became very clever at this work—some old, sharp, buried talent for shrewd trading that had come to him from his mountain blood now aided him. He could get the finest, freshest meats and vegetables at the lowest prices. The circus people were tough and hard, they always had a fierce and ravenous hunger, they would not accept bad food and cooking, they fed stupendously, and they always had the best of everything.

Usually the circus would arrive at a new town very early in the morning, before daybreak. He would go into town immediately: he would go to the markets, or with farmers who had come in for the circus. He felt and saw the purity of first light, he heard the sweet and sudden lutings of first birds, and suddenly he was filled with the earth and morning in new towns, among new men. He walked among the farmers' wagons, and he dealt with them on the spot for the prodigal plenty of their wares—the country melons bedded in sweet hay, the cool, sweet pounds of butter wrapped in clean, wet cloths, with dew and starlight still upon them, the enormous battered cans foaming with fresh milk, the new-laid eggs which he bought by the gross and hundred dozen, the tender, limey pullets by the score, the delicate bunches of green scallions, the heavy red ripeness of huge tomatoes, the sweet-leaved lettuces, crisp as celery, the fresh-podded peas and the suc‑ culent young beans, as well as the potatoes spotted with the loamy earth, the winy apples, the peaches, and the cherries, the juicy corn stacked up in shocks of luring green, and the heavy, blackened rinds of the home-cured hams and bacons.

As the markets opened, he would begin to trade and dicker with the butchers for their finest cuts of meat. They would hold great roasts up in their gouted fingers, they would roll up tubs of fresh-ground sausage, they would smack with their long palms the flanks of beeves and porks. He would drive back to the circus with a wagon full of meat and vegetables.

At the circus ground the people were already in full activity. He could hear the wonderful timed tattoo of sledges on the driven stakes, the shouts of men riding animals down to water, the slow clank and pull of mighty horses, the heavy rumble of the wagons as they rolled down off the circus flat cars. By now the eating tent would be erected, and, as he arrived, he could see the cooks already busy at their ranges, the long tables set up underneath the canvas with their rows of benches, their tin plates and cups. There would be the amber pungency of strong coffee, and the smell of buckwheat batter.

Then the circus people would come in for breakfast. The food they ate was as masculine and fragrant as the world they dwelt in. It be‑ longed to the warmed, stained world of canvas, the clean and healthful odor of the animals, and the wild, sweet, lyric nature of the land on which they lived as wanderers. And it was there for the asking with a fabulous and stupefying plenty, golden and embrowned. They ate stacks of buckwheat cakes, smoking hot, soaked in hunks of yellow butter, which they carved at will with a wide, free gesture from the piled prints on the table, and which they garnished with ropes of heavy black molasses, or with maple syrup. They ate big steaks for breakfast, hot from the pan and thick with onions; they ate whole melons, crammed with the ripeness of the deep-pink meat, rashers of bacon, and great platters of fried eggs, or eggs scrambled with calves brains. They helped themselves from pyramids of fruit piled up at intervals on the table—plums, peaches, apples, cherries, grapes, oranges, and bananas. They had great pitchers of thick cream to pour on everything, and they washed their hunger down with pint mugs of strong, deep-savored coffee.

For their midday meal they would eat fiercely, hungrily, with wolfish gusto, mightily with knit brows and convulsive movements of their corded throats. They would eat great roasts of beef with crackled hides, browned in their juices, rare and tender; hot chunks of delicate pork with hems of fragrant fat; delicate young broiled chickens; twelve-pound pot roasts, cooked for hours in an iron pot with new carrots, onions, sprouts, and young potatoes; together with every vegetable that the season yielded—huge roasting ears of corn, smoking hot, piled like cordwood on two-foot platters, tomatoes cut in slabs with wedges of okra and succotash, and raw onions, mashed potatoes whipped to a creamy batter, turnips, fresh peas cooked in butter, and fat, strong beans seasoned with the flavor of big chunks of pork. In addition they had every fruit that the place and time afforded: hot crusty apple, peach, and cherry pies, encrusted with cinnamon; puddings and cakes of every sort; and blobbering cobblers inches deep.

Thus the circus moved across America, from town to town, from state to state, eating its way from Maine into the great plains of the West, eating its way along the Hudson and the Mississippi Rivers, eating its way across the prairies and from the North into the South.

Abroad in this ocean of earth and vision, the boy thought of his father's land, of its great red barns, its clear familiarity and its haunting strangeness, and its lovely and tragic beauty. He thought of its smell of harbors and its rumors of the sea, the city, and the ships, its wine-ripe apples and its brown-red soil, its snug, weathered houses, its lyric, unutterable ecstasy.

A wonderful thing happened. One morning he awoke suddenly to find himself staring straight up at the pulsing splendor of the stars. At first he did not know where he was. The circus train had stopped in the heart of the country, for what reason he did not know. He could hear the languid and intermittent breathing of the engine, the strangeness of men's voices in the dark, the casual stamp of the horses in their cars, and all around him the attentive and vital silence of the earth.

Suddenly he raised himself from the pile of canvas on which he slept. It was the moment just before dawn: against the east the sky had already begun to whiten with the first faint luminosity of day, the invading tides of light crept up the sky, drowning the stars out as they went. The train had halted by a little river, which ran swift and deep close to the tracks, and now he knew that what at first he thought had been the sound of silence was the swift and ceaseless music of the river.

There had been rain the night before, and now the river was filled with the sweet, clean smell of earthy deposits. He could see the delicate white glimmer of young birch trees leaning from the banks, and on the other side he saw the winding whiteness of a road. Beyond the road, and bordering it, there was an orchard with a wall of lichened stone. As the wan light grew, the earth and all its contours emerged sharply. He saw the worn and ancient design of lichened rocks, the fertile soil of the ploughed fields; he saw the kept order, the frugal cleanliness, with its mild tang of opulent greenery. Here was an earth with fences as big as a man's heart, but not so great as his desire, and this earth was like a room he once had lived in. He returned to it as a sailor to a small, closed harbor, as a man, spent with the hunger of his wandering, comes home.

Instantly he recognized the scene. He knew he had come at last into his father's land. Here was his home, brought back to him while he slept, like a forgotten dream. Here was his heart's desire, his father's country, the earth his spirit dwelt in. He knew every inch of the land-scape, and he knew past reason, doubt, or argument that home was not three miles away.

He got up at once and leaped down to the earth: he knew where he would go. Along the track there was the slow swing and dance of the brakemen's lamps. Already the train was in motion, its bell tolled, and the heavy trucks rumbled away from him. He began to walk back along the tracks, for less than a mile away, he knew, where the stream boiled over the lip of a dam, there was a bridge. When he reached the bridge a deeper light had come: the old red brick of the mill emerged sharply and fell sheer into bright, shining waters.

He crossed the bridge and turned left along the road. Here it moved away from the river, among fields and through dark woods—dark woods bordered with stark poignancy of fir and pine, with the noble spread of maples, shot with the naked whiteness of birch. Sharp thrum-mings, woodland flitters, broke the silence. The tongue-trilling chirrs arose now, and little brainless cries, liquefied lutings. Smooth drops and nuggets of bright gold they were.

He went along that road where, he knew, the house of his father's blood and kin lay hidden. At length, he came around a bending of the road, he left the wooded land, he passed by hedges, and saw the old white house, set in the shoulder of the hill, clean and cool below the dark shelter of its trees. A twist of morning smoke coiled through its chimney.

Then he turned into the road that led up to the house, and at this moment the enormous figure of a powerful old man appeared around the corner, prophetically bearing a smoked ham in one huge hand. And when the boy saw the old man, a cry of greeting burst from his throat, and the old man answered with a roar of welcome that shook the earth. The old man dropped his ham, and waddled forward to meet the boy: they met half down the road, and the old man crushed him in his hug. They tried to speak but could not, they embraced again and in an instant all the pain of loneliness and the fierce hungers of desire were scoured away like a scum of frost from a bright glass.

At this moment also, two young men burst from the house and came running down the road to greet him. They were powerful and heavy youths, and, like their father, they recognized the boy instantly, and in a moment he was engulfed in their mighty energies, borne up among them to the house. As they ate breakfast, he told them of his circus wanderings and they told him what had befallen them. And they understood all that he wanted to say but could not speak, and they surrounded him with love and lavish heapings of his plate.

Such were the twin images of the circus and his father's land which now, as he stood there looking at the circus, fused instantly to a living whole and came to him in a blaze of light. And in this way, before he had ever seen or set his foot upon it, he came for the first time to his father's earth.

Thus, day by day, in the taut and tangled web of this boy's life, the two hemispheres that touched but never joined, contended, separated, recombined, and wove again. First came the old dark memory of time-haunted man and the lost voices in the hills a hundred years ago, the world-lost and hill-haunted sorrow of the time-triumphant Joyners. Then his spirit flamed beyond the hills, beyond lost time and sorrow, to his father and his father's earth; and when he thought of him his heart grew warm, the hot blood thudded in his veins, he leapt all barriers of the here and now, and northward, gleaming brightly there beyond the hills, he saw a vision of the golden future in new lands.

4

The Golden City

ALWAYS AND FOREVER WHEN THE BOY THOUGHT OF HIS FATHER, AND OF the proud, the cold, the secret North, he thought, too, of the city. His father had not come from there, yet strangely, through some subtle chemistry of his imagination, some magic of his boy's mind and heart, he connected his father's life and figure with the bright and shining city of the North.

In his child's picture of the world, there were no waste or barren places: there was only the rich tapestry of an immense and limitlessly fertile domain forever lyrical as April, and forever ready for the harvest, touched with the sorcery of a magic green, bathed forever in a full-hued golden light. And at the end, forever at the end of all the fabled earth, there hung the golden vision of the city, itself more fertile, richer, more full of joy and bounty than the earth it rested on. Far-off and shining, it rose upward in his vision from an opalescent mist, upborne and sustained as lightly as a cloud, yet firm and soaring with full golden light. It was a vision simple, unperplexed, carved from deep substances of light and shade, and exultant with its prophecy of glory, love, and triumph.

He heard, far off, the deep and beelike murmur of its million-footed life, and all the mystery of the earth and time was in that sound. He saw its thousand streets peopled with a flashing, beautiful, infinitely varied life. The city flashed before him like a glorious jewel, blazing with countless rich and brilliant facets of a life so good, so bountiful, so strangely and constantly beautiful and interesting, that it seemed intolerable that he should miss a moment of it. He saw the streets swarming with the figures of great men and glorious women, and he walked among them like a conqueror, winning fiercely and exultantly by his talent, courage, and merit the greatest tributes that the city had to offer, the highest prize of power, wealth, and fame, and the great emolu-

91

ment of love. There would be villainy and knavery as black and sinister as hell, but he would smash it with a blow, and drive it cringing to its hole. There would be heroic men and lovely women, and he would win and take a place among the highest and most fortunate people on the earth.

Thus, in a vision hued with all the strange and magic colors of his adolescence, the boy walked the streets of his great legendary city. Sometimes he sat among the masters of the earth in rooms of manlike opulence: dark wood, heavy leathers of solid, lavish brown, were all around him. Again he walked in great chambers of the night, rich with the warmth of marble and the majesty of great stairs, sustained on swelling columns of a rich-toned onyx, soft and deep with crimson carpets in which the foot sank down with noiseless tread. And through this room, filled with a warm and undulant music, the deep and mellow thrum of violins, there walked a hundred beautiful women, and all were his, if he would have them. And the loveliest of them all was his. Long of limb and slender, yet lavish and deep of figure, they walked with proud, straight looks on their fragile and empty faces, holding their gleaming shoulders superbly, and their clear, depthless eyes alive with love and tenderness. A firm and golden light fell over them, and over all his love.

He also walked in steep and canyoned streets, blue and cool with a frontal steepness of money and great business, brown and rich somehow with the sultry and exultant smell of coffee, the good green smell of money, and the fresh, half-rotten odor of the harbor with its tide of ships.

Such was his vision of the city—adolescent, fleshly, and erotic, but drunk with innocence and joy, and made strange and wonderful by the magic lights of gold and green and lavish brown in which he saw it. For, more than anything, it was the light. The light was golden with the flesh of women, lavish as their limbs, true, depthless, tender as their glorious eyes, fine-spun and maddening as their hair, as unutterable with desire as their fragrant nests of spicery, their deep melon-heavy breasts. The light was golden like a morning light that shines through ancient glass into a room of old dark brown. The light was rich brown shot with gold, lavish brown like old stone houses gulched in morning on a city street. The light was also blue, like morning underneath the frontal cliff of buildings, vertical, cool blue, hazed with thin morning mist, cold-flowing harbor blue of clean, cool waters, rimed brightly with a dancing morning gold.

The light was amber-brown in vast, dark chambers shuttered from young light, where, in great walnut beds, the glorious women stirred in sensual warmth their lavish limbs. The light was brown-gold like ground coffee, merchants, and the walnut houses where they lived; brown-gold like old brick buildings grimed with money and the smell of trade; brown-gold like morning in great gleaming bars of swart mahogany, the fresh wet beer-wash, lemon rind, and the smell of Angostura bitters. Then it was full-golden in the evening in the theatres, shining with full-golden warmth and body on full-golden figures of the women, on fat red plush, and on the rich, faded, slightly stale smell, and on the gilt sheaves and cupids and the cornucopias, on the fleshly, potent, softly-golden smell of all the people. And in great restaurants the light was brighter gold, but full and round like warm onyx columns, smooth, warmly-tinted marble, old wine in dark, rounded, age-encrusted bottles, and the great blonde figures of naked women on rose-clouded ceilings. Then the light was full and rich, brown-golden like great fields in Autumn; it was full-swelling golden light like mown fields, bronze-red picked out with fat, rusty-golden sheaves of corn, and governed by huge barns of red and the mellow, winy fragrance of the apples.

That vision of the city was gathered from a thousand isolated sources, from the pages of books, the words of a traveler, a picture of Brooklyn Bridge with its great, winglike sweep, the song and music of its cables, even the little figures of the men with derby hats as they advanced across it. These and a thousand other things all built the picture of the city in his mind, until now it possessed him and had got somehow, powerfully, exultantly, ineradicably, into everything he did or thought or felt.

That vision of the city blazed outward not only from those images and objects which would evoke it literally, as the picture of the Bridge had done: it was now mixed obscurely and powerfully into his whole vision of the earth, into the chemistry and rhythm of his blood, into a million things with which it had no visible relation. It came in a woman's laughter in the street at night, in sounds of music and the faint thrumming of a waltz, in the guttural rise and fall of the bass violin; and it was in the odor of new grass in April, in cries half-heard and broken by the wind, and in the hot daze and torpid drone of Sunday afternoon.

It came in all the sounds and noises of a carnival, in the smell of confetti, gasoline, the high, excited clamors of the people, the wheeling music of the carousel, the sharp cries and strident voices of the barkers. And it was in the circus smells and sounds as well—in the ramp and reek of lions, tigers, elephants, and in the tawny camel smell. It came somehow in frosty Autumn nights, in clear, sharp, frosty sounds of Hallowe'en. And it came to him intolerably at night in the receding whistle-wail of a distant and departing train, the faint and mournful tolling of its bell, and the pounding of great wheels upon the rail. It came also in the sight of great strings of rusty freight cars on the tracks, and in the sight of a rail, shining with the music of space and flight as it swept away into the distance and was lost from sight.

In things like these, and countless others, the vision of the city would come alive and stab him like a knife.

Book II

THE HOUND OF DARKNESS

Until his sixteenth year, George Webber, whom the boys called "Monk"—a name that was to stick to him throughout his life and come to seem more natural than the one his parents gave him—grew up among his Joyner kin. And he was one of them, knit closely in the web and fabric of their narrow, mountain-rimmed, and self-sufficient world. And yet he was a Webber, too, a fact of family shame and secret pride to him, and something from beyond the mountains was at work within his spirit.

Thus the strong, conflicting pulls of Joyner and of Webber blood which met but never fused in his own veins produced a ceaseless ebb and flow within his mind and heart, and from these motions of his spirit came a strangely sentient vision of the world, a richly varied tapestry of life, woven in contrasting tones of light and dark, of sunshine and deep shadow.

5

Aunt Mag and Uncle Mark

FOR MARK JOYNER'S WIFE, AUNT MAG, THE BOY GEORGE HAD LITTLE LOVE. She was of a family of mountain peasants, and she had done everything she could to advance her position in life by a liberal use of Mark's purse.

"She needn't give herself airs," said Aunt Maw. "When Mark first saw her, she was hoein' corn in a field."

Childless at forty-five, Mag was a tall, rather gaunt, white-faced woman, with cold eyes, a thin nose, and a bitter, sneering mouth. She had been handsome, but for twenty years she had been under the spell of a neurosis which had held her in the unshakable conviction that she was suffering from consumption, cancer, heart disease, and pernicious anæmia. She was under constant medical attention. She spent half her waking hours extended in white terror on her bed, in a room chemical with shelves and tables full of bottles, and sealed against a draft of air.

She was, as a matter of fact, a strong, healthy, and well-nourished woman.

George sometimes went along with Aunt Maw when she crossed the intervening strip of lawn to visit Mag in her new and ugly house of bright red brick. They would find her in her sealed room in a sickening enervation of red-hot stove heat.

"Come here!" Aunt Mag would say in her harsh, sneering voice, drawing the boy's unwilling figure beside her bed. "Lord a' mercy!" she would add, staring up into his face with her bitter laugh. "He smells like a Webber! Do your feet stink, boy?"

These pleasantries, delivered to the accompaniment of sneering laughter, and a bending down of her thin, pious mouth as she pretended to sniff the air with disgust, did not increase George's love for his aunt.

"You don't know how lucky you are, boy!" she would scream at him. "You ought to get down on your knees every night and thank the

97

Lord for having a good Christian home like this! Where would you be if it wasn't for me? I made your Uncle Mark take you in! If it wasn't for me, you'd have been sent to an orphan asylum—that's where you'd be!"

Under this goading, the boy would mumble his gratitude, but in his heart he often wished he *had* been sent to an orphanage.

Mag was a Baptist, and very active in her church. She donated liberally; she fattened the preacher at her Sunday table; above all, she contributed large sums for the maintenance of the Baptist orphanage, and kept in her service at all times two or three children whom she had taken under her generous wing. This charity got the thick coatings of flattery which assure a Baptist of success on earth and favor in heaven. The minister, speaking to his Sunday hundreds, would say:

". . . And now I know we will all be glad to hear that the heart of another orphan child has been made happy through the generosity of Sister Joyner, who, in the great goodness of her heart, is giving a comfortable home to Betsy Belcher, a little girl who lost both her parents before she was eight years old. This makes the sixth orphan that the good woman has taken into her loving care. I know, when we see her giving to the Lord so freely, that there are others here who will be led to give a little in the furtherance of the great work which the good Brothers and Sisters at the orphanage are doing."

And as Mag, bridling and ludicrously humble, advanced to the pulpit after the preacher's harangue, he would bend with greased unction over her hand, saying:

"And how is the good woman today?"

Mag took in these wretched children and made them drudges of all trades about the house. One of them was a boy of fourteen whose name was Willie, a thick-headed, smiling, perpetually bewildered idiot. Willie never played with the boys in the neighborhood because he was always kept busy doing chores, and George rarely saw him except on his visits of duty to Aunt Mag, when the orphan boy would be summoned into her room on a fire-building errand.

"Did you ever see such an idiot?" Mag would say, with her sneering laugh. "Lord a' mercy!"

And the boy would smile back at her, doubtfully, idiotically, fearfully, not knowing why.

One time Willie was left with Aunt Maw when Mark and Mag went to Florida. He worked like a dog. Aunt Maw stuffed him with food and gave him a little room in which to sleep. She did not abuse him. She and George laughed constantly at him, and he was absurdly pleased and grateful to know that he amused them, smiling his wide, idiot grin.

His hair was a tangled, uncut jungle which fell in matted lengths almost to his shoulder. Nebraska Crane told him solemnly, one day, that he was an experienced barber, and Willie submitted joyfully to the operation. Nebraska capped his large head with an inverted chamber pot, and laughed quietly from time to time as he sheared off all the hair that fell below the edges of the pot. And Willie, under the pot, continued to smile at them in friendly, puzzled idiocy while Nebraska and George caved slowly inward with laughter.

Mag had two nephews who lived in the big house with her and Mark. They were the sons of her brother who had died, and when the mother of the boys died not long after their father, Mag had taken them in. Since they were her own blood, she had brought them up with as much misguided indulgence as though they had been her sons, and had lavished upon them all the affection of which her narrow and thwarted nature was capable. Mark's money was poured out for their benefit with a liberal hand, Mag having made it a cardinal point, in her system of educating them for their high position in life as her nearest kin, to deny them nothing.

The older, Earl, was a heavy, florid, coarsely handsome young man with a loud, vacant, infectious laugh. He was well liked in the town. He had devoted all his time to the study of golf as a fine art, and was one of the best players in Libya Hill. It pleased Mag to know that he was a member of the Country Club. Her conception of gentility was a life of complete idleness spent in the company of "the best people."

The other nephew, the little golden apple of Mag's delight, was named Tad. He was now a young man of seventeen or eighteen, with a shiny red, porky face and an annoying, satisfied laugh. Tad had avoided expertly all of the inconvenient toil of life. He had all his aunt's skill in calling on physical collapse to aid him, and Mag was convinced that a weak heart ran in her family and that the boy had inherited it.

Tad, too delicate for the rough uses of a school, received his instruction at home, peripatetically, in the Greek manner, between three and four o'clock in the afternoon, from a withered hack who ran a small school for boys, and who, for a substantial sum, winked considerately and assured Mag that her nephew had already received the equivalent of a university education.

A good part of his time Tad spent in his "laboratory," a little gabled room in the attic to which he brought the subjects of his experiments—small, panting birds, vibrating cats, stray curs—noting with minute curiosity their sensory responses when he drove pins into their eyes, cut off portions of their tails, or seared them with a heated poker.

"That boy's a born naturalist," said Mag.

Mark Joyner was frugal for himself, but open-handed with Mag. He had toast and two boiled eggs for breakfast, which he cooked on top of a little wood stove in his room, estimating among his friends the cost of kindling, eggs, and bread at twelve cents. Later he used the hot water for shaving.

"By God!" said the townsmen, "that's the reason he's got it!"

He sought for his clothing among the Jews; he smoked rank, weedy "threefers"; he cobbled his own shoes; he exulted equally in his parsimony to himself and his liberality to his household. From the first years of his marriage he had given Mag a generous allowance, which had increased as his business prospered, and she had turned over a considerable part of it to her two nephews. They were her own blood, and whatever she had was theirs.

Most of the time Mag held her husband in iron subjection, but there was a hidden volcano of anger in him that increased from year to year of his living with her, and when it was roused, all her weapons of harsh laughter, incessant nagging, and chronic invalidism were impotent. He would grow silent, doing his utmost to control himself, and in the effort contorting his lips in a terrible grimace; but finally his emotion would become too much for him, and he would storm out of the house, away from Mag and the sound of her voice, and, turning his gaunt face towards the western hills, he would tramp through the woods for hours until his spirit grew calm again.

6

The Street of the Day

WHEN GEORGE WEBBER WAS A CHILD, LOCUST STREET, THE STREET ON which he lived with his Joyner relatives, seemed fixed for him into the substance of immemorial antiquity. It had a beginning and a history, he had no doubt, but a history that began so long ago tha' countless men had come and lived and died and been forgotten since the street began, and no man living could remember when that was. Moreover, it seemed to him that every house and tree and garden had been framed to the pattern of an immutable design: they were there because they had to be there, they were built that way because that was the only way in which they could be built.

This street held for him a universe of joy and magic which seemed abundant for a thousand lives. Its dimensions were noble in their space and limitless surprise. Its world of houses, yards, and orchards and its hundred people seemed to him to have the incomparable grandeur of the first place on earth, the impregnable authority of the center of the universe.

In later years, George plainly saw that the world in which he lived had been a little place. All of the dimensions of the street had dwindled horribly. The houses that had seemed so imposing in their opulence and grandeur, the lawns that were so spacious, the backyards and the vistaed orchards that went on in limitless progressions of delight and new discovery that never had an end—all this had shrunken pitifully, incredibly, and now looked close, and mean, and cramped. Yet even then, years later, the street and all its million memories of a buried life awoke for him with the blazing and intolerable vividness of a dream. It was a world which he had known and lived with every atom of his blood and brain and spirit, and every one of its thousand images was rooted into the structure of his life forever, as much a part of him as his inmost thoughts.

At first it was just the feel of the grass and the earth and the ground under your naked feet in May when you were going barefoot for the first time and walking gingerly. It was the cool feel of the sand up through your toes, and the feel of the soft tar in the streets and walking on a wall of concrete blocks, and the feel of cool, damp earth in shaded places. It was the feel of standing on the low edge of a roof or in a barn loft opening or on the second story of a house that was being built and daring another boy to jump; and looking over, waiting, knowing you must jump; and looking down, and waiting, daring, taunting, with a thudding heart, until you jumped.

And then it was the good feel of throwing a small, round, heavy stone through the window of a vacant house when the red and ancient light of evening was blazing on its windows; and it was like feeling a baseball in your hands for the first time in the Spring, and its round and solid weight at the end of your arm and the way it shot away like a bullet the first time when you threw it with a feeling of terrific power and speed and it smacked into the odorous, well-oiled pocket of the catcher's mitt. And then it was like prowling round in dark, cool cellars, thinking you would come upon a buried treasure any moment, and finding rows of cobwebbed bottles and the rusty frame of an old bicycle.

Sometimes it was like waking up on Saturday with the grand feeling of Saturday morning leaping in your heart, and seeing the apple blossoms drifting to the earth, and smelling sausage and ham and coffee, and knowing there would be no school today, no dreadful, morning, schoolhouse bell today, no thudding heart, and pounding legs, and shuddering nerves and bolted and uneasy food, and sour, distressful coffee in your guts, because there would be no school today and it was golden, shining, and triumphant Saturday.

And then it was like Saturday night, and joy and menace in the air, and everyone waiting to get out on the streets and go "uptown," and taking a hot bath, and putting on clean clothes and eating supper, and going uptown on the nighttime streets of Saturday where joy and menace filled the air about you, and where glory breathed upon you, and yet never came, and getting far down towards the front and seeing

Broncho Billy shoot the bad men dead three times until the last show of the night was over, and a cracked slide was shone on the screen which said "Good Night."

Then it was like Sunday morning, waking, hearing the bus outside, smelling the coffee, brains and eggs, and buckwheat cakes, feeling peaceful, sweetly happy, not exultant as on Saturday, a slumberous, drowsy, and more mournful joy, the smell of the Sunday newspapers, and the Sunday morning light outside, bright, golden, yet religious light, and church bells, people putting on good clothes to go to church, and the closed and decent streets of Sunday morning, and going by the cool side where the tobacco store was, and the Sunday morning sports inside who didn't have to go to church, and the strong, clean, pungent smell of good tobacco, and the good smell and feel of the church, which was not so much like God as like a good and decent substance in the world—the children singing, "Shall we gather at the River the Bew-tee-ful the Bew-tee-ful R-hiv-er!"—and the drone of voices from the class rooms later on, and the dark walnut, stained-glass light in the church, and decent, never-gaudy people with good dinners waiting for them when they got home, and the remote yet passionate austerity of the preacher's voice, the lean, horselike nobility of his face as he craned above his collar saying "heinous"—and all remote, austere, subdued, and decent as if God were there in walnut light and a choker collar; and then the twenty-minute prayer, the organ pealing a rich benison, and people talking, laughing, streaming out from the dutiful, weekly, walnut disinfection of their souls into bright morning-gold of Sunday light again, and standing then in friendly and yet laughing groups upon the lawn outside, and streaming off towards home again, a steady liquid Sunday shuffle of good leather on the quiet streets—and all of it was good and godly, yet not like God, but like an ordered destiny, like Sunday morning peace and decency, and good dinners, money in the bank, and strong security.

And then it was the huge winds in great trees at night—the remote, demented winds—the sharp, clean raining of the acorns to the earth, and a demon's whisper of evil and unbodied jubilation in your heart, speaking of triumph, flight, and darkness, new lands, morning, and a shining city.

And then it was like waking up and knowing somehow snow was there before you looked, feeling the numb, white, brooding prescience of soft-silent, all-engulfing snow around you, and then hearing it, soft, almost noiseless, fluff and fall to earth, and the scraping of a shovel on the sidewalk before the house.

And then it was like stern and iron Winter, and days and nights that ate intolerably the slow grey ash of time away, and April that would never come, and waiting, waiting, waiting dreamily at night for something magical that never happened, and bare boughs that creaked and swayed in darkness, and the frozen shapes of limbs that swung stiff shadows on the street below a light, and your aunt's voice filled with the fathomless sea-depths of Joyner time and horror, and of a race that lived forever while you drowned.

And then it was like the few days that you liked school, when you began and ended in September and in June. It was like going back to school again in September and getting some joy and hope out of the book-lists that the teacher gave you the first day, and then the feel and look and smell of the new geography, the reader and the composition books, the history, and the smells of pencils, wooden rules, and paper in the bookstore, and the solid, wealthy feel of the books and bookstrap, and taking the books home and devouring them—the new, richly illustrated geography and history and reading books—devouring them with an insatiate joy and hunger until there was nothing new left in them, and getting up in the morning and hearing the morning schoolhouse bell, and hoping it would not be so bad this year after all.

And it was like waiting in May for school to end, and liking it, and feeling a little sad because it would soon be over, and like the last day when you felt quite sorrowful and yet full of an exultant joy, and watched the high school graduate, and saw the plaster casts of Minerva and Diana, the busts of Socrates, Demosthenes, and Caesar, and smelled the chalk, the ink, the schoolroom smells, with ecstasy, and were sorry you were leaving them.

And you felt tears come into your own eyes as the class sang its graduation song with words to the tune of "Old Heidelberg," and saw the girls weeping hysterically, kissing each other and falling on the neck of Mr. Hamby, the Principal, swearing they would never forget him, no, never, as long as they lived, and these had been the happiest days of their lives, and they just couldn't bear it—boo-hoo-hoo!—and then listened to the oration of the Honorable Zebulon N. Meekins, the local Congressman, telling them the world had never seen a time when it needed leaders as it does at present and go—go—go my young friends and be a Leader in the Great World that is waiting for you and God Bless You All—and your eyes were wet, your throat was choked with joy and pain intolerable as Zebulon N. Meekins spoke these glorious words, for as he spoke them the soft, bloom-laden wind of June howled gusty for a moment at the eaves, you saw the young green of the trees outside and smelled a smell of tar and green and fields thick with the white and yellow of the daisies bending in the wind, and heard far-faint thunder on the rails, and saw the Great World then, the far-shining, golden, and enchanted city, and heard the distant, murmurous drone of all its million-footed life, and saw its fabulous towers soaring upward from an opalescent mist, and knew that some day you would walk its streets a conqueror and be a Leader among the most beautiful and fortunate people in the world; and you thought the golden tongue of Zebulon Nathaniel Meekins had done it all for you, and gave no credit to the troubling light that came and went outside, from gold to grey and back to gold again, and none to the young green of June and the thick-starred magic of the daisy fields, or to the thrilling school-house smells of chalk and ink and varnished desks, or to the thrilling mystery, joy, and sadness, the numb, delicious feel of glory in your guts—no you gave no credit to these things at all, but thought Zeb Meekins' golden tongue had done it all to you.

And you wondered what the schoolrooms were like in Summer when no one was there, and wished that you could be there alone with your pretty, red-haired, and voluptuous-looking teacher, or with a girl in your class who sat across the aisle from you, and whose name was Edith Pickleseimer, and who had fat curls, blue eyes of sweet tranquillity, and a tender, innocent smile, and who wore short little skirts, clean blue drawers, and you could sometimes see the white and tender plumpness of her leg where the straps and garter buckles that held up her stockings pressed into it, and you thought of being here with her alone, and yet all in a pure way too.

And sometimes it was like coming home from school in October, and smelling burning leaves upon the air, and wading in the oak leaves in the gutter, and seeing men in shirt-sleeves with arm bands of a ruffled blue upon the sleeves raking the leaves together in their yards, and feeling, smelling, hearing ripeness, harvest, in the air, and sometimes frost at night, silence, frost-white moonlight through the windows, the distant barking of a dog, and a great train pounding at the rails, a great train going in the night, the tolling bell, the lonely and departing whistle-wail.

These lights and shapes and tones of things swarmed in the boy's mind like a magic web of shifting, iridescent colors. For the place where he lived was not just a street to him—not just a strip of pavement and a design of weathered, shabby houses: it was the living integument of his life, the frame and stage for the whole world of childhood and enchantment.

Here on the corner of Locust Street, at the foot of the hill below his uncle's house, was the wall of concrete blocks on which Monk sat at night a thousand times with the other boys in the neighborhood, conspiring together in lowered voices, weaving about their lives a huge conspiracy of night and mystery and adventure, prowling away into the dark to find it, whispering and snickering together in the dark, now prowling softly in the shadows, halting sharply, whispering, "Wait a minute!"—now in full, sudden, startled flight and terror with a rush of feet, going away from—nothing. Now talking, conspiring mysteriously again upon the wall of concrete blocks, and prowling off desperately into the dark of streets, yards, and alleys, filled exultantly with the huge and evil presence of the dark, and hoping, with a kind of desperate terror and resolve, for something wicked, wild, and evil in the night, as jubilant and dark as the demonic joy that rose wildly and intolerably in their hearts.

This also was the corner where he saw two boys killed one day. It was a day in Spring, in afternoon, and heavy, grey, and wet to feel, all of the air was cool, and damp, full of the smell of earth and heavy green. He was on his way uptown, and Aunt Maw was cleaning up in the dining room and looking after him as he went down Locust Street, past the Shepperton house and past the house across the street where Nebraska Crane lived. He had a good feeling because he was going to buy chocolate and maple syrup for candy making, and because the air was heavy, grey, and green, and he felt some intolerable joy was in the air.

Then he turned the corner into Baird Street, and Albert and Johnny Andrews were coming towards him, coasting in their wagon, Albert steering; and Johnny raised his hand and yelled at him as he went by, and Albert yelled but did not raise his hand. And then Monk turned to watch them as they whizzed around the corner and saw the high-wheeled Oldsmobile that young Hank Bass drove run over them. And he remembered that the car belonged to Mr. Pendergraft, the fine-looking lumber man, who was rich and lived out on Montgomery Avenue in the swell part of town, and had two sons named Hip and Hop who went to Sunday School with Monk and grinned at people and were tongue-tied and had harelips. He saw the car hit the boys, smash their wagon into splinters, and drag Albert on his face for fifty yards. And Albert's wagon had been painted bright yellow, and on the sides had been printed the word "Leader."

Albert's face was smashed to currant jelly on the street, and Monk could see it scrape for fifty yards along the pavement like a bloody rag before the car was stopped; and when he got there they were getting Albert out from beneath the car. He could smell the sultry odors of the car, the smell of worn rubber, oil and gasoline, and heavy leathers, and the smell of blood; and everywhere people were rushing from their houses shouting, and men were going down beneath the car to get Albert out, and Bass was standing there with a face the color of green blubber, and cold sweat standing on his forehead, and his pants staining where he'd messed himself, and Albert was nothing but a bloody rag.

Mr. Ernest Pennock, who lived next door to Uncle Mark, got Albert out and lifted him in his arms. Ernest Pennock was a big, red-faced man with a hearty voice, the uncle of Monk's friend, Sam Pennock. Ernest Pennock was in shirt-sleeves and wore arm bands of ruffled blue, and Albert's blood got all over Ernest Pennock's shirt as he held Albert in his arms. Albert's back was broken and his legs were broken and the raw splinters of the bones were sticking through his torn stockings, and all the time he kept screaming:

"O mama save me O mama, mama save me O mama save me!"

And Monk was sick to his guts because Albert had shouted at him and been happy just a minute ago, and something immense and merciless that no one understood had fallen from the sky upon him and broken his back and no one could save him now.

The car had run over Johnny but had not dragged him, and he had no blood upon him, only two blue sunken marks upon his forehead. And Mr. Joe Black, who lived two doors below the Joyners, at the corner, and was the foreman of the street-car men and stood up in the

Public Square all day and gave orders to the motormen every fifteen minutes when the cars came in, and married one of the daughters of Mr. McPherson, the Scotchman who lived across the street above the Joyners, had picked Johnny up and was holding him and talking gently to him, and saying in a cheerful voice, half to Johnny, half to himself and the other people:

"This boy's not hurt, yes, sir, he just got bruised a bit, he's going to be a brave man and be all right again before you know it."

Johnny moaned a little, but not loudly, and there was no blood on him, and no one noticed Johnny, but Johnny died then while Joe Black talked to him.

And then Mrs. Andrews came tearing around the corner, wearing an apron and screaming like a demented hag, and she clawed her way through the crowd of people around Albert, and snatched him out of Ernest Pennock's arms, and kissed him till her face was covered with his blood, and kept screaming:

"Is he dead? Is he dead? Why don't you tell me if he's dead?"

Then suddenly she stopped screaming when they told her that it was not Albert but Johnny who was dead—grew calm, silent, almost tranquil, because Albert was her own child, and Johnny was an adopted child; and although she had always been good to Johnny, all the people in the neighborhood said later:

"You see, don't you? It only goes to show you! You saw how quick she shut up when she heard it wasn't her own flesh and blood."

But Albert died anyway two hours later at the hospital.

Finally—and somehow this was the worst of all—Mr. Andrews came tottering towards the people as they gathered around Albert. He was an insurance salesman, a little scrap of a man who was wasting away with some horrible joint disease. He was so feeble that he could not walk save by tottering along on a cane, and his great staring eyes and sunken face and large head, that seemed too heavy for the scrawny neck and body that supported it, went waggling, goggling, jerking about from side to side with every step he took, and his legs made sudden and convulsive movements as if they were going to fly away beneath him as he walked. Yet this ruin of a man had gotten nine children, and was getting new ones all the time. Monk had talked about this with the other boys in lowered voices, and with a feeling of horror and curiosity, for he wondered if his physical collapse had not come somehow from all the children he had got, if some criminal excess in nature had not sapped and gutted him and made his limbs fly out below him with these movements of convulsive disintegration; and he felt a terrible fascination and revulsion of the spirit because of the seminal mystery of nature that could draw forth life in swarming hordes from the withered loins of a walking dead man such as this.

But finally he had come around the corner, goggling, waggling, jerking onward with his huge, vacant, staring eyes, towards the bloody place where two of his children had been killed; and this, together with the strong congruent smells of rubber, leather, oil and gasoline, mixed with the heavy, glutinous sweetness of warm blood, and hanging there like a cloud in the cool, wet, earthy air of that grey-green day that just a moment before had impended with such a wordless and intolerable prescience of joy, and now was filled with horror, nausea, and desperate sickness of the soul—this finally was the memory that was to fix that corner, the hour, the day, the time, the words and faces of the people, with a feeling of the huge and nameless death that waits around the corner for all men, to break their backs and shatter instantly the blind and pitiful illusions of their hope.

Here was the place, just up the hill a little way from this treacherous corner, right there in front of Shepperton's house, where another accident occurred, as absurd and comic as the first was tragic and horrible.

One morning about seven o'clock, in the Spring of the year when all the fruit trees were in blossom, George was awakened instantly as he lay in his room, with a vision of cherry blossoms floating slowly to the earth, and at the same time with the memory of a terrific collision —a savage grinding and splintering of glass, steel, and wood—still ringing in his ears. Already he could hear people shouting to one another in the street, and the sound of footsteps running. The screen door slammed in his uncle's house next door, and the boy heard his Uncle Mark howl to someone in an excited tone:

"It's down here on Locust Street! Merciful God, they'll all be killed!"

And he was off, striding down the street.

But already George was out of bed, had his trousers on, and, without stopping for stockings, shoes, or shirt, he went running onto the porch, down the steps, and out into the street as hard as he could go. People were running along in the same direction, and he could see his uncle's figure in the rapidly growing crowd gathered in front of Shepperton's about a big telephone post which had been snapped off like a match stick near the base and hung half-suspended from the wires.

As he pounded up, the fragments of the car were strewn over the pavement for a distance of fifty yards—a wheel here, a rod there, a lamp, a leather seat at other places, and shattered glass everywhere. The battered and twisted wreckage of the car's body rested solidly and squatly upon the street before the telephone post which it had snapped with its terrific impact, and in the middle of all this wreckage Lon Pilcher was solemnly sitting, with a stupid look upon his face and the rim of the steering wheel wrapped around his neck. A few feet away, across the sidewalk, and upon the high-banked lawn of the Shepperton house, Mr. Matthews, the fat, red-faced policeman, was sitting squarely on his solid bottom, legs thrust out before him, and with the same look of stupid and solemn surprise on his face that Lon Pilcher had.

Uncle Mark and some other men pulled Lon Pilcher from the wreckage of his car, took the steering wheel from around his neck, and assured themselves that by some miracle of chance he was not hurt. Lon, recovering quickly from the collision which had stunned him, now began to peer owlishly about at the strewn remnants of his car, and finally, turning to Uncle Mark with a drunken leer, he said:

"D'ye think it's damaged much, Mr. Joyner? D'ye think we can fix her up again, so she will run?" Here he belched heavily, covered his mouth with his hand, said, "Excuse me," and began to prowl drunkenly among the strewn fragments.

Meanwhile Mr. Matthews, recovering from his shock, now clambered down clumsily from the bank and pounded heavily towards Lon, shouting:

"I'll arrest ye! I'll arrest ye! I'll take ye to the lockup and arrest ye, that's what I'll do!"—a threat which now seemed somewhat superfluous since he had arrested Lon some time before.

It now developed that Lon had been cruising about the town all night with some drunken chorus girls in his celebrated Cadillac, model 1910; that the policeman had arrested him at the head of the Locust Street hill, and had commanded Lon to drive him to the police station; and then, during that terrific dash downhill which had ended in the smash-up near the corner, had screamed frantically at his driver

"Stop! Stop! Let me out! You're under arrest! Damn you, I'll arrest ye fer this, as sure as you're born!"

And, according to witnesses, at the moment of collision the fat policeman had sailed gracefully through the shining morning air, described two somersaults, and landed solidly and squarely upon his bottom, with such force that he was stunned for several minutes, but still kept muttering all the time:

"Stop! Stop! Or I'll arrest ye!"

Here was the house, across the street from Shepperton's and just above Nebraska Crane's house, where Captain Suggs lived. He was a cripple, with both legs amputated far above the knee. The rest of him was a gigantic hulk, with enormous shoulders, powerful, thick hands, and a look of brutal power and determination about his great, thick neck and his broad, clean-shaven, cruel-lipped mouth. He got about on crutches when he had his wooden stumps on him; at other times he crawled about on the stump ends of his amputated legs. which were protected by worn leather pads. He had had one leg shot off at Cold Harbor, and the other was mangled and had to be amputated. In spite of his mutilation and his huge bulk, he could move with amazing speed when he wanted to. When he was angered, he could use his crutch as a club and could floor anyone within a radius of six feet. His wife, a little, frail woman, was thoroughly submissive.

His son, "Fielder" Suggs, was a little past thirty and on his way to fortune. At one time in his career he had been a professional baseball player. Later, with money enough for one month's rent, Fielder leased a vacant store and installed there the first moving picture projection camera the town had known. Now he owned the Princess and the Gaiety on the Square, and his career was a miracle of sudden wealth.

Here was the place upon the street before McPherson's house where the horse slipped and fell on the icy pavement one cold night in January, and broke its leg. There were dark faces of men around the house, and presently George heard two shots, and his Uncle Mark came back with a sad look on his face, shaking his head regretfully and muttering, "What a pity! What a pity!"—and then began to de-nounce the city government bitterly for making the pavements so slip-pery and the hill so steep. And light and warmth went from the boy's life, and the terror of the dark was all about him.

Here was the alleyway that ran past his uncle's house on the lower side and was bordered by a lane of lonely pines, and there was the huge, clay-caked stump of a tree where the boys would go Christmas morning and on the Fourth of July to explode their firecrackers on the stump. Rufus Higginson, who was Harry's older brother, came there one Fourth of July with a toy cannon and a large yellow paper bag filled with loose powder, and he threw a match away into the powder bag, and even as he bent to get more powder it exploded in his face. He rushed screaming like a madman down the alley, his face black as a negro's and his eyes blinded, and he rushed through his house from room to room, and no one could quiet him or get him to stop running because the pain was so intense. The doctor came and picked the powder out, and for weeks he bathed his face in oil; and his face turned into one solid scab, which then peeled off and left no scar at all, when everyone said he "would be scarred for life."

On up the hill past his uncle's new, brick house, and beside it, and to the rear, the little frame house which his grandfather had built more than forty years before, and where George now lived with his Aunt Maw; on up the hill past Pennock's house and Higginson's old house; on up past Mr. McPherson's house across the street, which always looked new and clean and tidy, and bright with new paint; on up to the top of the hill where Locust Street came into Charles, and on the left hand, was the huge, old, gabled house of brown, with its great porches, parlors, halls of quartered oak, and carriage entrances, and the enormous, lordly oaks in front of it. Some wealthy people from South Carolina lived there. They had a negro driver and a carriage that came up the driveway for them every day, and they never spoke to the other people on the street because they were too fine for them and moved in higher circles.

Across Charles Street, on the corner, was a brick house in which a woman lived with her aged mother. The woman was a good soul, with fluffy, sandy-reddish hair, a hooked nose, a red face, and teeth that stuck out. Everyone called her "Pretty Polly" because she looked like a parrot and had a parrot's throaty voice. She played the piano for the moving picture shows at the Gaiety Theatre, and every night when she stopped playing the people in the audience would cry out:

"Music, Polly, music! Please, Polly, music, Polly! Pretty Polly, please!"

She never seemed to mind at all, and would play again.

"Pretty Polly" had a beau named James Mears, better known as "Duke" Mears, because he was always smartly dressed in correct riding costume, or at least what he believed to be the correct riding costume of the English aristocracy. He wore a derby hat, a stock, a fawn-colored weskit with the last and lowest button nonchalantly left unbuttoned, a close-fitting checked riding coat, riding trousers and magnificent, shining riding boots and spurs, and he carried a riding crop. He always wore this costume. He wore it when he got up in the morning, he wore it when he walked across the Square, he wore it when he went down the main street of the town, he wore it when he got into a street car, he wore it when he went to Miller and Cashman's livery stable.

Duke Mears had never been on a horse in his life, but he knew more about horses than anyone else. He talked to them and loved them better than he loved people. George saw him one Winter night at the fire which burned down the livery stable, and he yelled like a madman when he heard the horses screaming in the fire; they had to hold him and throw him to the ground and sit on him to keep him from going in to get the horses. Next day the boy went by and the stable was a mass of smoking timbers, and he could smell the wet, blackened embers, caked with ice, and the acrid smell of the put-out fire, and the sickening smell of roasted horse flesh. Teams were dragging the dead horses out with chains, and one dead horse had burst in two across the belly and its blue roasted entrails had come bulging out with a hideous stench he could not blow out of his nostrils.

On the other corner of Locust Street and Charles, facing the house where "Pretty Polly" lived, was the Leathergood house; and farther along Charles Street, up the hill in the direction of the Country Club, was Mrs. Charles Montgomery Hopper's boarding house.

Everyone knew Mrs. Charles Montgomery Hopper. No one had ever seen or heard of Mr. Charles Montgomery Hopper. No one knew where he came from, no one knew where she got him, no one knew where they had lived together, no one knew who he was, or where he lived and died and was buried. It may very well be that he did not exist, that he never existed at all. Nevertheless, by the vociferous use of this imposing and resounding name, year after year, in a loud, aggressive, and somewhat raucous voice, Mrs. Charles Montgomery Hopper had convinced everyone, bludgeoned, touted everyone into the unquestioning acceptance of the fact that the name of Charles Montgomery Hopper was a very distinguished one, and that Mrs. Charles Montgomery Hopper was a very distinguished person.

In spite of the fact that she ran a boarding house, it was never referred to as a boarding house. If one telephoned and asked if this was Mrs. Hopper's boarding house, one of two things was likely to happen if Mrs. Hopper was the one who answered. The luckless questioner would either have the receiver slammed up violently in his face, after having his ears blistered by the scathing invective of which Mrs. Hopper was the complete mistress; or he would be informed, in tones that dripped with acid, that it was *not* Mrs. Hopper's boarding house, that Mrs. Hopper did not *have* a boarding house, that it was Mrs. Hopper's *residence*—then, also, he would have the receiver slammed up in his face.

None of the boarders ever dared to refer to the fact that the lady had a boarding house, and that they paid her money for their board. Should anyone be so indelicate as to mention this, he must be prepared to pay the penalty for his indiscretion. He would be informed that his room was needed, that the people who had engaged it were coming the next day, and at what time could he have his baggage ready. Mrs. Hopper had even her boarders cowed. They were made to feel that a great and distinguished privilege had been extended to them when they were allowed to remain even for a short time as guests in Mrs. Hopper's residence. They were made to feel also that this fact had somehow miraculously removed from them the taint of being ordinary boarders. It gave them a kind of aristocratic distinction, gave them a social position of which few people could boast, enrolled them under Mrs. Hopper's approving seal in the Bluebook of the 400,

So here was a boarding house that was no boarding house at all. Call it, rather, a kind of elegant house party which went on perpetually, and to which the favored few who were invited were also graciously permitted to contribute with their funds.

Did it work? Whoever has lived here in America must know how well it worked, how cheerfully, how meekly, how humbly, with what servility, the guests at Mrs. Hopper's house party endured that lean and scrawny fare, endured discomfort, cold, bad plumbing, and untidy housekeeping, even endured Mrs. Hopper and her voice, her domination and her dirge of abuse, if only they could remain there in the circle of the elect, not boarders really, but distinguished people.

That small company of the faithful returned from year to year to Mrs. Hopper's palace. Season after season, Summer after Summer, the rooms were booked up solid. Occasionally a stranger tried to make an entrance—some parvenu, no doubt, trying to buy his way into the protected circles of the aristocracy, some low bounder with money in his pocket, some social climber. Well, they looked him over with a very cold and fishy eye at Mrs. Charles Montgomery Hopper's, remarked that they did not seem to remember his face, and had he ever been to Mrs. Charles Montgomery Hopper's house before. The guilty wretch would stammer out a confused and panicky admission that this, indeed, was his first visit. A cold silence then would fall upon the company. And, presently, someone would say that he had been coming there every Summer for the past fourteen years. Another would remark that his first visit was the year before the year the War with Spain broke out. Another one would modestly confess that this was just his eleventh year and that at last he really felt that he belonged; it took ten years, he added, to feel at home. And this was true.

So they came back year after year, this little circle of the elect. There were old man Holt and his wife, from New Orleans. There was Mr. McKethan, who stayed there all the time. He was a jeweler's assistant, but his folks came from down near Charleston. He belonged. There was Miss Bangs, an antique spinstress, who taught in the public schools of New York City and soon would have her pension, and thereafter, it was thought, would retire forever, four seasons of the year, to the elegant seclusion of Mrs. Hopper's house. And there was Miss Millie Teasdale, the cashier at McCormack's pharmacy. She came from New York also, but now she was a "permanent" at Mrs. Hopper's house.

In the kitchen at Mrs. Charles Montgomery Hopper's was Jenny

Grubb, a negro woman of forty who had been there fifteen years or more. She was plump, solid, jolly, and so black that, as the saying went, charcoal would make a white mark on her. Her rich and hearty laughter, that had in it the whole black depth and warmth of Africa, could be heard all over the house. She sang forever, and her rich, strong, darkly-fibered voice could also be heard all day long. During the week she worked from dawn till after dark, from six in the morning till nine at night. On Sunday afternoon she had her day of rest. It was the day she had been preparing for, the day she had been living for all week. But Sunday afternoon was really not a day of rest for Jenny Grubb: it was a day of consecration, a day of wrath, a day of reckoning. It was potentially always the last day of the world, the day of sinners come to judgment.

Every Sunday afternoon at three o'clock, when Mrs. Hopper's clients had been fed, Jenny Grubb was free for three hours and made the most of it. She went out the kitchen door and round the house and up the alley to the street. She had already begun to mutter darkly and forebodingly, to herself. By the time she had crossed Locust Street and got two blocks down the hill towards town, her broad figure had begun to sway rhythmically. By the time she reached the bottom of the Central Avenue hill and turned the corner, began to mount again at Spring Street towards the Square, she had begun to breathe stertorously, to moan in a low tone, to burst into a sudden shout of praise or malediction. By the time she got to the Square, she was primed and ready. As she turned into the Square, that torpid and deserted Sunday Square of three o'clock, a warning cry burst from her.

"O sinners, I'se a-comin'!" Jenny yelled, although there were no sinners there.

The Square was bare and empty, but it made no difference. Swaying with a rhythmical movement of her powerful and solid frame, she propelled herself rapidly across the Square to the appointed corner, warning sinners as she came. And the Square was empty. The Square was always empty. She took up her position there in the hot sun, on the corner where McCormack's drug store and Joyner's hardware store faced each other. For the next three hours she harangued the heated, vacant Square.

From time to time, each quarter of the hour, the street cars of the town came in and crossed, halted and stopped. The motormen got down with their control rods in their hands, moved to the other end; the conductors swung the trolleys around. The solitary loafer leaned against the rail and picked his teeth, half-listening idly to black Jenny Grubb's harangue. And then the cars moved out, the loafer went away, and Jenny still harangued the vacant Square.

7

The Butcher

EVERY AFTERNOON, UP THE HILL BEFORE MARK JOYNER'S HOUSE, WHEEZED and panted the ancient, dilapidated truck in which Mr. Lampley, the butcher, delivered his tender, succulent steaks and chops and roasts, and his deliciously fragrant home-made sausage, headcheese, liverwurst, and fat red frankfurters. To the boy, George Webber, this glamorous and rickety machine seemed to gain glory and enchantment as the years went on and the deposits of grease and oil, together with the warm odors of sage and other spices with which he seasoned his fresh pork sausage and a dozen more of his home-made delicacies, worked their way in and through the rich, stained texture of its weathered, winelike wood. Even years later, in the transforming light of time, it seemed to him strange, important, and immense to remember Mr. Lampley, to remember his wife, his daughter, and his son, the wholesome, fragrant, and delicate quality of their work—and something as savage and wild as nature in the lives of all of them.

Mr. Lampley had come to town as a stranger twenty years before, and a stranger he had always been since coming there. Nothing was known of his past life or origins. He was a small and hideously battered figure of a man, as compact and solid as a bullock, and with a deadly stillness and toneless quietness about all his words and movements that suggested a controlled but savagely illimitable vitality. His small, red face, which had the choleric and flaring color of the Irishman, had been so horribly drawn and twisted on one side by a hideous cut, inflicted, it was said, by another butcher with a meat cleaver in a fight long before he came to town, that it was one livid and puckered seam from throat to forehead, and even the corners of his hard lips were drawn and puckered by the scar. Moreover, the man never seemed to bat his eyelids, and his small black eyes—as hard, as black, as steady as any which ever looked out upon the light of day—glared at the world so unflinchingly, with such a formidable and deadly gaze that no man could stand their stare for long, that one's words trembled, stammered, and faltered foolishly away as one tried to utter them, and all attempts at friendliness or intimacy were blasted and withered in a second before those two unwinking eyes. Therefore no one knew him, no one sought his friendship twice; in all the years he had lived in the town he had made, beyond his family, not one intimate or friendly connection.

But if Mr. Lampley was formidable in his own toneless and unwinking way, his wife was no less formidable in quite another. He had married a woman native to that section, and she was one of those creatures of an epic animality and good nature whose proportions transcend the descriptive powers of language, and who can be measured by no scale of law or judgment. Of her, it could only be said that she was as innocent as nature, as merciful as a river in flood, as moral as the earth. Full of good nature and a huge, choking scream of laughter that swelled boundlessly from her mighty breast, she could in an instant have battered the brains out of anyone who crossed her or roused the witless passion of her nature; and she would never have felt a moment's pity or regret for doing so, even if she had paid the penalty with her life.

She was one of a large family of country people, all built on the same tremendous physical proportions, the daughter of an epic brute who had also been a butcher.

Physically, Mrs. Lampley was the biggest woman George had ever seen. She was well over six feet tall, and must have weighed more than two hundred pounds, and yet she was not fat. Her hands were ham like in their size and shape, her arms and legs great swelling haunches of limitless power and strength, her breast immense and almost depthless in its fullness. She had a great mass of thick, dark red hair; eyes as clear, grey, and depthless as a cat's; a wide, thin, rather loose, and cruel mouth; and a skin which, while clear and healthy-looking, had somehow a murky, glutinous quality—the quality of her smile and her huge, choking laugh—as if all the ropy and spermatic fluids of the earth were packed into her.

There was nothing to measure her by, no law by which to judge her: the woman burst out beyond the limit of all human valuations, and for this reason she smote terror to George's heart. She could tell stories so savage in their quality that the heart was sickened at them, and at the same time throw back her great throat and scream with laughter as she told them—and her laughter was terrible, not because it was cruel, but because the substance of which cruelty is made was utterly lacking in her nature.

Thus she would describe incidents out of the life of her father, the butcher, in a strangely soft, countrified tone of voice, which always held in it, however, a suggestion of limitless power, and the burble of huge, choking laughter that would presently burst from her:

"There used to be a cat down there at the market," she drawled, "who was always prowlin' and snoopin' around to git at his meat, you know," she went on confidentially in a quiet, ropy tone, and with a faint smile about her mouth. "Well," she said, with a little heaving chuckle of her mighty breasts, "the old man was gittin' madder an' madder all the time, an' one day when he found the cat had been at his meat again, he says to me—you know, I used to keep his books fer him—the old man turns to me, an' says, 'If I ketch that son-of-a-bitch in here again I'm goin' to cut his head off—'" Here she paused to chuckle, her great throat swelling with its burble of laughter and her mighty bosom swelling. "I could see he was gittin' mad, you know," she said in that almost unctuous drawl, "and I knew that cat was goin' to git in trouble if he didn't mind! . . . Well, sir," she said, beginning to gasp a little, "it wasn't ten minutes afore the old man looked up an' saw the cat over yonder on the chopping block fixin' to git at a great big side of beef the old man had put there! . . . Well, when the old man sees that cat he lets out a yell you could hear from here across the Square! 'You son-of-a-bitch!' he says, 'I told you I'd kill you if I caught you here again!'—and he picks up a cleaver," she gasped, "and throws it at that cat as hard as he could let fly, and —har!—har!—har!—har!"—she screamed suddenly, her great throat swelling like a bull's, and a wave of limitless laughter bursting from her and ending in a scream—"he ketches that damn cat as perty as anything you ever saw, an' cuts him plumb in two—har!—har!—har!— har!"—And this time her huge laughter seemed too immense even for her mighty frame to hold, and the tears ran down her cheeks as she sank back gasping in her chair. "Lord! Lord!" she gasped. "That was the pertiest thing I ever see! I liked to laffed myself to death," she panted, and then, still trembling, began to wipe at her streaming eyes with the back of one huge hand.

Again, one day, she told this merry story of her honored sire:

"A nigger came in there one day," she said, "an' told the old man to cut him off a piece of meat an' wrap it up for him. When the old man gave it to him, the nigger begins to argue with him," she said, "an' to give him some back-talk, claimin' the old man was cheatin' him on the weight an' tryin' to charge him too much fer it! Well, sir," she said, beginning to gasp a little, "the old man picks up a carving knife an' he makes one swipe across the counter at that nigger with it— and—har!—har!—har!"—her huge laugh burst out of her mighty breast again and welled upward to a choking, ropy scream, "—that nigger!—that nigger!—his guts came rollin' out into his hands like sausage meat!" she gasped. "I wish't you could have seen the look upon his face!" she panted. "He just stood there lookin' at them like he don't know what to do with them—and har!—har!—har!"—she cast her swelling throat back and roared with laughter, subsiding finally to huge, gasping mirth—"that was the funniest thing I ever see! If you could a-seen the look upon that nigger's face!" she panted, wiping at her streaming eyes with the back of her huge paw.

Whenever a tall, strong, powerfully-built man came for the first time into the butcher's little shop, Mrs. Lampley would immediately comment on his size and strength in a flattering and good-natured tone, but with something speculative and hard in her eye as she surveyed him, as if she was coldly calculating his chances with her in a knockdown fight. Many men had observed this look of appraisal, and George had heard men say that there was something so savagely calculating in it that it had made their blood run cold. She would look them over with a good-natured smile, but with a swift narrowing of her cat-grey eyes as she sized them up, meanwhile saying in a bantering and hearty tone of voice:

"Say! You're a right big feller, ain't you? I was lookin' at you when you came in—you could hardly git through the door," she chuckled. "I said to myself, 'I'd hate to git mixed up in any trouble with him,' I says, 'I'll bet a feller like that could hit you an awful lick if you git him mad. . . .' How much do you weigh?" she would then say, still smiling, but with those cold, narrowed, grey eyes measuring the unhappy stranger up and down.

And when the wretched man had stammered out his weight, she

would say softly, in a contemplative fashion: "Uh-huh!" And after going over him a moment longer with those merciless and slitlike eyes, she would say, with an air of hearty finality: "Well, you're a big 'un, sure enough! I'll bet you'll be a big help to your paw an' maw when you git your growth—har!—har!—har!—har!" And the choking scream of laughter would then burst from her Atlantean breasts and bull-like throat.

When she spoke of her husband she always referred to him as "Lampley," and this was the way she always addressed him. Her tone when she spoke of him certainly had in it nothing that could be described as affection, for such a feeling would have had no more place in her nature than a swan upon the breast of the flood-tide Mississippi, but her tone had in it a note of brutal and sensual satis-faction that somehow told plainly and terribly of a perfect marriage, of savage and limitless sexual energies, and of a mate in the battered figure of that little bullock man who could match and fit this mountain of a woman perfectly in an epic, night-long bout of lust and passion.

Mrs. Lampley spoke constantly, openly, vulgarly, and often with a crude, tremendous humor, of the sexual act, and although she never revealed the secrets of her own marriage bed—if a union so savage, complete, and obvious as the one between herself and her husband could be called a secret—she did not for a moment hesitate to publish her opinions on the subject to the world, to give young married couples, or young men and their girls, advice that would make them flush to the roots of their hair, and to scream with merriment when she saw their confusion.

Her son, Baxter, at this time a youth of eighteen, had just a year or two before taken a young girl by force, a well-developed and seductive red-haired girl of fourteen. This event, so far from causing his mother any distress, had seemed to her so funny that she had published it to the whole town, describing with roars of laughter her interview with the girl's outraged mother:

"Why, hell yes!" she said. "She came down here to see me, all broke out in a sweat about it, sayin' Baxter had ruined her daughter an' what was I goin' to do about it!—'Now, you look a-here!' I said. 'You jist git down off your high horse! He's ruined no one,' I says, 'for there was no one to ruin to begin with'—har!—har!—har!—har!"— the full, choking scream burst from her throat— "'Now,' I says, 'if she turns out to be a whore, she'll come by it natural'—har!—har!—har!—har!—'an' Baxter didn't make her one,' I says. 'What do you mean? What do you mean?' she says—oh! gittin' red as a ripe termater an' beginnin' to shake her finger in my face—'I'll have you put in jail fer slander,' she says, 'that's what I'll do!' 'Slander!' I says, 'Slander! Well, if it's slander,' I says, 'the law has changed since my day and time. It's the first time I ever knew you could slander a whore,' I says, 'by callin' her by her right name.' 'Don't you call my daughter no name like that,' she says, oh, madder'n a wet hen, you know—'Don't you dare to! I'll have you arrested,' she says. 'Why, God-damn you!' I says—that's just the way I talked to her, you know, 'everyone knows what your daughter is!' I says, 'so you git on out of here,' I says, 'before I git mad an' tell you something you may not like to hear!'—and I'm tellin' you, she went!" And the huge creature leaned back gasping for a moment.

"Hell!" she went on quietly in a moment, "I asked Baxter about it and he told me. 'Baxter,' I says, 'that woman has been here now an' I want to know: did you jump on that girl an' take it from her?' 'Why, mama,' he says, 'take it from her? Why, she took it from me!' says Baxter—har!—har!—har!—har!"—the tremendous laughter filled her throat and choked her. "'Hell!' says Baxter, 'she throwed me down an' almost broke my back! If I hadn't done like I did I don't believe she'd ever a-let me out of there!'—har!—har!—har!—har!—I reckon ole Baxter figgered it might as well be him as the next one," she panted, wiping at her streaming eyes. "I reckon he figgered he might as well git a little of it while the gittin' was good. But Lord!" she sighed, "I laffed about that thing until my sides was sore—har!—har!—har!—har!—har!"—and the enormous creature came forward in her creaking chair again, as the huge laughter filled her, and made the walls tremble with its limitless well of power.

Towards her own daughter, however, whose name was Grace, and who was fifteen at this time, Mrs. Lampley was virtuously, if brutally, attentive. In both the children the inhuman vitality of their parents was already apparent, and in the girl, especially, the measureless animal power of her mother had already developed. At fifteen, she was a tremendous creature, almost as tall as her mother, and so fully matured that the flimsy little cotton dresses which she wore, and which would have been proper for most children of her age, were almost obscenely inadequate. In the heavy calves, swelling thighs, and full breasts of this great, white-fleshed creature of fifteen years there was already evident a tremendous seductiveness; men looked at her with a terrible fascination and felt the wakening of unreasoning desire, and turned their eyes away from her with a feeling of strong shame.

Over this girl's life already there hung the shadow of fatality. Without knowing why, one felt certain that this great creature must come to grief and ruin—as one reads that giants die early, and things which are too great in nature for the measure of the world destroy themselves. In the girl's large, vacant, and regularly beautiful face, and in the tender, empty, and sensual smile which dwelt forever there, this legend of unavoidable catastrophe was plainly written.

The girl rarely spoke, and seemed to have no variety of passion save that indicated by her constant, limitlessly sensual, and vacant smile. And as she stood obedient and docile beside her mother, and that huge creature spoke of her with a naked frankness, and as the girl smiled always that tender, vacant smile as if her mother's words had no meaning for her, the feeling of something inhuman and catastrophic in the natures of these people was overwhelming:

"Yes," Mrs. Lampley would drawl, as the girl stood smiling vacantly at her side. "She's growed up here on me before I knowed it, an' I got to watch her all the time now to keep some son-of-a-bitch from knockin' her up an' ruinin' her. Here only a month or two ago two of these fellers down here at the livery stable—you know who I mean," she said carelessly, and in a soft, contemptuous voice—"that dirty, good-fer-nothin' Pegram feller an' that other low-down bastard he runs around with—what's his name, Grace?" she said impatiently, turning to the girl.

"That's Jack Cashman, mama," the girl answered in a soft and gentle tone, without changing for a second the tender, vacant smile upon her face.

"Yeah, that's him!" said Mrs. Lampley. "That low-down Cashman—if I ever ketch him foolin' around here again I'll break his neck, an' I reckon he knows it, too," she said grimly. "Why, I let her out, you know, one night along this Spring, to mail some letters," she went on in an explanatory tone, "an' told her not to be gone more'n half an hour—an' these two fellers picked her up in a buggy they was drivin' an' took her fer a ride way up the mountain side. Well, I waited an' waited till ten o'clock had struck, an' still she didn't come. An' I walked the floor, an' walked the floor, an' waited—an' by that time I was almost out of my head! I'll swear, I thought I would go crazy," she said slowly and virtuously. "I didn't know what to do. An' finally, when I couldn't stand it no longer, I went upstairs an' waked Lampley up. Of course, you know Lampley," she chuckled. "*He* goes to bed early. He's in bed every night by nine o'clock, and *he* ain't goin' to lose sleep over nobody. Well, I waked him up," she said slowly. " 'Lampley,' I says, 'Grace's been gone from here two hours, an' I'm goin' to find her if I have to spend the rest of the night lookin' for her.'—'Well how you goin' to find her,' he says, 'if you don't know where she's gone?'—'I don't know,' I says, 'but I'll find her if I've got to walk every street an' break into every house in town—an' if I find some son-of-a-bitch has taken advantage of her, I'll kill him with my bare hands,' " said Mrs. Lampley. " 'I'll kill the two of them together—for I'd rather see her layin' dead than know she's turned out to be a whore'—that's what I said to him," said Mrs. Lampley.

During all this time, the girl stood obediently beside the chair in which her mother sat, smiling her tender, vacant smile, and with no other sign of emotion whatever.

"Well," said Mrs. Lampley slowly, "then I heard her. I heard her while I was talkin' to Lampley, openin' the door easylike an' creepin' up the stairs. Well, I didn't say nothin'—I just waited until I heard her tiptoe in along the hall past Lampley's door—an' then I opened it an' called to her. 'Grace,' I said, 'where've you been?'—Well," said Mrs. Lampley with an air of admission, "she told me. She never tried to lie to me. I'll say that fer her, she's never lied to me yet. If she did," she added grimly, "I reckon she knows I'd break her neck."

And the girl stood there passively, smiling all the time.

"Well, then," said Mrs. Lampley, "she told me who she'd been with and where they'd been. Well—I thought I'd go crazy!" the woman said slowly and deliberately. "I took her by the arms an' looked at her. 'Grace,' I said, 'you look me in the eye an' tell me the truth—did those two fellers do anything to you?'—'No,' she says.—'Well, you come with me,' I says, 'I'll find out if you're telling me the truth, if I've got to kill you to git it out of you.' "

And for a moment the huge creature was silent, staring grimly ahead, while her daughter stood beside her and smiled her gentle and imperturbably sensual smile.

"Well," said Mrs. Lampley slowly, as she stared ahead, "I took her down into the cellar—and," she said with virtuous accents of slight regret, "I don't suppose I should have done it to her, but I was so worried—so worried," she cried strangely, "to think that after all the bringin' up she'd had, an' all the trouble me an' Lampley had taken tryin' to keep her straight—that I reckon I went almost crazy. . . . I reached down an' tore loose a board in an old packin' case we had down there," she said slowly, "an' I beat her! I *beat* her," she cried powerfully, "until the blood soaked through her dress an' run down on the floor. . . . I beat her till she couldn't stand," cried Mrs. Lampley, with an accent of strange maternal virtue in her voice, "I beat her till she got down on her knees an' begged fer mercy—now *that* was how hard I beat her," she said proudly. "An' you know it takes a lot to make Grace cry—she won't cry fer nothin'—so you may know I beat her mighty hard," said Mrs. Lampley, in a tone of strong satisfaction.

And during all this time the girl just stood passively with her sweet and vacant smile, and presently Mrs. Lampley heaved a powerful sigh of maternal tribulation, and, shaking her head slowly, said:

"But, Lord! Lord! They're a worry an' a care to you from the moment that they're born! You sweat an' slave to bring 'em up right—an' even then you can't tell what will happen. You watch 'em day an' night —an' then the first low-down bastard that comes along may git 'em out an' ruin 'em the first time your back is turned!"

And again she sighed heavily, shaking her head. And in this grotesque and horribly comic manifestation of motherly love and solicitude, and in the vacant, tender smile upon the girl's large, empty face there really was something moving, terribly pitiful, and unutterable.

Whenever George thought of this savage and tremendous family, his vision always returned again to Mr. Lampley himself, whose last, whose greatest secrecy, was silence. He talked to no one more than the barest necessity of business speech demanded, and when he spoke, either in question or reply, his speech was as curt and monosyllabic as speech could be, and his hard, blazing eyes, which he kept pointed as steady as a pistol at the face of anyone to whom he spoke or listened, repelled effectively any desire for a more spacious conversation. Yet, when he did speak, his voice was never surly, menacing, or snarling. It was a low, hard, toneless voice, as steady and unwavering as his hard black eyes, yet not unpleasant in its tone or timbre; it was, like everything about him save the naked, blazing eyes—hard, secret, and contained. He simply fastened his furious and malignant little eyes on one and spoke as brief and short as possible.

"Talk!" a man said. "Why, hell, he don't need to talk! He just stands there and lets those eyes of his do all the talkin' for him!" And this was true.

Beyond this bare anatomy of speech, George had heard him speak on only one occasion. This had been one day when he had come to make collections for the meat he had delivered. At this time it was known in the town that Mr. Lampley's son, Baxter, had been accused of stealing money from the man he worked for, and that—so ran the whispered and discreditable rumor—Baxter had been compelled to leave town. On this day when Mr. Lampley came to make collections, Aunt Maw, spurred by her native curiosity, and the desire that people have to hear the confirmation of their worst suspicions from the lips of those who are most painfully concerned, spoke to the butcher with the obvious and clumsy casualness of tone that people use on these occasions:

"Oh, Mr. Lampley," she said, as if by an afterthought when she had paid him, "say—by the way—I was meanin' to ask you. What's become of Baxter? I was thinkin' just the other day, I don't believe I've seen him for the last month or two."

During all the time she spoke, the man's blazing eyes never faltered in their stare upon her face, and they neither winked nor wavered as he answered.

"No," he said, in his low, hard, toneless voice, "I don't suppose you have. He's not livin' here any more. He's in the navy."

"What say?" Aunt Maw cried eagerly, opening the screen door a trifle wider and moving forward. "The navy?" she said sharply.

"Yes, ma'am," said Mr. Lampley tonelessly, "the navy. It was a question of join the navy or go to jail. I gave him his choice. He joined the navy," Mr. Lampley said grimly.

"What say? Jail?" she said eagerly.

"Yes, ma'am," Mr. Lampley replied. "He stole money from the man he was workin' for, as I reckon maybe you have heard by now. He done something he had no right to do. He took money that did not belong to him," he said with a brutal stubbornness. "When they caught him at it they came to me and told me they'd let him go if I'd make good the money that he'd stolen. So I said to him: 'All right. I'll give 'em the money if you join the navy. Now, you can take your choice—it's join the navy or go to jail. What do you want to do?' He joined the navy," Mr. Lampley again concluded grimly.

As for Aunt Maw, she stood for a moment reflectively, and now, her sharp curiosity having been appeased by this blunt and final statement, a warmer, more engaging sentiment of friendliness and sympathy was awakened in her:

"Well, now, I tell you what," she said hopefully, "I believe you did just the thing you should have done. I believe that's the very thing Baxter needs. Why, yes!" she now cried cheerfully. "He'll go off there and see the world and meet up with all kinds of people, and learn to keep the proper sort of hours and lead a good, normal, healthy sort of life—for there's one thing sure," she said oracularly, "you can't violate the laws of nature. If you do, you'll have to pay for it some day as sure as you're born," she said solemnly, as she shook her head, "as sure as you're born."

"Yes, ma'am," said Mr. Lampley in his low, toneless voice, keeping his little blazing eyes fixed straight upon her.

"Why, yes," Aunt Maw cried again, and this time with the vigorous accents of a mounting cheerful certitude, "they'll teach that boy a trade and regular habits and the proper way to live, and you mark my words, everything's goin' to turn out good for him," she said with heartening conviction. "He'll forget all about this trouble. Why, yes!—the whole thing will blow right over, people will forget all about it. Why, say! everyone is liable to make a mistake sometime, aren't they?" she said persuasively. "That happens to everyone—and I'll bet you, I'll bet you anything you like that when that boy comes back ——"

"He ain't comin' back," said Mr. Lampley.

"What say?" Aunt Maw cried in a sharp, startled tone.

"I said he ain't comin' back," said Mr. Lampley.

"Why what's the reason he's not?" she said.

"Because if he does," said Mr. Lampley, "I'll kill him. And he knows it."

She stood looking at him for a moment with a slight frown.

"Oh, Mr. Lampley," she said quietly, shaking her head with a genial regret, "I'm sorry to hear you say that. I don't like to hear you talk that way."

He stared at her grimly for a moment with his furious, blazing eyes.

"Yes, ma'am," he said, as if he had not heard her. "I'll kill him. If he ever comes back here, I'll kill him. I'll beat him to death," he said.

Aunt Maw looked at him, shaking her head a little, saying with a closed mouth: "Huh, huh, huh, huh."

He was silent.

"I never could stand a thief," he said at length. "If it'd been anything else, I could've forgotten it. But a thief!" for the first time his voice rose hoarsely on a surge of passion. "Ah-h-h!" he muttered, stroking his head, and now there was a queer note of trouble and bewilderment in his hard tone. "You don't know! You don't know," he said, "the trouble I have had with that boy! His mother an' me done all we could for him. We worked hard an' we tried to raise him right— but we couldn't do nothing with him," he muttered. "He was a bad egg." He looked at her quietly a moment with his little, blazing eyes. Then he said, slowly and deliberately, and with a note of strong rising virtue in his voice, "I beat him, I beat him till he couldn't stand up—I beat him till the blood ran down his back—but it didn't do no more good than if I was beatin' at a post," he said. "No, ma'am. I might as well have beaten at a post."

And now his voice had a queer, hard note of grief, regret, and resignation in it, as if a man might say: "All that a father could do for a son I did for mine. But if a man shall beat his son until the blood runs down his back, and still that son learns neither grace nor penitence, what more can a father do?"

He paused a moment longer, with his little eyes fixed hard upon her.

"No, ma'am," he concluded, in his low, toneless voice, "I never expect to see his face again. He'll never come back here. He knows I'll kill him if he does." Then he turned and walked off towards his ancient vehicle while Aunt Maw stood watching him with a troubled and regretful face.

And he had told the truth. Baxter never did come back. He was as lost to all of them as if he had been dead. They never saw him again.

But George, who heard all this, remembered Baxter suddenly. He remembered his part-brutal, part-corrupted face. He was a creature criminal from nature and entirely innocent. His laugh was throaty with a murky, hoarse, and hateful substance in it; there was something too glutinously liquid, rank, and coarse in his smile; and his eyes looked wet. He had too strange and sudden and too murderously obscure a rage for the clear, hard passions most boys knew. He had a knife with a long, curved blade, and when he saw negroes in the street he put his hand upon his knife. He made half-sobbings in his throat when his rage took hold of him. Yet he was large, quite handsome, well-proportioned. He was full of rough, sudden play, and was always challenging a boy to wrestle with him. He could wrestle strongly, rudely, laughing hoarsely if he flung somebody to the ground, enjoying a bruising struggle, and liking to pant and scuffle harshly with skinned knees upon the earth; and yet he would stop suddenly if he had made his effort but found his opponent stronger than he was, and succumb inertly, with a limp, sudden weakness, smiling, with no pride or hurt, as his opponent pinned him to the earth.

There was something wrong in this; and there was something ropy, milky, undefined in all the porches of his blood, so that, George felt, had Baxter's flesh been cut or broken, had he bled, there would have been a ropy, milkweed mucus before blood came. He carried pictures in his pockets, photographs from Cuba, so he said, of shining naked whores in their rank white flesh and hairiness, in perverse and Latin revels with men with black mustaches, and he spoke often of experiences he had had with girls in town, and with negro women.

All this George remembered with a rush of naked vividness.

But he remembered also a kindness, a warmth and friendliness, equally strange and sudden, which Baxter had; something swift and eager, wholly liberal, which made him wish to share all he had—the sausages and sandwiches which he brought with him to school, together with all his enormous and delicious lunch—offering and thrusting the rich bounty of his lunch box, which would smell with an unutterable fragrance and delight, at the other boys with a kind of eager, asking, and insatiable generosity. And at times his voice was gentle, and his manner had this same strange, eager, warm, and almost timid gentleness and friendliness.

George remembered passing the butcher shop once, and from the basement, warm with its waft of fragrant spices, he suddenly heard Baxter screaming:

"Oh, I'll be good! I'll be good!"—and that sound from this rough, brutal boy had suddenly pierced him with an unutterable sense of shame and pity.

This, then, was Baxter as George had known him, and as he remembered him when the butcher spoke of him that day. And as the butcher spoke his hard and toneless words of judgment, George felt a wave of intolerable pity and regret pass over him as he remembered Baxter (although he had not known him well or seen him often), and knew he never would come back again.

8

The Child by Tiger

ONE DAY AFTER SCHOOL, MONK AND SEVERAL OF THE BOYS WERE PLAYING with a football in the yard at Randy Shepperton's. Randy was calling signals and handling the ball. Nebraska Crane was kicking it. Augustus Potterham was too clumsy to run or kick or pass, so they put him at center where all he'd have to do would be to pass the ball back to Randy when he got the signal. To the other boys, Gus Potterham was their freak child, their lame duck, the butt of their jokes and ridicule, but they also had a sincere affection for him; he was something to be taken in hand, to be protected and cared for.

There were several other boys who were ordinarily members of their group. They had Harry Higginson and Sam Pennock, and two boys named Howard Jarvis and Jim Redmond. It wasn't enough to make a team, of course. They didn't have room enough to play a game even if they had had team enough. What they played was really a kind of skeletonized practice game, with Randy and Nebraska back, Gus at center, two other fellows at the ends, and Monk and two or three more on the other side, whose duty was to get in and "break it up" if they could.

It was about four o'clock in the afternoon, late in October, and there was a smell of smoke, of leaves, of burning in the air. Bras had just kicked to Monk. It was a good kick too—a high, soaring punt that spiraled out above Monk's head, behind him. He ran back and tried to get it, but it was far and away "over the goal line"—that is to say, out in the street. It hit the street and bounded back and forth with that peculiarly erratic bounce a football has.

The ball rolled away from Monk down towards the corner. He was running out to get it when Dick Prosser, Sheppertons' new negro man, came along, gathered it up neatly in his great black paw, and tossed it to him. Dick turned in then, and came on around the house,

142

greeting the boys as he came. He called all of them "Mister" except Randy, and Randy was always "Cap'n"—"Cap'n Shepperton." This formal address—"Mr." Crane, "Mr." Potterham, "Mr." Webber, "Cap'n" Shepperton—pleased them immensely, gave them a feeling of mature importance and authority.

"Cap'n Shepperton" was splendid! It was something more to all of them than a mere title of respect. It had a delightful military association, particularly when Dick Prosser said it. Dick had served a long enlistment in the U. S. army. He had been a member of a regiment of crack negro troops upon the Texas border, and the stamp of the military man was evident in everything he did. It was a joy just to watch him split up kindling. He did it with a power, a clean precision, a kind of military order, that was astounding. Every stick he cut seemed to be exactly the same length and shape as every other. He had all of them neatly stacked against the walls of the Shepperton basement with such regimented faultlessness that it almost seemed a pity to disturb their symmetry for the use for which they were intended.

It was the same with everything else he did. His little whitewashed basement room was as spotless as a barracks room. The bare board floor was always cleanly swept, a plain, bare table and a plain, straight chair were stationed exactly in the center of the room. On the table there was always just one object—an old Bible with a limp cover, almost worn out by constant use, for Dick was a deeply religious man. There was a little cast-iron stove and a little wooden box with a few lumps of coal and a neat stack of kindling in it. And against the wall, to the left, there was an iron cot, always precisely made and covered cleanly with a coarse grey blanket.

The Sheppertons were delighted with him. He had come there looking for work just a month or two before, "gone around to the back door" and modestly presented his qualifications. He had, he said, only recently received his discharge from the army, and was eager to get employment, at no matter what wage. He could cook, he could tend the furnace, he could do odd jobs, he was handy at carpentry, he knew how to drive a car—in fact, it seemed to the boys that there was very little that Dick Prosser could not do.

He could certainly shoot. He gave a modest demonstration of his prowess one afternoon, with Randy's "twenty-two," that left them gasping. He just lifted that little rifle in his powerful black hands as if it were a toy, without seeming to take aim, pointed it towards a strip of tin on which they had crudely marked out some bull's-eye circles, and he simply peppered the center of the bull's eye, putting twelve holes through a space one inch square, so fast they could not even count the shots.

He knew how to box, too. Randy said he had been a regimental champion. At any rate, he was as cunning and crafty as a cat. He never boxed with the boys, of course, but Randy had two sets of gloves, and Dick used to coach them while they sparred. There was something amazingly tender and watchful about him. He taught them many things, how to lead, to hook, to counter, and to block, but he was careful to see that they did not hurt each other. Nebraska, who was the most powerful of the lot, could hit like a mule. He would have killed Gus Potterham in his simple, honest way if he had ever been given a free hand. But Dick, with his quick watchfulness, his gentle and persuasive tact, was careful to see this did not happen.

He knew about football, too, and that day, as Dick passed the boys, he paused, a powerful, respectable-looking negro of thirty years or more, and watched them for a moment as they played.

Randy took the ball and went up to him.

"How do you hold it, Dick?" he said. "Is this right?"

Dick watched him attentively as he gripped the ball and held it back above his shoulder. The negro nodded approvingly and said:

"That's right, Cap'n Shepperton. You've got it. Only," he said gently, and now took the ball in his own powerful hand, "when you gits a little oldah, yo' handses gits biggah and you gits a bettah grip."

His own great hand, in fact, seemed to hold the ball as easily as if it were an apple. And, holding it so a moment, he brought it back, aimed over his outstretched left hand as if he were pointing a gun, and rifled it in a beautiful, whizzing spiral thirty yards or more to Gus. He then showed them how to kick, how to get the ball off of the toe in such a way that it would rise and spiral cleanly.

He showed them how to make a fire, how to pile the kindling, where to place the coal, so that the flames shot up cone-wise, cleanly, without smoke or waste. He showed them how to strike a match with the thumbnail of one hand and keep and hold the flame in the strongest wind. He showed them how to lift a weight, how to "tote" a burden on their shoulders in the easiest way. There was nothing that he did not know. They were all so proud of him. Mr. Shepperton himself declared that Dick was the best man he'd ever had, the smartest darky that he'd ever known.

And yet? He went too softly, at too swift a pace. He was there upon them sometimes like a cat. Looking before them sometimes, seeing nothing but the world before them, suddenly they felt a shadow at their back, and, looking up, would find that Dick was there. And there was something moving in the night. They never saw him come or go. Sometimes they would waken, startled, and feel that they had heard a board creak, the soft clicking of a latch, a shadow passing swiftly. All was still.

"Young white fokes—O young white gentlemen"—his soft voice ending in a moan, a kind of rhythm in his lips—"O young white fokes, I'se tellin' you—" that soft, low moan again—"you gotta love each othah like a brothah." He was deeply religious and went to church three times a week. He read his Bible every night.

Sometimes Dick would come out of his little basement room and his eyes would be red, as if he had been weeping. They would know, then, that he had been reading his Bible. There would be times when he would almost moan when he talked to them, a kind of hymnal chant, a religious ecstasy, that came from some deep intoxication of the spirit, and that transported him. For the boys, it was a troubling and bewildering experience. They tried to laugh it off and make jokes about it. But there was something in it so dark and strange and full of a feeling they could not fathom that their jokes were hollow, and the trouble in their minds and in their hearts remained.

Sometimes on these occasions his speech would be made up of some weird jargon of Biblical phrases and quotations and allusions, of which he seemed to have hundreds, and which he wove together in the strange pattern of his emotion in a sequence that was meaningless to them but to which he himself had the coherent clue.

"O young white fokes," he would begin, moaning gently, "de dry bones in de valley. I tell you, white fokes, de day is comin' when He's comin' on dis earth again to sit in judgment. He'll put de sheep upon de right hand and de goats upon de left—O white fokes, white fokes —de Armageddon day's a-comin', white fokes—an' de dry bones in de valley."

Or again, they could hear him singing as he went about his work, in his deep, rich voice, so full of warmth and strength, so full of Africa, singing hymns that were not only of his own race, but that were familiar to them all. They didn't know where he learned them. Perhaps they were remembered from his army days. Perhaps he had learned them in the service of former masters. He drove the Sheppertons to church on Sunday morning, and would wait for them throughout the service. He would come up to the side door of the church while the service was going on, neatly dressed in his good, dark suit, holding his chauffeur's hat respectfully in his hand, and stand there humbly and listen during the course of the entire sermon.

And then when the hymns were sung, and the great rich sound would swell and roll out into the quiet air of Sunday, Dick would stand and listen, and sometimes he would join quietly in the song. A number of these favorite hymns the boys heard him singing many times in a low, rich voice as he went about his work around the house. He would sing "Who Follows in His Train?"—or "Alexander's Glory Song," or "Rock of Ages," or "Onward, Christian Soldiers."

And yet? Well, nothing happened—there was just "a flying hint from here and there"—and the sense of something passing in the night.

Turning into the Square one day, as Dick was driving Mr. Shepperton to town, Lon Pilcher skidded murderously around the corner, side-swiped Dick, and took the fender off. The negro was out of the car like a cat and got his master out. Mr. Shepperton was unhurt. Lon Pilcher climbed out and reeled across the street, drunk as a sot in mid-afternoon. He swung viciously, clumsily, at the negro, smashed him in the face. Blood trickled from the flat black nostrils and from the thick, liver-colored lips. Dick did not move. But suddenly the whites of his eyes were shot with red, his bleeding lips bared for a moment over the white ivory of his teeth. Lon smashed at him again. The negro took it full in the face again; his hands twitched slightly but he did not move. They collared the drunken sot and hauled him off and locked him up. Dick stood there for a moment, then he wiped his face and turned to see what damage had been done to the car. No more now, but there were those who saw it, who remembered later how the eyes went red.

Another thing. The Sheppertons had a cook named Pansy Harris. She was a comely negro wench, young, plump, black as the ace of spades, a good-hearted girl with a deep dimple in her cheeks and faultless teeth, bared in a most engaging smile. No one ever saw Dick speak to her. No one ever saw her glance at him, or him at her—

and yet that dimpled, plump, and smilingly good-natured wench became as mournful-silent and as silent-sullen as midnight pitch. She sang no more. No more was seen the gleaming ivory of her smile. No more was heard the hearty and infectious exuberance of her warm, full-throated laugh. She went about her work as mournfully as if she were going to a funeral. The gloom deepened all about her. She answered sullenly now when spoken to.

One night towards Christmas she announced that she was leaving. In response to all entreaties, all efforts to find the reason for her sudden and unreasonable decision, she had no answer except a sullen repetition of the assertion that she had to leave. Repeated questionings did finally wring from her a statement that her husband wanted her to quit, that he needed her at home. More than this she would not say, and even this excuse was highly suspected, because her husband was a Pullman porter, home only two days a week, and well accustomed to do himself such housekeeping tasks as she might do for him.

The Sheppertons were fond of her. The girl had been with them for several years. They tried again to find the reason for her leaving. Was she dissatisfied? "No'm"—an implacable monosyllable, mournful, unrevealing as the night. Had she been offered a better job elsewhere? "No'm"—as untelling as before. If they offered her more wages, would she stay with them? "No'm"—again and again, sullen and unyielding; until finally the exasperated mistress threw her hands up in a gesture of defeat and said: "All right then, Pansy. Have it your own way, if that's the way you feel. Only for heaven's sake, don't leave us in the lurch. Don't leave us until we get another cook."

This, at length, with obvious reluctance, the girl agreed to. Then, putting on her hat and coat, and taking the paper bag of "leavings" she was allowed to take home with her at night, she went out the kitchen door and made her sullen and morose departure.

This was on Saturday night, a little after eight o'clock.

That same afternoon Randy and Monk had been fooling around the Shepperton basement, and, seeing that Dick's door was slightly ajar, they stopped at the opening and looked in to see if he was there. The little room was empty, and swept and spotless as it had always been.

But they did not notice that! They saw *it*! At the same moment their breaths caught sharply in a gasp of startled wonderment. Randy was the first to speak.

"Look!" he whispered. "Do you see it?"

See it? Monk's eyes were glued upon it. Had he found himself staring suddenly at the flat head of a rattlesnake his hypnotized surprise could have been no greater. Squarely across the bare boards of the table, blue-dull, deadly in its murderous efficiency, lay an automatic army rifle. They both knew the type. They had seen them all when Randy went to buy his little "twenty-two" at Uncle Morris Teitlebaum's. Beside it was a box containing one hundred rounds of ammunition, and behind it, squarely in the center, face downward, open on the table, was the familiar cover of Dick's old, worn Bible.

Then he was on them like a cat. He was there like a great, dark shadow before they know it. They turned, terrified. He was there above them, his thick lips bared above his gums, his eyes gone small and red as rodents'.

"Dick!" Randy gasped, and moistened his dry lips. "Dick!" he fairly cried now.

It was all over like a flash. Dick's mouth closed. They could see the whites of his eyes again. He smiled and said softly, affably, "Yes suh, Cap'n Shepperton. Yes suh! You gent-mun lookin' at my rifle?" —and he stepped across the sill into the room.

Monk gulped and nodded his head and couldn't say a word, and Randy whispered, "Yes." And both of them still stared at him with an expression of appalled and fascinated interest.

Dick shook his head and chuckled. "Can't do without my rifle, white fokes. No suh!" He shook his head good-naturedly again, "Ole Dick, he's—he's—he's an ole *ahmy* man, you know. He's gotta have his rifle. If they take his rifle away from him, why that's jest lak takin' candy away from a little baby. Yes suh!" he chuckled again, and picked the weapon up affectionately. "Ole Dick felt Christmas comin' on—he—he —I reckon he must have felt it in his bones," he chuckled, "so I been savin' up my money—I jest thought I'd hide this heah and keep it as a big surprise fo' the young white fokes," he said. "I was jest gonna put it away heah and keep it untwill Christmas morning. Then I was gonna take the young white fokes out and show 'em how to shoot."

They had begun to breathe more easily now, and, almost as if they were under the spell of the Pied Piper of Hamelin, they had followed him step by step into the room.

"Yes suh," Dick chuckled, "I was jest fixin' to hide this gun away and keep it hid twill Christmas day, but Cap'n Shepperton—hee!" he chuckled heartily and slapped his thigh—"you can't fool ole Cap'n Shepperton! He was too quick fo' me. He jest must've smelled this ole gun right out. He comes right in and sees it befo' I has a chance to tu'n around. . . . Now, white fokes," Dick's voice fell to a tone of low and winning confidence, "Ah's hopin' that I'd git to keep this gun as a little surprise fo' you. Now that you's found out, I'll tell you what I'll do. If you'll jest keep it a surprise from the other white fokes twill Christmas day, I'll take all you gent'mun out and let you shoot it. Now cose," he went on quietly, with a shade of resignation, "if you want to tell on me you can—but"—here his voice fell again, with just the faintest yet most eloquent shade of sorrowful regret—"Ole Dick was lookin' fahwad to this. He was hopin' to give all the white fokes a supprise Christmas day."

They promised earnestly that they would keep his secret as if it were their own. They fairly whispered their solemn vow. They tiptoed away out of the little basement room, as if they were afraid their very footsteps might betray the partner of their confidence.

This was four o'clock on Saturday afternoon. Already, there was a somber moaning of the wind, grey storm clouds sweeping over. The threat of snow was in the air.

Snow fell that night. It began at six o'clock. It came howling down across the hills. It swept in on them from the Smokies. By seven o'clock the air was blind with sweeping snow, the earth was carpeted, the streets were numb. The storm howled on, around houses warm with crackling fires and shaded light. All life seemed to have withdrawn into thrilling isolation. A horse went by upon the street with muffled hoofs.

George Webber went to sleep upon this mystery, lying in the darkness, listening to that exultancy of storm, to that dumb wonder, that enormous and attentive quietness of snow, with something dark and jubilant in his soul he could not utter.

Snow in the South is wonderful. It has a kind of magic and a mystery that it has nowhere else. And the reason for this is that it comes to people in the South not as the grim, unyielding tenant of the Winter's keep, but as a strange and wild visitor from the secret North. It comes to them from darkness, to their own special and most secret soul there in the South. It brings to them the thrilling isolation of its own white mystery. It brings them something that they lack, and that they have to have; something that they have lost, but now have found; something that they have known utterly, but had forgotten until now.

In every man there are two hemispheres of light and dark, two worlds discrete, two countries of his soul's adventure. And one of these is the dark land, the other half of his heart's home, the unvisited domain of his father's earth.

And this is the land he knows the best. It is the earth unvisited—and it is his, as nothing he has seen can ever be. It is the world intangible that he has never touched—yet more his own than something he has owned forever. It is the great world of his mind, his heart, his spirit, built there in his imagination, shaped by wonder and unclouded by the obscuring flaws of accident and actuality, the proud, unknown earth of the lost, the found, the never-here, the ever-real America, unsullied, true, essential, built there in the brain, and shaped to glory by the proud and flaming vision of a child.

Thus, at the head of those two poles of life will lie the real, the truthful image of its immortal opposite. Thus, buried in the dark heart of the cold and secret North, abides forever the essential image of the South; thus, at the dark heart of the moveless South, there burns forever the immortal splendor of the North.

So had it always been with George. The other half of his heart's home, the world unknown that he knew the best, was the dark North. And snow swept in that night across the hills, demonic visitant, to restore that land to him, to sheet it in essential wonder. Upon this mystery he fell asleep.

A little after two o'clock next morning he was awakened by the ringing of a bell. It was the fire bell of the City Hall, and it was beating an alarm—a hard, fast stroke that he had never heard before. Bronze with peril, clangorous through the snow-numbed silence of the air, it had a quality of instancy and menace he had never known before. He leaped up and ran to the window to look for the telltale glow against the sky. But it was no fire. Almost before he looked, those deadly strokes beat in upon his brain the message that this was no alarm for fire. It was a savage, brazen tongue calling the town to action, warning mankind against the menace of some peril—secret, dark, unknown, greater than fire or flood could ever be.

He got instantly, in the most overwhelming and electric way, the sense that the whole town had come to life. All up and down the street the houses were beginning to light up. Next door, the Shepperton house was ablaze with light, from top to bottom. Even as he looked Mr. Shepperton, wearing an overcoat over his pajamas, ran down the steps and padded out across the snow-covered walk towards the street.

People were beginning to run out of doors. He heard excited cries and shouts and questions everywhere. He saw Nebraska Crane come pounding up the middle of the street. He knew that he was coming for him and Randy. As Bras ran by Shepperton's, he put his fingers to his mouth and whistled piercingly. It was a signal they all knew.

Monk was already almost dressed by the time he came running in across the front yard. He hammered at the door; Monk was already there. They both spoke at once. He had answered Monk's startled question before he got it out.

"Come on!" he said, panting with excitement, his Cherokee black eyes burning with an intensity Monk had never seen before. "Come on!" he cried. They were halfway out across the yard by now. "It's that nigger! He's gone crazy and is running wild!"

"Wh-wh-what nigger?" Monk gasped, pounding at his heels.

Even before he spoke Monk had the answer. Mr. Crane had already come out of his house and crossed the street, buttoning his heavy policeman's overcoat and buckling his girdle as he came. He had paused to speak for a moment to Mr. Shepperton, and Monk heard Mr. Shepperton say quickly, in a low voice:

"Which way did he go?"

Then he heard somebody cry, "It's that nigger of Shepperton's!"

Mr. Shepperton turned and went quickly back across his yard towards the house. His wife and two girls stood huddled in the open doorway. The snow had drifted in across the porch. The three women stood there, white, trembling, holding themselves together, their arms thrust in the wide sleeves of their kimonos.

The telephone in Shepperton's house was ringing like mad but no one was paying any attention to it. Monk heard Mrs. Shepperton say quickly as her husband ran up the steps, "Is it Dick?" He nodded and passed her brusquely, going towards the phone.

At this moment, Nebraska whistled piercingly again upon his fingers, and Randy Shepperton ran past his mother and sped down the steps. She called sharply to him. He paid no attention to her. When he came up, Monk saw that his fine, thin face was white as a sheet. He looked at Monk and whispered:

"It's—it's Dick!" And in a moment, "They say he's killed four people!"

"With—?" Monk couldn't finish.

Randy nodded dumbly, and they both stared there for a minute, two white-faced boys, aware now of the full and murderous significance of the secret they had kept, the confidence they had not violated, with a sudden sense of guilt and fear as if somehow the crime lay on their shoulders.

Across the street a window banged up in the parlor of Suggs' house and Old Man Suggs appeared in the window clad only in his nightgown, his brutal old face inflamed with excitement, his shock of silvery white hair awry, his powerful shoulders and his thick hands gripping his crutches.

"He's coming this way!" he bawled to the world in general. "They say he lit out across the Square! He's heading out in this direction!"

Mr. Crane paused to yell back impatiently over his shoulder, "No, he went down South Main Street. He's heading for Wilton and the river. I've already heard from headquarters."

Automobiles were beginning to roar and sputter all along the street. Even at that time, over half the people on the street had them. Across the street Monk could hear Mr. Potterham sweating with his Ford. He would whirl the crank a dozen times or more, the engine would catch for a moment, cough and splutter, and then die again. Gus ran out of doors with a kettle of boiling water and began to pour it feverishly down the radiator spout.

Mr. Shepperton was already dressed. They saw him run down the back steps towards the carriage house. Randy, Bras, and Monk streaked down the driveway to help him. They got the old wooden doors open. He went in and cranked the car. It was a new Buick. It responded to their prayers and started up at once. Mr. Shepperton backed out into the snowy drive. They all clambered up onto the running board. He spoke absently, saying:

"You boys stay here. Randy, your mother's calling you."

But they all tumbled in and he didn't say a word.

He came backing down the driveway at top speed. They turned into the street and picked up Mr. Crane. As they took the corner into Charles Street, Fred Sanford and his father roared past them in their Oldsmobile. They lit out for town, going at top speed. Every house along Charles Street was lighted up. Even the hospital was ablaze with light. Cars were coming out of alleys everywhere. They could hear people shouting questions and replies at one another. Monk heard one man shout, "He's killed six men!"

Monk didn't know how fast they went, but it was breakneck speed with streets in such condition. It didn't take them over five minutes to reach the Square, but when they got there it seemed as if the whole town was there ahead of them. Mr. Shepperton pulled the car up and parked in front of the City Hall. Mr. Crane leaped out and went pounding away across the Square without another word to them.

Everyone was running in the same direction. From every corner, every street that led into the Square, people were streaking in. One could see the dark figures of running men across the white carpet of the Square. They were all rushing in to one focal point.

The southwest corner of the Square where South Main Street came into it was like a dog fight. Those running figures streaking towards that dense crowd gathered there made Monk think of nothing else so much as a fight between two boys upon the playgrounds of the school at recess time. The way the crowd was swarming in was just the same.

But then he *heard* a difference. From that crowd came a low and growing mutter, an ugly and insistent growl, of a tone and quality he had never heard before, but, hearing it now, he knew instantly what it meant. There was no mistaking the blood note in that foggy growl. And the three of them, the three boys, looked at one another with the same question in the eyes of all.

Nebraska's coal black eyes were shining now with a savage sparkle even they had never had before. The awakened blood of the Cherokee was smoking in him. "Come on," he said in a low tone, exultantly. "They mean business this time, sure. Let's go!" And he darted away towards the dense and sinister darkness of the crowd.

Even as they followed him they heard behind them, at the edge of Niggertown, coming towards them now, growing, swelling at every instant, one of the most savagely mournful and terrifying sounds that night can know. It was the baying of the hounds as they came up upon the leash from Niggertown. Full-throated, howling deep, the savagery of blood was in it, and the savagery of man's guilty doom was in it, too.

They came up swiftly, fairly baying at the boys' heels as they sped across the snow-white darkness of the Square. As they got up to the crowd they saw that it had gathered at the corner where Mark Joyner's hardware store stood. Monk's uncle had not yet arrived but they had phoned for him; he was already on the way. But Monk heard Mr. Shepperton swear beneath his breath in vexation:

"Damn, if I'd only thought—we could have taken him!"

Facing the crowd which pressed in on them so close and menacing that they were almost flattened out against the glass, three or four men were standing with arms stretched out in a kind of chain, as if trying to protect with the last resistance of their strength and eloquence the sanctity of private property.

George Gallatin was Mayor at that time, and he was standing there shoulder to shoulder and arm to arm with Hugh McPherson. Monk could see Hugh, taller by half a foot than anyone around him, his long, gaunt figure, the gaunt passion of his face, even the attitude of his outstretched bony arms, strangely, movingly Lincolnesque, his one good eye (for he was blind in the other) blazing in the cold glare of the corner lamp with a kind of cold, inspired, Scotch passion.

"Wait a minute! Stop! You men wait a minute!" he cried. His words cut out above the shouts and clamor of the mob like an electric spark. "You'll gain nothing, you'll help nothing if you do this thing."

They tried to drown him out with an angry and derisive roar. He shot his big fist up into the air and shouted at them, blazed at them with that cold single eye, until they had to hear. "Listen to me!" he cried. "This is no time for mob law. This is no case for lynch law. This is a time for law and order. Wait till the sheriff swears you in. Wait until Mark Joyner comes. Wait——"

He got no further. "Wait, hell!" cried someone. "We've waited long enough! We're going to get that nigger!"

The mob took up the cry. The whole crowd was writhing angrily now, like a tormented snake. Suddenly there was a flurry in the crowd, a scattering. Somebody yelled a warning at Hugh McPherson. He ducked quickly, just in time. A brick whizzed past him, smashing the plate-glass window into fragments.

And instantly a bloody roar went up. The crowd surged forward, kicked the fragments of jagged glass away. In a moment the whole mob was storming into the dark store. Mark Joyner got there just too late. He said later that he heard the smash of broken glass just as he turned the corner to the Square from College Street. He arrived in time to take out his keys and open the front doors, but as he grimly remarked, with a convulsive movement of his lips, it was like closing the barn doors after the horse had been stolen.

The mob was in and they looted him. They helped themselves to every rifle they could find. They smashed open cartridge boxes and filled their pockets with the loose cartridges. Within ten minutes they had looted the store of every rifle, every cartridge in the stock. The whole place looked as if a hurricane had hit it. The mob was streaming out into the street, was already gathering around the dogs a hundred feet or so away, who were picking up the scent at that point, the place where Dick had halted last before he had turned and headed south, downhill along South Main Street, towards the river.

The hounds were scampering about, tugging at the leash, moaning softly with their noses pointed to the snow, their long ears flattened down. But in that light and in that snow it almost seemed no hounds were needed to follow Dick. Straight down the middle, in a snow-white streak, straight as a string right down the center of the sheeted car tracks, the negro's footsteps led away. By the light of the corner lamps one could follow them until they vanished downhill in the darkness.

But now, although the snow had stopped, the wind was swirling through the street and making drifts and eddies in the snow. The footprints were fading rapidly. Soon they would be gone.

The dogs were given their head. They went straining on, softly, sniffing at the snow; behind them the dark masses of the mob closed in and followed. The three boys stood there watching while they went. They saw them go on down the street and vanish. But from below, over the snow-numbed stillness of the air, the vast, low mutter of the mob came back to them.

Men were clustered now in groups. Mark Joyner stood before his shattered window, ruefully surveying the ruin. Other men were gathered around the big telephone pole at the corner, measuring, estimating its width and thickness, pointing out two bullet holes that had been drilled cleanly through.

And swiftly, like a flash, running from group to group, like a powder train of fire, the full detail of that bloody chronicle of night was pieced together.

This was what had happened.

Somewhere between nine and ten o'clock that night, Dick Prosser had gone to Pansy Harris' shack in Niggertown. Some said he had been drinking when he went there. At any rate, the police had later found the remnants of a gallon jug of raw corn whiskey in the room.

What had happened in the shack from that time on was never clearly known. The woman evidently had protested, had tried to keep him out, but eventually, as she had done before, succumbed. He went in. They were alone. What happened then, what passed between them, was never known. And, besides, no one was greatly interested. It was a crazy nigger with a nigger wench. She was "another nigger's woman"; probably she had "gone with" Dick. This was the general assumption, but no one cared. Adultery among negroes was assumed.

At any rate, some time after ten o'clock that night—it must have been closer to eleven, because the train of the negro porter, Harris, was late and did not pull into the yards until 10:20—the woman's husband appeared upon the scene. The fight did not start then. According to the woman, the real trouble did not come until an hour or more after his return.

The men drank together. Each was in an ugly temper. Dick was steadily becoming more savagely inflamed. Shortly before midnight they got into a fight. Harris slashed at Dick with a razor. In a second they were locked together, rolling about and fighting like two madmen on the floor. Pansy Harris went screaming out of doors and across the street into a dingy little grocery store.

A riot call was telephoned at once to police headquarters at the City Hall. The news came in that a crazy nigger had broken loose on Valley Street in Niggertown, and to send help at once. Pansy Harris ran back across the street towards her little shack.

As she got there, her husband, with blood streaming from his face, staggered out across the little lean-to porch into the street, with his hands held up protectively behind his head in a gesture of instinctive terror. At the same moment, Dick Prosser appeared in the doorway of the shack, deliberately took aim with his rifle, and shot the fleeing negro squarely through the back of the head. Harris dropped forward on his face into the snow. He was dead before he hit the ground. A huge dark stain of blood-soaked snow widened out around him. Dick Prosser took one step, seized the terrified negress by the arm, hurled her into the shack, bolted the door, pulled down the shades, blew out the lamp, and waited.

A few minutes later, two policemen arrived from town. They were a young constable named Willis, who had but recently got on the force, and John Grady, a lieutenant. The policemen took one look at the bloody figure in the snow, questioned the frightened keeper of the grocery store, and then, after consulting briefly, produced their weapons and walked out into the street.

Young Willis stepped softly down onto the snow-covered porch of the shack, flattened himself against the wall between the window and the door, and waited. Grady went around to the side, produced his flashlight, flashed it against the house and through the window, which on this side was shadeless. At the same moment Grady said in a loud voice:

"Come out of there!"

Dick's answer was to shoot him cleanly through the wrist. At the same moment Willis kicked the door in with a powerful thrust of his foot, and, without waiting, started in with pointed revolver. Dick shot him just above the eyes. The policeman fell forward on his face.

Grady came running out around the house, crossed the street, rushed into the grocery store, pulled the receiver of the old-fashioned telephone off the hook, rang frantically for headquarters, and yelled out across the wire that a crazy nigger had killed Sam Willis and a negro man, and to send help.

At this moment Dick, coatless and without a hat, holding his rifle crosswise in his hands, stepped out across the porch into the street, aimed swiftly through the dirty window of the dingy little store. and shot John Grady as he stood there at the phone. Grady fell dead with a bullet that entered just below his left temple and went out on the other side.

Dick, now moving in a long, unhurried stride that covered the ground with catlike speed, turned up the snow-covered slope of Valley Street and began his march towards town. He moved right up the center of the street, shooting cleanly from left to right as he went. Halfway up the hill, the second-story window of a negro tenement flew open. An old negro man, the janitor of an office building in the Square, stuck out his ancient head of cotton wool. Dick swiveled and shot casually from his hip. The shot tore the top of the old negro's head off.

By the time Dick reached the head of Valley Street, they knew he was coming. He moved steadily along, leaving his big tread cleanly in the middle of the sheeted street, shifting a little as he walked, swinging his gun crosswise before him. This was the negro Broadway of the town, the center of the night life of the negro settlement. But where those pool rooms, barber shops, drug stores, and fried-fish places had been loud with dusky life ten minutes before, they were now silent as the ruins of Egypt. The word was flaming through the town that a crazy nigger was on the way. No one showed his head.

Dick moved on steadily, always in the middle of the street, reached the end of Valley Street and turned into South Main—turned right, uphill, in the middle of the car tracks, and started towards the Square. As he passed the lunchroom on the left he took a swift shot through the window at the counter man. The fellow ducked behind the counter. The bullet crashed into the wall above his head.

Meanwhile, the news that Dick was coming was crackling through the town. At the City Club on Sondley Street, three blocks away, a group of the town's leading gamblers and sporting men was intent in a haze of smoke above a green baize table and some stacks of poker chips. The phone rang. The call was for Wilson Redmond, the police court magistrate.

Wilson listened for a moment, then hung the phone up casually. "Come on, Jim," he said in casual tones to a crony, Jim McIntyre, "there's a crazy nigger loose. He's shooting up the town. Let's go get him." And with the same nonchalance he thrust his arms into the overcoat which the white-jacketed negro held for him, put on his tall silk hat, took up his cane, pulled out his gloves, and started to depart. Wilson, like his comrade, had been drinking.

As if they were going to a wedding party, the two men went out into the deserted, snow-white streets, turned at the corner by the post office, and started up the street towards the Square. As they reached the Square and turned into it they heard Dick's shot into the lunchroom and the crash of glass.

"There he is, Jim!" said Wilson Redmond happily. "Now I'll have some fun. Let's go get him." The two gentlemen moved rapidly across the Square and into South Main Street.

Dick kept coming on, steadily, at his tireless, easy stride, straight up the middle of the street. Wilson Redmond started down the street to get him. He lifted his gold-headed cane and waved it at Dick Prosser.

"You're under arrest!" Wilson Redmond said.

Dick shot again, and also from the hip, but something faltered this time by the fraction of an inch. They always thought it was Wilson Redmond's tall silk hat that fooled him. The bullet drilled a hole right through the top of Judge Redmond's tall silk hat, and it went flying away. Wilson Redmond faded into the doorway of a building and fervently wished that his too, too solid flesh would melt.

Jim McIntyre was not so lucky. He started for the doorway but Wilson got there first. Dick shot cleanly from the hip again and blew Jim's side in with a fast shot. Poor Jim fell sprawling to the ground, to rise and walk again, it's true, but ever thereafter with a cane. Meanwhile, on the other side of the Square, at police headquarters, the sergeant had sent John Chapman out to head Dick off. Mr. Chapman was perhaps the best-liked man on the force. He was a pleasant, florid-faced man of forty-five, with curling brown mustaches, congenial and good-humored, devoted to his family, courageous, but perhaps too kindly and too gentle for a good policeman.

John Chapman heard the shots and ran forward. He came up to the corner by Joyner's hardware store just as Dick's shot sent poor Jim McIntyre sprawling to the ground. Mr. Chapman took up his position there at the corner behind the telephone pole. From this vantage point he took out his revolver and shot directly at Dick Prosser as he came up the street.

By this time Dick was not over thirty yards away. He dropped quietly upon one knee and aimed. Mr. Chapman shot again and missed. Dick fired. The high-velocity bullet bored through the post a little to one side. It grazed the shoulder of John Chapman's uniform and knocked a chip out of the monument sixty yards or more behind him in the center of the Square.

Mr. Chapman fired again and missed. And Dick, still coolly poised upon his knee, as calm and steady as if he were engaging in a rifle practice, fired again, drilled squarely through the center of the pole, and shot John Chapman through the heart. Mr. Chapman dropped dead. Then Dick rose, pivoted like a soldier in his tracks, and started back down the street, right down the center of the car tracks, straight as a string, right out of town.

This was the story as they got it, pieced together like a train of fire among the excited groups of men that clustered there in trampled snow before the shattered glass of Joyner's store.

And the rifle? Where did he get it? From whom had he purchased it? The answer to this, too, was not long in coming.

Mark Joyner denied instantly that the weapon had come from his store. At this moment there was a flurry in the crowd and Uncle Morris Teitlebaum, the pawnbroker, appeared, gesticulating volubly, clinging to a policeman. Bald-headed, squat, with the face of an old monkey, he protested shrilly, using his hands eloquently, and displaying craggy nuggins of gold teeth as he spoke.

"Vell," he said, "vhat could I do? His moaney vas good!" he said plaintively, lifting his hands and looking around with an expression of finality. "He comes with his moaney, he pays it down like everybodies—I should say no?" he cried, with such an accent of aggrieved innocence that, in spite of the occasion, a few people smiled.

Uncle Morris Teitlebaum's pawn shop, which was on the right-hand side of South Main Street, and which Dick had passed less than an hour before in his murderous march towards town, was, unlike Joyner's hardware store, securely protected at night by strong bars over the doors and show windows.

But now, save for these groups of talking men, the town again was silent. Far off, in the direction of the river and the Wilton Bottoms, they could hear the low and mournful baying of the hounds. There was nothing more to see or do. Mark Joyner stooped, picked up some fragments of the shattered glass, and threw them in the window. A policeman was left on guard, and presently all five of them—Mr. Shepperton, Mark Joyner, and the three boys—walked back across the Square and got into the car and drove home again.

But there was no more sleep for anyone that night. Black Dick had murdered sleep. Towards daybreak snow began to fall again. It continued through the morning. It was piled deep in gusting drifts by noon. All footprints were obliterated. The town waited, eager, tense, wondering if the man could get away.

They did not capture him that day, but they were on his trail. From time to time throughout the day news would drift back to them. Dick had turned east along the river to the Wilton Bottoms and, following the river banks as closely as he could, he had gone out for some miles along the Fairchilds road. There, a mile or two from Fairchilds, he crossed the river at the Rocky Shallows.

Shortly after daybreak a farmer from the Fairchilds section had seen him cross a field. They picked the trail up there again and followed it across the field and through a wood. He had come out on the other side and got down into the Cane Creek section, and there, for several hours, they lost him. Dick had gone right down into the icy water of the creek and walked upstream a mile or so. They brought the dogs down to the creek, to where he broke the trail, took them over to the other side and scented up and down.

Towards five o'clock that afternoon they picked the trail up on the other side, a mile or more upstream. From that point on they began to close in on him. He had been seen just before nightfall by several people in the Lester township. The dogs followed him across the fields, across the Lester road, into a wood. One arm of the posse swept around the wood to head him off. They knew they had him. Dick, freezing, hungry, and unsheltered, was hiding in that wood. They knew he couldn't get away. The posse ringed the wood and waited until morning.

At seven-thirty the next morning he made a break for it. He almost got away. He got through the line without being seen, crossed the Lester road, and headed back across the fields in the direction of Cane Creek. And there they caught him. They saw him plunging through the snowdrift of a field. A cry went up. The posse started after him.

Part of the posse were on horseback. The men rode in across the field. Dick halted at the edge of the wood, dropped deliberately upon one knee, and for some minutes held them off with rapid fire. At two hundred yards he dropped Doc Lavender, a deputy, with a bullet through the throat.

The posse came in slowly, in an encircling, flank-wise movement. Dick got two more of them as they closed in, and then, as slowly and deliberately as a trained soldier retreating in good order, still firing as he went, he fell back through the wood. At the other side he turned and ran down through a sloping field that bordered on Cane Creek. At the creek edge he turned again, knelt once more in the snow, and aimed.

It was Dick's last shot. He didn't miss. The bullet struck Wayne Foraker, another deputy, dead center in the forehead and killed him in his saddle. Then the posse saw the negro aim again, and nothing happened. Dick snapped the cartridge breech open savagely, then hurled the gun away. A cheer went up. The posse came charging forward. Dick turned, stumblingly, and ran the few remaining yards that separated him from the cold and rock-bright waters of the creek.

And here he did a curious thing—a thing that in later days was a subject of frequent and repeated speculation, a thing that no one ever wholly understood. It was thought that he would make one final break for freedom, that he would wade the creek and try to get away before they got to him. Instead, arrived at the creek, he sat down calmly on the bank, and, as quietly and methodically as if he were seated on his cot in an army barracks, he unlaced his shoes, took them off, placed them together neatly at his side, and then stood up like a soldier, erect, in his bare feet, and faced the mob.

The men on horseback reached him first. They rode up around him and discharged their guns into him. He fell forward in the snow, riddled with bullets. The men dismounted, turned him over on his back, and all the other men came in and riddled him. They took his lifeless body, put a rope around his neck, and hung him to a tree. Then the mob exhausted all their ammunition on the riddled carcass.

By nine o'clock that morning the news had reached the town. Around eleven o'clock the mob came back, along the river road. A good crowd had gone out to meet it at the Wilton Bottoms. The sheriff rode ahead. Dick's body had been thrown like a sack and tied across the saddle of the horse of one of the deputies he had killed.

It was in this way, bullet-riddled, shot to pieces, open to the vengeful and the morbid gaze of all, that Dick came back to town. The mob came back right to its starting point in South Main Street. They halted there before an undertaking parlor, not twenty yards away from where Dick had halted last and knelt to kill John Chapman. They took that ghastly mutilated thing and hung it in the window of the undertaker's place, for every woman, man, and child in town to see.

And it was so they saw him last. Yes, they all had their look. In the end, they had their look. They said they wouldn't look, Randy and Monk. But in the end they went. And it has always been the same with people. It has never changed. It never will. They protest. They shudder. And they say they will not go. But in the end they always have their look.

Nebraska was the only one of the boys who didn't lie about it. With that forthright honesty that was part of him, so strangely wrought of innocence and of brutality, of heroism, cruelty, and tenderness, he announced at once that he was going, and then waited impatiently, spitting briefly and contemptuously from time to time, while the others argued out their own hypocrisy.

At length they went. They saw it—that horrible piece of torn bait—tried wretchedly to make themselves believe that once this thing had spoken to them gently, had been partner to their confidence, object of their affection and respect. And they were sick with nausea and fear, for something had come into their lives they could not understand.

The snow had stopped. The snow was going. The streets had been pounded into dirty mush, and before the shabby undertaking place the crowd milled and jostled, had their fill of horror, could not get enough.

Within, there was a battered roll-top desk, a swivel chair, a cast-iron stove, a wilted fern, a cheap diploma cheaply framed, and, in the window, that ghastly relic of man's savagery, that horrible hunk of torn bait. The boys looked and whitened to the lips, and craned their necks and looked away, and brought unwilling, fascinated eyes back to the horror once again, and craned and turned again, and shuffled in the slush uneasily, but could not go. And they looked up at the leaden reek of day, the dreary vapor of the sky, and, bleakly, at these forms and faces all around them—the people come to gape and stare, the pool-room loafers, the town toughs, the mongrel conquerors of earth—and yet, familiar to their lives and to the body of their whole experience, all known to their landscape, all living men.

And something had come into life—into their lives—that they had never known about before. It was a kind of shadow, a poisonous blackness filled with bewildered loathing. The snow would go, they knew; the reeking vapors of the sky would clear away. The leaf, the blade, the bud, the bird, then April, would come back again—and all of this would be as if it had never been. The homely light of day would shine again familiarly. And all of this would vanish as an evil dream. And yet not wholly so. For they would still remember the old dark doubt and loathing of their kind, of something hateful and unspeakable in the souls of men. They knew that they would not forget.

Beside them a man was telling the story of his own heroic accomplishments to a little group of fascinated listeners. Monk turned and looked at him. He was a little ferret-faced man with a furtive and uneasy eye, a mongrel mouth, and wiry jaw muscles.

"I was the first one to git in a shot," he said. "You see that hole there?" He pointed with a dirty finger. "That big hole right above the eye?"

They turned and goggled with a drugged and feeding stare.

"That's mine," the hero said, and turned briefly to the side and spat tobacco juice into the slush. "That's where I got him. Hell, after that he didn't know what hit him. The son-of-a-bitch was dead before he hit the ground. We all shot him full of holes then. The whole crowd came and let him have it. But that first shot of mine was the one that got him. But, boy!" he paused a moment, shook his head, and spat again. "We sure did fill him full of lead. Why, hell yes," he declared positively, with a decisive movement of his head, "we counted up to 287. We must have put 300 holes in him."

And Nebraska, fearless, blunt, outspoken, as he always was, turned abruptly, put two fingers to his lips and spat between them, widely and contemptuously.

"Yeah—*we*!" he grunted. "*We* killed a big one! *We*—we killed a b'ar, we did! . . . Come on, boys," he said gruffly, "let's be on our way!"

And, fearless and unshaken, untouched by any terror or any doubt, he moved away. And two white-faced, nauseated boys went with him.

A day or two went by before anyone could go into Dick's room again. Monk went in with Randy and his father. The little room was spotless, bare, and tidy as it had always been. Nothing had been changed or touched. But even the very bare austerity of that little room now seemed terribly alive with the presence of its recent black tenant

It was Dick's room. They all knew that. And somehow they all knew that no one else could ever live there again.

Mr. Shepperton went over to the table, picked up Dick's old Bible that still lay there, open and face downward, held it up to the light and looked at it, at the place that Dick had marked when he last read in it. And in a moment, without speaking to them, he began to read in a quiet voice:

"The Lord is my shepherd; I shall not want. He maketh me to lie down in green pastures: He leadeth me beside the still waters. He restoreth my soul: He leadeth me in the paths of righteousness for His name's sake. Yea, though I walk through the valley of the shadow of death, I will fear no evil: for Thou art with me. . . ."

Then Mr. Shepperton closed the book and put it down upon the table, the place where Dick had left it. And they went out the door, he locked it, and they went back into that room no more, forever.

The years passed, and all of them were given unto time. They went their ways. But often they would turn and come again, these faces and these voices of the past, and burn there in George Webber's memory again, upon the muted and immortal geography of time.

And all would come again—the shout of the young voices, the hard thud of the kicked ball, and Dick moving, moving steadily, Dick moving, moving silently, a storm-white world and silence, and something moving, moving in the night. Then he would hear the furious bell, the crowd a-clamor and the baying of the dogs, and feel the shadow coming that would never disappear. Then he would see again the little room, the table and the book. And the pastoral holiness of that old psalm came back to him, and his heart would wonder with perplexity and doubt.

For he had heard another song since then, and one that Dick, he knew, had never heard and would not have understood, but one whose phrases and whose imagery, it seemed to him, would suit Dick better:

> Tiger! Tiger! burning bright
> In the forests of the night.
> What immortal hand or eye
> Could shape thy fearful symmetry?

*   *   *

What the hammer? what the chain?
In what furnace was thy brain?
What the anvil? what dread grasp
Dare its deadly terrors clasp?

When the stars threw down their spears,
And water'd heaven with their tears,
Did he smile his work to see?
Did he who made the Lamb make thee?

What the hammer? *What* the chain? No one ever knew. It was a mystery and a wonder. It was unexplained. There were a dozen stories, a hundred clues and rumors; all came to nothing in the end. Some said that Dick had come from Texas, others that his home had been in Georgia. Some said it was true that he had been enlisted in the army, but that he had killed a man while there and served a term at Leavenworth. Some said he had served in the army and had received an honorable discharge, but had later killed a man and had served a term in the state prison in Louisiana. Others said that he had been an army man but that he had "gone crazy," that he had served a period in an asylum when it was found that he was insane, that he had escaped from this asylum, that he had escaped from prison, that he was a fugitive from justice at the time he came to them.

But all these stories came to nothing. Nothing was ever proved. Nothing was ever found out. Men debated and discussed these things a thousand times—who and what he had been, what he had done, where he had come from—and all of it came to nothing. No one knew the answer.

He came from darkness. He came out of the heart of darkness, from the dark heart of the secret and undiscovered South. He came by night, just as he passed by night. He was night's child and partner, a token of the wonder and the mystery, the other side of man's dark soul, his nighttime partner, and his nighttime foal, a symbol of those things that pass by darkness and that still remain, of something still and waiting in the night that comes and passes and that will abide, a symbol of man's evil innocence, and the token of his mystery, a projection of his own unfathomed quality, a friend, a brother, and a mortal enemy, an unknown demon—our loving friend, our mortal enemy, two worlds together—a tiger and a child.

9

Home from the Mountain

THE WINTER WHEN HE WAS FIFTEEN YEARS OF AGE, ON SUNDAYS AND IN the afternoons after school, George would go for long walks with his uncle on the mountains above the town and in the coves and valleys on the other side. There had always been a quality of madness in his uncle, and his years of living bound to Mag had sharpened it, intensified it, built it up and held it to the point of passion and demonic fury where at times he shook and trembled with the frenzy of it and had to get away, out of that house, to calm his tortured soul. And when this happened to Mark Joyner, he hated all his life and everything about it, and sought the desolation of the mountains. There, in bleak and wintry winds, he found as nowhere else on earth some strange and powerful catharsis.

These expeditions wrought upon the spirit of the boy the emotions of loneliness, desolation, and wild joy with a strong and focal congruence of desire, a blazing intensity of sensual image, he had never known before. Then as never before, he saw the great world beyond the wintry hills of home, and felt the huge, bitter conflict of those twin antagonists, those powers discrete that wage perpetual warfare in the lives of all men living—wandering forever and the earth again.

Wild, wordless, and unutterable, but absolutely congruent in his sense of their irreconcilable and inexplicable coherence, his spirit was torn as it had never been before by the strange and bitter unity of that savage conflict, that tormenting oneness of those dual and contending powers of home and hunger, absence and return. The great plantation of the earth called him forth forever with an intolerable longing of desire to explore its infinite mystery and promise of glory, power, and triumph, and the love of women, its magic wealth and joy of new lands, rivers, plains, and mountains, its crowning glory of the shining city. And he felt the strong, calm joy of evening for doors and fences, a light, a window, and a certain faith, the body and the embrace of a single and unwearied love.

The mountains in the Wintertime had a stern and demonic quality of savage joy that was, in its own way, as strangely, wildly haunting as all of the magic and the gold of April. In Spring, or in the time-enchanted spell and drowse of full, deep Summer, there was always something far and lonely, haunting with ecstasy and sorrow, desolation and the intolerable, numb exultancy of some huge, impending happiness. It was a cow bell, drowsy, far and broken in a gust of wind, as it came to him faintly from the far depth and distance of a mountain valley; the receding whistle-wail of a departing train, as it rushed eastward, seaward, towards the city, through some green mountain valley of the South; or a cloud shadow passing on the massed green of the wilderness, and the animate stillness, the thousand sudden, thrumming, drumming, stitching, unseen little voices in the lyric mystery of tangled undergrowth about him.

His uncle and he would go toiling up the mountain side, sometimes striding over rutted, clay-caked, and frost-hardened roads, sometimes beating their way downhill, with as bold and wild a joy as wilderness explorers ever knew, smashing their way through the dry and brittle undergrowth of barren Winter, hearing the dry report of bough and twig beneath their feet, the masty spring and crackle of brown ancient leaves, and brown pine needles, the elastic, bedded compost of a hundred buried and forgotten Winters.

Meanwhile, all about them, the great trees of the mountain side, at once ruggedly familiar and strangely, hauntingly austere, rose grim and barren, as stern and wild and lonely as the savage winds that warred forever, with a remote, demented howling, in their stormy, tossed, and leafless branches.

And above them the stormy wintry skies—sometimes a savage sky of wild, torn grey that came so low its scudding fringes whipped like rags of smoke around the mountain tops; sometimes an implacable, fierce sky of wintry grey; sometimes a sky of rags and tatters of wild, wintry light, westering into slashed stripes of rugged red and incredible wild gold at the gateways of the sun—bent over them forever with that same savage and unutterable pain and sorrow, that ecstasy of wild desire, that grief of desolation, that spirit of exultant joy, that was as glee-ful, mad, fierce, lonely, and enchanted with its stormy and unbodied promises of flight, its mad swoopings through the dark over the whole vast sleeping wintriness of earth, as that stormy and maniacal wind, which seemed, in fact, to be the very spirit of the joy, the sorrow, and the wild desire he felt.

That wind would rush upon them suddenly as they toiled up rocky trails, or smashed through wintry growth, or strode along the hardened, rutted roads, or came out on the lonely, treeless bareness of a mountain top. And that wind would rush upon him with its own wild life and fill him with its spirit. As he gulped it down into his aching lungs, his whole life seemed to soar, to swoop, to yell with the demonic power, flight, and invincible caprice of the wind's huge well until he no longer was nothing but a boy of fifteen, the nephew of a hardware merchant in a little town, one of the nameless little atoms of this huge, swarming earth whose most modest dream would have seemed ridiculous to older people had he dared to speak of it.

No. Under the immense intoxication of that great, demented wind, he would become instantly triumphant to all this damning and over-whelming evidence of fact, age, prospect, and position. He was a child of fifteen no longer. He was the overlord of this great earth, and he looked down from the mountain top upon his native town, a con-queror. Not from the limits of a little, wintry town, lost in remote and lonely hills from the great heart, the time-enchanted drone and distant murmur of the shining city of this earth, but from the very peak and center of this world he looked forth on his domains with the joy of certitude and victory, and he knew that everything on earth that he desired was his.

Saddled in power upon the wild back of that maniacal force, not less wild, willful, and all-conquering than the steed that carried him, he would hold the kingdoms of the earth in fee, inhabit the world at his caprice, swoop in the darkness over mountains, rivers, plains, and cities, look under roofs, past walls and doors, into a million rooms, and know all things at once, and lie in darkness in some lonely and forgotten place with a woman, lavish, wild, and secret as the earth. The whole earth, its fairest fame of praise, its dearest treasure of a great success, its joy of travel, all its magic of strange lands, the relish of unknown, tempting foods, its highest happiness of adventure and love—would all be his: flight, storm, wandering, the great sea and all its traffic of proud ships, and the great plantation of the earth, together with the certitude and comfort of return—fence, door, wall, and roof, the single face and dwelling-place of love.

But suddenly these wild, demonic dreams would fade, for he would hear his uncle's voice again, and see the gaunt fury of his bony figure, his blazing eye, the passionate and husky anathema of his trembling voice, as, standing there upon that mountain top and gazing down upon the little city of his youth, Mark Joyner spoke of all the things that tortured him. Sometimes it was his life with Mag, his young man's hopes of comfort, love, and quiet peace that now had come to nought but bitterness and hate. Again his mind went groping back to older, deeper-buried sorrows. And on this day as they stood there, his mind went back, and, turning now to George and to the wind that howled there in his face, he suddenly brought forth and hurled down from that mountain top the acid of an ancient rancor, denouncing now the memory of old Fate, his father. He told his hatred and his loathing of his father's life, the deathless misery of his own youth, which lived for him again in all its anguish even after fifty years had passed.

"As each one of my unhappy brothers and sisters was born," he declared in a voice so husky and tremulous with his passionate resentment that it struck terror to the boy's heart, "I cursed him—cursed the day that God had given him life! And still they came!" he whispered, eyes ablaze and furious, in a voice that almost faltered to a sob. "Year after year they came with the blind proliferation of his criminal desire —into a house where there was scarcely roof enough to shelter us— in a vile, ramshackle shamble of a place," he snarled, "where the oldest of us slept three in a bed, and where the youngest, weakest, and most helpless of us all was lucky if he had a pallet of rotten straw that he could call his own! When we awoke at morning our famished guts were aching!—*aching!*" he howled, "with the damnable gnawing itch of hunger!—My dear child, my dear, dear child!" he exclaimed, in a transition of sudden and terrifying gentleness— "May *that*, of all life's miseries, be a pang you never have to suffer!—And we lay down at night always unsatisfied—oh always! *always! always!*" he cried with an impatient gesture of his hand—"to struggle for repose like restless animals—crammed with distressful bread—swollen with fatback and boiled herbs out of the fields, while your honored grandfather—the *Major!* . . . The *Major!*" he now sneered, and suddenly he contorted his gaunt face in a grotesque grimace and laughed with a sneering, deliberated, forced mirth.

"Now, my boy," he went on presently in a more tranquil tone of patronizing tolerance, "you have no doubt often heard your good Aunt Maw speak with the irrational and incondite exuberance of her sex," he continued, smacking his lips together audibly with an air of relish as he pronounced these formidable words—"of that paragon of all the moral virtues—her noble sire, the *Major!*" Here he paused to laugh sneeringly again. "And perhaps, boylike, you have conceived in your imagination a picture of that distinguished gentleman that is somewhat more romantic than the facts will stand! . . . Well, my boy," he went on deliberately, with the birdlike turn of his head as he looked at the boy, "lest your fancy be seduced somewhat by illusions of aristocratic grandeur, I will tell you a few facts about that noble man. . . . He was the self-appointed Major of a regiment of backwoods volunteers, of whom no more be said than that they were, if possible, less literate than he! . . . You are descended, it is true," he went on with his calm, precise deliberation, "from a warlike stock—but none of them, my dear child, were Brigadiers—no, not even Majors" he sneered, "for the highest genuine rank I ever heard of them attaining was the rank of corporal—and that proud dignity was the office of the Major's pious brother—I refer, of course, my boy, to your great-uncle, Rance Joyner! . . .

"Rance! Rance!"—here he contorted his face again—"Gods! What a name! No wonder he smote fear and trembling to the Yankee heart! . . . The *sight* of him was certainly enough to make them stand stock-still at the height of an attack! And the *smell* of him would surely be enough to strike awe and wonder in the hearts of mortal men—I refer, of course," he said sardonically, "to the average run of base humanity, since, as you well know, neither your grandfather nor his brother, Holy Rance, nor any other Joyner that I know," he jeered, "could be compared to mortal men. We admit that much ourselves. For all of us, my boy, were not so much conceived like other men as willed here by an act of God, created by a visitation of the Holy Ghost, trailing clouds of glory as we came," he sneered, "and surely you must have discovered by this time that it is our unique privilege to act as prophets, messengers. and agents of the deity here on earth—to demonstrate God's ways to man—to reveal the inmost workings of His providence and all the mysterious secrets of the universe to other men who have not been so sanctified by destiny as we. . . .

"But be that as it may," he went on, with one of his sudden and astonishing changes from howling fury to tolerant and tranquil admissiveness, "I believe there was no question of your holy great-uncle's valor. Yes, sir!" he continued, "I have heard them say that he could kill at fifty or five hundred yards, and always wing his bullet with a gospel text to make it holy! . . . Why, my dear child," the boy's uncle cried, "there was as virtuous a ruffian as ever split a skull! He blew their brains out with a smile of saintly charity, and sang hosannas over them as they expired! He sanctified the act of murder, and assured them as they weltered in their blood that he had come to them as an angel of mercy bearing to them the gifts of immortal life and everlasting happiness in exchange for the vile brevity of their earthly lives, which he had taken from them with such sweet philanthropy. He shot them through the heart and promised them all the blessings of the Day of Armageddon with so soft a tongue that they fairly wept for joy and kissed the hand of their redeemer as they died! . . .

"Yes," he went on tranquilly, "there is no question of your great-uncle's valor—or his piety—but still, my boy, his station was a lowly one—he never reached a higher rank than corporal! And there were others, too, who fought well and bravely in that war—but they, too, were obscure men! Your great-uncle John, a boy of twenty-two, was killed in battle on the bloody field of Shiloh. . . . And there are many others of your kinsmen, who fought, died, bled, were wounded, perished, or survived in that great war—but none of them, my dear child, was a Major! . . . There was only one *Major!*" he bitterly remarked. "Only your noble grandsire was a *Major!*"

Then, for a moment, in the fading light of that Winter's day, he paused there on the mountain top above the town, his gaunt face naked, lonely, turned far and lost, into the fierce wintry light of a flaming setting sun, into the lost and lonely vistas of the western ranges, among those hills which had begotten him. When he spoke again his voice was sad and quiet and calmly bitter, and somehow impregnated with that wonderful remote and haunting quality that seemed to come like sorcery from some far distance—a distance that was itself as far and lonely in its haunting spatial qualities as those fading western ranges where his face was turned.

"The Major," he quietly remarked, "my honored father—Major Lafayette Joyner!—Major of Hominy Run and Whooping Holler, the martial overlord of Sandy Mush, the Bonaparte of Zebulon County and the Pink Beds, the crafty strategist of Frying Pan Gap, the Little Corporal of the Home Guards who conducted that great operation on the river road just four miles east of town," he sneered, "where two volleys were fired after the flying hooves of two of General Sherman's horse thieves—with no result except to hasten their escape! . . . The Major!" his voice rose strangely on its note of husky passion. "That genius with the master talent who could do all things—except keep food in the cupboard for a week!" Here he closed his eyes tightly and laughed deliberately again.

"Why, my dear boy!" his uncle said, "he could discourse for hours on end most learnedly—oh! *most* learnedly!" he howled derisively, "on the beauty and perfection of the Roman Aqueducts while the very roof above us spouted water like a sieve! . . . Was it the secret of the Sphinx, the sources of the Nile, what songs the sirens sang, the exact year, month, week, day, hour, and moment of the Field of Armageddon with the Coming of the Lord upon the earth, together with all judgments, punishments, rewards, and titles he would mete to us— and particularly to his favored son, the *Major!*" sneered the boy's uncle. "Oh, I can assure you, my dear child, he knew about it all! Earth had no mysteries, the immortal and imperturbable skies of time no secrets, the buried and sunken life of the great ocean no strange terrors, nor the last remotest limits of the sidereal universe no marvels which that mighty brain did not at once discover, and would reveal to anyone who had the fortitude to listen! . . .

"Meanwhile," his uncle snarled, "we lived like dogs, rooting into the earth for esculent herbs that we might stay our hunger on, gorging ourselves on wild berries plucked from roadside hedges, finding a solitary ear of corn and hugging it to our breasts as we hurried home with it as if we had looted the golden granaries of Midas, while the *Major*— the *Major*—surrounded by the rabble-rout of all his progeny, the youngest of whom crawled and scrambled in their dirty rags about his feet while the great man sat enthroned on the celestial lights of his poetic inspiration, his great soul untainted by all this earthly misery about him, composing verses," sneered his uncle, "to the lady of his dreams. 'My lady's hair!' " he howled derisively. " 'My lady's *hair!* ' " And for a moment, blind with his gaunt, tortured grimace, he kicked and stamped one leg convulsively at the earth— "Oh, sublime! *Sublime!*" he howled huskily at length. "To see him there lost in poetic revery—munching the cud of inspiration and the frayed end of a pencil —his eyes turned dreamily upon the distant hills—slowly stroking his luxuriant whiskers with the fingers of those plump white hands of which he was so justly proud!" his uncle sneered—"dressed in his fine black broadcloth suit and white boiled shirt that *she*—poor, patient, and devoted woman that she was—who never owned a store dress in her whole life—had laundered, starched, and done up for her lord and master with such loving care. . . .

"My dear child," he went on in a moment, in a voice that had become so husky, faint, and tremulous that it scarcely rose above a whisper, "My dear, dear child!" he said, "may your life never know the anguish, frenzy, and despair, the hideous mutilations of the soul, that passion of inchoate hatred, loathing, and revulsion, that I felt towards my father—my own *father!*—with which my own life was poisoned in my youth!—Oh! To see him sitting there so smug, so well-kept and complacent, so invincibly assured in his self-righteousness, with his unctuous, drawling voice of limitless self-satisfaction, his pleased laughter at his own accursed puns and jests and smart retorts, his insatiable delight in all that he—he *alone*—had ever seen, done, thought, felt, tasted, or believed—perched there on the mountainous summit of his own conceit—while the rest of us were starving—writing poems to his lady's hair—his lady's *hair*—while *she*, poor woman—that poor, dead, lost, and unsung martyr of a woman that I have the honor to acknowledge as my mother," he said huskily, "did the drudgery of a nigger as he sat there in his fine clothes writing verses—kept life in us somehow, those of us who managed to survive," he said bitterly, "when she had so little of her own to spare—scrubbed, sewed, mended, cooked—when there was anything at all to cook—and passively yielded to that sanctimonious lecher's insatiable and accursed lust—drudging, toiling, drudging to the very moment of our birth—until we dropped full-born out of our mother's womb even as she bent above her labors at the tub. . . . Is it any wonder that I came to hate the very sight of him—venerable whiskers, thick lips, white hands, broadcloth, unctuous voice, pleased laughter, smug satisfaction, invincible conceit, and all the brutal tyranny of his narrow, vain, inflexible, small soul?—Why, damn him," the boy's uncle whispered huskily, "I have seen the time I could have taken that fat throat and strangled it between my hands, blood, bone, body, father of my life though he might be—oh!" he howled, "damnably, in-dubitably, *was!*"

And for a moment his gaunt face burned into the western ranges, far, lost, and lonely in the red light, westering to wintry dark.

"The Major!" he muttered quietly at length. "You have heard your good Aunt Maw speak, no doubt, about the Major—of his erudition and intelligence, the sanctified infallibility of all his judgments, of his fine white hands and broadcloth clothes, the purity of his moral char-acter, of how he never uttered a profane word, nor allowed a drop of liquor in his house—nor would have let your mother marry your father had he known that your father was a drinking man. That paragon of morals, virtues, purities, and manners—that final, faultless, and in-spired judge and critic of all things!—Oh, my dear boy!" he howled faintly, with his husky and contemptuous laugh—"she is a woman—therefore governed by her sentiment; a woman—therefore blind to logic, the evidence of life, the laws of ordered reason; a woman—there-fore at the bottom of her heart a Tory, the slave of custom and con-formity; a woman—therefore cautious and idolatrous; a woman—therefore fearful for her nest; a woman—therefore the bitter enemy of revolt and newness, hating change, the naked light of truth, the destruc-tion of time-honored superstitions, however cruel, false, and shameful they may be. Oh! she is a woman and she does not know! . . .

"She does not *know!*" the boy's uncle howled with his contemptuous laugh. "My dear child, I have no doubt that she has told you of her father's wisdom, erudition, and his faultless elegance of speech. . . . Pah-h!" he sneered. "He was a picker-up of unconsidered trifles—a reader of miscellaneous trash—the instant dupe for every remedy, nos-trum, cure-all that any traveling quack might offer to him, and the gullible believer of every superstitious prophesy, astrological omen, ghost-story, augury, or portent that he heard. . . . Why, my boy," his uncle whispered, bending towards him with an air of horrified revela-tion, "he was a man who used big words when he had no sense of their real meaning—a fellow who would try to impress some back-woods yokel with fine phrases which he didn't understand himself. Yes! I have heard him talk so even in the presence of people of some educa-tion and intelligence—I have seen them nudge and wink at one another over the spectacle he was making of himself—and I confess to you I had to turn my head away and blush for shame," his uncle whispered fiercely, his eyes blazing, "for *shame* to think my own father could ex-pose himself in that degrading fashion."

And for a moment he stared gauntly into the fading ranges of the west, and was silent. When he spoke again, his voice had grown old and weary, bitter with quiet fatality:

"Moral virtues—purity of character—piety—fine words—no profanity—yes! I suppose my father had them all," said Uncle Mark wearily. "No liquor in the house—yes, that was true enough—and also it is true there was no food, no human decency, no privacy. Why, my dear boy," he whispered suddenly, turning to the boy again with that birdlike tilt of the head and that abrupt and startling transition to a shamefaced intimacy of whispered revelation—"do you know that even after I had reached the age of twenty years and we had moved to Libya Hill, we all slept together—eight of us—in the same room where my mother and my father slept?—And for three days!" he cried suddenly and savagely—"Oh! for three damnable, never-to-be-forgotten days of shame and horror that left their scar upon the lives of all of us, the body of my grandfather, Bill Joyner, lay there in the house and rotted—*rotted*!" his voice broke in a sob, and he struck his gaunt fist blindly, savagely into the air, "rotted in Summer heat until the stench of him had got into our breath, our blood, our lives, into bedding and food and clothes, into the very walls that sheltered us—and the memory of him became for us a stench of shame and horror that nothing could wash away, that filled our hearts with hatred and loathing for our blood and kind—while my father, Lafayette Joyner, and that damned, thick-lipped, drawling, sanctimonious, lecher of a nigger-Baptist prophet—your great-uncle, Holy Rance!" he snarled savagely, "sat there smugly with that stench of rotting death and man's corrupt mortality thick in their nostrils—calmly discussing, if you please, the lost art of embalming as it was practiced by the ancient Egyptians—which *they*, they alone, of course, of all men living," he snarled bitterly, "had rediscovered—and were prepared to practice on that rotting and putrescent corpse!"

Then he was silent for a moment more. His face, gaunt and passionate, which in repose, after its grotesque contortions of scorn, rage, humor, and disgust, was so strangely, nobly tranquil in its lonely dignity, burned with a stern and craggy impassivity in the red, wintry glow of the late sun.

"And yet there was some strangeness in us all," he went on in a remote, quiet, husky tone that had in it the curious and haunting quality of the distance and passion which his voice could carry as no other the boy had ever heard, "something blind and wild as nature—

a sense of our inevitable destiny. Oh! call it not conceit!" his uncle cried. "Conceit is such a small thing, after all! Conceit is only mountain-high, world-wide, or ocean-deep!—This thing we had in us could match its will against the universe, the rightness of its every act against the huge single voice and bitter judgment of the world, its moral judgments against God himself.—Was it murder? Why, then, the murder was not in ourselves, but in the very flesh and blood of those we murdered. Their murder rushed out of their sinful lives to beg for bloody execution at our hands. The transgressor assaulted the very blade of our knives with his offending throat. The wicked man did willfully attack the sharp point of our bayonet with his crime-calloused heart, the offender in the sight of God rushed on us, thrust his neck into our guiltless hands, and fairly broke it, in spite of all that we could do! . . .

"My dear child, surely you must know by now," his uncle cried, as he turned on him with the fixed, blazing glare of his eyes, his set grimace of scorn and fury—"surely you have learned by now that a Joyner is incapable of doing wrong. Cruelty, blind indifference to everything except oneself, brutal neglect, children criminally begotten in casual gratification of one's own lust, children born unwanted and untended into a world of misery, poverty, and neglect where they must live or die or sicken or be strong according to their own means, in a struggle to survive as barbarously savage as the children of an Indian tribe endure—why, these are faults that might be counted crimes in other men, but in a Joyner are considered acts of virtue!—No, he can see the starved eyes of his children staring at him from the shadows as they go comfortless and famished to their beds, and then go out upon his porch to listen to the million little sounds of night, and meditate the glory of the moon as it comes up across the hill behind the river! He can breathe the sweet, wild fragrance of a Summer's night and dreamily compose a lyric to the moon, the lilac, and his lady's hair, while his daughter coughs her life out from the darkness of the wretched house—and find no fault or error in his life whatever! . . .

"Oh, did I not live and know it all?" his uncle cried, "that agony of life and death, blind chance, survival or extinction—till the mind went mad, man's heart and faith were broken, to see how little was the love we had, how cruel, vile, and useless was the waste!—My brother Edward died when he was four years old: there in the room with all of us he lay for a week upon his trundle bed—oh! we let him die beneath our very eyes!" his uncle cried, striking his fist into the air with a kind of agony of loss and pain—"he died beneath the very beds we slept in, for his trundle bed was pushed each night beneath the big bed where my mother and my father slept. We stood there staring at him with the eyes of dumb, bewildered, foolish oxen, while his body stiffened, his heels drew backward towards his head in the convulsions of his agony—and that damned sanctimonious, well-pleased voice drawled on and on with the conceit of its interminable assurance, 'giving it as my theory,'" snarled the boy's uncle—"though all things else were lacking in that house, there never was a dearth of theory—that unplumbed well of wisdom could give theories till you died. And Edward died, thank God, before the week was out," his uncle quietly went on. "He died suddenly one night at two o'clock while the Great Theorist snored peacefully above him—while all the rest of us were sleeping! He screamed once—such a scream as had the whole blind agony of death in it—and by the time we got a candle lighted and had pulled his little bed out on the floor, that wretched and forsaken child was dead! His body was stiff as a poker and bent back like a bow even as the Noble Theorist lifted him—he was dead before our eyes before we knew it— dead even as that poor woman who had borne him rushed screaming out of doors like a demented creature—running, stumbling, God knows where, downhill, into the dark—the wilderness—towards the river—to seek help somehow at a neighbor's when the need for help was past. And his father was holding that dead child in his arms when she returned with that unneeded help. . . .

"Oh, my child," his uncle whispered, "if you could have seen the look on that woman's face as she came back into that room of death again— if you could have seen her look first at the child there in his arms, and then at him, and seen him shake his head at her and say, 'I knew that he was gone before you went out of the door, but I didn't have the heart to call you back and let you know'—oh! if you could have heard the sanctimonious, grief-loving unction of that voice, that feeding gluttony and triumphant vanity of sorrow that battened on its own child's life and said to me, as it had said a thousand times, more plain than any words could do: 'I! I! I! Others will die, but I remain! Death, sorrow, human agony, and loss, all the grief, error, misery, and mischance that men can suffer occurs here for the enlargement of this death-devouring, all-consuming, time-triumphant universe of I, I, I!'—Why, damn him," said his uncle huskily, "I had no words to nail him with a curse, no handle to take hold of my complaint—he had escaped as always like oil running through my fingers, speaking those unctuous words of piety and sorrow that none could challenge—but I hated him like hell and murder in my heart—I could have killed him where he stood!"

But now, as the boy and his uncle stood there on the mountain top looking into the lonely vistas of the westering sun, watching its savage stripes of gold and red as it went down in the smoky loneliness and receding vistas of the great ranges of the west, the wind would fill the boy's heart with unwalled homelessness, a desire for houses, streets, and the familiar words again, a mighty longing for return.

For now black night, wild night, oncoming, secret, and mysterious night, with all its lonely wilderness of storm, demented cries, and unhoused wandering was striding towards them like an enemy. And around them on the lonely mountain top they heard the whistling of the wind in coarse, sere grasses, and from the darkening mountain side below them they could hear the remote howlings of the wind as it waged its stern, incessant warfare in the stormy branches of the bare and lonely trees.

And instantly he would see the town below now, coiling in a thousand fumes of homely smoke, now winking into a thousand points of friendly light its glorious small design, its aching, passionate assurances of walls, warmth, comfort, food, and love. It spoke to him of something deathless and invincible in the souls of men, like a small light in a most enormous dark that would not die. Then hope, hunger, longing, joy, a powerful desire to go down to the town again would fill his heart. For in the wild and stormy darkness of oncoming night there was no door, and the thought of staying there in darkness on the mountain top was not to be endured.

Then his uncle and he would go down the mountain side, taking the shortest, steepest way they knew, rushing back down to the known limits of the town, the streets, the houses, and the lights, with a sense of furious haste, hairbreadth escape, as if the great beast of the dark was prowling on their very heels. When they got back into the town, the whole place would be alive with that foggy, smoky, immanent, and strangely exciting atmosphere of early Winter evening and the smells of supper from a hundred houses. The odors of the food were brawny, strong, and flavorsome, and proper to the Winter season, the bite and hunger of the sharp, strong air. There were the smells of frying steak, and fish, and the good fat fragrance of the frying pork chops. And there were the smells of brawny liver, frying chicken, and, most pungent and well-savored smell of all, the smell of strong, coarse hamburger and the frying onions.

The grand and homely quality of this hamburger-onion smell had in it not only the deep glow and comfort of full-fed, hungry bellies, but somehow it made the boy think also of a tender, buxom, clean, desirable young wife, and of the glorious pleasures of the night, the bouts of lusty, loving dalliance when the lights were out, the whole house darkened, and the stormy and demented winds swooped down out of the hills to beat about the house with burly rushes. That image filled his heart with swelling joy, for it evoked again the glorious hope of the plain, priceless, and familiar happiness of a wedded love that might belong to any man alive—to butcher, baker, farmer, engineer, and clerk, as well as to poet, scholar, and philosopher.

It was an image of a wedded love forever hungry, healthy, faithful, clean, and sweet, never false, foul, jaded, wearied out, but forever loving, lusty in the dark midwatches of the night when storm winds beat about the house. It was at once the priceless treasure and unique possession of one man, and it was, like hamburger steak and frying onions, the plain glory and impossible delight of all humanity, which every man alive, he thought, might hope to win.

Thus the strong and homely fragrance of substantial food smells proper to the Winter evoked a thousand images of warmth, closed-in security, roaring fires, and misted windows, mellow with their cheerful light. The doors were shut, the windows were all closed, the houses were all living with that secret, golden, shut-in life of Winter, which somehow pierced the spirit of a passer-by with a wild and lonely joy, a powerful affection for man's life, which was so small a thing against the drowning horror of the night, the storm, and everlasting darkness, and yet which had the deathless fortitude to make a wall, to build a fire, to close a door.

The sight of these closed golden houses with their warmth of life awoke in him a bitter, poignant, strangely mixed emotion of exile and return, of loneliness and security, of being forever shut out from the palpable and passionate integument of life and fellowship, and of being so close to it that he could touch it with his hand, enter it by a door, possess it with a word—a word that, somehow, he could never speak, a door that, somehow, he would never open.

Book III

THE WEB AND THE WORLD

When George Webber's father died, in 1916, the boy was left discon-solate. True, he had been separated from his father for eight years, but, as he said, he had always had the sense that he was there. Now, more strongly than before, he felt himself caught fast in all that web of lives and times long past but ever present in which his Joyner blood and kin enmeshed him, and some escape from it became the first necessity of his life.

Fortunately, John Webber left his son a small inheritance—enough to put the boy through college, and, with careful management, to help him get his bearings afterwards. So that Autumn, with sadness and with exultation, he bade good-bye to all his Joyner relatives and set forth on his great adventure.

And, after college, he dreamed a dream of glory in new lands, a golden future in the bright and shining city.

10

Olympus in Catawba

ONE SEPTEMBER DAY IN 1916, A SKINNY, ADOLESCENT BOY, TUGGING AT A cheap valise, and wearing a bob-tail coat and a pair of skin-tight trousers that made up in brevity and in anatomical frankness what they lacked in length, was coming up along one of the pleasant paths that bisect the lovely campus of an old college in the middle South, pausing from time to time to look about him in a rather uncertain and bewildered manner, and doubtfully to consult a piece of paper in his hand on which some instruction had evidently been written. He had just put down his valise again, and was looking at the piece of paper for the sixth or seventh time, when someone came out of the old dormitory at the head of the campus, ran down the steps, and came striding down the path where the boy was standing. The boy looked up and gulped a little as the creature of pantheresque beauty, moving with the grace, the speed, the delicacy of a great cat, bore down swiftly on him.

At that moment the overwhelmed boy was physically incapable of speech. If his life had depended on it, he could not have produced sounds capable of human hearing or understanding; and if he had been able to, he would certainly not have had the effrontery to address them to a creature of such magnificence that he seemed to have been created on a different scale and shape for another, more Olympian, universe than any the skinny, adolescent boy had ever dreamed of. But fortunately the magnificent stranger himself now took the matter in hand. As he came up at his beautiful pacing stride, pawing the air a little, delicately, in a movement of faultless and instinctive grace, he glanced swiftly and keenly at the youth with a pair of piercing, smokily luminous grey eyes, smiled with the most heartening and engaging friendliness—a smile touched with tenderness and humor—and then, in a voice that was very soft and Southern, a little husky, but for all its agreeable and gentle warmth, vibrant with a tremendous latent vitality, said:

"Are you looking for something? Maybe I can help you."

"Y-y-yes, sir," the boy stammered in a moment, gulped again, and then, finding himself incapable of further speech, he thrust the crumpled paper towards his questioner with trembling hand.

The magnificent stranger took the paper, glanced at it swiftly with that peculiar, keen intensity of his smoky eyes, smiled instantly, and said:

"Oh, McIver. You're looking for McIver. Freshman, are you?"

"Y-yes, sir," the boy whispered.

For a moment more the magnificent young man looked keenly at the boy, his head cocked appraisingly a little to one side, a look of deepening humor and amusement in his grey eyes and in the quality of his pleasant smile. At length he laughed, frankly and openly, but with such a winning and friendly humor that even the awed youth could not be wounded by it.

"Damned if you ain't a bird!" the magnificent young man said, and stood there a moment longer, shrewdly, humorously appraising his companion, with his powerful hands arched lightly on his hips in a gesture which was unconsciously as graceful as everything he did. "Here," he said quietly, "I'll show you what to do, freshman." He placed his powerful hands on the boy's skinny shoulders, faced him around, and then, speaking gently, he said, "You see this path here?"

"Y-yes, sir."

"You see that building down there at the end of it—that building with the white columns out in front?"

"Yes, sir."

"Well," the young Olympian said quietly and slowly, "that's McIver. That's the building that you're looking for. Now," he continued very softly, "all you got to do is to pick up your valise, walk right along this path, go up those steps there, and go into the first door on your right. After that, they'll do the rest. That's where you registah." He paused a moment to let this information sink in, then, giving the boy a little shake of the shoulders, he said gently: "Now do you think you've got that straight? You think you can do what I told you to do?"

"Y-yes, sir."

"All right!" and, with the amazing speed and grace with which he did everything, the Olympian released him, cast up his fine head quickly, and laughed a deep, soft, immensely winning laugh. "All right, freshman," he said. "On your way. And don't let those sophomores sell you any radiators or dormitories until you get yourself fixed up."

And the boy, stammering awed but grateful thanks, picked up his valise hastily and started off to do the bidding of the tall Olympian. As he went down the path he heard again the low, deep, winning laugh, and, without turning his head, he knew that Olympian was standing there, following him with his piercing, smoky eyes, with his hands arched on his hips in that gesture of instinctive and unconscious grace.

Monk Webber would never be able to forget that incident. The memory of it burned in his brain as vividly as ever after more than twenty years. For he was that skinny, adolescent boy, and the Olympian, although he did not know it then, was the magnificent creature known to his earthly comrades as Jim Randolph.

Years later, Monk would still affirm that James Heyward Randolph was the handsomest man he ever saw. Jim was a creature of such power and grace that the memory of him later on was like a legend. He was, alas, a legend even then.

He was a man who had done brilliant and heroic things, and he looked the part. It seemed that he had been especially cast by nature to fulfill the most exacting requirements of the writers of romantic fiction. He was a Richard Harding Davis hero, he was the hero of a book by Robert W. Chambers, he was a Jeffery Farnol paragon, he was all the Arrow collar young men one had ever seen in pictures, all the football heroes from the covers of the *Saturday Evening Post*, he was all the young men in the Kuppenheimer clothing ads—he was all of these rolled into one, and he was something more than all of these. His beauty was conformed by a real manliness, his physical perfection by a natural and incomparable grace, the handsome perfection and regularity of his features by qualities of strength, intelligence, tenderness, and humor that all the heroes of romantic fiction can counterfeit but do not attain.

Jim was a classic type of the tall, young American. He was perhaps a fraction under six feet and three inches tall, and he weighed 192 pounds. He moved with a grace and power that were incomparable.

Whenever one saw him walking along the street, one got an overwhelming impression that he was weaving and "picking his holes" behind the interference, and that he was just about to shake loose around the ends in a touchdown gallop. He moved by a kind of superb pacing rhythm that suggested nothing on earth so much as a race horse coming from the paddocks down to the starting line. He paced upon the balls of his feet, as lightly and delicately as a cat, and there was always the suggestion that his powerful arms and hands were delicately pawing the air, a gesture not pronounced but unmistakable, and, like his walk, his carriage, everything about him, suggested a tremendous catlike power and speed—pent, trembling, geared for action, ready to be unleashed, like the leap of a panther.

Everything about him had this fine-drawn, poised, and nervous grace of a thoroughbred animal. The predominant characteristics were leanness, grace, and speed. His head was well-shaped, rather small. He had black hair, which was closely cropped. His ears also were well-shaped and set close to the head. His eyes were grey and very deep-set, under heavy eyebrows. In moments of anger or deep feeling of any kind his eyes could darken smokily, almost into black. Ordinarily they had the luminous grey potency, the sense of tremendous latent vitality, of a cat. This well-shaped head was carried proudly upon a strong, lean neck and a pair of wide, powerful shoulders. The arms were long, lean, powerfully muscled; the hands also were large and powerful. The whole body was shaped like a wedge: the great shoulders sloped down to a narrow waist, then the figure widened out somewhat to the lean hips, then was completed with the ranging power and grace of the long legs. Jim's speech and voice also maintained and developed the impression of catlike power. His voice was rather soft and low, very Southern, a little husky, full of latent passion, tenderness, or humor, and indicative, as only a voice can be, of the tremendous pantheresque vitality of the man.

He was a member of a good South Carolina family, but his own branch of it had been impoverished. From his high school days the burden of self-support had rested on his own shoulders, and, as a result of this necessity, he had accumulated a variety of experience that few men know in the course of a whole lifetime. It seemed that he had done everything and been everywhere. When Monk first knew him at college, he was already twenty-two or twenty-three years old, several years older than most of the students, and in experience twenty years older.

The range and variety of his brief life had been remarkable. He had taught for a year or two in a country school. He had shipped for a year's cruise on a freighter out of Norfolk, had been in Rio and in Buenos Aires, had gone up and down the whole Ivory Coast of Africa, had made the round of the Mediterranean ports, had known and "had" women (he was given to this kind of boasting) "on four continents and in forty-seven states of the Union." He had peddled books in Summer through the sweltering grain states of the Middle West. He had even been a traveling salesman for a period, and in this capacity had "been in every state but one." This was Oregon, which was, of course, the state where he had failed to "have" a woman, a deficiency which seemed to trouble him no little, and which he swore that he would remedy if the good Lord spared him just a little more.

In addition to all this, he had played professional—or "semi-professional"—baseball for a season or two in one of the mill towns of the South. His description of this episode was riotous. He had played under an assumed name in order to protect as best he could his amateur standing and his future as a college athlete. His employer had been the owner of a cotton mill. His salary had been $150 a month and traveling expenses. And for this stipend it had been his duty to go to the mill offices once a week and empty out the waste paper baskets. In addition to this, every two weeks the manager of the team would take him to a pool room, carefully place a ball exactly in front of the pocket and two inches away from it, and then bet his young first baseman $75 that he could not knock it in.

Even at the time when Monk knew him first at college, Jim had become, for the youth of two states at any rate, an almost legendary figure. The event which sealed him in their hearts, which really gave him a kind of immortality among all the people who will ever go to Pine Rock College was this:

Twenty years ago, one of the greatest sporting occasions in the South was the football game which took place annually between Pine Rock and the old college of Monroe and Madison in Virginia. They were two small colleges, but two of the oldest institutions in the South, and the game on Thanksgiving day was sanctified by almost every element of tradition and of age that could give it color. It was a good deal more than a football game, a great deal more than a contest between two powerful championship teams, for even at that time there were in the South better football teams, and games which, from the point of view of athletic prowess, were more important. But the game between Monroe and Madison and Pine Rock was like the Oxford-Cambridge race along the Thames, or like the Army-Navy game, or like the annual contest between Yale and Harvard—a kind of ceremony, a historic event whose tradition had grown through a series that had lasted even then for almost twenty years and through the associations of two old colleges whose histories were inextricably woven into the histories of their states. For this reason, not only for hundreds of students and thousands of alumni, but for hundreds of thousands of people in both states, the game upon Thanksgiving day had an interest and an importance that no other game could have.

The greatest team Pine Rock ever knew was that team they had that year, with Raby Bennett, back, Jim Randolph hinged over with his big hands resting on his knees, and Randy Shepperton crouched behind the line calling signals for the run around end. Jim could run only to the right; no one ever knew the reason why, but it was true. They always knew where he was going, but they couldn't stop him.

That was the year that Pine Rock beat Monroe and Madison for the first time in nine years. That was the year of years, the year they had been waiting for through all those years of famine, the year they had hoped for so long that they had almost ceased to hope that it would ever come, the year of wonders. And they knew it when it came. They felt it in the air all Autumn. They breathed it in the smell of smoke, they felt it in the tang of frost, they heard it coming in the winds that year, they heard it coming as acorns rattled to the ground. They knew it, breathed it, talked it, hoped and feared and prayed for it. They had waited for that year through nine long seasons. And now they knew that it had come.

That was the year they really marched on Richmond. It is hard to tell about it now. It is hard to convey to anyone the passion, the exultant hope, of that invasion. They do not have it now. They fill great towns at night before the game. They go to night clubs and to bars. They dance, they get drunk, they carouse. They take their girls to games, they wear fur coats, they wear expensive clothing, they are drunk by game time. They do not really see the game, and they do not care. They hope that their machine runs better than the other machine, scores more points, wins a victory. They hope their own hired men come out ahead, but they really do not care. They don't know what it is to care. They have become too smart, too wise, too knowing, too assured, to care. They are not youthful and backwoodsy and naïve enough to care. They are too slick to care. It's hard to feel a passion just from looking at machinery. It's hard to get excited at the efforts of the hired men.

It was not that way that year. They cared a lot—so much, in fact, they could feel it in their throats, taste it in their mouths, hear it thudding in the pulses of their blood. They cared so much that they could starve and save for it, hoard their allowances, shave their expenses to the bone, do without the suit of clothes to replace the threadbare one they owned. They were poor boys, most of them. The average expenditure among them was not more than $500 a year, and two-thirds of them worked to earn the greater part of that. Most of them had come from the country, from the little country towns up in the mountains, in the Piedmont, down in the pine lands of the coast. A lot of them were hayseeds, off the farm. And the rest of them had come from little towns. There weren't any big towns. They didn't have a city in the state.

They were, in point of fact, the student body of an old, impoverished, backwoods college. And they had the finest life. It was the finest place with all its old provincialism, the bare austerity of its whitewashed dormitory rooms, its unfurnished spareness, its old brick and its campus well, its world remotion in the Piedmont uplands of an ancient state. It beat any other place "all hollow." It beat Harvard, it beat Princeton, it beat Yale. It was a better life than Cambridge or than Oxford had to offer. It was a spare life, a hard life, an impoverished kind of life, in many ways a narrow and provincial kind of life, but it was a wonderfully true and good life, too.

It was a life that always kept them true and constant to the living sources of reality, a life that did not shelter them or cloister them, that did not make snobs of them, that did not veil the stern and homely visage of the world with some romantic softening of luxury and retreat. They all knew where they had come from. They all knew where their money came from, too, because their money came so hard. They knew all about, not only their own lives, but about the lives of the whole state. It is true they did not know much about any other life, but they knew that through and through. They knew what was going on around them. They knew the life of the whole village. They knew every woman, man, and child. They knew the histories and characters of each. They knew their traits, their faults, their meannesses and virtues; they were full of knowledge, humor, and observation. It was a good life. It was a spare one, and perhaps it was a narrow one, but they had what they had, they knew what they knew.

And they knew that they were going to win that year. They saved up for it. They would have made that trip to Richmond if they had had to march there. It was not hard for Monk. He got to go by the exercise of a very simple economic choice. He had the choice of getting a new overcoat or of going to Richmond, and like any sensible boy he took Richmond.

I said that he had the choice of Richmond or of a *new* overcoat. It would be more accurate to say he had the choice of Richmond or *an* overcoat. He didn't have an overcoat. The only one that he had ever had had grown green with age, had parted at the seams a year before he came to college. But he had money for a new one now, and he was going to spend that money for the trip to Richmond.

Somehow Jim Randolph heard about it—or perhaps he just guessed it or inferred it. The team was going up two nights before the game. The rest of them were coming up next day. They had a bonfire and a rousing rally just before the team went off, and after it was over Jim took Monk in his room and handed him his own sweater.

"Put this on," he said.

Monk put it on.

Jim stood there in the old, bare dormitory room, his strong hands arched and poised upon his hips, and watched him while he did it.

"Now put on your coat," he said.

Monk put his coat on over it.

Jim looked at him a moment, then burst out in a laugh.

"God Almighty!" he cried. "You're a bird!"

And a bird he was! The big sweater engulfed him, swallowed him like an enormous blanket: the sleeves came out a good four inches longer than the sleeves of his own coat, the sweater hit him midway between his buttocks and his knees and projected shockingly below the coat. It was not a good fit but it was a warm one, and Jim, after looking at him again and slowly shaking his head with the remark, "Damned if you aren't a bird!" seized his valise and put on his hat. (He wore a black or grey felt hat with a wide brim, not quite the slouch hat of a Southern politician, for Jim was always neat and dignified in dress, but a hat that, like all his other garments, contributed to his appearance a manlike strength and maturity.) Then, turning to the boy, he said sternly:

"All right, freshman. You wear that sweater when you go to Richmond. If I catch you up there running around in the cold with that little shavetail coat of yours, I'll beat yo' ——— till you can't sit down." And suddenly he laughed, a quiet, husky, tender, and immensely winning laugh. "Good-bye, son," he said. He put his big hand on Monk's shoulder. "Go ahead and wear the sweater. Don't mind how it looks. You keep warm. I'll see you after the game." Then he was gone.

Wear it! From that time on Monk lived in it. He clung to it, he cherished it, he would have fought and bled and died for it as a veteran in Lee's army would have fought for his commander's battle flag. It was not only Jim's sweater. It was Jim's sweater initialed with the great white "P R" that had been won and consecrated upon the field of many a glorious victory. It was not only Jim's sweater. It was Jim's *great* sweater, the most famous sweater in the whole school—it seemed to Monk, the most famous sweater on earth. If the royal ermine of His Majesty the King-Emperor of Great Britain and India had been suddenly thrown around his shoulders, he could not have been more powerfully impressed by the honor of his investiture.

And everyone else felt the same way. All the freshmen did, at any rate. There was not a boy among them who would not have cheerfully and instantly torn off his overcoat and thrust it at Monk if he thought Monk would have swapped the sweater with him.

And that was the way he went to Richmond.

But how to tell the wonder and glory of that trip? George Webber has been wide and far since then. He has pounded North and South and East and West across the continent on the crack trains of the nation. He has lain on his elbow in the darkness in his berth, time and again, and watched the haunted and the ghost-wan visage of Virginia stroke by in the passages of night. So, too, he has crossed the desert, climbed through the Sierras in the radiance of blazing moons, has crossed the stormy seas a dozen times and more and known the racing slant and power of great liners, has pounded down to Paris from the Belgian frontiers at blind velocities of speed in the rocketing trains, has seen the great sweep and curve of lights along the borders of the Mediterranean on the coasts of Italy, has known the old, time-haunted, elfin magic of the forests of Germany, in darkness also. He has gone these ways, has seen these things and known these dark wonders, but no voyage he ever made, whether by nighttime or by day, had the thrill, the wonder, and the ecstasy of that trip when they went up to Richmond twenty years ago.

The bonfire and the leaping flames, the students cheering, weaving, dancing, the red glow upon the old red brick, the ivy sere and withered by November, the wild, young faces of eight hundred boys, the old bell tolling in the tower. And then the train. It was a desolate little train. It seemed to be a relic of the lost Confederacy. The little, wheezing engine had a fan-shaped funnel. The old wooden coaches were encrusted with the cinders and the grime of forty years. Half of the old red seats of smelly plush were broken down. They jammed into it till the coaches bulged. They hung onto the platforms, they jammed the aisles, they crawled up on the tender, they covered the whole grimy caravan like a swarm of locusts. And finally the old bell tolled mournfully, the whistle shrieked, and, to the accompaniment of their lusty cheers, the old engine jerked, the rusty couplings clanked and jolted—they were on their way.

Flashing away to the main line junction, fourteen miles away, the engine was derailed, but that did not faze them. They clambered out and swarmed around it, and by main strength and enthusiasm they helped the ancient engineer to crowbar, jack, and coax and lift her back onto the rusty track. They got there finally to the junction and found the train that had been chartered for them waiting. Ten dusty, grimy coaches of the Seaboard Air Line waited for them. They clambered in, found places if they could. Ten minutes later they were on the way to Richmond. All through the night they pounded up out of the South, across Virginia, and they came to Richmond with the first grey light of dawn.

George Webber has been to that old town a good many times since then, but never as he came there first, out of the South by darkness, out of the South with the unuttered hope, the unspoken wildness, the fever of the impossible unknown joy, burning, burning, burning through the night. They got to Richmond just at break of day. They swarmed out cheering. They swarmed out into the long-deserted stretch of Gay Street. And then they started out, the whole noisy, swarming horde of them, up that deserted street, past all the darkened stores and shops, mounting the hill, up to the capitol. The dome of the old capitol was being tinged with the first rays of morning light as they came up. The air was sharp and frosty. The trees in the park around the capitol and the hill had the thrilling, clean austerity of morning, of first light, of frost, and of November.

It was a thrilling experience, for many of them a completely new experience, the experience of seeing a great city—for to most of them old Richmond seemed to be a great city—waking into life, to the beginning of another day. They saw the early street cars rattle past and clatter over switch points with a wonder and a joy that no one who looked at street cars ever felt before. If they had been the first street cars in the world, if they had been thrilling and enchanted vehicles newly brought from Mars, or from the highways of the moon, they could not have seemed more wonderful to them. Their paint was brighter than all other paint, the brilliance of their light was far more brilliant, the people in them reading morning papers, stranger, more exciting, than any people they had ever seen.

They felt in touch with wonder and with life, they felt in touch with magic and with history. They saw the state house and they heard the guns. They knew that Grant was pounding at the gates of Richmond. They knew that Lee was digging in some twenty miles away at Petersburg. They knew that Lincoln had come down from Washington and was waiting for the news at City Point. They knew that Jubal Early was swinging in his saddle at the suburbs of Washington. They felt, they knew, they had their living hands and hearts upon the living presence of these things, and upon a thousand other things as well. They knew that they were at the very gateways of the fabulous and unknown North, that great trains were here to do their bidding, that they could rocket in an hour or two into the citadels of gigantic cities. They felt the pulse of sleep, the heartbeats of the sleeping men, the drowsy somnolence and the silken stir of luxury and wealth of lovely women. They felt the power, the presence, and the immanence of all holy and enchanted things, of all joy, all loveliness, and all the beauty and the wonder that the world could offer. They knew, somehow, they had their hands upon it. The triumph of some impending and glorious fulfillment, some impossible possession, some incredible achievement was thrillingly imminent. They knew that it was going to happen—soon. And yet they could not say how or why they knew it.

They swarmed into the lunchrooms and the restaurants along Broad Street; the richer of them sought the luxury of great hotels. They devoured enormous breakfasts, smoking stacks of wheat cakes, rations of ham and eggs, cup after cup of pungent, scalding coffee. They gorged themselves, they smoked, they read the papers. The humblest lunchroom seemed to them a paradise of gourmets.

Full morning came, and clean, cold light fell slant-wise on the street with golden sharpness. Everything in the world seemed impossibly good and happy, and all of it, they felt, was theirs. It seemed that everyone in Richmond had a smile for them. It seemed that all the people had been waiting for them through the night, had been preparing for them, were eager to give them the warmest welcome of affectionate hospitality. It seemed not only that they expected Pine Rock's victory, but that they desired it. All of the girls, it seemed to them, were lovely, and all of them, they felt, looked fondly at them. All of the people of the town, they thought, had opened wide their hearts and homes to them. They saw a banner with their colors, and it seemed to them that the whole town was festooned in welcome to them. The hotels swarmed with them. The negro bellboys grinned and hopped to do their bidding. The clerks who waited smiled on them. They could have everything they wanted. The whole town was theirs. Or so they thought.

The morning passed. At one-thirty they went out to the playing field. And they won the game. As Monk remembered it, it was a dull game. It was not very interesting except for the essential fact that they won it. They had expected too much. As so often happens when so much passion, fervor, hot imagination has gone into the building of a dream, the consummation was a disappointment. They had expected to win by a big score. They were really much the better team, but all their years of failure had placed before them a tremendous psychical impediment. They won the game by a single touchdown. The score was 6 to 0. They even failed to kick goal after touchdown. It was the first time during the course of the entire season that Randy's toe had failed him.

But it was better that the game ended as it did. It was Jim's game. There was no doubt of that. It was completely and perfectly his own. Midway in the third quarter he did exactly what he was expected to do. Pacing out to the right, behind the interference, weaving and pawing delicately at the air, he found his opening and shook loose, around the end, for a run of 57 yards to a touchdown. They scored six points, and all of them were Jim's.

Later, the whole thing attained the clean, spare symmetry of a legend. They forgot all other details of the game entirely. The essential fact, the fact that would remain, the picture that would be most vivid, was that it was Jim's game. No game that was ever played achieved a more classical and perfect unity for the projection of its great protagonist. It was even better that he scored just that one touchdown, made just that one run. If he had done more, it would have spoiled the unity and intensity of their later image. As it was, it was perfect. Their hero did precisely what they expected him to do. He did it in his own way, by the exercise of his own faultless and incomparable style, and later on that was all they could remember. The game became nothing. All they saw was Jim, pacing and weaving out around right end, his right hand pawing delicately at the air, the ball hollowed in the crook of his long left arm, and then cutting loose on his race-horse gallop.

That was the apex of Jim Randolph's life, the summit of his fame. Nothing that he could do after that could dim the perfect glory of that shining moment. Nothing could ever equal it. It was a triumph and a tragedy, but at that moment Jim, poor Jim, could only know the triumph of it.

Next year the nation went to war in April. Before the first of May, Jim Randolph had gone to Oglethorpe. He came back to see them once or twice while he was in training. He came back once again when school took up in Autumn, a week or two before he went to France. He was a first lieutenant now. He was the finest-looking man in uniform George Webber ever saw. They took one look at him and they knew the war was won. He went overseas before Thanksgiving; before the New Year he was at the front.

Jim did just what they knew he would do. He was in the fighting around Château-Thierry. He was made a Captain after that. He was almost killed in the battle of the Argonne Wood. They heard once that he was missing. They heard later that he was dead. They heard finally that he had been seriously wounded and his chances for re‧ covery were slight, and that if he did recover he would never be the same man again. He was in a hospital at Tours for almost a year. Later on, he was in a hospital at Newport News for several months. They did not see him again, in fact, till the Spring of 1920.

He came back then, handsome as ever, magnificent in his Captain's bars and uniform, walking with a cane, but looking as he always did. Nevertheless he was a very sick man. He had been wounded near the spine. He wore a leather corset. He improved, however; was even able to play a little basketball. The name and fame of him was as great as ever.

And yet, indefinably, they knew that there was something lacking, something had gone by; they had lost something, something priceless, precious, irrecoverable. And when they looked at Jim, their look was somehow touched with sadness and regret. It would have been better for him had he died in France. He had suffered the sad fate of men who live to see themselves become a legend. And now the legend lived. The man was just a ghost to them.

Jim was probably a member of what the intellectuals since have called "the lost generation." But Jim really was not destroyed by war. He was ended by it. Jim was really not a member of the generation that was lost, but of a generation that was belated. Jim's life had begun and had been lived before the war, and it was ended with the war. At the age of twenty-six or twenty-seven, Jim was out of date. He had lived too long. He belonged to another time. They all knew it, too, although none of them could speak about it then.

The truth is that the war formed a spiritual frontier in the lives of all the students at Pine Rock in Webber's day. It cut straight across the face of time and history, a dividing line that was as clear and certain as a wall. The life they had before the war was not the life that they were going to have after the war. The way they felt and thought and believed about things before the war was different from the way they felt and thought and believed after the war. The America that they knew before the war, the vision of America that they had before the war, was so different from the America and the vision of America they had after the war. It was all so strange, so sad, and so confusing.

It all began so hopefully. Monk can still remember the boys stripping for the doctors in the old gymnasium. He can remember those young winds that echoed the first coming of the blade and leaf, and all his comrades jubilantly going to war. He can remember the boys coming from the dormitories with their valises in their hands, Jim Randolph coming down the steps of South, and across the campus towards him, and his cheerful:

"So long, kid. You'll get in too. I'll be seeing you in France."

He can remember how they came back from the training camps, spotless, new-commissioned shavetails, proud and handsome with their silver bars and well-cut uniforms. He can remember all of it—the fire, the fever, the devotion and the loyalty, the joy of it, the pride of it, the jubilation and the thrill of it. The wild excitement when they knew that we were winning. The excitement—and the sorrow—when we won.

Yes, the sorrow. Does anyone really think that they were glad? Does anyone think they wanted the war to end? He is mistaken. They loved the war, they hung on to it, and they cherished it. They said the things with lips that lips were meant to say, but in their hearts they prayed:

"Dear God, please let the war continue. Don't let the war be over until we younger ones get in."

They can deny it now. Let them deny it if they like. This is the truth.

Monk can still remember how the news came that the war was over. He can remember swinging on the rope as the great bell itself began to ring. He can still feel the great pull of the rope and how it lifted him clear off the ground, and how the rope went slanting in its hole, and how the great bell swung and tolled the news there in the darkness far above him, and how all of the boys were running out of doors upon the campus, and how the tears rolled down his face.

Monk was not the only one who wept that night. Later on they may have said they wept for joy, but this is not the truth. They wept because they were so sorrowful. They wept because the war was over, and because they knew that we had won, and because every victory of this sort brings so much sorrow with it. And they wept because they knew that something in the world had ended, that something else had in the world begun. They wept because they knew that something in their lives had gone forever, that something else was coming in their lives, and that their lives would never be the same again.

I I

The Priestly One

GERALD ALSOP, AT THE TIME MONK CAME TO COLLEGE, HAD BECOME A kind of Mother Machree of the campus, the brood hen of yearling innocents, the guide and mentor of a whole flock of fledgeling lives.

At first sight he looked enormous. A youth of nineteen or twenty at this time, he weighed close to three hundred pounds. But when one really observed him closely, one saw that this enormous weight was carried on a very small frame. In height he could not have been more than five feet six or seven. His feet, for a person of his bulk, were amazingly small, and his hands, had it not been for their soft padding, were almost the tiny hands of a child. His belly, of course, was enor-mous. His great fat throat went right back in fold after fold of double chins. When he laughed, his laugh came from him in a high, chok-ing, explosive scream that set the throat and the enormous belly into jellied tremors.

He had a very rich, a very instant sense of humor, and this humor, with the high, choking laugh and the great, shaking belly, had given him among many students a reputation for hearty good nature. But more observant people would find out that this impression of hearty and whole-souled good nature was not wholly true. If Gerald's an-tagonism and prejudice were aroused, he could still scream with his great fat whah-whah of choking laughter, but this time the laugh had something else in it, for the great belly that shook with such convulsive mirth was also soured with bile. It was a strange and curi-ously mixed and twisted personality, a character that had much that was good, much that was high and fine, much that was warm, affec-tionate, and even generous in it, but also much that was vindictive and unforgiving, prejudiced and sentimental. It was, in the end, a character that had too much of the feminine in it to be wholly mascu-line, and this perhaps was its essential defect.

188

Pine Rock—the small Baptist college of red brick, in its setting of Catawba clay and pine—had released him. In this new and somewhat freer world, he had expanded rapidly. His quick mind and his ready wit, his great scream of belly laughter, and something comfortable about him that made him very easy company, also made him a considerable favorite. He came to college in the fall of 1914. Two years later, when Monk joined him there, he was a junior, and well-founded: the ruling member, as it were, of a coterie; the director of a clique; already priestly, paternal, and all-fatherly, the father-confessor to a group of younger boys, most of them freshmen, that he herded under his protective wing, who came to him, as just recently they must have come to mother's knee, to pour out on his receiving breast the burden of their woe.

Jerry—for so he was called—loved confession. It was, and would remain, the greatest single stimulus of his life. And in a way, it was the perfect role for him: nature had framed him for the receiving part. He was always fond of saying afterward that it was not until his second year at college that he really "found" himself; strictly measured, that process of finding was almost wholly included in the process of being confessed to. He was like a kind of enormous, never sated, never saturated sponge. The more he got, the more he wanted. His whole manner, figure, personality, under the inner impulsion of this need, took on a kind of receptive urgency. By his twentieth year he was a master in the art of leading on. The broad brow, the jowled face, the fat hand holding a moist cigarette, the great head occasionally turned to take a long, luxurious drag, the eyes behind their polished frames of glass a little misty, the mouth imprinted faintly by a little smile that can only be described as tender, a little whimsical, as who should say, "Ah, life. Life. How bad and mad and sad it is, but then, ah, me, how sweet!"—it was all so irresistible that the freshmen simply ran bleating to the fold. There was nothing of which they did not unbosom themselves, and if, as often happened, they had nothing in particular to unbosom themselves of, they invented something. In this process of spiritual evacuation, it is to be feared the temptations of carnal vice came first.

It was, in fact, simply astounding how many of Jerry's freshmen had been sorely tempted by beautiful but depraved women—if the siren was mysterious and unknown, all the better. In one variant of the story, the innocent had been on his way to college, and had stopped over for the night at a hotel in a neighboring town. On his way to his room, a door along the corridor was opened: before him stood a beautiful specimen of the female sex, without a stitch of clothing on, inviting him with sweet smiles and honeyed words into her nest of silken sin. For a moment the freshman was shaken, his senses reeled, all that he had learned, all he had been taught to respect and keep holy, whirled around him in a dizzy rout; before he realized what he was doing, he found himself inside the accursed den of wickedness, half-fainting in the embraces of this modern whore of Babylon.

And then—*then*—he saw the image of his mother's face, or the features of the pure, sweet girl for whom he was "keeping himself." The freshmen of Pine Rock were usually in a careful state of refrigeration—nearly all of them were "keeping themselves" for a whole regiment of pure, sweet girls, to whose virginity they would someday add the accolade of their own penil sanctification. At any rate, during Jerry's regime at Pine Rock the number of lovely but depraved females who were cruising around through the hotel corridors of the state in a condition of original sin and utter nakedness was really astonishing. The census figures for this type of temptation were never before, or after, so high.

The usual end was well, however: the redemptive physiognomies of the Mother or the Chosen Girl usually intervened fortuitously at the fifty-ninth minute of the eleventh hour—and all was saved. As for Jerry, his final benediction to this triumph of virtue was simply beautiful to watch and hear:

"I knew you would! Yes, suh!" Here he would shake his head and chuckle tenderly. "You're too fine a pusson evah to be taken in by anything like that! . . . And if you had, think how you'd feel now! You wouldn't be able to hold yoah haid up and look me in the eye! You know you wouldn't! And every time you thought of your Mothah"—(it is impossible to convey within the comparatively simple vocabulary of the English language just quite what Jerry managed to put into that one word "Mothah"; however, it can be said without exaggeration that it represented the final and masterly conquest of the vocal chords, beside which such efforts, say, as those of the late Senor Caruso striking the high C seem fairly paltry by comparison)— "Every time you thought of your Mothah, you'd have felt lowah than a snake's belly. Yes, suh! You know you would! And if you'd gone ahead and married that girl—" he pronounced it "gul," with a vocal unction only slightly inferior to this pronunciation of the sainted name of "Mothah" —"you'd have felt like a louse every time you'd look at her! Yes, suh, you'd have been livin' a lie that would have wrecked yoah whole life! . . . Besides that, boy . . . you look a-heah, you scannel! You don't know how lucky you are! You keep away hereafter from that stuff! Yes, suh! I know what I'm talkin' about!" Here he shook his big jowled head again, and laughed with a kind of foreboding ominousness. "You might have gone and got yourself all ruined for life!"

He was preparing himself eventually, he thought, although he later gave up the idea, for the practice of medicine, in which he had already done considerable isolated reading of his own; the chief effects of which, apparently, were now to warn guileless freshmen of the awful consequences of carnal indulgence. He fairly reveled in this form of grisly description. His descriptions of disease, death, and madness which resulted from stray encounters with unknown females in the corridors of hotels were so graphic and compelling that he had the hair standing up on their young pates "like quills upon the fretful porpentine."

In Gerald's picture of things as they were, there was no escape, no pardon for the erring. The wages of sin were not only always and inevitably death, but the wages of seduction were inevitably fatherhood, man's guilty doom, and the utter ruination of another "pure, sweet girl."

Thus, early, Gerald had formed a picture of the world that was pontifical in its absolute and unquestioning acceptance of all forms of established and respectable authority—not only as they affected man's civic and political conduct, but as they affected his inner and personal life as well. In this scheme of things— call it rather, this mythology —the saintly figure of The Mother was supreme. A female, by virtue of the fact that in the process of lawful matrimony she had created progeny, became, in some divinely mysterious way, not only the author of all wisdom, but the spotless custodian of all morality as well. To have suggested that a woman was not necessarily an incorruptible divinity because she had given birth to a child was a dangerous heresy; to have argued this point doggedly to more far-reaching conclusions would have branded one in Jerry's sight as a dissolute or irresponsible member of society. From that time on, Jerry's hand and his heart would be set stubbornly against the infidel.

True, his enmity would be devious. Openly, for Jerry really had a good mind, which was clear enough to see, but not brave enough to confess the falsehood of his sentiment, he would be tolerant—his tolerance consisting of a form of benevolent I-see-your-point-but-then-let's-try-to-look-at-all-sides-of-the-question attitude, which was really more intolerant than any form of open bigotry could have been, because it masked the unyielding and unforgiving hostility of his wounded sentimentality. But hiddenly and deviously, his enmity would be bitter and unpardoning from that time on. It would take the form of sly gossip, rumor, whispering, swift mockery masked behind a play of innocence, a sudden twist upon a word, a quick, apparently guileless, misinterpretation of a meaning, the pontifical face schooled in grave and even respectful attentiveness, the whole ending suddenly with the explosion of mirth, the high, choking scream of laughter, which, as anyone who had been its victim could testify, was more devastating and unanswerable than any logic of cold argument could be.

He was a creature who, first and foremost, above all other things, hated trouble and abhorred pain—as what decent man does not?—except that here, in this great belly of a man, his hatred and abhorrence were so great that he would never face the things he hated. Thus, from an early age, he had learned to wear rose-colored blinders against life, and it was only natural that his own stubborn and unyielding hostility should be turned against anything—any person, any conflict, any situation, any evidence, or any idea—that would tend to take those blinders off.

In spite of this, in so many rich and wonderful ways Gerald Alsop was an extraordinary man. The thing that was most attractive about him was his genuine and warm humanity. In the most true sense of the word, he was a man who loved "the good things of life"—good food, good conversation, good humor, good fellowship, good books, the whole sound and happy aura of good living. His fault was, he loved them so well that he was unwilling to admit or accept the presence of any conflict that might disturb his own enjoyment of them. He was probably wise enough to see, but too sentimental to admit, that his enjoyment of them would have been enriched immeasurably by his recognition of the elements of conflict and denial, even where "the good things of life" were concerned.

Hence, there was no single virtue of his nature—and his nature was with virtue generously endowed—that was not in the end touched

with this taint. He had, for example, a genuine and deep appreciation of good writing, a love of literature, an excellent and discriminating taste; but where his judgment warred with sentiment, his judgment came off second best. The result was chaos. He not only could
see no merit in the work of the great Russian writers—Tolstoy, Dostoevski, Turgenev, even Chekhov—he had never even made an effort
to understand them. In some strange way, his heart was set against
them; he was afraid of them. He had long ago conceived the prejudice that a Russian writer stood for unbroken gloom, grim tragedy,
what gradually he began to rationalize in a phrase that he called "the
morbid and distorted view of life," in contradistinction to the works
of those writers of whom he approved, and who, correspondingly of
course, represented "the more wholesome and well-rounded point of
view."

Of this latter kind, Dickens probably stood first and highest in his
affections. His knowledge of the works of Charles Dickens was almost
encyclopædic. He had read them all so many times, and with such devotion, that there was scarcely an obscure character in that whole
crowded and amazing gallery with which he was not instantly
familiar—which he could not instantly tag with the word, quote with
the exact and descriptive phrase, with which Dickens himself had
tagged him.

But, here again, the nature of Alsop's fault was evident. Equipped
with the intelligence, the knowledge, and the taste to form a true
and accurate judgment of the work of a great writer, his sentiment had
nevertheless contrived to create a completely false and spurious Dickens,
a Dickens world that never was. Dickens himself, in Gerald's view, was
a kind of enormous super-Mr. Pickwick; and the world he had created in his books was a Pickwickian world—a jovial world, a ruddy,
humorous, jolly, inn-and-tavern sort of world, full of good food and
musty ale, full of sunlight and good cheer, of fellowship and love and
friendship, of wonderful humorous characters, and of pleasing, somewhat misty sentiment—a total picture that Gerald had now framed
in the descriptive phrase, "the more wholesome and well-rounded view
of life." It was a world very much like that depicted in those jolly
Christmas cards one sees so often: shining stage coaches loaded with
red-cheeked passengers, bundled in red scarves, dashing up before the
gabled entrance of a cheerful inn, mine host with pipe in hand, to
greet them, and hollied sprigs above the postern doors.

Of the other Dickens—the greater Dickens—the Dickens who had seen so much sin and poverty and misery and oppression, who had been moved to deep compassion for the suffering and oppressed of life, and who had been roused to powerful indignation at the cruelty and injustice in the life he knew—Gerald knew almost nothing, or, if he did know, he had refused to see it as it was, had closed his heart against it, because it was unpleasant and distasteful to him, and because it did not fit in with his own rosy vision of "the more wholesome and well-rounded view of things."

The result was chaos. It might be likened, rather, to a few chips of truth swimming around in a sea of molasses. Alsop could grow lyrical in discussing and estimating the prodigious beauties of John Keats, of Shelley, Shakespeare, Chaucer, and Kit Marlowe; but he could also grow lyrical and ecstatic in the same way and to the same degree in estimating the prodigious beauties of Winnie the Pooh, Don Marquis, F.P.A., last night's moving picture show, and the whimsical little Lamb-kins of a man named Morley:

"Sure damn genius—yes, suh!—sheer, damn, elfin, whimsical genius!" Here, he would read some treasured bit, cast his jowled head upward until light shimmered on the glasspoints of his misty eyes, and, with a laugh that was half-sob, and all compact of wonder and the treacle of his own self-appeasement, he would cry: "Lord God! Lord God—it's sure damn elfin genius!"

Even in these early days of his apprenticeship at college he had begun to accumulate a library. And that library was an astounding picture of his mind and taste, a symbol of his inner chaos all congealed in the soothing and combining solvent of his own syrup:

It contained a large number of good books—books that one liked, others of which one had heard and would like to read, books that had been preserved and saved with the intelligence of a good mind and a discriminating taste. Alsop was a voracious reader of novels, and his bookshelves even at that Baptist college showed selective power, and an eager curiosity into the best of the new work that was being produced. It was astonishing in a man so young, and in such a place.

But his library also included a world of trash: towering stacks of newspapers, containing morsels of choice taffy that had appealed to him; great piles of magazines, containing pieces of whimsey or of sentiment that were preserved in the mothering fullness of his bosom; hundreds of newspaper clippings, embalming some sentiment that was particularly dear to him; as well as many other things which were really valuable and good, and showed a welter of bewildering contradictions—a good mind and a keen and penetrating sense of judgment swimming around upon a sea of slop.

Brought down to simple fact, "the more wholesome and well-rounded view of things" resolved itself into an utter acceptance of things as they were, because things as they were, no matter how ugly, wasteful, cruel, or unjust, were "life"—hence, inevitable, once one understood them "in their full perspective" and saw "how essentially fine and sweet" (a phrase that did him valiant service) "life" was.

Thus Jerry Alsop became the devoted champion of the conventions, the accepted and established scheme of things. If a picture could have been made of his mind during the war and post-war years, it would have revealed the following record of faith and of belief:

The President of the United States, Woodrow Wilson, was not only "the greatest man since Jesus Christ," but his career and final martyrdom—for so did Alsop speak of it—were also closely comparable to the career and martyrdom of Christ. The President had been the perfect man, pure in conduct, irreproachable in wisdom, and faultless in his management of affairs. He had been deceived, tricked, and done to death by villains—by unscrupulous and contriving politicians in his own land, jealous of his fame, and by the unprincipled charlatans of diplomacy in others.

"The second greatest man since Jesus Christ" was the president of the college, a tall, pale man with a pure and suffering face, who got up in Chapel and agonized over his boys, making frequent use of such words as "service," "democracy," and "ideals of leadership"—all popular evidences of enlightened—nay, inspired!—thought, in the jargon of the time. What it all meant, reduced to concrete terms of conduct, was a little puzzling. "Character," "education for the good life," seemed to boil down in practice to a non-drinking, non-smoking, non-gambling, non-card-playing, non-fornicating state of single blessedness, leading up eventually to "the life of service and of leadership for which Pine Rock prepares a man"—namely, the eventual sacrament of matrimony with a spotless female, variously referred to in the lexicon of idealism as "a fine woman," or "a pure, sweet girl."

"An intelligent and liberal interest in the affairs of government and politics" seemed to mean supporting the Democratic or Republican tickets and voting for the candidates which the political machines that dominated these two parties put up at election time.

"A serious and enlightened attitude towards religion" did not mean hide-bound fundamentalism, for Pine Rock under its idealistic president prided itself on the liberalism of its thought. God, for example, might be understood as "a great idea," or "an ocean of consciousness," instead of the usual old gentleman with the long beard—but one went to church on Sunday just the same.

In fact, in spite of all this high-sounding talk about "service," "ideals of leadership," and "democracy," one could not see that it made much actual difference in the way things were. Children still worked fourteen hours a day in the cotton mills of the state. Tens of thousands of men and women and children were born, suffered, lived, and died in damnable poverty, bondage, and the exploitation of the tenant farm. One million black inhabitants of the state, about a third of the entire population, were still denied the rights of free suffrage—even though "the second greatest man since Jesus Christ" frequently declared that that right was one of the proudest triumphs of Anglo-Saxon law, and of the nation's own great Constitution. One million black inhabitants of the state were denied the right to the blessings of the higher education—although "the second greatest man since Jesus Christ" often declared that it was for this ideal that Pine Rock College lived and had its being, and that the right of education would be denied to no fit person at old Pine Rock, "regardless of creed, color, race, or other distinction of any kind whatsoever." In spite of the sounding phrases, the idealism, the martyred look, the inspired assurances, and all the rest of it, life went on according to the old formula, and in the old way, pretty much as it had always done. Class after class of pure young idealists marched forth from Pine Rock bearing the torch, prepared to bare their breasts and to die nobly, if necessary, at the barricades, no matter what sinister influences menaced them, or what overwhelming forces outnumbered them—in defense of monogamy, matrimony, pure sweet women, children, the Baptist Church, the Constitution, and the splendid ideals of the Democratic and Republican parties; aye, resolved furthermore, if they were challenged, so great was this, their devotion to the right, to die there at the barricades in the defense of the splendid institution of child labor, cotton mills, tenant farmers, poverty, misery, squalor, damnation, death, and all the rest of it—rather than recant for a moment, be recreant for a single second to the pure ideals that had been fostered in them, the shining star of conduct to which their youthful gaze had been directed by "the second greatest man since Jesus Christ."

And in the idolatry of this reverence, Gerald Alsop, like his distinguished predecessor, Adhem, led all the rest.

"The third greatest man since Jesus Christ" was a clergyman, pastor of the Pine Rock Episcopal Church, affectionately known to the boys as "Preacher" Reed. It was a name he had encouraged them to use himself. In a way, Jerry Alsop always looked upon Preacher as one of his own private discoveries. He certainly regarded him as another proof of his own liberalism, for Pine Rock was admittedly and professionally Baptist in its sympathies, but Jerry had been big enough to leap across the wall of orthodoxy and to fold the new Messiah to his breast.

Not that Preacher would not have done very nicely for himself had he been left solely to his own devices. For his own devices were unusual ones. To the boys they seemed at first amazing, then sensational, finally enchanting—until there was hardly a student in the college who had not enthusiastically succumbed to them.

At the outset, one would have said that the odds were a thousand to one against Preacher's getting anywhere. He was an Episcopalian—no one seemed to know quite what that was, but it sounded risky. He had just a little church, and almost no congregation. In addition to this, he was "a Northern man." The situation looked hopeless, and yet before six months were out Preacher had the whole campus eating from his hand, and black looks and angry mutterings from every other preacher in the town.

No one knew exactly how he did it; he went about it all so quietly that the thing was done before they knew that it was done. But probably the greatest asset that he had was that from the very beginning no one thought of him as a preacher. And the proof of this was that they called him one. They would not have dared to take such liberties with any other clergyman in town. Besides this, Preacher didn't preach to them; he didn't sermonize in hour-long harangues; he didn't pray for them in twenty-minute invocations; he did not thunder at them from the pulpit, nor did he work all the stops upon his ministerial vocal chords: he did not coo like a dove, roar like a lion, or bleat like a lamb. He had a trick worth six or eight of these.

He began to drop in to see the boys in their rooms. There was something so casual and so friendly in his visits that he put everyone at ease at once. In the most pleasant way he managed to convey to them that he was one of them. He was a well-conditioned man of fifty years, with sandy hair, and a lean face that had great dignity, but also a quality that was very friendly and attractive. In addition to this, he dressed in rather casual-looking clothes—rough, shaggy tweeds, grey flannel trousers, thick-soled shoes—all somewhat worn-looking, but making the boys wish vaguely that they knew where he got them, and wonder if they could get some like them. He would come by and sing out cheerfully:

"Working? I'll not stay if you are. I was just passing by."

At this, there would be an instant scraping of chairs, the scramble of feet, and a chorus of voices assuring him most earnestly that no one was working, and would he please sit down.

Upon receiving these assurances, he would sit down, tossing his hat as he did so upon the top tier of the double-decker cot, tilt back comfortably against the wall in an old creaking chair, one foot hinged on the bottom round, and produce his pipe—a blackened old briar that seemed to have been seasoned in the forge of Vulcan—load it with fragrant tobacco from an oil-skin pouch, strike a match, and begin to puff contentedly, speaking in between the puffs:

"Now I—I—like—a pipe!"—puff, puff— "You—younger—blades"— puff, puff—"can—have—your—cigarettes"—puff, puff, puff—"but as for me"—he puffed vigorously for a moment—"there's—nothing—that— can—give me"—puff, puff, puff—"quite the comfort—of this—old— briar—pipe!"

Oh, the gusto of it! The appeasement of it! The deep, fragrant, pungent, and soul-filling contentment of it! Could anyone think that such a man as this would fail? Or doubt that within a week half the boys would be smoking pipes?

So Preacher would have got along anyway without Jerry Alsop's help, and yet Jerry surely played a part in it. It was Jerry who had largely inaugurated the series of friendly meetings in students' rooms, in which Preacher took the leading and most honored role. Preacher, in fact, was one of those men who at the time were so busily engaged in the work of "relating the Church to modern life"—in his own more pungent phrase, of "bringing God to the campus." His methods of doing so were, as Jerry said, "perfectly delightful."

"Christ," Preacher would begin in one of those charming gatherings in student rooms, which found eight or ten eager youths sprawled around the floor in various postures, a half-dozen more perched up on the rickety tiers of a double-decker cot, a few more hanging out the windows, eagerly drinking in the whole pungent brew of wit, of humor, of good-natured practicality, life, and Christianity, through shifting planes of pipe and cigarette smoke—"Christ," Preacher would continue, puffing on his pipe in that delightfully whimsical way of his, "was a fellow who never made a Six in philosophy. He was a fellow who started out on the scrub team, and wound up playing quarterback on the Varsity. But if He'd had to go on playing with the scrubs"—this was thrown out perhaps, as a kind of sop of encouragement to certain potentially permanent scrubs who might be within the range of hearing—"if Christ had had to go on playing with the scrubs, why," said Preacher Reed, "He would have made a go of it. You see"—here he puffed thoughtfully on his seasoned pipe for a moment—"the point is, fellows—that's the thing I want you to understand—Christ was a fellow who always made a go of everything. Now Paul"—for a moment more Preacher puffed meditatively on his blackened briar, and then, chuckling suddenly in his delightful way, he shook his head and cried—"now Paul! Ah-hah-hah—that's a different story! Paul was a bird of a different feather! There's a horse of quite another color! Paul was a fellow who flunked out."

By this time the eager young faces were fairly hanging on these inspired words.

"Paul was a fellow who started out on the scrub team, and should have stayed there," said Preacher Reed. "But he couldn't stand the gaff! He was eating his heart out all the time because he couldn't make the Varsity—and when there was a vacancy—when they needed a new quarterback, because, you see, fellows," said Preacher quietly, "the Old One had died"—he paused for a moment to let this subtle bit sink in—"they put Paul in his place. And he couldn't make the grade! He simply couldn't make the grade. And in the end—what did he do? Well, fellows, I'll tell you," said Preacher. "When he found he couldn't make the grade—he invented a new game. The old one was too tough. Paul couldn't play it— it was too much for him! And so he invented a new one he could play—and that's where Paul flunked out. You see, fellows, Paul was a fellow who made a Six where Christ always made a One. That's the whole difference between them," Preacher said with the easy and informative manner of "Now it can be told," and then was silent for a moment, sucking vigorously and reflectively on his old briar pipe.

"In othah words, Preachah," Jerry, who had made a One in Logic and was accounted no slouch himself in the Hegelian metaphysic, now took respectful advantage of the silence that had fallen—"in othah words, Paul was a man who was defeated by his own Moment of Negation. He failed to absawb it."

"Exactly, Jerry!" Preacher cried out instantly and heartily, with the manner of one saying, "You take the words right out of my mouth!"—"That's it exactly! Paul was a man who got licked by his own Moment of Negation. He couldn't absorb it. When he found himself among the scrubs, he didn't want to play. Instead of using his Moment of Negation—realizing that the Moment of Negation is really the greatest friend and ally that a man can have—Paul let it get him down. He flunked. Now, Christ," Preacher went on, paused a moment to suck reflectively at his pipe, and then abruptly—"You see, fellows, that's the Whole Thing about Jesus. Christ never flunked. He always made his One. It was first down with him every time whether he was playing with the scrubs or with the Varsity. He was just as happy playing with one side as with the other. It didn't matter to Him where he played . . and if Christ had been there," Preacher Reed went on, "everything would have been all right, no matter where He played."

And again Preacher puffed vigorously on his pipe before he spoke: "You see, Jesus would have kept Paul from making that Six. He'd have said to him, 'Now, see here, Paul, if you want to play quarterback on the Varsity, that's all right with Me. It doesn't matter to Me where I play—all I'm interested in is the Game.'" Preacher paused here just perceptibly to let this sink in. "'I'd just as lief—'" Preacher was noted for his gift of homely phrase—"'I'd just as lief play with the scrubs as with the Varsity. So let's change places if you want to. The only thing, Paul, *let's have a good Game.*'" Preacher puffed a moment. "'Let's play according to the rules.'" He puffed again. "'You may think you can change them, Paul—but, uh-uh, no you can't—ah-hah-hah—'" again Preacher shook his head with a sharp, short movement, with a sharp, short laugh—"'you can't do it, Paul. It won't work. You can't change the rules. That's not playing the Game. If the rules are changed, Paul, that's not up to us—that's up to Someone Else—so let's all get together now, no matter which team we're on, and play the game the way it should be played.' . . . But," his fine lean face was grave now, he paused and sucked his pipe a moment longer—then: "that didn't happen, did it? . . . Alas, alas, the real Quarterback was gone!"

And in the awed hush that followed, he knocked his pipe out smartly on his heel, then straightened briskly, and got up, saying jauntily:

"Well! So silent, gentlemen? Come, come! For lusty fellows of our kidney this is very sad!"

So signified, the whole gathering would break up in general discussion, excited voices, laughter, young figures shifting through the smoke, plates of sandwiches, and lemonade. And in the center of it all stood Preacher Reed, his spare figure splendidly erect, his lean face finely and attentively aware, the clamor of the younger voices broken by his deeper resonance, his sandy and engaging warmth, the jolly brevity of his short and sudden laugh. And like moths infatuated by a shining light, all these moving and gesticulating groups would return inevitably to the magic ring of which he was himself the center.

Monk didn't know what it was, but they all felt happy and elated and excited and raised up and inspired, and liberal and enlightened and in touch with life and the high truth; and getting at last what they had come to college for.

As for Jerry Alsop, he was simply content to wait and watch, his fat chuckle sounding out occasionally from one corner of the room, where he, too, would be engaged in conversation with a group of freshmen, and yet betraying just perceptibly, by the shadow of a little smile, a little moisture in the eye, an occasional quiet but observant glance out towards the center of the room, that he knew his beloved master was still there and functioning, and that this was all the glory he himself could ask.

And as Alsop would himself say later, when the last reluctant footsteps died away, and there were the last "good nights" upon the campus, and he stood there in the now deserted room, polishing his misty glasses, and a little husky in the throat:

". . . It was puffectly delightful! Puffectly God-damned delightful! Yes, suh! That's the only word for it!"

And it was.

12

The Torch

ALSOP HAD TAKEN MONK WEBBER UNDER HIS PROTECTIVE WING WHEN the younger boy had arrived at Pine Rock in his freshman year, and for a period the association between them was pretty close. The younger one had quickly become a member of the coterie of devoted freshmen who clustered about their leader like chicks around a mother hen. For some months, definitely he was sealed of the tribe of Alsop.

Evidences of what journalists call a "rift" began to appear, however, before the end of the first year—began to appear when the younger student began to look around him and ask questions of this small but new and comparatively liberal world in which, for the first time in his life, he began to feel himself untrammeled, free, the beginning of a man. The questions multiplied themselves furiously.

Monk had heard the president of the college, the late Hunter Griswold McCoy, described by Alsop not only as "the second greatest man since Jesus Christ," but as a thinker and philosopher of the first water, a speaker of the most eloquent persuasion, and the master of a literary style which, along with that of Woodrow Wilson, by which he was undoubtedly strongly influenced, was unsurpassed in the whole range of English literature. Now, having, as most boys of that age do have, a very active and questioning mind, he began to feel distinctly uncomfortable when Alsop said these things, to squirm uneasily in his chair, to keep silence, or to mumble respectful agreements, while all the time he asked himself rather desperately what was wrong with him. Because, the truth of the matter was that "the second greatest man since Jesus Christ" bored him passionately, even at the tender age of seventeen.

And as for that triumphant style which Alsop assured him was practically unsurpassed in the whole field of English letters, he had made repeated attempts to read it and digest it—it had been fittingly embalmed in a volume which bore the title of *Democracy and Leadership*—and he simply could not get through it. As for the famous Chapel talks, which were considered masterpieces of simple eloquence and gems of philosophy, he hated them. He would rather have taken a bitter laxative than sit through one of them; but sit through them he did, hundreds of times, and endured them, until he came to have a positive dislike for Hunter Griswold McCoy. His pale, pure face, somewhat gaunt and emaciated, a subtle air he conveyed always of bearing some deep, secret sorrow, and of suffering in some subtle, complicated way for humanity, began to afflict Monk with a sensation that was akin to, and in fact was scarcely distinguishable from, the less acute stages of nausea. And when Alsop assured him, and the rest of the reverent clique, that Hunter Griswold McCoy was and had always been "as pure and sweet as a fine, sweet gul—yes, suh!"—his dislike for Hunter Griswold McCoy became miserably acute. He disliked him because Hunter Griswold McCoy made him feel so unworthy, like the bird that fouls its own nest, and because he felt miserably and doggedly that there must be something monstrously wicked and base and perverse in his own life if he could not see the shining virtue of this perfect man, and because he realized that he could never be in any way like him.

In addition to this, the glittering phrases of Hunter Griswold McCoy, which, Alsop assured him, were not only pearls of eloquence and poetry, but the very sounding board of life itself—and that whoever was fortunate enough to hear one of these Chapel talks was not only being told about truth and reality, but was given a kind of magic pass key to the whole mystery of life and the complex problem of humanity which he could use forevermore—well, Monk sat miserably in his seat in Chapel day after day and week after week, and the blunt and bitter truth was, he could make nothing out of it. If the wine of life was here, he squeezed the grape desperately, and it shattered in his fingers like a rusty pod. "Democracy and leadership," "education for the good life," "service," "ideals," all the rest of it—did not mean a damn thing to him. He could not find out, although he strained desperately to hear, what "the good life" was, except when it was connected in some very intimate and personal way with Hunter Griswold McCoy, sexual chastity, matrimony, "fine women," drinking water, and Chapel talks. And yet he felt wretchedly that if he wanted any life at all it was assuredly "the good life"—except "the good life" for him, vaguely phrased and indefinitely etched, but flaming in his vision with all the ardor, passion, aspiration of his youth, had so much in it that Hunter Griswold McCoy had never spoken of, and that he dumbly, miserably felt, Hunter Griswold McCoy would not approve.

The shape, the frame, the pattern, the definition of this "good life" was still painfully obscure; but he did feel, inchoately but powerfully, that it had so much flesh and blood in it. It had in it the promise of thick sirloin steaks, and golden, mealy, fried potatoes. It had in it, alas, the flesh of lavish women, the quickening enigma of a smile, the thrilling promise of a touch, the secret confirmation of the pressure of a hand. It had in it great rooms sealed to rich quietness, and the universe of mighty books. But it had in it much tobacco smoke as well—alas, alas, such sinful dreams of fleshly comforts!—and the flavors of strong wine. It had in it the magic of the Jason quest: the thought of golden artisans; almost intolerably a vision of the proud breast, the racing slant, of the great liners as they swung out into the stream at noon on Saturday in their imperial cavalcade, to slide past the chasm slant, the splintered helms and ramparts of a swarming rock, world-appointed and delivered to the sea. It had in it, at last and always, the magic vision of the city, the painted weather of a boy's huge dreams of glory, wealth, and triumph, and a fortunate and happy life among the greatest ones on earth.

And in the words and phrases of the perfect man, there was no word of this. Therefore, dumbly, the youth was miserable. To make the matter worse, two months before the Armistice, Hunter Griswold McCoy up and died. It was the final consummation: Alsop said immediately that it was the story of the Savior and his final martyrdom upon the Cross all over again. True, no one knew exactly just how Hunter Griswold McCoy had been martyred, except by the deadly prevalence of the influenza germ, but the whole memory of his life, the sense of inner purity shining out through his pale and martyred face through all the tedium of a thousand Chapel talks, somehow lent conviction to the final impression of martyrdom. And when Alsop announced in a choking voice that "he had laid down his life for a great Cause—to make the world safe for democracy," and that no soldier who had died in France, stopped by a hail of bullets as he moved forth to the attack against the hordes of barbarism, had been more truly a sacrifice for the great Cause than had McCoy, no single word was raised in protest; there was no single voice to say him nay.

And yet, the wicked truth is that our young sinner had a secret feeling of overwhelming relief when he knew that Hunter Griswold McCoy was gone, that there would be no more Chapel talks—at least, not by McCoy. And the knowledge of this wicked consciousness filled him with such an abysmal sense of his own degradation, of his own unworthiness, that like so many other guilty souls before him, he went it the whole hog. He began to hang around with a crowd of dissolute idlers that infested the college pharmacy; he began to gamble with them for black cows. One false step led to another. Before long he was smoking cigarettes with a dissipated leer. He began to stray away from the Alsopian circle; he began to stay up late at night—but not with Alsop, and not among the devoted neophytes who feasted nightly on the master's words. On the contrary, he fell in with a crowd of lewd-tongued, lusty fellows, who stayed up to all hours and played the phonograph; and who crowned a week of shameful indolence with a week-end of disgusting debauchery in the town of Covington, a score of miles away. The upshot of the matter was that in no time at all these reprobates had taken the innocent, got him drunk, and then delivered him into the custody of a notorious strumpet named "Depot Lil." The story not only came back to the Pine Rock campus, it roared back—it was retailed about, guffawed and bandied back and forth by these same dissolute and conniving rascals who had deliberately contrived this tragedy of ruined innocence, and who now, of such degraded texture were they, apparently thought that the story of the fall of one of Alsop's angels was a matter fit for laughter by the gods.

This was almost the end, but not quite. Alsop did not cast him out without reprieve, without "giving him another chance," for, above all things, Alsop was tolerant—like Brutus, Alsop was an honorable man. Quietly, gravely, the master instructed his disciples not to be too hard upon their fallen brother; they were even instructed not to speak about it, to treat their erring comrade as if nothing had happened, as if he were still one of them; to let him see, by little acts of kindness, that they did not think of him as a social outcast, that he was still a member of the human race. So instructed and so inspired with Christian charity, everyone began to reek with mercy.

As for our fallen angel, it must be admitted that when the full consciousness of his guilt swept down on him, and almost drowned him—

he came crawling back to the fold. There was a three-hour conference with Alsop, all alone in Alsop's room, from which everyone kept religiously away. At the end of that time, Alsop opened the door, polishing his misty glasses, and everyone came trouping solemnly in; and Alsop was heard to say in a quiet but throaty voice, and with a tender little chuckle:

"Lord God! Lord God! Life is all right!"

It would be good to report here that the pardon was final and that the reformation was complete. Alas, this did not happen. Within a month, the reprieved—perhaps paroled is the better word—man had slid back into his former ways. He had begun to hang around the pharmacy again, to waste his time in the company of other wastrels, and to gamble for black cows. And, if he did not slide the whole way back, and there was no exact repetition of the first catastrophe, his ways were certainly now suspect. He began to show a decided preference for people who thought only of having a good time; he seemed to like their indolent ways and drawling voices, he was seen around idling in the sun on the front porch of two or three of the fraternities. And since Alsop and none of his group belonged to a fraternity, this was considered as another sign of dissolution.

In addition to this, Monk began to neglect his studies and to do a great deal of desultory reading. This was another bad sign. Not that Alsop disapproved of reading—he read constantly himself; but when he questioned the disciple as to the reading he was doing, in an effort to find out if it was sound, in accordance with "the more wholesome and well-rounded view of things"—that is, if he was "getting anything out of it"—Alsop's worst fears were realized. The fellow had begun to prowl around in the college library all by himself, and had stumbled upon certain suspect volumes that had, in some strange or accidental way, insinuated themselves into those respectable shelves. Notable among them were the works of one Dostoevski, a Russian. The situation was not only bad, but, when Alsop finally rounded up his erstwhile neophyte—for curiosity, even where the fallen were concerned, was certainly one of Alsop's strongest qualities—he found him, as he pityingly described the situation to the faithful later, "gabbling like a loon."

The truth of the matter was, the adventurer had first stumbled upon one of these books in pretty much the same way that a man groping his way through a woods at night stubs his toe against an invisible rock and falls sprawling over it. Our groping adventurer not only knew nothing about the aforesaid Dostoevski: if he had even heard of him it was in the vaguest sort of way, for certainly that strange and formidable name had never rung around the classroom walls of old Pine Rock—not while he was listening anyway. The plain truth is that he had stumbled over it because he was looking for something to read and liked big books—he was always favorably impressed with the size and weight of a volume; and this one, which bore the promising name of *Crime and Punishment*, was certainly large and heavy enough to suit his taste.

Thereupon, he began a very strange and puzzling adventure with the book. He took it home and began to read it, but after fifty pages gave it up. It all seemed so strange and puzzling to him; even the characters themselves seemed to have several different names apiece, by which they addressed one another, the whole resulting in such confusion that he did not always know who was speaking. In addition, he was not at all sure what was happening. The book, instead of following the conventional line and structure of story, plot, and pattern, to which his reading had accustomed him, seemed to boil outward from some secret, unfathomable, and subterranean source—in Coleridginal phrase, "as if this earth in fast, thick pants was breathing." The result was that the story seemed to weave out upon a dark and turbulent tide of feeling. He was not only not sure of what was happening; when he tried to go back and trace the thread of narrative, he could not always be sure that he had followed it back to its true source. As for the talk, the way the people talked, it was the most bewildering and disturbing talk he had ever heard: anyone was likely to pour out at any moment, with the most amazing frankness, everything that was in his mind and heart, everything that he had ever felt, thought, dreamed, or imagined. And even this would be broken in its full flood tide by apparently meaningless and irrelevant statements. It was all too hard and confusing to follow, and after reading forty or fifty pages he threw the book aside and looked at it no more.

And yet he could not forget it. Events, characters, speeches, incidents kept coming back to him like things remembered from some haunting dream. The upshot of it was that in a week or two he went back to the book, and in two days' time finished it. He was more amazed and bewildered than ever. Within another week he had read the book a second time. Then he went on and read *The Idiot* and *The Brothers Karamazov*. It was at this stage that Alsop hunted him out and cornered him, and, as a result of their conversation, that Alsop confided to his associates that the lost one was "gabbling like a loon."

Perhaps he was. At any rate, anything the discoverer might have said at that time did not make much coherent sense. He did not even affirm any enthusiastic conviction, or confess his passionate belief that he had discovered a great book or a great writer. None of these things occurred to him at the time. The only thing he did know and was sure of was that he had stumbled on something new and strange and overwhelming, whose existence he had never dreamed about before.

He was incoherent, but he was also now passionately eager to talk to someone and tell him all about it. When Alsop came to him, therefore, he fastened on him gratefully. Alsop was older, he was wiser, he had read a great deal, he loved literature, he knew a great deal about books. Surely, if anyone at all could talk to him about this one, it was Alsop. The result of it was that Alsop suggested that he come around, remarking good-naturedly that he had been too much a stranger lately: they would have an evening of the old-time discussion, and everyone would join in. He agreed to this most eagerly, and the time was set. Alsop, meanwhile, passed the word around quietly among the other members of the group that perhaps a useful work of rehabilitation might here be done—the phrase he used was "get him back on the right track." When the appointed time arrived, everyone had been properly and virtuously informed with a sense of duty, the consciousness of lending a helping hand.

It was an unhappy occasion. It all started out casually, as Alsop himself had planned it. Alsop sat in the center of the room, one fat arm resting on the table, and with an air of confessorial benevolence on his priestly visage, a quiet little smile that said: "Tell me about it. As you know, I am prepared to see all sides." The discipleship sat in the outer darkness, in a circle, dutifully intent. Into this arena the luckless innocent rushed headlong. He had brought the old battered copy of *Crime and Punishment* with him.

Alsop, amid general conversation, led up to the subject skillfully, and finally said:

"What's this—ah—new book you were telling me about the othah day? I mean," he said smoothly, "you were telling me—about a book you've been reading—by—some Russian writer, wasn't it?" said Alsop blandly, hesitating—"Dusty—Dusty—Dusty—whosky?" said Alsop with a show of innocence, and then, before there was a chance for reply, his great belly shook, the fat scream of laughter sounded in his throat. The disciples joined hilariously in. "Lord God!" cried Alsop, chuckling again, "I didn't mean to do that—it just popped out, I couldn't help it. . . . But how do you pronounce his name, anyhow?" said Alsop gravely. His manner was now serious, but behind his winking spectacles his eyes were narrowed into slits of mockery—"How do you spell it?"

"I—I don't know how you pronounce it—but it's spelled Dos-to-ev-ski."

"I guess that would be Dos—Dos—" Alsop began. . . .

"Oh hell, Jerry, why don't you just sneeze it and let it go at that?" said one of the disciples. And again the room sounded with their laughter, Alsop's great belly heaving and his half-phlegmy choke of laughter rising above the rest.

"Don't mind us," he now said tolerantly, seeing the other's reddened face. "We weren't laughing at the book—we want to hear about it—it's only that it seems funny to talk about a book when you can't even pronounce the name of the author." Suddenly he heaved with laughter again—"Lord God," he said, "it may be a great book—but that's the damnedest name I ever heard of." And the laughter of agreement filled the room. "But go on now," he said encouragingly, with an air of serious interest, "I'd like to hear about it. What's it about?"

"It's—it's—it's—" Monk began confusedly, suddenly realizing how difficult it would be to put into a scheme of words just what the book *was* about, particularly since he was by no means sure himself.

"I mean," said Alsop smoothly, "could you tell us something about the plot? Give us some idea about the story?"

"Well," the other began slowly, thinking hard, "the leading character is a man named Raskalnikoff——"

"Who?" said Alsop innocently. And again there was an appreciative titter around the room. "Raskal-ni-who?" The titter grew to open laughter.

"Well, that's the way it's spelled anyhow," said the other doggedly. "Ras-kal-ni-koff—I guess you call it Raskalnikoff!"

And again Alsop heaved with laughter, the phlegmy chuckle

wheezed high in his throat. "Damned if you don't pick out funny names!" he said, and then encouragingly: "Well, all right, then, go on. What does Raskal What's-His-Name do?"

"Well—he—he—kills an old woman," Monk said, now conscious of the currents of derision and amusement in the ring around him. "With an axe!" he blurted out, and instantly was crimson with anger and embarrassment at the roar of laughter that greeted his description, feeling he had told the story clumsily, and had begun his explanation in the worst possible way.

"Damned if he don't live up to his name!" wheezed Alsop. "Old Dusty—old Dusty knew what he was about when he called him Raskal What's-His-Name, didn't he?"

The other was angry now: he said hotly, "It's nothing to laugh about, Jerry. It's——"

"No," said Alsop gravely. "Killing old women with axes is not a laughing matter—no matter who does it—even if you do have to sneeze it when you say it!"

At the burst of approving laughter that greeted this sally, the younger man lost his temper completely, and turned furiously upon the group:

"You fellows make me tired! Here you're shooting off your mouths and making jokes about something you know nothing about. What's funny about it, I'd like to know?"

"It suttinly doesn't strike me as funny," Alsop quietly observed. "It sounds pretty mawbid to me."

This quiet observation was greeted by a murmur of agreement.

For the first time, however, the use of the word, which was one of Alsop's favorite definitions, stung Monk into quick and hot resentment.

"What's morbid about it?" he said furiously. "Good Lord, Jerry, you're always saying that something is morbid, just because you don't like it. A writer's got a right to tell about anything he pleases. He's not *morbid* just because he doesn't write about peaches and cream all the time."

"Yes," said Alsop with his infuriating air of instructive tolerance. "But a great writer will see all sides of the situation——"

"All sides of the situation!" the younger man now cried excitedly. "Jerry, that's another thing you're always saying. You're always talking about seeing all sides of the situation. What the hell does it mean? Maybe a situation doesn't have all sides. I don't know what you're talking about when you say it!"

At last, then, here was insurrection, open, naked insurrection, for the first time now clear and unmistaken! A kind of deadly silence had fallen on the group. Alsop continued to smile his little smile, he still maintained his air of judicial tolerance, but somehow his smile was pale, the warmth had gone out of his face, behind his spectacles his eyes had narrowed to cold slits.

"I just mean—that a great writer, a really great writer—will write about all types of people. He may write about murder and crime like this Dusty What's-His-Name that you're talking about, but he'll write about othah things as well. In othah words," said Alsop pontifically, "he'll try to see the Whole Thing in its true perspective."

"In what true perspective, Jerry?" the other burst out. "That's another thing you're always saying too—talking about the true perspective. I wish you'd tell me what it means!"

Here was heresy again, and more of it. The others held their breath while Alsop, still maintaining his judicial calm, answered quietly:

"I mean, a great writer will try to see life clearly and to see it whole. He'll try to give you the whole pictuah."

"Well, Dostoevski tries to, too," said Monk doggedly.

"Yes, I know, but does he really now? I mean does he really show you the more wholesome and well-rounded view of things?"

"Ah—ah—Jerry, that's another thing you're always saying—the more wholesome and well-rounded view of things. What does *that* mean? Who ever did give you the more wholesome and well-rounded view of things?"

"Well," said Alsop judicially, "I think Dickens gave it to you."

There was a dutiful murmur of agreement from the disciples, broken by the rebel's angry mutter:

"Ah—Dickens! I'm tired hearing about Dickens all the time!"

This was sacrilege, and for a moment there was appalled silence, as if someone had at last committed a sin against the Holy Ghost. When Alsop spoke again his face was very grave, and his eyes had narrowed to cold points:

"You mean to say that you think this Russian fellow presents as wholesome and well-rounded a pictuah of life as Dickens does?"

"I told you," the other said in a voice that trembled with excitement, "that I don't know what you're talking about when you say that. I'm only saying that there can be other great writers in the world besides Dickens."

"And you think, then," said Alsop quietly, "that this man is a greater writer than Dickens?"

"I haven't—" the other began.

"Yes, but come on now," said Alsop. "We're all fair-minded people here—you really think he's greater, don't you?"

Monk looked at him for a moment with a kind of baffled indignation; then, spurred to a boiling point of irrational resentment by the expression of the stern faces all about him, he suddenly shouted out:

"Yes! He was! A hell of a sight greater! It's like Pascal said—that one of the grandest surprises in life is to open a book expecting to meet an author, and to find instead a man. And that's the way it is with Dostoevski. You don't meet the author. You meet the man. You may not believe everything that is said, but you believe the man who is saying it. You are convinced by his utter sincerity, by the great, burning light of him, and in the end, no matter how confused or bewildered or unsure he may himself be, time and again you know that he is right. And you see also that it doesn't matter how people say things, so long as the feeling behind the things they say is a true one. I can give you an example of that," he went on hotly. "At the end of *The Brothers Karamazov*, where Alyosha is talking to the boys in the cemetery, the danger of falseness and sentimentality in such a scene as this is overwhelming. In the first place, the scene is in a graveyard, and Alyosha and the children are there to put flowers upon the grave of another child who has died. Then again, there is the danger of Alyosha, with his convictions of brotherly love, his doctrine of redemption through sacrifice, of salvation through humility. He makes a speech to the children, a confused and rambling speech, of which sentence after sentence could have been uttered by a Y. M. C. A. secretary or a Sunday School teacher. Why is it, then, that there is nothing sickly or disgusting about it, as there would be in the harangue of such men as these? It is because we know from the beginning that the words are honest and sincere, because we believe in the sincerity and truth and honesty of the character who is speaking the words, and of the man who wrote the words and created the character. Dostoevski was not afraid to use such words," Monk went on in the full flood of his passion, "because he had no falseness and sentimentality in him. The words are the same as the Sunday School teacher might use, but the feeling behind them is different, and that makes the difference. Therefore they express what Dostoevski wanted them to. Alyosha tells the children that we must love one another, and we believe him. He tells them never to forget their comrade who has died, to try to remember all the countless good and generous acts of his life, his love for his father, his courage and devotion. Then Alyosha tells the children that the most important thing in life, the thing that will expiate our sins, pardon all our mistakes and errors, make our lives prevail, is to have a good memory of someone. And these simple words move us more than the most elaborate rhetoric could do, because suddenly we know that we have been told something true and everlasting about life, and that the man who told it to us is right."

During the last part of this long speech, Alsop had reached over quietly to his bookshelves, taken a well-worn volume from the shelf, and, even while Monk talked, begun to thumb quietly through its pages. Now he was ready for him again. He had the book open in his hand, one fat forefinger marking the spot. He was waiting for Monk to conclude, with a patient and tolerant little smile.

"Now," he said quietly, when the other finished, "that situation which you described there interests me very much, because Charles Dickens deals with the same situation at the end of *A Tale of Two Cities*, and says the same thing that Dostoevski says." Monk noticed he got the name right this time. "Now," said Alsop, looking around at his congregation with a little misty smile that prefaced all these tributes to sentiment and, in especial, to that chief object of his idolatry, Charles Dickens—and which said to them plainer than any words could do: "Now I'm going to show you what a really great man can do with sweetness and light"—he said quietly: "I think you'll all be interested to see how Dickens handles that same situation," and immediately began to read the concluding passages of the book, which are devoted to Sidney Carton's celebrated utterance as he steps up to the guillotine to sacrifice his own life in order that the life of the man beloved by the woman he himself loves may be spared:

" 'I see the lives for which I lay down my life, peaceful, useful, prosperous and happy, in that England which I shall see no more. I see her with a child upon her bosom, who bears my name. I see her father, aged and bent, but otherwise restored, and faithful to all men in his healing office, and at peace. I see the good old man, so long their friend, in ten years' time enriching them with all he has, and passing tranquilly to his reward.

" 'I see that I hold a sanctuary in their hearts, and in the hearts of their descendants, generations hence. I see her, an old woman, weeping for me on the anniversary of this day. I see her and her husband, their course done, lying side by side in their last earthly bed, and I know that each was not more honored and held sacred in the other's soul, than I was in the souls of both.

"'I see that child who lay upon her bosom and who bore my name, a man, winning his way up in that path of life which once was mine. I see him winning it so well, that my name is made illustrious there by the light of his. I see the blots I threw upon it, faded away. I see him, foremost of just judges and honored men, bringing a boy of my name, with a forehead that I know and golden hair, to this place—then fair to look upon, with not a trace of this day's disfigurement—and I hear him tell the child my story, with a tender and a faltering voice.

"'It is a far, far better thing that I do, than I have ever done; it is a far, far better rest that I go to, than I have ever known.'"

Alsop read these famous lines in a voice husky with emotion, and, at the end, paused a moment before speaking, to blow his nose vigorously. He was genuinely and deeply affected, and there was no doubt that his emotion and the way in which he read the passage had produced a profound effect on his audience. At the conclusion, after the vigorous salute into his handkerchief, and a moment's silence, he looked around with a misty little smile and said quietly:

"Well, what do you think of that? Do you think that comes up to Mr. Dusty What's-His-Name or not?"

There was an immediate chorus of acclamation. They all agreed vociferously that that passage not only "came up" to Mr. Dusty What's-His-Name, but far surpassed anything he had ever accomplished.

In view of the fact that none of them knew anything about Mr. Dusty What's-His-Name and were yet willing to pass judgment with such enthusiastic conviction, Monk felt his anger rising hot and quick, and broke in indignantly:

"That is not the same thing at all. The situation is altogether different."

"Well, now," said Jerry persuasively, "you must admit that fundamentally the situation is essentially the same. It's the idea of love and sacrifice in both cases. Only it seems to me that Dickens' treatment of the situation is the superior of the two. He says what Dostoevski is trying to say, but it seems to me he says it much better. He presents a more rounded pictuah, and lets you know that life is going to go on and be just as fine and sweet as it ever was in spite of everything. Now," he said, quietly and persuasively again, "don't you agree, Monk, that Dickens' method is the best? You know you do, you scannel!" Here he chortled richly, shoulders and his great belly shaking with good-natured glee. "I know how you feel at the bottom of your heart. You're just arguing to hear yourself talk."

"Why not at all, Jerry," Monk came back with hot earnestness, "I mean everything I say. And I don't see any similarity at all between the two situations. What Sidney Carton says has no relation to what Alyosha is trying to say at the end of *The Brothers Karamazov*. One book is a skillful and exciting melodrama, which makes use of some of the events of the French Revolution. The other book is, in this sense, not a story at all. It is a great vision of life and of human destiny, as seen through the spirit of a great man. What Alyosha is saying is not that man dies for love, not that he sacrifices his life for romantic love, but that he lives for love, not romantic love, but love of life, love of mankind, and that through love his spirit and his memory survive, even when his physical self is dead. That's not the same thing at all as the thing that Sidney Carton says. What you have on the one hand is a profound and simple utterance of a great spiritual truth, and what you have on the other is the rhetorical and sentimental ending to a romantic melodrama."

"No suh!" Jerry Alsop now cried hotly, his face flushed with anger and excitement. "No suh!" he cried again, and shook his big head in angered denial. "If you call that sentimental, you just don't know what you're talking about! You've just gone and got yourself completely lost! You don't even know what Dickens is trying to do!"

The upshot of it was that a cat-and-dog fight broke out at this point, a dozen angry, derisive voices clashing through the air trying to drown out the rebel, who only shouted louder as the opposition grew; and it continued until the contestants were out of breath and the entire campus was howling for quiet from a hundred windows.

It wound up with Alsop standing, pale but righteous, in the center of the room, finally restoring quiet, and saying:

"We've all tried to be your friends, we've tried to help you out. If you can't take it the way it's meant, you don't need to bothah with us any more. We all saw the way that you were going—" he went on in a trembling tone; and Monk, stung by these final words into maddening and complete revolt, cried passionately:

"Going—going hell! I'm gone!" And he stormed out of the room, clutching the battered volume underneath his arm.

When he had gone the tumult broke out anew, the loyal cohorts gathering round their wounded chief. The end of it all, when the whole tumult of bitter agreement had quieted down, was summed up in the final dismissal of Alsop's words:

"He's just an ass! He's just gone and played hell, that's what he's done! I thought there was some hope for him, but he's just gone and made a complete damned ass of himself! Leave him alone! Don't fool with him any longer, he's not wuth it!"

And that was that.

"Get the Facts, Brother Webber! Get the Facts!"

The square Sphinx head, shaven, paunch-jowled, putty-grey; the grim, dry mouth, puckered with surly humor; the low rasp of the voice. He sat in squat immobility, staring at them ironically.

"I am a Research Man!" he announced finally. "I get the Facts."

"What do you do with them after you get them?" said Monk.

"I put salt on their tails and get some more," said Professor Randolph Ware.

His stolid, ironic face, iron lidded, enjoyed the puzzled worship of their stare.

"Have I any imagination?" he asked. He shook his head in solemn negation. "No-o," he said with a long grunt of satisfaction. "Have I any genius? No-o. Could I have written *King Lear*? No-o. Have I more brains than Shakespeare? Yes. Do I know more about English literature than the Prince of Wales? Yes. Do I know more about Spenser than Kittredge, Manley, and Saintsbury put together? Yes. Do I know more about Spenser than God and Spenser put together? Yes. Could I have written *The Faery Queen*? No-o. Could I write a doctoral thesis about *The Faery Queen*? Yes."

"Did you ever see a doctor's thesis that was worth reading?" asked Monk.

"Yes," said the implacable monotone.

"Whose was it?"

"My own."

They answered with a young yell of worship.

"Then what's the use of the Facts?" said Monk.

"They keep a man from getting soft," said Randolph Ware grimly.

"But a Fact has no importance in itself," said Monk. "It is only a manifestation of the Concept."

"Have you had your breakfast, Brother Webber?"

"No," said Monk, "I always eat after class. That's to keep my mind fresh and active for its work."

The class snickered.

"Is your breakfast a Fact or a Concept, Brother Webber?" He stared grimly at him for a moment. "Brother Webber made a One in Logic," he said, "and he has breakfast at noon. He thinks he is another convert to Divine Philosophy, but he is wrong. Brother Webber, you have heard the bells at midnight many times. I have myself seen you below the moon, with your eyes in a fine frenzy rolling. You will never make a Philosopher, Brother Webber. You will spend several years quite pleasantly in Hell, Getting the Facts. After that, you may make a poet."

Randolph Ware was a very grand person—a tremendous scholar, a believer in the discipline of formal research. He was a scientific utilitarian to the roots of his soul: he believed in Progress and the relief of man's estate, and he spoke of Francis Bacon—who was really the first American—with a restrained but passionate wisdom.

George Webber remembered this man later—grey, stolid, ironic—as one of the strangest people he had ever known. All of the facts were so strange. He was a Middle-Westerner who went to the University of Chicago and learned more about English literature than the people at Oxford knew. It seemed strange that one should study Spenser in Chicago.

He was gigantically American—he seemed almost to foreshadow the future. George met few people who were able to make such complete and successful use of things as they are. He was a magnificent teacher, capable of fruitful and astonishing innovation. Once he set the class in composition to writing a novel, and they went to work with boiling interest. George rushed into class breathlessly three times a week with a new chapter written out on the backs of paper bags, envelopes, stray bits of paper. And Randolph Ware had the power of communicating to them the buried magic of poetry: the cold sublimity of Milton began to burgeon with life and opulent color—in Moloch, Beelzebub, Satan, without vulgarity or impertinence, he made them see a hundred figures of craft and rapacity and malice among the men of their time.

Yet it always seemed to George that there was in the man a cruelly wasted power. There was in him a strong light and a hidden glory. He seemed with deliberate fatalism to have trapped himself among petty things. Despite his great powers, he wasted himself compiling anthologies for use in colleges.

But the students who swarmed about him sensed the tenderness and beauty below his stolid and ironic mask. And once George, going in to see him at his house, found him at the piano, his blunt, heavy body erect, his putty face dreaming like a Buddha, as his pudgy fingers drew out with passion and wisdom the great music of Beethoven. Then George remembered what Alcibiades had said to Socrates: "You are like the god Silenus—outwardly a paunched and ugly man, but concealing inwardly the figure of a young and beautiful divinity."

In spite of the twaddle that the prominent educators of the time were always talking about "democracy and leadership," "ideals of service," "the place of the college in modern life," and so on, there wasn't much reality about the direction of such "education" as George had had. And that's not to say there had been no reality in his education. There was, of course—not only because there's reality in everything, but because he had come in contact with art, with letters, and with a few fine people. Maybe that's about as much as you can expect.

It would also be unfair to say that the real value of this, the beautiful and enduring thing, he had had to "dig out" for himself. This wasn't true. He had met a lot of other young people, like himself, and this fact was "beautiful"—a lot of young fellows all together, not sure where they were going, but sure that they were going somewhere.

So he had this, and this was a lot.

13

The Rock

SOME FIFTEEN OR MORE YEARS AGO (AS MEN MEASURE, BY THOSE DIURNAL instruments which their ingenuity has created, the immeasurable universe of time), at the end of a fine, warm, hot, fair, fresh, fragrant, lazy, furnacelike day of sweltering heat across the body, bones, sinews, tissues, juices, rivers, mountains, plains, streams, lakes, coastal regions, and compacted corporosity of the American continent, a train might have been observed by one of the lone watchers of the Jersey Flats approaching that enfabled rock, that ship of life, that swarming, million-footed, tower-masted, and sky-soaring citadel that bears the magic name of the Island of Manhattan, at terrific speed.

At this moment, indeed, one of the lone crayfishers, who ply their curious trade at this season of the year throughout the melancholy length and breadth of those swamplike moors which are characteristic of this section of the Jersey coast, lifted his seamed and weather-beaten face from some nets which he had been mending in preparation for the evening's catch, and, after gazing for a moment at the projectile fury of the Limited as it thundered past, turned and, speaking to the brown-faced lad beside him, said quietly:

"It is the Limited."

And the boy, returning his father's look with eyes as sea-far and as lonely as the old man's own, and in a voice as quiet, said:

"On time, father?"

The old man did not answer for a moment. Instead, he thrust one gnarled and weather-beaten hand into the pocket of his pea-jacket, fumbled a moment, and then pulled forth an enormous silver watch with compass dials, an heirloom of three generations of crayfishing folk. He regarded it a moment with a steady, reflective gaze.

"Aye, lad," he said simply, "on time—or thereabouts. She will not miss it much tonight, I reckon."

But already the great train was gone in a hurricane of sound and speed. The sound receded into silence, leaving the quiet moors as they had always been, leaving them to silence, the creaking of the gulls, the low droning of the giant mosquitoes, the melancholy and funereal pyres of burning trash here and there, and to the lonely fisher of the moors and his young son. For a moment, the old man and the lad regarded the receding projectile of the train with quiet eyes. Then, silently, they resumed their work upon their nets again. Evening was coming, and with it the full tide, and, with the coming of the tide, the cray. So all was now as it had always been. The train had come and gone and vanished, and over the face of the flats brooded as it had always done the imperturbable visage of eternity.

Within the train, however, there was a different scene, a kind of wakening of hope and of anticipation. Upon the faces of the passengers there might have been observed now all the expressions and emotions which the end of a long journey usually evokes, whether of alert readiness, eager constraint, or apprehensive dread. And on the face of one, a youth in his early twenties, there might have been observed all of the hope, fear, longing, exultancy, faith, belief, expectancy, and incredible realization that every youth on earth has always felt on his approach for the first time to the enchanted city. Although the other people in the coach were already restless, stirring, busy with their preparations for the journey's end, the boy sat there by a window like one rapt in dreams, his vision tranced and glued against the glass at the rushing landscape of the lonely moors. No detail of the scene escaped the ravenous voracity of his attention.

The train rushed past a glue factory. With the expression of one drunk with wonder the young man drank the pageant in. He saw with joy the great stacks, the glazed glass windows, the mighty furnaces of the enormous works; the pungent fragrance of the molten glue came to him and he breathed it in with rapturous appeasement.

The train swept on across a sinuous stream, itself an estuary of the infinite and all-taking sea, itself as motionless as time, scummed richly with a moveless green; the sheer beauty of the thing went home into his mind and heart forever.

He raised his eyes as men against the West once raised their eyes against the shining ramparts of the mountains. And there before him, at the edges of the marsh, rose the proud heights of Jersey City—the heights of Jersey City blazing forever to the traveler the smoldering welcome of their garbage dumps—the heights of Jersey City, raised proudly against the desolation of those lonely marshes as a token of man's fortitude, a symbol of his power, a sign of his indomitable spirit that flames forever like a great torch in the wilderness, that lifts against the darkness and the desolation of blind nature the story of its progress —the heights of Jersey, lighted for an eternal feast.

The train swept on and underneath the crests of yon proud, battlemented hill. The hill closed in around the train, the train roared in beneath the hill, into the tunnel. And suddenly darkness was upon them. The train plunged in beneath the mighty bed of the unceasing river, and dumbness smote the youth's proud, listening ears.

He turned and looked upon his fellow passengers. He saw wonder on their faces and something in their hearts that none could divine; and even as he sat there, dumb with wonder, he heard two voices, two quiet voices out of life, the voices of two nameless ciphers out of life, a woman's and a man's.

"Jeez, but I'll be glad to get back home again," the man said quietly.

For a moment the woman did not answer, then, in the same quiet tone, but with a meaning, a depth of feeling, that the boy would never after that forget, she answered simply, "You said it."

Just that, and nothing more. But, simple as those words were, they sank home into his heart, in their brief eloquence of time and of the bitter briefness of man's days, the whole compacted history of his tragic destiny.

And now, even as he paused there, rapt in wonder at this nameless eloquence, he heard another voice, close to his ears, a voice soft, low, and urgent, sweet as honey dew, and suddenly, with a start of recognition and surprise, he realized the words were meant for him, for him alone.

"Is you comin', boss?" the soft voice said. "We'se gettin' in. Shall I bresh you off?"

The boy turned slowly and surveyed his dark interrogator. In a moment he inclined his head in a slight gesture of assent and quietly replied:

"I am ready. Yes, you may."

But even now the train was slowing to a halt. Grey twilight filtered through the windows once again. The train had reached the tunnel's mouth. On both sides now were ancient walls of masonry, old storied buildings, dark as time and ancient as man's memory. The boy peered through the window, up as far as eyes could reach, at all those tiers of life, those countless cells of life, the windows, rooms, and faces of the everlasting and eternal city. They leaned above him in their ancient silence. They returned his look. He looked into their faces and said nothing, no word was spoken. The people of the city leaned upon the sills of evening and they looked at him. They looked at him from their old walls of ancient, battlemented brick. They looked at him through the silent yet attentive curtains of all their ancient and historic laundries. They looked at him through pendant sheets, through hanging underwear, through fabrics of a priceless and unknown tapestry, and he knew that all was now as it had always been, as it would be tomorrow and forever.

But now the train was slowing to a halt. Long tongues of cement now appeared, and faces, swarming figures, running forms beside the train. And all these faces, forms, and figures slowed to instancy, were held there in the alertness of expectant movement. There was a grinding screech of brakes, a slight jolt, and, for a moment, utter silence.

At this moment there was a terrific explosion.

It was New York.

There is no truer legend in the world than the one about the country boy, the provincial innocent, in his first contact with the city. Hackneyed by repetition, parodied and burlesqued by the devices of cheap fiction and the slap-stick of vaudeville humor, it is nevertheless one of the most tremendous and vital experiences in the life of a man, and in the life of the nation. It has found inspired and glorious tongues in Tolstoy and in Goethe, in Balzac and in Dickens, in Fielding and Mark Twain. It has found splendid examples in every artery of life, as well in Shakespeare as in the young Napoleon. And day after day the great cities of the world are being fed, enriched, and replenished ceaselessly with the life-blood of the nation, with all the passion, aspiration, eagerness, faith, and high imagining that youth can know, or that the tenement of life can hold.

For one like George Webber, born to the obscure village and brought up within the narrow geography of provincial ways, the city experience is such as no city man himself can ever know. It is conceived in absence and in silence and in youth; it is built up to the cloud-capped pinnacles of a boy's imagining; it is written like a golden legend in the heart of youth with a plume plucked out of an angel's wing; it lives and flames there in his heart and spirit with all the timeless faery of the magic land.

When such a man, therefore, comes first to the great city—but how can we speak of such a man coming first to the great city, when really the great city is within him, encysted in his heart, built up in all the flaming images of his brain: a symbol of his hope, the image of his high desire, the final crown, the citadel of all that he has ever dreamed of or longed for or imagined that life could bring to him? For such a man as this, there really is no coming to the city. He brings the city with him everywhere he goes, and when that final moment comes when he at last breathes in the city's air, feels his foot upon the city street, looks around him at the city's pinnacles, into the dark, unceasing tide of city faces, grips his sinews, feels his flesh, pinches himself to make sure he is really there—for such a man as this, and for such a moment, it will always be a question to be considered in its bewildering ramifications by the subtle soul psychologists to know which city is the real one, which city he has found and seen, which city for this man is really there.

For the city has a million faces, and just as it is said that no two men can really know what each is thinking of, what either sees when he speaks of "red" or "blue," so can no man ever know just what another means when he tells about the city that he sees. For the city that he sees is just the city that he brings with him, that he has within his heart; and even at that immeasurable moment of first perception, when for the first time he sees the city with his naked eye, at that tremendous moment of final apprehension when the great city smites at last upon his living sense, still no man can be certain he has seen the city as it is, because in the hairbreadth of that instant recognition a whole new city is composed, made out of sense but shaped and colored and unalterable from all that he has felt and thought and dreamed about before.

And more than this! There are so many other instant, swift, and accidental things that happen in a moment, that are gone forever, and that shape the city in the heart of youth. It may be a light that comes and goes, a grey day, or a leaf upon a bough; it may be the first image of a city face, a woman's smile, an oath, a half-heard word; it may be sunset, morning, or the crowded traffics of the street, the furious pinnacle of dusty noon; or it may be April, April, and the songs they sang that year. No one can say, except it may be something chance and swift and fleeting, as are all of these, together with the accidents of pine and clay, the weather of one's youth, the place, the structure, and the life from which one came, and all conditioned so, so memoried, built up into the vision of the city that a man first brings there in his heart.

That year there were five of them. There were Jim Randolph and Monty Bellamy, a South Carolina boy named Harvey Williams and a friend of his named Perce Smead, and then Monk Webber. They were all living together in an apartment they had rented up at 123rd Street. It was on the down slope of the hill that leads from Morningside towards Harlem; the place was on the very fringes of the great Black Belt, so near, in fact, that borders interwove—the pattern of the streets was white and black. It was one of the cheap apartment houses that crowd the district, a six-story structure of caked yellow, rather grimy brick. The entrance hall flourished a show of ornate gaudiness. The floors were tile, the walls were covered halfway up with sheets of streaky-looking marble. On either side, doors opened off into apartments, the doors a kind of composition of dark-painted tin, resembling wood but deceiving no one, stamped with small numerals in dry gilt. There was an elevator at the end, and, by night, a sullen, sleepy-looking negro man; by day, the "superintendent"—an Italian in shirtsleeves, a hard-working and good-humored factotum who made repairs and tended furnaces and mended plumbing and knew where to buy gin and was argumentative, protesting, and obliging. He was a tireless disputant with whom they wrangled constantly, just for the joy his lingo gave them, because they liked him very much. His name—"Watta the hell!"—was Joe. They liked him as the South likes people, and likes language, and likes personalities, and likes jesting and protesting and good-humored bicker—as the South likes earth and its humanity, which is one of the best things in the South.

So there were the five of them—five younglings from the South, all here together for the first time in the thrilling catacomb, all eager, passionate, aspiring—they had a merry time.

The place, which opened from the right as one went in that marble hall, ran front to rear, and was of the type known as a railroad flat

There were, if counted carefully, five rooms, a living room, three bedrooms, and a kitchen. The whole place was traversed from end to end by a dark and narrow hall. It was a kind of tunnel, a sort of alleyway of graduated light. The living room was at the front and had two good windows opening on the street; it was really the only room that had any decent light at all. From there on, one advanced progressively into Stygian depths. The first bedroom had a narrow window opening on a narrow passageway two feet in width that gave on the grimy brick wall of the tenement next door. This place was favored with a kind of murky gloom, reminiscent of those atmospheres one sees in motion pictures showing Tarzan in the jungle with his friends, the apes; or, better still, in those pictures showing the first stages in the ancient world of prehistoric man, at about the time he first crawled out of the primeval ooze. Just beyond this was a bathroom, whose Stygian darkness had never been broken by any ray of outer light; beyond this, another bedroom, identical with the first in all respects, even to the properties of light; beyond this, the kitchen, a little lighter, since it was larger and had two windows; and, at the end, the last and best bedroom, since it was at the corner and had a window on each wall. This room, of course, as fitted a prince of royal blood, was by common and tacit agreement allotted to Jim Randolph. Monty Bellamy and Monk had the next one, and Harvey and his friend Perce shared the other. The rent was $80 a month, which they divided equally.

In the bathroom, when the electric light was not burning, the illusion of midnight was complete. This illusion was enhanced in a rather sinister and clammy fashion by the constant dripping of the bathtub faucet and the perpetual rattling leakage of the toilet. They tried to cure these evils a dozen times; each of them made his own private experiments on the plumbing. The results, while indicative of their ingenuity, were not any particular tribute to their efficiency. It used to worry them at first when they tried to go to sleep at night. The clammy rattling of the toilet and the punctual large drip of the faucet would get on someone's nerves at last, and they would hear him curse and hit the floor, saying:

"God-damn it! How do you expect a man to get to sleep with that damn toilet going all night long!"

Then he would pad out and down the hall and flush the toilet, pull off the lid and fume and fuss with the machinery, and swear below his breath, and finally put the lid back on, leaving the empty bowl to fill again. And he would come back with a sigh of satisfaction, saying he reckoned he got the damn thing fixed that time all right. And then he would crawl into bed again, prepare himself for blissful slumber, only to have that rattling and infuriating leak begin all over again.

But this was almost the worst of their troubles, and they soon got used to it. It is true, the two bedrooms on the hall were so small and cramped they couldn't get two single cots in them, and so had to fall back on their old college dormitory expedient of racking them boat-wise, one upon the other. It is also true that these little bedrooms had so little light that at no time of the day could one read a paper without the aid of electricity. The single window of each room looked out upon a dingy airshaft, the blank brick surface of the next-door building. And since they were on the ground floor, they were at the bottom of this shaft. Of course this gave them certain advantages in rent. As one went up, one got more light and air, and as one got more light and air, one paid more rent. The mathematics of the arrangement was beautifully simple, but none of them, coming as they all did from a region where the atmosphere was one commodity in which all men had equal rights, had quite recovered from their original surprise at finding themselves in a new world where even the weather was apportioned on a cash basis.

Still, they got used to it very quickly, and they didn't mind it very much. In fact, they all thought it pretty splendid. They had an *apartment*, a *real* apartment, on the fabulous Island of Manhattan. They had their own private bathroom, even if the taps did leak. They had their kitchen, too, where they cooked meals. Every one of them had his own pass key and could come and go as he pleased.

They had the most amazing assortment of furniture Monk had ever seen. God knows where Jim Randolph had picked it up. He was their boss, their landlord, and their leader. He had already had the place a year when Monk moved in, so the furniture was there when he arrived. They had two chiffonier-dressers in the best Grand Rapids style, with oval mirrors, wooden knobs, and not too much of the varnish scaling off. Jim had a genuine bureau in his room, with real bottoms in two of the drawers. In the living room they had a big, over-stuffed chair with a broken spring in it, a long davenport with part of the wadding oozing out, an old leather chair, a genuine rocking chair whose wicker bottom was split wide open, a book case with a few books in it and glass doors which rattled and which sometimes stuck together when it rained, and—what was most remarkable of all—a real upright piano.

That piano had been to the wars and showed it. It looked and sounded as if it had served a long apprenticeship around the burlesque circuit. The old ivory keys were yellowed by long years of service, the mahogany case was scarred by boots and charred by the fags of countless cigarettes. Some of the keys gave forth no sound at all, and a good number of the sounds they did give forth were pretty sour. But what did it matter? Here was a piano—*their* piano—indubitably and undeniably a genuine upright and upstanding piano in the living room of their magnificent and luxurious five-room apartment in the upper portion of the fabulous Island of Manhattan. Here they could entertain their guests. Here they could invite their friends. Here they could eat and drink and sing and laugh and give parties and have girls and play their piano.

Jim Randolph, to tell the truth, was the only one who could play it. He played it very badly, and yet he played it rather wonderfully, too. He missed a lot of notes and smashed through others. But his powerful hands and fingers held in their hard stroke a sure sense of rhythm, a swinging beat. It was good to hear him play because it was so good to *see* and *feel* him play. God knows where he learned it. It was another in that amazing list of accomplishments which he had acquired at one time or another and at one place or another in his journeyings about the earth, and which included in its range accomplishments as wide and varied as the ability to run 100 yards in less than eleven seconds, to kick a football 80 yards, to shoot a rifle and to ride a horse, to speak a little Spanish, some Italian and some French, to cook a steak, to fry a chicken, or to make a pie, to navigate a ship, to use a typewriter—and to get a girl when and where he wanted her.

Jim was a good deal older than any of the others. He was by this time nearing thirty. And his legend still clung to him. Monk never saw him walk across the room without remembering instantly how he used to look as he started one of his great sweeps around right end behind his interference. In spite of his years, he was an amazingly young and boyish person, a creature given to impulse, to the sudden bursts of passion, enthusiasm, sentiment and folly and unreason of a boy. But just as the man had so much of the boy in him, so did the boy have so much of the man. He exerted over all of them a benevolent but paternal governance, and the reason that they all looked up to him as they did, the reason that all of them, without thought or question, accepted him as their leader, was not because of the few years' difference in their ages, but because he seemed in every other way a mature and grown man.

What is it that a young man wants? Where is the central source of that wild fury that boils up in him, that goads and drives and lashes him, that explodes his energies and strews his purpose to the wind of a thousand instant and chaotic impulses? The older and more assured people of the world, who have learned to work without waste and error, think they know the reason for the chaos and confusion of a young man's life. They have learned the thing at hand, and learned to follow their single way through all the million shifting hues and tones and cadences of living, to thread neatly with unperturbed heart their single thread through that huge labyrinth of shifting forms and intersecting energies that make up life—and they say, therefore, that the reason for a young man's confusion, lack of purpose, and erratic living is because he has not "found himself."

In this, the older and more certain people may be right by their own standard of appraisal, but, in this judgment on the life of youth, they have really pronounced a sterner and more cruel judgment on themselves. For when they say that some young man has not yet "found himself," they are really saying that he has not lost himself as they. For men will often say that they have "found themselves" when they have really been worn down into a groove by the brutal and compulsive force of circumstance. They speak of their life's salvation when all that they have done is blindly follow through an accidental way. They have forgotten their life's purpose, and all the faith, hope, and immortal confidence of a boy. They have forgotten that below all the apparent waste, loss, chaos, and disorder of a young man's life there is really a central purpose and a single faith which they themselves have lost.

What is it that a young man does—here in America? How does he live? What is the color, texture, substance of his life? How does he look and feel and act? What is the history of his days—the secret of the fury that devours him—the core and center of his one belief—the design and rhythm of his single life?

All of us know what it is. We have lived it with every beating of our pulse, known it with every atom of our bone, blood, sinew, marrow, feeling. The knowledge of it is mixed insolubly into the substance of our lives. We have seen and recognized it instantly, not only in ourselves, but in the lives of ten thousand people all around us—as familiar as the earth on which we tread, as near as our own hearts, as certain as the light of morn. And yet we never speak of it. We cannot speak of it. We have no way to speak of it.

Why? Because the young men of this land are not, as they are often called, a "lost" race—they are a race that never yet has been discovered. And the whole secret, power, and knowledge of their own discovery is locked within them—they know it, feel it, have the whole thing in them—and they cannot utter it.

George Webber was not long in finding out that perhaps it is just here, in the iron-breasted city, that one comes closest to the enigma that haunts and curses the whole land. The city is the place where men are constantly seeking to find their door and where they are doomed to wandering forever. Of no place is this more true than of New York. Hideously ugly for the most part, one yet remembers it as a place of proud and passionate beauty; the place of everlasting hunger, it is also the place where men feel their lives will gloriously be fulfilled and their hunger fed.

In no place in the world can the life of the lonely boy, the countryman who has been drawn northwards to the flame of his lust, be more barren, more drab, more hungry and comfortless. His life is the life of subways, of rebreathed air, of the smell of burned steel, weariness and the exhausted fetidity of a cheap rented room in the apartment of "a nice couple" on 113th Street, or perhaps the triumph of an eighty-dollar apartment in Brooklyn, upper Manhattan, or the Bronx which he rents with three or four other youths. Here they "can do as they please," a romantic aspiration which leads to Saturday night parties, to cheap gin, cheap girls, to a feverish and impotent fumbling, and perhaps to an occasional distressed, drunken, and half-public fornication.

If the youth is of a serious bent, if he has thoughts of "improving" himself, there is the gigantic desolation of the Public Library, a cut-rate ticket at Gray's and a seat in the balcony of an art-theatre play that has been highly praised and that all intellectual people will be seeing, or the grey depression of a musical Sunday afternoon at Carnegie Hall, filled with arrogant-looking little musicians with silky mustaches who hiss like vipers in the dark when the works of a hated composer are played; or there is always the Metropolitan Museum.

Again, there is something spurious and unreal in almost all attempts at established life in the city. When one enters the neat little apartment of a young man or a young married couple, and sees there on neat gaily-painted shelves neat rows of books—the solid little squares of the Everyman, and the Modern Library, the D. H. Lawrence, the *Buddenbrooks*, the Cabell, the art edition of *Penguin Island*, then a few of the paper-backed French books, the Proust and the Gide, and so on—one feels a sense of embarrassment and shame: there is something fraudulent about it. One feels this also in the homes of wealthy people, whether they live in a "charming little house" on Ninth Street which they have rented, or in the massive rooms of a Park Avenue apartment.

No matter what atmosphere of usage, servants, habitude, ease, and solid establishment there may be, one always has this same feeling that the thing is fraudulent, that the effort to achieve permanence in this impermanent and constantly changing life is no more real than the suggested permanence in a theatrical setting: one would not be surprised to return the next morning and find the scene dismantled, the stage bare, and the actors departed. Sometimes even the simplest social acts—the act of visiting one's friends, of talking to them in a room, of sitting around a hearth-fire with them—oh, above all else, of sitting around a hearth-fire in an apartment in the city!—seem naked and pitiful. There is an enormous sadness and wistfulness about these attempts to simulate an established life in a place where the one permanent thing is change itself.

In recent years many people have felt this insistent and constant movement. Some have blamed it on the war, some on the tempo of the time, some have called it "a jazz age" and suggested that men should meet the rhythm of the age and move and live by it; but although this notion has been fashionable, it can hardly recommend itself to men who have been driven by their hunger, who have known loneliness and exile, who have wandered upon the face of the earth and found no doors that they could enter, and who would to God now that they might make an end to all their wandering and loneliness, that they might find one home and heart of all their hunger where they could live abundantly forever. Such men, and they are numbered not by thousands but by millions, are hardly prepared to understand that the agony and loneliness of the human spirit may be assuaged by the jerky automata of jazz.

Perhaps this sense of restlessness, loneliness, and hunger is intensified in the city, but if anyone remembers his own childhood and youth in America he is certain to remember these desires and movements, too. Everywhere people were driven by them. Everyone had a rocking chair, and in the months of good weather everyone was out on his front porch rocking away. People were always eager to "go somewheres," and when the automobile came in, the roads, particularly on Sunday, were choked with cars going into the country, going to another town, going anywhere, no matter how ugly or barren the excursion might be, so long as this terrible restlessness might in some measure be appeased.

In the city, it is appalling to think how much pain and hunger people—and particularly young men—have suffered, because there is no goal whatever for these feverish extravasations. They return, after their day's work to a room which, despite all efforts to trick it out with a neat bed, bright colors, a few painted bookshelves, a few pictures, is obviously only a masked cell. It becomes impossible to use the room for any purpose at all save for sleeping; the act of reading a book in it, of sitting in a chair in it, of staying in it for any period of time whatever when one is in a state of wakefulness, becomes intolerable.

Yet, what are these wretched people to do? Every instant, every deep conviction a man has for a reasonable human comfort is outraged. He knows that every man on earth should have the decency of space—of space enough to extend his limbs and draw in the air without fear or labor; and he knows that his life here in this miserable closet is base, barren, mean, and naked. He knows that men should not defile themselves in this way, so he keeps out of his room as much as possible. But what can he do? Where can he go? In the terrible streets of the city there is neither pause nor repose, there are no turnings and no place where he can detach himself from the incessant tide of the crowd, and sink unto himself in tranquil meditation. He flees from one desolation to another, he escapes by buying a seat "at some show," or snatching at food in a cafeteria, he lashes about the huge streets of the night, and he returns to his cell having found no doors that he could open, no place that he could call his own.

It is therefore astonishing that nowhere in the world can a young man feel greater hope and expectancy than here. The promise of glorious fulfillment, of love, wealth, fame—or unimaginable joy—is always impending in the air. He is torn with a thousand desires and he is unable to articulate one of them, but he is sure that he will grasp joy to his heart, that he will hold love and glory in his arms, that the intangible will be touched, the inarticulate spoken, the inapprehensible apprehended; and that this may happen at any moment.

Perhaps there is some chemistry of air that causes this exuberance and joy, but it also belongs to the enigma of the whole country, which is so rich, and yet where people starve, which is so abundant, exultant, savage, full-blooded, humorous, liquid, and magnificent, and yet where so many people are poor, meager, dry, and baffled. But the richness and depth of the place is visible, it is not an illusion; there is always the feeling that the earth is full of gold, and that who will seek and strive can mine it.

In New York there are certain wonderful seasons in which this feeling grows to a lyrical intensity. One of these are those first tender days of Spring when lovely girls and women seem suddenly to burst out of the pavements like flowers: all at once the street is peopled with them, walking along with a proud, undulant rhythm of breasts and buttocks and a look of passionate tenderness on their faces. Another season is early Autumn, in October, when the city begins to take on a magnificent flash and sparkle: there are swift whippings of bright wind, a flare of bitter leaves, the smell of frost and harvest in the air: after the enervation of Summer, the place awakens to an electric vitality, the beautiful women have come back from Europe or from the summer resorts, and the air is charged with exultancy and joy.

Finally, there is a wonderful, secret thrill of some impending ecstasy on a frozen Winter's night. On one of these nights of frozen silence when the cold is so intense that it numbs one's flesh, and the sky above the city flashes with one deep jewelry of cold stars, the whole city, no matter how ugly its parts may be, becomes a proud, passionate, Northern place: everything about it seems to soar up with an aspirant, vertical, glittering magnificence to meet the stars. One hears the hoarse notes of the great ships in the river, and one remembers suddenly the princely girdle of proud, potent tides that bind the city, and suddenly New York blazes like a magnificent jewel in its fit setting of sea, and earth, and stars.

There is no place like it, no place with an atom of its glory, pride, and exultancy. It lays its hand upon a man's bowels; he grows drunk with ecstasy; he grows young and full of glory, he feels that he can never die.

14

The City Patriots

JERRY ALSOP HAD COME TO NEW YORK STRAIGHT OUT OF COLLEGE SEVERAL years before. Monk knew that he was there, and one day he ran into him. Neither seemed disposed to remember Monk's apostasy of college days; in fact, Jerry greeted his former protégé like a long lost brother and invited him around to his place. Monk went, and later went again, and for a time their relationship was reestablished, on the surface at least, on something of its former footing.

Alsop lived in the same part of town, on a cross street between Broadway and the river, and not far from Columbia University. He had two basement rooms and a dilapidated kitchenette. The place was dark, and he had collected a congeries of broken-down furniture—an old green sofa, a few chairs, a couple of tables, a folding couch or day-bed, covered with a dirty cloth, for visitors, another larger bed for himself, and a dirty old carpet. He thought it was wonderful, and because he communicated this sense of wonder to all his friends, they thought so, too. What it really represented to him was freedom—the glorious, intoxicating freedom that the city gave to him, to everyone. So seen and so considered, his apartment was not just a couple of dirty, dark, old rooms, filled with a hodgepodge of nondescript furniture, down in the basement of a dismal house. It was a domain, an estate, a private castle, a citadel. Jerry conveyed this magic sense to everyone who came there.

When Monk first saw him there in all the strangeness of New York, the changes in Alsop's vision and belief appeared astonishing. Only, however, at first sight. The younger man's sense of shock, the result of the blinding clarity of his first impression after the years of absence, was only momentary. For Alsop had gathered around him now a new coterie, the descendants of the clique at old Pine Rock: he was their mentor and their guiding star, and his two dark basement rooms had

233

become their club. And so Monk saw that Alsop had not really changed at all, that below all the confusion of outer change his soul was still the same.

One of the chief objects of his hatred at this time was Mr. H. L. Mencken. He had become for Alsop the Beast of the Apocalypse. Mencken's open ridicule of pedagogy, of Mother-idolatry, of the whole civilization which he called the Bible Belt and which referred to that part of life of which Alsop was himself a member, and, most of all, perhaps, the critic's open and ungodly mockery of "the greatest man since Jesus Christ," to whom he referred variously as "the late Doctor Wilson," or "the martyred Woodrow"—all of this struck with an assassin's dirk at the heart of all that was near and dear to Alsop, and, it seemed to him, at the heart of civilization itself, at religion, at morality, at "all that men hold sacred." The result was that this smashing but essentially conservative critic, Mencken, became in Alsop's eyes the figure of the Antichrist. Month after month he would read the latest blast of the Baltimore sage with the passionate devotion of pure hate. It was really alarming just to watch him as he went about his venomous perusal: his fat and usually rather pale face would become livid and convulsed as if he were in imminent peril of an apoplectic stroke, his eyes would narrow into reptilian slits, from time to time he would burst out into infuriated laughter, the whole proceeding being punctuated by such comment as:

"Well, I'll be God-damned! . . . Of all the! . . . Why, he's just a damned ass . . . yes suh! . . . That's the only name for him! . . . A plain damned ass. For God's sake now, listen to this!" Here his voice would mount to a choking scream. "Why, he hasn't got the brains of a louse!"—the whole winding up inevitably with the final recommendation for vindictive punishment: "You know what they ought to do with a man like that? They ought to take him out and ——."

He mentioned this act of mutilation with a hearty relish. It seemed to be the first act of vengeance and reprisal that popped into his head whenever anyone said or wrote or did something that aroused his hatred and antagonism. And it was as if Mr. H. L. Mencken, whom Alsop had never seen, had been a personal enemy, a malignant threat in his own life, a deadly peril not only to himself but to his friends and to the world he had shaped about him.

And yet, all the time Alsop himself was changing. His adaptive powers were remarkable. Like a certain famous Bishop, "he had a large and easy swallow." And really, what mattered most to him was not the inner substance but the outer show. He could, with no difficulty whatever, have agreed that black was white, or that two and two make four and three-quarters, if the prevailing order of society had swung to that belief.

It was only that, in Alsopian phrase, his "sphere had widened." He had come from the provincial community of the Baptist college to the city. And that staggering transition, so painful, so perilous, and so confusing to so many other men, had been for Alsop triumphantly easy. He had taken to the city like a duck to water. And in that complete and rapturous immersion was revealed, along with all that was shapeless in his character, also all that was warm and imaginative and good.

Some come to the city, no doubt, with wire-taut nerves, with trembling apprehension, with a resolution of grim conflict, desperate struggle, and the conviction they must do or die. Some, shackled by old fears, still cumbered with the harness of old prejudice, come to it doubtfully and with mistrust. And for them, the city that they find will be a painful one. And some come to it with exultancy and hope, as men rush forward to embrace a beloved mistress, whom they have never seen but of whom they have always known, and it was in this way that Alsop—Alsop of the bulging belly and the butter-tub of fat— it was in just this way that Alsop came.

It never occurred to him that he might fail. And indeed with faith like his, with such devotion as he brought, the chance of failure was impossible. Other men might rise to greater summits in the city's life. Other men might rise to greater substance of success, of wealth, of fame, achievement, or reputation. But no man would ever belong more truly to the city, or the city's life to him, than Gerald Alsop.

He was made for it; it was made for him. Here was a pond that he could swim in, a pool where he could fish. Here was the food for all his thousand appetites, the provender for his hundred mouths. Here was living water for the quenchless sponge that was himself: the rumor with the million tongues that could feed forever his insatiate ear, the chronicle of eight million lives that could appease his ceaseless thirst for human history.

Alsop was a man who had to live through others. He was an enormous Ear, Eye, Nose, Throat, an absorptive sponge of gluttonous humanity—he was not a thrust or arm—and in such a way as this, and so perfectly, so completely, the city was his oyster. And in his way he was incomparable. All that was best in him was here revealed. He communicated to everyone around him the contagion of his own enthusiasm, the sense of magic and of rapture which the city gave to him. With him, an excursion of any sort was a memorable event. A trip downtown in the subway, the gaudy lights, the thronging traffics of Times Square, the cut-rate ticket basement of Gray's Pharmacy, the constant nocturnal magic of the theatres, the cheap restaurants, a cafeteria or a lunchroom, a chop suey place, the strange faces, signs, and lights, the foreign vegetables, the unknown edibles of Chinatown— all this was simply magic. He was living in an enchanted world, he carried it with him everywhere he went.

His was the temper of the insatiable romantic. In no time at all, instantly, immediately, he inherited the city's hunger for celebrity. If he could not be great himself, he wanted to be near those who were. He lapped up every scrap of gossip about celebrated people he could read or hear. The records, diaries, comments, observations of the newspaper columnists were gospel to him. The pronouncements of a certain well-known dramatic critic, Cotswold, were like holy writ: he memorized them down to the last whimsical caprice of ornate phrasing. He went religiously to see every play the critic praised. One night he saw the great man himself, a fat and puffy little butter-ball of a man, in the interim between the acts, with another celebrated critic and a famous actress. When Alsop returned home he was transported—if he had seen Shakespeare talking to Ben Jonson, his emotion could not have been so great.

He became a watcher around stage doors. It was the period of the Ziegfeld shows, the glorified chorines, the proud, lavish flesh draped in a fold of velvet. Alsop now was everywhere, he delighted in these glorified carnalities. The girls were famous, he watched till they came out, and, like some ancient lecher, he licked his chops and gloated while the Ziegfeld Beauties and their moneyed purchasers walked away. The meeting of expensive flesh with shirt front, tails, and tall silk hatdom now delighted him. Strange work for old Pine Rock?— By no means: it was enhaloed now, set like a jewel in the great Medusa of the night, privileged by power and wealth and sanctioned by publicity. The aged lecher licking his dry lips and waiting with dead eyes for his young whore of Babylon, delighted Alsop now. He told of such a one: the beauty, already famed in print, came by—the aged lecher fawned upon her— "Oh, for Christ's sake!" said the beauty wearily, passing on.

"She meant that thing," said Alsop gloatingly. "Yes, suh! She meant that thing!" His great belly heaved, his throat rattled with its scream of phlegm. "God! The most beautiful damn woman that you ever saw!" said Alsop appetizingly as he shook his great jowled head. "She sure did get him told!" The scene delighted him.

All others, too: the rumors of a thousand tongues, the fruitage of a thousand whispered gossips: who slept with so-and-so; whose wife was faithless unto Caesar; whose wit had uttered such unprinted jest; what famous names, what authors, had behaved in such-and-such a way at such-and-such a party, had grown drunk there, had disappeared, had locked themselves in bedrooms with attractive women, gone into bathrooms with them, quarreled, fought with whom; what rather aged actress, famous for her lustihood in roles, had gone with boys of apple-cheeked persuasion; and who the famous fairies were, and the dance halls where they went to dance with one another, and what they said, the mincing syllables of their fond intercourse with one another— here belly heaved and Alsop screamed with choking laughter—such wickedness, together with all whimsicalities, and Morley's columns in the purest vein of elfin whimsey— "Pure genius! Pure damned elfin genius!"—old London in the byways of New York, Dickensian by-lights of the city ways, and the thronging chaoses of Herald Square, Park Row; the grime of unrubbed brasses, never noticed by the man-hordes passing by, but seen now in a certain light, and properly, the true quaintness of the world around him: the shopgirls eating sand-wiches of pimento cheese among the drug store slops of luncheon hour were really like the clients of an inn in Eastcheap ninety years ago. So, all together—Ziegfeld, beautiful chorines, and ancient lechers in silk hats; hot gossip of the great, the rumor of drunken riot with the famed and few, what Miss Parker said, and so-and-so; together with the Great Heart of the town, the men in subways and park benches— Lamb redivivus, alive and prowling among unrubbed brass in the quaint byways of Manhattan—all such as this was meat, drink, breath of life to Alsop.

So the food. His taste, like Dr. Samuel Johnson's, was not fine—he liked abundance and he liked to slop it in. He had a love for China-town, chop suey, and the pungent sauce: it was abundant, it was cheap. The strange faces of the Chinks, the moisty vapors, Oriental and somewhat depressant, all delighted him. He loved to go with several other people—one could order several dishes and thus share. When it was over he would call for paper bags, slop the remainders into them, and wheeze and choke with laughter as he did so.

When all this palled, or when he felt the belly hungers for familiar food—for home to heart and stomach was still very near—he and his cronies would buy up "a mess of stuff." There were stores everywhere, around the corner in every city block were stores, and the crowded opulence of night, and lighted windows, slanting shelves of vegetables and fruit; and butcher shops, chain groceries, bakeries, every kind of vast provisioning. They would go out upon their errands, they would buy the foods of home: a package of ground hominy—otherwise known as grits; string beans, which really were the same as they had always been, except no one knew how to cook them here, a piece of fat salt pork to give them seasoning; flour for gravy and for biscuit dough— for Alsop paled not at such formidable enterprise; steak, no worse if it were cheap and tough, but with the flour gravy and the condiments; bread from the bakery, butter, coffee. Then back to the basement, the two-roomed flat, a chaos of young voices, laughter, humorous, accusal— Alsop chuckling, serious, and all-governing, giving directions, bustling about in slippered feet, from whose stale socks protruded the fat hinge of his dirty heels. And then the pungency of native foods again—grits, fried steak with thick brown gravy, string beans savory, deep-hued with fat-back, brown-hued biscuits, smoking hot, strong coffee, melting butter. The vigorous confusion of young, drawling voices, excited, Southern, ingrown each to each, tribal and most personal—the new adventure of each daily life told eagerly and to the common mall, with laughter, agreement, strong derision. They appraised the new world where they lived with critic tongue, and often with a strong and dis-approving mockery.

They had small thought of ever going home again. At least, they seldom told their love. Their love, in fact, was mainly here—for most of them, like Alsop, were immersed in glamor now, had cottoned to this brave, new world, had taken it for their own domain as only people from the South can take it—some strange and stiff-necked pride kept them from owning it. They lived in legend now: among the thrill of all this present pageantry, they loved to descant on their former glories. "The South"—for in quotation marks they saw it—was now an exiled glory, a rich way of life, of living, and of human values which "these people up here" could never know about.

Perhaps they set this glory as a kind of reassuring palliative to their shock sense, the thrilling and yet terrifying conflict of the daily struggle. It was an occasional sop to wounded pride. The customs and the mores of the new world were examined critically and came off second best. A chicanery of the Northern ways, the suspicion of the hardened eye, the itching of the grasping palm, the machinations of the crafty Jew— all were observed upon with scorn and frequent bitterness. People in "the South" were not like this. As Alsop said, one had to come "up here" in order to find out just "how fine and sweet and lovable" they were.

George Webber had observed that there is no one on earth who is more patriotically devoted—verbally, at least—to the region from which he came than the American from the Southern portion of the United States. Once he leaves it to take up his living in other, less fair and fortunate, sections of the country, he is willing to fight for the honor of the Southland at the drop of a hat, to assert her supremacy over all the other habitable parts of the globe on every occasion, to speak eloquently and passionately of the charm of her setting, the superiority of her culture, the heroism of her men, and the beauty of her women, to defend her, to protect her, to bleed and die for her, if necessary—to do almost everything, in fact, for dear old Dixie except to return permanently to her to live.

A great many, it must be owned, do return, but most of those are the sorrier and more incompetent members of the tribe, the failures, the defeated ones—the writers who cannot write, the actors who cannot act, the painters who cannot paint, the men and women of all sorts, of all professions, of all endeavors from law to soda water, who, although not wholly lacking in talent, lack it in sufficient degree to meet the greater conflict of a wider life, the shock of open battle on a foreign field, the intenser effort and the superior performances of city life. These are the stragglers of the army. They hang on for a while, are buffeted, stunned, bewildered, frightened, ultimately overwhelmed by the battle roar. One by one they falter, give way, and, dispirited, bitter, and defeated, straggle back to the familiar safety and the comforting assurance of the hinterland.

Once there, a familiar process of the South begins, a pastime at which the inhabitants of that region have long been adept—the subtle, soothing sport of rationalization. The humbler members of the routed troops—the disillusioned soda-jerkers, the defeated filing clerks, department store workers, business, bank, and brokerage employees—arrive rapidly at the conclusion that the great city is "no place for a white man." The unfortunate denizens of city life "don't know what living really is." They endure their miserable existences because they "don't know any better." The city people are an ignorant and conceited lot. They have no manners, no courtesy, no consideration for the rights of others, and no humanity. Everyone in the city is "out for himself," out to do you, out to get everything he can out of you. It is a selfish, treacherous, lonely, and self-seeking life. A man has friends as long as he has money in his pocket. Friends melt away from him like smoke when money goes. Moreover, all social pride and decency, the dignity of race, the authority of class is violated and destroyed in city life— "A nigger is as good as a white man."

When George was a child, there was a story that was current over all the South. Some local hero—some village champion of the rights of white men and the maintenance of white supremacy—told the gory adventure of his one and only, his first and last, his final, all-sufficient journey into the benighted and corrupted domains of the North. Sometimes the adventure had occurred in Washington, sometimes in Philadelphia or New York, sometimes in Boston or in Baltimore, but the essential setting was always the same. The scene for this heroic drama was always laid in a restaurant of a Northern city. The plumed knight from below the Mason-Dixon line had gone in to get something to eat and had taken his seat at a table. He had progressed no further than his soup, when, looking up, he found to his horror and indignation that a "big buck nigger" had come in and taken a seat opposite him, and *at his own table*. Whereupon—but let the more skillful small-town raconteurs of twenty years ago complete the tale:

"Well, ole Jim says he took one look at him and says, 'You black son-of-a-bitch, what do you mean by sitting at my table?' Well, the nigger begins to talk back to him, telling him he was in the North now, where a nigger was just as good as anyone. And ole Jim says, 'You black bastard you, you may be as good as a Yankee, but you're talking to a white man now!'—and with that, he says, he ups with a ketchup bottle and he just busts it wide open over that nigger's head. Jim says he reckoned he killed him, says he didn't wait to see, he just left him laying there and grabbed his hat and walked out. He says he caught the first train going South and he's never been North since, and that he don't care if he never sees the God-damn place again."

This story was usually greeted with roars of appreciative and admiring laughter, the sound of thighs smitten with enthusiastic palms, gleeful exclamations of "'Oddam! I'd 'a' given anything to've seen it! Whew-w! I can just see ole Jim now as he let him have it! I'll betcha anything you like he killed that black bastard deader'n a doornail! Yes sir! Damned if I blame him either! I'd 'a' done the same thing!"

George must have heard this gory adventure gleefully related at least a hundred times during his childhood and the adolescent period of his youth. The names of the characters were sometimes different—sometimes it was "ole Jim" or "ole Bob" or "ole Dick"—but the essential circumstance was always the same; an impudent black limb of Satan entered, took the forbidden seat, and was promptly, ruthlessly, and gorily annihilated with a ketchup bottle. This story, in its various forms and with many modern innovations, was still current among returned wanderers from the Southland at the time when George first came to the great city to live. In more modern versions the insolent black had been annihilated on busses and in subway trains, in railway coaches or in moving picture theatres, in crowded elevators or upon the street—wherever, in fact, he had dared impudently to intrude too closely upon the proud and cherished dignity of a Southern white. And the existence of this ebony malefactor was, one gathered, one of the large contributing reasons for the return of the native to his own more noble heath.

Another, and probably more intelligent, portion of this defeated—and retreated—group had other explanations for their retreat, which were, however, derived from the same basic sources of rationalized self-defense. These were the members of the more intellectual groups—the writers, painters, actors—who had tried the ardors of the city's life and who had fled from it. Their arguments and reasons were subtler, more refined. The actor or the playwright asserted that he found the integrity of his art, the authentic drama of the folk, blighted and corrupted by the baleful and unnatural influence of the Broadway drama, by artificiality, trickery, and cheap sensation, by that which struck death to native roots and gave only a waxen counterfeit of the native flower. The painter or the musician found the artist and his art delivered to the mercy of fashionable cliques, constricted with the lifeless narrowness of æsthetic schools. The writer had a similar complaint. The creator's life was menaced in the city with the sterile counterfeits of art—the poisonous ethers of "the literary life," the poisonous intrigues of the literary cliques, the poisonous politics of log-rolling and back-scratching, critic-mongering and critic-pandering, the whole nasty, crawling, parasitical world of Scribbleonia.

In these unnatural and unwholesome weathers of creation, the artist— so these rebellious challengers asserted—lost his contact with reality, forgot the living inspirations of his source, had been torn away from living union with what he had begun to call his "roots." So caught and so imperiled, held high, Antæus-wise, away from contact with his native and restoring earth, gasping for breath in the dead vapors of an enclosed and tainted atmosphere, there was only one course for the artist if he would be saved. He must return, return to that place which had given him life and from which the strengths and energies of his art had been derived. But must renounce utterly and forever the sterile precincts of the clique, the salon, and the circle, the whole unnatural domain of the city's life. He must return again to the good earth, to affirmation of his origins, to contact with his "roots."

So the refined young gentlemen of the New Confederacy shook off their degrading shackles, caught the last cobwebs of illusion from their awakened vision, and retired haughtily into the South, to the academic security of a teaching appointment at one of the universities, from which they could issue in quarterly installments very small and very precious magazines which celebrated the advantages of an agrarian society. The subtler intelligences of this rebel horde were forever formulating codes and cults in their own precincts—codes and cults which affirmed the earthly virtues of both root and source in such unearthly language, by such processes of æsthetic subtlety, that even the cult adepts of the most precious city cliques were hard put to it to extract the meaning.

All this George Webber observed and found somewhat puzzling and astonishing. Young men whose habits, tastes, and modes of thought and writing seemed to him to belong a great deal more to the atmospheres of the æsthetic cliques which they renounced than to any other now began to argue the merits of a return to "an agrarian way of life" in language which was, it seemed to him, the language of a cult, and which assuredly few dwellers on the soil, either permanent or returned, could understand. Moreover, as one who was himself derived from generations of mountain farmers who had struggled year by year to make a patch of corn grow in the hill erosions of a mountain flank, and of generations of farm workers in Pennsylvania who had toiled for fifteen hours a day behind the plow to earn a wage of fifty cents, it now came as a mild surprise to be informed by the lily-handed intellectuals of a Southern university that what he needed most of all was a return to the earthly and benevolent virtues of the society which had produced him.

The summation of it all, of course, the fundamental characteristic of this whole defeated and retreated kind—whether intellectual or creative, professional or of the working group—was the familiar rationalizing self-defense of Southern fear and Southern failure: its fear of conflict and of competition in the greater world; its inability to meet or to adjust itself to the conditions, strifes, and ardors of a modern life; its old, sick, Appomattoxlike retreat into the shades of folly and delusion, of prejudice and bigotry, of florid legend and defensive casuistry, of haughty and ironic detachment from a life with which it was too obviously concerned, to which it wished too obviously to belong.

So much, then, for these defeated ones—these too tender and inept detachments of the rebel horde who could not meet and take the shock of battle, and who straggled back. What of the others, the better and the larger kind, the ones who stayed? Were they defeated? Were they swept under? Were they dispersed and scattered, or routed in dismay and driven back?

By no means. Their success, in fact, in city life was astonishing. There is no other section of the country whose city immigrants succeed so brilliantly when they do succeed. The quality of the Southerner's success in city life is derived, to an amazing degree, from the very nature of his handicap. If he prevails, if he conquers, he is likely to do it not only in spite of his provincialism but because of it, not only in spite of his fear but by means of it, and because that terrible and lacerating consciousness of inferiority is likely to drive him on to superhuman efforts.

The Southerner is often inspired to do his best when the odds are the heaviest against him, when he knows it, when he knows further that the world knows it and is looking on. The truth of this was demonstrated again and again in the Civil War, when some of the South's most brilliant victories—it is possible also to say, when some of the South's most brilliant defeats—were *won* under these circumstances. The Southerner, with all that is sensitive, tender, flashing, quick, volatile, and over-imaginative in his nature, is likely to know fear and to know it greatly. But also, precisely on account of his sensitivity, quickness, imagination, he knows fear *of* fear, and this second kind of fear is often likely to be so much stronger than the first that he will do and die before he shows it. He will fight like a madman rather than like a man, and he will often attain an almost unbelievable victory against overwhelming odds, even when few people in the world believe that victory is possible.

These facts are true, and they are likewise admirable. But in their very truth there is a kind of falseness. In their very strength there is a dangerous weakness. In the very brilliance of their victory there is a lamentable defeat. It is admirable to win against terrific odds, but it is not admirable, not well for the health and endurance of the spirit, to be able to win only against terrific odds. It is thrilling to see men roused to such a pitch of desperation that they fight like madmen, but it is also thrilling to see them resolved and strong in their ability to fight like men. It is good to be so proud and sensitive that one is more afraid of showing fear than of fear itself, but these intensities of passion, pride, and desperation also take their toll. The danger is that though they may spur men to the feverish consummation of great heights, they may also drop them, exhausted and impotent, to abysmal depths, and that one attains the shining moment of a brilliant effort at the expense of the consistent and steady achievement of a solid and protracted work.

The transplanted Southerner is likely to be a very lonely animal. For that reason his first instinctive movement in the city is likely to be in the direction of his own kind. The first thing he does when he gets to the city is to look up old college chums or boys from his home town. They form a community of mutual interests and mutual self-protection; they build a kind of wall around themselves to protect them from the howling maelstrom of the city's life. They form a Community of the South which has no parallel in city life. Certainly one does not find a similar Community of the Middle West, or a Community of the Great Plains, or a Community of the Rocky Mountain States, or a Community of the Pacific Coast There are, perhaps, the faint rudiments of a New England Community, the section which, after the South, is most definitely marked by a native identity of culture. But the New England Community, if it exists at all, exists so faintly and so sparely as to be almost negligible.

The most obvious reason for the existence of this Community of the South within the city's life is to be found in the deep-rooted and provincial insularity of Southern life. The cleavage of ideas, the division of interests, of social customs and traditional beliefs, which were developing with a tremendous gathering velocity in American life during the first half of the nineteenth century, and which were more and more separating the life of an agrarian South from the life of the industrial North, were consummated by the bloody action of the Civil War, and were confirmed and sealed by the dark and tragic act of reconstruction. After the war and after reconstruction, the South retreated in behind its shattered walls and stayed there.

There was an image in George Webber's mind that came to him in childhood and that resumed for him the whole dark picture of those decades of defeat and darkness. He saw an old house, set far back from the traveled highway, and many passed along that road, and the troops went by, the dust rose, and the war was over. And no one passed along that road again. He saw an old man go along the path, away from the road, into the house; and the path was overgrown with grass and weeds, with thorny tangle, and with underbrush until the path was lost. And no one ever used that path again. And the man who went into that house never came out of it again. And the house stayed on. It shone faintly through that tangled growth like its own ruined spectre, its doors and windows black as eyeless sockets. That was the South. That was the South for thirty years or more.

That was the South, not of George Webber's life, nor of the lives of his contemporaries—that was the South they did not know but that all of them somehow remembered. It came to them from God knows where, upon the rustling of a leaf at night, in quiet voices on a Southern porch, in a screen door slam and sudden silence, a whistle wailing down the midnight valleys to the East and the enchanted cities of the North, and Aunt Maw's droning voice and the memory of unheard voices, in the memory of the dark, ruined Helen in their blood, in something stricken, lost, and far, and long ago. They did not see it, the people of George's age and time, but they remembered it.

They had come out—another image now—into a kind of sunlight of another century. They had come out upon the road again. The road was being paved. More people came now. They cut a pathway to the door again. Some of the weeds were clear. Another house was built. They heard wheels coming and the world was *in*, yet they were not yet wholly of that world.

George would later remember all the times when he had come out of the South into the North, and always the feeling was the same—an exact, pointed, physical feeling marking the frontiers of his consciousness with a geographic precision. There was a certain tightening in the throat, a kind of dry, hard beating of the pulse, as they came up in the morning towards Virginia; a kind of pressure at the lips, a hot, hard burning in the eye, a wire-taut tension of the nerves, as the brakes slammed on, the train slowed down to take the bridge, and the banks of the Potomac River first appeared. Let them laugh at it who will, let them mock it if they can. It was a feeling sharp and physical as hunger, deep and tightening as fear. It was a geographic division of the spirit that was sharply, physically exact, as if it had been cleanly severed by a sword. When the brakes slammed on and he saw the wide flood of the Potomac River, and then went out upon the bridge and heard the low-spoked rumble of the ties and saw the vast dome of the Capitol sustained there in the light of shining morning like a burnished shell, he drew in hot and hard and sharp upon his breath, there in the middle of the river. He ducked his head a little as if he was passing through a web. He knew that he was leaving South. His hands gripped hard upon the hinges of his knees, his muscles flexed, his teeth clamped tightly, and his jaws were hard. The train rolled over, he was North again.

Every young man from the South has felt this precise and formal geography of the spirit, but few city people are familiar with it. And why this tension of the nerves, why this gritting of the teeth and hardening of the jaws, this sense of desperate anticipation as they crossed the Potomac River? Did it mean that they felt they were invading a foreign country? Did it mean they were steeling themselves for conflict? Did it mean that they were looking forward with an almost desperate apprehension to their encounter with the city? Yes, it meant all of this. It meant other things as well. It meant that they were also looking forward to that encounter with exultancy and hope, with fervor, passion, and high aspiration.

George often wondered how many people in the city realize how much the life of the great city meant to him and countless others like him: how, long ago in little towns down South, there in the barren passages of night, they listened to the wheel, the whistle, and the bell; how, there in the dark South, there on the Piedmont, in the hills, there by the slow, dark rivers, there in coastal plains, something was always burning in their hearts at night—the image of the shining city and the North. How greedily they consumed each scrap of gossip adding to their city lore, how they listened to the tales of every traveler who returned, how they drank in the words of city people, how in a thousand ways, through fiction, newspapers, and the cinema, through printed page and word of mouth, they built together bit by bit a shining image of their hunger and desire—a city that had never been, that would never be, but a city better than the one that was.

And they brought that image with them to the North. They brought it to the North with all their hope, their hunger, their devotion, with all their lust for living and with all their hot desire. They brought it to the North with all their pride, their passion, and their fervor, with all the aspirations in their shining dreams, with all the energy of their secret and determined will—somehow by every sinew of their life, by every desperate ardor of their spirit, here in the shining, ceaseless, glorious, and unending city to make their lives prevail, to win for their own lives and by their talents an honored place among the highest and the noblest life that only the great city had to offer.

Call it folly, if you will. Call it blind sentiment, if you like. But also call it passion, call it devotion, call it energy, warmth, and strength, high aspiration and an honorable pride. Call it youth, and all the glory and the wealth of youth.

And admit, my city friends, your life has been the better for it. They enriched your life in ways you may not know, in ways you never pause to estimate. They brought you—the half million or more of them who came and stayed—a warmth you lacked, a passion that God knows you needed, a belief and a devotion that was wanting in your life, an integrity of purpose that was rare in your own swarming hordes. They brought to all the multiplex and feverish life of all your ancient swarming peoples some of the warmth, the depth, the richness of the secret and unfathomed South. They brought some of its depth and mystery to those sky-shining vertices of splintered light, to all those dizzy barricades of sky-aspiring brick, to those cold, salmon-colored panes, and to all the weary grey of all those stony-hearted pavements. They brought a warmth of earth, an exultant joy of youth, a burst of living laughter, a full-bodied warmth and living energy of humor, shot through with sunlight and with Africa, and a fiery strength of living faith and hope that all the acrid jests, the bitter wisdoms, the cynical appraisals, and the old, unrighteous, and scornmaking pride of all the ancient of the earth and Israel could not destroy or weaken.

Say what you will, you needed them. They enriched your life in ways you do not know. They brought to it the whole enormous treasure of their dreams and of their hopes, the aspiration of high purposes. They were transformed, perhaps, submerged or deadened, in some ways defeated later, maybe, but they were not lost. Something of all of them, of each of them, went out into your air, diffused among the myriad tangle of your billion-footed life, wore down into the granite dullness of your pavements, sank through into the very weather of your brick, the cold anatomy of your steel and stone, into the very hue and weather of your lives, my friends, in secret and unknown ways, into all you said and thought and did, into all that you had shaped and wrought.

There's not a ferry slip around Manhattan that is not grained a little with their passion. There's not a salmon flank of morning at the river's edge that does not catch you at the throat and heart a little more because the fierce excitement of their youth and of their wild imagination went into it. There's not a canyon gulch blued with the slant of morning light that lacks a little of their jubilation. They're there in every little tug that slides and fetters at the wharves of morning, they're there in the huge slant of evening light, in the last old tingeings of unearthly red upon the red brick of the harbor heights. They're there in winglike soar and swoop of every bridge and humming rail in every singing cable. They're there in tunnel's depths. They're there in every cobble, every brick. They're there upon the acrid and exciting tang of smoke. They're there upon the very air you breathe.

Try to forget them or deny them, if you will, but they brought your harsh flanks warmth around them, brothers. They are there.

And so those younglings from the South did not go home except for visits. Somehow they loved the poison they had drunk; the snake that stung them was now buried in their blood

Of all of them, Alsop played the surest role: they clustered round him like chicks about a mother hen and he was most comforting. He loved the South—and yet was not so cabined and confined as they. For while the others kept inviolate the little walls of their own province, their special language, and the safe circle of their own community, venturing forth into that great and outer strangeness day by day like Elizabethan mariners on a quest for gold, or looking for the passage to Cathay—it was, in fact, still Indian country so far as some of them could see, and at night they slept within the picket circle of their wheels—Alsop cast a wider circle. He was broadening. He was talking to new people day by day—people on park benches, on bus tops, in lunchrooms, drug stores, soda fountains; people in Manhattan and the Bronx, in Brooklyn, Queens, and Staten Island.

He had been stronger than all of them in his contempt and his derision of "damned foreigners." Now he knew Romano, a young Italian, a clerk by occupation, but a painter by profession. Now he brought him home, and Romano cooked spaghetti. He met other ones as well—Mr. Chung, a Chinese merchant on Pell Street, and a scholar of the ancient poetry; a Spaniard working as a bus boy in a restaurant; a young Jew from the East Side. Alsop was strong in the profession of his nativeness, but the new and strange—the dark, the foreign, and the mixed—appealed to him.

And yet he loved the South—no doubt of that. He went back every Christmas. First he stayed two weeks, and then ten days, and then a week, and presently he was back in three days' time. But he loved the South—and he never failed to come back with a fund of bright new stories, of warmth and sentiment and homely laughter; with the latest news of Miss Willsie, of Merriman, his cousin, and of Ed Wetherby, and of his aunt, Miss Caroline; and of all the other simple, sweet, and lovable people "down there" that he had found.

And yet, in his all-mothering nature, Alsop's soul had room for many things. He chuckled and agreed with all the others, he was himself sharp-tongued and scornful of the city ways, but suddenly he would heave and wheeze with a Pickwickian toleration, he would be filled with warm admissions for this alien place. "Still, you've got to hand it to them!" he would say. "It's the damnedest place on earth . . . the most glorious, crazy, perfectly wonderful, magnificent, god-damned town that ever was!" And he would rummage around among a pile of junk, a mountain of old magazines and clippings, until he found and read to them a poem by Don Marquis.

15

Götterdämmerung

IT WAS NOT A BAD LIFE THAT THEY HAD THAT YEAR. IT WAS, IN MANY WAYS, a good one. It was, at all events, a constantly exciting one. Jim Randolph was their leader, their benevolent but stern dictator.

Jim was thirty now, and he had begun to realize what had happened to him. He could not accept it. He could not face it. He was living in the past, but the past could not come back again. Monk and the others didn't think about it at the time, but later they knew why he needed them, and why all the people that he needed were so young. They represented the lost past to him. They represented his lost fame. They represented the lost glory of his almost forgotten legend. They brought it back to him with their devotion, their idolatrous worship They restored a little of it to him. And when they began to sense what had happened, all of them were a little sad.

Jim was a newspaper man now. He had a job working for one of the great agencies of international information, the Federal Press. He liked the work, too. He had, like almost all Southerners, an instinctive and romantic flair for news, but even in his work the nature of his thought was apparent. He had, as was natural, a desire for travel, an ambition to be sent to foreign countries as correspondent. But the others never heard him say that he would like to go to Russia, where the most important political experiment of modern times was taking place, or to England, Germany, or the Scandinavian countries. He wanted to go to places which had for him associations of romance and glamorous adventure. He wanted to be sent to South America, to Spain, to Italy, to France, or to the Balkans. He always wanted to go to a place where life was soft and warm and gallant, where romance was in the air, and where, as he thought, he could have the easy love of easy women. (And there, in fact, to one of these countries, he did go finally. There he went and lived a while, and there he died.)

Jim's feeling for news, although keen and brilliantly colorful, was, like his whole vision of life, more or less determined by the philosophy of the playing field. In spite of his experience in the World War, he was still fascinated by war, which he regarded as the embodiment of personal gallantry. A war to him was a kind of gigantic sporting contest, an international football game, which gave the star performers on both sides an opportunity to break loose around the flanks on a touchdown dash. Like a Richard Harding Davis character, he not only wanted to see a war and report a war, he wanted also to play a part in war, a central and heroic part. In his highly personal and subjective view of the news, Jim saw each event as somehow shaped for the projection of his own personality.

It was the same way with athletic contests, in which his interest was naturally keen. This was strikingly and amusingly evident at the time of the fight between Dempsey and Firpo for the heavyweight championship of the world.

The fighters were in training. The air was humming with excited speculation. The champion, Dempsey, destined later, after his defeat by Tunney, to become, according to the curious psychology of the American character, immensely popular, was at this time almost bitterly hated. For one thing, he was the champion, and the job of being champion in any walk of American life is a perilous and bitter one. Again, he enjoyed the unenviable reputation of being almost invincible. This, too, aroused hatred against him. People wanted to see him beaten. Finally, he was viciously assailed upon all sides on account of his war record. He was accused of being a slacker, of having stayed at home and worked in the shipyard while his contemporaries were risking their lives on the fields of France. And of course one heard on every hand the familiar American charge that he was "yellow." This was untrue.

Firpo, on the other hand, appealed to the popular imagination, although he had little to recommend him as a fighter except enormous physical strength and a clumsy but tremendous punch. This was enough. In fact, his very deficiencies seemed to increase the excitement over the uneven match. Firpo became, in the popular mind, "The Wild Bull of the Pampas," and it was believed he would rush in, bull-like, with head lowered, and try to annihilate his opponent with a punch of his powerful right hand.

The two men were now in training for the fight, and every day it was part of Jim's job to go out to Firpo's training camp and observe his progress. The South American took a great liking to Jim, who could speak understandable Spanish, and Jim became intensely interested in the man and in his prospects for the fight. Perhaps something helpless, dumb, and inarticulate in the big, sullen brute awakened Jim's quick sympathies. Every night, now, Jim would come in, swearing and fuming about the day's happenings at the training camp.

"Oh that poah, dumb son-of-a-bitch," he would softly swear. "He don't know any more about getting into condition than the fat woman at Barnum and Bailey's Circus. And no one around him knows anything. Christ!—they've got him out there skipping the rope!" He laughed softly and swore again. "You'd think they were training him to be Queen of the May. Why the hell should he skip the rope to get ready for Dempsey? He's not goin' to get out of Dempsey's way. Dempsey will nail him with that right before the fight has gone five seconds. This bird don't know anything about boxing. They're trying to teach him how to weave and bob when his only chance is to get in there and slug for all he's worth. . . . And condition? All I know is about conditioning a football team, but if I couldn't take him and get him in better shape in the next three weeks than he's ever been in before, you can kick me all the way from here to the Polo Grounds." Laughing softly, he shook his head. "God almighty, it's a crime to see it! Why, dammit, they let him eat anything he likes! Any football coach that saw a halfback eat like that would drop dead. I've seen him begin with soup, go right through two big porterhouse steaks, with smothered onions and French fried potatoes, and top that off with a whole apple pie, a quart of ice cream, and foah cups of coffee! After that they expect him to go out and skip rope for a few minutes to get that belly down!"

"But why doesn't he get a good trainer, Jim?" someone asked.

"Why?" said Jim. "I'll tell you why. It's because he's too damn tight, that's why. Why that cheap ——!" he laughed, shaking his head again, "—he's so tight that he's got the first nickel he ever earned when he came to this country. Dempsey may knock him the whole way from here to Argentina, but he's going to take every penny he ever made when he goes."

These daily accounts were thrilling news for the others. They became passionately excited over the career and progress of the bull-like Argentinian, and as the time for the great battle drew near they all devised and entered into a fascinating speculation for their enrichment. Under Jim's leadership, they all bought tickets for the fight. It was their plan to hold these until the very eve of battle, and then to sell them to fight enthusiasts for a fabulous profit. They hoped to get as much as fifty dollars for tickets which had cost only five or ten.

This hope might have been realized if, at the last moment, they had not committed one of their characteristic follies. None of them, of course, would admit to the others that he would like to see the fight himself. Any suggestion of this was greeted by hoots of scorn. Jim, in fact, almost exploded with outraged contempt when one of them hinted that *he* might prefer to *use* his ticket instead of selling it for fifty dollars.

And yet, they held on to the tickets until it was too late—until, at any rate, they would have had to try to sell them at the Polo Grounds to possible last-minute purchasers. They might have been able to do this, but really what they had wanted all along, the secret hope that each of them had cherished in his heart and that none of them would admit, was that they could see that fight themselves. And that is what they did. And in the light of retrospect Monk was glad they did it. That night made history in their lives, in a curious, poignant, and indefinable way, as only a popular song or a prize fight can do in America, evoking a time with blazing vividness, a host of memories that otherwise would later be only obscure, blurred fragments of a half-forgotten past.

An hour before the fight was scheduled to begin, and even after the preliminary contests had begun, they were all together in the living room of their apartment, debating with one another violently. Each accused the others of having failed to go through with the plan. Each denied vehemently that he had had any intention of weakening. Above the whole excited babble, Jim's voice could be heard passionately asserting that he was still out to sell his ticket, that he was going to the Polo Grounds for purposes of speculation only, that the rest of them could back down if they wished but that he would sell his ticket if it was the last thing he ever did on earth.

The upshot of it was that the more he argued and asserted, the less they believed him; and the more he shouted, the less he convinced himself. They all squabbled, argued, challenged, and denied until the final moment, which they knew somehow was coming. And then it came. Jim paused suddenly in his hot debate with himself, looked at his watch, ripped out an alarmed oath, and then, looking at them, laughed his soft and husky laugh, saying:

"Come on, boys. Who's going to this fight with me?"

It was perfect. And it was the kind of folly and unreason that was characteristic of them all: the great plans and projects and the protestations they were forever making, and their ultimate surrender to impulse and emotion when the moment came. And it was exactly like Jim Randolph, too. It was the kind of thing he did, the kind of thing that he had always done, the irrational impulse that wrecked his best-laid plans.

Now that the time had come, now that they had all surrendered, now that all of them had openly admitted at last what they were going to do, they went jubilantly and exultantly. And they saw the fight. They did not sit together. Their tickets were in different sections of the field. Monk's was over behind third base and well back in the upper tier. That square of roped-in canvas out there in the center of the field looked very far away, and that surrounding mass of faces was enormous, overwhelming. Yet his vision of the whole scene remained ever afterwards startlingly immediate and vivid.

He saw the little eddies in the crowd as the fighters and their handlers came towards the ring, then heard the great roar that rose and mounted as they climbed through the ropes. There was something terrific in the sight of young Dempsey. Over all the roar and tumult of that mighty crowd Monk could feel the currents of his savagery and nervous tension. Dempsey could not sit still. He jumped up from his stool, pranced up and down, seized the ropes and stretched and squatted several times, as skittish and as nervous as a race horse.

Then the men were called into the center of the ring to receive their last instructions. Firpo came out stolidly, his robe stretched across his massive shoulders, his great coarse shock of hair shining blackly as he stood and glowered. He had been well named. He was really like a sullen human bull. Dempsey could not be still. As he got his last instructions, he fidgeted nervously and kept his head down, a little to one side, not meeting Firpo's sullen and stolid look.

They received their instructions and turned and went back to their corners. Their robes were taken off. Dempsey flexed and squatted swiftly at the ropes, the bell clanged, and the men came out.

That was no fight, no scheduled contest for a title. It was a burning point in time, a kind of concentration of our total energies, of the blind velocity of the period, cruel, ruthless, savage, swift, bewildering as America. The fight, thus seen, resumed and focalized a period in the nation's life. It lasted six minutes. It was over almost before it had begun. In fact, the spectators had no sense of its beginning. It exploded there before them.

From that instant on, the battle raged and shifted with such savage speed, with such sudden and astounding changes of fortune, that later people were left stunned and bewildered, no one knowing clearly what had happened. No two could agree. The crowd milled and mobbed, the hundred thousand voices raised in argument. No one was certain just how many knockdowns there had been, how often Firpo had been driven to the floor by the thudding power of Dempsey's fists, or how long Dempsey had been out of the ring when Firpo drove him through the ropes. Some said there had been seven knockdowns, some said nine, some said four. Some asserted bitterly that Dempsey had been knocked out of the ring for more than fifteen seconds, that the count was late in taking up, that Firpo had been robbed of a just victory. Others asserted that Dempsey had fought with a vicious disregard for the rules, that the referee had allowed him to take ruthless and illegal openings.

Certainly it was no crafty exhibition of ring skill or strategy. It was a fight between two wild animals, each bent on the annihilation of the other, by any means, by any method, in the shortest time. What finally remained most vivid, in that kaleidoscopic whirl of violent images, was the memory of Dempsey's black and bobbing head, his teeth bared in a grin of passion, the incredible speed and power of his sledge-hammer fists, and the sound of blows that moved so swiftly that the eye could not perceive them. He was like a human riveting machine. Over the terrific roar and tumult of the crowd one could hear the steady thud, thud, thud, the sickening impact of blows delivered with the velocity of a bullet. Again and again, the great brute went down before those whizzing gloves as if he had been shot. He *had* been shot, too. He looked and acted just like a man who has received a bullet in the brain. For a moment, for an infinitesimal fraction of a second, he would stand erect. And then he would not fall, he would just collapse, as if his massive legs had been broken. He just looked stunned, bewildered, sullenly infuriated, like a baffled bull.

But suddenly, like a baffled and infuriated bull, he charged. He caught Dempsey solidly with a terrible right-hand blow that knocked him clear across the ring, and then he charged upon him and fairly flailed him through the ropes and out of the arena. And now, while the crowd insanely roared, Firpo was like a triumphant bull that has driven his antagonist into oblivion and has the whole arena to himself. Dempsey went hurtling through the ropes like a battered doll. The newspaper men thrust up their arms to protect themselves. The fighter came crashing down into a nest of typewriters, and, at the same moment, muttered thickly, with the instinct of a fighting animal, "Get me back in there!"

They pushed him up and back, in through the ropes. He reeled in glassy-eyed, tottering like a drunken man. He fell into a clinch and hung on desperately; his brain cleared, the fight was on again—and again the riveting thud, thud, thud of those relentless hands. The bull halted, stunned, and collapsed again like broken straw.

It was all over in the first round, really, a round that lasted for three minutes, but that had attained such a focal concentration of intensity that men asserted later that it seemed to last for hours. In the second round it was ended definitely. The killer had learned caution now. He came out craftily this time, with his black jaw tucked in below his shoulder. It was all over then. The great bull had no weapons for methods such as these. He lowered his head and charged. The riveter shot him down.

That night the city was a boiling of excitement. It was like a war, like the announcement of a general mobilization order. After the fight, Jim Randolph, Monty Bellamy, Harvey Williams, Perce Smead, and Monk got together again at one of the exits to the grounds and went downtown. By the time they reached midtown New York the news was there. Broadway and the triangulated space before the Times Building was a seething horde of wildly excited, milling, fiercely argumentative people. Monk had never seen anything like it before. It was passionately and desperately exciting, but it was also sinister.

The crowd was composed, for the most part, of men of the Broadway type and stamp, men with vulpine faces, feverish dark eyes, features molded by cruelty and cunning, corrupted, criminal visages of night, derived out of the special geography, the unique texture, the feverish and unwholesome chemistries of the city's nocturnal life of vice and crime. Their unclean passion was appalling. They snarled and cursed and raged at one another like a pack of mongrel curs. There were raucous and unclean voices, snarls of accusation and suspicion, with hatred and infuriating loathing, with phrases of insane obscenity and filth.

Monk could not understand it. He was so new to the city, and the image of those livid faces, those convulsed and snarling mouths, those feverish eyes shining there in the glare of night, evoked a sense of some sinister and yet completely meaningless passion. He listened to their words. He heard their epithets of hatred and of filth. He tried to find the meaning of it, and there was no meaning. Some hated Firpo, some hated Dempsey, some hated the fight and the result. Some charged that the fight had been "fixed," others that it should never have been held. Some asserted that Firpo had been doped, others that he had been bribed; still others, that he was "nothing but a tramp," that Dempsey was "a yellow bum," that a former champion could have beaten both of them at the same time.

But what was behind their snarling hatred? Unable to explain it any other way, Monk at last concluded that what they really hated was not so much the fight, the fighters, and the fight's result: it was themselves, one another, every living thing on earth. They hated for the sake of hate. They jeered, reviled, cursed one another because of the black poison in their souls. They could believe in nothing, and neither could they believe in themselves for not believing. They were a race that had been drugged by evil, a tribe that got its only nourishment from envenomed fruit. It was so blind, so willful, and so evil, so horrible and so meaningless, that suddenly it seemed to Monk that a great snake lay coiled at the very heart and center of the city's life, that a malevolent and destructive energy was terribly alive and working there, and that he and the others who had come here from the little towns and from the country places, with such high passion and with so much hope, were confronted now with something evil and unknown at the heart of life, which they had not expected, and for which all of them were unprepared.

Monk was to see it, feel it, know it later on in almost every facet of the city's life, this huge and baffling malady of man's brain, his spirit, and his energy. But now he witnessed it for the first time. He could see no reason for this idiot and blind malevolence. Yet it was there, it was everywhere, in the hateful passion of those twisted faces and the unwholesome radiance of those fevered eyes.

And now Monk heard Jim speaking. They had moved about from group to group and listened to these hate-loving men, and now Jim

Randolph began to speak, quietly, in his rather soft and husky tones, good-naturedly and yet commandingly, telling them they were mistaken, that the fighters were not drugged, that the fight had not been fixed, that the result had been inevitable and just. And then Monk heard one of those mongrel voices snarl back at him in hatred and derision, a twisted and corrupted mouth spat out at him a filthy epithet. Then, quicker than the eye could wink, the thing had happened. Jim seized the creature with one hand, draping his garments together in his powerful fingers, lifting him clear off his feet into the air, and shaking him like a rat.

"Listen, mister!" his husky voice was now charged with a murderous intensity of passion that struck silence through the whole raucous and disputing crowd and turned the creature's face a dirty grey, "No man alive is going to say that to me! Another word from you and I'll break your dirty neck!" And he shook him once again till the creature's head snapped like a broken doll's. And then Jim dropped him like a soiled rag, and, turning to his companions, said quietly: "Come on, boys. We'll get out of here." And the creatures of the night held back before him as he passed.

Poor Jim! He, too, was like a creature from another world. With all his folly and his sentiment, with all his faults and childish vanities, he was still the heroic remnant of a generation that had already gone, and that perhaps we needed. But he was lost

George Webber had grown into a youth somewhat above the middle height, around five feet nine or ten, but he gave the impression of being shorter than that because of the way he had been shaped and molded, and the way in which he carried himself. He walked with a slight stoop, and his head, which was carried somewhat forward with a thrusting movement, was set down solidly upon a short neck, between shoulders which, in comparison with the lower part of his figure, his thighs and legs, were extremely large and heavy. He was barrel-chested, and perhaps the most extraordinary feature of his make-up—which accounted for the nickname he had had since childhood—were the arms and hands: the arms were unusually long, and the hands, as well as the feet, were very big, with long, spatulate fingers which curved naturally and deeply in like paws. The effect of this inordinate length of arms and hands, which dangled almost to the knees, together with the stooped and heavy shoulders and the out-thrust head, was to give his whole figure a somewhat prowling and half-crouching posture.

His features, his face, were small, compact—somewhat pug-nosed, the eyes set very deep in beneath heavy brows, the forehead rather low, the hair beginning not far above the brows. When he was listening or talking to someone, his body prowling downward, his head thrust forward and turned upward with a kind of packed attentiveness, the simian analogy was inevitable; therefore the name of "Monk" had stuck. Moreover, it had never occurred to him, apparently, to get his figure clothed in garments suited to his real proportions. He just walked into a store somewhere and picked up and wore out the first thing he could get on. Thus, in a way of which he was not wholly conscious, the element of grotesqueness in him was exaggerated.

The truth of the matter is that he was not really grotesque at all. His dimensions, while unusual and a little startling at first sight, were not abnormal. He was not in any way a freak of nature, although some people might think so. He was simply a youth with big hands and feet, extremely long arms, a trunk somewhat too large and heavy, with legs too short, and features perhaps too small and compact for the big shoulders that supported them. Since he had added to this rather awkward but not distorted figure certain unconscious tricks and mannerisms, such as his habit of carrying his head thrust forward, and of peering upward when he was listening or talking, it was not surprising if the impression he first made on people should sometimes arouse laughter and surprise. Certainly he knew this, and he sometimes furiously and bitterly resented it; but he had never inquired sufficiently or objectively enough into the reasons for it.

Although he had a very intense and apprehensive eye for the appearance of things, the eager, passionate absorption of his interest and attention was given to the world around him. To his own appearance he had never given a thought. So when, as sometimes happened, the effect he had on people was rudely and brutally forced upon his attention, it threw him into a state of furious anger. For he was young—and had not learned the wisdom and tolerant understanding of experience and maturity. He was young—still over-sensitive. He was young—not able to forget himself, to accept the jokes and badinage good-naturedly. He was young—and did not know that personal beauty is no great virtue in a man, and that this envelope of flesh and blood, in which a spirit happened to be sheathed, could be a loyal and enduring, though ugly, friend.

All this—and many more important things besides—had got him into a lot of confusion, a lot of torture, and a lot of brute unhappiness. And the same thing was happening to a million other young men at that time. Monk was a hard-pressed kid. And because he was hard pressed, he had wangled himself into a lot of nonsense. It wouldn't be true to say, for example, that he hadn't got anything out of his "education." Such as it was, he had got a great deal out of it, but, like most of the "education" of the time, it had been full of waste, foolishness, and misplaced emphasis.

The plain, blunt truth of the matter was that, essentially, although he did not know it, Monk was an explorer. And so were a million other young people at that time. Well, exploring is a thrilling thing. But, even for the physical explorers, it is a hard thing, too. Monk had the true faith, the true heroism, of an explorer. He was a lot more lonely that Columbus ever was, and for this reason he was desperately confused, groping, compromising, and unsure.

It would be nice to report that he was swift and certain as a flame, always shot true to the mark, and knew what he knew. But this wasn't true. He knew what he knew, but he admitted that he knew it only seldom. Then when he did, he asserted it; like every other kid, he "went to town." He said it, he shot it home, he made no apologies— he was passionate and fierce and proud, and true—but the next morning he would wake up feeling that he had made a fool of himself and that he had something to explain.

He "knew," for example, that freight cars were beautiful; that a spur of rusty box cars on a siding, curving off somewhere into a flat of barren pine and clay, was as beautiful as anything could be, as anything has ever been. He knew all the depths and levels of it, all the time evocations of it—but he couldn't say so. He hadn't found the language for it. He had even been told, by implication, that it wasn't so. That was where his "education" came in. It wasn't really that his teachers had told him that a freight car was not beautiful. But they had told him that Keats, Shelley, the Taj Mahal, the Acropolis, Westminster Abbey, the Louvre, the Isles of Greece, were beautiful. And they had told it to him so often and in such a way that he not only thought it true—which it is—but that these things were everything that beauty is.

When the freight car occurred to him, he had to argue to himself about it, and then argue with other people about it. Then he would become ashamed of himself and shut up. Like everyone who is a poet, and there really are a lot of poets, he was an immensely practical young man, and suddenly he would get tired of arguing, because he knew there was not anything to argue about, and then shut up. Furthermore, he had the sense that some people who *said* that a freight car was beautiful were fake æsthetes—which they were. It was a time when smart people were going around saying that ragtime or jazz music were the real American rhythms, and likening them to Beethoven and Wagner; that the comic strip was a true expression of American art; that Charlie Chaplin was really a great tragedian and ought to play Hamlet; that advertising was the only "real" American literature.

The fellow who went around saying that advertising was the only "real" American literature might be either one of two things: a successful writer or an unsuccessful one. If he was a successful one—a writer, say, of detective stories which had had an enormous vogue and had earned the man a fortune—he had argued himself into believing that he was really a great novelist. But "the times were out of joint," and the reason he did not write great novels was because it was impossible to write great novels in such times: "the genius of America was in advertising," and since there was no use doing anything else, the whole spirit of the times being against it, he had become a writer of successful detective stories.

That was one form of it. Then there was the fellow who was not quite good enough to be good at anything. He sneered at the writer of detective stories, but he also sneered at Dreiser and O'Neill and Sinclair Lewis and Edwin Arlington Robinson. He was a poet, or a novelist, or a critic, or a member of Professor George Pierce Baker's playwriting class at Harvard or at Yale, but nothing that he did came off; and the reason that it didn't was because "the times were out of joint," and "the real literature of America was in the advertising in popular magazines." So this fellow sneered at everything from a superior elevation. Dreiser, Lewis, Robinson, O'Neill, and the advertising in the *Saturday Evening Post* were all the same, really—"*Plus ça change, plus c'est la même chose.*"

At that time in George Webber's life, amidst all the nonsense, confusion, torture, and brute unhappiness that he was subject to, he was for the first time trying to articulate something immense and terrible in life which he had always known and felt, and for which he thought he must now find some speech, or drown. And yet it seemed that this thing which was so immense could have no speech, that it burst through the limits of all recorded languages, and that it could never be rounded, uttered, and contained in words. It was a feeling that every man on earth held in the little tenement of his flesh and spirit the whole ocean of human life and time, and that he must drown in this ocean unless, somehow, he "got it out of him"—unless he mapped and charted it, fenced and defined it, plumbed it to its uttermost depths, and knew it to its smallest pockets upon the remotest shores of the everlasting earth.

The greater part of his life had been lived in the confines of a little town, but he now saw plainly that he could never live long enough to tell the thousandth part of all he knew about its life and people—a knowledge that was not merely encyclopædic and mountainous, but that was as congruent and single as one gigantic plant, which was alive in all its million roots and branches, and must be shown so, or not at all. It now seemed that what had been given to him was not only his father's sturdy, solid power, but that all the million fibrous arms and branches of his Joyner blood, which had sprung from the everlasting earth, growing, thrusting, pushing, spreading out its octopal feelers in unceasing weft and thread, were also rooted into the structure of his life; and that this dark inheritance of blood and passion, of fixity and unceasing variousness, of wandering forever and the earth again—this strange legacy which by its power and richness might have saved him and given him the best life anyone had ever had—had now burst from the limits of his control and was going to tear him to pieces, limb from limb, like maddened horses running wild.

His memory, which had always been encyclopædic, so that he could remember in their minutest details and from his earliest years of childhood all that people had said and done and all that had happened at any moment, had been so whetted, sharpened, and enlarged by his years away from home, so stimulated by his reading and by a terrible hunger that drove him through a thousand streets, staring with madman's eyes into a million faces, listening with madman's ears to a million words, that it had now become, instead of a mighty weapon with a blade of razored sharpness which he might use magnificently to his life's advantage, a gigantic, fibrous, million-rooted plant of time which spread and flowered like a cancerous growth. It mastered his will and fed on his entrails until he lost the power to act and lay inert in its tentacles, while all his soaring projects came to naught, and hours, days, months, and years flowed by him like a dream.

The year before he had grown sick and weary in his heart of his clumsy attempts to write. He began to see that nothing he wrote had anything to do with what he had seen and felt and known, and that he might as well try to pour the ocean in a sanitary drinking cup as try to put the full and palpable integument of human life into such efforts. So now, for the first time, he tried to set down a fractional part of his vision of the earth. For some time, a vague but powerful unrest had urged him on to the attempt, and now, without knowledge or experience, but with some uneasy premonition of the terrific labor he was attempting to accomplish, he began—deliberately choosing a subject that seemed so modest and limited in its proportions that he thought he could complete it with the greatest ease. The subject he chose for his first effort was a boy's vision of life over a ten-month period between his twelfth and thirteenth year, and the title was, "The End of the Golden Weather."

By this title he meant to describe that change in the *color* of life which every child has known—the change from the enchanted light and weather of his soul, the full golden light, the magic green and gold in which he sees the earth in childhood, and, far away, the fabulous vision of the golden city, blazing forever in his vision and at the end of all his dreams, in whose enchanted streets he thinks that he shall some day walk a conqueror, a proud and honored figure in a life more glorious, fortunate, and happy than any he has ever known. In this brief story he prepared to tell how, at this period in a child's life, this strange and magic light—this "golden weather"—begins to change, and, for the first time, some of the troubling weathers of a man's soul are revealed to him; and how, for the first time, he becomes aware of the thousand changing visages of time; and how his clear and radiant legend of the earth is, for the first time, touched with confusion and bewilderment, menaced by terrible depths and enigmas of experience he has never known before. He wanted to tell the story of this year exactly as he remembered it, and with all the things and people he had known that year.

Accordingly, he began to write about it, starting the story at three o'clock in the afternoon in the yard before his uncle's house.

Jerry Alsop was changing. More than any of the others, he had plunged into the sea of life. As he said, his "sphere had widened," and now it was ready to burst through the little clinging circle he had so carefully built up around himself. His disciples hung on for a time, then, one by one, like leaves straying in a swirling flood, were swept away. And Alsop let them go. The truth was that the constant devotions of the old fellowship had begun to bore him. He was heard to mutter that he was getting "damned tired of having the place used as a clubhouse all the time."

There was a final scene with Monk. The younger man's first story had been rejected, and a word that Monk had spoken had come back to Alsop and stung him. It was some bitter, youthful word, spoken with youth's wounded vanity, about "the artist" in a "world of Philistines," and of the artist's "right." The foolish word, just salve to wounded pride, with its arrogant implication of superiority, infuriated Alsop. But, characteristically, when he saw Monk again he did not make the direct attack. Instead, he referred venomously to a book that he had been reading by one of the æsthetic critics of the period, putting into his mouth, exaggerating and destroying, the foolish words of wounded vanity and youth.

" 'I'm an artist,' " Alsop sneered. " 'I'm better than these God-damned other people. Philistines can't understand me.' "

He laughed venomously, and then, his pale eyes narrowed into slits, he said:

"Do you know what he is? He's just an ass! A man who'd talk that way is just a *complete* ass! 'An artist!' " and again he laughed sneeringly, "My God!"

His eyes were really now so full of rancor and injured self-esteem that the other knew it was the end. There was no further warmth of friendship here. He, too, felt a cold fury: envenomed words rose to his lips, he wanted to sneer, to stab, to ridicule and mock as Alsop had; a poison of cold anger sweltered in his heart, but when he got up his lips were cold and dry, he said stiffly:

"Good-bye."

And he went out from that basement room forever.

Alsop said nothing, but sat there with a pale smile on his face, a feeling of bitter triumph gnawing at his heart that was its own reprisal. As the lost disciple closed the door, he heard for the last time the jeering words:

"'An artist!' Jesus Christ!"—then the choking fury of his belly-laugh.

Jim Randolph felt for the four youths who lived with him a paternal affection. He governed them, he directed them, as a father might direct the destinies of his own sons. He was always the first one up in the morning. He needed very little sleep, no matter how late he had been up the night before. Four or five hours' sleep always seemed to be enough for him. He would bathe, shave, dress himself, put coffee on to boil, then he would come and wake the others up. He would stand in the doorway looking at them, smiling a little, with his powerful hands arched lightly on his hips. Then in a soft, vibrant, and strangely tender tone he would sing:

"Get up, get up, you lazy devils. Get up, get up, it's break o' day." Jim would cast his head back and laugh a little. "That's the song my father used to sing to me every morning when I was a kid way down there in Ashley County, South Carolina. . . . All right," he now said, matter-of-factly, and with a tone of quiet finality and command: "You boys get up. It's almost half-past eight. Come on, get dressed now. You've slept long enough."

They would get up then—all except Monty, who did not go to work till five o'clock in the afternoon; he was employed in a midtown hotel and didn't get home until one or two o'clock in the morning. Their governor allowed him to sleep later, and, in fact, quietly but sternly enjoined them to silence in order that Monty's rest be not disturbed.

Jim himself would be out of the place and away by eight-thirty. He was gone all day.

They ate together a great deal at the apartment. They liked the life, its community of fellowship and of comfort. It was tacitly assumed that they would gather together in the evening and formulate a program for the night. Jim, as usual, ruled the roost. They never knew what his plans were. They awaited his arrival with expectancy and sharp interest.

At six-thirty his key would rattle in the lock. He would come in, hang up his hat, and without preliminary say with authority:

"All right, boys. Dig down in your pockets, now. Everyone's chipping in with fifty cents."

"What for, for God's sake?" someone would protest.

"For the best damn steak you ever sunk yo' teeth into," Jim would say. "I saw it in the butcher shop as I came by. We're going to have a six-pound sirloin for supper tonight or I miss my guess. . . . Perce," he said, "you go to the grocery store and buy the fixings. Get us two loaves of bread, a pound of butter, and ten cents' worth of grits. We've got potatoes. . . . Monk," he said, "you get busy and peel those potatoes, and don't cut away two-thirds of 'em like you did last time. . . . I'm going to get the steak," he said, "I'll cook the steak. That nurse of mine is coming over. She said she'll make biscuits."

And, having instantly energized the evening and dispatched them on the commission of their respective duties, he went off upon his own.

They were constantly having girls in. Each of them would bring in recruits of his own discovery, and Jim, of course, knew dozens of them. God knows where he picked them up or when he found the time and opportunity to meet them, but women swarmed around him like bees around a honeycomb. He always had a new one. He brought them in singly, doubly, by squadrons, and by scores. It was a motley crew. They ranged all the way from trained nurses, for whom he seemed to have a decided flair, to shop girls and stenographers, waitresses in Childs restaurants, Irish girls from the remotest purlieus of Brooklyn, inclined to rowdy outcries in their drink, to chorines, both past and present, and the strip woman of a burlesque show.

Monk never learned where he got this last one, but she was a remarkable specimen. She was a voluptuous creature, a woman of such carnal and sensuous magnetism that she could arouse the fiercest intensity of amorous desire just by coming in a room. She was a dark, luscious kind of woman, probably of some Latin or Oriental extraction. She might have been a Jewess, or a mixture of several breeds. She pretended to be French, which was ridiculous. She spoke a kind of concocted patter of broken English, interspersed with such classic phrases as *"Oo là là," "Mais oui, monsieur," "Merci beaucoup," "Par-*

donnez-moi," and *"Toute de suite."* She had learned this jargon on the burlesque stage.

Monk went with Jim to see her play one time when she was appearing at a burlesque house on 125th Street. Her stage manner, her presence, the French phrases, and the broken speech were the same upon the stage as when she visited them. Like so many people in the theatre, she acted her part continually. Nevertheless, she was the best thing in the show. She used her patter skillfully, with sensual and voluptuous weavings of her hips, and the familiar carnal roughhouse of burlesque comedy. She came out and did her strip act while the audience roared its approval, and Jim swore softly under his breath, and, as the old ballad of Chevy Chase has it, "A vow to God made he"—a vow which, by the way, was never consummated.

She was an extraordinary person, and in the end an amazingly chaste one. She liked all the boys at the apartment and enjoyed coming there. She had them in a state of frenzy. But in the end the result was the same as if they'd been members of her burlesque audience. It was the strip act, nothing more.

Jim also had a nurse who used to come to see him all the time. His struggles with this girl were epic. There was a naked bluntness of approach and purpose in his attack. She was immensely fond of him, and, up to a certain point, immensely willing, but after that he got no further. He used to rage and fume up and down the place like a maddened tiger. He used to swear his oaths and make his vows. The others would howl with laughter at his anguish, but nothing came of it.

In the end it began to be a shoddy business. All of them except Jim began to get a little tired of it, and to feel a little ashamed and soiled by this shoddy community of carnal effort.

Their life together could not go on forever. All of them were growing up, becoming deeper in experience, more confident and knowing in the great flood of the city's life. The time was fast approaching when each, in his own way, would break loose for himself, detach himself from the fold, assert the independence of his own and separate life. And when that time came, they knew that they would all be lost to Jim.

It was a fault and weakness of his nature that he could not brook equality. He was too much the king, too kingly Southern, and too Southern for a king. It was the weakness of his strength, this taint of manhood and this faulty Southernness. He was so shaped in the heroic and romantic mold that he always had to be the leader. He needed satellites as a planet needs them. He had to be central and invincibly first in all the life of which he was a part. He had to have the praise, the worship, and the obedience of his fellows or he was lost.

And Jim was lost. The period of his fame was past. The brightness of his star had waned. He had become only a memory to those for whom he once had been the embodiment of heroic action. His contemporaries had entered life, had taken it and used it, had gone past him, had forgotten him. And Jim could not forget. He lived now in a world of bitter memory. He spoke with irony of his triumphs of the past. He spoke with resentment against those who had, he thought, deserted him. He viewed with bitter humor the exploits of the idols of the moment, the athletic heroes who were now the pampered favorites of popular applause. He waited grimly for their disillusionment, and, waiting, unable to forget the past, he hung on pitifully to the tattered remnants of his greatness, the adoration of a group of boys.

Besides themselves, he had few intimates, and certainly none with men of his own age. His fierce and wounded vanity now feared the open conflict with the world, feared association with men of his own years, with men of his own or greater capacity. He feared and hated the possibility that he might have to yield to anyone, play second fiddle, admit the superior wisdom or ability of another person. In the whole city's life he had formed only one other intimate acquaintance. This was a little man named Dexter Briggs, and Dexter, appropriately enough, was a little, amiably good-natured newspaper drunk who lacked every heroic quality of character or appearance that Jim had, and who, accordingly, adored Jim to the point of idolatry for the possession of them.

As for the four youths, the fascination of apartment life in the great city was beginning to wear off. The freedom that had seemed so thrilling and so wonderful to all of them at first now had its obvious limitations. They were not so free as they had thought. They were getting tired of a freedom which always expressed itself in the monotonous repetition of sordid entertainments, of cheap girls or easy girls, of paid women or of unpaid women, of drunk Irish girls or half-drunk Irish girls, of chorines or burlesque queens or trained nurses, of the whole soiled and shoddy business, of its degraded lack of privacy its "parties," its Saturday-night gin-drinking and love-making, its constant efforts towards the consummation of a sterile and meaningless seduction.

The rest of them were growing tired of it. There were times when they wanted to sleep and a party would be going on. There were times when they wanted privacy and there was no privacy. There were times when they were so tired and fed up with it that they wanted to clear out. They had begun to get on one another's nerves. They had begun to wrangle, to snap back, to be irritable, to rub one another the wrong way. The end had come.

Jim felt it. And this final knowledge of defeat embittered him. He felt that all of them had turned against him, and that the last remnant of his tattered fame was gone. He turned upon them. He asserted violently and profanely that the place was his, that he was the boss, that he'd run the place as he pleased, and that anyone who didn't like it could clear out. As for his shoddy girls, he got small pleasure from them now. But he had reached the point where even such poor conquests as these gave some bolstering of confidence to his lacerated pride. So the parties continued, the rabble rout of shabby women streamed in and out. He had gone over the edge now. There was no retreat.

The end came when he announced one night that he had applied for and had received an appointment from the news agency to one of its obscure posts in South America. He was bitterly, resentfully triumphant. He was going, he said, to "get out of this damn town and tell them all to go to hell." In another month or two he'd be in South America, where a man could do as he blank, blank pleased, without being watched and hindered all the time. To hell with all of it anyway! He'd lived long enough to find out one thing for himself— that most of the people who call themselves your friends are nothing but a bunch of crooked, double-crossing blank, blank, blanks, who stabbed you in the back the moment your back was turned. Well, to hell with 'em and the whole country! They could take it and ——

Bitterly he drank, and drank again.

About ten o'clock Dexter Briggs came in, already half-drunk. They drank some more together. Jim was in an ugly mood. Furiously he asserted he was going to have some girls. He demanded that some girls be found. He dispatched the others to round up the girls. But even they, the whole shabby carnival of them, had turned on Jim at last. The nurse excused herself, pleading another engagement. The burlesque woman could not be reached. The Brooklyn girls could not be found. One by one the youths made all the calls, exhausted all the possibilities. One by one they straggled back to admit dejectedly their failure.

Jim raged up and down, while Dexter Briggs sat in a drunken haze above Jim's battered-up old typewriter, picking out upon the worn keys the following threnody:

> *"The boys are here without the girls—*
> *Oh God, strike me dead!*
> *The boys are here without the girls—*
> *Oh God, strike me dead!*
> *Strike, strike, strike me dead,*
> *For the boys are here without the girls—*
> *So, God, strike me dead!"*

Having composed this masterpiece, Dexter removed it from the machine, held it up and squinted at it owlishly, and, after a preliminary belch or two, read it slowly and impressively, with deep earnestness of feeling.

Jim's answer to this effort, and to the shouts of laughter of the others, was a savage curse. He snatched the offending sheet of paper out of Dexter's hands, crumpled it up and hurled it on the floor and stamped on it, while the poet looked at him wistfully, with an expression of melancholy and slightly befuddled sorrow. Jim assailed the boys savagely. He accused them of betraying and double-crossing him. A bitter quarrel broke out all around. The room was filled with the angry clamor of their excited voices.

And while the battle raged, Dexter continued to sit there, weeping quietly. The result of this emotion was another poem, which he now began to tap out with one finger on the battered old typewriter, sobbing gently as he did so. This dirge ran reproachfully as follows:

> *"Boys, boys,*
> *Be Southern gentlemen,*
> *Do not say such things to one another,*
> *For, boys, boys,*
> *You are Southern gentlemen,*
> *Southern gentlemen, all."*

This effort, which Dexter appropriately entitled "Southern Gentlemen All," he now removed from the typewriter, and, when a lull had come in their exhausted clamor, he cleared his throat gently and read it to them with deep and melancholy feeling.

"Yes, sir," said Jim, paying no attention to Dexter. He was now standing in the middle of the floor with a gin glass in his hand, talking to himself. "Three weeks from now I'll be on my way. And I want to tell you all something—the whole damn lot of you," he went on dangerously.

"Boys, boys," said Dexter sadly, and hiccoughed.

"When I walk out that door," said Jim, "there's going to be a little sprig of mistletoe hanging on my coat-tails, and you all know what you can do about it!"

"Southern gentlemen, all," said Dexter sadly, then sorrowfully belched.

"If anyone don't like my way of doing," Jim continued, "he knows what he can do about it! He can pack up his stuff right now and cart his little tail right out of here! I'm boss here, and as long as I stay I'm going to keep on being boss! I've played football all over the South! They may not remember me now, but they knew who I was seven or eight years ago, all right!"

"Oh, for God's sake!" someone muttered. "That's all over now! We're tired hearing of it all the time! Grow up!"

Jim answered bitterly: "I've fought all over France, and I've been in every state of the Union but one, and I've had women in all of 'em, and if anyone thinks I'm going to come back here now and be dictated to by a bunch of little half-baked squirts that never got out of their own state until a year ago, I'll damn soon teach 'em they're mistaken! Yessir!" He wagged his head with drunken truculence and drank again. "I'm a better man right now—physically—" he hiccoughed slightly "—mentally——"

"Boys, boys," Dexter Briggs swam briefly out of the fog at this point and sorrowfully began, "Remember that you're Southern——"

"—and—and—morally—" cried Jim triumphantly.

"—gentlemen all," said Dexter sadly.

"—than the whole damn lot of you put together—" Jim continued fiercely.

"—so be gentlemen, boys, and remember that you're gentlemen. Always remember that—" Dexter went on morbidly.

"—so to hell with you!" cried Jim. He glared around fiercely, wildly, at them, with bloodshot eyes, his great fist knotted in his anger. "The hell with all of you!" He paused, swaying for a moment, furious, baffled, his fist knotted, not knowing what to do. "Ahhh!" he cried suddenly, high in his throat, a passionate, choking cry, "To hell with everything! To hell with all of it!" and he hurled his empty gin glass at the wall, where it shivered in a thousand fragments.

"—Southern gentlemen all," said Dexter sadly, and collapsed into his cups.

Poor Jim.

Two of them left next day. Then, singly, the others went.

So all were gone at last, one by one, each swept out into the mighty flood tide of the city's life, there to prove, to test, to find, to lose himself, as each man must—alone.

16

Alone

GEORGE WENT TO LIVE BY HIMSELF IN A LITTLE ROOM HE RENTED IN A house downtown near Fourteenth Street. Here he worked feverishly, furiously, day by day, week by week, and month by month, until another year went by—and at the end of it there was nothing done, nothing really accomplished, nothing finished, in all that plan of writing which, begun so modestly the year before, had spread and flowered like a cancerous growth until now it had engulfed him. From his childhood he could remember all that people said or did, but as he tried to set it down his memory opened up enormous vistas and associations, going from depth to limitless depth, until the simplest incident conjured up a buried continent of experience, and he was overwhelmed by a project of discovery and revelation that would have broken the strength and used up the lives of a regiment of men.

The thing that drove him on was nothing new. Even in early childhood some stern compulsion, a burning thirst to know just how things were, had made him go about a duty of observing people with such fanatical devotion that they had often looked at him resentfully, wondering what was wrong with him, or them. And in his years at college, under the same relentless drive, he had grown so mad and all-observing that he had tried to read ten thousand books, and finally had begun to stare straight through language like a man who, from the very fury of his looking, gains a superhuman intensity of vision, so that he no longer sees merely the surfaces of things but seems to look straight through a wall. A furious hunger had driven him on day after day until his eye seemed to eat into the printed page like a ravenous mouth. Words—even the words of the greatest poets—lost all the magic and the mystery they had had for him, and what the poet said seemed only a shallow and meager figuration of what he might have said, had some superhuman energy and desperation of his soul,

273

greater than any man had ever known or attempted, driven him on to empty out the content of the ocean in him.

And he had felt this even with the greatest sorcerer of words the earth has ever known. Even when he read Shakespeare, that ravenous eye of his kept eating with so desperate a hunger into the substance of his lives that they began to look grey, shabby, and almost common, as they had never done before. George had been assured that Shakespeare was a living universe, an ocean of thought whose shores touched every continent in the world, a fathomless cosmos which held in it the full and final measure of all human life. But now it did not seem to him that this was true.

Rather, as if Shakespeare himself had recognized the hopelessness of ever putting down the millionth part of what he had seen and known about this earth, or of ever giving wholly and magnificently the full content of one moment in man's life, it now seemed that his will had finally surrendered to a genius which he knew was so soaring, so far beyond the range of any other man, that it could overwhelm men with its power and magic even when its owner knew he had shirked the desperate labor of mining from his entrails the huge substance of all life he really had within him.

Thus, even in the great passage in *Macbeth* in which he speaks of time—

> . . . . *that but this blow*
> *Might be the be-all and the end-all here,*
> *But here, upon this bank and shoal of time,*
> *We'd jump the life to come. . . .*

—in this tremendous passage where he mounts from power to power, from one incredible magic to another, hurling in twenty lines at the astounded earth a treasure that would fill out the works and make the fame of a dozen lesser men—it seemed to George that Shakespeare had not yet said the thousandth part of all he knew about the terror, mystery, and strangeness of time, dark time, nor done more than sketch the lineaments of one of time's million faces, depending on the tremendous enchantments of his genius to cover the surrender of his will before a labor too great for human flesh to bear.

And now as time, grey time, wore slowly, softly, and intolerably about him, rubbing at the edges of his spirit like a great unfathomable cloud, he thought of all these things. And as he thought of them, grey time washed over him, and drowned him in the sea-depths of its unutterable horror, until he became nothing but a wretched and impotent cipher, a microscopic atom, a bloodless, eyeless grope-thing crawling on the sea-floors of the immense, without strength or power ever to know a hand's breadth of the domain in which he dwelt, and with no life except a life-in-death, a life of drowning horror, as he scuttled, headless, eyeless, blind and ignorant and groping, his way to the grey but merciful extinction of death. For, if the greatest poet that had ever lived had found the task too great for him, what could one do who had not a fraction of his power, and who could not conceal the task, as he had done, behind the enchantments of an overwhelming genius?

It was a desperate and lonely year he lived there by himself. He had come to the city with a shout of triumph and of victory in his blood, and the belief that he would conquer it, be taller and more mighty than its greatest towers. But now he knew a loneliness unutterable. Alone, he tried to hold all the hunger and madness of the earth within the limits of a little room, and beat his fists against the walls, only to hurl his body savagely into the streets again, those terrible streets that had neither pause nor curve, nor any door that he could enter.

In the blind lashings of his fury, he strove with all the sinews of his heart and spirit trying to master, to devour, and utterly to possess the great, the million-footed, the invincible and unceasing city. He almost went mad with loneliness among its million faces. His heart sank down in atomic desolation before the overwhelming vision of its immense, inhuman, and terrific architectures. A terrible thirst parched his burning throat and hunger ate into his flesh with a vulture's beak as, tortured by the thousand images of glory, love, and power which the city holds forever to a starving man, he thought that he would perish—only a hand's breadth off from love if he could span it, only a moment away from friendship if he knew it, only an inch, a door, a word away from all the glory of the earth, if he only knew the way.

Why was he so unhappy? The hills were beautiful as they had always been, the everlasting earth was still beneath his feet, and April would come back again. Yet he was wretched, tortured, and forlorn, filled with fury and unrest, doing the ill thing always when the good lay ready to his hand, choosing the way of misery, torment, waste, and madness, when joy, peace, certitude, and power were his, were his forever, if only he would take and use them for his own.

Why was he so unhappy? Suddenly he remembered the streets of noon some dozen years ago, and the solid, lonely, liquid leather shuffle of men's feet as they came home at noon to dinner; the welcoming shout of their children, the humid warmth and fragrance of the turnip greens, the sound of screen doors being slammed, and then the brooding hush and peace and full-fed apathy of noon again.

Where were they now? And where was all that ancient certitude and peace: the quietness of summer evenings, and people talking on their porches, the smell of the honeysuckles, roses, and the grapes that ripened in thick leaves above the porch, the dew-sweet freshness and repose of night, the sound of a street car stopping on the corner of the hill above them, and the lonely absence of departure that it left behind it when it had gone, far sounds and laughter, music, casual voices, all so near and far, so strange and so familiar, the huge million-noted ululation of the night, and Aunt Maw's voice droning in the darkness of the porch; finally the sound of voices going, people leaving, streets and houses settling into utter quietness; and sleep, then, sleep—the sweet, clean mercy and repose of healthful sleep—had these things vanished from the earth forever?

Why was he so unhappy? Where had it come from—this mad coil and fury of his life? It was, he knew, in everyone, not only in himself, but in people everywhere. He had seen and known it in a thousand streets, a million faces: it had become the general weather of their lives. Where had it come from—this fury of unrest and longing, driven flight and agonized return, terrific speed and smashing movement that went nowhere?

Each day they swarmed into the brutal stupefaction of a million streets, were hurled like vermin through the foul, fetid air of roaring tunnels, and swarmed up out of the earth like rats to thrust, push, claw, sweat, curse, cringe, menace, or contrive, in a furious round of dirty, futile, little efforts that got them nowhere, brought them nothing.

At night they rushed out again with the idiot and unwearied pertinacity of a race that was damned and lost, and gutted of the vital substance of its life, to seek, with a weary, frenzied, exacerbated fury, new pleasures and sensations that, when found, filled them with weariness, boredom, and horror of the spirit, and that were viler and baser than the pleasures of a dog. Yet, with this weary hopelessness of hope, this frenzied longing of despair, they would swarm back into their obscene streets of night again.

And for what? For what? To push, thrust, throng, and jostle up and down past the thousand tawdry pomps and dreary entertainments of those streets. To throng back and forth incessantly on the grimy, grey, weary pavements, filling the air with raucous jibe and jeer, and with harsh, barren laughter, from which all the blood and life of mirth and cheer, the exultant, swelling goat-cry of their youth, or the good, full guffaw of the belly-laugh, had died!

For what? For what? To drive the huge exasperation of their weary bodies, their tortured nerves, their bewildered, overladen hearts, back to those barren, furious avenues of night again, spurred on forever by this fruitless hopelessness of hope. To embrace again the painted shell of the old delusion, hurling themselves onward towards that huge, sterile shine and glitter of the night as feverishly as if some great reward of fortune, love, or living joy was waiting for them there.

And for what? For what? What was the reward of all this frenzied searching? To be shone on lividly by the lights of death, to walk with jaunty swagger and a knowing wink past all the gaudy desolations of the hot-dog, fruit-drink stands, past the blazing enticements, the trickster's finery of the eight-foot hole-in-the-wall Jew shops, and to cram their dead grey jaws in the gaudy restaurants with the lifeless husks of dead grey food. Proudly to thrust their way into the lurid maws, the dreary, impotent escapes, the feeble, half-hid nastiness of the moving picture shows, and then to thrust and swagger it upon the streets again. To know nothing, yet to look with knowing looks upon the faces of their fellow nighttime dead, to look at them with sneering lips and scornful faces, and with hard, dark, slimy eyes, and jeering tongues. Each night to see and be seen—oh, priceless triumph! —displaying the rich quality of their wit, the keen humor of their fertile minds, with such gems of repartee as:

"Jesus!"

"*Ho*-ly Chee!"

"Oh, yeah?"

"Yeah!"

"*Wich* guy?"

"*Dat* guy! Nah—not *him*! Duh *otheh* guy!"

"*Dat* guy? *Je*-sus! Is dat duh guy yuh mean?"

"Wich guy?"

"Duh guy dat said he was a friend of yours."

"A *friend* of mine! *Je*-sus! Who said he was a friend of mine?"

"He said so."

"*G'wan*! Where d'yah get dat stuff? Dat son-of-a-bitch ain't no friend of mine!"

"No?"

"No."

"Holy *Chee*!"

"*Je*-sus!"

Oh, to hurl that stony gravel of their barren tongues forever, forever, with a million million barren repetitions into the barren ears of their fellow dead men, into the livid, sterile wink of night, hating their ugly, barren lives, their guts, and the faces of their fellow dead men— hating, hating, always hating and unhappy! And then, having prowled the streets again in that ancient, fruitless, and unceasing quest, having hugged the husks of desolation to the bone, to be hurled back into their cells again, as furiously as they had come!

Oh, dear friends, is that not the abundant life of glory, power, and wild, exultant joy, the great vision of the shining and enchanted city, the fortunate and happy life, and all the heroic men and lovely women, that George Webber dreamed of finding in his youth?

Then why was he unhappy? Great God, was it beyond their power— a race that flung up ninety-story buildings in the air, and shot projectiles bearing twenty thousand men through tunnels at every moment of the day—to find a little door that he could enter? Was it beyond the power of people who had done these gigantic things to make a chair where he could sit, a table where he might be fed on food and not on lifeless husks, and a room, a room of peace, repose, and certitude, where for a little moment he could pause from all the anguish, fury, and unrest of the world around him, drawing his breath calmly for a moment without agony, weariness, and damnation of the soul!

At other times his mood would change, and he would walk the swarming streets for hours at a time and find in the crowds that thronged about him nothing but delight, the promise of some glorious adventure. At such a time he would sink himself wholly and exultantly into the city's life. The great crowds stirred him with a feeling of ecstasy and anticipation. With senses unnaturally absorptive, he drank in every detail of the mighty parade, forever alert for the pretty face and seductive figure of a woman. Every woman with a well-shaped leg, or with a strong, attractive, sexual energy in her appearance, was invested at once with the glamorous robe of beauty, wisdom, and romance which he threw around her.

He had a hundred unspoken meetings and adventures in a day. Each passed and was lost in the crowd, and the brevity of that meeting and departure pierced him with an intolerable sense of pain and joy, of triumph and of loss. Into each lovely mouth he put words of tenderness and understanding. A sales girl in a department store became eloquent and seductive with poignant and beautiful speech; the vulgar, loose mouth of an Irish waitress uttered enchanted music for him when it spoke. In these adventures of his fancy, it never occurred to him that he would have any difficulty in winning the admiration of these beauties—that he was nothing but an ungainly youth, with small features, large shoulders, legs too short, a prowling, simian look about the out-thrust head, and an incredible length of flailing arms. No: instead he cut a very handsome and heroic figure in these fantasies, and dreamed of an instant marriage of noble souls, of an immediate and tremendous seduction, ennobled by a beautiful and poetic intensity of feeling.

Sometimes, in these golden fantasies, it was a great lady who yielded herself to him—a lady rich, twenty-four or five years of age (for he could not stand them younger than he was), and widowed recently from an old man that she did not love but had been forced to marry by some bitter constraint and hard occasion dear. The circumstances of his meeting with her varied from repelling with a single annihilating blow of the fist the proffered violence of some Irish thug, to finding quite by accident in the gutter, already half obscured by the dead leaves of Autumn, a wallet or a mesh-bag containing not only ten or twenty thousand dollars in bank notes of huge denominations, but also a rope of pearls, some loose, uncut gems, an emerald of great size mounted on a ring, and a number of stocks or bonds, together with letters of the most valuable and distressing privacy. This form of meeting he preferred to any other, for, although it deprived him of heroism, it enabled him to show equivalent virtues of honesty and manly dignity. Also by means of it he could pay his way.

Thus, having picked up the bag on a lonely walk in Central Park, he would see at once the value of its contents—so huge as to make even a modest reward a substantial thing—and, thrusting it quickly into his pocket, he would go at once, though by a rather circuitous route which he had all planned out, to his room, where carefully and exactly he would itemize everything upon the back of an envelope, noting that the initials upon the clasp agreed with the name upon the visiting card he should find within.

This done, he would summon a taxicab and drive at once and at great speed to the indicated address. It would be a modest house in the East Sixties, or again it would be a large, grim pile on Fifth Avenue. He preferred the modest house, high storied, but with a narrow façade, not glaringly obtrusive, but almost gloomily mellow and dark. The furnishings would be masculine, the house still bearing the mark of its dead master's character—walnut and mahogany, with heavy, worn leather cushions on the chairs. To the right of the entrance hall would be the library, a gloomy room in walnut, completely lined up to its high ceiling with ten or fifteen thousand books save for the interstices of recessed, narrow windows.

Having arrived before the house, he would dismiss the taxicab and mount the steps. The door would be opened by a maid, a well-made girl of twenty-one or two, who obviously bathed frequently, and who wore expensive black silk stockings—which her mistress gave her—on her heavy but shapely legs. Smiling, she would usher him into the library, pausing, before she went to inform her mistress, to poke up the glowing coals in a small grate, revealing as she bent before him, the heavy white flesh of her under leg, just above the knee, where her garters of ruffled green silk (probably a gift from her mistress) furrowed deeply into the smooth column of her thigh. Then she would depart, one side of her face prettily flushed by the heat, casting him a swift and provocative glance as she went, while he grew conscious of the rhythmical undulations of her heavy breasts.

Presently he would hear the maid's low voice upstairs, and the nervous, irritable voice of another woman:

"Oh, who is it? Some young man? Tell him I can't see him today! I'm much too upset by this whole affair!"

Ablaze with fierce but righteous anger at this unhandsome return for his labor and honesty, he would stride to the foot of the stairway in time to find the maid descending, and to address her in a proud, harsh voice, not loud but almost metallic—a voice of great carrying power.

"Tell your mistress that it is imperative she give me the honor of her attendance. If I am intruding here, it is certainly against my will, and at a cost of considerable anxiety, care, and labor to myself. But I have information concerning a loss she may have sustained, which I believe may be of the greatest interest to her."

He would get no further. There would be a sharp cry above, and she would come down the stairs regardless of safety, her tense face very pale, her voice almost stricken. She would seize him so fiercely with her small, strong hands that she made a white circle around his wrists, speaking in a tone that was no more than a trembling breath:

"What is it? You must tell me at once, do you hear? Have you found it?"

Gently, soothingly, but with implacable firmness, he would answer:

"I have found something which may be your property. But so serious are the possibilities of this matter, to me, that I must ask you first of all to submit yourself to a few questions that I am going to ask you."

"Anything—anything you like!"

"You have suffered a loss. Describe that loss—the time and the place."

"I lost a silver mesh-bag two days ago between 8:20 and 8:35 in the morning, while riding in Central Park, just back of the Museum. The bag had been put in the right-hand pocket of my riding jacket; it was dislodged during my ride."

"Describe as carefully and exactly as you can the contents of the bag."

"There were $16,400 in bank notes—140 hundred dollar bills, the rest in fifties and twenties. There was also a necklace with a platinum clasp, containing ninety-one pearls of graduated size, the largest about the size of a large grape; a plain gold ring set with a diamond-shaped emerald ——"

"Of what size?"

"About the size of a lump of sugar. There were, in addition, eight Bethlehem Steel stock certificates, and, what I value most of all, several letters written by friends and business associates to my late husband, which contain matter of the most private sort."

Meanwhile he would be checking the list off, envelope in hand,

Now he would say quietly, taking the bag from his pocket and presenting it to her:

"I think you will find your property intact."

Seizing the bag with a cry, she would sink quickly upon a leather divan, opening it with trembling fingers and hastily counting through the contents. He would watch her with nervous constraint, conscious of the personal risk he took, the unanswerable suspicion that might be attached to him if everything was not there. But everything would be!

Finally looking up, her voice filled with fatigue and unutterable relief, she would say:

"Everything is here! Everything! Oh! I feel as if I had been born again!"

Bowing coldly and ironically, he would answer:

"Then, madam, you will pardon me the more willingly if I leave you now to enjoy the first happy hours of your childhood alone."

And, taking his battered but adventurous-looking old hat from a table, he would start for the door. She would follow immediately and interrupt his passage, seizing him again by the arms in her excitement:

"No, you *shall not* go yet. You shall *not* go until you tell me what your name is. What is your name? You *must* tell me your name!"

Very coldly he would answer:

"The name would not matter to you. I am not known yet. I am only a poor writer."

She would see, of course, from his ragged clothing—the same suit he was now wearing—that he was neither a wealthy nor fashionable person, but she would also see, from the great sense of style with which his frame carried these rags, as if indifferent or unconscious of them, that there was some proud royalty of nature in him that had no need of worldly dignities. She would say:

"Then, if you are a poor writer, there is one thing I can do—one very small return I can make for your splendid honesty. You must accept the reward that I have offered."

"*Reward?*" He would say in an astounded tone. "Is there a *reward?*"

"Five thousand dollars. I—I—hope—if you wouldn't mind—" she would falter, frightened by the stern frown on his forehead.

"I accept, of course," he would answer, harshly and proudly. "The service I rendered was worth it. I am not ashamed to take my wage. At any rate, it is better invested with me than it would be among a group of Irish policemen. Let me congratulate you on what you have done today for the future of art."

"I am so glad—so happy—that you'll take it—that it will be of any help to you. Won't you come to dinner tonight? I want to talk to you."

He would accept.

Before he left they would have opportunity to observe each other more closely. He would see that she was rather tall for a woman—about five feet six or seven inches, but giving the impression of being somewhat taller. She would have a heavy weight of rather blondish hair, but perhaps with a reddish tint in it, also—perhaps it would be the color of very pale amber. It would be piled compactly and heavily upon her head, so as to suggest somewhat a molten or malleable weight, and it would be innumerably various with little winking lights.

This weight would rest like a heavy coronal above a small, delicately-moulded face, remarkably but not unhealthily pale, and saved from unpleasant exoticism by the rapid and boyish daring of its movements, a smile like a flick of golden light across a small, full, incredibly sensitive mouth—a swift, twisted smile, revealing small, milk-white, but not too even teeth. The face would usually be cast in an intense, slightly humorous earnestness. Her conversation would be boyishly direct and sincere, delivered half while looking seriously at the auditor, and half with the eyes turned thoughtfully away; at the conclusion of each remark, however, the eyes, of a luminous blue-grey depth, a cat-like health and sensuousness, would steal thievishly sideways up to the face of the listener.

She would be dressed in a close-fitting blouse of knitted green silk, with pockets into which she occasionally thrust her small, brown, competent hands (unjeweled). Her breasts would not be like the slow, rich melons of the maid, but eager and compact—each springing forward lithely and passionately, their crisp and tender nozzles half defined against the silk. She would wear a short, straight skirt of blue serge; her long, graceful legs would be covered with silk hose; her small feet sheathed in velvet shoes clasped by old buckles.

Before he left, she would tell him that he must come as often as he liked—daily, if possible—to use the library: it was rarely used now, and that he might have it all to himself. He would depart, the door being closed behind him by the voluptuous and softly smiling maid.

Then, in a fever of excitement and rapt contemplation, he would walk, a furnace of energy, through the streets and up the broad promenade in the middle of Central Park. It would be a slate-colored day in late Autumn, dripping with small, cold rain, pungent with smoke, and as inchoate as Spring with unknown prophecy and indefinable hope. A few lone, wet, withered leaves would hang from bare boughs; occasionally he would burst into a bounding run, leaping high in the air and tearing with tooth or hand at some solitary leaf.

Finally, late in the afternoon, he would become conscious of delightful physical exhaustion, which, ministered by the golden wine of his fancy, could easily be translated into voluptuous ease, just as the flesh of certain fowl becomes more dainty when slightly old. Then turning towards Lexington Avenue, his face chill with beaded rain, he would take the subway to Fourteenth Street, go home to his room, enjoy the soaking luxury of a hot bath, shave, put on clean underwear, socks, shirt, and tie; and then wait with trembling limbs and a heart thudding with strong joy for the impending meeting.

Then, at half-past eight, he would present himself at her door again. The rain would fall coldly and remotely from bare branches, and from all the eaves. The first floor of the house would be dark, but behind drawn curtains the second floor would be warm with mellow light. Again the maid would open the door for him, leading him past the dark library, up the broad, carpeted stairs, where a single dim lamp was burning at the landing. He would follow, not too close, but a step or two behind, in order to watch the pleasant rhythm of her hips and the slipping back and forth of her rather tight skirt up her comely but somewhat heavy legs.

At the top of the stairs, waiting to greet him, the lady would be waiting. Taking him quickly by the hand with a warm, momentary pressure, and drawing him slightly towards her, she led the way into the living room, probably without saying a word, but with only the liquid stealth of the eyes. There would be none of that cold, remote, well-bred iciness of courtesy that chills and freezes up the warm glow of affection, such as "I'm *so* glad you could come!" or "It's *so* nice of you to come"—they would have begun almost instantly with a natural and casual intimacy, full of dignity and ease and beauty.

The boyishness of her morning garb and manner would have disappeared entirely. In unadorned but costly evening dress, of heavy, pearl-colored silk, with silver hose, and black, jeweled slippers, she would reveal an unsuspected maturity, depth of breast, and fullness of limb. Her sloping shoulders, round, firm arms, and long throat, in which a pulse would be beating slowly and warmly, in that light would be pearl-tinted, suffused, however, with a delicate bone color.

The living room would be a high, spacious room, masculine in its dimensions, but touched by her delicate taste, as the library had not been, into a room which was, although not frillishly, obviously, or offensively so, feminine.

There would be a huge divan, a chaise-longue, several large, deep chairs, luxuriously upholstered and covered with a dull, flowered pattern of old satin. A warm, bright fire of coals would be burning in a hearth of small dimensions, with a sturdy and sensible alignment of shovels, pokers, and tongs to one side, their brass very highly polished, and with no revolting antiquey-ness of pseudo-Revolutionary bed warmers. The mantel would be an unadorned piece of creamy marble; above, extending the entire distance to the ceiling, there would be an eighteenth-century French mirror, with a simple gilded border, somewhat mottled with small brown patches at the lower edges. The sole object upon the mantel would be an ornate, gilded, eighteenth-century clock, very feminine and delicate. All of the furniture would have strong but delicate proportions. There would be a table behind the divan—a round leaf of polished walnut. Scattered about its surface would be several periodicals and magazines: a copy of *The Dial, Vanity Fair*, which he might pick up without comment, tossing them back carelessly with a slight ironical lifting of the eybrows, copies of *The Century, Harper's*, and *Scribner's*, but none of *The Atlantic Monthly*. There would also be copies of *Punch*, of *Sketch, The Tatler*, or sporting and dramatic magazines, filled with pictures of hunt and chase, and many small photographs showing members of the English aristocracy, gaunt, toothy men and women, standing, talking, tailored into squares and checks with the toes of their large feet turned inwards, or caught walking, with their open mouths awry, and an arm or leg cutting angularly the air, with such legends below as, "Captain McDingle and the Lady Jessica Houndsditch caught last week enjoying a chat at the Chipping-Sodbury Shoot."

On a small table at one end of the divan there would be materials for making various kinds of cocktails and iced drinks—a rich, squat bottle of mellow rum, a bottle of Kentucky Bourbon whiskey matured for more than twenty years in oaken casks, and pungent gin, faintly nostalgic with orange bitters. There would be as well a cocktail shaker, a small bucket of cracked ice, and dishes of olives and salted almonds.

After drinking a chill and heady liquor, infused with her own certain intoxication, he would have another, his senses roused to controlled ecstasy, his brain leaping with a fiery and golden energy. Then they would go in to dinner.

The dining room, on the same floor, would be in semi-darkness, save for the golden light that bathed a round table, covered with a snowy and capacious cover, and two small, shaded lamps upon a huge buffet, gleaming with glassware, and various bottles containing whiskey, wines, liqueurs, vermouth, and rum. They would be attended at table by the maid. There would be only one other servant, the cook, a middle-aged New Hampshire woman, who had added to her native art things she had learned when the family had spent the Summer on Cape Cod, or in Paris, where the lady would have lived for several years. In the daytime there would be a man as well, who tended the furnace and did the heavier chores.

This would be all the service. The estate would not be unhappily and laboriously wealthy, extending into several millions of dollars: there would only be seven or eight hundred thousand dollars, solidly founded in tax-free bonds, yielding an annual income of twenty or twenty-five thousand, the whole intention and purpose of the fortune being total expenditure of the income for simple luxury.

The dishes would be few in number; the food would be man's food, simply and incomparably cooked. They would begin with a heavy tomato soup, the color of mahogany, or with a thick pea soup of semi-solid consistency, or with a noble dish of onion soup with a solid crust of toasted bread and cheese upon it, which she had made herself. There would be no fish, but, upon a huge silver platter, a thick sirloin or porterhouse, slightly charred and printed with the grid at the edges and center. Small pats of butter previously mixed with chopped mint and a dash of cinnamon would be dissolving visibly upon its surface. She would carve the steak into tender three-inch strips, revealing the rich, juicy, but not pasty, red of its texture. Then she would help his plate to mealy fried potatoes and tender, young boiled onions, exfoliating their delicate and pungent skins evenly at the touch of a fork. She would cover them with a rich butter sauce, touched with paprika.

There would be as well a salad—a firm heart of lettuce, or an artichoke, or, better still, crisp white endive. She would prepare the dressing in a deep mixing bowl, cutting small fragments of mint or onion into the vinegar, oil, and mustard to give it pungency. Finally, there would be deep-dish apple pie, spiced with nutmeg and cinnamon, and gummed with its own syrups along its crisped, wavy crust; this would be served with a thick hunk of yellow American cheese. They would have also a large cup of strong, fragrant coffee, with heavy cream. He would watch the cream coil through the black surface like thick smoke, changing finally into mellow brown. He would say little during the course of the meal. He would eat his food decently, but with enthusiastic relish, looking up from time to time to find her eyes fastened upon him with a subtly humorous and yet tender look.

Later, in the living room, they would sit before the fire, he in a deep upholstered chair, she on the chaise-longue, where they would have small cups of black coffee, a glass of green Chartreuse, or of Grand Marnier, and cigarettes. He would smoke fragrant, toasted, loose-drawing Lucky Strikes; she would smoke Melachrinos. From time to time she would move her limbs slightly, and her silken calves, sliding gently apart or together, would cause an audible and voluptuous friction.

There would be little other sound save the enveloping and quieting drip of rain from eaves and boughs, a brief gaseous spurt from the red coals, and the minute ticking of the little clock. From time to time he would hear the maid clearing the table in the dining room. Presently she would appear, ask if anything more was wanted, say good-night, and mount the stairs to her room on the top floor. Then they would be left alone.

They would begin to talk at first, if not with constraint, at least with some difficulty. She would speak of her education—in a convent— of her life abroad, of stupid and greedy parents, now dead, of her great devotion to an aunt, a wise and kindly woman, her only friend against her family in her difficult youth, and of her marriage at twenty to a man in his late forties, good, devoted, but vacant of any interest for her. He had died the year before.

Then she would ask him about his life, his home, his childhood, his age, and his ambition. Then he would talk, at first in short spurts and rushes. At length, language bursting like a torrent at the gates of speech, he would make a passionate avowal of what he had done, believed, felt, loved, hated, and desired, of all he wanted to do and be. Then he would light another cigarette, get up restlessly before the fire, sit down again beside her on the chaise-longue, and take her hand in a natural and casual way, at which she would give a responsive squeeze to his. Then, throwing his cigarette into the grate, he would put his arms around her quite naturally and easily, and kiss her, first for about forty seconds upon the mouth, then in a circle upon the cheeks, eyes, forehead, nose, chin, and throat, about the place where the pulse was beating. After this, he would gently insinuate his hand into her breasts, beginning near the deep and fragrant channel that parted them. Meanwhile, she would ruffle his hair gently and stroke his face with her delicate fingers. Their passion would have them chained in a silent drunkenness; she would submit to every action of his embrace without thought of resistance.

Lying beside her now, wound in her long arms, he would pass his hand along her silken, swelling hips, down the silken seam of her calf, and gently up her thigh below her skirt, lingering for a moment upon the tender, heavy flesh of her under leg. Then he would loosen one breast over the neck of her gown, holding its tender weight and teat gently and lovingly in one hand. The nipples of her firm breasts would not be leathery, stained brown, and flaccid, like those of a woman who has borne children; they would end briefly in a tender pink bud, as did those of the ladies in old French paintings—those of Boucher, for example.

Then he would lift her arms, observing the delicate silken whorls and screws of blonde hair in the arm pits. He would kiss and perhaps bite her tender shoulder haunch, and smell the pungent but not unpleasant odor, already slightly moist with passion. And this odor of an erotic female would have neither the rank stench of a coarse-bodied woman, nor some impossible and inhuman bouquet, disgusting to a healthy taste. It would be delicately vulgar: the odor of a healthy woman and a fine lady, who has not only been housed, clothed, fed, and attended with the simple best, but has been derived from ancestral loins similarly nourished, so that now the marrow of her bones, the substance of her flesh, the quality of her blood, the perspiration of her skin, the liquor of her tongue, the moulding of her limbs—all the delicate joinings and bindings of ligament and muscle, and the cementing jellies, the whole incorporate loveliness of her body—were of rarer, subtler, and more golden stuff than would be found elsewhere the world over.

And lying thus, warmed by the silent, glowing coals, he would perform on her the glorious act of love. He would dedicate to her the full service of his love and energy, and find upon her mouth double oblivion.

Later, reviving slowly, he would lie in her embrace, his head heavily sunk upon her neck, feel the slow, unsteady respiration of her breast, and hear, his senses somewhat drugged, the faint, incessant beating of the rain.

And he would stay with her that night, and on many nights thereafter. He would come to her in the darkness, softly and quietly, although there was no need for silence, conscious that in the dark there was waiting a central energy of life and beauty; in the darkness they would listen to the million skipping feet of rain.

Shortly after this night, he would come and live with her in the house. This would be all right because he would insist on paying for his board. He would pay, against all protests, fifteen dollars a week, saying:

"This is all I can afford—this is what I would pay elsewhere. I could not eat and drink and sleep as I do here, but I could live. Therefore, take it!"

His days would be spent in the library. There he would do stupendous quantities of reading, going voraciously and completely through those things he desired most to know, but effecting combinations, mélanges, woven fabrics of many other books, keeping a piled circle about him and tearing chunks hungrily from several at random.

The library would be based solidly, first, on five or six thousand volumes, which would cover excellently but not minutely the range of English and American literature. There would be standard editions of Thackeray, the Cruikshank and Phiz Dickenses, Meredith, James, Sir Walter Scott, and so on. In addition to the well-known literature of the Elizabethans, such as Shakespeare, the handy Mermaid collection of the dramatists, and the even more condensed anthologies with Jonson's *Volpone, The Alchemist,* and *Bartholomew Fair,* Dekker's *Shoemaker's Holiday,* Chapman's *Bussy d'Ambois,* there would be several hundred of the lesser-known plays, bad, silly, and formless as they were, but filled with the bawdy, beautiful, and turbulent speech of that time.

There would be prose pamphlets, such as the romances after Bandello of Robert Greene, the dramatist, or his quarrel with Gabriel Harvey, or his confessions, Dekker's *Guls Horne-booke,* the remnant of Jonson's *Sad Shepherd*, his *Underwoods*. There would be such books as Coleridge's *Anima Poetae*, the *Biographia Literaria*, *The Table Talk of S. T. C.*, and the sermons of the Puritan divines, particularly of Jonathan Edwards. There would be books of voyages, Hakluyt, Purchas, Bartram's *Travels in North America*.

And there would be facsimile reproductions of all the scientific manuscripts of Leonardo da Vinci, the great *Codice Atlantico*, written backwards and reversed across the page, scribbled with hundreds of drawings, including his flying machines, canals, catapults, fire towers, spiral staircases, anatomical dissections of human bodies, diagrams of the act of copulation while standing erect, researches in the movement of waves, fossilized remains, sea shells on a mountain side, notes on the enormous antiquity of the world, the leafless and blasted age of the earth which he put in the background of his paintings—as he did in Mona Lisa. With the aid of mirrors and of Italian grammars and dictionaries, he would spell out the words and translate them, using as a guide the partial deciphering already made by a German. Then, in his spare moments between writing novels, he would show how Leonardo regarded painting only as a means of support for his investigation into all movement, all life, and was only incidentally an artist and an engineer, and how what he was really doing was tracing with a giant's brush the map of the universe, showing the possibility of Man becoming God.

There would also be books of anatomical drawings, besides those of Leonardo, of the fifteenth and sixteenth centuries, showing ladies lying on divans, gazing wistfully through their open bellies at their entrails, and maps out of the medieval geographers, compounded of scraps of fact, hypothesis, and wild imaginings, with the different quarters of the sea peopled by various monsters, some without heads, but with a single eye and with a mouth between the shoulders.

Then there would be some of those books that Coleridge "was deep in" at the time he wrote *The Ancient Mariner*, such as Iamblichus, Porphyry, Plotinus, Josephus, Jeremy Taylor, "the English Metaphysicum"—the whole school of the neoplatonists; all the works that could be collected on the histories of demons, witches, fairies, elves, gnomes, witches' sabbaths, black magic, alchemy, spirits—all the Elizabethans had to say about it, particularly Reginald Scott; and all the works of Roger Bacon; all legends and books of customs and superstition whatever, and works of quaint and learned lore, Burton's

Anatomy of Melancholy, Frazer's *Golden Bough, The Encyclopædia Britannica,* in which, when he was tired of other reading, he could plunge luxuriously—picking out first the plums, such as Stevenson on Bérenger, or Theodore Watts-Dunton on poetry, or Carlyle, if any of him was left, on various things, or Swinburne on Keats, Chapman, Congreve, Webster, Beaumont and Fletcher.

He would have the *Magnalia* of Cotton Mather, the *Voyages of Dr. Syntax,* with illustrations, Surtees' sporting novels. He would have the complete works of Fielding, Smollett, Sterne, and Richardson, and everything of Daniel Defoe's he could lay his hands on. He would have the entire corpus of Greek and Latin literature, so far as it might be obtained in Loeb's library and in the coffee-colored india paper Oxford classical texts, with footnotes and introduction all in Latin, as well as cross-references to all the manuscripts. And he would have several editions each of the *Carmina* of Catullus (with Lamb's translations and settings to verse); Plato, with Jowett's great rendering— in particular, of the *Apology* and the *Phaedo;* the histories of Herodotus, and in general all lying and entertaining histories and voyages whatever, as Strabo, Pausanias, Froissart, Josephus, Holinshed, Marco Polo, Swift, Homer, Dante, Xenophon in his *Anabasis,* Chaucer, Sterne, Voltaire in his voyage to England, *With Stanley in Africa,* Baron Munchausen.

There would be as well the Oxford and Cambridge University texts of the poets, with other editions when lacking for men like Donne, Crashaw, Herbert, Carew, Herrick, Prior. And in the drama there would be several hundred volumes besides the Elizabethans, including everyone from the early Greeks to the liturgical plays of the Middle Ages, to the great periods in France, Germany, Spain, Italy, Scandinavia, Russia, including all newer dramatists of the art theatre— Ibsen, Shaw, Chekhov, Benavente, Molnar, Toller, Wedekind, the Irish, Pirandello, O'Neill, Sardou, Romains, including others from the Bulgarian, Peruvian, and Lithuanian never heard of. There would also be complete bound editions of *Punch, Blackwood's, Harper's Weekly, L'Illustration, The Police Gazette, The Literary Digest,* and *Frank Leslie's Illustrated Weekly.*

Walled by these noble, life-giving books, he would work furiously throughout the day, drawing sustenance and courage, when not reading them, from their presence. Here in the midst of life, but of life flowing in regular and tranquil patterns, he could make his rapid and violent sorties into the world, retiring when exhausted by its tumult and fury to this established place.

And at night again, he would dine with rich hunger and thirst, and, through the hours of darkness, lie in the restorative arms of his beautiful mistress. And sometimes at night when the snow came muffling in its soft fall all of the noises of the earth and isolating them from all its people, they would stand in darkness, only a dying flicker of coal fire behind them, watching the transforming drift and flurry of white snow outside.

Thus, being loved and being secure, working always within a circle of comfort and belief, he would become celebrated as well. And to be loved and to be celebrated—was there more than this in life for any man?

After the success of his first book, he would travel, leaving her forever steadfast, while he drifted and wandered like a ghost around the world, coming unknown, on an unplanned journey, to some village at dusk, and finding there a peasant woman with large ox eyes. He would go everywhere, see everything, eating, drinking, and devouring his way across the earth, returning every year or so to make another book.

He would own no property save a small lodge with thirty acres of woodland, upon a lake in Maine or New Hampshire. He would not keep a motor—he would signal a taxi whenever he wanted to go anywhere. His clothing, laundry, personal attentions, and, when he was alone at the lodge, his cooking, would be cared for by a negro man, thirty-five years old, black, good-humored, loyal, and clean.

When he was himself thirty or thirty-five years old, having used up and driven out all the wild frenzy and fury in him by that time, or controlled it somehow by flinging and batting, eating and drinking and whoring his way about the world, he would return to abide always with the faithful woman, who would now be deep-breasted and steadfast like the one who waited for Peer Gynt.

And they would descend, year by year, from depth to depth in each other's spirit; they would know each other more completely than two people ever had before, and love each other better all the time. And as they grew older, they would become even younger in spirit, triumphing above all the weariness, dullness, and emptiness of youth. When he was thirty-five he would marry her, getting on her blonde and fruitful body two or three children.

He would wear her love like a most invulnerable target over his heart. She would be the heart of his desire, the well of all his passion. He would triumph over the furious welter of the days during the healing and merciful nights: he would be spent, and there would always be sanctuary for him; weary, a place of rest; sorrowful, a place of joy.

So was it with him during that year, when, for the first time and with their full strength, the elements of fury, hunger, thirst, wild hope, and savage loneliness worked like a madness in the adyts of his brain. So was it when, for the first time, he walked the furious streets of life, a manswarm atom, a nameless cipher, who in an instant could clothe his life with all the wealth and glory of the earth. So was it with him that year when he was twenty-three years old, and when he walked the pavements of the city—a beggar and a king.

Has it been otherwise with any man?

Book IV

THE MAGIC YEAR

With the last remnant of the little money he had inherited on his father's death, George Webber now went to Europe. In the fury and hunger which lashed him across the earth, he believed that he would change his soul if only he could change his skies, that peace, wisdom, certitude, and power would come to him in some strange land. But loneliness fed upon his heart forever as he scoured the earth, and he awoke one morning in a foreign land to think of home, and the hoof and the wheel came down the streets of memory again, and instantly the old wild longing to return came back to him.

So was he driven across the seas and back again. He knew strange countries, countless things and people, sucked as from an orange the juice out of new lives, new cities, new events. He worked, toiled, sweated, cursed, whored, brawled, got drunk, traveled, spent all his money—and then came back with greater fury and unrest than ever before to hurl the shoulder of his strength against the world, desiring everything, attempting much, completing little.

And forever, in this fury of his soul, this unresting frenzy of his flesh, he lived alone, thought and felt alone among the manswarm of the earth. And in these wanderings, this loneliness, he came to know, to love, to join no other person's life into his own. But now at last the time for that had come.

17

The Ship

TOWARDS SUNDOWN ON A DAY IN AUGUST 1925, A SHIP WAS APPROACHING the coast of the North American continent at her full speed of twenty knots an hour. She was the *Vesuvia*, a vessel of thirty thousand tons, of Italian registry, and this was her first voyage.

Now ships, like young men, are amorous of fame: they want to make their mark at their first encounter; they are shy and desperate under the cold eye of the world. And the *Vesuvia* was making a test run.

There had been doubt that the great ship would reach port on schedule. For five days the sea had thrust and hammered at her plates, for five days the sea had uncoiled its fury, with that mounting endlessness, that increasing savagery, that says to the sick heart: "I am the sea. I have no end or limit. There is no shore, no coast, no harbor at the end. This voyage will never finish—there is no end to weariness, to sickness, to the sea."

Since the great ship had strode calmly from the bay of Naples at night, lit by the last lights of Europe, that with the strong glint of sparkle, of bright glimmering, winked up and down the magic coasts, the seas had mounted day by day in power and tumult, until the memory of earth grew dear and incredible, as strange as a memory of life and flesh must be to spirits. A long swell from the Gulf of Lyons took the ship as she came out below Sardinia, and she lunged down upon Gibraltar with a heavy swinging motion. There was a breathing spell of peace late in the night as, steadily, on even keel, the ship bore through the straits, and people lying in their berths felt a moment's hope and joy. They thought: "Is it over? Is the sea calm at last?" But soon there was a warning hiss and foam of waters at her sides again, a big wave jarred her with a solid blow, and tons of water broke across

297

her thousand little windows. The ship steadied for a moment, trembling and still, while the long waters foamed and coiled along her sides: then slowly she swept forward into the limitless and plangent deep, heaving steadily and majestically up and down like some proud caracoling horse.

Then, for the first time, many people lying in that ship's dark hull felt the power and the terror of the sea. The ship, spruce and limber as a runner's sinew, gave lithely to the sea, creaked softly with oiled ease and suppleness, dipped and plunged gracefully with a long and powerful movement, rose and fell slowly in the sea's plangent breast. Then many men lying in their berths knew the sea for the first time: in the dark, the sea was instantly revealed to them. The experience is one that can never be imagined and never forgotten. It comes but once to the sons of earth, but wherever it comes, though they be buried in some ship's dark hold, they know that they have met the sea. For it is everything that the earth is not, and in that moment men know the earth as their mother and friend; they feel the great hull in the dark plunge down into the heaving waste, and instantly they feel the terrible presence of miles of water below them, and the limitless, howling, mutable desert of the sea around them.

The great ship, as if pressed down by some gigantic finger from the sky, plunged up and down in that living and immortal substance which gave before it, but which gave like an infinite feel of mercury, with no suggestion of defeat, giving to itself and returning to itself unmarred, without loss or change, with the terrible indifference of eternity. The great ship rose and fell upon the sinister and unrelenting swell like some frail sloop that leans into the wind. Men felt those thirty thousand tons of steel swing under them like ropes, and suddenly that great engine of the sea seemed small and lonely there, and men felt love and pity for her. Their terror of the ocean was touched with pride and joy—this ship, smelted from the enduring earth, this ship, wrought and riveted from the everlasting land, this ship, ribbed and hinged and fused and delicately balanced by the magic in the hands and heads of men, would bring them through the awful seas to safety on strange shores.

They believed in that ship, then, and suddenly they loved her. They loved her delicate, bending strength, her proud undulance that was like the stride of a proud, beautiful woman. They loved the quiet song, the healthful music, of her motor's thought; among the howling and unmeted desolation of the ocean, it was there like reason on the waters. They loved her because she filled their hearts with pride and glory: she rode there on the deep an emblem of the undying valiance, the unshaken and magnificent resolution of little man, who is so great because he is so small, who is so strong because he is so weak, who is so brave because he is so full of fear—man, that little match-flare in the darkness, man, that little, glittering candle-end of dateless time who tries to give a purpose to eternity, man, that wasting and defeated tissue who will use the last breath in his lungs, the final beating of his heart, to launch his rockets against Saturn, to flash his meanings at unmindful stars. For men are wise: they know that they are lost, they know that they are desolate and damned together; they look out upon the tumult of unending water, and they know there is no answer, and that the sea, the sea, is its own end and answer.

Then they lay paths across it, they make harbors at the end, and log their courses to them, they believe in earth and go to find it, they launch great ships, they put a purpose down upon the purposeless waste. Their greatness is a kind of folly, for with wisdom in their hearts they make merry—their sketches, books, constructions, their infinite, laborious skill, are a kind of merriment, as soldiers seize each possible moment to carouse and whore before going into battle, nor do they want to talk of death or slaughter.

The brain, the old, crafty, wearing brain, that had conceived this ship, that had, out of a fathomless knowledge of ships, foreseen her lines, given balance to her hull, gauged her weights and ten thousand interwoven proportions, was the brain of an old man dying of cancer. That subtle mind that made no error in its million calculations, that shell of eaten fibre, forever cut off now from voyages, chained to a few tottering steps and a quiet room in a small German town, had yet foreseen each movement of this ship upon the water, and had seen great waves storming at her plates. That princely craft that had shaped and launched all this now sat in a chair with rugs about its knees, and drooled porridge from its flaccid mouth, wept with a senile quaver, nagged querulously at children or servants, was pleased and happy as a baby in moments of warmth and ease, wet itself and had to be cleaned, was lost and broken, gabbling now of childhood in Silesia, again of romance with some fat, blowzy waitress of his student days at Bonn.

And yet this rotting core could lift itself out of its decaying infancy and flicker into fire and craftiness again, and make a ship!

The ship was a token of her nation's pride, a great panther of the sea, a proud, swift cat of Italy. Her engines, it is true, were Swedish. Her plates had been forged of British steel upon the Clyde. Her superstructure was the work of Scottish engineering. A German had designed her. Her plumbing was American. And all the rest of her—rich upholstery, murals, the golden chapel where Holy Mass was celebrated, the Chinese Room where one drank drinks, the Renaissance Room where one also drank drinks and smoked, the Pompeian Room where one danced, the English Grill, paneled with oak and hung with sporting prints—all of this was the product of the art of many nations, but the ship unquestionably was Italian.

She was a mighty ship. Each day the master and the crew and all the passengers measured up the record of her deeds. They exulted in her speed. They boasted of her endurance. They watched her proud undulance and her balanced rhythm in the waters. She was their darling and their joy, and they loved her. The officers walked along her decks talking in low, excited voices. Sometimes one could see them alone together, gesticulating, debating passionately, pausing in silence to observe the ship again, then continuing with more vehemence and pride than before.

And the ship plunged forward through the storm, trembling like a cat. They watched her swing and dip into the mountainous waters. They saw the smoky mother of the waves boil up across her bows and whip along the decks in sheets of spray that cut like lashes: they felt the ship pause under them, as she got ready for her plunge, or as she rose with proud and dripping head. Then a thousand tons of water smote against her plates, she shuddered like a boxer who has had a body blow, then steadied once again and plunged ahead into the mountainous welter of sea and sky that besieged her like a howling beast. There was no distance and no horizon; there was only this howling welter of sea and sky in which that ship was struggling like an alien presence—in a hell of waters that smoked and boiled, and sent her into deep valleys and rushed down upon her terribly from great heights, that poised her on the Alpine peaks of waves, then fell away below her with the speed of an express train, as if the bottom had fallen from the universe and the sea was plunging down through space. The water was thick and green, and hissing with sheets of foam; and farther off it was grey-black and cold and vicious, and the tops of waves exploded into windy white. The clouds were thick and grey and joined the sea smokily in a living, savage element.

As day followed day, and the storm mounted in violence and fury, and the great ship lengthened to its stride, meeting its first test grandly and surpassing itself, the suppressed and nervous manner of the officers was supplanted by an air of open jubilation. There were great sudden bursts of laughter among them. They began to look at the stormy sea with insolence and indifference. When questioned about the weather by the passengers, they affected a tone of cool unconcern: Oh yes, it wasn't bad; there *was* a bit of a storm on, but they only wished there was some really savage weather so that the ship could show what she could do.

And this ship was the latest of them all upon the timeless seas. She set a day, and fixed a mark on history. She was the child of all other ships that had made their dots of time and that had brought small, vivid men and all their history upon the water—the Greeks, and the Phœnician traders, the wild, blond Norsemen with their plaited hair, the hot Spaniards, the powdered Frenchmen with their wigs, and the bluff English, moving in to close and board and conquer. These men were lords and captains on the sea, and they had given mortal tongue, and meters of mortal time, to timelessness. Yes! they made strong clocks strike sweetly out upon the ocean; they took the timeless, year-less sea and put the measure of their years upon it; they said, "In such-and-such a year we made this sea our own and took her for our ship and country."

This was the ship, and she was time and life there on the ocean. If from sea-caves cold the ageless monsters of the deep had risen, the polyped squirm and women with no loins and seaweed hair, they could have read her time and destiny. She cared for none of this, for she was healthy with the life of man, and men care little for the sea-cave cold. In their few million years what do they know of the vast swarming kingdoms of the sea, or of the earth beyond their scratchings on it?

The storm had reached the peak of its fury on the fifth day out, and then subsided quickly. Next morning the sun shone full and hot, and the great ship had settled down to a gentle rocking motion.

A little before noon that day, the third-class smoking room was crowded with a noisy throng of card players, on-lookers, talkers, and pre-luncheon drinkers. At one of the tables in a corner a young man was reading a letter. What he read apparently did not please him, for he scowled morosely, stopped abruptly, and impatiently thrust the letter back into his pocket. And yet, that battered document seemed to have a gloomy fascination for him, too, for presently he took it out again, opened it, and again began to read, this time more intently, with a kind of concentrated bitterness which indicated that his former mood was now tempered by a spirit of truculent denial. And this display of hostile feeling would have seemed doubly curious to an observer had he known that the passage which most aroused the reader's ire was an apparently innocent remark about the color of the sod.

The letter had been written by his uncle. And the sentence that the young man could not quite get over, that stuck there in his craw like a distressful fish bone every time he came to it, ran as follows: "You've been over there a year, and by this time you must have found out that the wherewithall don't grow on bushes. So if you've seen enough of it, my advice to you would be to come on back home where the grass is green."

"Where the grass is green." This pastoral phrase, with all its implications, was the thing that rankled and hurt. The youth's face darkened with a look of bitter irony as he reflected that his uncle had imputed to the grass—to the American grass—the very quality in which, by comparison with its European equivalent, it was most lacking.

His uncle's phrase, he knew, was figurative. The greenness of the grass was metaphorical. And the metaphor was not wholly pastoral. For, in America—and again, his mind was touched with irony—even the greenness of the grass was reckoned in terms of its commercial value.

And that was what had hurt. That was where the hook had gone in deep.

So he sat there scowling at the letter—a young man driving through the grassless main at twenty knots an hour, truculently defiant over just *whose* grass was green.

The youth, if not the type and symbol of the period, was yet a symptom of it. He was single, twenty-four years old, American. And, if not like millions of others of his own age and circumstance, at least, like certain tens of thousands of them, he had gone forth to seek the continental Golden Fleece; and now, after a year of questing, he was coming "home" again. Therefore again, the scowl, the hard lip, and the scornful eye.

Not that, by any means, the insides of our scornful hero were so assured, so grim, so resolutely confident in their high defiance, as the young man's outer semblance might have led one to believe. He was, to tell the truth, a sullenly lonely, frightened, and unhappy young animal. His uncle's letter had advised him bluntly to come on "home." Well, he was coming "home," and the rub was there. For suddenly he realized that he had no home to come to—that almost every act of his life since his sixteenth year had been a negation of the home which he had had, an effort to escape from it, to get away from it, to create a new life of his own. And now he realized that it would be all the more impossible to return to it.

His family, he knew, was even more bewildered by his conduct than he was. Like most American families of their class, they were accustomed to judge conduct and accomplishment only in terms of its local and accepted value. And according to these standards his own behavior was absurd. He had gone to Europe. Why? They were astounded, a little awed, and also a little resentful of it. None of his people had ever "gone to Europe." Going to Europe—so now his lacerated pride gave language to their own opinion—was all very well for people who could afford it. Humph! They just wished *they* could afford to go "flying off" to Europe for a year or so. Did he think that he—or they— were millionaires? For "going to Europe" was, he knew, in their eyes an exclusive privilege of the monied class. And, although they would have resented any suggestion that they were "not as good" as anybody else, still, according to the moral complex in America, they also accepted without question that there were some things that it was moral for a rich man to do, but immoral for a poor man. "Going to Europe" was one of these.

And the knowledge that his people felt this way, and the baffled and infuriated sense that he had no reasonable argument to oppose to it— only a rankling sense of outrage and injustice which was all the stronger because his conviction that he was somehow "right" could find no articulate reason to oppose to what were, he knew, the standards of accepted fact—increased his own feeling of solemn arrogance and hostility, his aching sense of homesickness, which was acute, and which derived even more from the feeling that he had no home than from the feeling that he had one.

Here, too, he was a familiar symptom of the period—a desperately homesick wanderer returning desperately to the home he did not have, a shorn Jason, still seeking and still unassuaged, returning empty-handed with no Golden Fleece. Reviewed with the superior knowing of a later time, it is easy to deride the folly of that pilgrimage, easy to forget the merit of the quest. For the quest was really livened with the Jason touch, blazoned with the Jason fire.

For this youth, and for many others of his kind, it had not been merely a voyage of easy and corrupt escape, like those with which the rich young people sought diversion and employment for their idleness. Nor had it been like those expeditions of the eighteenth century, the celebrated "Grand Tours," with which young gentlemen of wealth rounded out their education. His pilgrimage had been a sterner and more lonely one. It had been conceived in the ecstasy of a wild and desperate hope; it had been carried on in the spirit of a desperate adventure, a fanatical exploration that had no resource of strength or of belief except its own lonely and half-tongueless faith. Not even Columbus could have dared the unknown with such desperate resolution or such silent hope, for he at least had had the company of wild adventurers, and the backing of imperial gamblers—these young men had none. Columbus, too, had had the pretext of a Northwest Passage, and he had returned with a handful of foreign earth, the roots and herbage of unknown flowers, as token that perhaps indeed there was beyond man's hemisphere the promise of another paradise.

And these? Poor, barren these—these young Columbuses of this latter time—so naked, lonely, so absurd—and with no tongue, no language of their own to meet the jabs, the scorn, the stern reproof of their own kind, or the easy scathing of a later ridicule—this uncertain, famished little crew that had been so unsure even of its own purposes, so defiant in its desperate hope, that it did not even dare to utter it—this desperate little crew had lacked even the security of its own consent, had forborne, through pride and fear, to reveal itself even to its own small company—had gone forth, each by each, in his frail scallop shell of hope, to battle stormy seas alone. to reap there in the unknown world the magic of his own discovery—there, from the leaden vacancy of foreign skies to derive the substance of his own America—and, losing home, to find anew the home that he had lost—so naked, homeless, yet not utterly forlorn—here to return, still tongueless, still unfound, and still seeking—still seeking home.

And yet not utterly forlorn. Not utterly forlorn. The shorn Jason turned into the West again. The young Columbus was sailing home again without even the clink of a golden coin in his worn pocket, and not even a hand's breadth of the earth of his America. It was a sorry figure that he cut. And yet—he was not utterly forlorn.

As the young man sat there at his table he was joined presently by another man who had just entered the smoking room, and who now, after speaking to the youth, took a seat across from him and signaled to a waiter. The newcomer was a man of thirty years or more. He was of somewhat stocky build, with reddish hair, and with a florid, fresh complexion which, although it gave him a healthy "outdoors" kind of look, also showed traces of alcoholic stimulation. He was well-dressed, and his well-cut and even fashionable costume had a kind of easy casualness that can only be achieved through long custom and through association with the most expensive tailors. He might perhaps be best described as a "sporting" type, the type of man one often sees in England, whose chief interest in life seems to be sport—golf, hunting, horses—and the consumption of large quantities of whiskey. By the same token, indefinably and yet unmistakably, this man belonged to the American branch of the family. One could almost call him "post-collegiate." It was not that he actually seemed to be trying to be young beyond his years. As a matter of fact, his reddish hair was already growing thin on top, he had a bald spot, and more than a suggestion of a paunch about his waist, but he seemed to be cheerfully and healthily unconcerned with either. It was only that, having presumably finished his college years, he seemed never to have graduated into responsibilities of a maturer and more serious manhood. Thus, if he was not an old college boy, he was obviously the kind of man that college boys are often attracted to. One might have inferred from looking at him that he was the kind of man who habitually, and perhaps unconsciously, associated with men somewhat younger than himself—and this inference would have been correct.

Jim Plemmons was, as a matter of fact, one of those men that one can always find on the outskirts of the more fashionable universities. He was just over thirty—a kind of hangover from one of the recent college generations—and he was still getting his living and his life out of the college life and the association of college men. Usually such men have a somewhat rusty axe to grind. Their means are devious and unsure. They are kept employed by some business or other as a kind of extra-curricular bond salesman—their value to the business presumably lying in the "contacts" they can make: their personal agreeableness, their ability to "mix," their acquaintanceship with students, and their familiarity with the more fashionable ways of student life being relied upon to grease the skids of commerce with the oil of fellowship. In this capacity they serve a varied enterprise. Some work for fashionable tailors or purveyors of men's clothing. Some sell automobiles, some tobacco. Plemmons himself was employed by a sporting goods concern.

He was skilled, as men of his type often are, in the arts of "going along" with people of superior wealth. He had, as a matter of fact, a wide and extensive acquaintanceship among the passengers in the first-class cabins, and a large part of his time since coming aboard had been spent "up there." Monk suspected he had been there now.

"Oh, here you are," said Plemmons with an air of casual discovery as he came up and dropped into a chair. He fumbled in his pocket for his pipe and an oiled tobacco pouch, and, pausing briefly, said, "What's yours?" as the steward approached the table.

Monk hesitated just a moment: "Oh—scotch and soda, I suppose."

"Two," said Plemmons briefly, and the steward departed. "I have been looking for you out on deck," said Plemmons as he stuffed his pipe and lighted it. "Where have you been all morning? I didn't see you."

"No. I slept until eleven. I just came up."

"You should have been with me," the older man remarked. "I looked for you. I thought you might like to come along."

"Why? Where have you been?"

"I went up and took a swim."

He did not say where "up" was. There was no need to. "Up" meant first-class, and for a moment the younger man felt a touch of anger at the calm assurance with which the other took possession of all the perquisites of wealth and luxury while paying only for the modest accommodations of the poor. And perhaps that moment's anger was touched with just a trace of envy, too. For the younger man perceived in Plemmons a social assurance which he himself certainly did not have, and although he more than suspected that there was a good deal of shoddy in the older man's life—a good deal of pretense for which he must inevitably pay at times at the cost of his self-respect—he found himself more than once impressed by this show of easy manners and by this assumption of monied privilege which his own pride and constraint would prevent him from taking. Moreover, to his occasional annoyance, he found himself at times responding unconsciously to Plemmons' casual manner—playing up to it, assuming himself an air of easy knowingness which he was far from feeling, and acting in a way that was false and unnatural to him. And the base of the whole thing—what he really resented—was the implied arrogance of it.

Plemmons treated his entire existence among the third-class passengers as a kind of jolly slumming expedition. Not that he acted as if he thought himself in any way superior to it. On the contrary, he took pains to make himself agreeable to everybody. He was the "life" of the table at which both of them were seated in the dining salon. His full-blooded geniality dominated the whole group, that humble and familiar little group which included an old Jew, an Italian laboring man, a German butcher, a little middle-class English woman married to an American—just an average slice of third-class humanity, the kind of people one sees everywhere, upon the streets and in the subways, plying their humble traffic across the great seas on visits home, the whole dense weft and web of plain humanity everywhere that weave the homely threads of this great earth together. All these, of course, were delighted with Plemmons. There was an air of expectancy at the table before he came: he always arrived, of course, a half-hour late, but it is likely that they would have waited for him anyway through the course of a full meal, just for the pleasure that he gave them. He represented for them all, perhaps, the embodiment of some warmer, gayer, and more care-free life—the kind of life they would themselves have liked to lead if they could have afforded it, if the hard, sheer needs of poverty, family, and employment had permitted them. Already he was a kind of semi-legendary figure among them—a type of the rich young man without a care, or, if not a rich young man, almost the same thing, a fellow who went with rich young men, who spent his money like a rich young man, who was himself so much a part of that distant and enchanted world of wealth that he felt and acted "rich."

There was no doubt about it, he was a fine fellow, generous, genial, "democratic"—just like "all the rest of us"—and yet, as anyone could see, a gentleman. So it was no wonder that the humble, hodden little gathering at his dining table always waited for him expectantly, with a sense of pleasure and of glee—always looked forward happily to his arrival a half-hour behind but four good drinks ahead. They wouldn't have missed him for the world: the whole table was on the grin as he approached. He radiated so much ruddy warmth, so much cheerful casualness, such care-free, pleasant, slightly bibulous good spirits.

But now, in spite of all these engaging qualities—or perhaps because of them—Monk was conscious of a moment's flare of quick resentment, a feeling that this genial "democracy" of his companion which most of these simple people found so charming, and into which, to his own chagrin, he felt himself betrayed when in the company of Plemmons, was at bottom a spurious and rather shoddy thing, and all of its aspects, really, so far from being what it pretended—a feeling of real fellowship and of true respect for one's fellow man—no such thing at all; but, essentially, the shabby self-indulgence of a snob.

And yet, he too was conscious of a pleasant warmth in the man's persuasive charm as Plemmons tamped his pipe and lighted it, and in a moment, puffing comfortably, said casually:

"What are you doing tonight?"

"Why—" a little puzzled, the other considered for a moment—"nothing, I suppose. . . . Of course," he grinned a little, "there's a ship's concert, isn't there? I suppose I'll go to that. Are you going?"

"Yes." Plemmons puffed vigorously for a moment until he drew his pipe into a steady glow. "As a matter of fact," he continued, "that's what I came to speak to you about. Are you going to be free?"

"Yes, of course. Why?"

"Because," said Plemmons, "I have just come down from first. And I have two friends up there." He was silent for a moment, puffing at his pipe, and then, his ruddy face suffusing with a pleasant humor, and with a twinkle in his eye, he glanced quickly at the younger man and chuckled quietly. "If I may say so—two extremely beautiful and lovely ladies. I have been telling them about you," he said, and made no further explanation, although the other wondered what the man could "tell" about him that could possibly be of any interest to two utter strangers—"and they would like very much to meet you." Again he gave no explanation to this eagerly mysterious desire, but, as if sensing the other's quick, inquiring look, he went on rapidly: "I am going up there again tonight to meet them. I told them about the ship's concert down here, and all the people, and they said they would like to come down. So if you are not doing anything, I thought you might like to come along with me." He said all this quickly, and very casually. But now he was silent for a moment, and then, looking seriously towards the younger man, he said quietly and with a note of paternal kindliness: "I think I would do it if I were you. After all, if you are trying to write, it won't hurt you to know people. And one of these women is a very fine and talented person herself, who takes a great interest in the theatre and knows all kinds of people in New York that you might like to know. I wish you would meet her and talk to her. What do you say?"

"Of course," the other said, and was instantly conscious of a thrill of pleasure and excitement as, boylike, his imagination began to build glowing pictures of the two lovely strangers he was going to meet that evening. "I'd be delighted. And it is awfully nice of you to ask me, Plemmons." And sensing the genuine kindliness of the act, he felt a warm feeling of affection and gratefulness for the other man.

"Good," said Plemmons quickly and with an air of satisfaction. "We'll go up after dinner. You don't need to dress of course," he said quickly, as if to relieve any apprehension in the other's mind. "I'm not going to. So come just as you are."

As this moment the gong rang for luncheon and the noisy groups of people at the tables began to get up and leave the room. Plemmons raised his hand and signaled to the steward:

"Two more," he said.

Shortly after half-past eight of the same evening the two young men made the venturesome expedition "up to first." The crossing of the magic line proved very simple: it was achieved merely by mounting a flight of steps that led to an upper deck, vaulting across a locked gate, and trying a door that Plemmons knew from past experience would be unlocked. The door yielded instantly: the two young men stepped quickly through and, for the younger man at least, into the precincts of another world.

The change was instant and overwhelming. Not even Alice in her magical transition through the looking glass found a transformation more astounding. It was not that the essential materials of the two worlds had changed. Both had been wrought out of the same basic substances of wood, of iron, of steel, of bolted metal. But the difference was dimensional. The effect upon the explorer from the other world was one of miraculous enlargement. The first thing that one felt was a sense of tremendous release—a sense of escape from a world that was crowded, shut-off, cluttered, and confined, into a world that opened up with an almost infinite vista of space, of width, of distance, and of freedom. They had emerged upon one of the decks of the great liner, but to the younger man it was as if they had stepped suddenly into a broad and endless avenue. There was a sense of almost silent but tremendously vital dynamic energy. After the fury of the storm, and the incessant jarring vibration that never ceased below, one had here the feeling of a world as solid and as motionless as a city street. There was almost no vibration here, and no perceptible motion of the ship.

The sense of space, of silence, and of secret and mysterious power was enhanced by the almost deserted appearance of the deck. Far away, ahead of them, a man and woman, both attired in evening dress, were pacing slowly, arm in arm. And the sight of these two distant, moving figures, the slow and graceful undulance, the satiny smoothness of the woman's lovely back, gave to the whole scene a sense of wealth, of luxury, and of proportion that nothing else on earth could do. A little page, his red cheeks shining above the double rows of brass on his jacket, moved briskly along, turned in at an entrance way, and disappeared. A young officer, with his cap set at a jaunty angle on his head, walked past, but no one seemed to notice them.

Plemmons led the way; they went along the deck and turned in at a door that entered into another world of silence, a tremendous corridor of polished wood. Here the experienced guide quickly found another flight of stairs that led up to an upper deck, and now again they stepped out upon another tremendous promenade, a promenade even more astounding in its atmosphere of space, of width, of vista, and of luxury than the one below. This promenade was glass-enclosed, which added to the impression of its wealth. More people were to be seen here, pacing, the white shirt-fronts and evening black of men, the pearl-hued nakedness of women's shoulders. And yet there were not many people—a few couples making the great promenade around the deck, a few more stretched out in their steamer chairs. Broad windows flanked beside, and through these windows one could see the interiors of tremendous rooms—great lounges and salons, and cafés as large as those one would see in a great hotel, as solid-seeming also, as luxurious. Plemmons led the way quickly and confidently back along this deck in the direction of the stern, and finding here another flight of stairs, he mounted swiftly, and presently led the way around into a small verandah-like café, covered on top but open at the end, so that one had a clear view backward out across the broad wake of the ship. Here they seated themselves at a table and ordered a drink.

In response to Plemmons' inquiry, the steward replied that most of the passengers were still at dinner. Plemmons scrawled a note and dispatched it by a page. Presently the boy returned with a message that the ladies had not yet got up from dinner, but would join them presently.

The young men sat and drank their drinks. Shortly before nine o'clock they heard steps approaching along the passageway that led to the café. Plemmons looked around quickly, then got up.

"Oh, hello, Lily," he said. "Where is Mrs. Jack?"

Then he made introductions. The young woman whom he had just greeted turned and shook hands with Monk coldly, then turned again to Plemmons. She was a woman of thirty years or more, of sensational and even formidable appearance. Perhaps not many people would have called her beautiful, but everybody certainly would have admitted that she was astoundingly handsome. She was quite tall for a woman, with big limbs and large proportions. In fact, she just escaped massiveness, but her bigness was curiously mingled with an almost fragile delicacy. Monk noticed when he shook hands with her that her hand was almost as small and slender as a little girl's, and in her manner also, which was almost repellantly sullen and aloof, he noticed something timid, almost shrinking and afraid. She had a dark and Slavic face, and a mane of dark black hair which somehow contrived to give a cloudlike, wild, and stormy look to her whole head. Her voice was fruity, and had in it also a note of protest, as if she was impatient with nearly everything—with being bored by the people she met and by the things they said to her, of being weary and impatient with almost everyone and everything. It was quite a mannered voice, as well, and by its accents suggested the mannerisms of a person who had lived in England and had aped their way of speech.

While the young woman stood there talking to Plemmons in her fruity, mannered, and half-sullen voice, they heard steps again along the passageway, this time brisker, shorter, and half running. They turned, the young woman said, "Here's Esther now," and another woman now came in.

Monk's first impression of her was of a woman of middle age, of small but energetic figure and with a very fresh, ruddy, and healthy face. If his own mental phrase at the moment could ever have been recaptured or defined, he would probably have described her simply as "a nice-looking woman," and let it go at that. And this is probably the way she would have impressed most people who saw her for the first time or who passed her on the street. Her small but business-like figure, her brisk steps, the general impression she conveyed of a healthy and energetic vitality, and her small, rosy, and good-humored face would have given anyone who saw her a pleasant feeling, a feeling of affectionate regard and interest—and nothing more. Most people would have felt pleasantly warmed by the sight of her if they had passed her on the street, but few people would have paused to look back at her a second time.

At the moment when she entered the verandah café, although she had been looking for them and knew that they had been waiting for her, her manner at seeing them was surprised and even a little bewildered. She stopped and then cried: "Oh, hello, Mr. Plemmons, *there* you are. Did I keep you waiting—hah?"

This was spoken in a rapid and even excited tone. It was evident that the words required no answer, but were rather a kind of involuntary expletive of the excitement and surprise which were apparently qualities of her personality.

Plemmons now made introductions. The woman turned to Monk and shook hands with a brief, firm grasp and a friendly look. Then she turned immediately to Plemmons with a brightly inquiring and hopeful smile, "Well, are you going to take us down to see the show—hah?"

Plemmons was a little flushed from drink and in good spirits. Banteringly, he said: "So you really think you want to see how the other half lives, do you?"—and, looking at her for a moment, laughed.

Apparently she did not understand him at first, and said "Hah?" again.

"I say," he said somewhat more pointedly, "do you think you can stand it down there with all us immigrants?"

Her response to this was very quick, spontaneous, and charming. She shrugged her shoulders, and raised her hands in a gesture of comical protest, at the same time saying with a droll solemnity: "Vell vy nod? Am I nod mine-self an immi-grunt?"

The words were not themselves very funny or witty, but her improvisation was so quick and natural that the effect of them was irresistible. She conceived the part so instantly, and threw herself into it at once with so much earnestness, like a child absorbed in its own play-acting, and finally her own delight in her performance—for immediately she was shaken by a gale of laughter, she put her handkerchief to her mouth and shrieked faintly, as if in answer to some unspoken protest—"I know but it *was* funny, wasn't it?"—and then set off again in hysterical tremors—all this was so engaging in its whole-hearted appreciation of itself that the two young men grinned, and even the sullen and smoldering face of the tall, sensational-looking woman was lighted by an unwilling laugh and she said protestingly, "Oh, Esther, honestly, you are the most—" and then broke off with a helpless shrug of defeat.

As for Plemmons, he too laughed, and then said concedingly, "Well after that I think we had all better have a drink."

And, pleasantly warmed and drawn together by the woman's quick and natural display of spontaneous humor, they all sat down at one of the tables.

From that night on, Monk was never able again to see that woman as perhaps she really was, as she must have looked to many other people, as she had even looked to him the first moment that he saw her. He was never able thereafter to see her as a matronly figure of middle age, a creature with a warm and jolly little face, a wholesome and indomitable energy for every day, a shrewd, able, and immensely talented creature of action, able to hold her own in a man's world. These things he knew or found out about her later, but this picture of her, which was perhaps the one by which the world best knew her, was gone forever.

She became the most beautiful woman that ever lived—and not in any symbolic or idealistic sense—but with all the blazing, literal, and mad concreteness of his imagination. She became the creature of incomparable loveliness to whom all the other women in the world must be compared, the creature with whose image he would for years walk the city's swarming streets, looking into the faces of every woman he passed with a feeling of disgust, muttering:

"No—no good. Bad . . . coarse . . . meager . . . thin . . . sterile. There's no one like her—no one in the whole world who can touch her!"

So did the great ship come to port at last, and there four hundred people who had been caught up in the lonely immensity of the sea for seven days left her, and were joined to the earth and men again. The familiar noises of life rang in their ears again; the great roar of the city, and of its mighty machines, by which man has striven to forget that he is brief and lost, rose comfortingly around them.

Thus they were mixed and scattered in the crowd. Their lives began their myriad weavings. Through a million dots of men and masses they were woven—some to their dwellings in the city, some on vast nets of rails and by great engines through the land.

All went their ways and met their destinies. All were lost upon the enormous land again.

But whether any found joy or wisdom there, what man knows?

18

The Letter

AMONG THE WHOLE COMPLEX OF REASONS THAT HAD BROUGHT MONK back to America was one of the most distressing practicality. He had spent all his money, and now would have to earn his living. This problem had caused him much anxiety during his year abroad. He did not know what he was fitted for, unless it was some kind of academic post, and he wanted, if possible, to stay in New York. So he had made application and submitted his qualifications to one of the large educational factories in the city. There had been much cor-respondence, and a few friends had also been active in his behalf, and, shortly before he sailed from Europe, word had come that the job was his. The School for Utility Cultures, Inc., was downtown, and when Monk got off the boat he engaged a room at a small hotel near by that would be convenient to his work. Then, with the good feeling that he was at last established and "on his own," he took the train for Libya Hill to pay his duties to Aunt Maw and Uncle Mark in the brief interim before school opened.

When he returned to New York after this short visit, the city seemed deserted. He saw no one he knew, and almost immediately the great exhilaration of return was succeeded by the old feeling of haunting homelessness, of looking for something that was not there. Everyone who has ever returned to New York after an absence must have had this feeling; it is so overwhelming and characteristic of the city's life that people feel it even when they have been away only for a month or two.

And in a way it is this very quality that makes the life of the city so wonderful and so terrible. It is the most homeless home in all the world. It is the gigantic tenement of Here Comes Everybody. And that is what makes it so strange, so cruel, so tender, and so beautiful. One belongs to New York instantly, one belongs to it as much in five minutes as in five years, and he who owns the swarming rock is not he who died on Wednesday—for he, alas, is already forgotten—but he who came to town last night.

It is such a cruel, such a loving friend. It has given to many people fleeing from the little towns, from the bigotry and meanness of a constricted life, the bounty of its flashing and passionate life, the mercy of its refuge, the hope, the thrilling inspiration of all its million promises. And it gives them its oblivion, too. It says to them: "Here I am, and I am yours; take me, use me as you will; be young and proud and beautiful here in your young might." And at the same time it tells them that they will be nothing here, no more than a grain of dust; that they can come and sweat and swink and pour into the vortex of the city's life all of the hope, the grief, the pain, the passion, and the ecstasy that youth can know, or that a single life can hold, and, so living, die here and be charioted to swift burials and at once forgot, and leave not even a print of a heel upon these swarming pavements as a sign that a blazing meteor has come to naught.

And herein lies the magic and the mystery and the wonder of the immortal city. It offers all, and yet it offers nothing. It gives to every man a home, and it is the great No Home of the earth. It invites all human drops of water to the grand oblivion of its ceaseless tides, and yet it gives to every mother's son the promise of the sea.

All this returned to Monk at once, and so possessed him with terror and fascination. Save for casual nods, a word or two now spoken in half-friendly greeting, a face or two that he had seen before, it was all as if he had never been here, never lived here, never spent two whole years of his youth, his ardor, passion, and devotion within the laneways of this monstrous honeycomb. His stunned mind praised it, and words made echoes in his ears: "I've—I've been away—and now I'm home again."

During the two weeks that he had remained in Libya Hill he found himself thinking of Esther a great deal—far more than he was willing to admit. When he had returned to New York and asked for mail at the hotel desk, he was aware of a crushing feeling of disappointment when the clerk told him there was none, and this feeling, so over-whelming that for an hour or so it left him with a sick heart, was succeeded quickly by one of fierce contempt and hard impermeability —the natural and instinctive response of youth to the disappointment into which its own romantic hope and lacerated pride have betrayed it. He told himself savagely that it did not matter. Deliberately, he now tried to take the most cynical view of the whole thing: the experience, he told himself, was nothing but the familiar one of a wealthy woman toying with a lover during the secure isolation of a voyage. Now that she was back home again, she had resumed her former life of unchallenged respectability with her family, her husband, and her friends, and now butter wouldn't melt in her mouth for quite another year until she got away upon another trip. Then, of course, there would be more romance, more promises, a whole succession of new lovers.

He was so fiercely and grievously hurt that he now told himself that he had known this all along, that this was just what he had expected. Because he felt such a rankling sense of wounded pride and personal humiliation at the knowledge of how deeply his own feelings had been involved, and of how much he had hoped and looked forward to a different sort of consummation, he now tried to convince himself that he had been completely, toughly detached from the whole thing from the beginning—that he had had his fun as she had hers and that now it was all over, it had all turned out according to prophecy, and he had nothing to regret.

With this hard resolution, he plunged into his work and tried to forget about it. For a few days, almost he succeeded. It was the beginning of the term, there were classes to meet, new names to know, new faces to learn, the whole program of new work to lay out, and for a while this kept her buried in his thoughts.

But she came back. He kept putting her away, but he found he could no more banish her out of his life than he could banish memory out of his blood. She kept coming back incessantly—the memory of her flower face, her jolly look, her voice, her laugh, the brisk movement of her small but energetic figure, the whole memory of their last night together on the ship with the promise of its half-realized embrace —all this came back to haunt his mind, to burn there in his memory with the intolerable brightness of a vision. What made the memory of all this even harder to endure was a sense of its overwhelming reality, together with the maddening sense that all of it had happened in another world—a world now lost and unapproachable forevermore.

It had all happened in that haunting other world 'twixt land and land, in that strange and fated cosmos of a ship. And now he was baffled and maddened by the sense that this world with all its beauty, loveliness, and impossible reality was lost to him forever, had been fractured like a bubble at the moment of its contact with the land; and that now—with its huge cargo of longing and unrealized desire, for all its reality, now stranger, more insubstantial than a dream—it must live forever now uncaptured, to burn, to sear, to hackle in his heart.

Well, then, he must forget it. But he could not. It kept coming back to haunt him all the time, together with that flower of a face.

The upshot of it all was that he sat down one night and wrote her a letter. It was one of those pompous, foolish, vainglorious letters that young men write, that seem so fine when they write them, and that they writhe over when they recall them later. Instead of telling the woman the truth, which was that he had missed her and thought about her and wanted earnestly to see her again, he struck a very high and mighty attitude, cleared his epistolary throat, and let the periods roll.

"Dear Mrs. Jack," he began—he all but started it "Dear Madam"— "I do not know if you remember me or not"—although he knew she would. "It has been my experience along life's way"—he liked the sound of "it has been my experience," it had a ring of mature authority and casual knowingness that he thought was quite impressive, but he went back and crossed out "along life's way" as being trite and probably sentimental. "I believe you spoke of seeing me again. If by chance you should remember me, and should ever feel inclined to see me, my address is here at this hotel." He thought this part was pretty neat: it salved his pride a bit, since it put him in the position of graciously conferring a privilege on someone who was fairly clamoring to meet him again. "However, if you do not feel inclined, it does not matter; after all, ours was a chance acquaintance of the voyage— and these things pass. . . . In a life which for the most part has been lived alone, I have learned to expect or ask for nothing. . . . Whatever else the world may say of me, I have never truckled to the mob, nor for a moment bent the pregnant hinges of the knee to flatter the vanity of the idle rich." It is hard to say just what this had to do with his desire to see this woman again, but he thought it had a fine, ringing note of proud independence—particularly the part about not truckling to the mob—so he let this stay. However, upon reëxamination, the part about bending the pregnant hinges of the knee to flatter the vanity of the idle rich seemed to him a little too harsh and pointed, so he modified this somewhat to read, "to flatter the vanity of the individual."

When he had finished this high piece of thumping rhetoric it was seventeen pages long, and as he read it over he felt a sense of vague but strong unhappiness and discontent. To inform a lady casually that he would be graciously pleased to see her again if she liked, but that if she didn't it was all one to him and didn't matter, was very well. But he felt that seventeen pages to express this casual disinterest was laying it on a bit thick. Assuredly he was not satisfied with it, for he rewrote it several times, striking out phrases here and there, condensing it, modifying some of the more truculent asperities, and trying to give the whole creation a tone of casual urbanity. The best he could finally achieve, however, was an epistle of some eleven pages, still pretty high in manner, and grimly declaratory of his resolve not to "truckle," but of a somewhat more conciliating texture than his early efforts. Having accomplished this, he sealed it, addressed it, started to drop it in the box—withdrew—began—withdrew—and wound up by thrusting the envelope morosely in his inner breast pocket and walking around with it a day or two, wearing it sullenly, so to speak, until the document was soiled and dog-eared from much use, and then, in a fit of furious self-contempt, thrusting it into a letter-box one night and banging down the lid—after which fatal and irrevocable clangor, he realized he had made a fool of himself, and wondered miserably why he had concocted this gaudy and pretending fanfaronade, when all that had been needed was plain speech.

Whereat, his darkened mind got busily to work upon this painful mystery—how he had done this thing before in letters to his family or friends, and how a man could feel so truly and yet write so false. It made the heart sink down to see how often in such ways he had been self-betrayed and had no one but himself to blame.

But, of such is youth. And he was young.

19

The Ride

THE PHONE RANG NEXT MORNING BEFORE HE WAS OUT OF BED. HE WOKE, rolled over drowsily, reached for the instrument, and, as consciousness began to dawn, grunted with the unpleasant awareness of a man who has done something the night before which he would like to forget, and which he knows he will presently remember plainly. In another moment he sat bolt upright, taut as a wire, and listening—he had heard her voice upon the phone:

"Hello! . . . Oh, hello! . . ."

Even in the electric thrill of recognition, he was conscious of a feeling of disappointment and regret. Over the phone her voice seemed sharper than he had remembered it. It was, he saw, a "city" voice, a little cracked, impatient, and a trifle shrill.

"Oh—" she said less loudly, when she was sure that she had reached him. "Hello. . . . How are you?" She seemed a little nervous now, and ill at ease, as if some memory of their last meeting had now come back to embarrass her in this plain work-of-morning style. "I got your letter," she went on quickly and a little awkwardly. "I was glad to hear from you. . . . Look!" after a brief pause, she spoke abruptly, "How'd you like to see the show tonight?"

The friendly words both reassured him and relieved him, and also gave him the vague shock of disappointment and disillusion he had felt before. He did not quite know why, but probably he had expected something more "romantic." The rather sharp voice, the sense of awkwardness and constraint, and the homely sound of "How'd you like to see the show tonight?" were not what he had expected at all.

But all the same he was overjoyed to hear from her, and he stammered out that of course he would like to see the show.

"All right, then," she said, concluding the matter rapidly, with a suggestion of relief. "Do you know where the theatre is? . . . Do you know how to get there—hah?" Before he had a chance to answer, she had gone right on with her directions, telling him what to do. "And I'll meet you there at twenty after eight. . . . I'll have a ticket for you. . . . I'll meet you there in front of the theatah"—even in his excitement he noticed her quick, neat pronunciation of the last word. Then, after quickly repeating her instructions, and, even while he was still blundering out his thanks, she said quickly, nervously, and impatiently, as if somehow eager to conclude the matter before anything more could be said: "Well, then . . . good . . . I'll be expecting you. . . . Will be nice to see you again"—and before he could say anything else, she had hung up.

That day was to be forever after printed on his memory as a day that was divided in two moments—one in the early morning, one at night. Of what happened in between he later on would have no recollection. Presumably, he got up and dressed and went about the business of the day. He met his classes and he did his work, he wove his way among the million others of the never-ending streets—but all these things, these acts, these tones and lights and weathers, all these faces, were later as blank and as unmemoried as if they never had occurred.

Curiously, he was later to remember with a poignant and haunting vividness the details of the ride he took that evening as he went to meet her.

The theatre, one of those little theatres that had their inception as a kind of work of charity, as a sort of adjunct to "settlement work" among "the poor classes," was supported largely by the endowments of wealthy females, and had grown quite celebrated in recent years. In the beginning, no doubt, its purposes had been largely humanitarian. That is to say, certain yearning sensitivenesses had banded together in a kind of cultural federation whose motto might very well have been: "They've *got* to eat cake." At the inception, there was probably a good deal of nonsense about "bringing beauty into their lives," ennobling the swarming masses of the East Side through the ballet, "the arts of the dance," "the theatre of ideas," and all the rest of the pure old neurotic æstheticism that tainted the theatre of the period.

As the years had passed, however, these aspirations had undergone a curious and ironic transformation. The ideals were much the same, but the personnel had changed. The most considerable portion of the audiences that now packed this little theatre nightly were, it is true, from the East Side, but the East Side had now moved uptown, and the struggling masses were derived from the fashionable apartment houses of that district. They arrived in glittering machines in which large areas of bare back and shirt front were visible, and although the masses still struggled, their struggles were now largely confined to getting in—"Six for tonight down front, if you've got them—and this is Mr. Mæcenas Gotrox speaking."

Yes, the Community Guild had moved uptown, although it still did business in the same old place. It had grown fashionable, and it was thriving on its blight. It still did "finer things," of course, but it did them with eye cocked on the boiled-shirt trade. And the boiled-shirt trade was ready—nay, was eager—to be eyed. Indeed, the fashionable success of the little theatre in the last year or two had been so great that it was now in the comfortable position to which the Lady Harlot always aspires when she is having a run of luck—she could pick and choose, fix her own price, and roundly sneer at all her victims even as she took their money—which is to say, that for all its fine pretenses, its cultural programs, its "brave experiments," and all the rest of it, the Painted Jade was sitting in the saddle, in the playhouse, and from the look of things the Painted Jade had come to stay. For Fashion cracked the whip, and Fashion had decreed that trips into the lower East Side were now not only in order but compulsory; there could be no dinner talk hereafter without an excursion to the lower East.

And yet a trip down to the lower East Side was always a curiously memorable and moving experience, and the young man felt this more than ever as he was driven there this evening at the appointed time. It had always seemed to him, he did not know why, the real New York—for all its poverty, its squalor, its swarming confinement, the essential New York; by all odds the richest, the most exciting, the most colorful New York that he had known. And now, upon this evening, the thrilling reality and vitality of the great East Side was revealed to him as it had never been before. The taxicab wheeled swiftly along the almost deserted pavement of lower Broadway, turned east along an intersecting street, and at length turned south again on Second Avenue. Here, it seemed that one had entered into another world. The street was, in the phrase of the city, "a little Broadway"—

"the Broadway of the whole East Side." It seemed to him that the description did not do justice to the street. If it was a Broadway, it was, he thought, a better Broadway—a Broadway with the warmth of life, the thronging sense of the community, a Broadway of a richer and a more secure humanity.

It is just this quality that makes the lower East Side of Manhattan so wonderful, and tonight he was able to define it for the first time. Suddenly he understood that this, of all the sections of the city, was the only one where the people seemed to belong, where they were "at home." Or, if it was not the only one, it was preëminently and dominantly the first. The great salmon-hued apartment houses of the fashionable uptown districts lacked humanity. One look at them— the clifflike walls of Park Avenue, the ceaseless flight of motor cars, the cheaper bourgeois gaudiness of the great façades along the Drive —brought a sense of desolation. They brought into the soul of man the heartless evocations of a ruthless world—a world of lives that had no earth in them, a world of burnished myrmidons, each with the same hard polish, the varnish of the same hard style—lives that had come from God knows where, and too often were trying to conceal the places where they did come from, and lives that were going God knows where—a rattle of dry rice along the pavement, a scamper of dead leaves along the barren ways, a handful of smooth gravel flung against a wall—oh, call it anything you like, but it was not a Place.

Place! That was the word he had needed, and now that single, simple word defined the image of his thought. The East Side was a Place—and that was the thing that made it wonderful. It was a Place that people came from, where men were born and lived and worked and sweated and died. God knows, in so many hard and different ways it was not a pleasant Place, not a lovely Place, not an easy Place in which to live. It was a Place in which there had been crime and poverty, squalor and disease, violence and filth and hate and hell and murder and oppression. It was a Place into which the rulers of the Great Land of Canaan had taken millions of the oppressed, the stricken, the suffering, and the fleeing of mankind who had been drawn hither by the hope of their own desperate need, and had here confined them, here exploited them, here betrayed them, here distilled their blood into the golden clink of profit, here compelled the creatures of their fellow flesh and blood to eat the bread of misery and to dwell in habitations that were unfit for swine.

And the East? Had it been beaten in this bloody moil? Had all the life been taken from the East? Was the great East now wrecked and riddled utterly? No—for suddenly he looked, and for the first time there "saw the East," and knew the heart of the East was invincible; and that, for some inscrutable past of irony, the masters of the East had grown barren on their stolen fat, and the East had grown stronger on the blood it bled.

It was as if, somehow, every drop of blood that ever had been shed here in the East, every drop of sweat and every cry, every step of every weary way, the whole huge and intolerable compost of poverty, violence, brutal work, and human wretchedness—yes, and every cry that was ever shouted in the East, in the crowded streets, every burst of laughter, every smile, and every song—the whole vast fellowship of need, of hardship, and of poverty that bands the stricken of the earth together with its living nerves had got into the very substance of the East, had given it a thrilling life and warmth and richness that no other Place that he had seen had had.

Call it an old saddle, worn by an old rider and sweat-cured by an old horse; call it an old shoe, a battered hat, a worn chair, the hollowed roundness of an old stone step that has been worn by seven centuries of feet—in these things you will find some of the qualities that made the East. Each drop of sweat, each drop of blood, each song, each boy's shout, each child's cry, had worked its way into the lintels of the East, had got into each dark and narrow hallway, was seasoned there into the creaking of each worn step, the sagging of each spare rail, had gotten somehow, God knows how again, into the rusty angularity of those bleak architectures in the East, the façades of those grim and grimy tenements, the very texture of the stone— yes, even the very color of the old red brick that was so thrilling, so wonderful, that just to look at it was enough to touch the heart with an electric thrill, to knot and catch the throat in a sudden clutch of nameless and unknown but powerful excitement. Yes, all of this had got into the East, and because of all of this the East had got to be a Place. And because it was a Place, the East was wonderful.

Second Avenue was swarming with its nocturnal life. The shops, the restaurants, and the stores were open; the place was charged with the real vitality of night, a vitality that is not happy but that is burning with an insatiable hope, a feeling of immediate expectancy, the overwhelming sense that the thrilling, the exciting, the wonderful thing is just there within touch, and may be grasped at any moment. In this way again, the street was most American, and it occurred to the young man that the true cleavages, differences, and separations in American life are not really those of color, race, section, or class distinction, but simply those of kind; and that in all its essential elements this street was an "American" street in its nocturnal excitement, its love of nighttime, the thrilling expectancy that night arouses in all of us, closely akin to the essential life of any American street—of a street on Saturday night in a Colorado town when the farmers, the Mexicans, the big sugar workers have come in, to life in a town in South Carolina, or in the Shenandoah Valley of Virginia, when the farmers and cotton planters have come in, or in a Piedmont mill town when the mill hands throng the street and crowd the aisles of the 5-and-10-cent stores, or of a Pennsylvania Dutch town, or of any town throughout the length and breadth of the whole country where people go "downtown" on Saturday night—expecting "it" to happen, thronging around, milling around, waiting for—nothing.

Well, this was "it." He knew it, had seen it, lived it, breathed it, felt its strange and nameless thrill, its sharp, throat-gathering excitement, like an ache there in the throat, ten thousand times, in his own small town. Yes, this was "it"—but unmistakably itself, in its own way—Saturday night here every night and all the time—but just the same "American"—the real American—with the everlasting hope in darkness that never happens but that *may* arrive. Here was the American hope, the wild, nocturnal hope, the hope that has given life to all our poetry, all our prose, all our thoughts, and all our culture—the darkness where our hope grows, out of which the whole of what we are will be conceived. The Place was simply boiling with the heart, the hope, the life of nighttime in America; and in this way—yes, even to its rusted cornices, its tenemented surfaces, its old red brick, it was American—"a damn sight more American," so he phrased it, than Park Avenue.

They turned the corner, they were in between the tenements again, they halted to a stop—and there, beside him at the corner curb, were a battered, rusty ash can, the splintered lathings of a broken box, the crackling whippings of a fire, and, sharp playing, leaping with uneven legs, a group of tough street urchins; and suddenly he sensed the sharpness in the air, the wild, dark hope, the sadness, and the knowledge that October was soon here—that October would come back again, would come again. It was all so quick, so thrilling, and so wonderfully complete—fire, crackle, flame, rusty can, curb, corner, the thrilling, fitful red of flame-lit, tenemented brick, and wild and fitful fire across the urchins' faces—the whole of it was there—and there is nothing more of it to say, except that this was never any place except America.

Meanwhile, the flame-lit urchins knotted their debate: there was a dark Italian, with his raven chief, a Jew, a little tousled Irishman, pug-nosed and freckled, lengthy in the upper lip—the small pack faces, and the hard, small bodies, compact as a ball, and tightened in debate—young, tough, a little hoarse, unmusical, but righteously in-dignant—thus the Celt:

"Dere *is* too! Dere is so! Dere *is* a chorch deh!"

"Ah-h, you're wise!"

And this was all—the shifting of the gears, and darkness, and the tenemented street again.

20

The Theatre

HE FOUND HER WAITING FOR HIM, AS SHE HAD SAID, IN FRONT OF THE theatre. It was a handsome little building, bathed in light, and the red brick, the thrilling, harsh façades, of the old tenements was all around. There was a throng of business—expensive-looking people driving up and getting out of expensive-looking cars—but for him she stood there nakedly, projected on the grey curb and into his memory. She had come out of the theatre and was waiting for him. She was coatless, hatless, and she looked like a busy person who had just come out from a place where she had been at work. She was wearing a dress of dark red silk, and on the waist and bosom it had a lot of little winking mirrors wrought into the fabric. The dress was also a little wrinkled, but somehow he liked it because it seemed to go with her. It was one of the wonderful saris which women in India wear, and which she had made into a dress. He did not know this then.

She wore small velvet shoes, with plain, square buckles of old silver. Her feet were small and beautiful, like her hands, and had a look that was like the strength of an arch of a wing. Her ankles, too, were delicate and lovely, and well-shaped. Her legs, he thought, were rather ugly. They were too thin and straight, the calves were knotted up too high. Her dress, square-cut at the neck and shoulders, revealed her warm neck; he noticed again that her neck was a little worn and had small lines and pleatings in it. Her face was ruddy and healthy-looking, but her eyes were somewhat worn and worried, as of a person who led a busy life, and whose face was marked by the responsibility of work. Her hair, which was lustrous, dark, and of a rather indefinite quality, was parted on the side, and he noticed a few coarse strands of grey in it. She was waiting for him with one foot tilted to one side, giving the impression of her delicate ankles and her rather thin, nervous-looking lower legs. She was slipping the ring rapidly on and off her finger with one hand; her whole appearance was one of waiting, of slight impatience, even of perturbation.

She greeted him as she had done that morning, in a friendly manner, and yet with a kind of nervous and uneasy haste, a businesslike matter-of-factness that showed traces of concern.

"Oh, hello," she said quickly, "I've been looking for you. It's nice to see you"—as they shook hands. "Look. Here's your ticket," she had it in a small envelope. "I got them to give it to me on the aisle. . . . It's in the back of the house, but there are some vacant seats behind it, and I thought I would come out and join you later on. . . . I've been terribly busy ever since I got back. . . . I'm afraid I'll have to be backstage until the curtain goes up, but after that I can come sit with you. . . . I hope you don't mind."

"No, of course not. You go on back to work. I'll see you later."

She walked into the small lobby of the theatre with him. There were a number of people here. Some of them were fashionably dressed, others wore ordinary clothes but had the look, he thought, of theatre intellectuals. Most of them seemed to know one another. They were gathered together in chattering groups, and as he passed he heard one man say, with an air of complete dismissing knowingness that somehow annoyed him:

"Oh, no. The play is nothing, of course. But you really ought to see the sets."

In another group he heard someone else speak with this same air of assured and casual knowingness of a play then running uptown:

"It's a rather good O'Neill. I think you might be interested."

All these remarks, with their assumption of assured authority, annoyed him past a reasonable degree. It seemed to him that such talk was false and dishonest, and against the true spirit of what the theatre should try to be; and because he had no words to answer to such cold, smart talk as this, he again felt baffled and infuriated. The remark about it's being "a rather good O'Neill" angered him because of its implied patronage; and although he himself had been skeptical and critical of the playwright, he now found himself rushing hotly to the man's defense, feeling that a genuine creative talent was being patronized and smoothly patted on the head and dismissed by some bloodless and talentless nonentity, whose only ability in life was to feed, to chew, to live upon the spirit and the life of better people than himself. This stiffened him with the feeling of cold insult and outrage, as if the attack had been made upon himself; and he found himself in a moment drawn fiercely in conflict with the people here.

This feeling of hostility was undoubtedly increased by the fact that he had approached this place and this meeting with the woman with a chip upon his shoulder. He had come here in a spirit truculently prepared, and the words and phrases he had heard flicked him rawly like a whip. They angered him because he had always thought of the theatre as a place of enchantment, a place where one might forget himself in magic. So, at any rate, it had been with him in his childhood, when "going to see the show" had been a miraculous experience. But now all of this seemed to have been lost. Everything these people did and said strove to defeat the magic and the illusion of the theatre. It seemed to him that instead of going to the theatre to watch people act, they went to act themselves, to see one another and be seen, to gather together in the lobbies before the show and between the acts, exhibiting themselves and making sophisticated and knowing remarks about the play, the acting, the scenery, and the lights. The whole place seemed to prickle and to reek with the self-consciousness of these sophisticated people. They seemed to enjoy the excitement of this unwholesome self-consciousness, to get some kind of ugly thrill and pleasure from it, but it made him writhe, gave him a feeling of naked discomfort, of being observed and criticized by unfriendly eyes and mocking tongues, of feeling sullen, sick at heart, and forlorn.

Although his imagination had fashioned or exaggerated some of this, yet at the bottom of his heart he knew he was not wholly wrong. Somehow, again and again, he was made to feel that he, and such as he, must, in a society such as this, walk forever along the cold and endless streets, and pass endless doors, none of which could ever be open to him. He saw that this group of hard and polished people, the very institution of this building, while pretending that they were for the support of such as he, were not so at all: harsh and terrible as the admission was, they were the true enemies of art and life, who would really undermine and wreck his work if he allowed them to.

The little lobby was breached, and had it been a thicket of dense cactus it could not have stuck or prickled harder in his outraged head. Mrs. Jack seemed to have many friends and acquaintances among this great gathering. She introduced him to a man with a swollen, Oriental-looking face: this was Sol Levenson, the well-known stage designer. He received the young man's greeting without a word, turning his face upon him for a moment, and then turning his attention to Mrs. Jack again. As they were entering the door, she also introduced him to a meager, emaciated little woman with a big nose and a drawn and tormented-looking face. This was Sylvia Meyerson, the director of the theatre, a woman of great wealth, whose benefactions were largely responsible for its existence. He sat down then in his appointed seat, Mrs. Jack departed, and presently the lights were darkened, and the show began.

The show was an amusing one—an intimate revue which had been a great success and had won a critical and popular esteem. But here again the corrosive fault of æsthetic enterprises such as this was manifest. The revue, instead of drawing its life from life itself, or instead of being a pungent and weighty criticism of the events of life and of society, was really just a clever parody of Broadway, of plays which had won a fashionable success. There was, for example, a satire on the Hamlet of a famous actor. Here Mrs. Jack had done good service. She had designed a flight of high, ladderlike steps similar to those down which the actor had made his appearance, and the comedian was forever going up and down these steps, cleverly satirizing the vanity of the tragedian himself.

There was another parody on a Stravinsky concert, a parody of one of O'Neill's plays, some topical songs, which were just fairly good, but had in them an appropriate note of smart satire on events and persons of the times—Coolidge, the Mayor of New York, the Queen of England—and a series of female impersonations. This last performer scored the triumph of the evening. He was apparently a great favorite of the audience, a pet-of-fashion, because they would begin to laugh even before he spoke a word, and his impersonations, which seemed to the youth to derive most of their effectiveness not from true mimicry but rather from a certain twist, an exaggeration, a kind of lewdness and vulgarity which the man contrived to give to all of his impersonations, provoked storms of applause.

Halfway through the first part of the show Mrs. Jack came in and slipped into a seat behind Monk, and remained there until the intermission. When the people arose to file up the aisles into the lobby and out into the street, she tapped him on the arm and asked him if he would not like to get up too, at the same time saying brightly: "Do you like it—hah? Are you having a good time?"

Meanwhile, people began to come up to her, to greet her, and to congratulate her on the work she had done for the revue. She seemed to have dozens of friends in the audience. It seemed to Monk that two-thirds of the people there knew her, and even those who did not know her knew about her. He could see people nudge each other and look towards her, and sometimes strangers would come up to her and introduce themselves and tell her how much they had enjoyed her work in the theatre. She was apparently a kind of celebrity, much more of one than he had dreamed, but it was very pleasant to see how she received the flattering attention that was being heaped upon her. She neither simpered with false modesty nor did she receive praise with an affectation of haughty indifference. Her response to everyone was warm and natural. She seemed to be delighted at her success, and when people came up to praise her she showed the eager pleasure and interest of a child. When several people would come to her at once, her manner was divided between happiness and eager curiosity. Her face would be rosy with pleasure at what someone had just said to her, at the same time she would have a slightly troubled and concerned look because she could not hear what someone else was saying, so that she was always turning from one person to another, bending forward in her flushed excitement and eagerness not to miss a single word of it.

To see her thus in the lobby, surrounded by a cluster of congratulating people, was one of the pleasantest things that he had ever seen, and by far the pleasantest moment he had had since he had come into the theatre. The picture of this flushed, rosy, and excited little person, surrounded by a cluster of fashionable and sophisticated-looking people, made him think of some kind of strange and lovely flower surrounded by a swarm of buzzing bees, save that this flower seemed to draw honey to itself as well as give it off. The contrast between Mrs. Jack and all these other people was so startling that for a moment he wondered by what strange trick of chance she had been thrust among them. For a moment, she seemed almost to belong to another world, a world of simple joy, of childlike faith, of sweetness and of naturalness, of innocence and morning. In this sophisticated gathering, each person stamped in his own way with the city's mark, each touched with the sickness of the nerves which seems to be a tribute that the most favorite and most gifted of the city's children pay—the hard smile and the bloodless tone, the jaded and most weary eye—she seemed to have intruded like some accidental Alice of the noon-day world, who had wandered in and out of green fields and flowery meadows, suddenly to find herself *through* the looking glass in a whole world of—mirrors. And the transition seemed to delight her. It all seemed so gay, so brilliant, so exciting, and so wonderfully good and friendly. She opened to it like a flower, she beamed and beaconed to it like an enchanted child, she couldn't seem to get enough of it, and her flushed face, her eager interest, her constant air of bewildered and yet delighted surprise, as if her wonder grew with every breathing step, as if she could no longer quite take all of it in, but was sure that each new moment would be even more enchanting than the last—it was all the happiest and most appealing contrast to this hard and polished world imaginable—and yet?

And yet. "And yet" would come back many times to rend, to battle, and to haunt him in the years to come. It was great Coleridge who a hundred years before had asked this haunting question—and could not find the answer: "But if a man should sleep and dream that he had been in heaven and on waking find within his hand a flower as a token that he really had been there—ay, and what then, what then?" New times had wrought a newer and a darker image, for if a man should sleep and dream that he had been in hell and waking find within his hand a flower as a token that he really had been there —what *then?*

The contrast, seen here for the first time in these hard mirrors of the night, was at first enchanting, but in the end incredible. Had she been born but yesterday? Had she just come from the crib with the taste of her mother's milk fresh on her lips? Was she indeed so overwhelmed with rapture at this brave new world that presently she must simply clap her little hands with joy—and ask the pretty lady there what was that stuff she had upon her lips, and why each separate, several lash upon her lids stuck out so independently—"What makes your pretty eyes so big, Grandmaw?" Or now, the funny man in the play tonight, why had they laughed so hard when he came out in woman's dress, and worked his hips, and rolled his painted eyes? —and said—in *such* a funny tone—"You *must* come over." There were so many things she simply had to find out about—and all of them so wonderful—and she did hope the lovely people wouldn't mind if she asked questions.

No, no—it was unthinkable. Such dewy innocence as that did not exist—and if it had it would have been intolerable. No, she indeed—meshed in this world, and fibered to its roots, herself adeptive to the arts of it, a brilliant thread in the web of all its dense complexity—might be superior, but could never be a stranger, to it. This was no child of morn. This rosy innocence had not been fashioned yesterday, this impelled loveliness had kept its dewy freshness not wholly by the arts of simple nature—but here surrounded, here enthroned in these strange and troubling catacombs of night, it flourished here and aped the hues of morning. How could it be believed that the legend written on these faces—the fine etching of the soul's decease, the sickness of the nerves, the bloodless subtlety of the polished words, the painful complication of these lives, themselves so much the product of the waste, the loss, the baffled, blind confusion of the times—which was so plain to him, could yet be a total mystery to her who was a part of it. With a sick heart he turned away—baffled and tormented, as he was to be so many times, by the enigma of that flower face.

She came to him presently through the crowd, still flushed with pleasure, beaming with excitement and delight, and took him with her into the strange and fascinating world backstage. This transition was accomplished simply by opening a small door. Now they were in a corridor which flanked the theatre on one side and which led back into the wings and to the stage. The corridor was filled with the performers: many of them had come out here to smoke and gossip, and the place was filled with their noisy chatter.

He noticed that most of the performers were quite young. He passed a pretty girl whom he recognized as one of the young dancers in the show. She had been charming on the stage, a quick and graceful dancer and a comedienne, also, but now the illusion of the stage was shattered. She was bedaubed with make-up and paint, he noticed that her costume was somewhat soiled, and the lashes of her eyes had been so brilliantly lighted and the lids and under surfaces so heavily darkened with some purplish substance that the whole face had a drugged and hectic look, the eyes especially having the feverish brilliance of a cocaine addict. She was surrounded by two or three young men whom he also recognized as performers. Their faces, too, were heavily rouged, which gave them the appearance of a feverish flush. They all turned to greet Mrs. Jack as she went past, and although she referred to them later as "those kids," there was in their appearance something that belied these words. Certainly, all of them were still quite young, but already they had lost a good deal of the freshness and the eager and naïve belief that is a part of youth. Monk felt powerfully that they "knew" too much—and that in knowing too much they did not know enough: had lost a good part of the knowledge that should be a part of life before they had ever had a chance to gain it through experience, and now must live blind on one side and confirmed in error.

He noticed that the girl off stage had a strong quality of sexual attraction. And this, too, potent and unmistakable now, was too wise, too shameless, and too old. The young men who had clustered around her also showed the tarnish of this corrupt experience: there was something soft and loose about their eyes, their mouths, their faces, and somehow in their rouged cheeks and lidded eyes something unnatural and unmanly. The comedian in the show had just come up and joined them. He was wearing the costume he was going to wear in the next act. It was a woman's dress, he wore a woman's wig of fluffy, carroty-looking hair, and his face, seen in this light, was hideously painted and bedaubed. His manner off stage was just the same as it was on: as he approached his companions, he flounced his skirts and wiggled his shoulders, glared at them with his lidded eyes in a gesture of lewd refinement, and said something to them in a throaty, suggestive tone that made them all laugh. As Mrs. Jack and the young man approached, he glanced up quickly at them, then murmured something out of the corners of his mouth that made them all laugh again. Aloud, however, he raised his voice and said, "Oh, hello," to Mrs. Jack in his suggestive parody and yet also in a friendly way.

"Oh, hello, Roy," she cried eagerly, then turning to the other young people with her eager smiling look of slight surprise and inquiry, she said, "What are you kids up to now—hah?"

They greeted her affectionately. It was evident they were all very fond of her. They all called her "Esther," and one of the young actors put his arm around her affectionately and called her "darling."

This familiar use of hands and bestowing of caresses filled Monk with a hot surge of anger and dislike, but Mrs. Jack did not seem to notice it at all, or, if she did, she accepted it naturally and almost unconsciously as part of the easy fellowship that existed backstage.

In fact, now when she had entered through that door into this familiar world, there had been a subtle yet a pronounced change in her whole manner. She seemed to be just as happy and as eagerly excited as before, but now her manner was more familiar and assured. If anything, she had dropped off just that veil of "party manner" which people inevitably assume in more formal social relations. Her manner now was more accustomed: this whole world back here fitted her like an old shoe. She stepped right into it, and for the first time now Monk noticed a quality in her that he was to discover came from the truest and finest source of her whole character. It was evident that she had now left the world of play and entered the world of work, and that it was the world of work that meant most to her. Her conversation now with these young people was different from what it had been with the people outside. It was a matter of quiet familiarity and complete informality, and in its simplest accent one could somehow read a deep feeling of affection and understanding. This was evident every time she spoke to any of the people who kept passing along the corridor—"Oh, hello, Ed"—"Hello, Mary"—"Sorry, was the coat all right?—Yes, it looked perfect in front." And in the way these people spoke to her, calling her "darling," "Esther," and touching her familiarly with their hands when they passed, as the others had done, there was this same feeling of quiet affection and understanding.

She introduced Monk to some of the performers. In response to his greeting, the comedian tilted his head to one side and surveyed him languourously through his lidded eyes.

The others laughed and Monk's face burned with anger and embarrassment. A moment later, when he and Mrs. Jack had gone on back into the wings, she turned to him brightly, with a smile, and said: "Well, are you enjoying it, young fellow? Do you like to meet show people—hah?"

His face was still smouldering, and he muttered, "I know, but that damn fellow——"

She looked at him startled for a moment, then she understood, and said quietly: "Oh—Roy. Yes, I know." He made no reply, and in a moment, still quietly, she went on: "I've known all these people for years. Roy—" she was silent for a moment and then added very simply: "in many ways he is a very fine person. . . . Those other kids," she went on smiling, after a brief pause, "I watched most of them grow up. A lot of them are just kids from the neighborhood here. We've trained them all."

He knew that she had intended no reproof in her quiet words, but had simply been trying to tell him something that he did not understand; and, suddenly remembering the painted faces of the young actors, he remembered also, beneath their bright, unnatural masks, something that was naked and lonely. And he was touched with pity and regret.

They had reached the wings of the stage now. Here all seemed to be action, confusion, and excited haste. He could see the scene shifters rushing across the stage, wheeling into place with amazing speed the wings of a big set. Still further back in the mysterious depths, there were thumping noises. He could hear the foreman of the stage hands shouting orders in a thick Irish tone, people were scuttling back and forth, dodging each other nimbly, jumping out of the way of big flats as they shot past. It seemed to be a case of every man for himself. For a moment he felt bewildered and confused, like a country fellow caught smack out in the middle of the four corners of a city square, not knowing where to turn, and feeling that he is about to be run down from all directions.

And yet it was a thrilling scene as well. The whole thing reminded him of a circus. In spite of the apparent disorder, he noticed that things were slipping miraculously into structural form. It was a wonderful place. It had the beauty of all great instruments, of all great engines built for fluent use. Back here, the flim-flam and flummery of the front was all forgotten. The truth of the matter was, "the illusion of the stage" did not elude him. It never had. He had never been able to fool himself into believing that the raised platform before him, with one side open, was really Mrs. Cartwright's drawing room, or that the season, as the program stated, was September. In short, "realism" in the theatre had never seemed very real to him, and it got less real all the time.

His was increasingly the type of imagination which gains in strength as it grows older because it is rooted to the earth. It was not that since his childhood he had grown disillusioned, nor that the aerial and enchanted visions of his youth had been rubbed out by the world's coarse thumb. It was now just that Pegasus no longer seemed to him to be as interesting an animal as Man-O'-War—and a railroad roundhouse was more wonderful to him than both of them. In other words, as he grew older his efforts to escape were directed *in* instead of *out*. He no longer wanted to "get away from it all," but rather to try "to get into it all"—and he felt now powerfully, as he stood there in the wings, that here again he was in contact with the incredible, the palpable, the real, the undiscovered world—which was as near to every man alive as a touch of his hand, the beat of his heart, and farther away from most men's finding than the rivers of the moon.

Mrs. Jack was now in the center of her universe. She was no longer smiling. Her manner, as she stood there in the wings, rapidly snapping the old ring on and off her finger, taking in every detail of that confused but orderly activity with an experienced eye, was serious, quietly concerned. And again he noticed a rather worn look about the woman's eyes and head that he had observed when he first saw her that evening, waiting for him on the curb.

Above her, on a kind of raised platform, one of the electricians was manipulating a big spotlight that was to do service in the next act. In her quick and intent inspection of the stage she had not seemed to notice him at all, but now she looked up quickly, and said: "No. Up." As she spoke the words, she raised her hand a little. "You want it up more."

"Like this?" he said, and raised it.

"A little more," she said, and watched. "Yes, that's better."

At this moment, the stage manager came up to her with an air of haste.

"Mrs. Jack," he said, "you've got that new backdrop too small. There is that much left," he measured quickly with his hands, "between it and the wings."

"Oh, no," she said impatiently, "there's not, either. The thing's all right. I made the measurements myself. You've got the wing too far out. I noticed it tonight. Try bringing it in a bit."

He turned and shouted to two shifters. They moved the wing in, and the scene closed up. She studied it a moment, then she and the man walked out upon the stage, stepped over a tube of insulated wiring, and turned, facing the set, in the center of the curtain. For a moment they both looked at it, she turned and said something to the man, he nodded his head curtly, but in a satisfied way, then turned away and began to give orders. Mrs. Jack came back into the wings, turned, and began to watch the stage again.

The appearance of the stage from this position—behind the proscenium—was wonderful. To one side there was a complication of great ropes that extended far up into the vaulted distance overhead. Looking up, one saw suspended a series of great drops which somehow gave a sense of being so perfectly hung in balance that they could drop or rise swiftly and without a sound. On the other side there was the dynamic complication of the switchboard. A man was manipulating the switches, keeping his eye upon the row of footlights. Mrs. Jack watched this intently for a moment: the lights brightened, softened, suffused, changed, and mixed with a magic fluency. She said:

"A little more blue, Bob—no, towards the center more—no, you've got too much now—there!" She watched them while that magic polychrome of light like a chameleon changed its qualities, and presently, "Hold it there," she said.

In a moment she turned and, smiling, touched the young man lightly on the arm and led him back into a little corridor and up a flight of stairs. Some of the performers, costumed for the new act, were clattering down the steps. All called out greetings to her as they passed, in the same casual and affectionate way he had observed before. Upstairs, there was a row of dressing rooms, and as he went by he could hear the voices of the performers, excited, busy, occasionally laughing.

They mounted another flight of stairs that led up to the third floor, and entered a large room that opened at the end of the corridor. The door was open and the room was lighted.

This was the costume room. Compared to the sharp excitement, the air of expectation and of hurried activity which he had observed in other parts of the theatre, the atmosphere of this room was quiet, subdued, and even, after so much electric tension, just vaguely melancholy. The room had in it the smell of goods and cloth; it had also the kind of gentle warmth that goes with women's work—with the hum of sewing machines, the sound of the treadle, and the quiet play of busy hands—an atmosphere that is apparently a happy one for a woman, but that is likely to be a little depressing to a man. To the youth, the room, although a large one, and on the scale of ordered enterprise, nevertheless evoked somehow an instant memory of all these other more domestic things. Long rows of costumes were hung on hooks from the walls, and on two or three long tables, such as tailors use, were strewn other garments, dresses, jackets, bits of lace or trimming, the varied evidence of work and of repair.

There were three women in the room. One, a small, plump, dark young woman, wearing glasses, was seated cross-legged at one of the tables, with a piece of cloth spread out across her knees and sewing quickly. She was a wonderfully deft and nimble-fingered person; her small, plump hands were busy as a pair of beavers, and one could see the needle flashing through the air like a flight of arrows. Facing them under a bright light and seated at a sewing machine, was a woman stitching a piece of cloth. Seated farther away, behind these two women, was a third. She also was working on a piece of goods and had a needle in her hand. She was wearing a pair of horn-rimmed spectacles, and these emphasized the lean and sunken silence of her face. Even seated as she was, engaged in homely work and somberly attired in a dress of dark material, the woman gave an impression of fastidious elegance. Perhaps this was partly due to her costume, which was so sober that a man would not even notice it, and yet so perfectly correct that he would not forget it later. But, even more, the impression was probably due to the sunken quietness of the woman's thin yet not unattractive face, the thinness of her figure which looked rather tired and yet capable of constant work, and the movement of her white and rather bony hands.

As they entered the room, the woman at the sewing machine looked up and stopped her work; the other two did not. As they approached, she smiled and called out a greeting. She was somewhat younger than Mrs. Jack, and yet, by some indefinable token, she was also an "old maid." She immediately conveyed to one, however, a sense of warmth and humor, and of kind good nature. She was certainly not pretty, but she had beautiful red hair; it was fine-spun as silk, and it had all kinds of wonderful lights in it. Her eyes were blue and seemed full of wit, of shrewdness, and of humor, and her voice had this quality also. She got up as she spoke to them, and came around her machine and shook hands with the young man. The two other women acknowledged the introduction simply by raising their heads and speaking, and then returned to their work again. The little plump one seated cross-legged at the table seemed almost sullen in the muttered brevity of her response. The other woman, whom Mrs. Jack introduced as her sister, Edith, simply looked up for a moment through her bony spectacles, regarding him with her large, somewhat sunken, and army-silent eyes, said, "How do you do," in a voice so toneless that it halted all communication, and then returned to her work again.

Mrs. Jack turned to the red-haired woman and for some moments they talked to each other about the costumes. It was evident, just by the unspoken affection and intimacy of the conversation, that they were good friends. The red-haired woman, whose name was Mary Hook, paused suddenly in her conversation, and said:

"But you two had better be getting back, hadn't you? The act has started."

They listened. All below was silent. The actors had departed for the stage. All here was now silent, too, and yet waiting. All life had for the moment been *here* withdrawn; but meanwhile, it had all concentrated *there*. Meanwhile, *here* waited and was still.

Mrs. Jack, after a startled moment, said quickly:

"Yes—oh, well then—we must go."

They hurried down the stairs, along the corridor, and out to the now-deserted lobby. When they got back into the theatre, the house was dark again, the curtain had gone up. They slipped into their seats and began to watch.

This act was better than the first. At the conclusion of each scene, Mrs. Jack leaned forward in her seat and whispered bits of information to her guest about some of the performers. One of them, a tough yet dapper little fellow, was a tap dancer who moved his legs and shot his feet out with astonishing agility, and scored a great success. She bent forward and whispered:

"That's Jimmy Haggerty. We won't be able to keep him after this season. He's going on." She did not explain what she meant by "on," there was no need to: it was evident she meant that his star was now in its ascendency.

In another scene, the star performer was a young girl of twenty. She was not pretty, but her quality of sexual attractiveness was such that, in Mrs. Jack's own phrase, "it hit you in the eye." It was shocking and formidable in its naked power. When the act was over and the girl walked forward to acknowledge the storm of applause, there was an arrogant and even insolent assurance in the way she received it. She neither bowed nor smiled, nor gave any sign that she was pleased or grateful. She simply sauntered out and stood there in the center of the stage with one hand resting lightly on her hip, and with a sullen and expressionless look on her young face. Then she strolled off into the wings, every movement of her young body at once a provocation and a kind of insult, which seemed to say, "I know I've got it, so why should I thank anybody?"

Mrs. Jack bent forward in her seat, and, her face flushed with excitement and laughter, whispered:

"Isn't it awful! Did you ever see such a brazen, sexy little trollop? And yet—" her face grew thoughtful as she spoke—"she's got it too. She'll make a fortune."

He asked her about one or two of the others, about Roy Farley, the comedian.

"Oh, Roy," she said—and for a moment her face showed regret. "I don't know about Roy." She spoke now with a trace of difficulty, looking away, as if she knew what she wanted to say but was having trouble in finding words to phrase it: "Everything he does is just— just—a kind of imitation of someone else, and so he's having a kind of—vogue—right now—but—" she turned and looked at him seriously—"you've got to have something else," she said, and again her low brow was furrowed by that line of difficulty between the eyes as she sought for an answer. "I don't know—but—it's something that *you've* got to have yourself—inside of you—something that is *yours*, and that no one else has. Some of those others had it—even that little slut with her hand on her hip. It may be cheap, but it's hers— and its kinda wonderful." For a moment longer she was silent, looking at him. "Isn't it strange," she whispered, "and wonderful—and— and sort of sad?" She paused, and then said very quietly: "It is just the way things are. Just something you can't help, and that no one can do anything about, and that nothing can make better." Her face was touched for the moment with sadness, and then, irrelevantly it seemed, she said: "Poor things." And the quiet pity in those words did not need a definition.

When the show was over, they went out again into the lobby. Here some more people greeted her, and others said good-bye, but the place was clearing swiftly now as the cabs and motors drove away, and soon the house was almost empty. She asked him if he would go uptown with her, and invited him to come with her while she got her coat and hat and some costume drawings which she had left in what she called her "work room." Accordingly, they went backstage again. The stage hands were quickly dismantling the set, stowing the flats, the sections, and the properties away into the dim and cavernous reaches of backstage. The performers had all hurried off to their dressing rooms, but as they mounted the stairs again they could hear their voices, this time gayer and more noisy, with a sense of release.

Mrs. Jack's "work room" was on the third floor, not far away from the costume room. She opened the door and went in. It was a place of ordinary dimensions with two windows at one end. There was no carpet on the floor, and, save for a drawing table near one of the windows, a chair and locker, there were no furnishings. Behind the table, a sheet of tracing paper with some geometric designs of a set had been pinned against the wall with thumb tacks, and beside this, hanging from a nail, was a T-square. Against the whitewashed wall it looked very clean, exact, and beautiful. Upon the table, which was a level sheet of white, beautifully perfect wood, a square of drawing paper had also been pinned down to the board by means of small brass-headed tacks. This sheet was also covered with designs, and elsewhere on the table were other sheets that were covered with swift, sketchy, and yet beautiful costume drawings. These little drawings, so full of quickness and sureness, were remarkable because, although they did not show the figure they were destined to portray, yet it seemed as if the figure was always there. There would be just the jaunty sketching of a jacket, an elbowed sleeve, or perhaps just the line and pleating of the skirt. Yet the sketches could not have been more eloquent and moving in their portraiture of life if a whole gallery of men and women had been drawn in. There was also a little cardboard model of a setting, pressed and folded into shape, a row of drawing pencils, each sharpened to the perfection of a point, of equal length, and perfectly in line, a little jar containing long-stemmed brushes, feathery as hair, and a little white fat pot, full of gold paint.

She began to put some drawings and some tracing sheets into a brief case; then she opened her pocketbook and fumbled about in it, as women do, until she found her key. She laid the key down on the able, and then, before she closed her purse, she took out something white and crumpled that had been smoothed out and folded carefully, and just for a moment she held it against her bosom and patted it affectionately, at the same time looking at him with a childlike smile.

"My letter," she said proudly, and patted it again with her gloved hand.

For a moment he stared at her, puzzled; then, as he remembered what accursed nonsense he had written her, his face flamed red, and he started around the table after her.

"Here, give me that damn thing."

She moved quickly away, out of his reach, with an alarmed expression, and at the other end she paused again, and, holding it against her breast, she patted it with two hands now.

"My letter," she said softly again, and in an enrapt tone that a child uses, but speaking to herself, she said, "My beautiful letter where he says he will not truckle."

The words were deceptively innocent and for a moment he glared at her suspiciously, baffled. And then, like a child repeating to herself the sound of a word that fascinates her, she murmured: "He does not truckle. . . . He is no truckler. . . ."

She slipped quickly around the table as he started after her again, his hand outstretched, his face the color of a beet: "Here, if you don't give me that damn ——"

She slipped out of reach, across to the other side, and, still holding that damning piece of folly to her breast, like a child absorbed by some nonsense rhyme of its own fashioning, she murmured, "Britons never will be trucklers. . . ."

He chased her around the table in dead earnest now. Her shoulders shaking with laughter, she tried to escape from him, shrieking faintly. But he caught her, forced her back against the wall, and for a moment they struggled for the letter. She tried to keep it away from him, thrust it behind her back. He pinioned her arms and slid one hand down over hers until he had his hand upon the letter. Finding herself captured, and the letter being forced out of her grip, she paused and looked at him, and said reproachfully:

"Ah—you wouldn't be so mean! Give me my letter—please."

Her tone was now so earnest and reproachful that he released her, and stood back, glaring at her with a look of guilty and yet angry shame. "I don't blame you for laughing," he said. "I know it sounds as if a damn fool wrote it. Please let me have it and I'll tear it up. I'd like to forget about it."

"Oh, no," she said, softly and gently. "It was a beautiful letter. Let me keep it." She put it back in her purse again, and closed it; and then, as he still glared at her with a guilty, baffled face, as if not understanding what to do, she held the purse against her breast and patted it with her gloved hand, looking at him and smiling with the proud, childlike smile he had seen before.

Then they started to go out. She looked around and took the farewell look that people always take of rooms where they have worked, each time they leave them. Then she picked up her key, handed him the brief case, thrust her purse beneath her arm, and turned out the light. A corner lamp from the street outside threw some of its radiance into the room, and across the white board of the table.

They paused there, just for a moment, and then awkwardly he put his arm around her waist. It was the first time during the whole evening, the first time since the last meeting on the ship, that they had been alone and silent with each other, and now, as if some recognition of that fact was in the minds and hearts of each, they felt a sense of deep and strong embarrassment. He tightened his hold around her waist and made a half-hearted effort to embrace her, but she moved clumsily and uneasily, and murmured indefinitely, "Not here —all these people." She did not say who "all these people" were, and indeed most of the people in the theatre were now gone, for the place was now silent; but he understood that her embarrassment and confusion came from the sense of this intimacy here where her associations with her friends and her fellow workers were still so recent; and he, too, feeling—he did not know why—a strong sense of embarrassment and impropriety, made no further effort, and in a moment clumsily withdrew his hand.

They said no more, but opened the door and went out. She locked the door, and both of them went down the stairs together, still with that strange feeling of confusion and constraint, as if a barrier had suddenly been imposed between them and neither of them knew what to say. Below, the house was dark and quiet, but the old night watchman, an Irishman with a thick brogue, let them out into the street through the stage entrance. The streets around the theatre also looked barren and quiet, and after the so recent gaiety and brilliance of the performance and the crowd, the place seemed cold and sad. He hailed a taxi cruising past; they got in and were driven uptown through the almost deserted streets of the East Side and the darkened stretch of lower Broadway. She would not let him take her home, but left him in front of his hotel.

They shook hands and said "good night" almost formally. They paused and looked at each other for a moment with a troubled and confused look, as if there was something that they wanted to say. But they could not say it, and in a moment she was driven away; and with a sad, bewildered, and disappointed sense of something baffled, incomplete that had eluded both of them, he went into the hotel and up to his small room.

21

The Birthday

OUT OF THE NAMELESS AND UNFATHOMED WEAVINGS OF BILLION-FOOTED life, out of the dark abyss of time and duty, blind chance had brought these two together on a ship, and their first meeting had been upon the timeless and immortal seas that beat forever at the shores of the old earth.

Yet later, it would always seem to him that he had met her for the first time, had come to know and love her first, one day at noon in bright October. That day he was twenty-five years old, she had said that she would meet him for his birthday lunch; they had agreed to meet at noon before the Public Library. He got there early. It was a fine, shining day, early in October, and the enormous library, set there at the city's furious heart, with its millions of books, with the beetling architectures that towered around it, and the nameless brutal fury of the manswarm moving around it in the streets, had come to evoke for him a horrible mockery of repose and study in the midst of the blind wildness and savagery of life, to drown his soul with hopelessness, and to fill him with a feeling of weariness and horror.

But now his excitement and happiness over meeting her, together with the glorious life and sparkle of the day, had almost conquered these feelings, and he was conscious of a powerful, swelling certitude of hope and joy as he looked at the surging crowds upon the street, the thronging traffic, and the great buildings that soared up on every side with a sheer and dizzy frontal steepness.

It was the day when for the first time in his life he could say, "Now I am twenty-five years old," and, like a child who thinks that he has grown new muscle, a new stature over night, the magic numerals kept beating in him like a pulse, and he leaned there on the balustrade feeling a sense of exultant power inside of him, a sense of triumph for the mastery, the conviction that the *whole* of this was his.

346

A young man of twenty-five is the Lord of Life. The very age itself is, for him, the symbol of his mastery. It is the time for him when he is likely to feel that now, at last, he has really grown up to man's estate, that the confusions and uncertainties of his youth are behind him. Like an ignorant fighter, for he has never been beaten, he is exultant in the assurance of his knowledge and his power. It is a wonderful time of life, but it is also a time that is pregnant with a deadly danger. For that great flask of ether which feels within itself the illusions of an invincible and hurtless strength may explode there in so many ways it does not know about—that great engine of life charged with so much power and speed, with a terrific energy of its high velocity so that it thinks that nothing can stop it, that it can roar like a locomotive across the whole continent of life, may be derailed by a pebble, by a grain of dust.

It is a time when a man is so full of himself, of his own strength and pride and arrogant conceit that there is not much room left at the center of his universe for broad humanity. He is too much the vaunting hero of his cosmic scheme to have a wise heart for the scheme of others: he is arrogant and he does not have a simple heart, and he is intolerant and lacks human understanding, for men learn understanding—courage also!—not from the blows they give to others, but from those they take.

It is the time of life when a man conceives himself as earth's great child. He is life's darling, fortune's pet, the world's enhaloed genius: all he does is right. All must give way to him, nothing must oppose him. Are there traces of rebellion there among the rabble? Ho, varlets, scum—out of the way! Here's royalty! Must we rejoice, then, at the beatings which this fool must take? Not so, because there is so much virtue in the creature also. He is a fool, but there's a touch of angel in him too. He is so young, so raw, so ignorant, and so grievously mistaken. And he is so right. He would play the proud Lord, brook no insolences, and grind his heel into the world's recumbent neck. And inside the creature is a shaft of light, a jumping nerve, a plate so sensitive that the whole picture of this huge, tormented world is printed in the very hues and pigments of the life of man. He can be cruel, and yet hate cruelty with the hate of hell; he can be so unjust, and give his life to fight injustice; he can, in moments of anger, jealousy, or wounded vanity, inflict a grievous hurt upon others who have never done him wrong. And the next moment, thrice wounded, run through and pinioned to the wall upon the spear of his own guilt, remorse, and scalding shame, he can endure such agonies that if there really were a later hell there would be no real damnation left in it.

For at the end the creature's spirit is a noble one. His heart is warm and generous, it is full of faith and noble aspiration. He wants to be the best man in the world, but it is a good world that he wants to be the best man in. He wants to be the greatest man on earth, but in the image of his mind and heart it is not among mean people, but among his compeers of the great, that he wishes to be first. And remember this thing of this creature too, and let it say a word in his defense: he does not want monopoly, nor is his fire expended on a pile of dung. He does not want to be the greatest rich man in the world, to beetle up out of the blood-sweat of the poor the gold of his accretions. It is not his noble, proud ambition to control the slums, to squeeze out in his own huge ciderpress the pulp of plundered and betrayed humanity. He does not want to own the greatest bank on earth, to steal the greatest mine, to run the greatest mill, to exploit the labor and to profit on the sweat of ninety thousand lesser men. He has a higher goal than this: at very least he wants to be the greatest fighter in the world, which would take courage and not cunning; and at the very most he wants to be the greatest poet, the greatest writer, the greatest composer, or the greatest leader in the world—and he wants to paint instead of own the greatest painting in the world.

He was the Lord of Life, the master of the earth, he was the city's conqueror, he was the only man alive who ever had been twenty-five years old, the only man who ever loved or ever had a lovely woman come to meet him, and it was morning in October; all of the city and sun, the people passing in the slant of light, all of the wine and gold of singing in the air had been created for his christening, and it was morning in October, and he was twenty-five years old.

And then the golden moments' wine there in the goblet of his life dropped one by one, the minutes passed, and she did not come. Some brightness had gone out of day. He stirred, looked at his watch, searched with a troubled eye among the thronging crowd. The minutes dropped now like cold venom. And now the air was chilled, and all the singing had gone out of day.

Noon came and passed, and yet she did not come. His feeling of jubilant happiness changed to one of dull, sick apprehension. He began to pace up and down the terrace before the library nervously, to curse and mutter, already convinced that she had fooled him, that she had had no intention of coming, and he told himself savagely that it did not matter, that he did not care.

He had turned and was walking away furiously towards the street, cursing under his breath, when he heard a clatter of brisk, small feet behind him. He heard a woman's voice raised above the others, calling a name, and though he could not distinguish the name, he knew at once that it was his own. His heart gave a bound of the most unspeakable joy and relief, and he turned quickly, and there across the pavement of the court, threading her way through the fast weavings of the crowd, he saw her coming towards him eager and ruddy as an apple, and clad in rich, russet, autumnal brown. Bright harvestings of young October sun fell over her, she trotted towards him briskly as a child, with rapid step and short-paced runs. She was panting for breath: at that moment he began to love her, he loved her with all his heart, but his heart would not utter or confess its love, and he did not know of it.

She was so lovely, so ruddy, and so delicate, she was so fresh and healthy-looking, and she looked like a good child, eager and full of belief in life, radiant with beauty, goodness, and magic. There was an ache of bitter, nameless joy and sorrow in him as he looked at her: the immortal light of time and of the universe fell upon her, and the feet swarmed past upon the pavements of the street, and the old hunger for the wand and the key pierced to his entrails—for he believed the magic word might come to unlock his heart and say all that he felt as he saw Esther there at noon in bright October on the day when he was twenty-five years old.

He went striding back towards her, she came hurrying up, they came together in a kind of breathless collision and impulsively seized each other by the hands, and stood there so, panting, and for a moment too excited to speak.

"Oh!"—she gasped when she could speak. "I *ran* so! . . . I saw you walking away—my heart jumped so!" And then, more quietly, looking at him, with a shade of reproach, "You were going away," she said.

"I thought—" then paused, groping, not knowing what, in this intoxication of joy and relief, he *had* thought. "I waited for you," he blurted out. "I've been here almost an hour—you said twelve."

"Oh, no, my dear," she answered quietly. "I told you I had an appointment at the costumer's at twelve. I'm a few minutes late, I'm sorry—but I said twelve-thirty."

The emotion of relief and happiness was still so great that he scarcely heard her explanation.

"I thought—I'd given you up," he blurted out. "I thought you weren't coming."

"Oh," she said quietly but reproachfully again, "how could you think that? You must have known I would."

For the first time now, they released each other from the hard clasp in which, in their excitement, they had held each other fast. They stepped back a little and surveyed each other, she beaming, and he grinning, in spite of himself, with delight.

"Well, young fellow," she cried in a jolly tone, "how does it feel to be twenty-five years old?"

Still grinning, and staring at her foolishly, he stammered: "It—it feels all right. . . . Gosh!" he cried impulsively, "you look swell in brown."

"Do you like it—hah?" she said, eagerly and brightly. She stroked the bosom of her dress, which was like the red one she had worn the first night at the theatre, with the kind of pride and satisfaction a child might take in its belongings. "It is one of my Indian dresses," she said, "a sari. I'm glad if you like it."

Arm in arm, still looking at each other and so absorbed that they were completely oblivious of the crowd, the people passing, and the city all around them, they had begun to walk along, and down the steps that led to the street. On the curb they paused, and for the first time became aware of their surroundings.

"Do you know?"—she began doubtfully, looking at him— "Where are we going?"

"Oh!" He recollected himself, came to himself with a start. "Yes! I thought we'd go to a place I know about—an Italian place on the West Side."

She took her purse from under her arm and patted it.

"This is to be a celebration," she said. "I got paid this morning."

"Oh, no you don't! Not this time. This is my party."

Meanwhile, he had stopped a taxicab and was holding the door open for her. They got in, he gave the driver the address, and they were driven across town towards the place that he had chosen.

It was an Italian speakeasy on West 46th Street, in a row of brownstone houses, of which almost every one harbored an establishment similar to this. Certainly New York at that period must have contained thousands of such places, none of which differed in any essential detail from Joe's.

The setting and design of the establishment was one which a few years under the Prohibition Act had already made monotonously familiar to millions of people in New York. The entrance was through the basement, by means of a grated door which opened underneath the brownstone steps. To reach this door one went down a step or two from the sidewalk into what had formerly been the basement areaway, pressed a button, and waited. Presently the basement door was opened, a man came out, peered through the grating of the gate, and, if he recognized the visitor, admitted him.

Within, too, the appearance of the place was one that had already grown familiar, through thousands of duplications, to city dwellers. The original design of a city house had not been altered very much. There was a narrow hallway which led through the place from front to rear, and at the end of it there was a kitchen; to the left, as one entered, there was a very small room for the hat-check woman. On the right-hand side, in a larger but still very dark and narrow room, there was a small bar. From the bar one entered through a door into a small dining room of about the same dimensions. Across the hall there was a larger dining room, which had been created by knocking out the wall between two rooms. And upstairs on what had once been the first floor of the house, there were still other dining rooms, and private ones, too, if one desired them. On the floors above were—God knows what!—more rooms and lodgings, and shadowy-looking lodgers who came in and out, went softly up and down the carpeted tread of the old stairs, and, quickly, softly, through the entrance of the upper door. It was a life secret, flitting, and nocturnal, a life rarely suspected and never felt, that never intruded upon the hard, bright gaiety, the drunken voices, and the raucous clatter of the lower depths.

The proprietor of this establishment was a tall, thin, and sallow man with a kind of patient sadness, a gentle melancholy which one somehow liked because he felt and understood in the character of the man a sense of decency and of human friendliness. The man was an Italian, by name Pocallipo, and since he had been christened Giuseppe, the patrons of the place referred to it as "Joe's."

The history of Joe Pocallipo was also, if one could probe that great catacomb of life that hives the obscure swarmings of the city millions, a familiar one. He was one of those simple, gentle, and essentially decent people whom circumstance, occasion, and the collusions of a corrupt period had kicked upstairs, and who did not really like this ruthless betterment.

Before the advent of the Prohibition Act, he had been a waiter in a large hotel. His wife had run this same house as a lodging house, her clientele being largely derived from actors, vaudeville performers, and somewhat down-at-the-heels theatrical people of all sorts. As time went on, the woman began to provide some of her guests with an occasional meal when they would ask for it, and Joe, whose skill as a chef was considerable, began himself, on his "off day," to prepare a Sunday dinner, to which paying guests were invited. The idea, begun really as a kind of concession to the lodgers in the house, caught on: the meals were cheap, the food was excellent, people came and came again, returning often with their friends, until Joe's Sunday dinners had achieved a kind of celebrity, and the man and his wife were sorely taxed to accommodate the numbers that now came.

This involved, of course, the taking on of extra service and the enlargement of the dining space; meanwhile, the Prohibition Act had gone into effect, and now people at these Sunday dinners began to suggest the advisability of his serving wine to those who wanted it. To an Italian, this request seemed not only simple, but completely reasonable; he found, moreover, that although prohibition was a law, the supply of wine, both new and old, was plentiful to those who could afford to pay for it. Although the price was high, as he soon found from investigation carried on among his friends and colleagues, who had also been led in some such way as this into the labyrinth of this strange profession, the profit, once the corks were pulled, was great.

The remainder of the road was certain. There was a moment—just a moment—when Joe was faced with a decision, when he saw the perilous way this casual enterprise had led him into, when it was plain to him the kind of decision he had to make; but the dice were loaded, the scales too weighted down upon one side to admit a balanced judgment. Before him lay the choice of two careers. On the one hand, he could continue working as a waiter in a big hotel, which meant the insecurity of employment, subservience, and dependence for his living on a waiter's tips; and this way, as Joe well knew, the end was certain —old age, poverty, and broken feet. Before him on the other hand lay a more perilous and more ruthless way, but one made tempting by its promise of quick wealth. It was a way that would lead him, if not into full membership in the criminal underworld, at least into collusion with it; into a bought-and-paid-for treaty with the criminal police; and to violence, dishonesty, and crime. But it promised to him also wealth and property and eventual independence, and, like many another simple man of the corrupted period, it seemed to him there was no choice to make.

He made it, and the results within four years had been more glittering than he had dared to hope. His profit had been enormous. Now he was a man of property. He owned this house, and a year before he had bought the next one to it. He was even now considering the purchase of a small apartment house uptown. And if not in actual fact a rich man now, he was destined to be a very rich one soon.

And yet—that sad, dark face, that tired eye, the melancholy patience with a quiet tone. It was all so different from the way he thought it would turn out—so different from the life that he had thought he would have. It was, in some ways, so much better; it was, wearily and sadly, so much worse—the dense enmeshment of that tangled scheme, the dark, unhappy weavings of the ugly web, the complications of this world of crime, with its constantly growing encroachments, its new and ever uglier demands, the constant mulctings of all its graft, of blackmail, and of infamy, the fear of merciless reprisal, the knowledge that he was now imprisoned in a deadly world from which he could never hope again to escape—a world controlled by criminals, and by the police, each in collusion with the other, and himself so tarred now with the common stick of their iniquity that there was no longer any appeal left to him to any court of justice and authority, if there had been one. And there was none.

So here he stood today, peering out behind the grating of his basement gate, a sad and gentle man with weary eyes, looking out between the bars of his own barricade to see what new eventuality the ringing of the bell had brought to him, and whether enemy or friend.

For a moment he stood there, looking out through the bars with a look of careful anxiousness; then, when he saw the young man, his face brightened, and he said: "Oh, good morning, sir. Come in."

He unlocked the door then and held it open for his visitors as they came in, smiling in a gentle, kindly way, as they passed him. He closed the gate behind them and stood aside while they went in. Then he led the way along the narrow little corridor into a dining room. The first one they came to had some people in it, but the smaller one behind was empty. They chose this one, and went in and took a table, Joe pulling back the chairs and standing behind Mrs. Jack until she was seated, with the air of kind and gentle dignity that, one felt, was really a part of the decency and goodness of the man.

"I have not seen you for so long, sir," he said to the young man in his quiet voice. "You've been away?"

"Yes, Joe, I've been away a year," said the young man, secretly warmed and pleased that the man should have remembered him, and a little proud, too, that this mark of recognition should be given in front of Mrs. Jack.

"We've missed you," Joe said with his quiet smile. "You've been in Europe?"

"Yes," the other said casually, but quite pleased just the same that the proprietor had asked him, for he was at that age when one likes to boast a little of his voyages. "I was there a year," he added, and then realized that he had said something of this sort before.

"Where were you?" Joe inquired politely. "You were in Paris, sir, I am sure," he said and smiled.

"Yes," the other answered carelessly, with just a trace of the non-chalance of an old boulevardier, "I lived there for six months," he said, tossing this off carelessly in a tone of casual ease, "and then I stayed in England for a while."

"You did not go to EEtaly?" inquired Joe, with a smile.

"Yes, I was there this Spring," the traveler replied in an easy tone that indicated that this season of the year was always the one he preferred when taking his Italian holiday. He did not think it worth mentioning that he had gone back again in August to sail from Naples: that trip hardly counted, for he had gone straight through by train and had seen nothing of the country.

"Ah, EEtaly is beautiful in Spring," Joe said. "You were at Rome?"

"Not long," said the voyager, whose stay in Rome, to tell the truth, had been limited to a stop between trains. "In the Spring I remained in the North"—he tossed this off with some abandon too, as if to say that at this season of the year "the North" is the only portion of the Italian peninsula that a man of cultivated taste could tolerate.

"You know Milano?" said Joe.

"Oh, yes," the other cried, somewhat relieved to have some place mentioned at last that he could honestly say he did know. "I stayed there for some time"—a slight exaggeration of the fact, perhaps, as his sojourn had been limited to seven days. "And Venezia," he went on quickly, getting a lascivious pleasure from his pronunciation of the word.

"Venezia is very beautiful," said Joe.

"Your own home is near Milano, isn't it?"

"No, near Turino, sir," Joe replied.

"And the whole place here," the youth went on, turning eagerly to Mrs. Jack—"all the waiters, the hat-check girl, the people out in the kitchen, come from that same little town—don't they, Joe?"

"Yes, sir, yes, sir," said Joe smiling, "all of us." In his quiet and gentle way he turned to Mrs. Jack and with a movement of the hand explained: "First one man came—and he writes back that he is doing" —he moved his shoulders slightly—"not so bad. Then others came. Now, I think we are more here than we are left at home."

"How interesting," murmured Mrs. Jack, pulling off her gloves and looking around the room. "Look," she said quickly, turning to her companion, "could you get a cocktail—hah? I want to drink to your health."

"Well, of course," said Joe. "You can have anything you like."

"It's my birthday, Joe, and this is my birthday party."

"You shall have everything. What will the lady drink?"—he turned to her.

"Oh, I think—" she meditated a moment; then, turning to the youth, said brightly, "A nice Martini—hah?"

"Yes, I'll have that too. Two of them, Joe."

"Two Martinis. Very good, *very* good," said Joe, with an air of complaisance, "and after that ——?"

"Well, what have you?"

He told them what he had, and they ordered the dinner—antipasto, minestrone, fish, chicken, salad, cheese, and coffee. It was too much, but they had the spirit of true celebrants: they ordered a quart flask of Chianti to go with it.

"I'm not doing anything else all afternoon," said Mrs. Jack. "I saved it for you."

Joe disappeared and they could hear him giving orders in fast Italian. A waiter brought two cocktails on a tray. They clinked glasses and Mrs. Jack said, "Well, here's to you, young fellow." She was silent for a moment, looking at him very seriously, then she said: "To your success—the real kind—the kind you want inside of you—the best."

They drank, but her words, her presence here, the feeling of wonderful happiness and pride that the day had brought to him, a sense that somehow this was the true beginning of his life, and that a fortunate and happy life such as he had always visioned now lay immediately before him, gave him an exalted purpose, the intoxication of a determined and irresistible strength that even drink could add nothing to. He leaned forward across the table and seized her hand in both of his: "Oh, I'll do it!" he cried exalted, "I'll do it!"

"You will," she said, "I know you will!" And putting her other hand on top of his, she squeezed it hard, and whispered: "The best! You are the best!"

The wild happiness of that moment, the mounting total of that enchanted day left now only the overpowering sense of some miraculous consummation that was about to be realized immediately. It seemed to him that he had "the whole thing" within his grasp—what, he did not know, and yet he was sure that he had it. The concrete distillation of all this overwhelming certainty, this overwhelming joy—that the great success, the magnificent achievement, the love, the honor, and the glory were already his—lay there palpable, warm and heavy as a ball does, in his hand. And then, feeling this impossible realization so impossibly near that he already had it in his grasp, feeling this certitude so exultantly, the sense of purpose so powerfully, that he was sure he knew exactly what certitude and purpose were—feeling the language he had never uttered so eloquently there at the very hinges of the tongue, the songs that he had never sung, the music he had never heard, the great books, the novels, the poems he had never fashioned—they were all so magnificently, so certainly his that he could utter them at any moment—now—a moment after—within five minutes—at any moment that he chose to make them his!

That boiling confidence of wild elements proved too much for the fragile tenement of flesh, of bone, of thinking, and of sense that it inhabited, and he began to talk "a blue streak." As if every secret hope, every insatiate desire, every cherished and unspoken aspiration, every unuttered feeling, thought, or conviction that had ever seethed and boiled in the wild ferment of his youth, that had ever rankled, eaten like an acid in the secret places of his spirit, that had ever been withheld, suppressed, pent-up, dammed, concealed through pride, through fear of ridicule, through doubt or disbelief, or because there was no other ear to hear him, no other tongue to answer back, to give them confirmation —this whole tremendous backwater of the spirit burst through its walls and rushed out in an inundating flood.

The words rushed from him in wild phrases, hurled spears, flung and broken staves of thought, of hope, of purpose, and of feeling. If he had had a dozen tongues, yet he would not have had the means to utter them, and still they charged and foamed and thrust there at the portals of his speech, and still not a thousandth part of what he wished to say was shaped or uttered. On the surface of this tremendous superflux he was himself whirled and swept away like a chip, spun round and car-ried onward, helpless on his own raging flood; and finding all the means at his disposal insufficient, failing him, like a man who pours oil on a raging fire, he ordered one drink after another and gulped them down.

He became very drunk. He became more wild, more incoherent all the time. And yet it seemed to him that he must say it finally, get it out of him, empty himself clean, get it all clear and straight and certain.

When they got out in the street again, darkness had come and he was still talking. They got into a cab. The thronging streets, the jammed congestion of the traffic, the intolerable glare, the insane kaleidoscope of Broadway burned there in his inflamed and maddened vision, not in a blur, not in a drunken maze, but with a kind of distorted and in-sane precision, a grotesque projection of what it really was. His baffled and infuriated spirit turned against it—against everyone, everything— against her. For suddenly he realized that she was taking him home to his hotel. The knowledge infuriated him, he felt that she was deserting him, betraying him. He shouted to the driver to stop, she caught hold of his arm and tried to keep him in the car, he wrenched free, shouted at her that she had gone back on him, sold him out, betrayed him— that he wanted to see her no more, that she was no good—and even while she pled with him, tried to persuade him to get back into the car with her, he told her to be gone, slammed the door in her face, and lunged away into the crowd.

The whole city now reeled past him—the lights, the crowds, the glittering vertices of night, now bedimmed and sown with a star-flung panoply of their nocturnal faëry—it all burned there in his vision in a pattern of grotesque distortion, it seemed cruel and insane to him. He was filled with a murderous fury, he wanted to batter something into a pulp, to smash things down, to stamp them into splintered ruin. He slugged his way through the streets like a maddened animal, he hurled himself against the crowd, lunged brutally against people and knocked them out of his way, and finally, having stunned himself into a kind of apathy, he reached the end of that blind and blazing passage, he found himself in front of his hotel, exhausted, sick, and with no more hope for a singing in his heart. He found his room, went in, and fell senseless and face downward on the bed.

The flask of ether had exploded.

22

Together

SHE TELEPHONED NEXT MORNING A LITTLE AFTER NINE O'CLOCK. HE stirred, groaned, and sat up dizzily with a head full of splitting rockets, sick at heart and sick at stomach, and buried at the bottom of a pit of shame.

"How are you?" she said quietly, at once, in the tone people always use on such occasions, which is neither very sympathetic nor forgiving, but just a flat interrogation of a fact.

"Oh . . . well, pretty bad," he said morosely. "I . . . guess I was pretty bad yesterday."

"Well—" she hesitated, and then laughed a little. "You were a little wild," she said.

He groaned to himself, and he said miserably and without much hope, "I'm sorry," having the feeling a man has on such occasions that mere sorrow does not make things right.

"Have you had any breakfast yet?" she said.

"No." His stomach turned at the thought of it.

"Why don't you get up now and take a shower? Then go out somewhere and get your breakfast, you'll feel a lot better when you do. It's a beautiful day," she went on. "You ought to get out and take a walk. It would do you lots of good."

It seemed to him that he could never again take an interest in such things as breakfast, walking, or the weather, but he mumbled that he would do as she advised, and she went on at once as if outlining a practical working program for the day:

"And what are you going to be doing later on—I mean tonight?"

This seemed so impossibly far away, it conjured up such melancholy vistas of the miserable eternity that must elapse before night could come again to shelter his guilt in its concealing darkness that he could not

359

answer for a moment. He said: "Oh, I don't know—I hadn't thought of anything." And then, miserably, "Nothing, I guess."

"Because," she went on quickly, "I was wondering if you would care to meet me tonight?—That is, if you weren't doing something else."

For the first time, excitement stirred him, he felt hope.

"But, of course I would," he stammered. "You mean you would like to——"

"Yes," she said quickly and decisively. "Look—I wonder if you could do this. Could you come down here tonight after the show? I mean—I didn't think you would want to sit through the whole thing again, and I'll be free after that—and I thought if you could come down a little after eleven, there'd be more time and—maybe we could go off somewhere and talk."

"At what time shall I come?"

"About a quarter after eleven?—Is that all right?"

"Yes, I'll be there. And . . . and I'd just like to say about yesterday . . . about the way I——"

"Well, that's all right," she interrupted him, laughing. "You get up now and do what I told you to do, and you'll feel better."

He felt immensely better already, still dizzy and still queasy in the flesh, but with a tremendous lift and relief of the whole spirit, and he felt more hopeful of his life when he went downstairs.

The performance was over and the theatre empty when he got to it that night. She was waiting for him in the lobby. They shook hands with a sense of formal constraint, and started backstage through the corridor. The stage hands had almost finished with their work, a few men were still about, but there was only a single light burning on the stage, a very big, bright one which cast a great light, but which gave to the shadows all around, in the vaulted spaces and the depths behind, the mysterious distance of a shadowy and unexplored dominion.

Almost all the performers had departed. One of them had paused for a moment at the bulletin board and was scanning the announcements. As they started up the stairs, two more came swiftly down; all spoke quick greetings as they passed and then hurried away, with the look of people who have finished their work. Upstairs, all was silent and deserted. She got out her key and unlocked the door of her own room, and they went in. The sound they made was the sound that people make when they are entering an empty place.

"Look," she said, "I thought I'd get my coat and hat and we could go uptown—to a Childs restaurant, or some place like that. I'm simply starved. I had only time to get a sandwich before the show, and I've been going ever since."

She put her purse down on the table and turned to get her coat off the hook upon the wall.

"I'd like to say—" he began.

"I'll only be a moment," she said quickly. "We can get started then."

He stopped her as she started to move away, and said:

"I'd like to tell you about yesterday."

The woman turned to him and took him by the hands.

"Listen," she said, "there is nothing to tell between you and me. There is nothing to explain. When I saw you on the boat I knew that I had always known you, and it has been the same way ever since. When I got your letter—" he winced, and she went on quickly—"when I saw the writing on the letter, I knew it was from you. I knew again that I had found you and that I had always known you, and that it would always be the same. Yesterday, when I came to meet you, when I saw you, and you were walking away, the thought came to me you were leaving me. It was as if a knife had been turned and twisted in the heart, and then you turned, and you were there again, and then we were together and there were just you and I. And that's the way it is, and I have always known you, and we are together. There's nothing to explain."

A heavy door had slammed below, and for a moment there was the lean and lonely sound of footsteps walking away upon an empty pavement. Then there was nothing, just the hushed, still silence in the house. They stood there, holding each other by the hands, as they had done the day before, and this time there was nothing more to say, as if that stormy meeting of the day before had somehow erased, wiped out for each of them, all confusion, all constraint, the need of any further explanation. They stood there with held hands and looked each other in the eye, and knew that there was nothing more to say.

Then they came together and he put his arms around her and she put her arms around his neck and they kissed each other on the mouth.

23

Esther's House

M RS. JACK LIVED IN A HOUSE ON THE WEST SIDE, BETWEEN WEST END
Avenue and the river. At night she could hear the boats blowing
in the river, and she could hear the ships putting out to sea. It was a
five-story building of that familiar reddish brownstone which is now
disappearing, but of which there were even then many miles left in the
city. The material is ugly, but it is ugly with an evocative memory
that is much more poignant and wonderful than most things that are
considered beautiful. For in these ugly and desolate blocks of buildings
of which the old New York was made, are the memories of primitive
America, of "1887," of "1893," of "1904,"—that lost time which is more
remote, more strange, and, to some men, more beautiful, than the
Middle Ages—and the sounds of those times are more lost than
Persepolis.

But the house in which Mrs. Jack lived was not ugly. It had an
elegant and luxurious look. It was not lumpy and involved, with deep
and dull indentures, or stiff, harsh, and angular, as many of these structures are. The front was flat, plain, and delicate-looking, and to the
left of the entry door there was one big, gleaming window of sheeted
glass, in which there was always set an enormous bottle. The bottle
was of green, delicate texture, so thin that it trembled to the touch, and
gave forth a quivering, crystalline resonance.

Whether this ornament had been set there deliberately by the expert
and subtle theatricalism of its owner, or whether the magic intuition
of her taste, which was no less certain, but less conscious, accounted
for it, it is impossible to say, but it remained in the memory forever
after. That flat and elegant façade, set with its one great sheet of glass
and its immense green bottle, was like a picture of its owner's talent,
which was delicate, opulent, and pure.

Before this house Monk now stopped. He had come uptown by

the subway; with eager stride, he had walked down one of the streets that lead to the river, and walked along the Drive past Mrs. Jack's street, trying to guess which house was hers. Then he had made a complete circuit of the block, and now he was here before her house. He mounted a step or two, rang the bell, and in a moment a young Irish woman in maid's dress opened the inner door and let him in. He asked the girl if Mrs. Jack was there, told her his name, and in a thick, rich voice she said he was expected, and would he come with her.

The entrance hall was large, darkly paneled, and floored with a walnut tiling. Before he followed the girl upstairs he looked through a door she had left open and caught a momentary glimpse of young Irish maids around a table, and a big policeman with his coat off. They turned flushed and merry faces on him for a moment, there was a burst of music from a phonograph, the door was closed. Then he mounted the broad, dark stairs behind the girl.

The house was somewhat narrowly built, but it was deep. There was just space for one big, nobly-proportioned room across its width; those big rooms ran back three deep, there was an air of spaciousness and calm; and the lovely and certain touch of the woman, which was at once delicate and immensely strong, was everywhere in the house.

The furniture was old, and of a dozen different styles and periods. There were chairs, tables, chests of drawers marked with the incomparable clean simpleness of colonial America, there was a great chest from fourteenth-century Italy, there was a piece of old green Chinese silk upon the mantel, and a little green figure of one of the lovely and compassionate goddesses of infinite mercy, there were magnificent drinking glasses from Vienna, there were cupboards from the farmhouses of the Pennsylvania Dutch, and cabinets with the gay, crude little figures of the Bavarian peasants, there were wonderful knives and forks and spoons, heavy and plain, from eighteenth-century England.

There was this great variety of times and fashions, and yet the result was not a hodgepodge of ill-assorted relics, but a living unity. These things fused warmly and beautifully into the unity of the house; they had been chosen slowly, at many different times and places, because they were beautiful and useful, and because she had known they were right for her house. Everything in the house seemed to have been put there to give joy and comfort to people, nothing was there simply as a museum piece to be stared at, everything was in use, and everywhere there was the sense of tranquil dignity, ease, and abundance.

The impression they gave, which would certainly have been justified, was that no one who ate or drank here ever went away hungry or thirsty. The house was one of the most hospitable and abundant places in the world. One of the finest elements in the Jewish character is its sensuous love of richness and abundance: the Jew hates what is savorless and stingy in life, he will not stand for bad food or dreary discomfort, he will not make jokes about them, or feel it a fine thing to cheat the senses. He feels there is something mean and degraded about poor living, he loves warmth and opulence, and he is right.

This wonderful house, therefore, was one of the finest places in the world. Although modest in size and appearance, it was certainly unlikely that anything to approach its warmth and beauty could have been found among the great establishments of England, where people have dozens of ancient rooms and scores of servants, but rub their raw, chapped hands over Brussels sprouts and mutton, and huddle miserably over half-pint fires; nor in France, where things are too gilt and brittle; nor in Germany, where there is an immensely high, but immensely heavy, standard of good living.

American joy is the sharpest and most exultant joy on earth: a house like this is set in a magical ether, and the belief in success and golder wealth and glory touches everything. So does it seem to a young man. For him, it is much better to know rich people than to be rich himself; for youth, it is not wealth but the thought of wealth that is wonderful. The youth does not want money: he wants to be invited to the homes of rich people and to eat rich dinners, he wants to know wealthy and beautiful women, and to have them love him, and he fancies that just as their clothes, their stockings, all their garments are of the finest and rarest textures, so the texture of their flesh, the spittle of their mouths, the hair of their heads, and all their combining sinews, tissues, and ligaments are fairer and finer than those of poorer people.

Monk had never seen the inside of such a house as this one, nor was he accustomed to its subtle, rather worn quality and flavor, and at first he was disappointed. He had formed lavish notions of Mrs. Jack's wealth. He had named sums to himself since the man on the boat had said she was "immensely wealthy"—he had thought of thirty or forty million dollars, and he had expected the house to be something immense and brilliant. Now it seemed to him old and a little shabby, but it also seemed friendly and comfortable. He was no longer afraid and awed by it as he had been before entering.

As he turned to ascend the second flight of stairs he had a moment's glimpse of the living room, with its worn and friendly look, and of low bookshelves all around the walls. There were hundreds, thousands of books, but they did not have the stiff-bound, sumptuous look of the unread treasures in the houses of rich, unlettered people. The books had the warm, worn smell and coloring of books which have been read and handled.

Then, more briskly and confidently, he went up after the maid, and they passed by bedrooms, spacious and bright, with great four-poster beds and thick quiltings; and finally, at the top of the house, they came to the little room which Mrs. Jack used as a workshop. The door was partly open, they went in, and Mrs. Jack, very businesslike and earnest, was leaning over her drawing table at work, and with one trim foot crossed jauntily before the other. She looked up as they entered. Monk was momentarily shocked because she was wearing horn-rimmed spectacles. They gave her small, delicate face a motherly appearance, and she peered at him comically over the top of the lenses, calling out in cheerful voice:

"There you are, young fellow! Come in!"

Then with a quick, nervous movement of her small hand she removed the spectacles, put them on the table, and came around to greet him. At once, now, she was the warm little creature he remembered. Her tender face glowed with its warm color, only, now, she became suddenly a little formal and embarrassed, she shook hands somewhat nervously and stiffly, and said: "Hello, Mr. Webber. How are you—hah?" in a somewhat cracked, shrill, and impatient city voice. Then she stood rapidly slipping the ring on and off her finger with the nervous and impatient movement that worried and somewhat annoyed him. "Would you like to have some tea—hah?" she said again in her somewhat protesting tone, and when he said "Yes," she said, "All right, Katy bring us some tea." The girl went out and closed the door.

"Well, Mr. Webber," said Mrs. Jack, still slipping the ring on and off, "this is my little room where I do my work. How do you like it—hah?"

He said that he thought it was a nice room, and added lamely, "It must be a fine place to work in."

"Oh," she said earnestly, "it's the most wonderful place you ever heard of. It's simply marvelous," she added solemnly. "You get the most wonderful light here all day long, but now they're going to ruin it all," she said, gesturing out the window where the gaunt framework of a large building was being erected. "They're putting up one of those big apartment houses, and it's simply going to smother us. Isn't it a shame?" she went on indignantly. "We've lived here for years, and now they're trying to drive us out."

"Who is?"

"Oh, these apartment house people. They want to tear down this whole block and put up one of those awful places. In the end I suppose they'll drive us out."

"How can they do that? Don't you own the place?"

"Oh yes, we own it, but what can you do about it if they want to force you out? They'll put up big buildings all around you, they'll shut out all light and air—they'll simply smother you. Do you think people have any right to do things like that?" she burst out with her plain, kind indignation, which with her jolly, wholesome, and indignantly flushed little face was tremendously appealing, and gave people a tender and humorous feeling towards her, even when she protested angrily. "Don't you think it's dreadful—hah?"

"It's too bad, it looks like a nice house."

"Oh, God, it's a *wonderful* house!" she said earnestly. "It is the most magnificent place you ever saw. Some day I want you to see it all—I'll show you all around. When we leave this place I'm going into mourning."

"Well, I hope you'll never have to."

"Oh, we'll have to," she said gravely and sadly. "That's New York. Nothing lasts here. . . . The other day I went by the house where I lived for a time as a girl. It's the only house left on the street—all around it are these enormous buildings now. God, it was like a dream! You know how time makes you feel? It's as if you've lived forever or only five minutes, you don't know which—there's something strange and terrible about it. I got frightened and gazooky," she said comically.

"What's gazooky?"

"You know—they way you feel when you are looking down from a high building. . . . I must have lived in that house a year or two. It was after my father died, and I was staying with my uncle. He was an enormous man, he weighed over three hundred pounds, and God! —how he loved to eat! You would have adored him. The *very* best was just about good enough for that fellow!" As she uttered these words her tender and delicate face was glowing with humor, and she emphasized the words by almost whispering them, and by pressing the thumb and forefinger of her strong little hand together and gesturing in a way that showed she meant something of almost superhuman excellence by "the *very* best." "Gee! he was a grand fellow! The doctors said he kept alive fifteen years longer by sticking to Scotch highballs. He used to start about eight o'clock in the morning and kept it up all day. You never saw anything like it in your whole life—the amount of liquor that fellow could consume. You just wouldn't believe it possible. And he was so smart—that was the strangest thing, it didn't seem to make any difference to his work. He used to be Police Commissioner, he was one of the best they ever had. He was great friends with Roosevelt, and Mr. Roosevelt used to come there to that house to see him. . . . God! it all seems so long ago, and yet I remember it all so well—I feel just like something in the museum," she went on, laughing. "One night he took me to the opera, I must have been about sixteen, and God! I felt so proud to be with him! It was one of those operas of Wagner's, and you know how everybody gets killed in them, and we were coming up the aisle just before the end and Uncle Bob came booming out, 'They're all dead except the orchestra!'" Here her voice imitated the full, booming quality of the enormous man in such a way that one saw him vividly. "God! I though they'd have to stop the show! You could hear him all over the place, his voice carried everywhere."

She paused, animated, laughing, flushed with the eagerness of her story. She paused by the river of life and time. And for a moment Monk had a blazing vision of lost time, he heard the strange, sad music that time makes. For here, delivered unto the punctual and unshadowed minutes, was this warm, breathing flesh stored with the memories of a lost world and the ancient days. The ghosts of the forgotten hours now moved about her, and the strange brown light of memory shed its unearthly glow upon the moment's actual light. A vision of old prints and readings, a potent and evocative memory of a past Monk had not seen but which was mixed with his blood like the foods of the earth he lived on flashed through his spirit its vivid and unspeakable sorrow.

He saw the moments of lost time, he felt the pang of hunger and intolerable regret that all lost time, and the thought of all the life that has been lived upon the earth, and that we have never seen, awakes in us. He heard the myriad sounds of the forgotten feet, the speech and movement of the tongueless dead, the vanished clatter of hoof and tire—things lost, and lost forever. And he saw forgotten fume-flaws of soft smoke about Manhattan, the vanished cleavings of bright ships upon the endless waters, the forest of masts about the magic island, the grave faces of the derbied men who, caught in some casual moment of a nameless day by an old camera, paused, in their broken stride, in queer and incompleted gestures, as they moved out of time across the Bridge.

All these had cast their shadows on this delicate and rosy-hued face, all these had left their echoes in her memory, and she stood here now, a child, a woman, a phantom, and a living being—the fleshly unity that bound him suddenly to the ghostly past, a miracle of deathling loveliness among great spires and ramparts, a jewel found by chance upon the seas, a part of the enormous wistfulness and lone-liness of America, where all men wander and are sick for home, where all things change but change itself, where even the memory and relic of love falls to the wrecker's hammer, gapes for a moment like a ruined wall upon the earth's blind eye, and then is drawn under and erased by the unrelenting tides of change and movement.

Mrs. Esther Jack was fair; she was fair, she had the flower face; it was October, nineteen twenty-five, and dark time was flowing by her like a river.

Shall we save one face from the million faces? Shall we keep one moment from the adyts of lost time? Was no love living in the wilderness, and was there nothing but the snarl and jungle of the streets, the rasp and driven fury of the town? No love? Was no love living in the wilderness, and was there nothing but unceasing dying and begetting, birth, growth, pollution, and the cat's great snarl for blood and honey? Was there no love?

We shall scorn scorners, curse revilers, mock at mockers. Have they grown wise on dust and alum? Do they speak truly because their tongues are bitter? Have they seen clearly because their eyes are blind? Is there no gold because the sands are yellow? It is not true. They'll build great bridges yet and taller towers. But a vow has lasted where a wall has fallen; a word has been remembered where a city perished; and faith has lived when flesh grew rotten.

Mrs. Jack was fair; she was fair, she had dove's eyes; and in all the world there was no one like her.

For a moment the woman paused, looking out of the window, smiling gently, and with that musing and tranquil expression touched with sadness that people have when they remember lost faces and lost laughter, and the innocence of old joy. The strong, delicate light of the late sun shone on her face without violence or heat, with its remote, fading, and golden glow, and for a moment she passed into a deeper revery, and he saw the look on her face that he had seen once or twice before on the ship, and which already had power to wound his suspicion and to awake in him a jealous curiosity.

It was a somber, dark, and passionate look that transformed her merry and eager face with an expression of brooding intensity. Suddenly, he noticed that the line of her mouth was curved downward like a wing, giving a masklike grief, an almost Slavic and undecipherable passion to her face, and he was pierced with a bitter desire to know the secret of this look. It had in it a strange, animal bewilderment. He noted her low skull, now contracted by a frown of perplexity, as if her brain was struggling with some grievous thing in life it could not fathom.

In a moment she had passed from the simple and eager interest, the lively and childish curiosity which drew her senses outward and seemed to fill her with a constant and sensuous delight in all the life and movement of the earth, into an inner and remote absorption from which the world was excluded. The look had in it so much perplexity and pain, so much dark grief and brooding passion, that it awakened in him a feeling of bitter mistrust.

He felt tricked and cheated and baffled by a cleverness and subtlety of living that was too old, too wise and crafty, for him to fathom or contend with. He wondered if her simple eagerness and apparent absorption in lively human things, even her merry and rosy face of a delicate and noble beauty, were not merely some apparatus of concealment and escape from this secret thing that dwelt in her, if they were not merely an appearance calculated to deceive the world, and if, left to herself, unoccupied by any work or amusement, she would not plunge immediately into this somber mood.

What was it? Was it the memory of some definite and painful loss, the thought of some lover who had left her, the recollection of some grief from which she had never recovered? Was it the thought of some man, some unknown lover, from whom, perhaps, she had parted that Summer in Italy? Was it some young man like himself, some boy, she coveted? Were her thoughts, from which he was now completely excluded, focused upon this passion and this person? Was he merely the substitute to this desire, the second-hand assuagement?

He told himself that he did not care, and surely the cynicism which he professed to himself at that moment, and which simply connected this woman to the great number of wealthy and fashionable women who are constantly seeking new loves and lovers, should have enabled him to accept such a situation without regret. But now he felt instead the stab of jealousy: without being willing now to admit either desire or love for her, he wanted her to admit them for him. He wanted to be loved and preferred above all others.

A sinister vision of the city blazed in his mind. Instead of the golden and exultant vision of the city which he had known in childhood, this vision was drawn in lines of lust and cruelty, peopled with faithless loves and treacheries, inhabited by the conspirators of passion— by a world of rich, sensuous, and unsated women, of professional Don Juans, of lesbians, pederasts, and the cruelly impotent, of sterility that battened on pain, of the jaded appetites that could be spurred only by the sight of grief and madness—these figures appeared to mock the faith and passion of youth, as a countryman is mocked when he discovers that his love has been made the spectacle of a peep-show audience.

Or was this woman's somber and passionate revery only a token of some less definite and less personal sorrow? Was it simply the sign of a state of brooding consciousness which, inarticulate and directed towards no thing or person, felt deeply and wordlessly the tragic underweft of life, the loss of youth, the approach of age and death, the inescapable horror of time?

He remembered now how quietly and with what fatal decision she had said the last night on the ship: "I want to die—I hope that I die in a year or two." And when he had asked her why, she said with this same look of animal-like perplexity on her face: "I don't know. . . . I just feel finished. . . . It seems that I've come to the end of everything. . . . There's nothing more that I can do."

The statement had exasperated and angered him inexplicably, because he hated death and wanted passionately to live, and because there had been no hysteria or sudden grief in the way she said it. The way in which she had spoken had a curious flatness, a desolate perplexity, as if she had really come to the end of all desire, and of all her resources, and as if she felt convinced that no new or beautiful thing could in the future be added to the sum of her life.

The contrast between this moment of desolate and hopeless resignation and Mrs. Jack's usual state of merry and joyful absorption with the details of living was so great that he felt anger and mistrust: if this sense of vacancy and tragedy dwelt in her always, then how far could one trust this simple and eager appearance she made before the world, this presentment that was so lovely, sensuous, so full of delight, sweetness, and humor, and that made people love her?

He could not feel that she was practicing some specious and complex fraud upon the world. Such an idea seemed ridiculous because there had never been an actress with enough talent to play such a part, and he felt the mistrust and pain one feels when he discovers unsuspected and bewildering depths and complexities in the character of a person he thought was simply and easily understood, and that he had come to know.

Now, even the plain, frank, and simple way she had of talking—her frequent, yet very straight and natural-sounding, use of such words as "fine," "grand," "marvelous," and occasionally "swell"—seemed, together with her jolly and rosy little face, and her whole manner of honesty, simplicity, and directness, to be part of the deceptive mechanism of an immensely complex, old, and sophisticated spirit.

Mrs. Jack not only made use of this kind of rough-simple argot that was at that time coming into fashion among sophisticated people, but it really seemed to be a part of her life and character, and she seemed to use it with complete honesty and sincerity, along with a speech that was plain, straight, and pungent, enriched by a meaty, homely, and colloquial metaphor, a concrete descriptive power that made use of the good, straight words of common speech, but that was absolutely her own, and that seemed to come out with an immense, spontaneous inventiveness as she talked, and to be drawn out of the experience and feeling of her own life.

For example, in describing the terrible heat on the pier the day the ship had docked, she said: "God, wasn't it awful! I thought I was going to melt away before I got out of there! I just wanted to unscrew my head from my shoulders and drop it down into a well of nice cold water to soak a while!" And this image of coolness and refreshment so delighted her that she went on, with her ruddy little face glowing with humor, delight, and eagerness as she described how it might be done: "Wouldn't it be wonderful if you could do a thing like that?" she cried. "I used to think about it when I was a kid. I always hated it when it got hot in the Summer; they made us wear so many clothes in those days, it was simply horrible! I used to think how fine it would be if I could just unscrew my head and drop it down a well to soak— I could see the whole thing just as plain as day," she went on with her face flushed with laughter. "I'd give my head a little turn—it would go 'Twirk!'" she said comically, "and there it would be all ready to go down into the well. Then after I'd let it soak a while I'd pull it back again, and put it on—and it would go 'Twirk'—and there I'd have it, cool and clean, back on my head again! Isn't it wonderful the things a kid can think of—hah?" she demanded, with a merry, glowing, and delighted face.

Her mind was full of all kinds of fantastic images like this, and she invented new ones all the time with a childlike fascination. Of some pompous actor, she would say with a disgusted scorn that yet had in it no real ill-humor or malice:

"Say! That fellow makes me sick with all the airs he gives himself. He's so damned fancy that you wouldn't believe it's possible till you see him. You know what his face looks like? Well, I'll tell you, it looks just like a piece of cold sliced ham!" and, her face glowing with good humor, she would break into a delighted yell of full, rich, woman's laughter.

Finally, she would say in a quiet and very earnest tone of some person of her acquaintance:

"Oh, he's a *very* fine person! He's one of the finest people that I've ever known!"—and she would say this with such a straight, open, and engaging look of frankness and conviction on her earnest little face that one felt convinced immediately, not only of her sincerity, but also of the "fineness" of the person she spoke about.

Yet, she made frequent use of these rough-simple words which fashionable and sophisticated people were beginning to use at that time, and in which there was something false, shameful, and sickening when *they* said them. But now he wondered with an incoherent perplexity and confusion of spirit if she did not use these words for the same reason the other fashionable people used them—to give an appearance of simplicity, plainness, and straightforward honesty to a complex and subtle character that had no simplicity in it, but which was so immensely talented and able that she could use all the words and phrases a thousand times and with a sophistication so assured and certain that it could mask itself at every point with an impregnable illusion of simplicity.

She was always using the word "fancy," and it was evident that about the worst comment she could make on anyone was to call him "fancy." Yet, remembering now things she had said to him on the ship, and always with this same straight, open, and utterly convincing look of sincerity—that she thought a play by James Joyce, *Exiles,* was "the greatest play that had ever been written," and knowing that this play was nothing but a fancy and obscure little play, and not in any way to be compared with *Ulysses*; and having heard her talk of D. H. Lawrence almost in the manner of a cult-adept, as if Lawrence had not only given men fine books and moving characters but was himself a second Jesus Christ offering us the way to life and everlasting truth; and having heard her say that she had been "psychoanalyzed," and speak of psychoanalysis as the greatest truth that men had ever discovered, and the sudden means of healing all the fury, unrest, and madness that had afflicted the souls of men for twenty thousand years—having heard all this, together with her comments on African sculptures, primitive paintings, Charlie Chaplin as a supremely great tragic artist, the modern dance, and all the other identifying paraphernalia with which the lives of sophisticated people were tricked out, and which, beneath its show of liberalness and alertness to new forms of art and life, was really itself nothing but a sterile, monotonous, and lifeless form of dutiful consent for people who had no power to make a new life for themselves, and whose greatest impulse was to keep in the swim—having already seen and observed in her all these disquieting signs of a familiar cult, he now wondered, in the distress and perplexity of his spirit, whether she was really an immensely competent "fancy" person pretending to be simple, or the simple, direct, and honest person that she seemed to be, who hated what was "fancy."

And his feeling on this point was so belligerent and resentful because every time she used the word he would apply it to his own life, and remember the letter he had written her. Then he would writhe with shame and loathing as he remembered how pompous, florid, and unnatural it was, and yet how it had come out of the passion and the substance of his life—how he had sweated real blood, and paid real anguish, desolation, and despair for something that was false.

Then he remembered suddenly, too, that during that last night on shipboard she had confessed a compassionate nature, had been distressed because she "did not want to see him suffer"—and as he remembered her words, and the casual circumstance of their meeting, an intolerably painful suspicion awoke in him that if it had not been he it might have been another youth, that an opportune chance had simply put him in the way of a romantic woman at a moment when she wanted adventure. The whole scene of their meeting on the ship returned to his memory bitterly. He winced and tried to withdraw from it. He realized now that he wanted to forget or change it.

A man can survey the general spectacle of living with the detachment of a philosopher or a cynic, he can be amused by its delusions, and follies, above all he can laugh at the madness of love and of the lover; but when he deserts the general spectacle to become an actor in the show, his detachment vanishes, and when his heart and interest are involved, the conflict between general truth and particular desire causes doubt, pain, and suffering. And Monk felt something of this conflict now. What was she—a woman approaching middle age who dreaded its coming and wanted a lover, any lover? No, a rare and beautiful woman who had preferred him above all others. What was his involvement with her—a part of the human comedy of folly and illusive desire, another repetition of the endless adventure of the infatuated youth, the gulled yokel, the country greenhorn for the first time in the city? No, the miracle of chance, the met halves of the broken talisman, the jointure of the two true hearts, the beautiful and faithful lovers who had made their way through all the maze and tumult of this earth's vast wilderness to find each other—the very proof and purpose of a destiny.

In all his confusion and doubt as he gazed at the woman plunged in her somber and disturbing revery, suddenly he wanted to cry out at her angrily and violently: "What are you thinking about? What is the meaning of this tragic and mysterious air? Do you think you are so subtle I cannot understand you? You're not so wonderful as all that! I have thoughts and feelings just as deep as yours!"

For some time, lost in this dark and brooding revery which he could not fathom, Mrs. Jack had been leaning on her drawing table where her designs and some sketches for costumes were scattered. And now, unconsciously, impatiently, Monk struck the smooth white board of the table a smart blow with the flat of his hand. Immediately she started out of her revery, looked in a startled manner at him, slipped the ring nervously on and off her finger, and then, with a kind and eager look, she came towards him smiling.

"What are you looking at, Mr. Webber? Do you like my design—hah?"

"Oh, yes! Very much," he said stiffly. "It's very good," although he had not looked at it.

"I love to work here," she said. "All the things you use to work with are so clean and beautiful. Look at these," she said, pointing to the wall behind the table, where several of her instruments—a T-square and a triangle—hung suspended from nails.

"Aren't they beautiful? It's as if they had a sort of life of their own, isn't it? They are so clean and strong. You can do such delicate and beautiful things with them. Aren't they noble and dignified things, though?" she continued. "It must be wonderful to be a writer like you are, and have the power to express yourself in words." He flushed, glancing at her sharply and suspiciously, but he said nothing. "I think it is the greatest power in the world," she continued earnestly. "There's nothing else that can touch it—it is so complete and satisfying. God, I wish I could write! If I only knew how to put it down I know I could write a wonderful book. I'd tell them a few things that would make their eyes stick out, all right."

"What sort of things?" he now asked with curiosity and interest.

"Oh," she said eagerly, "all sorts of things I know about. I see the most marvelous things every day. Here is all this glory and richness around you, and no one seems to do anything about it! Don't you think it's a shame—hah?" she said in the indignant and earnest tone that made people want to laugh. "I do. I'd like to tell people about my work. I'd like to tell them about these things I work with," she said, rubbing her fingers gently along the soft, smooth board of the table. "I'd like to tell them all the things you can do with these wonderful materials, and of the sort of life things have in them—the way they hang from the wall, or the way they feel. God, I wish I could tell people about my work! I should like to tell them what it's like when I design! The most wonderful and exciting thing goes on inside me, and no one has ever asked me about it, nobody has ever tried to find out what it is that happens," she said indignantly, as if she held some person responsible for this stupid neglect. "Isn't it a shame! . . . Gee, I'd love to put down the things I see every time I go out in the street. It gets richer and more beautiful all the time. I keep seeing new things now that I used not to notice at all. . . . Do you know what is one of the most wonderful things in the world?" she demanded abruptly.

"No," he said in a fascinated tone, "what is it?"

"Well," she said impressively, "I'll tell you—it's the window of a hardware store. . . . I passed by one going downtown the other day, and God!—it was so wonderful I stopped the car and got out. There were all these strong and beautiful instruments, they made a wonderful kind of pattern, it was just like some strange, new kind of poetry. . . . And oh, yes! I should like to tell the way the elevated structure looks when you come down some cross street to it. Sometimes at evening it makes the most wonderful design against the sky—I should like to paint it. . . . Then I should like to tell about all the different people I see, the clothes they wear. I should like to write down what I know about clothes. It is the most fascinating thing in the world, and nobody seems to know anything about it."

"Do *you*?" he said. "Do you know a lot about it? I suppose you do."

"Do I know a lot about it!" she cried. "And he asks me if I know a lot about it!" she exclaimed comically, and Jewishly raised her palms to the attendant universe. "Let me at him!" she said with a jolly burlesque of pugnacity. "Just let me at him! Well, young fellow, all I got to say is, if you find anyone who knows more about it than your old Esther, you're going to have to get up pretty early in the morning. That's all I've got to say about it!" He was somehow delighted by the joy she took in her skill and knowledge; her boastfulness was so gay and good-humored that no one could be displeased with it, and he felt sure now that it was entirely justified.

"Oh, I know the most marvelous things about clothes," she went on solemnly. "There's no one who knows the things about clothes that I do. Some day I'll tell you all about it. . . . You know, I've got a job working for a big dressmaking place downtown. I go in two mornings a week and design for them. It is the most wonderful place to work, I wish you could see it. It's so clean and spacious, they have these big, quiet rooms, and all around you everywhere they have bolts and bolts of beautiful material. There's something so magnificent about all this cloth, it is noble and beautiful, you can do such wonderful things with it. I love to go back to the work room and watch all the little tailors at work. You know, they're very fine workmen, some of them get paid two hundred dollars a week. And God!" she exclaimed suddenly, her little face deepening with a rich flush of humor, "how they stink! It's simply dreadful sometimes, you could cut the stink with a knife. But I love to watch them at their work. They have such delicate hands. When they draw the thread through and make a knot it is like a kind of dance."

As the woman talked, a feeling of immense joy, peace, and certitude entered his spirit. He got from her a sense of strength, ease, and happiness which he had not felt before, and the doubts and confusion of a moment before had vanished. Suddenly the life of the city seemed opulent, glorious, and full of triumph for him, he felt able to conquer and subdue any obstacle, he forgot his horror and fear of the swarming life of the streets, and the terrible loneliness and impotent desolation of a human atom threading its way among millions, trying to make its life prevail against the horror of gigantic crowds and architectures.

This little creature had found a way of life that seemed to him full of happiness and success: she was strong, small, and competent, she was also full of joy, tenderness, and lively humor, and she was immensely brave and gentle. He saw plainly that she was a product of the city. She had been born in the city, lived in it all her life, and she loved it; and yet she didn't have the harassed and driven look, the sallow complexion, the strident and metallic quality that many city people have. She was the natural growth of steel, stone, and masonry, yet she was as fresh, juicy, and rosy as if she had come out of the earth.

There are some people who have the quality of richness and joy in them and they communicate it to everything they touch. It is first of all a physical quality; then it is a quality of the spirit. With such people it makes no difference if they are rich or poor: they are really always rich because they have such wealth and vital power within them that they give everything interest, dignity, and a warm color. When one sees such a person in a lunchroom drinking a cup of coffee, one can almost taste and smell the full delicious flavor of the coffee: it is not simply one of a million cups of lunchroom coffee, it is the best cup of coffee that has ever been made, and the person who drinks it seems to possess to the utmost every drop of its essence and flavor. Yet this is done without affected gusto, gourmandising, sighs, or smackings and lickings of the lips. It is a real and vital power this person has for joy and richness, it comes from the texture of his life, it cannot be imitated.

A tramp, a hobo, or a beggar often has this quality. It is a joy to see such a man thrust his hand carelessly into the baggy pocket of a ragged old coat and draw out a loose cigarette, put it in his mouth, light it with twisted lips and a flame cupped in his hard palms, and then draw the first pungent draft of smoke deeply and deliciously into his lungs, exhaling it presently in slow fumings from his nostrils with a naked lift of his teeth.

The men who drive great trucks at night across the country often have this power. They lean against their fenders in the small green glow of lamps, they smoke; their lives are given then to speed and darkness, they enter towns at dawn. The men who rest from labor have this power. The masons coming from their work who sit in trains and smoke strong, cheap cigars—there is something simple and innocent about such men as they look at their cheap cigars, held in their great stiff fingers, with pleased smiles. The sharp fumes drug their tired flesh with deep content.

Those who have this quality are the young policemen sitting in shirt-sleeves in the all-night eating places, taxi drivers with black shirts, prize fighters, baseball players, and racing drivers, brave and gentle people; steel workers sitting astride a giddy spar, locomotive engineers and brakemen, lone hunters, trappers, most shy and secret people who live alone, whether in the wilderness or in a city room; in general, all people who deal with sensuous things, with what has taste, smell, hardness, softness, color, must be wrought or handled—the builders, the movers, the physical and active people, the creators.

The people who do not have this quality are the people who rustle papers, cap keys—the clerks, the stenographers, the college instructors, the people who eat lunch in drug stores, the countless millions who have lived meagerly in pallor and safety.

But when a person has in him the vitality of joy, it is not a meaningless extravagance to say that "nothing else matters." He is rich. It is probably the richest resource of the spirit; it is better than all formal learning, and it cannot be learned, although it grows in power and richness with living. It is full of wisdom and repose, since the memory and contrast of pain and labor are in it. It comes from competence, and it is touched with sadness, since the knowledge of death is on it. It has learned acceptance and regret, and it is nice because it sees that what is barren must be false.

Mrs. Jack had this vital quality of joy in its highest degree. With her it was not merely a physical and sensuous thing, it was a richly imaginative and delicately intuitive thing; it was full of faith and dignity, and she communicated it to everything she touched. Thus, as she drew his attention to the instruments and materials with which she worked—the drawing table, with its one smooth slab of soft white wood laid flat on trestles, the fat little pots of paint, the crisp squares of drawing paper, nailed with thumb tacks to the table, the neatly sharpened pencils and the delicate brushes, and the T-squares, sliding rules, and triangles—he began to feel the essence and vital beauty of these objects as he had never felt them before. Mrs. Jack loved these things because they were precise and delicate instruments, and because they served honestly and richly the person who knew how to use them.

This warm and lovely talent served her everywhere with an unfaltering directness and certainty. Mrs. Jack wanted what was best and most beautiful in life, she was always on the lookout for it, and she never failed to know and appreciate it when she found it. In everything, she wanted only the best. She would not make a salad of wilted leaves: if the outer parts were not crisp and fresh, she would strip them off and use the heart. If she had possessed only two dollars in the world, and had invited some people to dinner, she would not stingily spread her money out in little dabs of one thing and another. She would have gone to the markets and bought there the best steak she could find for two dollars, she would have brought it home and cooked it herself until it was informed with all the succulence and flavor her own rich character could give it, then she would have served it on a thick, creamy platter on a table adorned only by her big plates and the heavy and simple eighteenth-century knives and forks she had got in England. This would be all, but when her guests had eaten there would not be one of them who did not feel that he had richly banqueted.

People who have this energy of joy and delight draw other people to them as bees are drawn to ripe plums. Most people have little power for living in themselves, they are pallid and uncertain in their thoughts and feelings, and they think they can derive the strength, the richness, and the character they lack from one of these vital and decisive people. For this reason people loved Mrs. Jack and wanted to be near her: she gave them a feeling of confidence, joy, and vitality which they did not have in themselves.

Again, the world is full of people who think they know what they really do not know—other people have had their convictions and beliefs and feelings for them. With Mrs. Jack, it was at once obvious that she knew what she knew. When she spoke of the little tailors sitting cross-legged on their tables, and of the delicate and beautiful movements of their hands, or when she described the beauty and dignity of the great bolts of cloth, or when she spoke with love and reverence of the materials and instruments she worked with, one saw at once that she spoke in this manner because she had used and known all these things, she had worked and wrought with them, and her knowledge was part of her life, her flesh, her love, her marrow, her tissue, and was melted and mixed indissolubly with the conduits of her blood. This is what knowledge really is. It is finding out something for oneself with pain, with joy, with exultancy, with labor, and with all the little ticking, breathing moments of our lives, until it is ours as that only is ours which is rooted in the structure of our lives. Knowledge is a potent and subtle distillation of experience, a rare liquor, and it belongs to the person who has the power to see, think, feel, taste, smell, and observe for himself, and who has hunger for it.

As Mrs. Jack talked about herself and her life, and told in her vivid and glowing manner of her daily little discoveries in the streets, Monk began to get a vision of the city's life that was as different from the swarming horror of his own Faustine vision as anything could be. He saw that the city, whose immensity drowned him in confusion and impotence, was for her simply what rich woods and meadows might be for a country child. She loved the unending crowds as a child might love a river or tall, blown grass. The city was her garden of delight, her magic island, in which always she could find some new joy, some new rich picture to feed her memory.

She was like time, like the elfin light of time, because she gave the warm and magical color of distance and memory to things she had seen an hour before. In these stories to which her vivid and visual mind reduced experience, and in which her childhood and youth appeared so often, a picture of the old New York, and the old America, was already expanding and being given order and perspective in Monk's mind.

His own America was the America of the country man of the wilderness. The story of his potent and turbulent blood was a story of hundreds of men and women who had lived in loneliness, and whose bones were buried in the earth. The memory that lived in him was not the memory of men who had lived in paved and numbered streets, it was the memory of solitude and the distance and direction of the hunter and the frontiersman—a memory even now of men who "lived over yonder," a memory of "a feller I was talkin' to t'other day over in Zebulon," a memory of men who lived "jist before you git to the fork of the road where it turns off to go down into that holler—you'll see a big locust tree thar an' if you jist foller along that path hit'll take you right by his place—hit ain't fer, not more'n a mile, I reckon—you cain't miss hit."

Their greeting to strangers had been hearty, and their voices full of a deliberate kindliness, their gestures were slow and courtly, but their eyes were mistrustful and sharp, and flickered rapidly, and the smouldering embers of violence and murder were quickly fanned to fury in them. When they awoke at morning their eyes were fixed upon the calm and immutable earth, they watched the slow processional of the seasons, and fixed in their memory were always a few familiar things—a tree, a rock, a bell. The calm of the eternal earth and its elastic spring below man's foot had been his inheritance. He had the experience of the country boy who comes to the city—his feet were tired of the endless pavements, his eyes were weary of incessant change and movement, and his brain was sick with the horror of great crowds and buildings.

But now, in Mrs. Jack, he beheld a natural and happy product of the environment that terrified him, and in her warm little stories he began to get a picture of the city America he had not known, but had imagined. It was a world of luxury, comfort, and easy money; of success, fame, and excitement; of theatres, books, artists, writers; of delicate food and wine, good restaurants, beautiful fabrics, and lovely women. It was a world of warm, generous, and urbane living; and it all seemed wonderful, happy, and inspired to him now.

In his countless goings and comings about New York, his rides in the subways, his walks through the streets, each one of which had become a savage struggle with life, sound, movement, and design until he now faced the simplest excursion among a crowd with tightened nerves and a sense of horror and dislike, he had often observed an expression on the faces of middle-aged New Yorkers which repelled and depressed him. The expression was surly, sour, and petulant, the texture of the flesh was grey and sallow, and it sagged in a doughy fashion. Upon these countenances there was legible a common story of mean and ungenerous living, of bad food eaten dully without distaste or enjoyment in cafeterias, of homes in dismal single bedrooms or flats, of employment as night clerks in cheap hotels, ticket sellers in subways, cashiers in lunchrooms, as petty and ill-humored officials in uniform—the kind of men who snarl and bully and answer a civil question with an insolent reply, or who fawn in a whining and revolting manner when told that the stranger they have insulted is a person of importance to their employer:

"Why didn't yuh tell me yuh was a friend of Mr. Crawford's? I didn't know! If I'd known you was a friend of Mr. Crawford's yuh coulda had anything yuh like. Sure! Yuh can't blame us. Yuh know how it is," in a whining and confidential voice, intended to be ingratiating. "We gotta be careful. So many people comes here wantin' to see Mr. Crawford that ain't got no business to see him that he wouldn't have no time at all if we let 'em all in. Then if we let 'em in an' they ain't got no business to be let in, we get blamed for it. Yuh know how it is."

Upon these mean visages he had not been able to find any sign that would indicate any dignity or beauty in their lives. Their lives stretched back through a succession of grey and ugly days into that earlier New York of which he could get no picture except that it was dreary, and barren, and dull. He felt contempt, disgust, and pity for them. They were like small things that whine when threatened or beaten, and they belonged to that vast, drab horde who snarled, fawned, bickered, and whined their ways at length into nameless, numberless, and forgotten graves.

And he hated these people, too, because they gave the lie to all his early country visions of a warm, magnificent, and opulent life in the great city. It seemed impossible that they should have come out of the same time and the same city as Mrs. Jack. In her stories of her childhood and youth, of her wonderful, wild father who was an actor, of her beautiful, wasteful mother who bit diamonds from her necklace when she needed money, of her fat Rabelaisian Christian uncles who were enormously rich and ate the most succulent foods, which they themselves went to market for every day, poking and prodding at the meat and vegetables, of her beautiful and generous Jewish aunt, of her Christian aunt, of her English relatives, her Dutch relatives, of her husband's German relatives and her visits to them, of Mr. Roosevelt, and of actors, jolly priests, plays, theatres, cafés, and restaurants, of a great number of brilliant and interesting people—bankers, brokers, socialists, nihilists, suffragettes, painters, musicians, servants, Jews, Gentiles, foreigners, and Americans, he began to get fixed in his imagination an opulent and thrilling picture of the city in the Nineties and the early years of the twentieth century.

24

"This Thing Is Ours"

THEY HAD BEEN MEETING THREE OR FOUR TIMES EVERY WEEK. THESE hours and moments snatched from work, at noon time or late at night after the performance was over, and spent together on the ride uptown in a taxicab, over the plates at lunch somewhere in Greenwich Village, or over the polished slab, the almost vacant privacy, of a Childs restaurant late at night, were very eager, very precious ones. But, as is usual with most lovers in the city, they were both troubled by the lack of that essential need of love—a meeting place: a meeting place not on the corner, in a cab, before a window, or on the street, shared emptily beneath the naked sky with all blind and brute participations of the million-footed crowd, but a meeting place where they could be alone and which would be their own.

Both felt increasingly a sense of this unhappy lack. To meet her at her house now seemed impossible—not from fear or inexpediency, and assuredly not from any shame, but because both had the sense of their own integrity. What they were, they were, and they felt no concealment, but they also had the sense of their own decency and propriety. And this was also true about their meetings at the theatre: here the sense of all her active life, her work, her association with her friends was still too recent, it still clung to her and hung like a troubling veil of mist above the life of each.

As for the small hotel in which he lived, had meeting there been possible, the stupefactions of that place, the dreary contagion of its shabby lives, would have been too much for him.

She solved the problem in a characteristic way, in a manner typical of the indomitable purpose which, he was to find, that small figure housed. And, rather comically, she found it by a demonstration of one of those processes of a woman's mind by which she gets the thing

384

that she is looking for by pretending that she is looking for something else. She began to talk about "a place to work."

"Well, haven't you got one?"

"No, nothing that's really good enough. Of course, that was a lovely room I had at home. It faced north, and the light was always good. But now those wretched people have come along and built a big apartment house right in our backyard. So it has become too dark to work in now, and, besides, it's so hard to work at home. You're always being interrupted—you're always having to answer the phone, talk to one of the maids, or one of the family is always coming in."

"What's wrong with the room you've got at the theatre?"

"Oh, that never was intended as a place to work. It was just a room they had left over where they used to hang costumes they didn't need any longer. They let me have it because I had to have some place to work and that was all there was. But it's very difficult to work there, and it's getting worse all the time. Some of the girls leave their things in there and are always coming in and out. Besides, the light is very bad. . . . Anyway, now that I'm getting all these other jobs to do outside, I really need a place—some place more uptown so that I will not be so far away from all these places where I have to go."

This was probably true. At any rate, she kept referring to her need of a new working place every day or two when they would meet. Finally, one day she met him in a state of jubilant excitement.

"I've a place," she cried at once, even as she was pulling off her gloves, and before she sat down. "I've been looking around all morning—most of them were too depressing."

"You like this one?"

"It's simply wonderful," cried Mrs. Jack, with an air of astounded revelation. "In all your life you've never thought of such a place. It's up at the top of an old house," she went on. "The kind of old house that I used to live in when I was a child. Only this one is all rickety and gone to seed. You think the steps are going to give way on you, and it's very dirty. I don't know, the whole place is empty now, but it looks as if it's had a lot of sweatshops in it. But it's been a beautiful house," she cried, "a noble house. And I've taken the whole floor."

"A whole floor!" he exclaimed.

"The whole thing!" she gleefully affirmed. "In all of your life you've never seen such space. *There's* a place that you can spread yourself around in."

"Yes—but it must cost a fortune."

"Thirty dollars a month," she said triumphantly.

"*What!*"

"Thirty—dollars—a—month!" Mrs. Jack said slowly and impressively, and then, seeing a look of surprise and disbelief on his face, she went on quickly, "You see it is not fixed up at all. It's really very much run down and out of repair, and I suppose they are glad enough to rent it at any price. But, oh!" she cried rapturously, "Such noble space! Such wonderful light! Just wait until you see it!"

She was so eager to show him her great find that she could scarcely wait until he had finished with his lunch, and she seemed barely to touch hers. And he, too, stirred by her description and the elation of her discovery, felt a sharp excitement. After lunch they got up from their chairs immediately and went around to the new place.

It was an old four-story house on Waverly Place that had obviously fallen on evil days. One mounted from the street by a rusty flight of steps. On the first floor as one entered there was a dingy-looking tailor shop. The hall stood open to the winds, the door having been wrenched from its fastening and hanging by one hinge. Then one went up a flight of stairs that was so old and decrepit that it leaned crazily to one side as if its underpinning on that side was giving way. The stairs creaked heavily as one stepped on them, and the old rail sagged—it was as loose as an old tooth.

Upstairs the place was dark and completely deserted. The only illumination was provided by a gas jet in the narrow hallway, which was kept burning night and day. In the walls along the stairs were niches, hollowed in the plastering: they reminded her of a more prosperous and gracious day for the old house, when marble busts and statues had been stationed here. As they mounted they opened a door or two and looked in. The rooms were large and spacious, but they were very dirty and in a pitiable state of dilapidation. Apparently they had been used as work rooms of some sort, for there was a great tangle of electric wiring from the ceiling, and piles of rubbish on the bare floors, cardboard boxes, paper, bits of litter. Thus far the prospect was not very hopeful.

At length, up those steep, winding stairs, they reached the top floor.

They came up to a little landing, and stood before a door. The door was just a crude nailed-together kind of gate. It was fastened by a padlock and a bolted hinge. Mrs. Jack fumbled in her purse, produced a key, unlocked the door, and pushed it open. They went in.

The room they entered was really a discovery. Like all the others they had seen, the place was very dirty, but it occupied the whole floor. Like all the others, this room too had been used apparently as a kind of factory: there was again a great tangle of electric wiring on the ceiling, and the fixtures for a great many electric lights. An old, roughly-made, dilapidated-looking table had been left in the room in a good deal of rubbish which she had already swept up into a pile. In the middle of the room there was a skylight opening from the roof, and the ceilings sloped at either end, so that although there was great space and ample standing room in the central portion, one had to stoop a little as he approached the ends. The old whitewashed walls were dirty and in places pieces of plaster had been knocked out, leaving visible strips of dry brown plastering and dry lathing—the body and bones of the old house. The walls also bulged outward in places, and the bare wooden floor sagged and creaked as one walked across it. The whole place had the sag and lean of a old house, the worn modeling of time from which all sharp new edges and all solid holds have been worn away.

She turned proudly and stood looking at him with a bright and hopeful smile, as if to say: "There, now. What did I tell you? Isn't it fine?"

He didn't say anything for a moment, but he was conscious at first of a feeling of disappointment. He had expected something grander and better kept, and for a moment the shabby dilapidation of the whole place gave him a feeling of distress. Then he began to walk back and forth across the length of the whole floor: the great space of the room and the sense it gave him of unimpeded and expansive movement delighted him. After the cramped confinement of his own small room, and all the cramped confinements of the city, where space had become the last and dearest luxury, this delighted him. The old floor gave and creaked precariously, and in one place it was so loose and giving that it seemed unsafe. But the sense of release, of quietness, and of privacy was wonderful.

She watched him anxiously as he walked up and down:

"Do you like it? Of course, you have to stoop there at the end. But isn't it a wonderful room? The space is so grand. And the light!" she cried. "Isn't the light marvelous? It's such a perfect light to work by. Don't you think it's grand?"

Through the skylight over her, the light came down, soft, silent, steady, unperturbed; the brutal stultification of the streets, the unending tumults of the city were here stilled; and the effect upon his soul was like that quality of light itself, an effect of silence and of peace and of asylumage.

She was talking now, quickly and enthusiastically as she moved around, already full of busy plans of renovation:

"Of course, it's very dirty. . . . It's simply filthy! But I'm having a man in tomorrow to wash the windows and to scrub the floors. And I'm sending some things down from the house—my drawing table and my instruments, an old couch that we've no use for, and some chairs. You've no idea what a difference it will make when it looks clean and has a few things in it. . . . I thought I'd put my drawing table here? Below this light? Don't you think so?" She stood beneath the light and gestured to him. The strong, soft radiance came down from above and shone upon her fresh and ruddy face, so full of eagerness and hope, and for a moment he turned away, suddenly and deeply moved, he did not know why.

When they went out she locked the door behind her, and for a moment, before she put the key away into her purse, she shook it in his face with a gleeful and exultant little movement, which plainly said, "This thing is ours."

Then slowly, carefully, holding each other by the hand, as people unaccustomed do, they started down those old winding stairs. The floor treads creaked and sagged below their feet, and behind them in the dark there was a sound of a single drop of water that gathered, swelled, developed, dropped, in its steady, punctual monotone, like the sound of silence in the old house of life, alone.

25

A New World

A MIRACULOUS CHANGE HAD BEEN EFFECTED IN MONK'S LIFE, AND, AS SO often happens, he was scarcely aware at first that it had come. He did not see at first the meaning that Esther had for him. It was not merely the fact of romantic conquest that had wrought the change: in its essential values it was probably this fact least of all. Much more than this, it was the knowledge that for the first time in his whole life he mattered deeply, earnestly, to someone else.

Without being quite aware of it, this wonderful fact had an almost immediate effect on him. He was still likely to be crotchety, still too quick to take offense at a slight, whether real or imagined, still walking around with a chip on his shoulder daring someone to knock it off— but the chip was not so large now, nor so perilously tilted. He had a sense of inner security, of self-belief, that he had not had before. And he believed in himself because someone else believed in him. His war against the world was somewhat abated because his own war with himself was reconciled. As for all the minor grievances and annoyances, the surliness of nincompoops and the stupidity of fools, the tissue of paltry intrigues, envies, venoms, gossips, rumors, and petty politics that poisoned the life of the School for Utility Cultures, where he worked, and the little flicks and darts of daily life that had at first whipped his spirit into lacerated scorn—all this had now slipped back into its proper place. He saw them as the trivialities they were, if not with equanimity, at least more temperately, in their true proportion.

The woman had, in fact, begun to give a kind of frame, design, and purpose to his life that it had never had before. Although he did not know it at the time, she had herself become a kind of goal and purpose in his life, a kind of target at which his tremendous energies, so long exploded, scattered, misdirected, or diffused into thin air, could now be aimed. It would not be true to say that he actually "lived" for the times

389

when he would meet her. As a matter of fact, his life in between these times now passed more evenly, more temperately, and with a more proportionate judgment than it had done before. It was as if all the elements in his life had suddenly begun to take on the proportionate form, the balance in the distance, of a picture. He saw her now three or four times a week, but the sense of his contact with her life was daily, constant, and united.

She called him up every morning, usually before he was out of bed. The sound of her quick, bright voice, itself already so full of life, morning, and of business, awoke in him a healthy desire to be up and at his work, for he was now writing furiously every moment he could snatch from his duties at the school. She would always be full of her plans and projects for the day—the places where she had to be, the appointments that she had to meet, the work she had to do. If she was going to be in his "part of town" at lunch time, they would have lunch together; and since she loved the work she did, she always brought to these meetings a sense of healthy energy, of happy activity, of the movement, the excitement, the vitality of the world itself. Occasionally they would meet for dinner in the evening, but more often he would meet her later, after the performance. He would make the long, exciting drive into the East Side alone. Then they would leave the darkened theatre and come uptown together, usually stopping off at a Childs restaurant in a quiet neighborhood—their favorite one was on Fifth Avenue just above Madison Square—for a midnight lunch and an hour of talk together.

It was not merely that he was in love with her. In addition to that, through his association with her it seemed to him that now at last he had begun to "know" the city. For, in some curious way, the woman had come to represent "the city" to him. To him she was the city he had longed to know. Hers was not the city of the homeless wanderer, the city of the wretched, futile people living in the rooms of little cheap hotels, the city of the lost boy and the stranger looking at a million lights, the terrible, lonely, empty city of no doors, and of the homeless, thronging ways. Hers was the city of the native, and now it seemed to him that he was "in."

She was the city's daughter just as he had been the product of the town. The city's ways were not strange ways to her, nor were its crowded highways lonely ones, nor were its tongues and faces to her hard and cold and new. Rather, the city was the familiar neighborhood of her whole life—the yard in which she played when she was young, the place where she had gone to school, the "different parts of town" where she had lived, grown up, been married, moved to—and all of it was a province as warm, as friendly, as familiar, as were ever the cribbed horizons of a little town.

The woman really loved the city. She loved it not with ostentatious show, self-consciously; nor coldly, like feeble people who show off an old house which their ancestors built and, unable to make a real life in the world they have, trump up a false one of the world which they have lost. No, for Mrs. Jack the city was her living tenement; it was her field, her pasture, and her farm; and she loved it so because she was herself so much a part of it, because she knew and understood it so, because it was the stage and setting of her own life and work.

For her, the city was a living, breathing, struggling, hoping, fearing, hating, loving, and desiring universe of life. It was the most human place on earth because it had in it the most "humanity," the most American because it had in it the most Americans. All the grandeur and the misery; the high aspiration and the base desires; the noble work and the ignoble strivings for mean ends; the terror, violence, and brute corruption, and the innocence, the hope, the dreaming, and the loveliness; the huge accomplishment and a constant, raw unfinish of things still doing, never ended, getting done—all of it was here, and so to her the city *was* America. And in all of this, of course, because this vision and this understanding was so healthy, sound, and true, Mrs. Jack was right.

She carried this sense of health, of life, of work, of human understanding with her everywhere she went; it radiated from her like a strong and sweet vitality of happiness. It was as if, Antæuslike, Mrs. Jack derived her own strength, her own health, her own energy of work, of wanting, and of business, that radiated from her rosy face, that was legible in every movement of her energetic figure, that was described in every small, brisk step, in every gesture, from her constant, living contact with the bones and body of *her* native earth—which was that swarming and immortal rock on which she trod.

She brought this grand exhilaration of the city's life to all the meetings that she had with him. There on the parapets of furious noon, upon these mounting pinnacles of day, these two would meet, and instantly for him it would be as if the huge, sweet cargo of the morning had been borne in upon him too. A dozen tales of life and business would form upon the lips of this excited voyager, and suddenly it would seem to him that a vast and moving pageantry, the whole imperial chronicle of day, was there.

She had been "here and there" about the town. At nine o'clock she had been at work among the tailors in the garment district, where she was employed two mornings in the week to make designs. Even as she spoke, the whole scene spread before his eyes—the enormous buildings of the district, the huge "lofts," the great warehouse room, with its tables and its bolts of cloth, the coarse, clean smell of wool, the fitting rooms, and cutting rooms, with the tailors sitting cross-legged on the tables. "In all your life you've never seen such skill as these men have! The way they use their hands! It's all so swift, so sure, so delicate—it's—somehow it makes you think of some great orchestra!—But God!" suddenly her shoulders shook, her face turned crimson—"The way it smells! Sometimes I have to hang my neck out of the window!"

At half-past ten she had been to the costume fitter's. Here was the world backstage again, the life of the performers: "I got Mary Morgan fitted up. She's going to look lovely. The poor kid!" Suddenly her face was earnest and indignant, full of pity and concern: "She has been out of a job for almost a year. This is the first work that she has had to do! And she was so frightened, so ashamed when she came in. She pulled me by the arm and got me off into a corner and told me her underwear was simply in rags. She said, 'I simply can't let these people see me as I am, I'll drop dead if they do. What am I going to do?' The poor kid was almost crying. I gave her some money and told her to go out and buy herself some decent things. Honestly! if somebody had handed her the moon upon a silver platter she couldn't have been half so happy! She threw her arms around me and hugged me, and said, 'When you die and go to heaven they'll have to turn the Holy Mother out and give you the best room in the house.' She's a Catholic," said Mrs. Jack and laughed, but then her face grew earnest in its indignation, and she said: "Well, isn't it a shame! A kid like that pounding pavements for eight months until her shoes had holes in them, and her clothing is of rags! And God knows what she has lived on, how she has kept from starving! And then rehearsing her three weeks without a cent of pay! And if the show is a flop, she gets nothing and is out upon the street again, looking for a job! . . . But gee! You should have seen her when we fitted her! She was lovely! There's a girl for you, young fellow!" cried Mrs. Jack, with twinkling eyes.

"You should have seen her this morning when she got that dress on! She would have knocked your eye out! She's got the most beautiful arms and shoulders I have ever seen. She's playing the part of a society girl in this play——"

"A *society* girl!"

"Yes." She paused for a moment, not understanding the implication of surprise. Then as it came to her, she looked at him, her shoulders began to shake hysterically again, and she cried: "Can you beat it! Isn't it wonderful! The poor kid with no soles in her shoes and her underwear in rags playing the part of Marcia Coventry!"

"What did the dress cost—do you know?"

"Yes," again her face was serious and concerned, full of business, "I got the estimates this morning. I've tried to keep it down as much as possible—don't believe anybody else could have done half so well. If I had taken her to Edith's, I couldn't have touched it under five hundred dollars. But I've kept it down to just under three hundred, doing it this way. And it's a knock-out! I'll bet every little Junior Leaguer in the world will copy it this Winter."

"You've done a lot of work on it, haven't you?"

"You've *simply* no idea!" cried Mrs. Jack, looking very earnest. "The work I've done on this kid's clothes alone! She's a regular clothes horse in the play! And it's the damnedest tripe!" she said quite simply. Her face flushed, and her shoulders shook again with laughter: "We've got a name for it among ourselves. We call it—The Fall Showing."

"What is it?"

"Oh, it's a lot of junk someone has thrown together for that fellow Croswell."

"Cecil Croswell?"

"Yes, you know—the Lady Killer. In all your life—you've no idea"— she went on with an air of incredulity—"it's simply past belief!"

"What?"

"What these people—these actors—are like. They know simply nothing of what's going on—outside. If you spoke to that fellow about Mussolini, he'd ask you what did he ever play in. That's about as much as he knows about anything," she said in a tone of disgust. "And of all the nerve! Of all the conceit! If you knew what that fellow thinks of himself"—suddenly she choked and shrieked hysterically—"God! This morning—" she began, and could not go on.

"What happened this morning?"

"When he came for his fitting—" said Mrs. Jack. "He wears evening clothes all through the play—that's the kind of play it is. Well, I've designed a beautiful suit for him and he put it on. And then," Mrs. Jack had a hysterical lilt in her voice, "he would strut back and forth before the mirror, to and fro and up and down, wiggling his shoulders, and fooling with his collar, and giving it a tug here and a tweak there, until he almost drove me out of my mind. And then he began to hem and to haw, and, well, you see it was this way, and, well, you see it was that way, and the upshot of it," she cried indignantly, "was that the big ham didn't think this beautiful suit I had designed was good enough for him. The nerve of him! I could've killed him! Well, he cleared his throat and began to orate—you'd have thought he was doing *East Lynn* in a road show. 'On the whole,' says he, 'I think I like my own suit better.' He's got a fancy suit of evening clothes that he loves so much he wears it down to breakfast. 'Well, Mr. Croswell,' I said, 'all I can say is that this is a suit that fits the part and the one you ought to wear.' 'Yes,' says he, 'but the lapels,' he says—'the *lapels*'— he cries out in his tragic tone—'the lapels, dear lady, are not right'— with that he lets his voice drop down as if he was announcing the death of a child. The nerve of that guy!" she muttered angrily. "I knew more about lapels when I was six years old than he'll ever know. 'The lapels,' he says, drawing himself up and tweaking at them with his fingers, as if he was addressing Parliament, 'The lapels are too narrow!'—The ones he has, of course, on that fancy rig of his, are broad enough to drive a team of horses over. 'Well, Mr. Croswell,' I said, 'all I can say is that the lapels may not be right for Croswell but they are right for the part he is playing—and Croswell is not playing Croswell, but the part that has been written for him in the play'—which is a big lie, of course," she said disgustedly—"Croswell *is* playing Croswell—that's all he can play, all he ever played! Of course, he couldn't see this—these people have no quality!" she cried impatiently, in a kind of parenthesis. "You've simply no idea! You wouldn't believe that it was possible! The fool kept talking of his 'points.' 'Yes, I know,' he says, as if he were speaking to a child, 'I know. Still, all of us have our own points. And as for me—' he cried, slapping himself on the chest like a big piece of ham"—and with these words, Mrs. Jack, her eyes dancing and her face rosy with laughter, suited the action to the words and slapped herself on the breast with her small hand— "'As for *me*,' he cried"—she uttered the words in a tone of sonorous burlesque— "'As for me, I am noted for muh torso!'" She shook hysterically, with a last shriek faintly: "Can you beat it? Does it seem possible? Now, that will just give you an idea of what some of them are like!"

"And what else have you been doing? Is that all?"

"Oh, heavens no! I put in a full day's work before I met you here today. First, well, let's see—" she studied briefly, "Katy came in with coffee at seven-thirty. Then I bathed and took a cold shower. I take it so cold that it sends tingles all up and down my spine." And, indeed, her face always had that glowing freshness as if she had just come from a cold shower. "I dressed and had my breakfast, talked to Cook, told her what to order, and how many were coming to the house tonight. I talked to Barney—he's our driver—and told him where to come for me this afternoon. Then I read the mail and paid some bills and wrote some letters. I talked to Roberta on the phone about this new show I'm doing for the League. I saw Fritz for a moment, as he was leaving for the office. I looked in and talked to Edith for a moment in her room. And I was out of the house and on my way downtown before nine o'clock. Then I was at work at Stein and Rosen's for an hour—then to Heck's for costume fittings until twelve—then to the wig maker's on 47th Street at twelve-fifteen—" she laughed: "The strangest thing happened! You know where the wig maker's is—it's in what used to be an old brownstone house, and you go up a flight of steps and there is a big front window on the first floor with wigs and hats in it. Well!" she exclaimed with accented and excited finality. "What do you suppose I did? I went up the stairs and thought that I was right, and saw a door and opened it, and just walked in. And what do you suppose I found? I walked right in upon a bar. It seemed to run the whole way back, and a whole lot of men were standing at the bar drinking, and there was a man behind the bar mixing drinks. Well!" she cried again, "I was so surprised! Honestly, it was the strangest thing. I couldn't believe my eyes! I just stood there with my mouth wide open staring at them. And they were all so jolly. The man behind the bar called out: 'Come right on in, lady. There's always room for one more.' Well, I was so confused—I just didn't know what to say, and at last I said, 'I thought this was the wig maker's!' Well, you should have heard them laugh! The bartender said, 'No, lady, this ain't the wig maker's, but we've got some hair tonic here that'll grow hair better than a wig!' And another man said, 'You're in the wrong place.

This ain't the wig maker's, it's the Novelty Shop'—and then they all laughed again; I guess, because the place had a kind of fake window with some dirty old Christmas bells, and a few strips of red crêpe paper in it, and a sign that said, 'United Novelties Supply Company,' I guess as a kind of dodge—and that was the reason they laughed. They seemed awfully jolly. The bartender came out from behind the bar and took me to the door, and showed me where the wig maker's was, which was just next door, and the reason I had got confused was that there are two flights of steps and I was in a hurry and wasn't looking, and so I got mixed up—but isn't New York wonderful!"

She had delivered all of this in a tone of excited and almost breathless rapidity, but seemed to translate the confusion of the moment perfectly in her own breathless and bewildered face.

"After that," she went on, "I had to go and rummage through some old furniture shops up on Eighth Avenue. You simply have no idea the kind of junk that you can find. It's fascinating just to poke around. I was looking for some things that would go into a setting for a room in a Victorian house in the Seventies. I found some marvelous things: a picture in a kind of gilt frame, a sort of lithograph, I guess, showing a lady with blonde hair playing a spinet, and a gentleman, with ruffles at the neck and lacy sleeves, leaning on the spinet with a gloomy look, and three little gold-haired children, all with high waists and ruffled sleeves and long skirts like the lady had, waltzing around in a sort of dance, and marble flags upon the floor and a tiger skin—it couldn't have been more perfect for the kind of room I have in mind. I found some window hangings and some drapes of the kind that I was looking for—of an awful, faded, greeny plush—God! they looked as if all the germs and dust and microbes in the world had nested there—but they were just the things I wanted. And I would ask for other things as well, which it didn't seem that any living, breathing, mortal man could possibly have—and the old fellow would go poking and rummaging around in those piles of junk, and finally bring out just what I was looking for! . . . Look!" She took out a tiny folded scrap of tinfoil wrapping paper, and she spread it out for him: it had a winy, brilliant, and exotic color, and she said, "Don't you think that's beautiful?"

"What is it?"

"It's the wrapping off a piece of candy. I saw it this morning as I was passing by a little stationery shop. The color was so strange and beautiful that I went in and bought the candy, just to get this wrapping here. If I can, I'm going to see if I can match it somewhere with a piece of cloth—I've never seen this shade before, it would be beautiful." She was silent for a moment, then continued: "God! I wish I could tell you everything I've seen today. I am bursting with it, I want to bring it all to you, and give it to you, but there is so much of it, it gets away. When I was a little girl, I was fascinated by all the different shapes of things, by all the beautiful designs there are. I would go and get all different kinds of leaves: the shape and form of each one was so different, and so delicate, so beautiful, I would draw all the different kinds of leaves, with all the delicate little lines and forms they had in them. Sometimes the other kids laughed at me for doing it, but it was like having found a new and wonderful world that is all around us, and that most people never see. And it keeps getting richer and more beautiful all the time. I see things every day now that I never saw before—things that people pass by all the time without ever seeing."

She would meet him late at night sometimes, after she'd gone to a gay and brilliant dinner party, or had given one herself. And here, too, she would be flushed with happy energy, charged with gaiety and good spirits, full of news. And now the world she brought to him was no longer the world of morning work and business; it was the great world of the night, a golden world of pleasure, wealth, distinction, talent, and success. She was charged with it, still bubbling over with the bright champagne of all its heady gaiety, still sparkling with its brilliance and its joy.

This night world in which she moved and lived as a familiar and acknowledged denizen was a privileged world of high distinction. It included illustrious names and celebrated personalities that had long been famous through the length and breadth of the whole nation. It included great producers and famous actresses, well-known writers, painters, journalists, and musicians, and mighty financiers. And these great illuminati of the night seemed to move and live and breathe and have their being in a kind of golden colony that once, in the enchanted imaginings of his boyhood, had seemed impossibly far away, and that now, by the same enchantment, seemed miraculously near.

She brought it all to him, still warm with her recent contact, this magic world of fame, of beauty, wealth and power. She brought it to him with a casual touch of her own familiarity with it, and what was most incredible was the knowledge that she was herself a part of it.

God knows what he had expected to discover—to hear these creatures feasted on ambrosia, drank nectar from a golden cup, ate lampreys or strange foods the average man had never heard about. But it was somehow astounding to hear that this famous company went to bed, got up, and bathed and dressed, and ate and went about its business much the same as other people did, and that from the portals of these celebrated lips fell passages of speech not wholly different from his own.

The celebrated columnist whose winged jest, whose subtle wit, whose jabs and praises, whose graceful lyrics, and whose clever limericks had flashed forth for more than twenty years—this man whose daily chronicle of the city's life he had so often feasted on in his own college years, reading into that diary of the day's activity the whole glamorous pageantry of that distant Babylon, cloud-capped and rosy-hued there in the smoke of his imagination—this Aladdinlike enchanter who had so often rubbed his lamp and brought the magic of great Babylon to life for a hundred thousand boys like him—this magician alive and breathing in the flesh had been a guest at dinner on this very evening, had sat next to her, and talked to her, called her by her first name, as she called his, and would record that very date and day, the place, the person, and the time, in another portion of that endless diary, which other visionary youths in a thousand other little towns would read and feast upon, dreaming forever of great Babylon: "So, out and in a petrol waggon to Esther Jack's, and found a merry company, and S. Levenson the designer there, and S. Hook, the scrivener, and a mighty handsome girl in a red dress whom I had never seen, and straightway gave a buss upon the cheek, and many others there, as well, and mighty fine, but none so fine, methought, as Esther was."

Or she would bring to him the merry tidings of some glittering first night, some opening of a famous theatre, and the company of the famous and the beautiful who were there. The brilliant process of these happenings would babble from her lips with the gay, excited humor of a child. And, as if to give the whole thing naturalness— perhaps to put him more at ease, to make him feel that he, too, was a member of this favored group, himself initiate to all its privilege; or perhaps, just with a shade of affectation, to show she was herself of such a clear and simple spirit as not to be impressed or overawed by the resounding reputations of the great—she would preface her descriptions, qualify her golden calendar of names, with such modest phrases as "a man named ——."

She would say: "I wonder if you ever heard of a man named Karl Fine? He's a banker. I was talking to him at the play tonight. I have known him for years. And look!" here her manner changed to merry glee, "you'd never guess what he said to me when he came up and spoke. . . ."

Or: "I was seated tonight at dinner next to a man named Ernest Ross," mentioning a famous criminal lawyer. "His wife and I used to go to school together."

Or: "I wonder if you have ever heard of a man named Stephen Hook?" This was a writer who enjoyed a wide reputation as a critic and biographer. "Well, he was up to our house for dinner tonight, and I was telling him about you. He would like to meet you. He's one of the finest people I have ever known. I've known him for years."

Or, after an opening: "Guess who I saw tonight! Did you ever hear of a man named Andrew Cottswold?" mentioning the best-known dramatic critic of the time. "Well, he was there tonight, and he came up to me after the show and guess what he said!" With her eyes sparkling and her face flushed with laughter and happiness, she looked at him a moment, then said: "He told me that I was the best designer in America. That's what he said!"

Or: "I wonder if you ever heard of a woman by the name of Roberta Heilprinn?" This was the director of a famous art theatre. "Well, she came to dinner tonight. We are very old friends," said Mrs. Jack. "We grew up together."

The number of celebrated people with whom she "had grown up together" or "had known all her life" was really astonishing. Was the name of a famous producer in the theatre mentioned? "Oh, Hugh—yes. We grew up together. He used to live in the house next door to us. He's a very fine person," said Mrs. Jack, looking very earnest. "Oh, a *very* fine person." When she referred to someone as "a *very* fine person," with an air of great seriousness and conviction, it was as if she not only meant just that, but also derived a virtuous self-satisfaction from the knowledge that the "very fine person" was very successful to boot, and that she was herself on such excellently intimate terms with both fine persons and success.

Mrs. Jack sometimes gleefully asserted that she was like her uncle "for whom the very best of everything was just about good enough." And certainly her standard in men and women—as in foods, in work, in goods, construction, and material—was a very high one. The very best of everything, in men and women, did not include mere money grubbing, money getting, or social eminence. It is true that sometimes she would mention the names of great capitalists, friends of her husband, and their wives, and would even speak of their enormous wealth with a kind of satisfaction. "Fritz says there's literally no end to what he's worth! It's simply fabulous!"

And she would speak of the glittering beauty of some of the women in the same way. There was the wife of "a man named" Rosen, the famous merchant for whom she worked, and in whose great shop her sister, Edith, was vice-president and second in command. Rosen's wife had half a million dollars' worth of jewels— "And she wears them all!" cried Mrs. Jack, looking at the young man with a bewildered and inquiring expression. "They were at the house last night for dinner—she had all of it on—it was unbelievable!" said Mrs. Jack. "That woman glittered like a piece of ice! And she is very beautiful! I could hardly eat my dinner I was so fascinated. I couldn't keep my eyes off of her. I watched her, and I'm sure she was thinking about her jewelry all the time. The way she moved her hands and arms, the way she turned her neck—it wasn't like a person wearing jewelry, but like jewelry wearing the person. Isn't it strange?" said Mrs. Jack. And again the young man noticed that she had a troubled and inquiring look.

Occasionally when she spoke of this side of the city's life, describing it in quick and casual phrases, she evoked a picture that was stupendous in its wealth and power, and rather sinister. She would refer, for example, to a friend of her husband's, a millionaire named Bergerman whose wealth was "simply fabulous." Then she would tell of the evening in Paris when he had taken her and Roberta Heilprinn out to dinner, and later to a gambling club where first a boxing bout had been arranged for the delectation of the clients. "You would have thought you were in a drawing room! Everyone was dressed in evening clothes, and the women wore ropes of pearls, and there was a great, thick carpet on the floor, and you sat in the most delicate gold-leaf chairs with flowered satin seats. Even the ropes around the ring had velvet coverings! It was thrilling—and, somehow, a little terrible. It was all so strange, and when they turned the lights out you could see nothing but the two men in the ring—one of them a negro—their bodies were magnificent, the action of the black against the white so quick and swift, like a kind of dance." Later on, she told him, after the fight was over, the guests had scattered around the gaming tables, and Bergerman had lost a million francs at roulette in less than twenty minutes, or, at the rate of exchange that then existed, almost thirty thousand dollars. "And it meant absolutely *nothing* to him!" said Mrs. Jack, looking at the young man with a flushed and very earnest face. "Can you imagine it? Isn't it incredible?" And for a moment more she continued to look at him with a surprised and questioning kind of face, as if he, perhaps, might be able to supply the answer.

She had other stories of this kind—stories of men who won or lost fortunes at gambling every evening and who were not troubled, either with their losses or their gains; stories of women and young girls who came into Mr. Rosen's shop and within fifteen minutes spent more money for clothing than most people hoped to possess in a whole lifetime; of a famous courtesan who walked in with her elderly lover and bought a Chinchilla coat "right off the rack," paying for it in spot cash, taking from her purse a wad of thousand-dollar bills, "big enough," said Mrs. Jack, "to choke a horse," and tossing sixty of them out across the counter.

The effect of these stories was to evoke a picture of a world of wealth that was at first fabulous and fascinating in its Bagdadlike enchantments, but that quickly took on a more sinister hue as Monk read the meaning of its social implications. It shone there, written on the face of night, like a lurid and corrupted sneer. It was a world that seemed to have gone insane with its own excess, a world of criminal privilege that flouted itself with an inhuman arrogance in the very face of a great city where half the population lived in filth and squalor, and where two-thirds were still so bitterly uncertain of their daily living that they had to thrust, to snarl, to curse, to cheat, contrive, and get the better of their fellows like a race of mongrel dogs.

The obscene wink, so written there against the visage of the night, was intolerable in its damnable injustice. The knowledge of it choked him, turned his veins into a poison of cold fury, a murderous desire to smash and trample it to ruin. He wondered how men who drew the breath of life and did the work of day could let their enemy feed upon their blood, how they could allow themselves to forget the insecurity of their lives by gazing raptly at the mirage of "prosperity" towards which all seemed to think that they were turning, and which most of them were sure they already shared. Like those lost creatures in the Country of the Blind who thought the single man among them who had eyes was diseased with cancer of the brain, they were sure that heaven started just a little out of reach above their heads, and that presently they would scale a ten-foot ladder and be there. Meanwhile, these blind men lived in filth and went through a daily struggle just to get the barest means of life, and they swallowed down obediently all the vicious nonsense that any politician told them about the "high standard" of their living which, these wretches were solemnly assured, made them "the envy of the world."

And yet, although they were blind, surely they could smell. But they were so infatuated that they reveled in the general all-pervasive stink of rottenness. The blind men knew that government was rotten, that almost every branch of authority, from high office down to the lowest constable that patrolled the beat, was riddled through and through, like a putrescent honeycomb, with dishonesty and graft. And yet the most obscure of all the land, the smallest cipher in the subway's depths, could assure you that this was the way things ought to be, the way that things had always been, the way they would continue to the end of time. The blind were wise—with a wisdom celebrated in the city streets. Were politicians rogues? Were officials in the city's government grafters, thieves? Every man, the blind could tell you as they struggled through the subway door while there was still room for one more visionless sardine, was "getting his." And if one protested at the process over much, it was a sign the man was "sore"—"You'd do the same thing if you were in his place—*sure* you would!"

One's virtue, therefore, was only another name for one's envious chagrin. And if one was virtuous, did one think because he was that there would be no more cakes and ale—or, for that matter, chickens in the pot, or two cars in garages, or, to step it up a peg or two, Chinchilla coats from Mr. Rosen's, or roulette wheels for Mr. Bergerman, or many other splendid things like this—the blind assured each other as they struggled through the stiles—that had made them all "the envy of the world"?

The knowledge that she was a part of this life, too, went through him like a flash, and he would feel again the baffling torture of that doubt which in the years to come was to torment and trouble him so often—the enigma of this flower face. How *could* she be a part of it? This creature seemed to him so full of health and happiness, so full of work, of hope, of morning, and of high integrity. And yet, indubitably, she was a part of this thing, too—of this Midas world of night, of this reptilian wink, its criminal corruption and inhuman privilege, the impregnable arrogance of its living sneer.

And here, too, at night, she could blossom like a flower, a flower that had the look at night, even as it had by day, of innocence and morning; and that could live here, breathe here, blossom in the foul contagion of this air just as she blossomed in the day, and be a part of it, that never lost an atom of her freshness and her beauty—a flower that blossomed from a hill of dung.

He could not fathom it, it whipped his spirit to a frenzy, it made him turn on her at times and rend her, bitterly accuse her with unjust and cruel words—and leave him baffled and infuriated at the end, no nearer to the truth than he had ever been.

And the truth was simply that she was a woman, and that her way, like everyone's, had been a vexed and most uncertain one, and that, like everyone in that great honeycomb, she, too, was caught up in a web, and had come to these concessions in the end. The truth was also that the better part of her was loyal to the better part of life, but her loyalties, like everyone's, were mixed, and in this twin allegiance was the wrong. On one side was the worldly society and the duty it imposed, the responsibility it demanded, the obligations it entailed. And on the other side there was the world of work, and of creating, the world of friendship, aspirations, and the heart's true faith. And this side was the deeper, truer part of Mrs. Jack.

It was as worker and as doer that this woman was supreme. The true religion of her soul, the thing that saved her and restored her from the degradation of the wasteful idleness, the insane excess of self-adornment, the vanity of self-love, and the empty ruin of hollowness that most women of her class had come to know, was the religion of her work. It saved her, took her out of herself, united her life to a nobler image, which was external to her and superior to the vanities of self. There was no labor too great, no expenditure of time and care and patient effort too arduous and too exacting, if, through it, she could only achieve "a good piece of work."

And of all the things she hated most, the first one was a shoddy piece of work. To her this was original sin. She could overlook the faults and errors of a human personality, excuse its weaknesses, tolerate its vices, and the flaws it could not help. But she could not, would not, stand for shoddy work, for there was no excuse for it. An ill-cooked meal, an ill-kept room, an ill-made dress, an ill-painted piece of scenery, meant something more to her than haste or carelessness, something more than mere forgetfulness. They meant a lack of faith, a lack of truth, a lack of honesty, a lack of all integrity—a lack of everything "without which," as she said, "your life is nothing."

And that is what saved her in the end. She held steadfast to the faith of honest work. This was her real religion, and from it all the good things in her life and person came.

26

Penelope's Web

THE WOMAN HAD BECOME A WORLD FOR HIM—A KIND OF NEW AMERICA—and now he lived in it, explored it all the time. It was not merely love that accounted for this immolation. Or rather, with him, love had so much hunger in it. Perhaps, although he did not know it, there was destruction in him, too, for what he loved and got his hands upon he squeezed dry, and it could not be otherwise with him. It was something that came from nature, from memory, from inheritance, from the blazing energies of youth, from something outside of him and external to him, yet within him, that drove him forever, and that he could not help.

Seated beside him at the theatre one night, in the interval between the acts, Mrs. Jack looked suddenly at his knotted hands and said, "What have you got there?"

"What?" he looked at her bewildered.

"Oh, look!" She took it from him and shook her head. "Your program! See what you have done to it!"

He had rolled the thick and heavy pages of the program into a cylinder, and, during the first act, had twisted it in two. She smoothed the torn pages out and surveyed them with a rueful little smile.

"Why do you always do that?" she said. "I've noticed that you always do."

"Oh—I don't know. It's nervousness, I guess. I don't know why I do it but I tear up everything I get my hands on."

The incident was symbolic. The truth was, once a thing had touched his interest he fastened to it like a hound, his hunger for it insatiable, voracious, devouring, and consuming, and it drove him on until he reached the end. It had always been that way with him.

As a child, hearing Aunt Maw speak about the Civil War, and of the day the men came marching back, suddenly for the first time in his

405

life he saw the war, heard the voices of the men again, and he fell upon her like a beast of prey. What kind of day was it, at what time did it occur? Who were the men she saw, and how were they dressed, were they ragged, did all of them have shoes? Who were the people waiting there beside the road, what did the women say, and did they cry?

He would go for her with ceaseless questions until she was bewildered and worn out; then he would come pounding back at her again. What did they live on now that their money was all gone? Where did they get their clothes? They grew them. Who made them? The women spun them. How did women spin, and had she used a spinning wheel herself? What colors were the clothes, or did they have a color? Yes, they dyed them, and they made the dyes themselves. How did they make the dyes? What were they made of? From walnut hulls, from elderberries, and from sassafras which they gathered in the woods. What colors did they get from these, by what process were they got?—and so on, back and forth, making the old woman strain her memory until he had pumped her dry.

So, now, he was after Mrs. Jack like this. She would say:

"My father used to go to Mock's. . . ."

"Where was it? Never heard of it."

"It was a kind of restaurant—he used to go there almost every night."

"Where was this restaurant? Were you ever there yourself?"

"No, I was just a child, but I would hear him speak of it, and the name would fascinate me."

"Ah, that *would* fascinate. What kind of a place was Mock's?"

"Oh—I don't know. I was never there myself, but when he came in late at night I would hear him talking to my mother."

"How could you hear him? Why weren't you in bed?"

"Well, I was. But my room was just above the dining room, and there was a furnace ventilator in the wall. And when I turned this on I could sit there in the darkness and hear everything they said. They thought that I was sound asleep, but I would sit there listening to them like some invisible spirit, and I found this thrilled me and excited me. I would hear them talking down below, and often they would talk of Mock's. Sometimes my father would bring other actors, friends of his, with him; and I would hear my mother say, 'Where on earth have you all been?' And I would hear my father and the other actors laugh, and he would say, 'Why, we've been to Mock's.' 'Well, what have you been doing all this time at Mock's?' 'Well, we had a glass a beer,' father said. 'Yes, I can see that,' I would hear my mother say.

'It's pretty plain that all of you have had a glass of beer,' she said. And I would hear the voices and the talking, and the actors laughing, and all of it sounded so jolly, until it seemed to me that I was sitting there with them except they didn't know it because I was invisible—and I would hear them talking, telling that they had been to Mock's."

"And that's all you know—all you found out? You never found out where it was, nor what it looked like?"

"No, but I imagine it was more a place for men, with a bar and oysters—and sawdust on the floor."

"And the name of it was Mock's?"

"The name of it was Mock's."

In that way he kept after her, prying, probing, questioning about everything she told him, until at last he got from her the picture of her lost and vanished years.

"Long, long into the night I lay ——"
        (One!)
"Long, long into the night I lay awake ——"
        (Two!)
"Long, long into the night I lay awake, thinking how I should tell my story."

Oh how lovely those words are! They make a music in me just like bells.

(*One,* Two, Three, Four! One, *Two,* Three, *Four!*)

Oh there are bells, and that is time! What time is that? That was the half hour that the bells were striking. And that was time, time, time.

And that was time, dark time. Yes, that was time, dark time, that hangs above our heads in lovely bells.

Time. You hang time up in great bells in a tower, you keep time ticking in a delicate pulse upon your wrist, you imprison time within the small, coiled wafer of a watch, and each man has his own, a separate time.

And once upon a time there was a tiny little girl, and she was a mighty pretty, sweet little girl, too, and she was awfully smart, she learned to write before she was six years old, and she used to write her dear uncles John and Bob letters, and they were great, fat fellows—God, how those fellows could eat!—and they simply adored her, and she used to call them her Dere Uncle Honeys: We have a new Dog named Roy and he is swete but Bella says he is also messy Sister is lerning to talk and she can now say everything and I am taking french lessons and the tetcher says I can now talk it good I am awfely smart and good and I think of my dere Uncle Honeys all the time wel that is all Sister sends luv and we know our dere Uncle Honeys will not forget us and will bring something luvly yore darling litel Esther.

Oh, but that must have been much later, after we came back from England. Yes, I think it must have been a year or two later because all I can remember before is a big boat that went up and down and Mama got awfully sick—God, she was white! I got so frightened and began to cry, and Daddy was so lovely. He brought her champagne, I heard him say, "Here, drink this, you'll feel better," and she said, "Oh, I can't, I can't!" But she did. Everyone always did what he wanted them to do.

And I had a nurse called Miss Crampton—isn't that a funny name to have?—and at first we lived behind the Museum in Gower Street, then later we were in Tavistock Square. And the milkman had a little cart that he pushed before him, and he made a funny noise in his throat, and every morning when he came by they let me go out and sit upon the curb and wait for him, and the sun was like old gold and murky-looking, and I gave the man some money, two or three pennies, and he said in a loud voice, "There you are, Miss, fresh as a dyesy," and he gave me a *tiny* little bottle of cream, and I drank it all right there before him, and gave him back the bottle. God, I was proud! I think I was about three or four years old. And then when I asked Daddy why cream cost so much more than milk, he said, "Because it's so hard for the cow to sit down on those little bottles." And oh! I thought that was so wonderful I couldn't stop thinking about it, and Mama told him he ought to be ashamed of himself talking to a child like that, but there was something so wonderful about him, I believed everything he said.

Then, later, Daddy was away on a tour with Mansfield, and Mama went with him, and they left me with Auntie May. She had a house in Portman Square. God! What a lovely house that was! She was a writer. She wrote a book about a kid who grew up in the East End of London, it was damned good; the whole thing was done with the most enormous skill, it was trash, but it was awfully good trash.

Auntie May was awfully nice. She always let us have tea with her, I used to love that, all sorts of people came to see her, she knew a great many people; and one day when I came down to tea there was an old man there with a long white beard, and I was wearing my little apron, I must have been awfully sweet. And Auntie said, "Come here, my dear," and she took me and stood me between her knees, and turned my face towards the old man—and God! I was frightened, there was something so strange about it! And Auntie said, "I want you to look at this gentleman and remember his name, for some day you will know more about him and remember meeting him." Then Auntie said that the old man's name was Mister Wilkie Collins, and that he was a writer, and I thought that was an awfully funny name for anyone to have, and I wondered what an old man like that could write.

Then Cousin Rupert laughed at me and teased me because I was afraid of Mister Collins—Oh, he was dreadful! I used to hate him!— and I began to cry and Mister Collins got me to come and sit on his knee, and he was really an awfully nice old man. I think he died a year or so after that. He began to tell me some stories and they were simply fascinating, but I've forgotten what they were. But God! I used to love his books—oh, he wrote some wonderful books! Did you ever read *The Woman in White* and *The Moonstone?* Well, they're pretty swell.

So then I guess we must have been away two years in all, Daddy was on this tour with Mansfield, and when we got back to New York we all went to live with Bella. I think that was the only time she and Mama were separated, they simply adored each other. . . . Well, no, maybe we did not live with Bella at first. Mama still had some of those houses left downtown so maybe we went there at first, I don't know.

That was a good time then, for then the sun came out one day and the Bridge made music through the shining air. It was like a song: it soared like flight above the harbor, and there were men with derby hats upon it. It was like something you remember for the first time, it was like seeing something clearly for the first time in your life, and down below it was the river. I think it is like that when you are a kid, I am sure it must be just like that, you remember things but they are all confused and broken up and darkness is in them; and then one day you know what day it is, and you know what time it is, and you remember everything you see. And it was just like that. I could see all the masts of the sailing ships tied up below, and they were like a forest of young trees, they were delicate and spare and close together and they had no leaves upon them and I thought of Spring. And a ship was coming up the river, and there was a white excursion boat all jammed with people and a band was playing, and I could see and hear it all. And I saw all the faces of the people on the Bridge, and they were coming towards me and there was something strange and sad about it, and yet it was the most magnificent thing I had ever seen: the air was clean and sparkling like sapphires, and out beyond this was the harbor and I knew that the sea was there. And I heard the hoofs of all the horses, and the bells of the street cars, and all those heavy, trembling sounds as if the Bridge was all alive. It was like time, it was like the red brick houses that they have in Brooklyn, it was like being a kid in the early Nineties, and I guess that was when it was.

The Bridge made music and a kind of magic in me, it bound the earth together like a cry; and all of the earth seemed young and tender. I saw the people moving in two streams back and forth across the Bridge, and it was just as if we all had just been born. God, I was so happy I could hardly speak! But when I asked Daddy where we were going he kept singing in a kind of chant:

"To see the man who built the Bridge, who built the Bridge, who built the Bridge, to see the man who built the Bridge, my fair La-dee."

"O Daddy, we are not!" I said.

He was so wild and wonderful, he told so many stories I never knew when to believe him. We sat up front on one of those open cars behind the motorman. The man kept clanging on his bell with his foot, and Daddy was so happy and excited. When he got that way he had a wild, crazy look in his eye. God, he was handsome! He was all dressed up in a rich, dark coat with light grey trousers, he had a pearl in his necktie and a grey derby tilted sideways on his head, it was all so rich and perfect; his hair was like bright sand, it was thick and shiny. I was so proud of him, everyone stared after him wherever he went, the women were simply mad about him.

So when we got over there we got off and walked down a street and went up the steps of this wonderful old house, and an old nigger man came to the door and let us in. He had a white coat on and he was all white and black and clean-looking, and he made you think of good things to eat and drinks in tall, thin glasses, something with mint and frost and lots of ice in it. And we went back through the house behind the nigger, and it was one of those wonderful old houses that are so dark and cool and grand, with walnut stair rails a foot thick and mirrors up to the ceiling. Then this old nigger took us into a room in the back of the house, and it was one of the most magnificent rooms you ever saw. It was noble and high, and the air from the sea was in it. It had three great windows, all open, and a balcony outside, and beyond that you could see all of the harbor, and there was the Bridge where we had come from. It was like a dream—the Bridge soared through the air and seemed to be so near the window and yet it was so far away. And down below us was the river, and the sparkle of the water, and all the ships; and boats were coming in and boats were going out to sea; and there were delicate plumes of smoke above the boats.

And there was an old man in a wheel-chair by the window. His face was strong and gentle, his eyes were grey like Daddy's, but they were not wild; he had enormous hands, but they were delicate, and he used them in a wonderful way. And when he saw us he began to smile. He came towards us in the chair, he could not get up out of it: his face had an eager and wonderful look when he saw Daddy, because Daddy was so grand to people, they all loved him and wanted to be near him; he made them feel good. And Daddy began to talk at once, and God! I was so embarrassed I just didn't know what to say, I stood there pulling at my dress.

"Major," Daddy said, "I want you to meet the Princess Arabella Clementina Sapolio Von Hoggenheim. The Princess has appeared both in the flesh and by proxy here and abroad, and before all the crowned heads of Arope, Erop, Irop, Orop, and Urop."

"O Daddy!" I said, "I have not!" God! I didn't know what to say, I was afraid the old man would believe it.

"Don't listen to her, Major!" Daddy said. "She'll deny it if she can, but you mustn't believe her. The Princess is very shy and shuns publicity. She is hounded by reporters wherever she goes, the gilded youth pursue her with offers of marriage, and unwelcome suitors are constantly throwing themselves out of windows and under the wheels of locomotives when she passes just to attract her attention."

"O Daddy!" I said, "they do *not!*" Gee! I just stood there, not knowing what to say.

And then the old man took my hand in his, and his great hand was so strong and gentle, it closed around my hand and my hand was lost in it and I was not afraid of him. A kind of wonderful joy and strength went through me like a flame. It came out of him, and it was like being on the Bridge again.

And then Daddy said, "This is the man that built the Bridge, that built the Bridge, that built the Bridge, this is the man that built the Bridge, my fair La-dee."

And I knew that it was true! I knew the Bridge had come out of him, and that his life was in the Bridge. He could not move, because his legs were crippled, and yet his life soared up out of him; his eyes were calm and steady, yet they leaped through space like a cry and like a glory; he sat in his chair, but his great life sang a song, and I knew in my heart that it was true that he had built the Bridge. And I did not think of all the men who had worked for him, and had done what he had told them to do—I only knew that he was an angel and a giant who could build great bridges with his hands, and I thought that he had done it all himself. And I forgot that he was an old man crippled in his chair; I thought that if he had wanted to, he could have soared through space and back again just like the Bridge.

I had a feeling of the most unspeakable joy and happiness, it was as if I had discovered the world the day when it was made. It was like getting back to the place where all things come from, it was like knowing the source where all things start, and having it in you, so that there will always be immortal joy and strength and certainty, and no more doubting and confusion. Yes! I knew he was the man who built the Bridge, by the touch of his hand and the great life that soared out of him, but I was so confused that all I could say was, "O Daddy! He did *not!*" And then I turned to him and said, "You didn't, did you?"—just to hear him say he did.

And he was so grand and gentle, he kept smiling and he kept holding to my hand. He had a German way of talking, I think he had been born in Germany, and he said: "Vell, your fader says I did, unt you must alvays belief vat your fader says because he alvays tells the truth."

And he said this in such a solemn way, and then he looked at Daddy and they laughed.

And then I said: "Oh you didn't! How *could* you?" And I kept looking at his crippled legs.

And they both knew what I was thinking, and Daddy said: "What! How *could* he? Why, he just called out to them when he wanted anything done—he just hollered over and told them what he wanted, and they did it."

God! It was so silly that I had to laugh, but Daddy was so serious, he had such a wonderful way about him that he could make you believe anything he wanted, and I said, "Oh he did *not*!" And then I said to the old man, "Did you?"

And he said, "Vell, your Datty says I did, and you should alvays belief your Datty."

"What's that?" Daddy said. "What was the general drift and purport of that last remark, Major?"

"I told her," the old man said, "that you are a truthful man, Choe, and she must alvays belief her Datty."

Then Daddy threw his head back and laughed in that strange, wild way he had; there was a sort of fate and prophecy in it. "God, yes!" he said, "she must always believe her Daddy."

And I went to the window and kept looking at the Bridge, and sometimes it seemed so close you could almost touch it, and again it seemed miles away, and they were both watching me; and then I saw the wagons crawling back and forth across it, and little tiny dots of men upon it, and I said: "I don't believe it. The men couldn't hear you holler. It's too far."

"All right, I'll show you, then," said Daddy. And he went to the window and put his hands up to his mouth, and he had this powerful, magnificent voice, and he could do all sorts of things with it, he could throw it like a ventriloquist and make it come from somewhere else; and he called out in a tone that made the whole room tremble:

"HELLO OVER THERE! IS THAT YOU?"

Then he answered in a funny little voice that seemed to come from miles away, "Yes, sir."

"WHO GAVE YOU THAT BLACK EYE?" Daddy said.

Then the little voice said, "A friend of mine."

"HOW'S THE BRIDGE GETTING ON TODAY?" Daddy hollered.

"Very well, sir," the little voice said.

"WELL, TIE UP THEM LOOSE CABLES. WE DON'T WANT NO ACCIDENTS," Daddy said.

"All right, sir," the little voice said.

"CATCHING ANY FISH?" Daddy hollered.

"No, sir," the little voice said.

"WHAT'S THE MATTER?" Daddy hollered.

"They ain't bitin'," the little voice said.

There, tell me; tell me, there: where is lost time now? Where are lost ships, lost faces, and lost love? Where is the lost child now? Did no one see her o'er the tangled shipping? Did no one see her by light waters? Lost? Did no one speak to her? Ah, please, can no one find her, hold her, keep her—bring her back to me? Gone? Just for a moment, I beseech you, just for a moment out of measured, meted, and unmindful time!

Gone? Then is she lost? Can no one bring me back a child? You'll build great engines yet and taller towers, our dust will tremble to far greater wheels: have you no engines, then, to bring back sixty seconds of lost time?

Then she is lost.

You would have loved Daddy. He was so wild and beautiful, everybody adored him. That was the trouble: things came too easy for him, he never had to work for anything.

The year before he died, I was about sixteen. God, I was a beauty!—I was like peaches and cream, I don't think I've changed much. Don't you think I have a nice face? It's the same as it always was, people don't change much.

Daddy was playing in New York that year. Did you ever hear of a play called *Polonius Potts, Philanthropist*? Oh, it was a wonderful play! Daddy was so good in it—he took the part of Professor McGilligrew Mumps, of Memphis, D. D.—people began to roar as soon as he came on the stage. I have some pictures of him in his make-up: he had a bald wig and long side-whiskers that stuck out like hay, he had on a long frock coat, and he carried a big, floppy umbrella that kept coming open whenever he leaned on it. "Mumps is my name, McGilligrew Mumps of Memphis—" then he would pull out a big red handkerchief from his side pocket and blow his nose like a trumpet. He had only to do that to stop the show, the audience would howl for five minutes.

He was so beautiful. The corners of his mouth bent up as if they were trying to smile all the time, and when he smiled his whole face seemed to light up. There was something so delicate about it—it was just as if someone had turned on a light.

They don't have plays like that any more, I suppose people would think them too simple and foolish. I thought they were wonderful. I don't know, it seems to me people were more simple in those days. Most people are such smarties nowadays—everyone thinks he has to be saying or doing something smart all the time. They're all so fancy, they make me tired. Most of the young fellows are such trash, they're all sicklied o'er with the pale cast of someone else—a little false this and a little not quite that, it's all like imitation shredded wheat. Good heavens, what's the use of trying to be something you're not and throwing away whatever quality you have?

The next year Richard Brandell made a production of *Richard III*, and he sent my father tickets for the performance, with a very urgent and excited note asking us to come to see him before the show began. At this time my father had not played in the theatre for almost a year. His deafness had got so bad he could no longer hear his cues, and Uncle Bob had given him a job as his secretary at Police Headquarters. I used to go there to meet him every Saturday—the policemen were very nice to me and gave me bundles of pencils and great packages of fine stationery.

Mr. Brandell had not seen my father for several months. When we got to the theatre we went backstage for a few moments before the curtain. As my father opened the door and went into the dressing room. Brandell turned and sprang out of his chair like a tiger: he threw both arms around my father and embraced him, crying out in a trembling and excited voice as if he were in some great distress of mind and spirit:

"Choe! Choe! I am glad you have come! It's good to zee you!"

When he was excited he always spoke like this, with a pronounced accent. Although he insisted he was English by birth, he had been born in Leipzig, his father was a German; his real name was Brandl, which he had changed to Brandell after becoming an actor.

He had the most terrific vitality of any man I have ever seen. He was very handsome, but at the moment his features, which were smooth, powerful, and infinitely flexible, were so swollen and distorted by some convulsion of the soul that he looked like a pig. At his best, he was a man of irresistible charm and warmth: he greeted me in a very kind and affectionate way, and kissed me, but he was overjoyed to see my father. He stood for a moment without speaking, grasping him by the arms and shaking him gently; then he began to speak in a bitter voice of "they" and "them." He thought everyone was against him, he kept saying that Daddy was his only friend on earth, and he kept asking in a scornful and yet eager tone:

"What are *they* saying, Joe? Have you heard *them* talk?"

"All that I've heard," my father said, "is that it's a magnificent performance, and that there's no one on the stage today who can come anywhere near you—no, that there's no one who can touch you, Dick— and that's the way I feel about it, too."

"Not even His Snakeship? Not even His Snakeship?" Mr. Brandell cried, his face livid and convulsed.

We knew he was speaking of Henry Irving and we said nothing. For years, ever since the failure of his tour in England, he had been convinced that Irving had been responsible for his failure. In his mind, Irving was a monster who spent all his time conspiring how to ruin and betray him. He had become obsessed with the idea that almost everyone on earth hated him and was trying to get the best of him, and he seized my father's hand, and, looking very earnestly in his eyes, he said:

"No, no! You mustn't lie to me! You mustn't fool me! You are the only man on earth I'd trust!"

Then he began to tell us all the things his enemies had done to injure him. He began to curse and rave against everyone. He said the stage hands were all against him, that they never got the stage set in time, that the time they took between scenes was going to ruin the production. I think he felt his enemies were paying the crew to wreck the show. Daddy told him this was foolish, that no one would do a thing like that, and Mr. Brandell kept saying:

"Yes they would! They hate me! They'll never rest now until they ruin me! *I* know! *I* know!" in a very mysterious manner. "I could tell you things. . . . I know things. . . . You wouldn't believe it if I told you, Joe." Then, in a bitter voice, he said: "Why is it, then, that I've toured this country from coast to coast, playing in a new town every night, and I've never had any trouble like this before? Yes! I've played in every damned opera house and village auditorium on the North American continent and I always found the stage ready when it was time for the curtain! I've had my scenery arrive two hours before the performance and they always set it up for me on time! Yes! They'll do that much for you in any one-horse town! Do you mean to tell me they can't do as well here in New York?"

In a moment he said, in a bitter tone: "I've given my life to the theatre, I've given the public the best that was in me—and what is my reward? The public hates me and I am tricked, betrayed, and cheated by the members of my own profession. I started life as a bank clerk in a teller's cage, and sometimes I curse the evil chance that took me away from it. Yes!" he said in a passionate voice, "I should have missed the tinsel, the glitter, and the six-day fame—the applause of a crowd that will forget about you tomorrow, and spit upon you two days later—but I would have gained something priceless ——"

"What's that?" my father said.

"The love of a noble woman and the happy voices of the little ones."

"Now I can smell the ham," my father said in a cynical tone. "Why, Dick, they could not have kept you off the stage with a regiment of infantry. You sound like all the actors that ever lived."

"Yes," said Mr. Brandell with an abrupt laugh, "you're right. I was talking like an actor." He bent forward and stared into the mirror of his dressing table. "An actor! Nothing but an actor! 'Why should a dog, a horse, a rat have life—and thou no breath at all?'"

"Oh, I wouldn't say that, Dick," my father said. "You've got plenty of breath—I've never known you to run short of it."

"Only an actor!" cried Mr. Brandell, staring into the mirror. "A paltry, posturing, vain, vile, conceited rogue of an actor! An actor—a man who lies and does not know he lies, a fellow who speaks words that better men have written for him, a reader of mash notes from shop girls and the stage-struck wives of grocery clerks, a seducer of easy women, a fellow who listens to the tones of his own voice, a fellow who could not go into the butcher's to buy his dog a bone without wondering what appearance he was making, a man who cannot even pass the time of day without acting—an *actor*! Why, by God, Joe!" he cried, turning to my father, "when I look into the glass and see my face I hate the sight of it."

"Where's that ham?" said Daddy, sniffing about the place.

"An actor!" Mr. Brandell said again. "A fellow who has played so many parts that he can no longer play his own! A man who has imitated so many feelings that he no longer has any of his own! Why, Joe!" he said, in a whispering voice, "do you know that when the news came to me that my own mother was dead, I had a moment—yes, I think I really had a moment—of genuine sorrow. Then I ran to look at my face in the mirror, and I cursed because I was not on the stage where I could show it to an audience. An actor! A fellow who has made so many faces he no longer knows his own—a collection of false faces! . . . What would you like, my dear?" he said to me ironically, "Hamlet?"—instantly he looked the part. "Dr. Jekyll and Mr. Hyde?"— here his face went through two marvelous transformations: one moment he was a benevolent-looking gentleman, and the next the deformed and horrible-looking monster. "Richelieu?"—all at once he looked like a crafty and sinister old man. "Beau Brummel?"—he was young, debonair, arrogant, and a fop. "The Duke of Gloucester?"—and in a moment he had transformed himself into the cruel and pitiless villain he was to portray that night.

It was uncanny and fascinating; and there was something horrible in it, too. It was as if he was possessed by a powerful and fluent energy which had all been fed into this wonderful and ruinous gift of mimicry—a gift which may have, as he said, destroyed and devoured his proper self, since one got fleeting and haunting glimpses between these transformations of a man—a sense, an intuition, rather than a memory, of what the man was like and looked like—a sense of a haunted, lost, and lonely spirit which looked out with an insistent, mournful, and speechless immutability through all the hundred changes of his mask.

It seemed to me there was a real despair, a real grief, in Mr. Brandell. I think he had been tormented, like my father, by the eternal enigma of the theatre: its almost impossible grandeur and magnificence, its poetry and its magic which are like nothing else on earth; and the charlatanism and cheapness with which it corrupts its people. Richard Brandell was not only the greatest actor I have ever seen upon the stage, he was also a man of the highest quality. He possessed almost every gift a great actor should possess. And yet his spirit was disfigured as if by an ineradicable taint—a taint which he felt and recognized, as a man might recognize the action of a deadly poison in his blood without being able either to cure or control it.

He had an astounding repertory of plays which ranged all the way from the great music of *Hamlet* to grotesque and melodramatic trash which he had commissioned some hired hack to write for him, and he would use his great powers in these parts with as much passion and energy as he used in his wonderful portrayals of Iago, Gloucester, or Macbeth. Like most men who are conscious of something false and corrupt in them, he had a kind of Byronic scorn and self-contempt. He was constantly discovering that what he thought had been a deep and honest feeling was only the posturings of his own vanity, a kind of intoxication of self-love, an immense romantic satisfaction at the spectacle of himself having such a feeling; and while his soul twisted about in shame, he would turn and mock and jeer himself and his fellow actors bitterly. Thus he would corner one of them so that he could not escape, and bear down upon him relentlessly:

"Oh, *please* let me tell you all about myself. Let's just sit right down and have a good, long talk all about myself. I can see by the look in your eye that you are just dying to hear, but you're too polite to ask. I know you'd love to hear me talk about myself. Of course, you have nothing to say about yourself, have you?" he would sneer. "Oh, dear no! You're much too modest! But what shall it be now? What do you most want to hear about first? Would you like to hear about the house I had in Lima, Ohio? Or would you rather hear of Cairo, Illinois? I had them hanging to the edges of their seats there, you know. It was marvelous, old boy! Such an ovation! They stood and cheered for ten minutes! Women hurled flowers at me, strong men broke down and wept. Are you interested? I can see you are! I can tell by that eager look in your eye! Now *do* let me tell you some more. Don't you want to hear about the women? My dear fellow, they're mad about me! I had six notes in the mail this morning, three from Boston heiresses and two from the wives of prominent feed and hay merchants in Minnesota. . . . But I must tell you about the house I had in Cairo, Illinois. . . . I was playing in *Hamlet* that night. It's a good part, old boy—a little old-fashioned maybe, but *I* fixed that: I had to write a few of the speeches over here and there, but no one knew the difference. I made up some marvelous business for some of the scenes—absolutely marvelous! And my boy, they *loved* me! They adored me! I had sixteen calls at the end of the third act—they wouldn't let me go, old man; they kept calling me back—until finally I simply had to say a few well-chosen words. Of course, I hated to do it, old boy—you can imagine how I hated it—after all, the play's the thing, isn't it? We're not there to get applause for ourselves, are we? Oh, *dear* no!" he sneered. "But *do* let me tell you what I said to them in Cairo. I can see you are burning up to hear!"

That night was the last time Mr. Brandell ever saw my father. Just before we left he turned to me, took me by the hand, and said very simply and earnestly: "Esther, earn your living in the sweat of your brow, if you have to; go down on your hands and knees and scrub floors, if you have to; eat your bread in sorrow, if you have to—but promise me you will never attempt to go on the stage."

"I have already made her promise that," my father said.

"Is she as good as she's pretty? Is she smart?" said Mr. Brandell, still holding my hand and looking at me.

"She's the smartest girl that ever lived," my father said. "She's so smart she should have been my son."

"And what is she going to do?" said Mr. Brandell, still looking at me.

"She's going to do what I could never do," my father said. He lifted his great hands before him and shook them suddenly in a gesture of baffled desperation. "She's going to take hold of something!" Then he took my hands in his and said: "Not to want the whole earth, and to get nothing! Not to want to do everything, and to do nothing! Not to waste her life dreaming about India when India is around her here and now! Not to go mad thinking of a million lives, wanting the experience of a million people, when everything she has is in the life she's got! Not to be a fool, tortured with hunger and thirst when the whole earth is groaning with its plenty. . . . My dear child," my father cried, "you are so good, so beautiful, and so gifted, and I love you so much! I want you to be happy and to have a wonderful life." He spoke these words with such simple and urgent feeling that all the strength and power in him seemed to go out through his great hands to me as if all of the energy of his life had been put into his wish.

"Why, Dick," he said to Mr. Brandell, "this child was born into the world with more wisdom than either of us will ever have. She can go into the Park and come back with a dozen kinds of leaves and study them for days. And when she gets through she will know all about them. She knows their size, their shape and color—she knows every marking on them, she can draw them from memory. Could you draw a leaf, Dick? Do you know the pattern and design of a single leaf? Why, I have looked at forests, I have walked through woods and gone across the continent in trains, I have stared the eyes out of my head trying to swallow up the whole earth at a glance—and I hardly know one leaf from another. I could not draw a leaf from memory if my life depended on it. And she can go out on the street and tell you later what clothes the people wore, and what kind of people wore them. Can you remember anyone you passed by on the street today? I walk the streets, I see the crowds, I look at a million faces until my brain goes blind and dizzy with all that I have seen, and later all the faces swim and bob about like corks in water. I can't tell one from the other, I see a million faces and I can't remember one. But she sees one and remembers a million. That's the thing, Dick. If I were young again I'd try to live like that: I'd try to see a forest in a leaf, the whole earth in a single face."

"Why, Esther," Mr. Brandell said. "Have you discovered a new country? How does one get to this wonderful place where you live?"

"Well, I tell you, Mr. Brandell," I said. "It's easy. You just walk out in the street and look around and there you are."

"There you are!" Mr. Brandell said. "Why, my dear child, I have been walking out and looking around for almost fifty years, and the more I walk and look, the less I see that I care to look at. What are these wonderful sights that you have found?"

"Well, Mr. Brandell," I said, "sometimes it's a leaf, and sometimes it's the pocket of a coat, and sometimes it's a button or a coin, and sometimes it's an old hat, or an old shoe on the floor. Sometimes it's a tobacco store, the cigars tied up in bundles on the counter, and all of the jars where they keep the pipe tobacco, and the wonderful dark smell of the place. Sometimes it's a little boy, and sometimes it's a girl looking out a window, and sometimes it's an old woman with a funny hat. Sometimes it's the color of an ice wagon, and sometimes the color of an old brick wall, and sometimes a cat creeping along the backyard fence. Sometimes it's the feet of the men on the rail when you pass a saloon, and the sawdust floors, and the sound of their voices, and that wonderful smell you get of beer and orange peel and Angostura bitters. Sometimes it's people passing underneath your window late at night, and sometimes it's the sound of a horse in the street early in the morning, and sometimes it's the ships blowing out in the harbor at night. Sometimes it's the design of the elevated structure across the street where a station is, and sometimes it's the smell of bolts of new, clean cloth, and sometimes it's the way you feel when you make a dress—you can feel the design go out of the tips of your fingers into the cloth as you shape it, and you feel yourself in it and it looks like you, and you know nobody else on earth could do it that way. Sometimes it's the way Sunday morning feels when you wake up and listen to it—you can smell it and feel it, and it smells like breakfast. Sometimes it's the way Saturday night is. Sometimes it's the way Monday morning feels, you get all excited and nervous, and your coffee goes bouncing around inside you, and you don't enjoy your breakfast. And sometimes it's like Sunday afternoon, with people coming from a concert—this feels terrible and makes you blue. Sometimes it's the way you feel at night when you wake up in Winter time and you know it's snowing, although you can't see or hear it. Sometimes it's the harbor, sometimes the docks, and sometimes it's the Bridge with people coming across it. Sometimes it's the markets and the way the chickens smell; sometimes it's all the new vegetables and the smell of apples. Sometimes it's the people in a train that passes the one you're in: you see all the people, you are close to them, but you cannot touch them, you say good-bye to them and it makes you feel sad. Sometimes it's all the kids play ing in the street: they don't seem to have anything to do with the grown-ups, they seem to be kids, and yet they seem to be grown up and to live in a world of their own—there is something strange about it. And sometimes it's like that with the horses, too—sometimes you go out and there is nothing but the horses, they fill the streets, you forget about all the people, the horses seem to own the earth, they talk to one another, and they seem to have a life of their own that people have nothing to do with. Sometimes it's all the different kinds of carriages—the hansoms, the four-wheelers, the victorias, the landaulets. Sometimes it's the Brewster Carriage Works on Broadway: you can look in and see them making them down in the basement—everything is very delicate and beautiful, you can smell the shavings of the finest wood, and new leather and harness, and the thills, the springs, the wheels, and the felloes. Sometimes it's all the people going along the streets, and sometimes there's nothing but the Jews—the old men with the beards, and the old women poking and prodding at ducks, and the girls and the kids. I know all about this and what is going on inside them, but it's no use telling you and Daddy—you're both Gentiles and you wouldn't know what I was talking about. Well—there's a lot more—do you give up?"

"Good God, yes!" said Mr. Brandell, picking up a towel from his dressing table and waving it at me, "I surrender! Oh, brave new world that has such wonders in it! . . . O Joe, Joe!" he said to my father, "will that ever happen to us again? Are we nothing but famished beggars, weary of our lives? Can you still see all those things when you walk the streets? Would it ever come back to us that way again?"

"Not to me," my father said. "I was a Sergeant, but I've been rejuced."

He smiled as he spoke, but his voice was old and tired and weary. I know now he felt that his life had failed. His face had got very yellow from his sickness, and his shoulders stooped, his great hands dangled to his knees; as he stood there between Mr. Brandell and me he seemed to be half-erect, as if he had just clambered up from all fours. And yet his face was as delicate and wild as it had ever been, it had the strange, soaring look—as if it were in constant flight away from a shackling and degrading weight—that it had always worn, and to this ex-pression of uplifted flight there had now been added the intent listening expression that all deaf people have.

It seemed to me that the sense of loneliness and exile, of a brief and alien rest, as if some winged spirit had temporarily arrested flight upon a foreign earth, was more legible on him now than it had ever been. Suddenly I felt all the strangeness of his life and destiny—his remoteness from all the life I knew. I thought of his strange child-hood, and of the dark miracle of chance which had brought him to my mother and the Jews—an alien, a stranger, and an exile among dark faces—with us but never of us. And I felt more than ever before a sense of our nearness and farness; I felt at once closer to him than to anyone on earth, and at the same time farther from him. Already his life had something fabulous and distant in it; he seemed to be a part of some vanished and irrevocable time.

I do not think Mr. Brandell had noticed before how tired and ill my father looked. He had been buried in his own world, burning with a furious, half-suppressed excitement, an almost mad vitality which was to have that night its consummation. Before we left him, however, he suddenly glanced sharply and critically at my father, took his hand, and said with great tenderness:

"What is it, Joe? You look so tired. Is anything wrong?"

My father shook his head. He had become very sensitive about his deafness, and any reference to the affliction that had caused his retirement from the stage or any suggestion of pity from one of his former colleagues because of his present state deeply wounded him. "Of course not," he said. "I never felt better! I used to be Joe the Dog-Faced Actor, now I'm Joe the Dog-Faced Policeman, and I've got a badge to prove it, too." Here he produced his policeman's badge, of which he was really very proud. "If that's not a step up in the world, what is it? Come on, daughter," he said to me. "Let's leave this wicked man to all his plots and murders. If he gets too bad, I'll arrest him!"

We started to go, but for a moment Mr. Brandell stopped us and was silent. The enormous and subdued excitement, the exultant fury which had been apparent in him all the time, now became much more pronounced. The man was thrumming like a dynamo, his strong hands trembled, and when he spoke it was as if he had already become the Duke of Gloucester: there was a quality of powerful cunning and exultant prophecy in his tone, something mad, secret, conspiratorial, and knowing.

"Keep your eyes open tonight," he said. "You may see something worth remembering."

We left him and went out into the theatre. It was the last time Brandell ever saw my father.

When we got out into the auditorium the house was almost full, although the people were still going down the aisles to their seats. Because of my father's deafness, Brandell had given us seats in the front row. For a few minutes I watched the people come in and the house fill up, and I felt again the sense of elation and joy I have always felt in the theatre before the curtain goes up. I looked at the beautiful women, the men in evening clothes, and at all the fat and gaudy ornamentation of the house; I heard the rapid and excited patter of the voices, the stir and rustle of silks, the movement—and I loved it all.

Then in a few minutes the lights darkened. There was a vast, rustling sigh all over the theatre, the sound of a great bending forward, and then, for a moment, in that dim light I saw the thing that has always seemed so full of magic and beauty to me: a thousand people who have suddenly become a single, living creature, and all the frail white spots of faces blooming like petals there in a velvet darkness, upturned, thirsty, silent, and intent and beautiful.

Then the curtain went up, and on an enormous and lofty stage stood the deformed and solitary figure of a man. For a moment I knew the man was Brandell; for a moment I could feel nothing but an astounded surprise, a sense of unreality, to think of the miracle of transformation which had been wrought in the space of a few minutes, to know that this cruel and sinister creature was the man with whom we had just been talking. Then the first words of the great opening speech rang out across the house, and instantly all this was forgotten: the man was no longer Brandell, he was the Duke of Gloucester.

That evening will live in my memory as the most magnificent evening I ever spent in the theatre. On that evening Richard Brandell reached the summit of his career. That night was literally the peak. Immediately after the performance Brandell had a nervous collapse: the play was taken off, he never appeared as Richard again. It was months before he made any appearance whatever, and he never again, during the remainder of his life, approached the performance he gave that night.

With the opening words, the intelligence was instantly communicated to the audience that it was about to witness such a performance as occurs in the theatre only once in a lifetime. And yet, at first, there was no sense of characterization, no feeling of the cruel and subtle figure of Richard—there was only a mighty music which sounded out across the house, a music so grand and overwhelming that it drowned the memory of all the baseness, the ugliness, and the pettiness in the lives of men. In the sound of the words it seemed there was the full measure of man's grandeur, magnificence, and tragic despair, and the words were flung against immense and timeless skies like a challenge and an evidence of man's dignity, and like a message of faith that he need not be ashamed or afraid of anything.

> *Now is the winter of our discontent*
> *Made glorious summer by this sun of York;*
> *And all the clouds that lour'd upon our house*
> *In the deep bosom of the ocean buried.*

Then, swiftly and magnificently, with powerful developing strokes of madness, fear, and cruelty, the terrible figure of Richard began to emerge; almost before the conclusion of the opening speech it stood complete. That speech was really a speech of terror, and set clearly the picture of the warped, deformed, agonized Gloucester, for whom there was no beautiful thing in life, a man who had no power to raise himself except by murder. As the play went on, the character of Richard had become so real to me, the murders so frightful, the lines filled with such music and such terror, that when the curtain rose on that awful nightmare scene in the tent, I felt I could not stay there if one more drop of blood was shed. Then, just as the ghosts of the little princes appeared to Richard, just as he started up crying, "The lights burn blue"—there occurred one of the most extraordinary experiences of my life.

Suddenly, I heard in my ears the faint rumbling of wheels, far, far away, and gradually coming nearer. The king's tent faded from my view, and suddenly before my eyes there stretched a long band of hard, silvery sand and a calm ocean beyond. The water was of a delicate blue tint known as aquamarine, the sun shone low in the sky from the land side. The beach near the water was perfectly flat, no human had trod there since the tide had washed out.

I felt the land was an island, the beach curved round a high cliff of earth and growth quite far down. Then I heard the wheels come nearer, and saw a chariot moving with great speed, drawn by three horses. The rumble of the wheels grew very loud and the chariot, which was of Greek form, came before my vision. It was driven by a woman who filled my being at once with warmth and familiarity. She was of medium height, her head rather small, and her face I can only describe as heart-shaped: it was wide at the temples and tapered to a delicate pointed chin. She had fine, silky, wavy hair, bound with a chaplet of leaves made of beaten gold, the chaplet tied at the back with a red-purple ribbon. Neither face nor figure was of the classic type, as we conceive it. The face was beautiful in its own way and touched a chord within me that answered with all the warmth of my nature.

I had known this woman forever. Sometimes a certain set of vibrations will make a crystal goblet ring when nothing has really touched it. That is what this woman did to my heart. If I had come into a room filled with the most beautiful women on earth, and among them I had seen her face, I would have exclaimed, "There she is!" She meant home, love, delight to me. Her figure was rounded, but not developed like the Greek statues, and not particularly beautiful except for her noble and perpendicular carriage. She handled the reins and horses with a swift, sure grace, with one hand, and with the other patted the heads of two children who stood at her left side—a girl of about ten, skinny, and a tiny boy about four, whose eyes just cleared the rim of the chariot. Her dress was ivory white, laced in infinitesimal pleats of that clinging yet flowing material worn by the Greeks. She wore high-laced cothurns of white leather, trimmed with gold.

So they raced along, the wind whipping her dress close to her form. The wheels thundered in my ears, and the thud of the horses' hoofs upon the hard, wet sand. I could see the wheel revolving on the axle. They passed by, and soon had turned the promontory. She was gone. I felt a sense of irreparable loss. I have felt nothing like it, before or since.

Then I became aware of the theatre full of people. I saw the scene on the stage again, and I heard a sound coming from my own throat. My father had taken my outstretched hands in his and was speaking gently to me. The vision, or whatever it was, seemed to me to have lasted fully five minutes, but in reality it must have been much less.

I wrenched my mind from my vision to watch the stage. The play was drawing to its magnificent close. But the dream stayed with me for many days, and for months I would feel that wonderful sense of recognition and love, and smell the beach, the sea, the shore, and see everything as clearly as events that passed around me. Then, in course of time, it faded; but from time to time, in years to come, it would return, as clearly as when first I saw it that night in the theatre.

What do you think it was?

"Long, long into the night I lay awake, thinking how I should tell my story."

(One!)

Now in the dark I hear the boats there in the river.

(Two!)

Now I can hear the great horns blowing in the river.

Time! Where are you now, and in what place, and at what time? Oh now I hear the whistles on the river! Oh now great ships are going down the river! Great horns are baying at the harbor's mouth, great boats are putting out to sea!

And in the nighttime, in the dark, in all the sleeping silence of the earth, the river, the dark rich river, full of strange time, dark time, strange tragic time, is flowing, flowing out to sea!

God, the things I'd like to tell! I wish I could write! I'd like to write a book and tell people about the things that happen inside me, and about all the things I see.

First, I should tell them all about the clothes people wear. You can't know what a person is like until you have seen what he is wearing. People are like the clothes they wear. They may think it's all an accident, but it's not. There is the way that actors and preachers and politicians and quack doctors and psychologists dress: everything they wear sort of goes forward, they are turning everything in them out for the world to see. You can tell if people turn inward or outward by their shoes, neckties, shirts, socks, and hats.

The most wonderful people are the old women you see who wear about a million little things. There are a lot of them in England. They live in all those horrible little hotels up in Bloomsbury and places like that. There are also a lot of them in Boston. They have strange faces, they are lost.

Gee, I saw a wonderful old woman in Boston once! It was in a restaurant. She must have had about a thousand little things on. She had on a long black dress and it was all covered with beads and bangles and glittering ornaments. God! It must have weighed a ton! Then she had all sorts of lace things on over that, it all sort of dripped down from her arms, and fell over her wrists, and got into her soup. And then she had a lot of rings and loose bracelets and beads and necklaces, and a whalebone collar with a lot more lace, and earrings, and all sorts of combs in her hair, and a hat all covered with masses of things, feathers, fruit, birds. God! That woman was a walking museum! It was one of the strangest things I ever saw in my life, and I was so excited. I got as close as I could to her and tried to hear what she was saying, but I couldn't. I'd have given anything to know what it was. There was something so tragic about her. Isn't it a strange thing? It comes from something inside them, something all fancy and broken up like beads, something all cluttered up that can't bear to throw anything away and that is smothering in oceans of junk.

Then there are the things people wear underneath. I should like to tell about that, too. There was poor old Todd that time she was staying at our house and got bronchitis, and we thought she was going to die. She was simply burning up with fever and shivering, and Edith and I undressed her and put her to bed.—Good God! Would you believe it? She was wearing three pairs of those old-fashioned cotton drawers!

"O Todd!" I cried, "Todd! In God's name, what's the matter?"

"Oh don't let them see me!" she said. "They're after me!"

"They?" I said, "Who do you mean, Todd? There's no one here but us."

The poor old thing, she was simply terrified. She told me later she'd been afraid for years that some man was going to attack her, and that's why she wore all those things.

God, it's sad! When I first knew her she was a young and very beautiful woman, she had just come from the hospital, and Bella was her first case. Then later, when I had my little Alma, we had her again. That was the time I almost died. She was simply wonderful, and since then she always came and stayed with us. Isn't it a strange thing? I remember her when she had lots of beaus, and several men wanted to marry her, and she had this other terrible thing in her all the time.

Oh yes! And then I should like to write about the way you feel when you have a child, and what it was like when my little Alma came, for I had lain on the earth upon green hillsides all that Summer with my child inside me, and I felt the great earth move below me and swing eastward in the orbits of the sun. I knew the earth, my body was the earth, I grew into the earth, and my child was stirring in me as I lay there on that green hillside.

And Todd came, and old Dr. Roth—he was a great surgeon—and I seemed to be out of my head. And yet I knew everything that was going on around me. It was about eleven o'clock in the morning and it was August and it was hot as hell, and I could hear the people going by in the street, I heard the clank of the iceman's tongs and the children shouting, and all of a sudden I could hear all the birds singing in the trees outside, and I cried out, "Sweet is the breath of morn, her rising sweet, with charm of earliest birds," and that was the way it was.

It was so lovely—God!—and I was mad with the pain. It is beyond anything you could ever imagine. It becomes a kind of exquisite and unbearable joy, and one part of you, the upper part, seems to be floating around way up above you, and the other part seems chained to the earth, and they are rending and stabbing you with knives, and great waves of it roll over you, and you feel yourself come and go from it, and when it came I kept crying out:

"*Who* would fardels bear? *Who* would fardels bear? *Who* would fardels bear?"

And I could see Todd and Dr. Roth moving about through it all, and it was all so strange because their faces bloomed and faded with the pain. And then there was Todd with her enormous, gentle hands that were everlasting and merciful, they were as big and strong as a man's under me, and I was not afraid but I thought I was dying, I was sure I was dying, and I cried:

"O Todd! Todd! Good-bye, I am going!"

And she said: "O my darling! My dear! You're not! You will be all right!"

She loved me so, and God! but I was lovely then, I was so small and lovely then. But there was something so strange and terrible about Todd and Dr. Roth. I had never seen them that way before, he was always so gentle. He told me later he was awfully worried, but now he was bending over me and barking in my face:

"Push! You've got to push, mother! You're not trying hard enough! You've got to try harder than that, mother! Come on, mother! We can't have it for you, you know! Push! Push hard, mother! You're not trying!"

And Todd said: "Oh she is trying, too!" She got so mad at him, and they were both terribly worried, it had been so long. And then it was all over and I was floating on clouds of peace, I was floating in a lovely and undulant ocean of bliss.

And yes! I should like to tell all about my little Alma, and how tiny she was, and of the things that child said! Gee, she was a funny kid! We were having tea one day and she came by the door, and we had guests there, and she couldn't have been more than four years old, and I called out:

"O Alma, Alma, where are you going?"

And she said, "I am going out, out, brief candle!"

O God! I thought they'd kill themselves laughing, but there was something so wonderful about it, too. Wasn't that a strange thing for a child that age to say? It popped right out of her mouth, I suppose she had heard some of us quoting Shakespeare.

And then one time when Edith and I came in we found her doing her lessons. She had all her books around her in the middle of the floor and she was doing her spelling lesson. She was simply biting each word off as if she were scolding it:

"O-u-n-c-e, ounce! O-u-n-c-e, ounce! O-u-n-c-e, ounce!"

Then she changed to another one:

"P-u-a-r-t, quart! P-u-a-r-t, quart! P-u-a-r-t, quart!"

God, we had a fit! The poor kid thought the "q" was a "p." And whenever anything went wrong after that, we used to say, "O-u-n-c-e, ounce!"—it was like saying damn, only better.

Gee, that kid's a scream! You have never in your life heard anything like the way she goes on at the table. We get to laughing so sometimes that we can hardly eat. She says the funniest things you ever heard, I wish I could remember some of them. . . . Oh yes! The other night we were talking about the house in the country and what name we would call it by, and Alma said:

"We will call the side that Father sleeps on the Patri-side, and the side that Mother sleeps on the Matri-side."

God, she's so wonderful! She is my darling and my dear, she is my little Alma, she is the most delicate and lovely thing that ever lived.

And, oh yes! I should like to tell about Jews and Christians, and about Jews who change their names. There's this fellow Burke! Doesn't it make you want to laugh? Nathaniel Burke my eye! Why didn't he go pick a real fancy Christian name while he was about it? Montmorency Van Landingham Monteith, or Reginald Hilary Saltonstall, or Jefferson Lincoln Coolidge, or something like that? Nathaniel Burke! Can you beat it? His real name is Nathan Berkovich, I've known his people all my life.

The nerve of that fellow! I got so tired of his goings on that I said to him once: "Look here, Burke. You'd just better be glad you *are* a Jew. Where would you be if it weren't for the Jews, I'd like to know? It's too bad about you."

His mother and father were such nice old people. The old fellow had a store on Grand Street. He wore a beard and a derby hat, and washed his hands in a certain way they have before eating. There's something awfully nice about old Jews like that. They were orthodox, of course, and I think it almost killed them the way he's acted. He won't go near them any more. Isn't it a shame—to throw that wonderful thing away in order to become an imitation Christian?

We're fine people. They sneer at us and mock us, but we're fine people just the same. "Many a time and oft in the Rialto you have rated me . . . and spit upon my Jewish gaberdine." Daddy was a Christian, but he was so beautiful. He loved all the things we do. He loved food so much, I don't think he could have stood this anæmic Christian cooking. No wonder he got away from them.

And yes! Yes! I should like to tell how it is the mornings I go to Stein's and Rosen's to design, and Mr. Rosen is walking up and down on big, thick carpets, and God! richness and power and goose grease seem to be oozing out of every pore of him. And there is something so clean and lovely about the place, and wonderful, too, with the Grand Duchess Somebody-or-Other selling one thing and this Princess Piccatitti selling something else. If I had a name like that I'd change it to Schultz or something. Even Edith has to laugh when she says it. Imagine being called Ophelia Piccatitti! Wouldn't it be awful to be one of the Piccatitti children and have them call you one of the little Piccatittis?

Gee, I have to laugh sometimes when I see their names in the social columns. New York must be simply full of these people. Where do you suppose they all come from? When you read about it, it doesn't seem possible, you think somebody made all the names up: "Mrs. H. Stuyvesant O'Toole entertained at dinner last night in honor of the Prince and Princess Stephano di Guttabelli. Among those present were Mr. and Mrs. Van Rensselaer Weisberg, Count Sapski, Mr. R. Mortimer Shulemovitch, and the Grand Duchess Martha-Louise of Hesse Schnitzelpuss."

And then there's Mr. Rosen in his shop, walking up and down and giving orders and bowing and shaking hands with people in his striped pants and rich black coat with the pearl in his necktie. He is so well-kept and sleek, and everything about the place sort of purrs with luxury, everything seems so quiet, but everything seems to be going on just the same, and they're calling for Edith all over the place. You hear them asking for her everywhere. And there she is, looking like a very elegant piece of limp celery, with that pedometer strapped around her ankle. She told me she walked seventeen miles one day, and sometimes she is simply dead when she gets home. The poor thing is as thin as a rail. Sometimes she won't say three words during the entire evening, even when there are people coming to dinner. But God, she is smart! They couldn't do without her, she is smarter than any of them.

"Long, long into the night I lay awake ——"
(One!)
Come, mild sleep, seal up the porches of our memory. . . .
(Two!)
Come, magnificent sleep, blot out the vision of lost days. . . .
(Three!)
For we are strange and beautiful asleep, we are all strange and beautiful asleep. . . .
(Four!)
For we are dying in the darkness, and we know no death, there is no death in sleep. . . .
O daughter of unmemoried hours, empress of labor and of weariness, merciful sister of dark death and all forgetfulness, enchantress and redeemer, hail!

27

Stein and Rosen's

ONE EVENING WHEN THE WORLD WAS A GREAT DEAL YOUNGER THAN IT IS now, Mr. Rosen, who then had only a modest shop in lower Fifth Avenue, was at the theatre with his wife. Mr. Rosen saw a great many people he knew in the audience. This was not surprising, for the star of the piece was a very brilliant Russian actress named Alla Nazimova who had recently come to America, and the piece in which she was playing was *A Doll's House*. Mr. Rosen walked about during the interval between the acts, greeting his friends and noting what the ladies were wearing. His friends were, for the most part, wealthy and cultivated Jews. The women were very elegant and fashionable, beautifully gowned, dark, tall, some of them exotically lovely. Most of these people had known one another since childhood, they belonged to a very limited and exclusive group; some of them valued fine intelligence and the ability to create more than they valued money, but most of them had both.

Moving among this brilliant crowd on his soft and powerful tread, Mr. Rosen saw the two Linder girls. He always thought of them as "the two Linder girls," although the older one, Esther, was now a very beautiful woman of thirty, and married to a man named Frederick Jack. The other sister, Edith, was five years younger than Esther. People liked her and thought she was "a clever girl," although she had never been known to say anything. She went about a great deal with Esther. She was always perfectly composed, and absolutely silent—if she contributed a half dozen words to an evening's conversation, she had been talkative.

Mr. Rosen knew the Linder girls very well, and was a little in awe of them. His own position had been won with difficulty—he had come from plodding Jews of the middle class. But there was a reckless and

434

romantic strain in the Linder family that he admired and mistrusted: they did difficult things with brilliant ease, spent money extravagantly, made fortunes, lost them, remade them.

He had known the father of the two girls—Joe Linder. Joe had been an actor, well known in his day, but he had died before his fiftieth year. Mr. Rosen remembered him vividly as a handsome man with hair which had been silver since his youth—a man who was always making a joke of everything. He had played with Mansfield, and when he was drinking he would quote Shakespeare by the yard with tears in his eyes. Joe Linder had been half Christian—his mother was a Gentile—and it was to this foreign strain that Mr. Rosen attributed his instability and downfall. Mr. Rosen remembered that two of Joe's boon companions had been Catholic priests—Father O'Rourke and Father Dolan. They used to meet Joe after the theatre and go to White's, where they all drank as much as they could before midnight. Then, if the priests were conducting Mass the next morning, they stopped. And, with somewhat troubled spirit, Mr. Rosen now recalled that Edith, the younger of Joe Linder's girls, had been educated in a Catholic convent in the Bronx.

Mr. Rosen remembered the girls' mother. She had died before her husband when the children were very young. She had been entirely Jewish, and of the finest stock—her parents were Dutch. Her father, a lawyer, had made a fortune in New York and left her whole blocks of houses. But she had been even more extravagant than Joe. If she wanted a diamond necklace, she sold a house; if she wanted a dress, she sold the necklace, or part of it. With keen pain Mr. Rosen remembered that she used to bite the diamonds off one at a time and send them to the pawnbroker when she wanted money. At the memory he shook his head sadly.

But now, with dark excitement, he approached the two young women, closing his eyes with rapture as he came near to them.

"Where—where—" he whispered somewhat hoarsely to Esther, clasping his hands and shaking them prayerfully before him, for want of adequate tribute, "—where did you get that dress?"

"Do you like it?" she said.

"My dear, it's a dream."

"Well, as Daddy used to say," said Esther, "it's better than a kick in the eye, isn't it?"

Mr. Rosen groaned at the sacrilege, then demanded impatiently: "But where did you get it? You must tell me."

"Will you promise not to tell anyone if I let you know?" she asked, "Yes, of course," said Mr. Rosen feverishly.

"Well," said Esther solemnly, "I'll tell you then. I got it in Macy's bargain basement."

Mr. Rosen groaned loudly and smote his forehead. This was the way Joe Linder used to talk, and, in Mr. Rosen's opinion, it had probably had something to do with his untimely death. There was a time and place for levity, but one must not trifle with sacred things.

"Macy's!" said Mr. Rosen. "You insult my intelligence! There's not a shop in New York making frocks like that."

"Well, I did just the same," said Esther, laughing. "I bought the material there."

"Damn the material!" said Mr. Rosen. "Who made the dress?"

"My sister Edith," said Esther triumphantly. "You didn't know she was so smart, did you?" She took Edith's hand affectionately. "You know, Mr. Rosen," she said happily, "I haven't got any sense myself, but Edith's awfully smart. She can do anything. She's just like Daddy."

And she stood there holding Edith by the hand, and looking up at Mr. Rosen, flushed, radiant, happy, and delighted "not to have any sense" as long as everyone was so nice and one had such a smart sister.

Mr. Rosen turned slowly and commandingly upon the other young lady, who had kept her silence during this entire conversation with perfect composure, and who now stood with her hand in her sister's, looking from one to the other with a very calm glance of her large, dark eyes.

"Edith!" said Mr. Rosen, sternly. "Did you make that dress?"

"Yes," said Edith, in her talkative way.

"Edith," said Mr. Rosen, his tone becoming soft and winning, "how would you like a job?"

"Doing what?" said Edith, with a burst of eloquence.

"Designing dresses," said Mr. Rosen tenderly. "Designing dresses," he murmured luxuriously, "like this one here."

"I should like it," said Edith, fatigued by so much speech-making.

Mr. Rosen's soul rushed out of him. He enveloped them all in his blessing.

"Come to my shop," he whispered hoarsely. "Come to my shop Monday morning."

Then he left them.

By Monday morning, however, both sisters had completely forgotten the incident, and Edith came as near the animation of surprise as she ever did when her maid came to her room at ten o'clock to tell her Mr. Rosen had telephoned and wanted to talk to her at once. She got out of bed and went into Esther's room, where there was a phone extension.

"Well?" the impatient voice of Mr. Rosen demanded. "Why didn't you come to the shop?"

"For what?"

"For the job I offered you."

"I forgot about it. I didn't think you meant it."

"Of course I meant it. Why should I waste my time if I didn't mean it?"

"Do you still want me?"

"Yes!" he shouted. "Come down at once!"

Edith dressed, and went downtown.

In this leisurely, half-accidental way Edith had started to work for Mr. Rosen. She was now vice-president, and she also owned a share in the business.

The firm of Stein and Rosenberg had moved a long way uptown, from Grand Street to Fifth Avenue, and in its prosperous migration had lost its name. Mr. Stein was dead, and Mr. Rosenberg—well, Mr. Rosenberg was now Mr. Rosen, with a son at Oxford, and a daughter who preferred to live in Paris.

Mr. Rosen was now fifty-five, a handsome and powerful man, very Jewish-looking, dark, fiercely Oriental. He had changed his name, but he had made no effort to change his race or his identity. A photograph of his dead partner, Saul Stein, had never left the desk top in his office: the wide, grinning face, with its immense, putty-colored nose, smiled down on him, evoking pictures full of pain and tenderness, of a time when he had sat next to this dead man cross-legged on a tailor's table, and of other days when they had stood outside their East Side shop inviting to come buy all the dark swarm of Jewry that the fine, warm days of May had drawn out.

No; he had not forgotten, and he was not ashamed. He walked with soft and powerful tread along the rich carpets of his big shop, he wore pin-stripe trousers and a cutaway coat, and he bowed and spoke gently to his clients, the fabulously rich of the nation—but he had not forgotten. There was in him a vast pride of race, a vast pride in the toil and intelligence which had brought him wealth. For this reason, Mr. Rosen had a very princely quality—the princely quality that almost all rich Jews have, and that few rich Christians ever get. Wealth is difficult to attain, but it is good, pleasant, desirable—therefore let those with wealth enjoy it.

There is, of course, no greater fallacy than the one about the stinginess of Jews. They are the most lavish and opulent race on earth. Mr. Rosen went to Paris twice a year on the *Ile de France*: he had a suite and a private deck, and his wife was the best and most expensively dressed woman on the ship. In Summer, Mr. Rosen must spend a great deal of time in Paris buying clothes, but his wife and children went to Deauville. Mr. Rosen flew down to join them in the evening, and the family swam and danced and drank cocktails.

Further, Mr. Rosen had always lived over his shop. He began it in two rooms on Grand Street, and he continued it now in two floors and eighteen rooms on Fifth Avenue. And he will continue it, also, in the new and more splendid building now being erected farther uptown. There he will have the top three floors, twenty-four rooms, and the best view in town. When a Christian makes money out of his shop, or another man's shop, he moves out as soon as he can. He goes up the Hudson, buys a thousand acres and forty rooms, and gets gardeners and hostlers from England. Not so Mr. Rosen. His ideas went back to the Fuggers, the Cabots, the early Rothschilds. He lived over his shop and had lots of the very best champagne for dinner.

As for Stein and Rosen's, it had become one of the most fashionable and expensive shops in the country, and its victorious journey uptown was shortly to be consummated when it moved into its magnificent new building. The authors of society novels made their characters speak of it: Rita (or Leila or Sheila) is going along thinking about Bruce, with her fine, dark head "and strong, brown hands," and of the disquieting way Hilary, the artist, looked at her "out of his slanting, almost Oriental eyes" the night before, when suddenly she sees Jenifer Delamar going into Stein and Rosen's.

Under this success, Mr. Rosen had burst into a full, rich bloom. His well-fed body took on an added richness of hue. He was of a princely tissue, and as he walked up and down with soft and powerful tread he suggested a fine prize bull. The presence of this strong, luxurious flesh in the French elegance of the shop, surrounded by gossamer webs and smoky silks, was not at all incongruous: the delicate fabrics might have come from this rich body like an ectoplasm. And the great ladies who bought at Stein and Rosen's must have felt a delicious sensation of comfort and mystery when they looked at him, for his dark, smiling face, with its perfection of large, pearl teeth, and full nose, with the wide, fleshy volutes of the nostrils, gave him a touch of Oriental wizardry. They felt that in his inexhaustible princeliness he had only to clap his large, pink hands together, and a procession of slaves would enter, balancing treasure of baled stuffs upon their heads.

This, in fact, he could and did do, although in place of ebony eunuchs he offered something better—slim, luscious houris clothed in magic.

A good part of the magic, he knew, was Edith Linder's. Mr. Rosen's voice when he mentioned her name had a husk of religious sanctity— he called her "a great woman" and felt the mild inadequacy of language. The feeling of awe which he had always had in reference to the Linders had grown deeper. They could do anything, and they could do anything with ease. Although he knew very well how indefatigably Edith had worked in developing the business, there was for him in everything she did magic and ease. And this was the impression everyone got.

She had grown more silent and more emaciated as she grew older. Her silence had turned in upon her and devoured her. Perpetual weariness rested on her flesh like a subtle perfume, but she never rested. She worked ceaselessly, silently, doing the magic, costly things with her hands that brought great wealth to Stein and Rosen's. Throughout the day one heard her name on every floor of the shop. Where was she? Could she come at once? She came, saying nothing—a weary, meager elegance dressed in eight hundred dollars' worth of simple black. Around her small, bony ankle was strapped a pedometer, and around her fragile wrist, netted with veins in fine blue ink and drawn taut like the bones of a bird, was a diamond-encrusted wrist watch, a miracle of delicate workmanship, that ticked off time—strange, tragic time—in a faultless shell no bigger than a thimble.

Mr. Rosen's dark face was radiant with power and pleasure. He had two handsome children. He had a beautiful wife. He was himself as handsome as a prize bull. They all loved one another dearly. Yes, Mr. Rosen had come far, far uptown, since those old hard days of first endeavor. . . . Softly, softly, on dark, powerful tread, he moved up and down his shop.

He was very, very happy.

28

April, Late April

AUTUMN WAS KIND TO THEM, WINTER WAS LONG TO THEM—BUT IN April, late April, all the gold sang.

Spring came that year like magic and like music and like song. One day its breath was in the air, a haunting premonition of its spirit filled the hearts of men with its transforming loveliness, working its sudden and incredible sorcery upon grey streets, grey pavements, and on grey faceless tides of manswarm ciphers. It came like music faint and far, it came with triumph and a sound of singing in the air, with lutings of sweet bird cries at the break of day and the high, swift passing of a wing, and one day it was there upon the city streets with a strange, sudden cry of green, its sharp knife of wordless joy and pain.

Not the whole glory of the great plantation of the earth could have outdone the glory of the city streets that Spring. Neither the cry of great, green fields, nor the song of the hills, nor the glory of young birch trees bursting into life again along the banks of rivers, nor the oceans of bloom in the flowering orchards, the peach trees, the apple trees, the plum and cherry trees—not all of the singing and the gold of Spring, with April bursting from the earth in a million shouts of triumph, and the visible stride, the flowered feet of the Springtime as it came on across the earth, could have surpassed the wordless and poignant glory of a single tree in a city street that Spring.

Monk had given up his tiny room in the dingy little hotel and had taken possession of the spacious floor in the old house on Waverly Place. There had been a moment's quarrel when he had said that from that time on he would pay the rent. She had objected that the place was hers, that she had found it—she wanted him to come, she would like to think of him as being there, it would make it seem more "theirs"—but she had been paying for it, and would continue, and it didn't matter. But he was adamant and said he wouldn't come at all unless he paid his way, and in the end she yielded.

And now each day he heard her step upon the stairs at noon. At noon, at high, sane, glorious noon, she came, the mistress of that big, disordered room, the one whose brisk, small step on the stairs outside his door woke a leaping jubilation in his heart. Her face was like a light and like a music in the light of noon: it was jolly, small, and tender, as delicate as a plum, and as rosy as a flower. It was young and good and full of health and delight; its sweetness, strength, and noble beauty could not be equaled anywhere on earth. He kissed it a thousand times because it was so good, so wholesome, and so radiant in its loveliness.

Everything about her sang out with hope and morning. Her face was full of a thousand shifting plays of life and jolly humor, as swift and merry as a child's, and yet had in its always, like shadows in the sun, all of the profound, brooding, and sorrowful depths of beauty.

Thus, when he heard her step upon the stairs at noon, her light knuckles briskly rapping at the door, her key turning in the lock, she brought the greatest health and joy to him that he had ever known. She came in like a cry of triumph, like a shout of music in the blood, like the deathless birdsong in the first light of the morning. She was the bringer of hope, the teller of good news. A hundred sights and magical colors which she had seen in the streets that morning, a dozen tales of life and work and business, sprang from her merry lips with the eager insistence of a child.

She got into the conduits of his blood, she began to sing and pulse through the vast inertia of his flesh, still heavied with great clots of sleep, until he sprang up with the goat cry in his throat, seized, engulfed, and devoured her, and felt there was nothing on earth he could not do, nothing on earth he could not conquer. She gave a tongue to all the exultant music of the Spring whose great pulsations trembled in the gold and sapphire singing of the air. Everything—the stick-candy whippings of a flag, the shout of a child, the smell of old, worn plankings in the sun, the heavy, oily, tarry exhalations of the Spring-warm streets, the thousand bobbing and weaving colors and the points of light upon the pavements, the smell of the markets, of fruits, flowers, vegetables, and loamy earth, and the heavy shattering *baugh* of a great ship as it left its wharf at noon on Saturday—was given intensity, structure, and a form of joy because of her.

She had never been as beautiful as she was that Spring, and sometimes it drove him almost mad to see her look so fresh and fair. Even before he heard her step upon the stair at noon he always knew that she was there. Sunken in sleep at twelve o'clock, drowned fathoms deep at noon in a strange, wakeful sleep, his consciousness of her was so great that he knew instantly the moment when she had entered the house, whether he heard a sound or not.

She seemed to be charged with all the good and joyful living of the earth as she stood there in the high light of noon. In all that was delicate in her little bones, her trim figure, slim ankles, full, swelling thighs, deep breast and straight, small shoulders, rose lips and flower face, and all the winking lights of her fine hair, jolliness, youth, and noble beauty—she seemed as rare, as rich, as high and grand a woman as any on earth could be. The first sight of her at noon always brought hope, confidence, belief, and sent through the huge inertia of his flesh, still drugged with the great anodyne of sleep, a tidal surge of invincible strength.

She would fling her arms around him and kiss him furiously, she would fling herself down beside him on his cot and cunningly insinuate herself into his side, presenting her happy, glowing little face insatiably to be kissed, covered, plastered with a thousand kisses. She was as fresh as morning, as tender as a plum, and so irresistible he felt he could devour her in an instant and entomb her in his flesh forever. And then, after an interval, she would rise and set briskly about the preparation of a meal for him.

There is no spectacle on earth more appealing than that of a beautiful woman in the act of cooking dinner for someone she loves. Thus the sight of Esther as, delicately flushed, she bent with the earnest devotion of religious ceremony above the food she was cooking for him, was enough to drive him mad with love and hunger.

In such a moment he could not restrain himself. He would get up and begin to pace the room in a madness of wordless ecstasy. He would lather his face for shaving, shave one side of it, and then begin to walk up and down the room again, singing, making strange noises in his throat, staring vacantly out of the window at a cat that crept along the ridges of the fence; he would pull books from the shelves, reading a line or page, sometimes reading her a passage from a poem as she cooked, and then forgetting the book, letting it fall upon the cot or on the floor, until the floor was covered with them. Then he would sit on the edge of the cot for minutes, staring stupidly and vacantly ahead, holding one sock in his hand. Then he would spring up again and begin to pace the room, shouting and singing, with a convulsion of energy surging through his body that could find no utterance and that ended only in a wild, goatlike cry of joy.

From time to time he would go to the door of the kitchen where she stood above the stove, and for a moment he would draw into his lungs the maddening fragrance of the food. Then he would fling about the room again, until he could control himself no longer. The sight of her face, earnestly bent and focused in its work of love, her sure and subtle movements, and her full, lovely figure—all that was at once both delicate and abundant in her, together with the maddening fragrance of glorious food, evoked an emotion of wild tenderness and hunger in him which was unutterable.

Meanwhile the cat crept trembling at its merciless stride along the ridges of the backyard fences. The young leaves turned and rustled in light winds of April, and the sunlight came and went with all its sudden shifting hues into the pulsing heart of enchanted green. The hoof and the wheel went by upon the street, as they had done forever, the manswarm milled and threaded in the stupefaction of the streets, and the high, immortal sound of time, murmurous and everlasting, brooded forever in the upper air above the fabulous walls and towers of the city.

And, at such a time, as the exultancy of love and hunger surged up in them, these were the things they said, the words they spoke:

"Yes! He loves me now!" she cried out in a jolly voice. "He loves me when I cook for him!" she said. "I know! I know!" she went on, with a touch of knowing and cynical humor. "He loves me then, all right!"

"Why—you!" he would say, shaking her deliberately to and fro as if he could speak no more. "Why . . . my . . . delicate . . . darling!"

he continued, still slowly, but with a note of growing jubilation in his voice. "Why . . . my little . . . plum-skinned wench! . . . Love you! . . . Why, damn you, my darling, I adore you! . . . Let me kiss your pretty little face for you!" he said, brooding prayerfully over her. "I will kiss you ten thousand times, my sweet girl!" he now yelled triumphantly in his rapture. "I am so mad about you, my sweet, that I shall have you for my dinner!"

Then for a moment he would step back, releasing her, and breathing slowly and heavily. Her flushed face was eager and insatiate. His eye fed on her for a moment, a heavy surge of blood began to thud thickly along his veins, beating slow and heavy at his pulse and temples, making his thighs solid with potency, and impending warmly in his loins. Deliberately he would step forward again, bending over her; then, tentatively, he would take her arm and pull it gently like a wing.

"Shall it be a wing?" he would say. "A tender wing done nicely with a little parsley and a butter sauce? Or shall it be the sweet meat of a haunch done to a juicy turn?"

"*Und ganz im Butter gekocht,*" she cried, with a merry face.

"*Ganz im besten Butter gekocht,*" he said. . . . "Or shall it be the lean meat of the rib?" he continued in a moment, "or the ripe melons that go ding-dong in April?" he cried exultantly, "or shall it be a delicate morsel now of woman's fingers? . . . O you damned, delectable, little plum-skinned trollop! . . . I will eat you like honey, you sweet little hussy!"

Then they would draw apart once more, and for a moment she would look at him with a somewhat hurt and reproachful look, and then, shaking her head with a slight, bitter smile, she said:

"God, but you're a wonder, you are! How have you got the heart to call me names like that?"

"Because I love you so!" he yelled exultantly. "That's why! It's love, pure love, nothing on earth but love!"

Then he fell to kissing her once more.

Presently they drew apart again, both flushed and breathing hard. In a moment she said in a soft and yet eager voice:

"Do you like my face?"

He tried to speak, but for a moment he could not. He turned away, flinging his arms up in a wild, convulsive movement, and suddenly cried out extravagantly in a mad, singing tone:

"I like her face, and I like her pace, and I like her grace!"

And she too, now as extravagantly beyond reason as he was, would lift her glowing face and say:

"And he likes my chase, and he likes my place, and he likes my base!"

Then, separately, each of them would begin to dance about the room —he leaping and cavorting, flinging his head back in goatlike cries of joy, she more demurely, singing, with hands spread wing-wise, and with the delicate wheelings and pacings of a waltz.

Suddenly he paused as the purport of her words came clearly to him for the first time. He came back to her seriously, accusingly, but with laughter welling up in him and an inclination to convulsive mirth at the corners of his mouth.

"Why, what is this? What did you say, girl? Like your base?" he said sternly.

She grew serious for a moment, considering, then her face grew beet-red with a sudden wave of choking laughter:

"Yes!" she screamed. "O God! I did not know how funny it would sound!" and then rich, yolky screams of laughter filled her throat, clouded her eyes with tears, and echoed about the high, bare walls of the room.

"Why, this is shocking talk, my lass!" he would say in chiding tones. "Why, woman, I am shocked at you." And then, with a sudden return to that mad and separate jubilation in which their words, it seemed, were spoken not so much to each other as to all the elements of the universe, he would lift his head and sing out again: "I am astounded and confounded and dumbfounded at you, woman!"

"He is astonished and admonished and demolished and abolished!" she cried.

"You missed that time, it doesn't rhyme!" he cried, and, putting his arms around her, he would fall to kissing her again.

They were filled with folly, love, and jubilation, and they would not have cared how their words might sound to anyone on earth. They loved and clung, they questioned, imagined, denied, answered, believed. It was like a great fire burning all the time. They lived ten thousand hours together, and each hour was like the full course of a packed and crowded life. And always it was like hunger: it began like hunger, and it went on forever, never satisfied. When she was with him, he was mad with love of her, and when she had left him, he would go mad with thinking of her.

And what did he do? How did he live? What did he enjoy, possess, and make his own in April, late April, of that year?

At evening, when he was alone, he would rush out on the streets like a lover going to meet his mistress. He would hurl himself into the terrific crowds of people that swarmed incredibly, uncountably, from work. And instead of the old confusion, weariness, despair, and desolation of the spirit, instead of the old and horrible sensation of drowning, smothering, in the numberless manswarm of the earth, he knew nothing but triumphant joy and power.

Everything seemed fine and wonderful to him. Over the immense and furious encampment of the city there trembled the mighty pulsations of a unity of hope and joy, a music of triumph and enchantment, that suddenly wove all life into the fabric of its exultant harmonies. It quelled the blind and brutal stupefaction of the streets, it pierced into a million cells, and fell upon ten thousand acts and moments of man's life and business, it hovered above him in the air, it gleamed and sparkled in the flashing tides that girdled round the city, and with a wizard's hand it drew forth from the tombs of Winter the grey flesh of the living dead.

The streets were bursting into life again, they foamed and glittered with new life and color, and women more beautiful than flowers, more full of juice and succulence than fruit, appeared upon them in a living tide of love and beauty. Their glorious eyes were shining with a single tenderness, they were a red rose loveliness of lip, a milk-and-honey purity, a single music of breast, buttock, thigh, and lip and flashing hair. But not a one, he thought, as lovely as his Esther.

He wanted to eat and drink the earth, to swallow down the city, to let nothing escape from him, and it seemed to him that he was going to succeed! Each little moment was crammed with an intolerable joy and glory, so rich with life that all eternity seemed packed into it, and to see it pass, to lose it, to be unable to fix and hold it, was an intolerable and agonizing loss. And he thought that he was going to discover something no one else on earth had ever known—the way to own, to keep, to fix, and to enjoy forever all of the beauty and the glory of the earth.

Sometimes it was just the brave, free shout of children in the street, a sound of laughter, an old man, the *baugh* of a great ship in the harbor, or the slow, sliding movement of two green lamps upon a liner's mast as they passed at night, above the roof of a great pier, down the river towards the sea. Whatever it was, and whenever it happened, it struck music from the earth until the city rang like a single minted coin for him, and lay in his hand with the weight and heaviness of living gold.

And he would come in from the streets wild with delight and longing, with a sense of victory, pain, and joy, of possession and of having nothing. And instead of being a madman who had coursed furiously and uselessly through a hundred streets, and who had found no door to enter, no one to speak to, no end or goal to all his infuriated seeking, it now seemed to him that he was the richest man on earth, the possessor of something more precious and glorious than anyone on earth had ever seen before. And he would walk the floor with it, unable to sit or rest or be content. And then he would fling out of his room and from the house, and rush out in the streets again with a feeling of wild longing, pain, and joy, believing that he was missing something rare and precious, that he was allowing some superb happiness and good fortune to escape from him by staying in his room.

The city seemed carved out of a single rock, shaped to a single pattern, moving forever to a single harmony, a central, all-inclusive energy—so that not only pavements, buildings, tunnels, streets, machines, and bridges, the whole terrific structure that was built upon its stony breast, seemed made from one essential substance, but the tidal swarms of people on its pavements were filled and made out of its single energy, moving to its one rhythm. He moved among the people like a swimmer riding on the tide; he felt their weight upon his shoulders as if he carried them, the immense and palpable warmth and movement of their lives upon the pavements as if he were the rock they walked upon.

He seemed to find the source, the well-spring, from which the city's movement came, from which all things proceeded—and, having found it, his heart rose with a cry of triumph, and it seemed to him that he possessed it all.

And just as this tremendous fugue of hunger and fulfillment, of wild longing and superb content, of having everything and owning nothing, of finding the whole glory of the city in one small moment of his seeing, and of being maddened with desire because he could not be everywhere at once and see everything—just as these great antagonists of wandering forever and the earth again worked furiously in him all the time, in a conflict of wild forces which strove constantly with each other and yet which were all coherent to a central unity, a single force —so now did the city seem to join the earth it rested on, and everything on earth to feed the city.

Therefore, at any moment on the city streets, he would feel an intolerable desire to rush away and leave the city, if only for the joy he felt in being there, and for the joy of coming back to it. He would go out in the country for a day and come back at night; or, at the weekend when he had no class to teach, he would go away to other places— to Baltimore, to Washington, into Virginia, to New England, or among his father's people in a country town near Gettysburg in Pennsylvania. And at every moment when he was away, he would feel the same longing to return, to see if the city was still there, and, still incredible, to find it once more blazing in all its fabulous reality, its eternal unity of fixity and variousness, its strange and magic light of time.

He ate and drank the city to its roots—and through all that Spring not once did it occur to him that he had left not even a heel print on its stony pavements.

Meanwhile, a fool walked carefully by a newsstand in the Bronx, he dodged a taxi, heard three voices, looked wearily at the Hampshire Arms Apartments, and he made a note. It was the twenty-first of April, and he resented it: he thought of ancient times when light fell differently, his heart was barren for a glory that was gone. Therefore he thought of nightingales in Newark, and muttered of his ruins; he knew six words of Greek and spoke of Clytemnestra. He muttered bitterly, was elegant and lost, and yet he did not die: he watched the windows, wore his rubbers when it rained, wept when his wife betrayed him, and went abroad to live—a royalist from Kansas City, a classicist from Nebraska, a fool from nowhere and from nothing.

But on that very day George Webber and his Esther touched the earth and found it tangible, they looked at life and saw it could be seen. They went out in the streets together, and everywhere they went was food and richness. Spring comes up in bright flowers below the feet of April, and below the feet of lovers the earth yields up all its glory and its opulence. Therefore they drew up ripeness out of stone and steel, beauty from shambles of old brick. The earth blazed with its potent and imperial colors because they were so fit and equal for it, and because there was no falseness in their hearts.

They bought food with the passionate intensity of poets, and they found the lost world not in Samarkand but on Sixth Avenue. The butchers straightened up and grew in stature when they saw them: they slapped their straw hats with their thick hands, they arranged the folds of their bloody aprons; they got the choicest meat they had, held it up proudly, slapped it with a rough but loving palm, and said to her:

"Lady, that's prime, now. That's the best bit o' meat I got in the place. Look at it, lady! If that ain't the finest cut you ever saw, you bring it back and I'll eat it raw right here in front of you."

And the grocers would find their finest fruits for them. George, with his out-thrust lip and dark-browed earnestness, would poke at the meat, tweak the legs of chickens, feel the lettuces, plunk at great melons with his finger, read all the labels on the canned goods with a lustful eye, and breathe all the sharp and spicy odors of the shops. And they walked home together with great bags and packages of food.

She was now central, like an inexorable presence, to every action, every feeling, every memory of his life. It was not that he thought directly of her at all times. It was not that he was unable for a moment to free his brain of an all-obsessing image on which the whole energy of his life was focused. No. Her conquest was ten thousand times more formidable than this. For, had she dwelt there in the courts of the heart only, or as some proud empress throned in the temporal images of the brain, she could perhaps have been expelled by some effort of the will, some savage act of violence and dismissal, some oblivion of debauch, or some deliberate scourging of the soul to hate. But she had entered in the porches of the blood, she had soaked through all the tissues of the flesh, she had permeated the convolutions of the brain, until now she inhabited his flesh, his blood, his life, like a subtle and powerful spirit that could never again be driven out, any more than a man could drive out of him the blood of his mother, secrete unto himself the blood and tissue of his father.

Whether he thought of her with deliberate consciousness or not, she was now present, with a damnable and inescapable necessity, in every act and moment of his life. Nothing was his own any more, not even the faintest, farthest memories of his childhood. She inhabited his life relentlessly to its remotest sources, haunting his memory like a witness to every proud and secret thing that had been his own. She was founded in the center of his life now as if she had dwelt there forever, diffused through all its channels, coming and going with every breath he took, beating and moving in every pulse.

And when he stood there in the room and looked at her, he would smell suddenly and remember again the food which she was cooking in the kitchen, and a wild and limitless gluttony, which somehow identified her with the food, would well up in him. Then he would seize her in his powerful arms, and cry out jubilantly in a hoarse and passionate tone:

"Food! Food! Food!"

Then he would loosen her from the viselike grip and would hold her hand gently. She would kiss him and say, tenderly and eagerly:

"Are you hungry? Are you hungry, my dear?"

"Oh, if music be the food of love, play on Macduff, and damned be him that first cries, 'Hold, enough!'"

"I'll feed you," she said eagerly. "I'll cook for you, I'll get the food for you, my dear."

"You are my food!" he cried, seizing her again with singing in his heart. "You are meat, drink, butter and bread and wine to me! . . . You are my cake, my caviar, you are my onion soup!" he cried.

"Shall I make you some onion soup?" she then said eagerly. "Is that what you would like?"

"You are my dinner and my cook in one. You are my girl with the subtle soul and the magical hand, you are the one who feeds me, and now, my sweet pet, now, my delicate darling," he cried, seizing her and drawing her to him, "now my jolly and juicy wench, I am going to have my dinner!"

"Yes!" she cried. "Yes!"

"Are you my delicate damned darling and my dear?"

"Yes," she said, "I am your darling and your dear!"

"Is that my arm?"

"Yes," she said.

"Is that my neck? Is that my warm, round throat, are these my delicate fingers and my apple-cheeks? Is that my red rose lip, and the sweet liquor of my juicy tongue?"

"Yes!" she said. "Yes! It is all yours!"

"Can I eat you, my sweet pet? Can I broil you, roast you, stew you?"

"Yes," she said, "in any way you like!"

"Can I devour you?" he would say with swelling joy and certitude. "Can I feed my life on yours, get all your life and richness into me, walk about with you inside me, breathe you into my lungs like harvest, absorb you, eat you, melt you, have you in my brain, my heart, my pulse, my blood forever, to confound the enemy and to laugh at death, to love and comfort me, to strengthen me with wisdom, to make my life prevail, and to make me sound, strong, glorious, and triumphant with your love forever?"

"Yes!" she cried out strongly. "Yes! . . . Yes! . . . Yes! . . . Forever!"

And both of them were certain it was true.

Book V

LIFE AND LETTERS

That magic year with Esther passed and was given unto time, and now another year had come and gone.

And now George Webber was engulfed in a tremendous labor. It had all grown out of his endeavor to set down the shape and feel of that one year in childhood which he called, "The End of the Golden Weather." From that beginning, he had conceived the plan for a book, in which he wanted to present the picture, not merely of his youth, but of the whole town from which he came, and all the people in it just as he had known them. And as he labored on it, the thing took life beneath his hand and grew, and already he could dimly see the substance of a dozen other books to carry on the thread, moving out, as he had moved, from that small town into the greater world beyond, until in the end, as the strands increased, extended, wove, and crossed, they would take on the denseness and complexity of the whole web of life and of America.

Meanwhile his life with Esther went on as before. That is, it seemed the same in outward shows. But there had been a change. It puzzled him at first, and only gradually he came to understand its meaning.

29

The Ring and the Book

ANOTHER YEAR HAD GONE, ANOTHER SPRING HAD COME, AND MONK WAS writing, writing, writing with the full intensity of creative fury. The room was littered now with great piles and heaps of finished manuscript, and still he wrote.

His mind was ablaze with a stream of swarming images, stamping a thousand brilliant pictures on his brain with the speed of light, the flare of a soaring rocket. And in each of these flaming and instant pictures there was buried entire and whole the fruit of every long and painful ardor of his mind and memory.

For the first time, now, his memory seemed to be in complete and triumphant possession of every moment of its life. He could not only see and remember to their remotest detail every place where he had lived, every country he had visited, every street he had ever walked upon, everyone he had ever known or spoken to, together with the things they said and did: he remembered as well a thousand fleeting and indefinable things which he had seen for the flick of an eye in some lost and dateless moment of the swarming past. He could remember a woman's voice and laughter in a leafy street at home, heard twenty years ago, in darkness and the silence of an unrecorded night; the face of a woman passing in another train, an atom hurled through time somewhere upon the inland immensity of the nation; the veins that stood out on an old man's hands; the falling of a single drop of water in a dank, dark, gloomy hall; the passing of cloud shadows on a certain day across the massed green of the hills at home; the creaking of a bough in winter wind; a corner light that cast its livid glare upon the grey, grimed front of a dismal little house. These and a thousand other memories now returned, for what reason he did not know, out of the furious welter of the days.

The majestic powers of memory, synthesis, and imagination which

455

now exerted a beneficent and joyful dominion over his life, sharpening and making intensely vivid every experience of each passing day, had attained this maturity and certainty at the beginning of that season which, more than any other, is able to extend over man's spirit the sense of his temporal brevity against the eternity of the earth. No other season has the power of evoking in the same degree as Spring the whole temporal unity of life, the brief, piercing, and instant picture of the entire human destiny, with its fabric of exultant and wordless joy and unutterable grief, of youth that can never die and that yet is dying with each flitting moment, of beauty that is deathless and that yet appears and vanishes with the viewless speed of light, of love that is immortal and that dies with every breath we draw, of the eternity of corruptible things, of the everlasting and ephemeral life-in-death, the undying passing at each moment into death, the absolute and immortal glory tainted with the marks of finite imperfection, the goat-cry of exultant joy and ecstasy torn from the heart of ageless grief and tragic destiny.

The whole passionate enigma of life, the living contradiction, the undemonstrable but overwhelming unity which comprises every antithesis by which men live and die, is evoked by the spirit of Spring as by no other season. And yet, to the young man, this time of year often seems to be the time of chaos and confusion. For him it is the time of the incoherence of the senses, the wild, tongueless cries of pain, joy, and hunger, the fierce, broken wanderings of his desire, the lust for a thousand unknown and unnameable things which maddens his brain, disturbs his vision, and rends his heart asunder.

And so it was with Monk that year. Along with the new-found certainty of his work and his creation came other things as well. Suddenly as he stood by the window, twenty-six years old, and looked out on the magical enchantments of that new April, he thought of his father, and of all the other people who had died, and there rose up in him a wordless pity, an aching loneliness, a memory of something lost and slain. And at such times his hope and joy would vanish, and there came to him a conviction of unutterable loss and ruin. The work he had begun with such exultant certitude now lay before him like a limb of a shattered sculpture on the table, and with a revulsion of infinite disgust he put it away out of his sight.

He had no heart or interest in it any more. He now hated and was ashamed of it. He could not return to it, nor did he want to see it again. And yet he could not destroy it. He put it away in trunks and boxes, he piled it in tottering heaps upon his bookshelves, and the sight of it filled his heart with weariness and horror. These evidences of the unfinished book were like epitaphs of dissolution, tombstones to ruin and disintegration.

And yet, marvelously, incredibly, within a day or two his heart would waken into hope again, his life grow green with April. An impulse to new labor would surge up in him triumphantly once more, and he would plunge with furious joy into the forge-fires of creation. Then he would work day and night, almost without a pause except for the necessities of the school, and the time so spent he resented bitterly. He yielded stubbornly and irritably to snatches of a fevered sleep, where the whole enormous weight of time and memory worked constantly, unrestingly, shaping itself into a vast, congruent structure of experience. The heightened activities of his mind fed always at repose and energy with a vulture's beak, so that he woke exhausted in the morning, only to hurl himself into his work again.

And always when this happened, when he worked with hope, with triumph, and with power, he would love the woman more than he loved life. He could not hold it in him. It would burst out of its tenement of blood and bone like the flood tide bursting through a dam, and everything on earth would come to life again. He would start up from a furious burst of work, tired but with a huge joy pulsing in him, when he heard her step upon the stairs.

Each day at noon she came as she had always come. Each day she came and cooked for him. And sometimes they would both go out, when his supplies ran low, to shop and forage and come home again with boxes, bags, and packages of good food.

Once, in a wonderful store where all things could be bought together—the meat upon one side, the groceries on the other, the fruits and vegetables and all the green things of the season heaped up in the center—there was a young and lovely woman. Esther saw him follow the curve of her hip, the slow movements of her breasts, the delicate screw of hair upon her neck, the undulant movement of her body as she walked among the vegetables; and when she saw how beautiful the woman was and how much younger than herself, and when she saw his eye gleam as he looked at her, she knew what his desire was. She knew he wanted her, and for a moment it was as if a knife had twisted in her heart.

Later, she said: "I saw you!"

"Saw what?" he said.

"I saw you looking at that woman in the store."

"What woman?" he said, beginning to grin.

"You know," she said. "That little Christian wench that you were looking at! I saw you!"

"Haw!" he cried exultantly, and tried to seize her.

"Yes, haw, yourself," she said. "I know what you were thinking."

"Haw!" he yelled with a crazy chortle, and took hold of her.

"The little slut knew that you were ogling her," she said. "That's why she bent over the way she did, pretending to look at the carrots. I know what they are like. She uses cheap perfume instead of washing."

"Haw, haw!" he yelled and almost crushed her with his hug.

"I know what you've been doing," she said. "You think you're fooling me, don't you? But you're not. I know when one of them has been here."

"How do you know?" he said.

"I know, all right. You think you're pretty smart, young fellow, but I always know. I've found their hairpins on the pillow, and you always hide my apron and my slippers away on the top shelf of the closet."

"Haw, haw!" he yelled. "Whee! Woman, you lie," he said.

"This is *our* place," she said with a flushed face, "and I don't want anyone else coming up here. You leave my things alone. I want my slippers right out there where every little wench can see them. Don't you dare bring any more of them up here," she said. "If I ever catch one of them here I'll smash your face in, I'll claw her eyes out."

He laughed like a madman. "That's big talk, woman!" he said. "You can't. I'm free. You have nothing to do with it now, I'll do as I please."

"You're not free!" she said. "You belong to me and I belong to you forever."

"You have never belonged to me," he said. "You have a husband and a daughter. Your duty is to your family, Sister Jack," he said, in an oily tone. "Try to rectify the mistakes of your past life before it is too late. There is yet time if you will only repent sincerely."

"I repent nothing," said Esther. "I have been honest and decent all my life. The only thing I repent is that you are not worthy of this great love I feel for you. That's all I've got to repent, you low fellow. You don't deserve it."

"Get right with God, sister," he said in a pious tone. "Oh, I know, sister, I know what you are thinking. You're thinking it's too late. But it's never too late, sister. It's never too late with Jesus, sister. Fifty-three long and bitter years ago this Michaelmas I was leading almost as wicked and sinful a life as you are, Sister Jack. I thought of nothing all day long but eating and drinking and the lusts of the flesh. I was tortured by carnal desires, sister. I was sorely tried and tempted, sister. I not only danced and played cards, sister, and gorged myself on big dollar dinners, but I coveted my neighbor's wife and wanted to commit adultery with her. Did you ever hear of anything so wicked, Sister Jack? But I kept it to myself. I never told anyone of the evil thoughts I had inside me. I thought no one knew my secret. But someone did know. There was someone with me all the time who knew what I was thinking. Do you know who it was, sister? It was Jesus. Jesus knew, sister. I thought that I was all alone with my sinful thoughts, but Jesus was right there looking at me all the time. I didn't know he was there, sister. He saw me, but I didn't see him. Do you know why I didn't see him, sister? Because my heart was so black with sin I couldn't see out of it, sister. And if you see Jesus, you've got to see him with your heart, Sister Jack. Then one day he spoke to me. I was sore tempted and tried, sister. I was about to give in to my temptations. I was on my way to meet my neighbor's wife, Sister Jack, and we were going out to eat a big dollar dinner together. I heard him calling to me, sister. I heard him calling a long way off. I turned around, sister, but there was no one behind me, and I thought I had been mistaken. I walked on down the road a little farther, Sister Jack, and then I heard him calling once again. This time he was close up on me, sister, and I could hear what he was saying."

"What was he saying?" she asked.

Because it was fiendish and blasphemous, his eyes had a crazy fire in them: for a moment the fanatic madness of Rance Joyner was in him, and he believed it.

"He was calling my name, sister. He was calling me by name. He was calling to me to stop and listen to him."

"What did you do?" she asked.

"I got scared, sister. I thought of my sinful life, and I lit out down the road as hard as I could, Sister Jack. I tried to get away from him, sister, but I couldn't. There he was right on my heels, getting closer all the time. I could feel his hot breath on my neck, Sister Jack. And then he spoke right in my ear. Do you know what he said?"

"What did he say?" she asked.

"He said, 'It's no use, son. You might as well save your breath. No matter how fast you run I can always run just a little bit faster. You can't get away from me, brother. I'm a hot Christian. Are you going to talk to me now, or do I have to chase you a little farther?'"

"What did you say?" she asked in a fascinated tone.

"I said: 'Speak, Lord, for thy servant heareth.' And he spoke to me, Sister Jack, and his voice was sweet. Sometimes it was like the gentle tinkle of falling waters, and again it was like the balmy breeze of April in the dogwood bushes. He said: 'Brother, let's sit right down here on a rock and talk things over. I want to talk to you as man to man, son. I got a proposition to make to you. I've been watching you, son. I've had my eye on you. I know what's been going on, boy.' I said: 'Lord, I know I've done wrong. I guess you're pretty mad at me, ain't you?' And the Lord said: 'Why no, son. I'm not mad at you. That's not my way, brother. You've got me wrong. That's not the Lord's way, son. He doesn't get mad and want to fight. If you hit me in the face right now as hard as you could, I wouldn't get mad. That's not my way. I'd say: "Hit me again, boy! If you feel that way, just hit me again."' 'Why, Lord,' I said, 'you know I wouldn't do nothing like that.' Then the Lord said: 'Hit me, son! If it makes you feel any better, just haul off and hit me as hard as you can, brother.' The way he said them words just tore my heart wide open, Sister Jack. I began to cry like a baby—my eyes filled up and tears as big as hen's eggs began to trickle down my cheeks. And the Lord shouted out: 'Hit me, boy! It may hurt, but if you want to do it, go ahead.' And I said: 'Why, Lord, I'd rather cut my right hand off than lay a finger on you. You hit me, Lord. I done wrong and I deserve a beating. Hit me, Lord.' And, sister, by that time we were both crying like our hearts would break, and the Lord yelled: 'I'm not mad at you, boy. That's not my way. I'm just hurt, son. You've hurt my feelings. I'm disappointed in you. I thought you'd act better than that, son.' And, sister, I yelled right back at the Lord, 'O Lord, I'm sorry for the way I've done.' And the Lord yelled, 'Glory be, boy! Amen!' And I yelled: 'O Lord, I know I've been a wicked sinner. My heart was black as hell.' 'Now you're talking!' the Lord shouted, 'Hallelujah!' 'O Lord, forgive me for what I've done. I know I've been a bad man, but give me one more chance and I'll do right.' 'Glory to God!' the Lord yelled, getting off his rock, 'You are forgiven and your soul is saved. Arise and sin no more!' "

He paused—his eyes burned and his face was dark. For a moment he believed his story which he had begun in mockery. For a moment he believed that there were gods to medicine one's pain; he believed there was a brain of pity and of wisdom which could weigh each atom of bruised flesh that walked the streets, pierce to the swarming cells of rooms, of tunnels, and of little skulls, unweave the chaos of forgotten tongues and feet, redeem, remember us, and heal.

Then his lip twisted with its mockery again; he said: "Get right with Jesus, sister. He's here, he's watching you. He's standing at your shoulder this very minute, Sister Jack. Do you hear him? He's speaking to me now, sister. He's saying: 'The woman has sinned and is sorely tempted. She may yet be saved if she will only repent. Tell her to consider her grey hairs and meditate her wifely duties. Tell her to sin no more, and to return again to lawful wedlock. Remove temptation from the path, my son. Arise and leave her.' "

He paused for a moment; he stared at her with a madman's burning love.

"The Lord is speaking to me, Sister Jack. He is telling me to leave you."

"You go to hell," she said.

One day Monk sat and watched Esther as she leaned quietly on the clean white board of her table, arms folded, and with one trim foot briskly cocked across the other. Upon the wall behind her the crisp sheets of tracing paper rattled clearly, and below her, on the stiff square of drawing paper which had been fastened with thumb tacks to the board, three boldly penciled little figures had leaped into a life of rich and vivid color. She stood, poised trimly, in the midst of all her work: her brushes, pencils, paints, and drawing instruments were strewn in clean confusion all about her. Behind her, from a nail driven in the wall, the T-square hung the clean precision of its length, and farther off, near the window, a good photograph of one of Cranach's little naked women was fixed at top and bottom with a tack. The lovely little figure, thin-limbed and girdled with a chain around its slender waist, with its small and narrow breasts, its swelling belly, and its incomparable union of a beauty at once strong and delicate, childlike and maternal, lovely and strange, might well have been the picture of Esther's working spirit. It seemed to embody perfectly the whole swift grace and certainty of her labors, as well as their energy, delicacy, and beauty.

And the whole effect of this one corner that was hers, and where she worked, was like that: a spirit that was certain, strong, and graceful, full of energy and delight, seemed to dwell there. She had gained out of life, somehow, not only the joy of work, but the ease of work. She could work like a happy little fury, and yet everything she did seemed done with ease and certainty. When Monk saw her there in her corner working happily away, she seemed beyond all comparison to be the most fortunate and the most gifted person he had ever known. For she seemed to have triumphed over chance, and to work with perfect clearness, without the confusion, the error, the miserable blind fumbling which he and most other people knew.

If a man has a talent and cannot use it, he has failed. If he has a talent and uses only half of it, he has partly failed. If he has a talent and learns somehow to use the whole of it, he has gloriously succeeded, and won a satisfaction and a triumph few men ever know. And it was exactly here, Monk thought, that Esther had won the greatest victory from life. With her, the act of creation seemed to follow a clean, constant arc, and to complete itself in a single stroke, from the moment of inception in her mind to the final moment of its manual completion. She was able to effect the creative act—the act that releases from the secret earth of the spirit the elements of the thing which is to be created and which then gives to them an objective and crystalline union—with no confusion, no waste of the first energy, no loss whatever.

And that the act was partly physical, that it depended as much on muscular coördination as on a corresponding unity of spirit, she was herself assured. She insisted that the sense of timing and rhythm which the greatest athletes have had—the timing of Dempsey at Toledo, of Tilden, Babe Ruth, or the runner, Nurmi—was really "a thread of gold" which ran through all the works of the greatest painters, poets, and composers, as well.

Monk knew that this was true. The greatest works of art are inevitable from their inception. Each is a single developing act, as inexorable in its unity as the swing of Ruth's great bat. In Degas' pictures of race horses and ballet girls, in *The Iliad*, in Peter Breughel's "Icarus" and his picture of "The Playing Children," and finally, in as complete and perfect a form as it may be found on earth, in Mathius Grünewald's tremendous panels for the Issenheim altar, this single stroke and rhythm of the artist, with all the brilliant variations in spacing, balance, and design that enrich its unity, is evident from first to last.

But it is not, unhappily, evident in everything they do. Some great men have achieved this triumph almost constantly—as did Herrick, Shakespeare, and Chekhov. And these men must have been among the happiest people who ever lived. Herrick had a small, sweet, perfect voice, and it never faltered in its song. His life must have been a gloriously happy and triumphant one. Shakespeare, about whom we know nothing, but who understood and suffered everything, had probably the finest life that any man upon this earth has lived. Chekhov attempted suicide and died fairly early of consumption; nevertheless, he must have had a fine life. If a woman was sick and called the doctor, or if Chekhov saw a young student coming across the fields at evening, this made a story for him, and instantly he touched it and the thing was turned to gold.

Esther's quality seemed to be that of the painter. The genius of the painter has a physical, a manual, a technical quality which the genius of the poet does not have. Thus when a painter attains his full power, he seems then not to lose what he has gained; he continues to do good work until he dies.

But the poets, who have been the greatest men that ever lived, have failed most often. Coleridge had the greatest genius of any poet since Shakespeare's time, but he has left us only a few magnificent fragments. He completed and fulfilled his powers one time, and in one poem. That poem is as good as anything on earth, but the man who wrote it lived wretchedly and died in ruin and defeat. For genius such as his, unless its owner learns the way to use it, will turn and rend him like a tiger: it can bring death to men as surely as it brings them life.

Esther was not a genius; Monk did not even know whether she was "a fine artist," as she proudly said she was; but her life had the same quality of control, clearness, and energy that the lives of many great artists had. Monk's dislike of the theatre was growing, and he could not see that designing settings for the stage was any art whatever, better than a kind of skillful carpentry, or that the art theatre, with all its leers and knowing winks, was better than a rubbishy sort of thing. But he did see that everything she touched, every bit of work she did, if it were nothing but a brave and jaunty drawing for a sleeve, was infused immediately with all the strong, delicate, and beautiful strength of her spirit.

Sometimes the thought that the truest reflections of her life were to be shown and exhibited before a crowd of perfumed apes, pawed over and sat upon by an accursed trash of actors, leered at and ogled and applauded by pretending and dishonest fools, choked him with a feeling of shame and bitterness. It seemed to him, at such a time, that if she had come out on the stage and exhibited herself naked, she could not have done a more vulgar and shameful thing. The fleshly vanity and boastings, the cheap personal egotism of the people of the theatre, and their constant desire to exhibit themselves stank foully in his nostrils, and he wondered how so high and rare a woman could be tainted by so vile a thing.

As he sat there watching her at work, the sight of her and the train of thought it started now awakened a whole swarm of associations with things and people he despised. And he recalled a curious vanity in her that seemed somehow both innocent and childish.

He remembered the first night of a play which he had gone to because she had designed it, and he remembered it because that night had given him the first sense he had that there was something wrong, for him at least, in their relationship. That night, there in the theatre, he suddenly had a strange, uncomfortable feeling of something closing in on him, as if a magic and invisible ring had been drawn round him, encircling him, shutting him in, making him against his will a part of this world to which she belonged.

He could see her daughter, strikingly gowned; her sister, silent, with the straight eye and the impassive face; and her husband, short, plump, ruddy, with a faultless dress and grooming, gently glowing with a quiet satisfaction, a deep material contentment, at this opulent and public evidence of his wife's success in the world of fashion, wealth, and art.

And between the acts, Esther, richly and beautifully dressed, with a chain of great, dark, Eastern jewels around her neck, had walked up and down the aisles, glowing like a rose, beaming with delight and satisfaction at the praise and compliments that were heaped on her from every side. The audience, brilliant in dress and reeking with power and wealth, seemed to compose a whole community, a little town, all of whom she knew. This, then, was her "city"—the city that she knew, a city as small, as confined, and as absorbed in its own life and scandals as any country village. It was peopled with rich men and their wives, famous actors and actresses, the most successful writers, critics, and painters, and the fashionable patrons and pretenders of the arts.

Esther knew them all, and as she walked up and down the aisles he could see her greeted everywhere by people eager to grasp her hand and praise her. And he could hear her voice, a trifle high, Jewish, a little bewildered and protesting, but full of delighted eagerness, saying in a friendly manner: "Oh, hello there, Mr. Fliegelheimer. Did Mrs. Fliegelheimer and Rosy come along? . . . Oh, do you really think so? . . . Do you like it—hah?" Her tone was eager and almost gleeful, and she leaned forward hungrily as if she would lap up more if more was given.

Then, still beaming rosily and answering greetings everywhere, she had started down the aisle towards him. Just before she reached his seat there was a commotion in the row behind him, and a big, beak-nosed Jew arose. He had a moon of oily face and sensual nostril volutes, lit with a blaze of diamond studs and emerging from the lavish acre of his evening shirt, and he almost fell into the laps of the other people in his eagerness to reach her. He pressed his way towards her, seizing her hand prayerfully and tenderly between his own, and began to whisper gutterally a torrent of flattery while he stroked her arms and fingers.

"O Esther!" he whispered loudly. "Your sets!" He rolled his eyes aloft in speechless awe and then whispered with a gutteral rapture, "Your sets are lufly! Lufly!"

"Oh, do you really think so, Max?" she cried in a high, excited voice, beaming with pleasure. "Do you like them—hah?" she cried.

Max lowered his voice to an even more portentous whisper, looking craftily around before he spoke.

"The best thing in the show!" he whispered. "So help me God, I wouldn't kid you if I didn't mean it! I was saying the same thing to Łena just before you came. I said to her—you ask her yourself if I didn't—I said, 'By God, Lena, she's got the rest of them beat a city block, there's no one in the business who can touch her!' "

"Oh, I'm awfully glad you like it, Max!" Esther cried happily.

"Like it!" he swore passionately. "Say! I'm mad about it! Honest to God, I love it! It's the finest thing I ever saw!"

Then, as the lights darkened in the house and she came and sat down by Monk, he seized her hands and muttered to her in an ironic parody:

"Oi! Your sets are lufly! Lufly!"

He felt her body tremble with laughter, and she turned towards him a face so red with its mirth that even the fading light could not destroy its bloom.

"Sh-h!" she said in a choked whisper. "I know! I know!" She went on with a pretense at pitying gravity: "Poor things! They mean so well—they don't know how it sounds."

But her delight was so evident that he muttered in derision:

"And you hate it, don't you? God, how you hate it! Your sets are lufly!" he muttered. "Hell, you eat it up!"

She tried to look at him with an expression of protest and denial, but her delight and jubilation were too much for her. A gleeful smile was straining at the corners of her mouth, she laughed a little crooning laugh of triumph and squeezed hard on his hands.

"I tell you!" she whispered exultantly, "they've got to get up pretty early in the morning if they want to get ahead of your little Esther!" Then, with a grin, she said quietly, with calm confession: "Well, we all like it, don't we? Say what you will, it sounds pretty good when you hear it!"

And suddenly he felt an immense wave of love and tenderness for her. She filled him with hope and joy. He loved her because she was so small, so strong, so jolly and beautiful, and so talented, and because she exulted in these tributes to her industry and competence with the eager and gleeful happiness of a child.

When the play was over, he saw her again for a moment in the lobby, receiving the greetings and compliments of people with a happy face, and surrounded by the members of her family. And, seeing them there, he had a feeling of affection and respect for all of them. They stood around her, trying to appear casual and urbane, but in each of them—husband, sister, daughter—there was evident an immense and quiet pride, a sense of joy, a tender and loyal union.

Dark with authority, scornful with pride and money, the great Jews and Gentiles of the earth passed by her attended by the insolent beauty of their women, evoking as they passed an image of a menaceful and overwhelming power. But by the literal and cruel comparison of his eye, he saw that all their pride and scorn and power came to nothing before the one small atom of her face, and all their insolent beauty faded and grew hard and barren before the radiance of her little figure.

It seemed to him she had more wealth in one small corner of her heart than they had stored up in all their vaults and treasuries, more living strength in every breath she drew than they had built into the overwhelming strongholds of their power, more greatness in that little living house of blood and bone and fire than in all the spires and ramparts of their tremendous city. And as he saw this, all of them, with all their scornful pomp and pageantry, went grey and shabby in his eye, and he knew that there was no one on the earth who could compare with her.

He did not know, or care, how fine an artist she might be, or the nature of the art, if art it was, she followed. But, by literal and innumerable comparison, he was certain that she was a great woman, as one is sometimes sure a woman or a man is "great" regardless of their fame or lack of it, and no matter whether they have any power or talent in them that could bring them fame.

He did not care what work she did: it only seemed to him, as he saw her there, that any work she did, anything she touched—food, clothing, color, costume, the books and papers in a room, the set and hang of pictures on a wall, the arrangement of the furniture, even the brushes, rules, and compass with which she worked—would be filled at once with the direct and single magic of her touch, with the radiance, clarity, and beauty of her character.

And yet, with all his love for her, he had felt for one brief moment the cold and chilling shadow of that ring around his heart.

30

First Party

MRS. JACK KNEW EVERYBODY WHO WAS ANYBODY IN THE ARTS, AND NOW Monk was to see this brilliant world in its real texture. She came to him one day quite flushed with eagerness, and told him he had been invited to a party: would he come?

At first he was hostile and suspicious. With youth's fierce shyness, he held himself scornful and aloof from such imagined splendors because his heart had been so close to them. But as she talked, he relented to consent. Her eager excitement touched him, he felt its warm contagion, and his pulse was quickened by its glow.

"If only you liked parties more!" she said. "There's such a pleasant life that you could have! There are so many gay and interesting people who would be so happy to invite you if you would only come!"

"Am I invited to this one?" he asked suspiciously.

"Oh, of course!" she said impatiently. "Frank Werner would love to have you. I spoke to him of you, and he said to be sure to bring you along."

"Bring me along? Just like something that the cat dragged in, I guess. Bring me along because he thinks I'm tied to you and he can't help himself."

"Oh, don't be such a fool! How ridiculous!" And her face looked indignant. "Honestly, you expect the whole world to be handed to you on a silver platter! I guess the next thing you will begin to complain because he didn't send you a gold-engraved invitation!"

"I don't want to go to places where I'm not invited."

"Oh, of course you are invited! Everybody wants you! People would adore you, if you would only let them."

"Who's going to be there—do you know?"

"Oh, everybody!" she exclaimed rather extensively. "Frank knows all kinds of people—the most interesting people—you know, he's a very cultivated person—he knows all kinds of literary people, and some of them are going to be there. I don't know—but, somehow, I thought it would be rather nice for you to meet some people like that. I don't know who he will have—but he mentioned Van Vleeck"—this was a fashionable writer of the period—"of course, they are great friends," she said, looking very serious, with just a trace of pomp, "and Claude Hale, who writes the books—I don't know, but I thought one of them was rather good—and, I suppose, some people from the theatre, and—oh, yes—that poet everyone is talking of, you know— that woman, Rosalind Bailey."

" 'The greatest master of the sonnet that has lived since Shakespeare's day,' " he said sinisterly, repeating one of the more restrained encomiums that had been recently made about this woman's book of verse.

"I know!" said Esther, pityingly. "It's ridiculous! These people are such fools, you'd think they had never read a thing—they have no quality. . . . Still, don't you think it would be rather nice to meet them?" she said, looking at him quietly and hopefully. "To find out what she's really like? They say she is simply beautiful . . . and all these other people will be there . . . and I don't know, it all sounds sort of jolly . . . and people really are so nice . . . and everyone would love you if they knew you as I do—ah, come!" she cried swiftly, coaxingly, as she came close to him and took him by the arms.

"All right—I might as well be there, I guess, as up here in this freezing room, alone."

"Ah, me!" said Esther in a melodramatic tone, and then, striking a pose and smiting herself upon the breast, she cried out throatily, "Strike home, strike home!" in the celebrated phrase and style of Mr. Turvey-drop.

He glowered sullenly at her, but as she began to shake with laughter, and to shriek with appreciation of her own wit, the contagion of her self-enjoyment was so infectious that after a moment he grinned sheepishly and shook her by the arms.

"I know—" she gasped—"but that's the way you sound—like Mr. Turveydrop—freezing in this cold garret, all alone!" Again she struck a melodramatic pose as she pronounced the words with sonorous resignation.

"Ah—h," he protested, "I didn't say 'garret,' I said 'room.' "

"I know," said Esther, "but you meant garret, yes you did!" she cried.

seeing a look of denial on his face, and then went off again in laughter. "God, you are a wonder—you are!" she said when she had recovered. "I wonder if there was ever anybody like you. It doesn't seem possible."

"There won't be anyone like me when you are done with me," he predicted gloomily.

"Strike home!" cried Esther.

He seized her, and they wrestled, and he flung her on the couch.

As the time for the great party approached, there was excitement about it. Now that he had made the decision, taken the first step, committed at length his pride and youth to the ordeal of its own desire, he felt a tension, nervous, sharp, electric, like that a runner feels when he is teetering at the mark. The group of persons she had named were, he knew, among the most fashionable and sophisticated of the literary people of the day. The circle that they kept was touched with magic: the glamour of their names embodied the glamour of the whole city at the time.

Now that the thing was settled, they both went at it with a will. He had no suit of evening clothes, but now he decided that he ought to get one, and the matter was confirmed.

"I think it'd be a good investment," said Esther. "Now that you're meeting people, you'll probably be going out more and more all the time"—great vistas of social glory opened up before him—"and you'll find you can always use it. Besides," she added loyally, "you'll be simply beautiful."

They went to one of the great stores at Herald Square and, under her discerning and appraising eye, he got fitted up. It was not perhaps the best of fits, he got it out of stock, and it had not been designed for such variations from type as his heavy shoulders and long arms and short waist and legs signified. Nevertheless, like Mercutio's wound, it would serve. Esther made him revolve while she inspected him; she put deft fingers in the lapel here, made chalk marks there across the sleeves and shoulder blades, surveyed the waist and legs, and gave instructions to the fitter that left the man quite silent, humble, and amazed.

Downstairs, on their way out, they stopped and shopped for evening shirts and collars, links and studs, and a black tie. She decided that he didn't have to purchase evening pumps:

"Lots of people never use them," she said. "You'll look well enough without them. Besides," she smiled at him, "you'll be so beautiful now that no one will ever look at your feet. You wait and see."

Even so it was a dear economy. By the time he had finished his modest purchases he had consumed the better part of a month's salary. Going abroad among the great ones of the city, even when the great were poets, was coming high.

The great night had arrived. He was to dine with Mrs. Jack at home, and later take her to the party, which was not scheduled until ten.

He dressed with tense, excited care in his new regalia. His sumptuous black and white sat awesomely against his gaze at first, and he was almost overwhelmed by his own splendor.

He reached the street and breached the foot traffic to the corner like a man who walks out for the first time upon an enormous stage before a mighty audience. But almost instantly he saw that the look of people was friendly and approving, and after that he felt glittering and fine. And James, the negro bootblack on the corner, flashing solid white teeth at him from the compact ebon of his face, said, "Steppin' out among 'em, huh?"—the words were full of glamorous excitement and cheerful happiness—then the darkey nimbly sprang ahead of him and signaled for a cab.

He felt fine. He had been in the city a long time and felt he knew it—knew it as only one can know it who has walked the streets alone at all hours of the day and night. But now he was going to see and be a part of it for the first time.

The experience of being "dressed up" is a healthy and invigorating one. To be formally attired for the first time in the conventional appointments of society is one of the memorable experiences in a man's life. And to be young, and in love, and so beautifully arrayed, and on one's way to meet one's love through the sky-flung faëry of the night, and thence to join in the companionship of poets, and of the loveliest women that this jeweled rock, this central and imperial gem of all the earth could offer—the magic of this wine, this golden draft, this glory and this triumph—there is no pinnacle of life so dizzy and intoxi-cating, and, happens once, it will burn there in the mind forever.

He was not merely young, in love, and going to a party so arrayed for the first time in his life. There beat in him that night the pulse of Tamerlane, and he thought that it was passing great to be a king and ride in triumph through Persepolis.

And it was not merely that he had been a stripling boy led moth-wise, like a million others, from the outer darkness of the province to the great blaze of this imperial light, into familiar patterns of desire and custom as old as cities and as ageless as the earth.

He was a poet, the flung spear of their immortal life, and he sang the songs of all the poets that had ever sung and died. He was a poet, and upon his tongue there rolled the swelling tide of song of all the poets that had ever sung and lived. He was a poet, and he was the brother and the son, and the undying tongue, of all the poets that had ever sung and lived and died since time began. He was a poet, and the son of poets dead and gone, and a mighty poet in his own domain, and in his wild, unuttered blood there sang that night the wild, unuttered tongues of darkness and America. He was a poet, and all of the wild, unuttered tongues that he must sing were singing in his blood that night. And he stood here on the lid of night, upon this shore of the immortal dark, upon the undiscovered edge of all the brave new world of this America; and knew that still the tide was coming in upon the full, and that even yet, the Muses yet, had not yet reached their prime.

That hour, that moment, and that place struck with a peerless co-incision upon the very heart of his own youth, the crest and zenith of his own desire. The city had never seemed as beautiful as it looked that night. For the first time he saw that New York was supremely, among the cities of the world, the city of the night. There had been achieved here a loveliness that was astounding and incomparable, a kind of modern beauty, inherent to its place and time, that no other place nor time could match. He realized suddenly that the beauty of other cities of the night—of Paris spread below one from the butte of Sacré Cœur, in its vast, mysterious geography of lights, fumed here and there by drowsy, sensual, and mysterious blossoms of nocturnal radiance; of London with its smoky nimbus of fogged light, which was so peculiarly thrilling because it was so vast, so lost in the illimitable—had each its special quality, so lovely and mysterious, but had yet produced no beauty that could equal this.

The city blazed there in his vision in the frame of night, and for the first time his vision phrased it as it had never done before. It was a cruel city, but it was a lovely one; a savage city, yet it had such tenderness; a bitter, harsh, and violent catacomb of stone and steel and tunneled rock, slashed savagely with light, and roaring, fighting a constant ceaseless warfare of men and of machinery; and yet it was so sweetly and so delicately pulsed, as full of warmth, of passion, and of love, as it was full of hate.

And even the very skies that framed New York, the texture of the night itself, seemed to have the architecture and the weather of the city's special quality. It was, he saw, a Northern city: the bases of its form were vertical. Even the night here, the quality of darkness, had a structural framework, an architecture of its own. Here, compared with the qualities of night in London or in Paris, which were rounder, softer, of more drowsy hue, the night was vertical, lean, immensely clifflike, steep and clear. Here everything was sharp. It burned so brightly, yet it burned sweetly, too. For what was so incredible and so lovely about this high, cool night was that it could be so harsh and clear, so arrogantly formidable, and yet so tender, too. There were always in these nights, somehow, even in nights of clear and bitter cold not only the structure of lean steel, but a touch of April, too: they could be insolent and cruel, and yet there was always in them the suggestion of light feet, of lilac darkness, of something swift and fleeting, almost captured, ever gone, a maiden virginal as April.

Here in this sky-hung faëry of the night, the lights were sown like flung stars. Suddenly he got a vision of the city that was overwhelming in its loveliness. It seemed to him all at once that there was nothing there but the enchanted architecture of the dark, star-sown with a million lights. He forgot the buildings: all of a sudden, the buildings did not seem to exist, to be there at all. Darkness itself seemed to provide the structure for the star dust of those million lights, they were flung there against the robe of night like jewels spangled on the gown of the dark Helen that is burning in man's blood forevermore.

And the magic of it was incredible. Light blazed before him, soared above him, mounted in linkless chains, was sown there upon a viewless wall, soared to the very pinnacles of night, inwrought into the robe of dark itself, unbodied, unsustained, yet fixed and moveless as a changeless masonry, a world of darkness, the invisible, lighted for some immortal feast.

He was as naked and as perfect as a flame: his face glowed with all the clarity of its high youth. He was exalted with that supreme and noble exaltation of man's youth, which comes so seldom, and which he can never later on regain. It was a moment when the whole wine of life seemed to have been distilled and poured into his veins, when his very blood was the wine of life itself, when he possessed the whole of life—its power, beauty, pity, tenderness, and love, and all its overwhelming poetry—when all of it was his, fused to a perfect center in the white heat of his youth, the triumphant knowledge of his own success.

The hour spoke to him its unuttered tongues, and suddenly he heard the song of the whole land:

Smoke-blue by morning in the chasmed slant, on, quickening the tempo of the rapid steps, up to the pinnacles of noon; by day, and ceaseless, the furious traffics of the thronging streets; forever now, forevermore, upbuilding through the mounting flood crest of these days, sky-hung against the crystal of the frail blue weather, the slamming racketing of girdered steel, the stunning riveting of the machines. So soon the dark, the sky-flung faëry, and the great Medusa of the night; 'twixt beetling seas, the star-flung crustaceans of the continent, and darkness, darkness, and the cool, enfolding night, and stars and magic on America. And across the plains the Overland, the continental thunders of the fast express, the whistle cry wailed back, the fire box walled and leveled on eight hundred miles of wheat; the stiff rustling of the bladed corn at night in Indiana; down South, beside the road, the country negro, clay-caked, marching, mournful, and the car's brief glare; the radiance of the mill at night, the dynamic humming behind light-glazed glass, then the pines, the clay, the cotton fields again; fast-heard, soon-lost, the wheeling noises of the carnival; and sinners wailing from a church; and then dumb ears beneath the river bed, the voices in the tunnel stopped for Brooklyn; but hackled moonlight on the Rocky Mountains, time silence of the moon on painted rock; in Tennessee, among the Knobs, down by the Holston River, the last car coming by upon the road above, sounded horn, and someone surely listening: "That's those fellows. They've been to town. They're coming in"—and silence later and the Holston River; but in Carlisle, a screen door slammed and voices going and "Goodnight, goodnight, Ollie.

Goodnight, May. . . . Where's Checkers? Did you let him out?"—and silence, silence, and "Goodnight, goodnight"; the cop in Boston, twirling at the stick, "Just one lone bum"—and ruminant—"Just one lone bum upon the Common—that was all tonight; well, goodnight, Joe"—the windows fogged with pungent steam—"Goodnight"; and moonlight on the painted buttes again—"Meestaire. . . . Oh—h, Meestaire"—so eager, plaintive, pleading, strange—and off the road, in the arroyo bed a shattered Ford, a dead man, two drunk Mexicans—"Meestaire"—and then the eerie nearness of the wild coyote yelp—"Meestaire"—and it is seven miles to go to Sante Fe.

And the rustle of young leaves across America, and, "Say it!" fierce, young, and low—and fierce and panting, "Oh, I won't!"—insistent, fierce, "You will! Now say it! Say it!"—and the leaves softly, *say it, say it*—and half-yielding, desperate, fierce, "Then . . . if you promise!"—the leaves, then, sighing, *'promise, promise'*—quickly, fiercely, "Yes, I promise!"—"I'll say it!"—"Then say it! Say it!"—and quickly, low, half-audible, ". . . Darling! . . . There! I said it!"—fierce, exultant, the boy's note, "Darling! Darling! Darling!"—wild and broken, "Oh, you promised!"—wild and fierce, "Oh, darling, darling, darling, darling, darling!"—despairing, lost, "You promised!"—and the leaves, sadly, *'promised, promised, promised'*—"Oh darling, but you promised!"—*'promised promised promised promised promised,'* say the leaves across America.

And everywhere, through the immortal dark, something moving in the night, and something stirring in the hearts of men, and something crying in their wild, unuttered blood, the wild, unuttered tongues of its huge prophecies—so soon the morning, soon the morning: O America.

The people who build apartment houses had won a double victory: Mrs. Jack had at last given up her lovely old house near the Drive and had moved into a large apartment on Park Avenue. As Monk's cab drew up before the entrance, the liveried doorman stepped smartly out to the curb, opened the door, and said, "Good evening," with just a shade more warmth than the young man had expected from so grand a creature. Inside at the desk, the telephone girl looked up from the switchboard for a moment and smiled quietly at him as she told him the apartment number. He stepped into the elevator and was whisked noiselessly aloft.

Mrs. Jack's family had gone out, and a quiet dinner had been arranged for four. Stephen Hook was there, with his sister, Mary.

Hook's fragile body had been set beyond the glittering stir and shock of life. He had lived a hermit's life, incurred by filial devotion to his mother. He was remote, detached, amorous of all the rich life of the senses, with his iron brain knowing what joy was without the power to feel it. He lived almost completely in the lives of others. Only his bright, sharp mind was bold and fierce.

For ten years Hook had turned more and more to certain Jews in New York for companionship. His mind, with its hunger for the rich and sumptuous, drew back wearily and with disgust from the dry sterility and juiceless quality of his own Puritan inheritance. All around him, he thought, he saw this drying up of the warmth and savor of life. "Things flat and stale in hand" possessed the earth, and he thought this universal saplessness, especially in the life of the artist and the intellectual, was false.

The Jews loved what was beautiful and pleasant in life. Rich Jews and poor Jews were full of life and curiosity. The rich Jews had saved themselves from the inanity of the Yankee plutocrats with their imitation of English high life. While the Smart Set gravitated with the routine imbecility of the seasons between New York, Newport, Palm Beach, and Nice, the rich Jews were going everywhere, seeing everything. They established art theatres and made them pay, they spent week-ends with Bernard Shaw, they got analyzed by Sigmund Freud, they bought paintings by Pablo Picasso, they endowed radical magazines, they flew to Russia in airplanes, and they explored the fjords of Norway in yachts rented from decayed royalty. They had a glorious time, and their wives were dark and beautiful, covered with rich gems.

As for the poor Jews, they were a low-down, swarming lot, and Hook never got tired watching them—his face like a homesick ghost pressed to the window of a taxi as it wove drunkenly among the pillars of the elevated in the Bronx and on the East Side. They swarmed, they fought, they haggled, they pinched the vegetables and prodded the meat, they talked with dirty fingers, they swore that they were being robbed or swindled—they ate, drank, and fornicated with a will. The poor Jews also enjoyed life.

Hook was often sorry he had not been born a Jew.

Later, Monk was always to remember the wonder of that meal—the fine dining room and the lovely table, and the faces of four people lit so purely and so hauntingly by the candles' silent flame. He knew somehow it was *his* dinner—his and Esther's—and the other two, as if they knew it also, seemed to share in the communion of his happiness and youth. Mary Hook's blue eyes danced with sparkles of amusement, she looked shrewdly at him and laughed her wise, infectious laugh, and in the candle light her red hair was astoundingly lovely. He had seen her once before, but, being with her now, the quality of her spinsterhood was completely evident. One felt and saw that she was an old maid, but an old maid of such great charm that for a moment it seemed to Monk that every woman in the world ought to be an old maid like Mary Hook.

Until he looked at Esther. And then he knew that every woman in the world should be like her. She was radiant. He had never seen her so beautiful as she was that night. His eyes kept going to the portrait behind her on the wall that Henry Mallows had painted of her in her loveliness of twenty-five, and then with wonder back to her face, and, "God, she's beautiful!" was all his mind could say. And between the living portrait and the living woman he was haunted by the miracle of time.

She was dressed in a simple but magnificent evening frock of plum-colored velvet, her smooth shoulders and her arms were bare, and she wore a cluster or a brooch of gems against her breast. Her eyes danced and sparkled, and her tender face, as always, was as flushed and rosy as a flower. She was so radiant, merry, happy, and so full of life and health that it was fascinating just to look at her. He became so absorbed in the spectacle that he almost forgot to eat the delicious food. He looked at her with a kind of fascinated interest, as a parent might regard the self-absorbed activity of a child; he was enchanted by it, and even the gusto of her appetite, the gusto of a healthy person interested in good food, somehow delighted and amused him. She had just opened her mouth and was about to take a greedy little bite when she looked up, their eyes met, and they roared with laughter.

It was the gayest, merriest meal he had ever known. Mary Hook looked on and laughed at the radiant elation of these other two. And even Hook, behind his customary mask of bored indifference, which was really just a kind of protective shield to his excruciating shyness and sensitivity and which could not conceal the real warmth and generosity of the man's character, could not wholly hide the amusement and interest that the energy and love of these two people had for him.

The women began to talk to each other, and the young man glanced quickly from one to the other. Then his eyes met Hook's, and for a moment there was a flash of amused communication between them, the communication of two men looking at the world of women, which is wordless and perhaps untranslatable, but which seems to say: "Oh, well. You know how they are!"

As for the women themselves, they were delightful. He had never felt before so happily and so completely the purely enchanting quality of female companionship, a quality that is assuredly conveyed by sex, since it is only in the presence of women that one feels it, but that is divorced from crude desire, or the animal magnetism of seduction.

It was half-past nine before they got up from the table, and almost ten o'clock before, farewells having been said, Monk and Esther departed for the party. Her happiness and elation continued during the drive downtown.

Mrs. Jack's friend, Frank Werner, was a bachelor, and had an apartment in a house on Bank Street in Greenwich Village. The house was a pleasant one, of a familiar type, one of the better sort of houses that are to be found in that part of town. It was a modest three-story structure of red brick, with neat green blinds, a flight of steps, and a graceful arched doorway of Colonial white. It belonged to the good style of architecture that was being followed eighty or ninety years ago, before the harsh and ugly brownstone front had begun to dominate the city. So conceived, it was, of course, Victorian, but it had still managed to retain some of the grace and simplicity of its Colonial predecessors. Even if the simplicity of this kind of structure was not the result of the deliberation of high art, at least it was infinitely superior to the calculated ugliness of a later and more ornate style. The neat green blinds, so bright and gay, and the spotless white of the arched doorway, the polished doorknob, and the shining brass of the neat stair rails were, if not an innovation of more recent time, at least an afterthought. The flavor of this place, therefore, was Colonial— Greenwich Village Colonial—just a little bit too quaint, and artfully contrived.

It was a very pleasant house to look at. Monk had seen its like many times before. To a young man, alone and friendless, and living in a rented room, it gave a pleasant feeling of warmth, of friendship, and of quiet luxury. More than this, it suggested, in the roaring vortex of the city's life, the security of quiet retreat, the sense of homely comfort and of modest living. It seemed to be the kind of house in which "writers and artists" ought to live. His glimpses into houses of this sort, with their pleasant rooms, their shelves of books, and warm yet quiet lights, had touched him with a desire to know these houses and their inmates better, a feeling that here were people living sanely, soundly, quietly, as the artist should.

For it still seemed to him that the life of the creative man should represent an achievement into this kind of security. It still seemed to him that the mature artist could, in a life like this, achieve an escape from—he would have called it a triumph over—the savage conflicts of the world, the harsh and violent grappling with reality. With the ignorance and the hope of youth, the warm and cozy little light that such a house as this suggested, seemed to him to be a consummation devoutly to be wished, the kind of life an artist ought to have. His untried youth was not able to understand, would perhaps have been unwilling to face the grim fact, that man's conflict with the forces of reality is unceasing, that life is an ordeal to which a true man must expose and steel himself with ever-increasing fortitude, that for the artist most of all in this hard world there is no security, that he, above all other men, must draw his nourishment from stone, win through to glory and his soul's salvation with a taste of steel upon his lips—and that there is for him no comfortable retreat behind green shutters and warm lights as long as life waxes in him and endures.

Frank Werner's apartment was on the second floor of this pleasant house. They mounted the street steps, and in the vestibule they found his name and bell in a neat row of other names and bells. They pushed the button, the lock clicked, they went in. The hall within was carpeted, there was a polished table and a mirror, and a silver tray. They climbed a graceful flight of stairs, and as they did so a door above was opened, they heard the warm, exciting medley of fused voices, Frank Werner came out on the landing and waited for them, and they heard his cheerful voice raised in greeting.

He was a well-kept, pleasant-looking man of middle years, and his costume suggested a casual yet rather foppish elegance. He wore grey flannel trousers, thick-soled shoes, a well-cut coat of English tweed, a white shirt with a turn-down collar, and a red tie. He had a pleasant, agreeable, sensitive, and intelligent face. He was somewhat above the average height, and rather slight of build, but his face was ruddy and healthy-looking, and his high forehead and partially bald head was browned and freckled as if he went much out of doors. He was holding a very long and costly-looking amber cigarette holder with a lighted cigarette, and his whole manner radiated good cheer and a state of elated good spirits, which one guessed was habitual with him.

As they came up, he raised his voice in cheerful greeting, chuckling and smiling as he did so, and displaying pearly, well-kept teeth. He patted Mrs. Jack lightly on the hand as he welcomed her, kissed her lightly upon one rosy cheek, and said: "Darling, how beautiful you are tonight. I quite think," he said, smiling and turning to the young man, "she has discovered that magic fountain of youth that the rest of us are always looking for in vain, don't you?" He smiled winningly at his guest, and then, turning to Mrs. Jack again, he laughed with exuberant good spirits. "Hah, hah! Yes indeed!" he cried. His tone was rather mannered and over-cultivated, but his good nature was genuine enough.

The room which they now entered was fine and large, the first impression was of warmth, of comfort, and of peace. There were thousands of beautiful books, one whole wall being built up to the ceiling with shelves. Their rich bindings seemed to receive and to return the warmth and color of the whole room. Behind a screen, there was a fire of snapping pine, the furniture was simple and Colonial, there were a few fine etchings of the city on the walls, the shaded lamps gave off an orange glow.

A door led from this room to another one behind of about the same dimensions as the first. There was a small room up front in which Frank Werner kept his bed, and to the rear, upon one side, a kitchenette, upon the other, a bath.

Everything about the place gave the effect of comfort, culture, and a quiet taste. A closer and practised eye might have found the scheme a little foppish for a man's apartment. There was too fine and too precise an eye for everything: the andirons and the meaningless and useless warming pan were just a little bit too precious, and suggested the touch of the interior decorator.

There were several people in the front room, and a sound of voices from the room behind. A young man and a young woman were standing talking with highball glasses in their hands. The girl was pretty and had an air about her of the young heroines in smart novels. The young man was fair-haired, and when he spoke he had an effeminate lisp. Two men were seated by the fire. One was heavy-looking, with a red face, very fine-spun white hair, and buck teeth which showed constantly through a mouth that was always partly open. The other man, smaller and darker, suggested amber: he had a silky little mustache on his upper lip and a Semitic cast of countenance. Everyone except the host was formally attired, although there was no apparent reason why people should have dressed for such quiet surroundings, and the fact that the host alone had failed to do so now gave a trace in affectation to his own simplicity.

Frank Werner now made introductions. The amber-looking man got up and greeted Mrs. Jack very warmly. He was Maurice Nagle, and he was a director of the famous Play League in which so many of her friends were intimately concerned.

The man with the buck teeth, whom Werner addressed as Paul, was Van Vleeck, the novelist. His books were enjoying a great celebrity. They were very sophisticated books about tattooed duchesses, post-impressionist moving picture actresses, and negro prize fighters who read Greek, and they were a sufficient indication to the world that when it came to sophisticated knowingness America could hold her own.

Van Vleeck did not get up to greet the newcomers, nor did he even speak. He simply turned his pink and heavy face upon them and stared with unwinking eyes. In this stare there was a kind of calculated simplicity as of a person of such complex and subtle feelings that he was always looking for something complex and subtle in other people. Apparently he did not find it here among these new arrivals, for, after looking at them heavily for a long moment, he turned his head away and went on talking to Nagle.

The young woman said, "How do you do," without friendliness or warmth, and turned away, as though she felt there was some kind of uncompromising honesty in her rude manner. But the young man with her was lush and effusive: he was the son of a well-known actress and he immediately began to tell Mrs. Jack rather gushingly that he knew about her work in the theatre and thought it was "too marvelous!"

At this moment Rosalind Bailey entered the room from the door which led from the room behind. There was no doubt at all who she was. Her cold beauty was celebrated, her picture was well known, and, in justice to her, it must be said that she was one author who fully lived up to her photographs. Although she was well past forty, her appearance was astonishingly youthful. The impression she gave was virginal and girlish, and it was not contrived. She had the long, straight, lovely legs of a young girl, she was tall, and she carried herself proudly. Her neck and the carriage of her head were young and proud and beautiful, her dark hair was combed in the middle and framed her face in wings, her eyes were very dark and deep, and her glance was proud and straight. Anyone who ever saw her would always retain the memory of her lovely, slender girlishness, her proud carriage, the level straightness of her glance, and a quality of combined childishness and maturity, of passion and of ice.

Immediately, however, she began to behave in a strange manner. Taking no notice of the newcomers, she swept through the doorway and then stood there before Werner with a proud and outraged look.

"Frank," she said, in a cold, decisive voice, "I will *not*"—her voice rose strongly on the word—"stay here in this room as long as Paul remains."

Monk was struck by the absurdity of the statement, for she had just come into the room of her own accord, and obviously in search of trouble, and she must have known all the time that Van Vleeck was there.

"Now, Rosalind," said Van Vleeck, looking up and staring at her heavily, and speaking petulantly, "I'm not going to talk to you."

"I am *not* going to stay here where he is, as long as he says such things!" she declared strongly and loudly, without looking at Van Vleeck, and seeming a very goddess of outraged injury.

"I am not going to talk to her any more," said Van Vleeck, turning away, and speaking in the same aggrieved tone as before.

"I will *not* stay here," she declared, "if Paul is going to get in one of his insulting moods."

"But darling," protested Werner gently, obviously alarmed, and doing what he could to pacify her, "I'm sure he didn't mean to ——"

"I will *not* listen to him!" she cried again, imperiously. "I am *not* going to be insulted in this way!"

"But Rosalind!" protested Werner mildly, "I'm sure he had no intention of insulting you."

"Yes, he did!" she cried, and then in a tone of outrage, "He said that Eleanora Duse was the most beautiful woman he had even seen!" And with this astounding statement a black ice of fury seemed fairly to crackle from her blazing eyes.

"I'm not going to talk to her any more," said Van Vleeck, staring petulantly into the fire.

For the first time she turned on him in a cold voice: "Did you or did you *not*," she cried, "say that Duse was the most beautiful woman you had ever seen?"

"I'm not going—" said Van Vleeck again.

"Answer me!" the goddess cried like an awakened wrath. "Did you say it, or didn't you?"

"I'm not going—" he began again, then he turned slowly in his chair, and for a moment stared at her sullenly. "Yes," he said.

She burst into tears, and, turning, fell into the comforting arms of her husband, who had just come in, sobbing convulsively like a child. "I can't stand it! I can't stand it!" she sobbed. "He said—he said—" words choked in her and she sobbed more bitterly than ever, "I can't endure it!"

They gathered about her in a hovering brood, coaxing, petting, pleading, praying, cajoling—her husband, the pretty girl, Werner, Maurice Nagle—everyone except Van Vleeck, who sat heavily and solemnly impassive, staring into the fire.

It was a precious coterie—a group of privileged personalities who had won for themselves an intoxicating position in the life of the city. They had formed themselves into a clique, which at that moment was supreme, and at the head of this clique, crown jewel of its reverence, object of its idolatry, was the poetess, Rosalind Bailey.

She was at once the idol and the victim of the time that had produced her. One of those people who live to witness their own immortality, she was assured of it, and she did not know how fast and fleeting was her fame.

Poor Keats cried out, "Here lies one whose name was writ in water," and died. The cultists of Rosalind cried, "Here lives one whose name is writ in tablets of enduring bronze"—but she was to die. It was perhaps a symbol of the time that they needed some such image as this winged fame to preserve for them the illusion of eternity. At a time when all seemed to come, to go, to vanish, and to be forgotten with tragic haste— when today's enthusiasm would tomorrow be as dead and stale as last week's news—they felt the need of some more certain value that was sacred and that would endure.

And the woman was the queen of that impassioned incarnation. There had been a time on earth when poets had been young and dead and famous—and were men. But now the poet as the tragic child of grandeur and of destiny had changed. The child of genius was a woman now, and the man was gone.

31

Dark Interlude

WHERE THE DAYS AND MONTHS HAD GONE, MONK NEVER KNEW, BUT the seasons passed in their appointed rounds, he worked, he loved, he walked the furious streets of night, and now his book was rounding to the finish.

Meanwhile, and almost imperceptibly, his relations with Mrs. Jack had taken on a different tone and color. There was still gold and singing in their love, but now, with increasing frequency, there were also patches of grey shadow, and sometimes, in the fury and unreason of his restless, tortured soul, there were streaks and spots of bloodshot red. Time, dark time, washed over them, and worked its subtle changes in their lives.

His conquest of the woman was no longer new, but a familiar thing. And, even more, he now began to feel that he himself was caught up in the web which they had spun together. He loved her still, loved her as he knew he'd never love another; but the more he loved her, the more he felt she had become the single great necessity of his life, the more he also felt that he, the trapper, had been trapped. And as he felt this, he would see her as the author of his doom, and he would lash out at her even while he knew he loved her, and while a mounting sense of shame and anger rose up in him to crush him as he did it.

Then, too, although he demanded faithfulness of her, and often drove himself half-mad with groundless fears and vague imaginings that she was being false and wanton, yet his own desires and hungers strayed and would not stay on leash. He loved no other woman, certainly; all the love that he could give was hers, and hers alone: but still he was unfaithful.

But Esther did not change. She was just the same. The fault was in himself, and in his growing knowledge that, for him at least, love was not enough, and that a love which made him so dependent on her, which made him feel, without her, hopeless, helpless, and a thing of no account, was, for such a man as he, a prison of the spirit—and his spirit, needing freedom, now began to hurl itself against the bars.

And yet their life went on. Sometimes he loved her wholly, as he had loved her in those first rare months when love was gold and green and still untarnished, and then she came to him like morning, joy, and triumph, and the lights of April. Again, when driven in upon himself by his dark thoughts, she seemed to him the subtle, potent bait of life, the fabled lure of proud and evil cities, cunningly painted with the hues of innocence and morning, the evil snare that broke the backs of youth, and spread corruption in the hearts of living men, and took all of their visions and their strength in fee.

Sometimes, suddenly, this black convulsion of madness, shame, and death would sweep through his brain even as he spoke his love for her, and he would cry out savagely the burden of his despair.

"Oh, you are mad!" she would say. "And your mind is black and twisted with its evil!"

But instantly the wave of death and horror would pass out of him as quickly as it came, as if he had not heard her voice, and he would tell her then with swelling joy and certitude the depth and fullness of the love he felt for her.

And still the cat crept trembling at its merciless stride along the ridges of the backyard fence. The hoof and wheel went by upon the street. And high above the fabulous walls and towers of the city, the sound of time, murmurous and everlasting, brooded forever in the upper air.

32

The Philanthropists

WE HAVE NOW REACHED THAT PORTION OF OUR NARRATIVE WHERE IT becomes our agreeable privilege to inform the reader of an event which he must have been eagerly anticipating for some time—namely, the entrance of our young hero into the literary life of the great city, or, as those of us who have been to France and know the language would prefer to say, his initiation into the mysteries of *La Vie Littéraire*.

It is true that the young man's entrance—if so it may be described— was an extremely modest one, and bore few of the aspects of an invasion. In fact, if he got in at all, it might be said he got in by a side door, and—to put it brutally—only after he had been kicked downstairs, had picked up his bruised behind from the cobblestones, and limped off, muttering, no doubt, that Rome would *yet* live to hear of Caesar!

It happened in this way:

The book on which Monk had been employed for three years or more was completed very early in that fat year of Our Lord and Calvin Coolidge, 1928, and Mrs. Jack suggested to him that so pure a gem should not be left to glitter in obscurity. In short, she said the time had now arrived when "We ought to show it to someone."

This had been the author's notion all the time, but now that his work was done, he was stricken with a sense of complete helplessness, and all he could do was to look at the lady rather stupidly, and say:

"Show it to someone? Who?"

"Why," said Mrs. Jack impatiently, "to someone who knows about these things."

"What things?"

"Why, about books!"

"*Who* knows about them?" he inquired.

"Why—critics, publishers—people like that!"

487

"Do you know any publishers?" the young man said, staring at her with a dull yet fascinated eye, as who should say, "Are you acquainted with any hippogriffs?"

"Why—let me see!" said Mrs. Jack, reflecting. "Yes, I know Jimmy Wright—I used to know him very well."

"Is he a publisher?" Monk said, still looking at the lady with an expression of fascinated disbelief.

"Yes, of course he is!" said Esther. "He's a partner in the firm of Rawng and Wright—you must have heard of them!"

He had heard of them, everyone had heard of them; nevertheless, he did not believe in their existence. In the first place, now that his book was finished, he did not believe in the existence of any publisher. A publisher was a figment of the romantic imagination, an agreeable fiction conceived by young men writing their first book in order to tide them over their darker moments! But seriously to believe now, in the cold light of reality, while his appalled eye rested on the huge pile of his completed manuscript, that such a creature as a publisher really existed—that a publisher could be found who would publish *this* leviathan—no, it was too much! It was impossible! To believe that a publisher actually lived and moved and had his being somewhere in the canyoned precincts of the mighty city was like believing in ghosts and fairies! Such a creature and the whole world he moved in was a myth, a fable, and a legend.

If it was hard to believe in the existence of *any* publisher, it was especially hard to believe in the existence of the firm of Rawng and Wright. True, he had heard of them; they were, at the moment, one of the most famous publishing houses in existence, but everything that he had ever heard had been unbelievable, fascinating but impossible, matter for amusing anecdotage over one's cups—but in the cold grey dawn of soberness, incredible.

In the first place, from all that he had heard about the firm of Rawng and Wright, it appeared that they were a firm that published books but never read them. Mr. Rawng, in fact—the fabulous Mr. Hyman Rawng, a large and Oriental-looking gentleman who had been born Rawngstein but had changed his name, in the interests of brevity, no doubt—Mr. Rawng was a familiar figure at first nights, cocktail parties, the better class of speakeasy, and other public gatherings where food and drink were available—but no one had ever known him to read a book. Moreover, he admitted it. It was Mr. Rawng himself who had conceived the famous *mot*:

"I don't read books, I *publish* 'em!"

The firm of Rawng and Wright belonged, indeed, to the youngei and more unconventional element of the publishing profession. The stodgy business of print was agreeably enlivened by long and frequent intervals of women, wine, and song. Their publishing judgments may have erred at times, but their cuisine was always excellent. One saw few books about their cheerful offices, but there was a large and well-appointed bar. They gave parties, teas, and dinners to their authors, to which a large part of the public was invited; there may have been, conceivably, a dearth of plain thinking at these gatherings, but of high living there was no end.

It will be seen, then, that this enterprising house belonged to the new school of what might be called "publishing by intuition." While Mr. Rawng boasted openly that he never read a book, Mr. Wright, who made great store of all his erudition, asserted frequently that so far as reading was concerned, he didn't have to read, because he had "done all his." As for reading any of their *own* books, or reading an author's manuscript when it was sent in for their inspection, that, of course, was out of the question, absurdly out of date, ridiculous—the kind of thing, really, that had ruined the whole publishing profession, the kind of stodgy, unimaginative procedure to be expected from what the Messrs. Rawng and Wright called "old-line houses"—such as Scribner, Harper, or Macmillan—but from the Messrs. Rawng and Wright, by heaven, never!

"Read a manuscript!" cried Mr. Rawng one time when questioned on the point—"*Me* read a manuscript!" he cried again, and tapped his bosom with fat fingers, and dilated fleshly nostrils with rich scorn. "Don't make me *leff!*" cried Mr. Rawng, unmirthfully. "Vy the hell *should* I read a manuscript? I don't *have* to read it! All I have to do is pick it up and *feel* it!"—here he wagged four fat fingers feelingly— "All I have to do is hold it up and *smell* it"—here he dilated his fat nostrils with odorous appraisal—"If if *feels* good—*good*! I publish it! If it smells good—*good*! I publish it! If it feels bad and smells *lousy*—" Mr. Rawng's voluptuous features writhed with disgust, he pointed downward with a fat, condemning thumb— "R-r-raus mit it!" he growled. "The thing stinks! I wouldn't have it on a bet!"

Moreover, it was a theory of the house—call it rather an unspoken but nevertheless passionate conviction—that business should never be discussed at the offices of the firm. Let the "old-line houses" go in for that sort of thing! Let the "old-line houses" proceed along these lines of conventional commerce which had stultified the imagination and impeded the free expansion of the whole profession. Let the "old-line houses" proceed on the assumption that publishing was a business rather than a branch of the fine arts, and that the delicate and shrinking soul of the artist could not be lacerated by talk of contracts, royalties, publication dates, etc., as if he were some dull-witted Philistine upon the Stock Exchange! Let *them*—these "old-line houses"—carry on in the sinister privacy of their business offices the old, old game of stealth and slyness, whispering intrigue, secret agreements, hidden diplomacy! Such methods as these did nothing but breed suspicion and future misunderstandings; they were ruinous—ruinous!—would these crafty old ones never learn?—and had brought the publishing profession to its present wretched state.

As for the Messrs. Rawng and Wright, they would have none of it. They had brought new life to publishing. As they admitted, they had entered the publishing business "like a fresh breeze"—and they were blowing across it now like a tornado! Let others have their business offices and their stodgy atmospheres; the Messrs. Rawng and Wright, who understood the delicate adjustments of the artistic temperament better than any of their competitors, had studios, reception rooms, and couches with lots of cushions on them. The note they sounded was æsthetic, not commercial.

If business with an author *had* to be discussed—and the Messrs. Rawng and Wright regretted personally that the necessity ever had to arise—let the discussion be carried on without concealment or suspicion, in a free, frank, and wholesome manner, and let the public be invited. In accordance with this principle, all of the business negotiations and arrangements of the firm took place in a well-known speakeasy conveniently located in the basement of a brownstone house three doors down the street. Here, at almost any hour of the day or night, some member of the organization might be found discussing the plans, projects, and accomplishments of the house to anyone inclined to listen. One of the most delightful features of the personnel of Rawng and Wright was that it had no secrets. A delightful air of camaraderie prevailed throughout. The office boy was almost as well informed on all the affairs of the firm as were the two great heads themselves, and within a quarter of an hour of any new development the matter was being amiably talked over with waiters, bartenders, bar-flies, and anyone within a hearing radius of one hundred yards.

All negotiations with authors were made as agreeable as possible. Knowing the nature of the artistic temperament as they did, and understanding to the full—nay! wincing in sympathy with—its exquisite sensitivity, any matter of contracts, royalties, or advances was never even mentioned until after the sixth round of drinks. If the business to be discussed was a simple one—some matter of routine dispatch such as getting an author's signature to a contract calling for "the usual terms," together with an option on his next eight books— nothing more was needed than six or seven stiff Scotch highballs and the hypnotic compulsions of Mr. Hyman Rawng's persuasive voice to make the owner of the temperament succumb, see light, and get the unpleasant business signed and over with without delay.

In more difficult problems, of course, where the artistic temperament was inclined to be more vexed and hostile, a longer period of persuasive preparation was at times essential. If there was some dispute —and, unhappily, we must admit, these unfortunate disputes do sometimes happen—if there was, on the part of the artistic temperament, some over-sensitive tendency to truculent suspiciousness, Mr. Hyman Rawng's sympathetic pity was as wide as nature, as deep as the Atlantic, as tender in its mercy as the love of God.

"My dear boy," he could be heard, after the eleventh round of drinks, speaking as gently, tenderly, and sweetly as one speaks to little children, "My dear boy, vat do you think I'm in the publishing business for anyway?—To make money?"

"Well," the Temperament might answer, surveying his benefactor with truculent surprise, mixed in between a hiccup and a belch—"hic! —aren't you?"

Here Mr. Hyman Rawng would laugh gently, gutturally, understandingly—a laugh mixed equally of pity and reproach. Then, wagging a fat forefinger sidewise before his fleshy nose, he would say:

"Nah! Nah! Nah! Nah! Nah! . . . My dear boy, you don't understand! . . . Money! My dear boy, I don't care for money! It means nothing to me! If I cared for *money*," he cried triumphantly, "vy the hell should I be in the publishing business? . . . Nah! Nah! Nah! You got it all wrong! It's not money that I'm after! No publisher is! If I was after money I wouldn't be in this business. My dear boy . . . you got it all wrong! *Publishers* don't make money! . . . Nah! Nah! Nah! . . . I thought you *knew* that!"

"Oh, I see!" the Temperament might now say bitterly. "Just a bunch of—hic!—big-hearted philanthropists, hey?—in business—hic!—for your health!"

Mr. Rawng's manner now became immensely grave and confidential. Leaning over and tapping his companion on the knee with a fat fore-finger he would say in a low but very impressive whisper:

"You said it! . . . You got it eggs-ackly! . . . You hit the nail right on the head! . . . That's what we are—philantropists!"

"Yeah!"—this with a decided shade of cynical aspersion—"Then what about those royalties of mine? Where's all that dough you made on my last book?"

"Royalties?" said Mr. Hyman Rawng in a thoughtful and abstracted tone, as if he had heard this curious word somewhere in his childhood long ago. "Royalties? . . . Oh, royalties!" he cried suddenly, as if the meaning of the word had just dawned on him. "It's *royalties* you're talking about? That's what's worrying you?"

"You bet your cock-eyed life that's what's worrying me! What about 'em, huh?"

"My dear boy," Mr. Rawng now said in a commiserating tone, "why didn't you say so before? Why didn't you get it off your chest? Why didn't you come to me and *tell* me about it? *I'd* have under-stood! That's what we're here for—because we *understand* these things! So when anything of this sort comes up again . . . when it begins to worry you . . . for *God's* sake, come to *me*, and spill it! . . . Don't let it *eat* on you! . . . That's the trouble with you fellows—you're all so God-damn sensitive! . . . Of course, you wouldn't be *writers* if you weren't! . . . But don't be that way with me, Joe! . . . You got noth-ing to be afraid of where *I'm* concerned. . . . You know that, don't you? . . . So don't be so sensitive!"

"*Sensitive!* Why, you— *Sensitive!* . . . What the hell do you mean by *sensitive?*"

"Just what I say," said Mr. Rawng. "I mean you got nothing to worry about at all. That's what I brought you in here to tell you—I could see you had begun to let it eat on you—so I just wanted to bring you in here for a drink or two to tell you everything was all right!"

"*Tell* me! Tell me what's all right? It's *not* all right! Not by a damn sight!"

"It *is* all right! If it's not all right, I'll *make* it all right! . . . Listen to me, Joe," again the low and quiet reassurance, Mr. Rawng's dark, compelling eye, the finger tapped impressively on the author's knee. "Forget about it! . . . I could see you've let it eat on you—but forget it! Life's too short! We want you to feel right. . . . So I just brought you in here to let you know that it's all settled as far as *we're* concerned! . . . You owe us nothing!"

"Owe you! Why, you old—why, *owe* you! What the hell do you mean by *owe* you?"

"Just what I say! . . . I mean that from now on . . . today! . . . right now! . . . this minute! . . . we're starting out with a clean slate! . . . What's done is done! . . . What's over is over! . . . We're banking on your future, and we want you to have a mind free from worry, so you can do the work we know you're going to do. . . . So just forget about it! . . . The coast is clear, the slate is clean—that's the way *we* feel about it!"

"The way *you* feel about it, is it! The slate is clean, is it? Not by a damn sight! That's not the way *I* feel about it!"

"I know you don't," said Mr. Rawng quietly, "but that's because you're so sensitive! You think you owe us something! You think you're under some sort of obligation to us. But that's just your pride!"

"Owe! Obligation! Pride! Why——"

"Listen, Joe," said Mr. Rawng in his quiet and earnest tone again. "That's what I tried to tell you a while ago, but you wouldn't listen to me! I told you I wasn't in this business to make money! . . . If I wanted to make money, I wouldn't be in this business! . . . I'm in this business because—" Mr. Rawng's voice faltered huskily, for a moment his dark eye shone humidly, but he mastered himself, and concluded simply—"well, I'm in this business because I *love* it . . . because of the friendships I have made . . . because, maybe . . . well, Joe, I didn't mean to say this . . . I know it will embarrass you . . . I know how you hate it when anyone talks to you about your work . . . but I got to say it! . . . I know that a hundred years from now no one will remember me," said Mr. Rawng with a sad but manly resignation, "I know I'm just one of the *little* guys of the world. . . .

It don't matter much whether I live or die, they won't remember me. . . . But if someone a hundred years from now picks up one of your books and sees my mark on it, and says, 'Well, I don't know what that guy was like, but he *was* the guy who first discovered Joseph Doaks, and gave him his first chance' . . . why, then, I would consider that my life had not been lived in vain! . . . That's just how much it means to me, boy!" Mr. Rawng's voice was now distinctly husky. "That's why I'm in this game! It's not the money! . . . Nah! Nah!" He smiled moistly, painfully, and shook a fat finger before his nose. "It's the thought that maybe I've been of some use here on earth . . . that maybe I've been able to be of some use to guys like you . . . helped you on your way a little . . . made things a little easier for you so you could realize your genius. So you don't owe me *one red cent*! Not a *penny*! You're not under any obligation to me *what-so-ever*! . . . Your friendship means too much to me for that—the pride I take in the knowledge that I am your publisher! . . . So forget about it! You owe me nothing!"

"Owe you nothing! . . . Why—you—" the voice rose to a maddened scream, the Temperament tore papers from his pockets and smashed them viciously upon the table—"Take a look at this royalty report!"

"Wait a minute!" Mr. Rawng's voice was now low, controlled, imperative. "I said what I meant, and I meant what I said! . . . I said you didn't owe me anything and I meant it! I meant that we wanted you to forget all that money we've been advancing to you to live on for years now——"

"All that money! . . . Why, do you mean to say——"

"I mean to say we did it because we were willing to invest to that extent in your future as a writer. I mean to say we did it because we believed in you . . . and that we are willing to cancel the debt because we still believe in you and your work, and don't want to see you worrying about your debts. . . . And still you're not satisfied? You're not yet convinced? You're still worried over royalty statements, are you? . . . Good!" said Mr. Rawng with harsh decision—"That's all I want to know! Then—here!" with these words he picked up the offending royalty sheets, tore them in two, then tore them cross-wise, folded and refolded them, and tore them finally and carefully into a thousand little bits. Then, looking at his companion quietly, he said:

"Now—will that do? Do you believe me now when I tell you that you owe us nothing? Are you convinced?"

Not to pain the reader with further elaboration, it must be admitted that there were, even among the authors of the Messrs. Rawng and Wright, those whose artistic temperaments refused to be convinced, even after the most benevolent persuasions.

Such people there are, alas, in every walk of life, and, hard though it is to believe, such people as these are not unknown to the philanthropists who conduct that great and benevolent institution known as the publishing business. Nay, incredible as it may seem, my friends, these snakes, unworthy of the name of men, may be found coiled in the grass of even the oldest and most dignified publishing establishments, ever willing to doubt the charity of purpose, the devotion to principle, and the holy reverence for pure letters which, as every unbiased person knows, are the motives which control every publisher worthy of the name—even willing to doubt that publishing is not carried on in the spirit of pure philanthropy which Mr. Rawng has so feelingly described, willing to suspect publishers of taking an occasional business advantage of an author, driving hard bargains, and putting cunning clauses in a contract—in short, to feel suspicion, distrust, and indignation towards these holy custodians of *print* without whose aid the mere writers of books are nothing. Of such unworthy wretches as these, it is impossible to speak too harshly. They are like the bird that fouls its nest, like the mongrel cur that bites the hand that feeds him. But they do exist—even in the houses of such devoted, idealistic, and nobly generous purpose as the great house of Rawng and Wright.

When the Messrs. Rawng and Wright discovered the presence of such a viper in their midst, there was just one course left open to them—they cast the viper out. They cast him out gently, quietly, sadly, and regretfully; nevertheless, they cast him out utterly. In their own words, he no longer saw things "eye to eye" with them. They were compelled, therefore, to "let him go," "seek opportunities in another publishing field," "develop elsewhere"—but they "let him go."

He went, and often, we regret to say, he went in bitterness, mouthing evil words against his former philanthropic guardians. He went, and often he said harsh things of them—aye! and wrote them, too— as witness the following regrettable lines, written by one of the disgruntled vipers, and repeated here solely to show how sharper than a serpent's tooth is base ingratitude:

Poems are made by fools who write,
And books are published by Rawng and Wright;

Poems are made by flame and song,
But God knows who made Wright and Rawng!

Whenever I see the two of them
I'm glad there are so few of them.

Whenever Rawng doth to me nod,
I'd rather be Wright than Rawng, by God!

Until Wright comes, and I see light
And know I'd rather be Rawng than Wright.

33

Waiting for Glory

THE FOREGOING FACTS ABOUT THE CELEBRATED FIRM OF RAWNG AND Wright were, of course, unknown to Monk, although he had, no doubt, heard rumors of them. But perhaps ignorance at this time was fortunate, since the ordinary pains of the expectant author are bad enough, and if, to the torment of expectancy and doubt which now possessed him, there had been added a certain knowledge of the standards and requirements of the Messrs. Rawng and Wright, his anguish during this trying period would have been extreme.

Five weeks passed before he heard anything from them, and during that time——

But how can we describe that period of impassioned waiting? It is like having given birth to one's first-born, and now, the birth-pangs over, the parent waits in anguished tension for the doctor's verdict. Is the child sound, and of good weight? Does it have all its wits and faculties about it? Is it well-made? Are there any blemishes or disfigurements? Does it have a harelip or a cleft palate? Is it cross-eyed or club-footed? Does it have the rickets? Is it marked by a caul, a mole, a rash, a wart, a birthmark of any fashion whatsoever? Or has it come full-limbed and well-proportioned to the world, alive and well and vigorously kicking? Will the doctor presently come in and say, "It is my happy privilege to inform you that you have given birth to a bouncing, healthy son!"

Yes, the pangs of birth are over, but the pangs of anguished waiting have only just begun. The author goes through torment! He sees signs and symbols everywhere; becomes insanely superstitious; will not get out of bed on the left side in the morning for fear it will bring him bad luck; goes through one door and comes out through another; changes his brand of cigarettes, then changes back again; can't make up his mind to anything—whether to cross the street or not to cross the street, whether to buy a newspaper at this newsstand or at that; guesses the number of steps across his room and shortens his stride to make it come out even—becomes, in short, a whole madhouse of compulsions, numbers, omens, portents, superstitious emanations, and magnetic influences—all directed prayerfully towards the Messrs. Rawng and Wright and his manuscript, whose fate now hangs in the precarious scales of hair-line fortune, and may be made—or ruined—by a sneeze! He hopes and prays and sweats and fears and holds his breath and counts his steps, in order somehow, even if he cannot *influence*, at least not to disturb, the processes of destiny.

So the young author waits and goes through—no! he does not go through Hell; he goes through worse than Hell: he goes through Limbo. For Hell, at least, is fairly certain and decisive: one is burned by fire eternally, frozen by ice, scourged by devils, tormented by thirst and hunger and impossible desire. But in Limbo one just floats around: he has not roots—not even hellish roots!—he is tossed about upon a sea of doubts; he doesn't know where he is; or where the end or the beginning of anything is!

It will soon be the Springtime of the year. Our author looks and watches for it, hopeful for a sign before the season's due. It won't be long before the trees will burst in poignant green just overnight—oh, God is good! And so are Rawng and Wright!

Night comes, frosty and star-brilliant skies of February, the windswept darkness of young March—our hero soars the rockets of young fame, the blazing constellations of first triumph. Morning comes, night's wild chemistries are faded—grey dejection now. Then flashing noon, a sapphire sky, and everything in life a-sparkle—how can there be a minute's doubt on earth with the immortal "yes!" of all this shining clearness! Then, swift as light, a shadow passes, and the shining goes; the street is darkened and the light fades out—and Rawng and Wright have given their last word, secure Despair has ended Doubt!

But then the shadow passes! Light comes back again, the old red brick of the house across the street is bright with life and March again, all of the shining sparkle of the day, the sapphire skies, have come again.—No, no! they have not given their last word, their last word is not stern Rejection, their last word is still undecided—Mr. Rawng has merely frowned reflectively; Mr. Wright has had a moment's doubt—but now their heads are bent earnestly again, they turn the thumb-worn pages of the great manuscript with feverish interest —they read with breathless fascination—Rawng breathes hoarsely, reading, saying—"God, Jim! What a writer this boy is! Listen to this passage, will you!"—And then Wright, exploding suddenly in a shout of laughter—"Great God! What bawdy, lusty humor! There's been nothing like it since old Rabelais!"

And Rawng, slowly, with conviction: "The book America has been waiting for!"

And Wright: "The writer that this country *had* to have!"

And Rawng: "We've got to publish it! I'd publish it if I had to set the type with my own fingers!"

And Wright: "I'd help you do it!—Yes, we've got to bring it out!"

And Rawng, exultantly: "And the beauty of it is the boy has just begun!"

And Wright, rapturously: "He hasn't even started yet! He's got a hundred books in him!"

And Rawng: "A treasure!"

And Wright: "A gold mine!"

And Rawng: "A wonderful property!"

And Wright: "The best our house has ever had!"

And Rawng: "It's like stumbling over a gold mine!"

And Wright: "It's like picking money up out of the street!"

And Rawng: "It's like dew from heaven!"

And Wright: "It's like bread upon the waters!"

And Both Together: "It's like manna! . . . It's like mercy! . . . It is grand!"

Meanwhile the light still comes and goes, the shadows pass, and shining day comes back again, the sapphire sky a single shell again, the sparkle of the day again—all of the hope, joy, terror, doubt, and misery, all of the triumph and the certitude, all of the death, defeat, all sodden, dull despair—all of the glory and the singing, and—oh, life of life, and heart of hearts, fond, foolish, sinful, proud, and innocent— potential, lovely, and mistaken youth!

And while the light comes and goes, and the cat creeps trembling at its merciless stride along the ridges of the backyard fence, every day at noon he hears her steps upon the stairs:

And Esther, her jolly apple-cheeks aglow with morning, bright and eager as a bird: "Any news? Any news today, boy?"

And Monk, now gruff, glowering, grumbling as a bear: "Naw."

She: "Did you get a letter from them yet?"

He: "Naw! No letter from them yet!"

She: "Well, of course you can't expect to hear so soon. You've got to give them time."

He, hands clasped together, leaning forward, staring at the floor: "I've given 'em time. I don't expect to hear at all."

She, impatiently: "Oh, don't talk like such a fool! You *know* you'll hear from them!"

He: "You're the one who's talking like a fool! You know I won't hear from them!"

She, her voice rising a little with annoyance: "Honestly, I don't see how a person with your capacity can talk such rot."

He: "Because I don't have any capacity and I have to spend eight hours a day listening to *your* rot!"

She, in a high, excited, warning kind of voice: "Now you're beginning again!"

He, bitterly: "I wish to God you were ending again! But I know there's no hope of that!"

She, more high and excited than ever, her voice trembling a little: "Oh, so you want me to go, do you? You want to get rid of me, do you? That's what you're after?"

He, muttering: "*All* right! *All* right! *ALL* right! You're wrong! I'm right! *You* win!"

She, her voice trembling dangerously: "Because if that's what you want, I'll do it! I'll not stay a moment longer if I'm not wanted! Do you want me to go, or not?"

He, muttering sullenly as before: "*All* right! *All* right! *All* right! Have it your own way."

She, her voice squeaking a little at the end now: "Is that what you're after? Is that what you want me to do? Are you trying to get rid of me? Do you want me to go—hah?"

He, muttering disgustedly: "Oh, for God's sake!" Gets up and walks towards window, muttering: "Do anything you damn please—just leave me alone, that's all." Leans on his arms across the window sill, and gazes dejectedly out into the backyard, and the light comes and fades and passes, comes again and passes, brightens, shines, and pierces, and goes dead.

She, her voice breaking dangerously towards hysteria: "Is that what you want—hah? Is that what you're after? Are you trying to get rid of me? Is this your way of telling me you're through with me? Do you want me to leave you—go away and leave you—leave you alone?"

He, turning with a maddened shout, clapping his hands against his tortured ears: "For God's sake—yes! . . . Get out of here! Go away! . . . Do anything you like!"—yelling now—"Leave me alone, for Christ's sake!"

She, in a high, cracked tone: "I'm going now! . . . I'm going now! . . . Good-bye . . . I'm going! . . . I'll not bother you again! . . . I'll leave you alone, if that's what you want." To this there is no answer. She wanders confusedly about, talking to Someone in a confiding, Ophelialike, here's-roses-for-you, theatrical kind of tone: "Good-bye! . . . Over! . . . Done for! . . . No good any more! . . . He's through with her! . . . He's tired of her! . . . She loved him, she came and cooked for him. . . . She stood all of his abuse, because she worshipped him. . . . But it's all over now! . . . He's had enough of her! . . . He got what he wanted from her . . . used her for what she was worth to him. . . . Now she's no use to him any more!"

He, turning suddenly like a maddened animal at bay, with a snarl in his throat: "Used *you!* Why, you—you—you hussy, you—what do you mean by used *you!* Used *me,* you mean!"

She, now very Ophelialike, tenderly distrait, brokenly resigned and forgiving, wagging her head with eerie understanding, as she confides to Someone in the Solar Spaces of the Universe: "It's all right! . . . *I* understand! . . . He's through with her! . . . She slaved for him all these years . . . stood by him, comforted him, believed in him. . . . She thought he loved her, but she sees now it was all a mistake. . . . All right! All right! She's going now! . . . He has no more use for her, so he's telling her to get out! . . . Throw her out! . . . She's no good any more! . . . He's had all he wanted from her! . . . She's given him all her love and devotion. . . . She thought he wanted it, but he doesn't want it any more. . . . He's used her for all she was worth to him. . . . Now he's through using her. . . ."

He, stamping insanely back and forth across the room, and jeering to his own Particular Confidant Up There Somewhere in the Solar System: "Used *her!* Taken all *she* had to give! Why, God-damn my soul to hell, it's perfectly delightful! Used *her*! Through using *her* now!" with a jeering, mincing daintiness of tone, "Now ain't that nice! Now ain't that just too God-damned sweet for words! Used *her*! Now wouldn't that give a preacher's ——— the heartburn, now!" Then with a sudden return to the snarling intimacies of direct address: "Why, God-damn it, the only way I ever used *you* was to give you my youth—my life—my strength—my faith—my loyalty—and my devotion; to give you all the passion, poetry, and pride of youth, its innocence and purity—and for what purpose! For what! . . . Why, God-damn my ill-starred, miserable, and ill-fated life to hell—because I loved her—because I loved her more than my own life! . . . *Using* her! Yes, by God, using her by loving her—this woman who should have her thoughts turned upon serene middle age—as any other woman *would*!—who should be trying to spend her few remaining years in making her peace with God! Yes, I say, using her by feeding her with the adoration and devotion of youth, and lighting her talents with the passion, the poetry, the genius, and the inspiration of a young man's life! Using her! Yes, God-damn me for the moon-struck, hypnotized, and opium-eating cuckold that I was and am! That's the way that I used *you*—and I got what I deserved!"

She, in a controlled, quiet, slightly panting voice: "No, no! . . . That's not true, George! . . . I loved you. . . . It's all over now, I'm leaving, since that's what you seem to want . . . but at least be fair about it now. . . . Be honest about it. . . . You've got to admit that I loved you." With a very controlled and ladylike quietness of dignity, she continued: "I had supposed, of course, that you loved me, too. . . . I had supposed that you returned my love . . . but—" with a little twisted smile, and the same quiet dignity—"I see now I was wrong. . . . I see now that I was mistaken. . . . But at least you might be fair about it, now that you're casting me out." Then with a slight gesture of the hands and shoulders, a slight return of her former manner of speaking quietly to Someone Way Up There, but with the greatest and most ladylike refinement: "I loved you, it is true. . . . I always will! . . . Of course, with you it's apparently on one day and off the next, but . . . well—" again the little twisted smile—"*I'm* just not built that way. . . . Love is not a thing that comes and goes, is hot and cold, can be turned on and off like a water tap." With a note of pride— "My people are loyal! . . . With us love is a thing that lasts!" With bitterness—"We're not like you fine and noble Christians . . these great and wonderful Gentiles." She began to pant and heave loudly with excitement: "Oh, a fine lot they are, all right, all right! I know! *I* know!" nodding her head sagely, "I know what you are like. . . . You told me all about it . . . your loose women, sleeping with your pick-ups, having your promiscuous relations with your little strumpets before you met me. . . . *I* know! I know all about it! You told me all about your father, didn't you? . . . Oh! a wonderful father he must have been, wasn't he! . . . Leaving your mother for a prostitute!"

He, in a low, strangled tone: "Now, listen, *you!* You leave my father out of it! . . . You get out of here!"

She, still quietly, but with rising excitement again: "I'm going . . . I'm going now! . . . I'll leave you alone, if that's what you want. . . . But before I go, I want to tell you something. . . . You'll remember this some day! You'll see what you have done to me! You'll understand then that you've turned your back on the best friend you ever had . . . thrown the one who loved you out into the gutter . . . deliberately spat upon and trampled the greatest love that any man has ever had!"

He, breathing hoarsely, ominously: "Are you going now, or not?"

She, her voice now high and trembling again: "I'm going! I'm going! . . . But before I do, I want to tell you that I hope you live to see the day when you will understand what you have done to me." Her voice was trembling with the hysteria of tears: "I hope you live to see that day . . . and suffer what I'm suffering now."

He, breathing hoarsely, swinging her by the arms and shoulders, propelling her towards the door: "Get out of here! You're getting out of here, I say!"

She, her voice breaking in a cry, half sob, half scream: "George! George! . . . No, no, for God's sake, not like this! . . . Don't lay this black crime on your soul! . . . Don't say good-bye like this! . . . A little love, a little mercy, a little pity, tenderness, I beg of you, for God's sake! . . . Don't end it all like this!" She screams: "No, no! For God's sake!" She seizes at the edges of the now-opened door and hangs on, sobbing hoarsely: "No, no! I beg of you—don't let it end like this!" One hand is brutally ripped away from the door—she is pushed out, sobbing hoarsely, into the hall, he slams the door shut, and leans against it panting like an animal at bay.

In a moment he lifts his head, listening intently. There is no sound outside in the dark hall. He looks worried and ashamed. he winces like an animal and his lip sticks out, he puts his hand upon the door knob, is about to open it, his jaw hardens, he turns and sits down on his cot again, bent over, staring sullenly at the floor, more gloomily dejected than ever before.

And again light comes and passes, comes, passes, fades, and comes again. And there is silence, the little ticking and interminable minutes of slow silence, wearing the ash of slow, grey time away—and at last a sound! Outside a board creaks softly, the door knob slowly turns. He looks up quickly; then bends his head again, looks doggedly and sullenly at the floor. The door opens, Esther is standing there, very red in the face, her eyes very bright, her little figure very determined, but very ladylike, the picture of dignified restraint, refined control.

And Esther, very quietly: "I am sorry to have to disturb you again. . . . But there are a few things which I have left here . . . some designs I made, and my drawing materials. . . . If I'm not coming back here any more, I shall need them."

And Monk, looking at the floor dejectedly and muttering: "All right! *All* right!"

She, going to her drawing table, opening the drawer, and taking out designs and instruments: "Since that's what you seem to want, isn't it? . . . You told me to go away and leave you, and not bother you any more. . . . If that's what you want. . . ."

He, wearily as before: "*All* right! *All* right! *You* win!"

She, quietly, but with acid sarcasm: "I suppose that's meant for wit, isn't it? . . . The young author with his great command of language and his brilliant repartee!"

He, heavily, dejectedly, staring downward: "O.K. Y*ou're* right! Y*ou* win, *all* right!"

She, flaring sharply: "Oh, for heaven's sake! Say something different, won't you? Don't sit there mumbling 'all right,' like an idiot!" Then sharply, commandingly: "Look at me when you speak to me!" Impatiently: "Oh, for God's sake, pull yourself together and try to talk and act like a grown-up human being! Stop acting like a child!"

He, as before: "*All* right! *All* right! *You* win!"

She, slowly, pityingly: "You — poor — blind — fool! . . . To think that you have no more sense than to turn on the one person who loves you . . . who adores you . . . who has so much to give you! . . . That you would throw that priceless treasure away! . . . When I know so much—" she smites herself on the bosom—"when I have this Great Thing all stored up in me—*here! here!* . . . ready to pour it out to you . . . this Great Treasure of all I see and feel and know . . . yours for the asking . . . yours, all yours . . . no one's but yours . . . the greatest treasure any man could have . . . all that richness and beauty that might feed your genius . . . and all thrown away, all wasted . . . just because you're too big a fool to take it! . . . Just because you are so blind and ignorant that you will not see it, use it, take what's offered to you! . . . Oh, the wicked, wanton, *sinful* waste of it—when I am willing to pour it all out to you—empty my soul for you—give you the whole rich treasure of my being—and you throw it away just because you're so *stupid—blind—*and *ignorant!*"

He, heavily, with a dejected sigh: "O.K! *O-KAY! You* win! *You're* right! Everything you say's O.K."

She, looking at him intently, keenly, challengingly for a moment, then very quiet and direct: "Listen! Have you been drinking? . . . Have you had a drink?"

He, wearily, dejectedly: "Nope. Nary a drink. Not a drop—" gloomily— "There's nothing in the house."

She, sharply, inquiringly: "Are you sure?"

He: "Sure I'm sure."

She: "Because you act as if you had."

He: "Well, I *haven't.*" He broods sullenly for a moment, then suddenly smites a clutched fist on his knee, and, looking upward with grim determination written on his face, cries out: "But by God, I'm going to have one! . . . I'm going to have several!" Then slowly, with bitter, ever-growing resolution: "I'm going out and get as drunk as the whole God-damned British navy! So help me God, I will, if it's the last thing I ever do!"

She: "Did you have any breakfast?"

He, morosely: "Naw!"

She: "Haven't you had anything to eat all day?"

He, as before: "Naw."

She: "You ought to eat, of course. You're a fool to abuse your health this way. . . . Now that you're putting me out, I shall worry about you. . . . At any rate, I *did* see that you got your food on time—you'll have to admit that! . . . Who's going to do that for you now? . . .

You'll never do it, I know that." Then sarcastically: "Maybe one of the little wenches you bring up here will do it for you—" bitterly— "Like *hell* they will!—" muttering sarcastically— "I can just *see* them doing it!"

He makes no answer.

She, hesitantly: "Would you like it if I fixed you a little lunch?—" hastily— "I wouldn't stay, I could go right afterwards. . . . I know you don't want me here with you any longer . . . but if I could fix you up a bite before I go . . . at least, I'd know you had been *fed*. . . . I wouldn't worry so much about it later." Then with a quiet note of regret in her voice: "Of course, it seems such a shame for all that good food to go to waste . . . such a wicked waste when there are so many people going hungry in the world. . . . But—" with a slight shrug of the shoulders, the little twisted smile, the note of resigned acceptance—"since you feel the way you do about it—why, that's all there is to it, isn't it?"

He, looking up after a moment's silence: "What good food do you mean?"

She, with an attempt at casual lightness: "Oh, the food I bought when I came downtown today. . . . I thought we were going to have lunch together. . . . I thought we had agreed on it . . . I was looking forward to it . . . but since you feel the way you do, since you want me to go—" she sighs—"all right, then—*there* it is!" With a movement of her head she indicates a big market bag on the table. "Do what you like with it—throw it in the garbage can—give it to the janitor. . . . Only I wish you had let me know in advance if that's what you intended to do. . . . It would have saved me all that trouble."

He, after another moment's heavy silence, looking up and staring at the bag curiously: "What's in that bag?"

She, lightly: "Oh, nothing much! Nothing elaborate! Nothing that it would have taken me long to prepare! . . . You know—you may have forgotten, but I told you I planned on having a very simple lunch. . . . So I stopped off on the way down at that nice butcher's shop on Sixth Avenue—you know the one where all the butchers know us— and they always have such beautiful cuts—and I asked the butcher if he had anything extra-special in the way of a sirloin steak—and he showed me a really beautiful inch-thick cut—so I got that. . . . And—" with a little descriptive movement of thumb and finger to indicate exquisite perfection—"some little Spring potatoes . . . the kind that *simply* melt in your mouth. . . . You know how much you used to like them the way I fix them . . . with a dressing of melted butter and a few sprigs of young parsley. . . . Then I saw some lovely, crisp, green lettuce and I bought a head, and a few oranges, and apples, a couple of pears, and a grapefruit—you know how much you like a fruit salad the way I make it with *my* kind of French dressing—not too sweet or sour, the way you like it. . . . And I also saw some wonderful strawberries that had just come in—I thought you might like them later on, so I bought a basket of them, and a pint of cream." She smiled a little rueful smile: "Well, it's too bad to see it go to waste—but I suppose it can't be helped! . . . That's the way things are, isn't it? . . . That's life!"

He, after a moment's pause, while he scratches himself reflectively through the stubble of his whiskers: "How long would it take to broil the steak?"

She: "Oh, only a few minutes after I get it on the broiler. . . . Of course the potatoes take a little longer. . . . But—well—after what's happened you wouldn't want them now, anyway, would you?" She turns as if to go, but lingers on.

He, rising, and putting a restraining hand upon her arm, licking his lips reflectively: "Did you remember to get some butter?"

She: "Oh, yes, the butter situation is all right—I remembered we were out and bought two sticks."

He, dreamily, rubbing his hand a little up and down her arm: "Ah-hah! . . . And what about oil for the salad dressing?"

She, quickly: "Oh, yes, that's right too! I remembered we were out of olive oil—so I stopped off at that nice Italian store and got some. . . . Oh, yes, and I forgot—just a *tiny* little sprig of garlic—you know, if you know how to use it—the way I do!—not too much—just a *delicate* little fragrance of it rubbed about the edges of the bowl—" again the descriptive gesture of the thumb and finger— "there's nothing like it to give a salad *just* the proper touch! . . . And, oh! I wish you'd see the *fruit* I bought—you've never in your life *beheld* such things as they have in the markets this season—that lovely, crisp, green lettuce-head—and the apples! . . . and the pears! . . . and the vegetables!" she whispers rapturously, "the beans and peas and radishes! . . . the lovely little bunches of carrots! . . . Oh, how *delicate* they are! . . . Isn't it a delicate food? . . . And the *new* asparagus! . . .

I could just see them lying on a dish, dripping in the kind of butter sauce I know how to make for them. . . . And the cauliflower! . . . In all your days you never saw such cauliflower as they have this season in the markets. . . . And—oh!—the onions! . . . the *delicate* little onions . . . like big pearls they are!" earnestly, "Aren't *onions* wonderful? . . . Isn't it marvelous that onions should be so cheap and plentiful! . . . The things you can *do* with them! . . . The dozens of ways you can use them! . . . The way they simply *melt* in your mouth when they are cooked the right way—the way I know how to! . . . If onions were rare, don't you know that people would pay almost any price to *get* them! . . . Isn't it wonderful that they're such a common vegetable?"

He, meditatively: "Hm! Yes." He licks his lips slowly and thoughtfully.

She, with just the proper shade of regret: "Of course, what I had really been planning on doing all the time—" with a little rueful smile, touched faintly by a question—"but it's no use going into all that now, is it? . . . That's all done for, now that you're sending me away."

He, as before, reflectively: "Hm! Planning what? What was it you were planning?"

She, regretfully: "Well, I had planned on coming down early Thursday night . . . that is, if you wanted me to—if you weren't doing anything else—about five o'clock, say, and cooking you a pot roast—you know, the way *I* fix one——"

He, broodingly, in a far-off tone: "Hm—yes! . . . A pot roast, you say?"

She: "Yes, you know the way I do it—about eight pounds of the finest larded beef—of course, I won't use anything except the *very best.* . . . I was speaking to the butcher about it just this morning— he assured me he would give me nothing but the *finest* cut. . . . Of course, it takes time! . . . You ought to have at least three or four hours to do it right—you know, in my big iron pot. . . . If you get a girl to cook for you after I'm gone, you should always *insist* that she cook in an iron pot. Oh, it's *much* better! *Much* better! The only way if you're to do it properly—but, then, so few women understand that—not one in a thousand. . . . Then, you let it cook *slowly*—oh, *very* slowly, for several hours—it's a *very* delicate operation—you've got to keep your eye on what you're doing all the time—so few of these women you meet nowadays will take the trouble. . . . But it's got to be done *very* slowly and carefully until the flavor of the beef has got into all the vegetables and the flavor of the vegetables has got into the beef." She went on in a very earnest tone, a lowered voice: "It's like a masterpiece—a symposium, you know—all the parts so delicately blended that each is *all* and all is *each*."

He, tenderly, in a gently tranced tone: "The vegetables, you said?"

She: "Yes, of course—the vegetables I was telling you about! . . . Those tender, fresh, Spring vegetables!"

He, in an abstracted tone: "All kind of mixing and melting into the roast, you say?"

She, quickly: "Yes—and of course there's butter, too—lots of it! You should *always* cook with butter! . . . Tell your girls that. . . . And a touch of paprika!—there's nothing like it if you know how to use it —just a dash, you know—so few people know how it's done. . . . Then pepper and salt! . . . Oh, well, it's no use telling you—it's no use now, anyway, is it?—now that we're not going to see each other again."

He, with dreamy and abstracted contemplation: "Ye-e-s! . . . Hm-m! . . . Butter, you say?" By this time, he has his arm around her. "A dash of paprika?"

She, suddenly beginning to protest vigorously, making as if to pull away but not doing so: "No! . . . No! . . . You can't start *that* now! . . . It's too late for that! . . . You told me to go away and leave you! . . . You put me out! . . . No! . . . No! . . . I won't let you! . . . It's all over now!" Firmly she shakes her head: "Too late! . . . All over now!"

He, attempting to laugh it off jovially, but with an uneasy note: "Why—ah-hah—hah!—pshaw! . . . I was just joking. . . . *You* knew that! . . . I was just having a little fun. . . . It was just a joke. . . . You *know* I didn't mean it!"

She, very red in the face, panting: "Yes, you did! . . . You meant every word of it!—" indignantly— "A fine joker you are! . . . You use such dainty and elegant language when you joke, don't you?—" bitterly, almost tearfully— "To the one who adores you, the one who would do anything for you! . . . Throwing her out into the gutter and calling her a hussy when she would lay down her life for you!— Oh, a fine joker you are!—I suppose you learned all those lovely words at that Baptist college!" Panting, struggling, she pushes at him with her hands: "No! No! . . . You can't do that! . . . You can't turn on me and revile me and call me dirty names one minute, and . . . **and** . . . and start doing *this* the next.—No! . . . No!"

He, slowly, with gloating jubilation, seizing her arms and shaking her back and forth with slow and swelling exultation: "Why—you— you—delicate—little—plum-skinned—wench—you! Why—you ——"

She, panting. "Oh, a fine one! . . . Such fine words! . . . Such elegant expressions!"

He, exultantly: "Why—my delicate damned darling and my dear! Why-y— Why-y—" he glowers around uncertainly, searching about for language, breathing strenuously; suddenly he crushes her to him, and cries out with savage joy: "Why—you little plum-skinned angel—I will *kiss* you—that's what I'll do! . . . By God, I will!" He kisses her fiercely. Then he breathes hoarsely and uncertainly again, and glowers around for more language: "I . . . I . . . I'll kiss you all over your damned jolly little face!" He does so, while she makes gestures of protest; he breathes stertorously a few moments longer, then suddenly cries out with savage conviction, as if he has found the solution to the problem that has been troubling him: "I will kiss you about ten thousand times, by God!" He does so. She shrieks faint protests and struggles feebly. "Steak, hey?—I'll steak you!" He does so. "Pot roast, hey?—Why you—*you're* my pot roast!"

She, shrieking faintly: "No! No! . . . You've no right! . . . It's too late now! . . ."

But is it ever too late for love?

At length he goes to the window, and leans his arms upon the open sill, staring out. And the light comes and goes and comes again; all of the singing of the shining day returns.

And Esther, raptly, in a low, tranced voice: "Was there ever love like ours! . . . Was there ever anything like it in the *world* since time began?"

And Monk, in a low tone, to himself, as he stares out the window, slowly: "I believe—by *God,* I just *believe* ——"

She, still raptly, to herself, and to the Universe: "Do you suppose any two people have ever felt the way we feel about each other? Could anyone on earth who didn't *know* ——"

He, as before, staring fixedly out the window, but with growing exultation: "I believe—yes, sir, I just *believe*——"

She, to her Celestial Confidant: "—possibly understand what it is like—the great poetry of it, the everlasting beauty that fills me like a star—the truth—the glory—and the magic of this tremendous—this soul-consuming—this—this all-engulfing——"

He, suddenly, with soaring and triumphant conviction: "Yes, sir! By God, I *know* that's what they're going to do! I *know* it!" He turns and drives his clenched fist in his palm, and shouts: "I tell you that I *know* it! I *know* it just as well as I know I'm standing here!"

She: "—this mighty, sweet, and powerful——"

He, with a jubilant yell: "By God, *they're going to take it!*"

She: "—this glorious and everlasting——"

And Monk, casting his head back, and laughing with savage joy and hunger: "Steak! . . . Steak! . . . Steak!"

And Esther, brooding raptly: "Love! . . . Love! . . . Love!"

And the light comes and goes, and fades and passes, the cat creeps trembling at his merciless stride across the ridges of the backyard fence, the light fades and comes again and passes—and all is, and is forever, as it always was.

34

Glory Deferred

FIVE WEEKS PASSED—FIVE WEEKS WOVEN OF ALL THIS LIGHT AND SHADOW, five weeks of soaring hope and bitter and dejected hopelessness, five weeks of joy and sorrow, gloom and glory, tears and laughter, love and—steak!

The most Monk could legitimately hope for was that his manuscript had fallen into the hands of an intelligent person, and was being given a careful reading. He did not know about Mr. Rawng's feeling and smelling test. Had he known of the smelling test, he could only have hoped and prayed that all that he had written might smell sweet and wholesome to Mr. Rawng's voluptuous nostrils. But as for the feeling test—how could a manuscript ten inches thick, and fourteen hundred pages long, *feel* anything but appalling to a publisher? The very sight of it was enough to make a reader tremble, an editor turn pale, and a printer recoil in horror.

And, as a matter of fact, the book had not survived this preliminary test. Its fate had been decided within an hour after its arrival at the offices of the Messrs. Rawng and Wright. Mr. Rawng, coming out of his office, had suddenly halted, clapped a pudgy hand to his forehead, and, pointing to the leviathan on the office boy's table, had cried:

"My God! What's this?"

He was informed it was a manuscript, and groaned. He walked around it carefully, surveying it from every angle with suspicious, unbelieving eyes. He edged closer to it cautiously, reached out and poked it with a finger—and it never budged. Finally, he got his fat hand gripped upon it, tugged and heaved and lifted—felt its weight and groaned again—and then let it drop!

"Nah!" he cried, and scowled darkly at the office boy.

"Nah!" he said again, and took two steps forward, one step back, and paused.

"Nah!" he shouted with decision, and waved his fat hand rapidly before his features in a gesture eloquent of malodorous disgust and furious dismissal.

"Nah! Nah! Nah!" he shouted. "Take it away! The whole thing stinks! Pfui!"—and, holding his nostrils with his fingers, he fled.

Thus was the matter decided.

And now the forgotten and unread manuscript was gathering dust on top of a pile of old ledgers, and the Messrs. Rawng and Wright were gulping highballs three doors down the street in Louie's Bar.

Monk, by now, was reduced to a state of madman's frenzy. He no longer knew whether he waked or slept, walked or sat down, ate or did not eat. The twenty-four hours of each diurnal round were lived through in nightmare chaos, tortured by mad dreams. He lived from one day to the next for the coming of the mail—for the arrival of a single fatal, dreaded, wildly longed-for letter—which was awaited hourly, and which never came.

At the end of five weeks of this, when it seemed that flesh and blood and brain and spirit could no longer endure, when he thought that he had given up hoping, yet could not bear the utter loss of hope, when nothing, no opiate of food or drink or books or words or work or writing or love for Esther could longer bring a moment's rest, an instant of oblivion to his tormented soul—he sat down and wrote the Messrs. Rawng and Wright a letter, asking if they had read his book, and what their intentions were concerning it.

His answer came within two days, with unexpected swiftness. He ripped the letter open with numb fingers—and read it with set face. Before he had finished the first dozen words he knew the answer, and his face was white. The letter ran as follows:

"Dear Sir:

"We have read your manuscript and regret to say we cannot use it. While the writing shows an occasional trace of talent, it seems to us that the work as a whole is without sufficient merit to justify its publication, and moreover, of such enormous length that even if a publisher were found who was willing to print it, it would be extremely difficult to find readers who would be willing to read it. The book is obviously autobiographical—" (Although neither Rawng nor Wright had read the manuscript, and although neither was very sure in his mind what "autobiographical" meant, or in what way any creative work was more or less "autobiographical" than another, they felt it safe to assume that this manuscript *was*, since it was a young man's first book, and all first books by all young men are, obviously, of course, "autobiographical.") "The book is obviously autobiographical, and since we published at least a half dozen books just like this last year, and lost money on all of them, we don't see how we could risk money on your book, particularly since the writing is so unskillful, amateurish, and repetitive as practically to annihilate what small chances of success such a book might have. It is probably true that the novel form is not adapted to such talents as you have—" (which, by this time, did not even seem microscopic to their stricken owner) "but should you ever attempt another book—" (he shuddered with convulsive horror at the thought of it!) "we can only hope you will choose material of a more objective nature, and thus avoid one of the worst pitfalls into which the novice is likely to fall. If you ever write such a book, we should, of course, be glad to see it.

"Meanwhile, with regrets that we are not able to give you a more encouraging answer, I am

Ever sincerely yours,

James N. Wright."

And what now?—tears, curses, fights, brawls, drunkenness, imprecations, savage rage, insane despair? No, that was over; the sullen apathy of a stalled ox, the drugged eye of an opium addict, the set visage of a sleepwalker—an eye that no longer saw, an ear that no longer heard, a hand that no longer felt, a brain, a spirit, sunk—not fathoms deep in blind despair, but fathoms deeper in a kind of eyeless, tongueless, soundless, tasteless, and unfeeling ocean bed of black and bottomless oblivion.

He sat there on his rumpled cot, one leg sprawled out, mouth sullenly, stupidly ajar, with that little scrap of paper—the sentence of his execution—in his fingers. And still light came and passed and faded, the cat crept trembling, and the light, quick steps trod on his stairs at noon again. The door was opened. He stared like some brute animal that has just been slugged at the base of the brain with the butcher's sledge, and he felt nothing.

And Esther, snatching the letter from his hand and reading like a flash, sharply, with a little cry: "Oh!—" then quietly— "When did this come?"

And Monk, mumbling thickly: "This morning."

She: "Where's the manuscript?"

He: "In the closet."

She goes to the closet and opens the door. The manuscript, face down and opened, a sheaf of spreading leaves, is on the closet floor. She picks it up tenderly, smoothes the rumpled leaves, closes the binding, and presses it against her. Then she puts it down upon the table.

She: "Is that the way you treat your own manuscript—your own blood and sweat? Is that all the respect you have for it?"

He, thickly and numbly: "Don't want to look at it! Throw it in the closet! Close the door!"

She, sharply: "Oh, for heaven's sake! Brace up and act like a man! Have you got no more faith or self-respect for what you do than this— that you're willing to give up the ghost without trying—the first bit of hard luck you have!"

He, dumbly: "He says I'm no good!"

She, impatiently: "Oh, stop talking bilge! Who says you're no good?"

He: "Wright says so."

She, contemptuously: "Oh, who gives a damn what *he* says! What does *he* know about it? You don't know if he's even read your manuscript!"

He: "He says he has, and that I'm no good!"

She: "Oh piffle! Who cares what he says! You ought to have more sense than to pay any attention to him!" Then sharply, after a pause: "When did your manuscript come back?"

He, dully: "It didn't come, I went."

She: "Went where?"

He: "Went and got it."

She: "Did you see anyone?"

He: "Yes."

She: "Who did you see?—" snapping her fingers impatiently—

"Don't sit there staring at me like an idiot! Speak up and tell me! *Who did you see up there?*"

He: "Rawng."

She: "You didn't see Wright?"

He: "No, I saw Rawng."

She, exasperated: "Well, then, for heaven's sake, tell me what he said!"

He: "He didn't say anything."

She, impatiently: "Oh, nonsense! He must have said something! People just don't look at you and say nothing when you go to see them, do they?"

He, sullenly: "Yes, they do. *He* did!"

She, angrily: "Well, then, what did he do? He must have been doing something."

He: "Yes, he was. He was coming out of his office."

She: "Was someone with him?"

He: "Yes."

She, triumphantly: "That explains it! He was with someone. He was busy." Then angrily: "Oh, you *are* a fool!"

He: "I know it. I'm no good."

She, snapping her fingers impatiently: "Well then, go on and tell me! Don't sit there like an imbecile! You must have talked to someone."

He: "Yes, I did."

She: "Well, who was it?"

He: "A Jew."

She, in an excited and warning tone of voice: "Now you're beginning again!"

He: "I'm not beginning again. You asked me and I told you."

She: "Well, then, what did *he* do? For *heaven's* sake, you'll drive me *mad* if you don't speak up!"

He: "He looked at me and said, 'Vell, vat is it?'"

She, warningly and excitedly again: "I've *told* you now! If you're going to begin again, I'm leaving."

He: "I'm not beginning again. You asked me what he did, and I told you."

She, not wholly mollified: "Well, you'd better look out! That's all I've got to say! If you're going to start in on your abuse, I'm not going to stand for it!" Then abruptly and impatiently: "Well, and then what? What happened then?"

He: "Well, he said, 'Vat is it?'—and I told him what it was."

She, impatiently: "Oh, told him what *what* was! You're talking like an idiot."

He: "I told him what it was I wanted—my manuscript."

She: "Well? And what happened then? What did he say when you told him?"

He: "He said, 'Oh, you're the guy! Jesus!'"

She: "Well, and then? What happened next?"

He: "He got the manuscript and gave it to me."

She: "Well? And what happened next?"

He: "I blew the dust off the manuscript."

She: "Well, go on! Go on! What happened then?"

He: "I went out."

She: "Went out where?"

He: "Out the door!"

She, incredulously: "And nothing else happened?"

He: "Nothing else, no."

She: "And you talked to no one else?"

He: "To no one. No."

She: "Oh, you fool, you! And to think you'd have no more sense than to let a thing like this get you down! To think that you have no more pride or self-respect—no more faith in what you do!"

He: "I'm no good. And I want to be left alone. I wish to God you'd go away. And throw that manuscript away before you go—throw it anywhere—in the garbage pail—down the privy—into the closet— only for Christ's sake get it out of my sight where I won't have to look at it." He gets up wearily—"Here, I'll do it!"

She, snatching up the imperiled manuscript, and hugging it to her bosom: "No you won't either! . . . This manuscript's *mine*! . . . Who stood by you all these years, and stood over you, and made you do it, and had faith in you, and stuck to you? . . . If you've got no more faith in it now than to throw it away, I won't let you! . . . I'll save it! . . . It's mine, I tell you, mine!" She cries out sharply: "George! What are you doing?"

He, wearily as before, but doggedly: "Here, give me the God-damned thing—I'll put it where I'll never look at it again!"

She, panting, hugging it to her: "No! No! . . . You mustn't! . . . George, I tell you——"

They struggle for the manuscript, they tug and wrench and wrestle;

the binding rips apart in their hands, he gets one part and she another. He takes his part and hurls it at the wall, the pages fly and scatter everywhere. He opens the closet door, cursing and kicking viciously at the offending manuscript, until he has kicked it into the dark oblivion of the closet. Then he slams the door, and comes back across the room, and sits down dejectedly on his cot again.

And Esther, gasping for breath, glaring at him with tearful eyes, clutching her part of the manuscript to her breast, breathless, aghast: "Oh . . . you . . . you *wicked* fellow! . . . Oh! . . . What a *wicked* thing to do! . . . It's like . . . like kicking your own child! . . . *Oh!* . . . How *vile!*" Tears begin to trickle down her cheeks, she scuttles around the room snatching up loose pages of manuscript, she darts into the closet and comes out clutching the other battered fragment to her breast—she hugs the whole confused mass of it to her, weeping, saying: "You had no right to do it! . . . It's *mine!* . . . Mine! . . . Mine!"

And Monk, stretching out wearily on the cot, hanging his feet over the end, speaking wearily: "Please go away. Do me a slight favor, won't you? Kindly get the hell out of here. I'm no good, and I don't want to have you around."

She, excitedly, with a rising note of hysteria in her voice: "Oh, so that's it, is it? . . . That's what you want! . . . You're trying to get rid of me again, are you?"

He, as before: "Please go away."

She: "It's all my fault, I suppose! . . . Just because someone writes you a letter saying you're no good, you blame it all on me!"

He, with profound apathy: "Yes. You're right. You got it. It's all your fault."

She, tearful and indignant: "All my fault because someone says you're no good? Is that what you mean? Is that what you're accusing me of now—hah?"

He, with an immensely weary calm: "Yes, that's it. You got it. You're right. Everything's your fault. It's your fault that I'm no good. It's your fault I've got to look at you. It's your fault I ever met you. It's your fault I'm alive when I ought to be dead. It's your fault I ever kidded myself into thinking I was a writer. It's your fault I ever thought I was any good!"

She, hysterically: "I'm going! I'm going! . . . You've done this to me! . . . You've driven me out! . . . You're the one!"

He, turning his face to the wall, with weary quietness: "Please get the hell out of here, won't you? I'm no good, and I'd like to die in peace—if you don't mind."

She: Oh, *vile* . . . oh, wicked fellow that you are!" Then wildly— "Good-bye! Good-bye! . . . You'll never see me any more! . . . This time it is good-bye!"

He, dully, with face turned to the wall: "Good-bye."

She rushes out, cheeks bright with anger, clutching the manuscript to her breast. The door slams after her, then her feet upon the stairs, and then the street door slams. He turns over on his back and listens wearily, muttering:

"I'm no good—Rawng thinks so and he's right. No; Wright thinks so, but he can't be wrong." He sighs wearily: "Well, no matter which— I knew I was no good anyway. This just proves it. How can I wear time out from now on? It seems too long to wait."

Time passes—day, night, morning—and the sparkle of bright noon again. All is as it always was. He sees, feels, hears, knows, cares for none of it—not even for the light, quick step at noon upon his stairs again.

Esther opens the door and comes over and sits down beside him on the cot. She says quietly:

"Have you had anything to eat since I was here?"

He: "Don't know."

She: "Have you been lying here all that time?"

He: "Don't know."

She: "Have you been drinking?"

He: "I don't remember. Hope so. Yes."

She, taking his hair in her hands and pulling it with quiet intensity: "Oh, you *fool!* Sometimes I feel like *choking* you! Sometimes I wonder why I adore you so. . . . How can so great a person be so big a fool!"

He: "I don't know. Don't ask me. Ask God. Ask Rawng and Wright."

She, quietly: "Do you know I sat up half the night putting your manuscript together again ——"

He: "Did you?" His hand tightens on hers a little.

She: "—after you had so wickedly attempted to destroy it." A pause, then quietly: "Aren't you ashamed of yourself?"

Another pause.

He, with a trace of a grin: "Well—you know, I have two extra copies of it anyway."

She, after a moment's startled silence: "Oh, you *villain*!" Suddenly she throws back her head and shouts with laughter, a rich, full-throated, woman's yell: "God, was there ever anyone like you! I wonder if anyone who didn't know you would believe you were possible! . . . Well, anyway, I got it all together again, and this morning I took it to Seamus Malone. Do you know who he is?"

He: "Yes. He's that visiting Irishman who writes pieces in the magazines, isn't he?"

She, impressively: "And a *very* brilliant man! The things that fellow knows! He has *read* everything! And, of course, he knows *everyone* in the publishing profession. . . . He has contacts *everywhere.*" Then casually, but a trifle importantly, she adds: "Of course, he and his wife are *very* old friends of mine—I've known them for years."

He, remembering that she seems to have known everyone for years, but curiously interested at last: "What's he going to do with my book?"

She: "He's going to read it. He told me he'd begin at once, and let me know about it in a few days." Then earnestly, with intense conviction: "Oh, I know it's going to be all right now! Malone knows *everybody*—if anybody knows what to do with a book he's the man! He'll know right away what to do with your manuscript—where to send it!" Then scornfully: "Jimmy Wright! What does *he* know—*that* fellow! How could a person like *that* understand your quality! You're too big for them—they are *little* people!" She mutters scornfully, her jolly little face flushed and indignant: "Why, it's ridiculous! The nerve of him sending you a letter like that, when he couldn't begin to know about you if he lived a thousand years!" In a low, quiet tone, charged with adoring tenderness, she continues: "You're my George, one of the great ones of the earth!" Then, in a kind of rapt, brooding chant: "George, the Great George! . . . Great George, the poet! . . . Great George, the mighty dreamer!" She whispers, her eyes suddenly shot with tears, kissing his hand: "You're my great George, do you know that? . . . You're like no one else that ever lived! . . . You are the greatest person I have ever known . . . the

greatest poet . . . the greatest genius—" then raptly, to herself—
"and someday the whole world will know it as I do now!"

He, in a low tone: "Do you mean that? . . . Do you really believe
it?"

She, quietly: "My dear, I know it."

There is a silence.

He: "When I was a child, sometimes I used to see myself, and feel
that there were great things in me. I would look at myself and see
my nose, the way it turned up at the end, and the way my ears stuck
out, and the way my eyes looked. I would look at my eyes a long time,
until I felt naked, and it seemed that I was talking to the naked
heart of me—to the naked spirit. Then I would say to the eyes: 'I
think I am going to be a great man. I am here alone with you, and it
is three o'clock—I hear the wooden clock upon the mantel tocking—
and I feel that I am going to be a great man and find Perfection. I
think the whole thing is inside me now. What do you think?' And the
eyes, so naked, brown, and grave and honest, would speak back and
say, 'Yes, you will be!'—'But,' I would say, 'maybe every boy feels this
way about himself. I look at Augustus Potterham, at Randy Shepperton, and at Nebraska Crane—and all of them think well of themselves, they know they are good, they are convinced of their unique
and special quality. Is that all I feel when I look at myself? I feel I am
some kind of genius—sometimes I am sure of it—yet I have no way of
knowing that I am—no way of being *for dead sure* that I'm not the
same as all the other boys.' And the eyes would look back, grave and
naked, saying: 'No, you're not the same. You are a genius. You will
do great things and reach Perfection.' . . . (a pause). . . . Well, that
was a long time ago, and now Perfection's gone. I know I never can
attain it now; I know I've already done things that I can't atone for
or expiate; I know there are black marks upon me; I know I've
marred the record, blotted the sheet. . . . I know I'm no longer twenty
and a leaping flame; I know I'm almost thirty, often tired. . . . Yet
still the thing keeps climbing in me. I want to do a great thing yet.
I want to balance up the record somehow before I finish, strive always
for Perfection though I never reach it, grow stronger, braver, better
wiser, as an artist and a man. . . . (another pause). . . . Nothing is
the way you thought that it would be; nothing turns out as you
thought it would. . . . I thought that I would be a great man in the
world by the time I was thirty. Now I'm almost thirty, and the world

has never heard of me. I dreamed of shining deeds and golden countries, young, glorious women, glorious love, and everlasting and unwearied marriage! . . . It has not happened! Deeds are not shining, but they are sometimes good. No country that I ever saw was golden— yet each of them has had some gold in it. No woman, young or old, that I ever knew, was wholly glorious; nor was love. . . . The whole record is streaked and spotted as I never dreamed that it would be. The shining city of my youth and dream is a warren of grimed brick and stone. Nothing shines the way I thought it would—there is no Perfection. And instead of the proud Gibson girl of childhood fancy, I met—you."

She, warningly: "Are you beginning again?"

He: "No. The world is a better place than I thought it was—for all its spots and smudges—for all its ugliness, drabness, cruelty, terror, evil—a far, far better and more shining place! And life is fuller, richer, deeper—with all its dark and tenemented slums—than the empty image of a schoolboy's dream. And Mrs. Jack, and other women, too—poor, leaky, addled, half-demented wenches that most of them are—are greater, stronger, richer people than a Gibson girl. . . . (pause). . . . Poor Mrs. Jack! Poor Mrs. Jack with the grey hairs in her head, and her nice, respectable family—Mrs. Jack with her tears, her sobs, her protestations—Mrs. Jack threatening suicide one moment, talking of eternal love the next—Mrs. Jack leaving here with sobs and tears and moanings, arriving home twenty minutes later wreathed in jolly smiles—Mrs. Jack talking about Forever and forgetting Five Minutes Ago—Mrs. Jack with her innocent and jolly little face, and her eye that misses nothing—Mrs. Jack moving about in a world peopled with lesbians, pederasts, actors, actresses, slander, lying, infidelity, Broadway, and the slime of an evil, secret, jubilantly unclean laughter, pretending to see nothing, finding happiness, good humor, sweetness and light everywhere—and Mrs. Jack with her strategies, her ruses, her vanity, her egotism—Mrs. Jack with her clever woman's brain, her childish cunning—and Mrs. Jack with her warmth, her richness, her enormous beauty, her love, her devotion, her loyalty, her honesty, her lovely, certain talent. . . . I did not foresee you, Mrs. Jack— nothing in life has turned out the way I expected—but, like God, if you had not existed, it would have been necessary to invent you. You may be right about me, or you may be wrong—they say you're wrong. I may be a genius and a great man, as you say I am; or I may be a nonentity and a nincompoop, a pitiable fool deluding himself into thinking he possesses talents he never had. Certainly, the child-hood dream has vanished. Sometimes I feel I never will do any of the great things I thought I would do. And the record has been marred, the scutcheon has been blotted; the life of shining, golden deeds and spotless purity has been attainted. I have soiled my soul and scarred my spirit by inexpiable crimes against you. I have reviled you, Mrs. Jack, been cruel and unkind to you, repaid your devotion with a curse, and put you out of doors. Nothing is the way I thought it was going to be, but, Mrs. Jack, Mrs. Jack—with all your human faults, errors, weak-nesses, and imperfections, your racial hysteria, and your possessiveness —you are the best and truest friend I ever had, the only one who has ever stuck to me through thick and thin, stood by me and believed in me to the finish. You are no Gibson Girl, dear Mrs. Jack, but you are so much the best, the truest, noblest, greatest, and most beautiful woman that I ever saw or knew, that the rest are nothing when compared to you. And, God help my unhappy and tormented soul, with all the crimes and guilts and errors that are piled upon it—you are the woman that I love, and no matter where I go, or when I leave you, as I shall, down at the bottom of my soul I'll keep on loving you forever."

35

Hope Springs Eternal

ONE MORNING, SEVERAL DAYS LATER, ESTHER TELEPHONED HIM TWO hours before she put in her usual noon appearance. It was at once evident from the excitement of her voice that she had news of considerable importance to communicate.

"Oh, look!" she cried without preliminary, "I have news for you. I've just been talking to Seamus Malone over the phone and he's *terribly* excited about your book."

This, as he was later to discover, was a very considerable enlargement of the fact, but under the depressing circumstances of the moment, almost any straw that could be grasped at looked like an oak tree, and Esther had seized it as if it were.

"Yes," she was now saying, in a rapid and exciting tone, "he wants very much to see you and talk to you. He has some suggestions to make. He tells me that a friend of his is just starting out as a literary agent, and he thinks it might be a good idea if he turned the manuscript over to her to see if she can't do something with it. She knows people everywhere—I think she might be a very good person for this kind of thing. Do you mind if she looks at the manuscript?"

"No, of course not. Something's better than nothing. If we could only get someone to read it, that *would* be something, wouldn't it?"

"Yes, I think so, too. And don't you worry any more, my dear. I'm sure that something will come of this. Seamus Malone is a *very* old friend of mine—and a *very* cultivated man—he has a *very* high standing as a critic—and if he says a thing is good, he knows what he's talking about. . . . And Lulu Scudder—that's this friend he was telling me about—he say's she's *very* energetic! If you let her take your manuscript she'll probably show it around everywhere! Don't you think it's a good idea if we let her—hah?"

524

"Yes, I do. I don't see what harm it could do, and something might come out of it!"

"I think so, too. At any rate, it looks like our best bet at the moment, and there can be no harm in letting her try. And I know something is *bound* to happen sooner or later. It's *got* to! What you do is—is—is too fine—to be ignored! Sooner or later they've got to recognize you! You wait and see! I know what I'm talking about—I've known it all along!" Then with abrupt and rapid decision: "Well, then, look! Here's what I've done. I'm giving a little party to some people that I know on Thursday night—and Seamus Malone and his wife are coming. Why don't you come, too? It will be just a very simple and informal little affair—there'll only be the family, a few old friends, some people from the theatre, Steve Hook and his sister, Mary, and the Malones. It'll give you a chance to meet Seamus and have a talk with him. Why don't you do it?"

He agreed to come, of course.

When Monk arrived at Mrs. Jack's at nine-thirty on the evening of the party, a considerable number of the invited ones had already gathered. This was immediately apparent when he stepped from the elevator into the reception hall of the magnificent apartment. There was the excitingly confused clamor of many voices, a kind of woven texture of bright sound, a pleasantly confused noise—laughter, the tinkle of ice in tall glasses, the resonant depth of men's voices, the silvery sweetness of the women's.

Mrs. Jack met the young man in the hall. She was dressed in one of her splendid saris, and she was very beautiful. Her eyes sparkled, her jolly face was wreathed in smiles, her whole figure was charged with the added joy which the presence of her friends, the happy occasion of a party, always gave her. Flushed with happiness, rosy with pleasure, she took his hand and squeezed it tenderly, and then led him immediately into the great living room.

Here, a brilliant scene greeted him. The lady's "simple little party" had turned into a very glittering and splendid affair. There must have been at least thirty or forty people, most of them in evening dress.

As he entered the room, he had the feeling of having stepped right into a Covarrubias drawing and having all the figures come to life, looking even more like their own cartoons than life itself. There was Van Vleeck, with his buck teeth, over in a corner talking to a negro; there was Stephen Hook, leaning against the mantel with that air of bored nonchalance that was really just the screen for his excruciating shyness; there was Cottswold, the critic, a little puffball of a man, a lover of dear whimsey, a polished adept of envenomed treacle; and many other famous ones of art and letters and the theatre.

They all looked so much like themselves, and as Monk knew that they *must* look, that he squared his shoulders, drew a breath, and muttered to himself, "Well, here we are."

Stephen Hook was standing by the hearth talking to someone, his portly figure turned half away from his companion, his white, fat face, with its amazingly sensitive features, half averted and fixed in its customary expression of bored and weary detachment. Looking up quickly as Monk entered, he said, "Hello, how are you?"—extended his fat hand briefly and desperately, then turned away, leaving, however, a curious sense of friendliness and warmth.

Elsewhere in the brilliant crowd Monk saw other people that he knew. There was Mary Hook, with hair of flaming red, much more at ease with life, more friendly and direct and practical than was her brother, but giving the same sense of charm, integrity, and hidden warmth. There was Mr. Jack, and the daughter, Alma.

And everywhere there was the sound of voices—that curious, haunting medley of three dozen voices, all together, a woven fabric of bright sound, a murmurous confluence as strange as time. But over all these voices, through them and above them, instantly distinguishable from all the others, there was a single all-pervading, all-compelling, all-conclusive, and all-dominating Voice.

It was certainly by all odds the most extraordinary voice that Monk had ever heard. In the first place, it was distinguished by a perfectly astounding richness and an indescribable sonority that seemed to have in it the compacted resonance in the voice of every Irishman who ever lived. But this magnificently full-bodied voice of Celtic richness was charged through and through with hell-fire. One felt, with every word this great voice uttered, a kind of imminent flood of malevolent feeling for all mankind that seemed to swell up from some bottomless well of fury inside him and make instant strangulation inevitable.

The possessor of this remarkable voice was Mr. Seamus Malone, and Mr. Malone's appearance was fully as remarkable as his voice.

He was a man somewhere in his early fifties, of rather fragile physical mold, but giving a spurious impression of ruggedness through the possession of an astonishing beard. This beard covered all his face; it was square-cut, not long, but luxuriant, and of an inky, blue-black color. Above this beard a pair of pale-blue eyes surveyed the world with scorn; the total effect was to give Mr. Malone something of the appearance of an embittered Jesus Christ.

Mr. Malone's full-bodied voice, of course, surged through the black luxuriance of this beard. When he talked—and he talked constantly— one became uneasily aware of the presence of two pale-red lips, thick and rubbery-looking, concealed in the black foliage. These lips were characterized by an astonishing flexibility; as Mr. Malone talked they writhed and squirmed and twisted about in the beard like a couple of snakes. Sometimes they parted in a travesty of a smile, sometimes they writhed clear around his face in a convulsive snarl. But they were always busy, never silent for a moment; through them poured a flood tide of envenomed speech.

Mr. Malone was seated at the end of a sofa, and like many of the other guests, he held a highball glass in his hand. He was surrounded by an attentive audience of several people. Prominent among them were a young man and his beautiful young wife, both of whom—mouths slightly parted, eyes shining with hypnotized fascination—were leaning forward and listening with breathless attentiveness to the impassioned flood of Mr. Malone's erudition.

"Obviously," Mr. Malone was saying, "obviously!" Oh, how to convey the richness, the sonority, the strangling contempt that was packed into that single word! "*Obviously*, the fellow has read nothing! All that he's read, apparently, are two books that every schoolboy is familiar with—namely, the *Pons Asinorum* of Jacopus Robisonius, which was printed by Parchesi in Bologna in the Spring of 1497, and the *Pontifex Maximus* of Ambrosius Glutzius, which was printed in Pisa in the following year! Beyond that," snarled Mr. Malone, "he knows nothing! He's read nothing! Of course—" and his rubber lips did a snake dance all through the thicket of his beard—"of course, in a so-called civilization where the standard of refined and erudite information is governed by the lucubrations of Mr. Arthur Brisbane and the masterly creations of the *Saturday Evening Post*, the pretensions of such a fellow pass, no doubt, for encyclopædic omniscience! , . . But he *knows* nothing!" choked Mr. Malone, and at the same time he threw both hands up as a final gesture of exasperated futility. "He's read nothing! In God's name, what *can* you expect?"

And gasping, exhausted by his effort, he did a kind of mad devil's jig for a moment with one foot. He took a hasty sip from his glass, set it down, and then, still gasping but a little appeased, he panted out: "The whole thing's absurd—the sensation he has made! The fellow is an ignoramus—an imbecile—he knows nothing!"

During the concluding passages of this tirade, Mrs. Jack and Monk had approached the place where the master was sitting, and waited in respectful silence until the conclusion of his remarks. Now, when he had somewhat composed himself, and the devil's jig of toe and knee had ceased, Mrs. Jack bent over him and spoke quietly:

"Seamus."

"Eh? Hey? What is it?" he said, startled, looking up and breathing heavily. "Oh, hello, Esther. It's you!"

"Yes. I want to introduce the young man I was speaking to you about—Mr. Webber, the one whose manuscript you have been reading."

"Oh—eh—how are you?" said Seamus Malone. He extended a clammy hand, his pale-red lips twisted in a ghastly attempt at a friendly smile. And in this smile there was something that was likewise pitiable, something that spoke of a genuine warmth, a genuine instinct for friendship down below the whole tortured snarl of his life, something really engaging that peered out for just an instant behind the uncontrollable distemper of his race. It was there beneath all his swarming hatreds, jealousies, his self-pity, his feeling that life had somehow betrayed him, which it had not done, and that his talents had not had their due, which they had and more, and that infamous charlatans, fools, ignoramuses, dolts, dullards, mountebanks of every description were being acclaimed as geniuses, surfeited with applause, fatted-up with success, lavished-over with all the honied flatteries, the adoring cajoleries, the sickening adulations of a moronic populace which should have been *his! his! his!*—no one's but *his*, great God!—if there was an atom of truth, of honor, of character, intelligence, and fair-dealing in this damnable, accursed, imbecilic Judas Iscariot of a so-called world!

But now, having spoken to Monk with a brief and painful effort at friendly greeting, an "Oh, yes! How are you? . . . I've been reading your manuscript," the confession was too much for him, and the old note of scorn began to appear in the richly sonorous tones.

"Of course, to tell the truth, I haven't read it," boomed Mr. Malone, beginning to tap impatiently upon the edges of the sofa. "*No* one who has an atom of intelligence would *attempt* to read a manuscript, but I've looked into it! . . . I've—I've read a few pages." This admission obviously cost him a great effort, but he wrenched it out at length. "I've—I've come across one or two things in it that—that didn't seem *bad*! Not bad, that is—" he was snarling in good form now—"compared to the usual nauseating drivel that gets *published*, and that passes in this Noble and Enlightened Land of Yours for Belles-Lettres!" By this time his pale-red lips were twisted around sideways in his beard, almost over to the lobe of his right ear. "Not bad," he cried chokingly, "when compared to the backwoods bilge of Mr. Sinclair Lewis! Not bad when compared to the niggling nuances of that neurotic New Englander from Missouri, Mr. T. S. Eliot, who, after baffling an all-too-willing world for years by the production of such incomprehensible nonsense as *The Waste Land* and *The Love Song of J. Alfred Prufrock*, and gaining for himself a reputation for perfectly *enormous* erudition among the æsthetes of Kalamazoo by the production of verses in dog-Latin and rondels in bastard French that any convent schoolgirl would be ashamed to acknowledge as her own, has now, my friends, turned prophet, priest, and political revolutionary, and is at the present moment engaged in stunning the entire voting population of that great agnostic republic known as the British Isles with the information that *he*—God save the mark!—Mr. Eliot from Missouri, has become a *Royalist*! A *Royalist*, if you please," choked Mr. Malone, "and an Anglo-Catholic! . . . Why, the news must have struck terror to the heart of every Laborite in England! The foundations of British atheism are imperiled! . . . If the great Mr. Eliot continues to affront the political and religious beliefs of every true-blue Englishman in this way, God knows what we can expect next, but we must be prepared for anything! . . . I should not be at all surprised to hear he had come out in favor of parliamentary government, and was demanding the instant establishment of a police force for the City of London, to put an end to the lawlessness, the rioting, the revolutionary violence that is raging through the streets!

"No," said Mr. Malone, after a brief pause to catch his breath, "I have not read much of this young man's book—a few words here

and there, a passage now and then. But compared to Mr. Eliot's portentous bilge, the perfumed piffle of Mr. Thornton Wilder—" he cleared
his throat and began to rock back and forth with the old red glitter
in his eyes—"the elephantine imbecility of Mr. Theodore Dreiser—
the sentimental slops and syrups of the various verse-mongering Mil-
lays, Robinsons, Wylies, Lindsays, and others of their ilk—the moon-
struck, incoherent idiocies of the Sherwood Andersons, the Carl Sand-
burgs, the Edgar Lee Masterses—the Ring Lardner-Ernest Hemingway
'I Am Dumb' school—the various forms of quackery purveyed by the
various Frosts, O'Neills, and Jefferses, the Cabells, Glasgows, Peterkins,
and Cathers, the Bromfields and Fitzgeralds—together with the lesser
breeds of mountebanks that flourish through the length and breadth
of this Great Land as nowhere else on earth, the Kansas Tolstois, the
Tennessee Chekhovs, the Dakota Dostoevskis, and the Idaho Ibsens—"
he choked—"compared to all the seven hundred and ninety-six varieties
of piffle, treacle, bilge, quack-salvery and hocus-pocus that are palmed
off upon the eager citizens of this Great Republic by the leading purveyors of artistic hogwash, what this young man has written is not
bad." Rocking back and forth again, he struggled stertorously for
breath, and at last exploded in a final despairing effort. "It's all *swill!*"
he snarled. "Everything they print is swill! . . . If you find *four* words
that are *not* swill, why then—" he gasped, and threw his hands up
in the air again—"print it! *Print* it!"

And having thus disposed of a large part of modern American writing, if not to his utter satisfaction, at least to his utter exhaustion,
Mr. Malone rocked back and forth for several minutes, breathing like
a porpoise and doing the devil's jig of knee and toe.

There was a rather awkward pause at the conclusion of this tirade.
Few people were hardy enough to attempt to interpose an answer to
Mr. Seamus Malone. There was in his approach to such matters a
kind of tornadolike completeness that rendered argument, if not
impotent, at least comparatively useless. It would have been like
clearing up the shattered remains of several dozen Humpty-Dumpties,
and debating their value had they not had a great fall.

After a painful silence, however, more to restore the aspects of
polite conversation than for any other reason, one of the audience—
the young man with the beautiful wife—inquired with just the right
note of respectful hesitancy:

"What—what do you think of Mr. Joyce?" Mr. Joyce, indeed,

amid the general wreckage seemed at the moment one of the few undemolished figures left in modern literature. "You—you know him, don't you?"

It was evident at once that the question was unfortunate. Red fire began to flame again in the Malone eye, and he was already rubbing his hands back and forth across the hinges of his bony knees.

"What—" Mr. Malone began in an extremely rich, foreboding tone of voice—"*what* do I think of Mr. Joyce? . . . And do I *know* him? Do I *know* him? . . . I presume, sir," Mr. Malone continued, very slowly, "that you are asking me if I know Mr. James Joyce, formerly a citizen of Dublin, but at present, I believe—" here his pale lips writhed around in a meaningful smile—"at the present moment, if I mistake not, a resident of the Left Bank of Paris. You ask me if I know him. Yes, sir, I do. I have known Mr. James Joyce for a very long time—a very long time, indeed—too, too long a time. I had the honor—call it, rather, the Proud Privilege—" the choking note was evident—"of watching young Mr. Joyce grow up in the years after I moved to Dublin. And surely, my friends, it is a proud privilege for one so *humble* as *myself*—" here he beckoned sneeringly to his frail breast—"to be able to claim such glorious intimacy with the Great Mumbo Jumbo of Modern Literature, the holy prophet of the Intelligentsia, who in one single, staggering tome exhausts everything there is to write about—to say nothing of *everyone* who has to read it. . . . Do I *know* Mr. Joyce? Sir, I think I may modestly claim that happy distinction," Mr. Malone remarked, with a slight convulsion of the lips. "I have known the gentleman in question for thirty years, if *not* exactly like a brother—" jeeringly—"at least *quite* well enough! . . . And what do I think of Mr. Joyce, you ask? . . . *What* do I think of Mr. *Joyce*? . . . Well," Mr. Malone went on in a tone of sonorous reflectiveness, "let me see, what *do* I think of Mr. Joyce? . . . Mr. Joyce, first of all, is a little bourgeois Irishman of provincial tastes who has spent a lifetime on the continent of Europe in a completely *fruitless* attempt to overcome the Jesuit bigotry, prejudice, and narrowness of his childhood training. Mr. Joyce began his literary career as a fifth-rate poet," Mr. Malone continued, rocking back and forth, "from there proceeded to become a seventh-rate short-story writer, graduated from his mastery of this field into a ninth-rate dramatist, from this developed into a thirteenth-rate practitioner of the literary Mumbo-Jumboism which is now held in high esteem by the Cultured Few," Mr. Malone sneered, "and I believe is now en-gaged in the concoction of a piece of twenty-seventh-rate incoherency—as if the possibilities in this field had not already been exhausted by the master's preceding opus."

In the pause that followed, while Mr. Malone in a manner composed himself, some person of great daring was heard to murmur that he *had* thought that parts of *Ulysses* were rather good.

Mr. Malone took this mild dissension very well. He rocked back and forth a little, and then, waving his thin white hand with a gesture of pitying concessiveness, remarked:

"Oh, I suppose there is some slight talent there—some minor vestiges, at any rate. Strictly speaking, of course, the fellow is a schoolteacher—a kind of small pedant who should be teaching the sixth form some-where in a Jesuit seminary. . . . But," Mr. Malone remarked, waving his hand again, "he has *something*—not a great deal, but something. . . . Of course—" here the gorge began to rise again, and red, baleful lightnings shot out from his eyes—"of course, the amazing thing is the reputation the fellow has gotten for himself when he had no more to start with. It's extremely amusing," cried Mr. Malone, and his lips writhed again in a mirthless attempt at laughter. "There were at least a dozen people in Dublin at the time who could have done the job Joyce tried to do in *Ulysses*—and done it *much* better!" he choked. "Gogarty, who is twenty times the man Joyce is, could have done it. A.E. could have done it. Ernest Boyd could have done it. Yeats could have done it. Even—even Moore or Stephens could have done it." He rocked back and forth, and suddenly snarled: "*I* could have done it! . . . And why didn't I?" he demanded furiously, thus asking a question that was undoubtedly in everybody's mind at the moment. "Why, because I simply wasn't interested! It didn't matter enough to any of us! We were interested in—in other things—in liv-ing! . . . Of course," he choked, "that is the history of all modern lit-erature, isn't it? It explains the barrenness of output, the dullness, the sterility. All of the people who really *could* write stay out of it. Why? Because," boomed Mr. Malone, "they're not interested in it! They're interested in other things!"

He was interested in his whiskey glass at the moment; he looked around and found it, reached for it, and took another sip. Then, with an effort at a smile, he turned to the young man with the beautiful wife, and said:

"But come! Let's talk of something else—something pleasanter! I hear you're going abroad soon?"

"Yes," the young man answered quickly, with a suggestion of relief. "We're going over for a year."

"We're *terribly* thrilled over going," the young woman remarked. "We've been before, of course, but never for so long a time. We know you've lived there such a lot, and we'd be *awfully* grateful for any advice you'd give us."

"Where are you going?" said Malone. "Are you—are you just traveling around—" his lips twisted, but he controlled himself—"or are you going to settle down and live in one place?"

"Oh, we're going to live in one place," the young man said quickly. "That's part of our idea in going. We thought we'd like to get the experience of European life—really live into it, so to speak. We're going to settle down in Paris."

There was a pause; then the young wife leaned forward towards the great man a little anxiously and said:

"Don't you think that's a good idea, Mr. Malone?"

Now, if Mr. Malone had been expressing his own opinion, five minutes or five months before, he certainly *would* have thought it was a good idea to go to Paris and live there for a year. He had said so himself on many occasions—occasions when he had denounced American provincialism, American puritanism, American crassness, and American ignorance of Continental life. Moreover, he had frequently demanded *why* Americans, instead of racing all over the map and trying to gulp all Europe down at once, didn't settle down in *Paris* for a year, live quietly, observe the people, and learn the language. Moreover, if the young man and his wife had announced their intention of settling down in *London* for a year, the effect on Mr. Malone would have been easily predictable. His pale, rubbery lips would have twisted around scornfully in his whiskers, and he would have ironically inquired:

"Why London? Why—" here he would have begun to breathe hoarsely—"why inflict upon yourself the dull provincialism of English life, the dreary monotony of English food, the horrible torpor of the English mind, when only seven hours away across the Channel you have the opportunity of living *cheaply* in the most beautiful and civilized city in the world, of living comfortably, luxuriously, in *Paris* for a fraction of what your living would cost you in London, and, furthermore, of associating with a gay, intelligent, and civilized people instead of with the provincial Babbitts of the British bourgeoisie?"

Why, then, did the old red flood of scorn rise up in Mr. Malone now that the young people had expressed their intention of doing the very thing he would himself have urged them to do?

Well, first of all, they were telling *him*—and Mr. Malone could not brook such impudence. Second, he rather regarded the city of Paris as his own private discovery, and too many damned Americans had begun to go there. Certainly no one could go there without his consent.

So, now that these two young people had decided, all by *themselves*, to go to Paris for a year, he found their puppylike insolence insupportable. For a moment after the young man and his wife had spoken there was silence; red fire began to flash from the Malone eye, he rocked gently back and forth and rubbed his knees, but for the nonce controlled himself.

"Why *Paris?*" he inquired, quietly enough, but with a note of ironic sarcasm in the rich timbre of his voice. "Why *Paris?*" he repeated.

"But—don't you think that's a good place to go to, Mr. Malone?" the young woman anxiously inquired. "I don't know," she went on rapidly, "but—but Paris sounds so gay—and jolly—and sort of exciting."

"Gay? . . . Jolly? . . . Exciting?" said Mr. Malone, slowly and gravely, and with an air of serious reflection. "Oh, I suppose some gaiety is left," he conceded, "That is, if Midwestern tourists, avaricious hotelkeepers, and the Messrs. Thomas Cook have not utterly destroyed what was left of it. . . . I suppose, of course," he went on with a slight choke, "that you'll do all the things your compatriots usually do—sit twelve hours a day among the literati at Le Dôme, or on the terrace of the Café de la Paix, and come back at the end of your year having seen *nothing* of Paris, *nothing* of the French, nothing of the *real* life of the people, utterly, thoroughly convinced that you know *all!*" He laughed furiously, and said: "Really, it's *most* amusing, isn't it, the way all you young Americans nowadays flock to Paris? . . . Here you are—young people *presumably* of some intelligence, and, at any rate, of sufficient means to allow you to travel—and where do you go?" sneered Mr. Malone. "Paris!"—he snarled the word out as if the stench of it disgusted him—"*Pa-a-ris,* one of the *dullest, dreariest,* most *expensive, noisiest,* and most *uncomfortable* cities in the world . . . inhabited by a race of penny-pinching shopkeepers, cheating taxi-drivers and waiters, the simply *appalling* French middle class, and the excursions of Cook's tourists."

There was a stricken silence for a moment; the beautiful young wife looked crushed, bewildered; then the young man cleared his throat and said a trifle nervously:

"But—but where would *you* go, Mr. Malone? Can you think of any—any better place than Paris?"

"Better place than Paris?" said Mr. Malone. "My dear fellow, there are dozens of more interesting places than Paris! Go anywhere, but don't go there!"

"But where?" the young woman said. "Where would you suggest, Mr. Malone? What other city can you think of?"

"Why—why—why, *Copenhagen!*" Mr. Malone suddenly boomed triumphantly. "By all means, go to *Copenhagen!* . . . Of course," he sneered, "the news has probably not yet reached the Greenwich Village Bohemians on the Left Bank, Midwestern schoolteachers, or other great globe-trotters of that ilk. They've probably never *heard* of the place, since it's a little off their beaten route. They would probably be surprised to know that Copenhagen is the *gayest, pleasantest,* most civilized city in Europe, populated by the most charming and intelligent people in the world. The news, no doubt," he jeered, "would come as a distinct shock to our Bohemian friends on the Left Bank, whose complete conception of the geography of Europe does not extend, apparently, beyond the Eiffel Tower. But Copenhagen *is* the place! Go to Copenhagen, by all means. *Pa-a-ris*—" he snarled—"not in a million years! Copenhagen! Copenhagen!" he yelled, threw his hands up in a gesture eloquent of exasperated futility over the spectacle of human idiocy, did the devil's jig of toe and knee, and gasped stertorously for breath.

Then suddenly, seeing the stricken figure, the somewhat appalled face, of young Mr. Webber, so swiftly and so sharply caught there among imagined great ones of the earth and finding all of it so strange, Mr. Malone, as if the face of young Webber brought sharply back, and instantly, the memory of the young Malone, and of all Webbers, all Malones that ever were, turned towards him and cried out warmly, richly:

"But I thought that what I read was—was—" Just for a moment the pale lips writhed tormented in his inky, blue-black beard, and then—oh, tormented web of race and man!—he got it out. He smiled at young Webber quite winningly and said: "I liked your book. Good luck to you!"

Such a man as this was Mr. Seamus Malone.

And, in such a way as this, was George Webber's modest entrance into the great literary life at length accomplished. It was an entrance which, as we have said, bore few of the aspects of an invasion, but which was, nevertheless, had he but known it, fraught with portent. How runs the maxim? "Great oaks from little acorns grow." Well, not to bridle further the straining curiosity of the reader, here's how it grew:

Mr. Malone gave the young man's manuscript to Lulu Scudder, and she, in turn, did with it whatever it is that literary agents do, and in the end—yes, in the end—something came of it. But weary months were still to pass before that something happened, and meanwhile Monk—young hopeless, hopeful, hapless Monk—was sunk down fathoms deeper than he'd ever been before in sea-depths of self-doubt and black despair beyond all caring.

Book VI

LOVE'S BITTER MYSTERY

The party had had an unexpectedly depressing effect on Monk. He came away from it feeling more strongly than ever that he was no good, and that his book would never achieve the consummation of print.

But it was more than that—much more. For he knew that Esther was in some way inextricably involved in the web and weft from which his bitter and despairing mood was spun. There in the luxury of her home he had rubbed elbows with the great ones of the earth whose rare and glorious lot had been the object of his distant envy and ambition. And now that he had moved among them, seen and talked to them, what he observed had filled him with dismay, a cold constriction of the heart.

Still too close to the event to sort out and make clear just what it was that so affected him, yet he knew, with an instant, certain, deadly knowledge, that a dear illusion had been shattered. And so strong had been the pull of this illusion, so central since his childhood to all his hopes, that now he had the sense that he himself—all his directing energies, his work, his very life—was broken, shattered, torn asunder, and destroyed, inescapably laid low in the wreckage of his golden dream.

36

A Vision of Death in April

THAT SPRING—IN THE GREEN SORCERY OF THAT FINAL, FATAL, AND RUINOUS April--a madness which was compounded of many elements took possession of him and began to exert completely its mastery of death, damnation, and horror over the whole domain of his body, mind, and spirit. He thought that he was lost, and he looked on life with the eye, not of a dead man, but of a man who had died against his will, who had been torn bitterly out of the glorious music of the day, and who, out of the shades of death, revisits all the glory he has lost and feeds upon it with a heart of fire, a tongueless cry, a passion of soundless grief, an agony of regret and loss.

And in the tortured, twisted crevices of his brain, he felt, with a wave of desolating self-pity and despair, that Esther had contrived this ruin against him. He saw her at the center of a corrupt and infamous world, inhabited by rich, powerful, and cynical people—great, proud, and potent beak-nosed Jews, their smooth-skinned wives who made a fashion and a cult of books and plays and nigger carvings, the so-called leaders in the arts themselves, the painters, writers, poets, actors, critics, sly and crafty in their knowingness and in their hate and jealousy of each other—and in this picture of her world, the only thing, he thought, that gave joy to these dead, sterile, and hateful lives in their conspiracy of death was the castration of the spirit of a living man. They had used Esther as a bait to snare the yokel. And it seemed to him that they had succeeded. It seemed that he was fairly caught at last in the trap which they had laid, and into which his own folly had led him, that his ruin was complete and incurable, that he was shorn of his strength forever, and that for him there was no hope of recovery or salvation.

He was now twenty-seven years old, and like a man who has waited too long before the approaching hoof beats of disaster, who has watched with too dull, too careless, or too assured an eye the coming of a flood, the approach of the enemy, or like an ignorant young fighter who, having never been hurt, having never tested the full strength of an immense and merciless power, having never been stung by the bitter asp of defeat, having never been made wary by a blow of incredible, unrealizable force, and who thinks in his insolence and pride that he is the measure of all things and will be triumphant in every conflict, so, now, it seemed to him he had been overtaken by disaster, and was fairly, fatally engulfed in an abyss of ruin he had not foreseen.

And yet he thought that no Spring ever came more sweetly or more gloriously to any man than that one came to him. The sense of ruin, the conviction that he was lost, the horrible fear that all the power and music in his life, like the flying remnants of a routed army, had been blown apart into the fragments of a ghastly dissolution so that they would never come back to him, never again the good times, the golden times, the nights his spirit prowled with the vast stealth and joy of a tiger across the fields of sleep, and the days when his power leaped on from strength to strength, from dream to dream, to the inevitable and sustained accomplishment of a great, exultant labor—the sense of having lost all this forever, so far from making him hate the Spring and the life he saw around him, made him love it more dearly and more passionately than he had ever done before.

In the backyard of the old brick house in which he lived, one of those small, fenced backyards of a New York house, a minute part in the checkered pattern of a block, there was, out of the old and worn earth, a patch of tender grass, and a single tree was growing there. That April, day by day, he watched the swift coming of that tree into its glory of young leaf again. And then one day he looked into its heart of sudden and magical green and saw the trembling lights that came and went into it, the hues that deepened, shifted, changed before one's eye to every subtle change of light, each delicate and impalpable breeze, and it was so real, so vivid, so intense that it made a magic and a mystery, evoking the whole poignant dream of time and of man's life upon the earth, and instantly, it seemed to Monk, the tree became coherent with his destiny, and his life was one with all its brevity from birth to death.

The peculiar power and property of Spring for evoking the whole sense of man's unity with all the elusive and passionate enigmas of life came, Monk felt, from the effect of the color green upon his memory and his sense of time. The first green of the year, and particularly the first green in the city, had a power not only of drawing all the swarming chaos and confusion of the city into one great lyrical harmony of life, it had also such a magical power over all his memories that the life that moved and passed around him became an instant part of all the moments of his life. So, too, the past became as real as the present, and he lived in the events of twenty years ago with as much intensity and as great a sense of actuality as if they had just occurred. He felt that there was no temporal past or present, no *now* more living than any reality of *then*; the fiction of temporal continuity was destroyed, and his whole life became one piece with the indestructible unity of time and destiny.

Thus over his whole mind that Spring there hung the sorcery of this enchanted green, and for this reason his life that Spring attained the focal intensity of a vision. And it was a vision of death and dissolution, ever present in a thousand images that swarmed incredibly in his brain. He saw the world in the hues of death, not because he was trying to fly from reality, but because he was trying to embrace it, not because he wanted to escape out of a life that he had found unendurable into some pleasing fable of his own devising, but because for years the hunger that had driven him with a desire for knowledge so insatiate that he wanted to pluck the final core and essence out of every object still moved him forward towards an escape *into* life. But now it seemed to him that life itself had played him false.

Save for those hours each day when Esther stayed with him, and the hours when he had to go to the school to meet his classes, he spent his time either in a mad and furious walking of the streets from night to morning, or at home in a contemplation of complete solitude. For hours at a time he would sit immovable in a chair, or lie extended on his cot with his hands folded beneath his head, apparently sunk in senseless apathy, but in reality, although he did not stir a muscle, every faculty was engaged in the most furious activity he had ever known. The images of the past and present swept through his mind in a stream of blinding light.

As he thought of Esther, of her world, and of the ruin in which he felt she had involved him, suddenly he would be roused by the sound of deathless birdsong in the tree. Then he would start up from his cot and go to the window, and as he looked into the magic heart of the green tree, the moments of lost time awoke with all their tragic memories, as actual as the room in which he stood.

Suddenly he thought of the time in his childhood when he had seen a man shaken like a rat, slapped in the face, retreating and cringing before his enemy while his wife and young son looked on with white and staring faces. And he knew that from that moment that man's spirit and his life were broken. He remembered the day, the time, the ghastly and unnatural silence of the neighborhood which heard and saw it all. And for months thereafter the man had walked by all the curious, staring, and quietly contemptuous faces of the town with a lowered head, and when he spoke to anyone, when he tried to smile, his smile was horrible—a pitiful grimace, an ingratiating and servile smirk rather than a smile. And his wife and his son went silently and alone thereafter, with furtive glances, frightened, stricken, and ashamed.

Again, when he was twelve years old, he had seen a man publicly whipped and slapped by his wife's lover. The man was a shabby little creature, the husband of a bold and sensual woman, whose lover, a strong, handsome, brutal-looking man of wealth and authority, came to fetch her in his motor every evening after dinner. When this happened, the husband, who at this time would be watering the lawn before the house, would keep his pallid face fixed on the ground before him, never speaking to the lover, or to his own wife as she passed by him on the walk.

One night, however, when the lover came and halted his car before the house and signaled for the woman to come out, the husband had suddenly thrown down his hose, rushed across the lawn and down the cement steps to the place where the car was halted, and begun to speak to the other man in a high, trembling, and excited voice. In a moment there was a low roar of anger and surprise from the big man in the car, he had thrown open the door so violently that the husband was hurled back, and then he had seized the husband, shaken, mauled, and slapped him, cursing him foully and savagely, and with a deliberate arrogance publishing his relations with the man's wife to the neighborhood and to the whole audience of the silent, staring street.

It was a sight unutterable in its naked shame, and the most shameful thing was the hideous fear of the husband, who, after his first wild impulse of courage, was now squeaking like a rat with terror, pleading to be let go and not to be slapped again. Finally, in his frenzy, he had wrenched free from the other man, and scrambled and stumbled backward up the steps in horrible retreat, his thin hands held out in a protesting and pleading manner before him as the other man followed him heavily, cursing him and mauling at him with clumsy blows that somehow seemed more shameful because of their clumsiness, the man's heavy panting breath, and the wet and naked silence of the air.

Then the woman had come swiftly from the house, assailed her cowering husband furiously, saying he had disgraced her and himself by "acting like a fool," and then ordered him into the house like a beaten child. And the man had gone, he had taken it all with a cringing and whimpering apology, and then had half-run, half-stumbled into the merciful concealment of the house, his head lowered and tears streaming down the reddened flanks of his thin, slapped face. Then the woman had got into the car with her cursing and boastfully threatening lover, and had talked to him in a low, earnest, and persuasive voice until he was pacified.

The car drove off, and as it turned the corner at the foot of the hill, Monk could hear the woman's sudden, rich, and sensual burst of laughter. Then darkness had come, and all the far sounds and brooding mystery of the night, the great stars had flashed into the sky again, and on the porches up and down the street he could hear once more the voices of the neighbors, quiet, sly, and immensely greedy, breaking from time to time into coarse, sudden shouts of laughter. And he had hated that night forever, and it seemed to him there was no darkness in it deep enough to cover his own shame.

These memories and many others now came back to him, and the result was a nightmare vision of man's cruelty, vileness, defeat, and cowardice so unendurable that he writhed upon his cot, ripping the sheets between convulsive hands, and cursing with a twisted mouth, and finally smashing his bloody knuckles at the wall as the black horror of man's cruelty and fear writhed like a nest of vipers in his brain.

These things he had seen and known in his childhood, and he had sworn, as every other boy has sworn, that he would die or be beaten to a senseless pulp before he let them happen to him. And he had steeled his heart and set his teeth against the coming of the enemy, and he had sworn he would be ready for him when he came.

But now, at the beginning of that fatal April, it seemed to him that the enemy had come, but not as he expected him, not from the direction where he looked for him, not in the fierce shape and manner he had visioned him. For it seemed to him that the enemy had come on him from an unknown quarter, and that he had not known him when he came, and that he had wrought upon him a defeat, a humiliation, a ruin more horrible and irrevocable than had happened to either of these two men.

And yet, like a man who has been overpowered by his enemies and had the organs of his virility torn from him, he still knew every furious desire, every soaring hope of creation and fulfillment that he ever had. The plans and projects for a dozen books, a hundred stories, worked in his brain like madness: the whole form and body of a book, complete from start to finish, would blaze suddenly and entire within him, and he would hurl himself into it with savage and complete absorption. And this surge of new creation might continue for a week.

At such a time, in the intervals between his furious bursts of writing, he would walk the streets again with something like a return of the joy he once had felt in all the life around him. And just as his whole complex of bitter and confused feelings about Esther had become entwined and interwoven with everything he thought or felt or said that Spring, so, too, he looked now with an eye of wild desire at every other woman that he saw.

One day he saw a handsome, strong, and brawny Irish girl, with the coarse, wild beauty of her race as she came round an ugly corner beneath the brutal rust and slamming racket of the elevated structure. And as she turned the corner a gust of wind drove suddenly at her, thrusting her dress back through her legs, and in a minute her whole figure was stamped and printed nakedly against the wind—broad, potent belly, heavy breasts, and great columnar thighs coming forward with a driving sensual energy. And instantly a feeling of such power rose up in him that he felt he could tear the buildings up by the roots like onions from the earth. The blazing image of the brawny, lusty beauty of the woman was stamped into his brain forever, giving its savage memory of joy to the hideous clamor of the ugly street and all the crowds of grey-faced people that swarmed round her.

Again, in one of the narrow, crowded little streets near lower Broadway, full of the old, rusty, and gloomy-looking buildings of another time, but also filled with the sensuous and basic substances of life and commerce—with bales and crates and powerful machinery, with a smell of coffee, leather, turpentine, and rope, and with the clopping sound and the movement of great, slow-footed horses, the rumble of wheels upon the cobbles, the oaths, cries, and orders of drivers, packers, movers, and bosses—a young woman passed him as he stood before a leather store.

She was tall and slender, yet her figure was tremendously seductive, and she walked with a proud and sensual stride. Her face was thin and delicate, her eyes were clear and radiant, yet a vague and tender look dwelt in them, and her hair was carrot-colored, blown, spun like silk, escaping with a kind of witchcraft from the edges of her hat. She walked past him with a slow and undulant step, her mouth touched faintly with a smile at once innocent and corrupt, benignant and yet filled with a compassionate and seductive tenderness, and he watched her go with a feeling of wild joy and lust, a sense of unutterable loss and pain.

He knew that she was gone forever, that he would never see her again, and at the same moment he was certain he would find her and possess her. It was like magic, and the magic came not only from the lovely girl, but from the old and narrow street with its rich, dingy, and thrilling compost of the past, with its strong, clean odors of sensuous materials, and raw and honest substances, and especially the clean and glorious smell of leather from the leather shop—the smell of the big valises, bags, and cases piled before the shop which came to him strongly as the woman passed—all of this, together with the delicate, strange, and lovely light of April, made a scene of joy and magic which he thought would last forever.

He never forgot the girl, the street, the odor of the leather. It was part of the intolerable joy and pain of all that Spring. And somehow the thought of her, though for what reason he never knew, was joined forever with the thought of ships, the smell of the sea, the slant and drive and frontal breast of a great racing liner, and the wild prophecy of a voyage.

So it was with him in the brief intervals when, for no apparent reason, his spirits rose again and swept him upward for a day or two with new impulses back to life, to love, and to creation. And then, suddenly, out of the heart of joy, and the magical gold and glory and exultant music of the earth, the white blind horror of his madness would return again to stun him and to shatter the sequence of his energy into a thousand pieces.

Sometimes the wave of death and horror came upon the insane impulses of a half-heard word, a rumor of laughter in the street at night, the raucous shout and gibe of young Italian thugs as they passed by below his window in the darkness, or a look of mockery, amuse-ment, curiosity from some insolent face at a restaurant table, some whispered, unheard communication. And sometimes it came from sourceless depths, from no visible or tangible cause whatever. It would come as he sat quietly in a chair at home, as he stared at the ceiling from his cot, from a word in a poem, from a line in a book, or simply as he looked out of the window at that one green tree. But whenever it came, and for whatever cause, the result was always the same: work, power, hope, joy, and all creative energy were instantly engulfed and obliterated in its drowning and overwhelming tide. He would rise with it inside him and hurl himself insanely against the world like a man maddened by an agony of physical pain, like a man stamping and stumbling blindly about a room in an insanity of pain, with every tissue of his life drawn and fed into the maw of a cancerous tumor, or clutching between his frantic hands a whole horrible hell of abscessed and aching teeth.

And always now, when the convulsion of pain and horror drove him mad, he sought again the spurious remedy of the bottle. The raw gin gurgled down his tilted throat like water down a gully drain, numbing and deadening the mad particles of the brain, the raging tumults of blood, heart, and leaping nerves with its temporary illusions of power, deliberation, and control. Then it would begin to burn and seethe like a slow oil in his blood. His brain burned slowly and literally like a dull fire smouldering in a blackened, rusty brazier, and he would sit numbed and silent in the sullen darkness of a slowly mounting and murderous rage until he went out in the street to find the enemy, to curse and brawl and seek out death and hatred in dive and stew, among the swarms of the rats of the flesh, the livid, glittering dead men of the night.

And then from night to morning, like a creature destined to live for-ever in a hideous nightmare, seeing all things and persons of the earth in kaleidoscopic shapes of madness, he would prowl again the huge and obscene avenue of night, shone upon forever with its immense and livid wink. He would go along rat's alley where the dead men were, while the street, the earth, the people, even the immense and cruel architectures, reeled about him in a demented and gigantic dance, and all the cruel and livid faces of its creatures seemed to burn up at him suddenly with the features of snakes, foxes, vultures, rats, and apes —while he looked forever for a living man.

And morning would come again, but with no light and singing. He would recover out of madness and see with sane, untroubled eyes once more, but out of weary and fathomless depths of the spirit, into the heart of a life which he thought he had lost forever.

When Esther came again at noon, sometimes she seemed to him the fatal root of all his madness, which now could be plucked out of him no more than the fibrous roots of a crawling cancer from the red courses of the blood. At other times the green of that first April of their life together would come back again, and then she was united to the heart of joy, to all that he loved in life, to all the gold and singing of the earth.

But then at night when she had gone, he could remember her no longer as she had looked at noon. The dark and fatal light of absence, the immense and velvet night, menaced with its thousand intangible treacheries, fell upon her, and the radiant face of noon, the light of certitude, possession, and health, had vanished utterly. Fixed in an arrogant power, her face as he saw it then flamed like a strange and opulent jewel; in his feverish imagination it smouldered drowsily with all the slumberous and insatiate passions of the East, it spoke of a desire illimitable as the ocean, a body to be taken by all men, and never to be possessed by any.

Again and again, a mad, distorted picture blazed within his mind. He saw a dark regiment of Jewish women in their lavish beauty, their faces melting into honey, their eyes glowing, their breasts like melons. Seated in power and wealth, and fitly walled by the arrogant and stupendous towers of the city, he saw their proud bodies opulently gowned and flashing with the somber fires of ancient jewels as they paced with the velvet undulance of an intolerable sensuality the proud and splendid chambers of the night. They were the living rack on which the trembling backs of all their Christian lovers had been broken.

the living cross on which the flesh and marrow of Christian men had been crucified. And they were more lost than all the men whom they had drowned within the sea-gulf of their passion, their flesh more tormented than the flesh of all the men whose lives had been nailed upon their lust, and whose wrung loins hung dry and lifeless like a withered stalk from the living wall of their desire. And behind them always in the splendor of the night were the dark faces of great, beak-nosed Jews, filled with insolence and scorn, with dark pride and an unutterable patience, with endurance and humility and an ancient and unspeakable irony as they saw their daughters and their wives yield their bodies into the embraces of their Gentile lovers.

Thus when Esther left him, the madness passed into him instantly, and instantly he knew that he was mad and yet was powerless to check it. He stood there looking at the tree and watched that black abomination of death and hatred sweep upon him like a wave. It soaked first into the deep folds and convolutions of his brain its damnable slime of poison, and then it channeled out its blackened tongues along the veins and arteries of his flesh. It heated and inflamed his brain with a dull, sweltering fire that was like a smear of blood and murder, but all else within the house of the flesh it chilled, froze, and constricted with a reptile's fangs. It shriveled up his heart in a ring of poisonous ice, it deadened the feeling in his fingers, his flesh withered and turned numb, dead, and sallow-looking, his cheeks were tinged with a greenish hue, his mouth got dry, the tongue was thick and pulpy, the edges of the lips had an acrid and bitter taste, the thighs and buttock felt weak and flabby, the sockets of the knee bent down beneath the body's weight and felt watery and feeble, the feet and toes grew cold, white, phthisic, the guts got sick, numb, and nauseously queasy, and the loins which once had leaped and quivered with a music of joy and life, under the poisonous and constricting fury grew sterile, sour, and dry.

And in the seizures of his madness he felt that there was no remedy, no relief, and no revenge for the falseness of women, their tender cruelty, and their corrupt innocence. The frenzied curses, oaths, and prayers of the lover could not prevail over the merciless necessity of a woman's nature. Nor could all a woman's tears, protests, and passionate avowals change it. Nothing could stop or control a woman's insatiate desires as she faced her hated doom of old age and death. For all the good it would do, the lover might as well shout at a wall, spit off the bridge into the river, attempt to tie a rope around a hurricane, or build a picket fence upon the middle of the ocean as expect to make a woman faithful.

Could women not lie, and lie, and lie, and yet still think that they had spoken truth? Could they not beat their breasts and tear their hair, smash their accusing lovers in the face, and scream that such purity, fidelity, steadfastness as theirs had never been known since the beginning of time? Yes! Could they not sweat nobility at every pore and with every moan and sob of protest until they lay blear-eyed, bedraggled, red-faced, blown, and panting on the bed, exhausted with these ardors of their pure, innocent, and womanly natures—and yet could they not lie, betray, and cheat you in the flick of an eye, the turn of a corner, in any one of the million blind, undiscoverable, and unknowable cells of the trackless jungle of the city, where your rivals lay coiled like snakes to poison faith and spread corruption at the heart of love?

The evil splinter of a shameful memory passed like a poisoned arrow through his brain. He remembered suddenly the vile and cunning words that one of Esther's friends in the theatrical world had spoken to him almost three years before, the only open words of accusation and indictment that anyone had ever spoken, that anyone had ever dared to speak, to him against Esther. And as the hateful words came back to him, he remembered also the time, the place, the street, the very hand's breadth of grey, rootless city pavement where they had been spoken.

He had been walking with this girl along the street where she lived, at about eleven o'clock in the evening. And as she spoke the words, they were passing below the striped sidewalk awning of a new apartment house. And even as the words struck numbly their envenomed fangs into his heart, he looked up into the loose, tough, pustulate face of a young flunkey in the door of the building, he saw the heavy braid upon his uniform, his brass buttons, his insolent grin, and the man's face had been fixed forever in his memory with a sense of hatred and of loathing.

The girl, looking at him with a sly and secret malice in her starved and ugly little face, had warned him of the woman he had met only a month before, saying, in a careful and regretful tone that ended with a sudden burst of venom and of bitterness:

"She *likes* young men. I'm sorry, but that's what they say about her. I'm afraid that's the way it is, I really am, you know."

And now, in an instant of black horror, the words returned to him with all their poisonous and rankling connotations. In the hot anger that surged up in him when he first heard them, he had regarded what the girl had said as an act of ugly malice, the jealous hatred of the grey, fleshless dead for the beautiful, warm, and glorious living. But he could not forget them. Again and again the words returned to fester at the roots of his heart like foul, cureless sores.

They evoked a picture of the whole horrible world of the theatre, the livid, glittering, nighttime world of Broadway, a world of weariness, of death, hatred, and a sterile prostitution, eager to slime all living things with its own filth. And as he thought of this great rat's alley where the dead men were, the great street of the night lit with its obscene winks of sterile light and swarming with a million foul, corrupt, and evil faces—the faces of rats, snakes, vultures, all the slimy crawls and sucks and eyeless reptiles of the night, the false and shoddy faces of the accursed actors, with all the sly communication of their obscene whispering—he was driven mad again with horror, doubt, and unbelief. It seemed incredible that this vital, beautiful, and wholesome-looking woman with her fresh, jolly, noonday face of flowerful health and purity and joy could be joined in any way, could be connected by any filament, however small, to this evil nighttime world of shoddy, filth, and death.

And now, in one stunned instant of his madness, the foul and rankling memory of the unforgettable words had passed across his brain, evoking a poisonous breed of viper thoughts and insane fabrications. He saw again some casual glance upon her face, remembered a hundred casual words and acts and intonations, and, however trivial and momentary, they all seemed blackly pregnant now with revelations of falseness, treachery, and evil. Now for the first time, in the darkness of his tortured mind, he thought he understood them at their true and shameful value.

And suddenly a dozen images of betrayal blazed through his mind with stabbing intensities of hatred and despair, no less torturing to his spirit for being pictures projected out of nothing but the madness of his own enfevered brain. He saw her secure against detection in all the swarming immensity of the city, guarded and protected by the power of the arrogant, insolent wealth that surrounded her. Or again he saw her buried safely in the cruel loveliness of Spring somewhere in the country, at the homes and estates of rich and sensual Jewish women, who aided and abetted her.

He saw her quilted in the silken tapestries of wealth and lust, and melting into tenderness in the embrace of some accursed boy. Sometimes it was a stripling with blond hair and downy apple-cheeks. Sometimes it was some sensitively obscure and artistic youth, who pined above the tea cups of æsthetic women, expiring with pale languor the limp lily of his energy into an embrace of jade earrings and exquisite yearnings. And sometimes it was some accursed actor in the theatre, some youth with a thin, poisonous face and hateful sideburns, some insolent darling of erotic theatrical females—"one of our best young actors," who did the youthful lover in some merry jest of bawdry in Budapest, some light-hearted chronicle of whoredom in Vienna, or some pleasant little squib of native fornication in the suave purlieus of Newport's Younger Set, almost as good, if you please, in the "civilized" refinements of its humor as the merry urbanities of plays about the European whores and cuckolds.

As his maddened brain invented these images of self-torture, tongueless words of hate and scorn twisted his features in a writhing and convulsive snarl. Oh, was she merry, was she gay, was she witty and quick and light, in these delicate engagements of love and treason? Did she carry it off with the celebrated "light touch" of the fashionable art-theatre comedy? Tell me, was it light and delicate, sweet sirs, was it with a hey, now, noble dames, with a hey and a ho and a hi-nonny-neigh, my gentles all? Deary me, now! Could she sit on her delicate tail and banter away about the light refinements of adultery? Was it all done gracefully to the tune of jolly jokes about the fairies and the lesbians?

Oh, tell me, tell me, now! Were she and her friends, the rich and sensual Jewish women he had seen at her apartment—were they merry about adultery, pale green toilet paper, cellophane, Cal Coolidge, the talkies, the Shubert brothers, prohibition, and the culinary patios of Alice Foote McDougall? Were they impressed, as they ought to be, by the plays of Pirandello? Were they sealed, as was most fit and fashionable, of the tribe of Lawrence? Had they read all the latest books, sweet friends? Had they looked with sneering smiles of intellectual arrogation upon the faces of their fellow subscribers in those delightful mid-act promenades that gave the final touch of triumph and disdain to those evenings of ripe culture at the Guild? Did they know "Lynn and Alfred," good my lord? Had they seen this, had they read that, and was it "swell" or "grand" or "lousy," son of man?

Did they know all the words and remember all the answers, know all the places for the painting of a laugh, all of the touchstones of a sneer, as well as all the proper things for reverence and worship? Oh, were they all, sweet friends, wise, witty, brave, and modern, the last latest miracle of time and better than their fathers ever were, too good, too fine, and too enlightened for the common grief and agony of such base clay as his, too rare for all the sorrow of such men as ever once had drawn in below immense and timeless skies the burden of their grief and agony? Were they not released by the miracle of the age and science from all the blights of hatred, love, and jealousy, of passion and belief, which had been rooted in the structure of man's life and soul for twenty thousand years? Oh, could they not tell you who were made of baser earth the place where you might take your packed and overladen hearts (if only you were rich enough!), the physician who could analyze your error, medicine your woe in forty stylish treatments, instruct you in deep damnation of an ancient grief three times a week, mend and repair your sorrowful and overladen spirits out of the chaos of their grief and folly in an eight months' alchemy of fashionable redemption?

Yes! Had she not herself been saved and freed forever from all the fears and phantoms flesh is heir to by this same magic, grown sublimely healthy, sane, and knowing on this same medicine? And now did she not sob, pray, plead, and entreat, threaten suicide and vengeance, show jealousy, rage, pain, sorrow, indignation, swear she was the noblest and most unfortunate woman that ever walked the earth, that such sorrow, tragedy, and love as hers had never before been known—all with as much unreason, passion, intemperance, and confusion as if she were only some ignorant and suffering child of Eve who wore a bloody clout twelve times a year, and whose tumultuous, unenlightened soul had never known the healing light at all?

Yes! They were a rare and subtle breed, the liberated princelings of the age, beyond the bloody imperfections of his own base, sweating, stinking earth of toil and agony. And suddenly he wondered if he was going to strangle to death like a mad dog in the darkness, hurl his strength against a world of bloodless phantoms, madden and die desperately of grief among the corrupt and passionless dead, a horrible race of rootless ciphers who *felt* that they felt, *thought* that they thought, *believed* that they believed, but who were able to feel, think, and believe nothing. Had he loved a woman who never had loved him, and had he now gone mad, was he ruined, lost, and broken because of the frailties of a toy, the inconstancies of dough and tallow, the airy frolics of butterflies and sparrows?

Or was the treason consummated darkly, without the gay and lightsome touch of delicate banter? Did she in some green and cruel loveliness of Spring melt with a poppied tenderness into the arms of some fleshly and swarthy youth, some actor with full lips and the flowing volutes of a sensual nostril, some dark, moist creature with a full, white, hairless body and a thick, spermatic neck?

Or was it some dark and sullen youth who irritably tapped on tables and had "lived in Paris," and who scowled with a febrile discontent at the images of his misprized talents? Did she look at him with an eye of glowing tenderness, gently stroke his thin, dark features, and say in tones of wonder that his face was "lovely," "so delicate," and "like an angel's"? Did she tell him that "no one could ever know how beautiful you are"? Did she say: "You have the greatest and most beautiful quality in you of anyone I have ever known, the greatest power, the greatest genius. No one could ever know how grand and rich and beautiful your spirit is the way I do."

And then did she speak of the tragic difference in the years that divided them and made true happiness impossible? Did she speak of the sorrows of her life, and weep as she spoke of them, and swear this was "the great love of her life," that all the love and living that had gone before were nothing when compared to it, that she had never dreamed, had never been able to believe it possible, that such a glory of love as this could exist on earth, and that in all the history of the world there had never before been anything to equal it? Did she use the big words, the grand words, and yield herself into easy surrender as she spoke nobly of high love and holy purity, eternal faithfulness, physical and spiritual consecration?

The accursed images streamed through his maddened mind their black processional of death and shame as he stared blindly into the heart of the pulsing and magical green. He was caught in a trap of folly, ruin, and madness, hating his life and the abomination of shame in which his life lay drowned, stripped to his naked woe before the staring and merciless eye of the earth, and nowhere able to avoid it or hide himself out of its sight, and in no way able to utter to any man the weight of evil and horror that lay upon his heart.

Sometimes at noon, in the presence of Esther's rosy, healthful face of love, all the gold and singing of the past came back to him with exultant joy and sanity, but always, always, when she had gone, this cruel and sinister vision of Esther at night and in absence, the potent and evil flower of a corrupt and infamous world, would awake in him again with a searing vividness of horror. The madness would swarm into him again, poisoning his bone, brain, and blood with its malignant taint.

Then he would call Esther on the phone, and if he found her in her room he would curse and taunt her foully, ask her where her lover was, and if she had him by her at that moment, and believe he heard him whispering and snickering behind her even as she swore no one was there. And then, cursing her again, he would tell her never to come back to him, and rip the phone out of its moorings in the wall, hurl it on the floor, and smash and trample it underneath his feet, as if the instrument itself had been the evil and malignant agent of his ruin.

But if he could not find her when he called for her, if her Irish maid should answer and tell him she was out, his despair and madness knew no bounds. He would ask the woman a hundred furious questions. Where had her mistress gone? When would she return? How could he find her at once? Who was with her? What message had she left for him? And if the maid could not answer all these questions exactly and at once, he was convinced he was being duped and mocked at with a jeering contempt and arrogance. He would read into the rich and rather unctuously respectful tone of the Irish maid an undernote of mockery, the evil amusement of the hireling, lewd and confident, her own life bribed, tainted, and polluted with the wage of silence and collusion.

And he would leave the phone to drain the bottle to its last raw drop, then rush out in the streets to curse and fight with people, with the city, with all life, in tunnel, street, saloon, or restaurant, while the whole earth reeled about him its gigantic and demented dance.

And then, in the crowded century of darkness that stretched from light to light, from sunset until morning, he would prowl a hundred streets and look into a million livid faces seeing death in all of them, and feeling death everywhere he went. He would be hurled through tunnels to some hideous outpost of the mighty city, the ragged edge of Brooklyn, and come out in the pale grey light of morning in a wasteland horror of bare lots and rust and rubbish; of dismal little houses flung rawly down upon the barren earth, joined each to each in blocks that duplicated one another with an idiot repetition.

Sometimes, in such a place, the madness and the shapes of death would leave him as suddenly and mysteriously as they had come, and he would come back in the morning, come back from death to morning, walking on the Bridge. He would feel below him its living and dynamic tremble, its vast winglike sweep and flight. Then he would smell the fresh, half-rotten river smell, the glorious spermy sea-wrack with its exultant prophecy of the sea and voyages, and the sultry fragrance of the roasted coffee. He could see below him the great harbor with its flashing tides, its traffic of proud ships, and before him he could see the great frontal cliff of the terrific city, with morning, bright, shining morning, blazing again upon its thousand spires and ramparts.

So it was with him in the green sorcery of that final, fatal, and ruinous April. He was a hater of living men who saw nothing but death and cold corruption in everything and everyone around him, and who yet loved life with so furious and intolerable a desire that each night he seemed to revisit the shores of this great earth like a ghost, an alien, and a stranger, his brain filled with its wild regret of memory, and with insatiable thirst for all the joy and glory of a life that he thought he had lost forever.

37

The Quarrel

UNDERLYING ALL THE MADNESS OF HIS LIFE THAT APRIL, CENTRAL TO IT, touching it at every point, was his love for Esther, a love which now, through self-inflicted jealousy, his loathing of the world she moved in, his sense of ruin and lost hope, had been converted into bitter hate. It had been almost three years since he first met Esther and since he had begun to love her, and now, like a man who emerges from the blind rout and fury of a battle and, looking back across the field, sees clearly for the first time that he is party to a broken force, sees legible at last the news of his own defeat, so now it was possible for Monk to see all of the emergent and consecutive stages through which his love for her had run.

There had been the time, in the beginning, when he had felt a young man's exultant pride and vainglory in what he thought of as a brilliant personal conquest—the possession of the love of a beautiful and talented woman—a tribute to his vanity.

Then his vanity and joy of sensual conquest gave way to the humility and adoration of love, until every pulse, energy, and passion of his life became obsessed by her.

And then, before he knew it, the trapper was trapped, the conqueror conquered, the proud and the insolent laid low, and she was entombed in his flesh, fatally absorbed in his blood until it seemed that he would never get her out of him again, never look out on life again with his own proper vision, never recover again the exultant solitudes of his youth, never again distill out of his flesh and spirit the terrible invasions of love which rob men of their unshared secrecy, their deep-walled loneliness, the soaring music of their isolation. And when he first began to realize the deep exclusiveness of love, the extent to which it was absorbing all his thoughts and energies, he felt the price he paid for it was too exorbitant, and he began to fret and chafe against the shackles which his heart had forged.

And now, finally, all the proud, triumphant music of this love which had possessed and conquered him was being broken, corrupted, made dissonant and harsh by these recurring waves of doubt, suspicion, hate, and madness which had at last exerted a final and ruinous dominance over all his life.

In the furious chronicle of this passion, with its innumerable memories of things done, its countless intertwisted shades and moments, thoughts and feelings, each of which was so alive with a wordless fabric of pain, joy, tenderness, love, cruelty, and despair that it seemed to feed itself with the whole packed pageant of the earth, the reality of measured and recorded time had been exploded and these three years were really longer than any ten that Monk had ever known before. All that he had seen, done, felt, read, thought, or dreamed in all his former life seemed but the food and substance of this present time.

And as Monk's thoughts made all this clear to him, the full and conscious knowledge of her invasion of his life and his subjection to her conquest seemed intolerable. The conviction of his ruin and defeat was now rooted in his heart, and he swore that he would free himself, and draw his breath alone as he had once, or die.

These thoughts and resolutions Monk had formed one night as he lay the long dark hours through upon his cot, staring up at the ceiling of his room. The next day when Esther came to him as usual, the sight of her jolly, rosy face was like a challenge to him. It seemed to him a suspicious circumstance that she should be so radiant when he was so depressed, and instantly the worm was eating at his heart again. As she came in and greeted him in her usual cheerful way, all the images of betrayal that his madness had ever fashioned now flashed in his brain once more; he passed his hand blindly and clumsily before his eyes, his vision reeled with swimming motes, and he began to speak in a voice grown hoarse with rending hate.

"So!" he said, with exaggerated emphasis. "You've come back to me, have you? You've come back, now that day is here, to spend an hour or two with me! I suppose I ought to be grateful that you haven't forgotten me altogether!"

"Why, what on earth?" she said. "In God's name, what is it now?"

"You know damn well what it is!" he flung back brutally. "You can't go on forever playing me for a fool! I may be just a country yokel, but I do catch on after a while!"

"Oh, come now, George," she said soothingly, "don't be such a fool just because I wasn't in when you telephoned last night. Katy told me you called, and I'm sorry I wasn't there. But, good heavens! Anybody would think from the way you talk that I was carrying on with other men."

"Think!" he said in a thick tone, and suddenly he began to snarl with brutal laughter. "Think! Why, God-damn you, I don't *think*, I *know!* . . . Yes! Every time my back is turned!"

"So help me God, I never have," she said in a trembling voice, "and you know it! I have been good and faithful to you since the first moment that I met you. No one has come near me, no one has touched me, and in your evil, lying heart you know it!"

"God, how can you say it!" he said, shaking his head with a kind of sullen wonder. "How can you stand there and look at me and say the words! It's a wonder you don't choke to death on them!"

"It's the living truth!" she said. "And if your mind wasn't poisoned by evil and vile suspicions you'd know it! You mistrust everyone because you think everyone is as vile and base as you are!"

"Don't you worry about that!" he shouted furiously. "I'll trust anyone that's worth it! I know when people can be trusted, all right!"

"Oh, you *know*, you *know*," she said bitterly. "God, you know nothing! You wouldn't know the truth if it stopped you on the street!"

"I know *you*, all right!" he shouted. "And I know that damned crowd you run around with, too!"

"Listen to me!" she cried warningly. "You may not like the people I work with——"

"You're damned right I don't like the people you work with!" he shouted. "Nor any of their crowd—those fine Jewish ladies on Park Avenue with their million-dollar soul yearnings and their fancy fornications!" Then, quietly, dangerously, he turned to her and said: "I should like to ask you a single question." He stood facing her. "Tell me, Esther, do you know what a whore is?"

"Wh-a-a-t?" she said, in a faltering and uncertain voice that ended on a high note of hysteria. "What did you sa-a-y?"

He leaped savagely upon her, gripping her arms, pinning her and thrusting her back against the wall.

"Answer me!" he snarled insanely. "You heard me! You're good enough at using words like faith, and truth, and love, and loyalty! But you don't even know what I'm saying, do you, when I ask you if you know what a whore is! That's not a word to use about those fine ladies on Park Avenue, is it? That doesn't apply to the like of them, does it? You're God-damned right it doesn't!" he whispered slowly, with all the choking passion of his hate.

"Let me go!" she said. "Take your hands off me!"

"Oh, no—not yet! You're not going yet. You're not going till I instruct your pure, sweet innocence!"

"Oh, I have no doubt that you can tell me," she said bitterly. "I have no doubt that you're an authority on the subject! That's the trouble with you now! That's the reason that your mind's so full of filth and evil when you speak of decent women! You never knew a decent woman till you met me. You've gone with dirty, rotten women all your life—and that's the only kind of woman that you know about. That's the only kind you understand!"

"Yes, I know about them, Esther, and I understand them better than I do all the fancy soul yearnings of your million-dollar friends. I've known two hundred of the other kind—the common street and house and gutter whore—I've known them in a dozen countries, and there never was one yet like these fine Park Avenue ladies!"

"You can bet your life they weren't!" she said quietly.

"They didn't have a million dollars, and they didn't live in twenty-room apartments. And they didn't whine and whimper about their souls, and say their lovers were too coarse and low to understand them. They were not fine and dainty in whatever light you saw them, but they knew that they were whores. Some were fat, worn-out old rips with pot bellies and no upper teeth, and a snuff stick dripping from the edges of their mouth."

"You can save your precious knowledge for those who want to hear it," Esther said. "But it only sickens me! I don't want to know any more about this great wisdom you've dug out of the gutter."

"Oh, come, now!" he jeered quietly. "Is this the fine artist who sees life clearly and who sees it whole? Is this the woman who finds truth and beauty everywhere? Since when have you begun to turn your nose up at the gutter? But maybe you don't like my kind of gutter? Now, if it were only a fine art-theatre gutter—if it were only a fine old gutter from Vienna or Berlin—that would be a different matter, wouldn't it? Or a nice, juicy, running sewer of a gutter in Marseilles? That's the real stuff, isn't it? In fact, you made designs one time for a fine gutter in Marseilles, didn't you? The one about the whore who was the mother of all men living, and who mothered the waifs and outcasts of the earth into her all-engulfing belly— Madame Demeter! I could have told you something of that gutter, too, because I have been there on my travels, pet, although I never happened to run into that particular lady! And of course my vile, low nature could not appreciate the deep, symbolic beauty of the play," he snarled, "although it might have given you a few pointers about the stinks and smells of the Old Quarter and the bits of rotten fish and fruit and excrement in the alleyways! But you didn't ask me, did you? I have a good eye and a splendid nose, and the memory of an elephant—but I lack the deeper vision, don't I, darling? And besides, my base soul could never rise to the high beauties of a fine old gutter in Marseilles or Budapest—it could not rise above the gutter of a Southern Niggertown! And of course, that's only common, native clay—that is not *art*!" he said in a strangling voice.

"Now, quiet, quiet, quiet!" she said gently. "Don't lash yourself into a frenzy. You're out of your head and you don't know what you're saying." For a moment she stroked his hand tenderly and looked sorrowfully at him. "In God's name, what is it? What is all this wild talk about gutters and alleyways and theatres? What has it got to do with you and me? What has it got to do with how I love you?"

His lips were blue and trembled stiffly, and his face had grown livid and was twisted in a convulsion of mad, mindless fury, and it was true that he was no longer fully conscious of what he said.

Suddenly she grasped him by the arms and shook him fiercely. Then she seized him by the hair and furiously pulled his stunned, drugged stare around to her.

"Listen to me!" she said sharply. "Listen to what I'm going to tell you!" He stared at her sullenly, and for a moment she paused, her eyes shot angrily with tears and her small figure trembling with the energy of a dogged and indomitable will.

"George, if you hate the people that I work with and the work I do—I'm sorry for it. If the actors and the other people working in the theatre are as vile and rotten as you say they are, I am sorry for that, too. But I did not make them what they are, and I have never found them that way. I have found many of them vain and pitiful and shabby, poor things without a grain of talent or of understanding, but not vile and evil as you say they are. And I have known them all my life. My father was an actor and he was as wild and mad as you are, but he had as glorious and beautiful a spirit as anyone that ever lived."

Her voice trembled, and the tears began to flow from her eyes. "You say we are all base and vile and have no faithfulness! Oh, you fool! I heard him crying for me in the middle of the night—I rushed in and found him lying on the floor and the blood was pouring from his mouth! I felt the strength of ten people and I lifted him up and put him across my back and carried him to his bed." She paused, her voice was trembling so she could not continue for a moment. "His blood soaked through my nightgown on my shoulders—I can feel it yet—he could not speak—he died there holding to my hand and looking at me with his great grey eyes—and that was almost thirty years ago. You say we are all base and vile and have no love for anyone except ourselves. Do you think I could ever forget him? No, never, never, never!"

She closed her eyes, raising her flushed face slightly, and tightly pressing her lips together. In a moment she went on, more quietly:

"I'm sorry if you do not like my work, or the people that I have to work with. But it's the only work I know—the work I like the best—and George, no matter what you say, I am proud of the work I do. I am a fine artist and I know my value. I know how cheap and trashy most plays are—yes! and some of the people who play in them, too! But I know the glory and the magic is there just the same, and that nothing in this world can beat it when you find it!"

"Ah! The glory and the magic—rot!" he muttered. "All of them talk their bilge about the glory and the magic! It's the glory and magic of bitches in heat! All of them looking for some easy love affairs! With our best young actors, hey?" he said savagely, seizing her by the arm. "With our would-be Ibsens under twenty-five! Is that it? With our young scene designers, carpenters, electricians—and all the other geniuses with their boyish apple-cheeks!" he said chokingly.

"Is that the glory and the magic that you talk of? Yes! the glory and the magic of erotic women!"

She wrenched herself away from his hard grasp, and suddenly she held her small, strong hands up before his face.

"Look at these hands," she said quietly and proudly. "You poor fool, look at them! Are those the hands of an erotic woman? They have done more work than any man's you ever knew. There's strength and power in them. They have learned how to sew and paint and design and create—and they can do things now that no one else on earth can do. And they cooked for you! They cooked the finest meals for you that you have ever eaten." She seized him fiercely by the arms again and drew him to her, and looked up at him with a flaming face. "Oh, you poor, mad fool," she whispered in the rapt tone of a woman in a trance. "You tried to throw me over—but I stuck to you. I stuck to you," she whispered in an exultant and triumphant chant. "You tried to drive me away from you, you cursed me and reviled me—but I stuck to you, I stuck to you! You've tortured and abused me and made me go through things that no one else on earth would have endured—but you couldn't drive me off," she cried with an exultant laugh, "you couldn't get rid of me because I love you more than anything on earth and it will never change. Oh, I've stuck to you! I've stuck to you! You poor, mad creature, I have stuck to you because I love you, and there's more beauty and more glory in your mad, tormented spirit than in anyone I ever knew! You are the best, the best," she whispered. "You are mad and evil, but you are the best, and that's the reason that I've stuck to you! And I'm going to get the best, the highest out of you if I have to kill myself in doing it! I'll give my strength and knowledge to you. I'll teach you how to use the best in you. Oh, you'll not go wrong!" she said with almost gleeful triumph. "I'll not let you go wrong or mad or false or cheap, or lower than the best on earth. In God's name, tell me what it is," she cried out as she shook him desperately. "Tell me what there is that I can do about it—and I'll help you. I'll show you the clear design, the thread of gold, and you must always stick to it! I'll show you how to get it out of you. I'll not let you lose the pure gold that you have in you below a mass of false and evil things. I'll not let you throw your life away on drunkenness and wandering and cheap women and low brothels. Tell me what it is and I will help you." She shook him fiercely. "Tell me! Tell me!"

He stared thickly at her through the blind, swimming glaze of madness, and as it passed and he saw her face before him once again, his mind picked up wearily and obscurely, and with a stunned, uncertain consciousness, the broken thread of what he had been saying, and he proceeded in the dull, dead, toneless recitation of an automaton:

"They live in little houses in the nigger districts of a Southern town, or they live across the railroad tracks, and they have chains upon their blinds—that is their trade-mark—and they have a lattice all around the house. Sometimes you went there in the hot afternoon, and your shoes were covered with white dust, and everything was hot and quiet and raw and foul and ugly in the sun, and you wondered why you had come and felt that everyone you knew was looking at you. And sometimes you went there in the middle of the night in Winter. You could hear the niggers shouting and singing in their shacks and see their smoky little lights behind old dingy yellow shades, but everything was closed and secret and all the sounds were shut away from you, and you thought a thousand eyes were looking at you. And now and then a negro would prowl by. You would wait and listen in the dark, and when you tried to light a cigarette your fingers trembled so the light went out. You could see the street lamp at the corner wink and shutter with its hard, cold light, and the stiff, swinging shadows of bare branches on the ground, and the cold, raw clay of Niggertown below the light. You prowled around a dozen corners in the dark and went back and forth before the house a dozen times before you rang the bell. And inside the house, it was always hot and close and smelled of shiny furniture and horsehair and varnish and strong antiseptics. And you could hear a door that opened and shut quietly and someone going out. One time there were two of them who were sitting cross-legged on a bed and playing cards. They told me to choose between them, and they kept on playing cards. And when I left, they grinned and showed their toothless gums at me and called me 'son.' "

She turned away with a burning face and a bitter and contracted mouth.

"Oh, it must have been charming . . . charming!" she said quietly.

"And sometimes you were sitting all night long on a rickety bed in a little cheap hotel. You gave a dollar to the nigger and you waited till the night clerk went to sleep, and the nigger brought the woman to you or took you to her room. They came in on one train and they went out on another in the middle of the night, and the cops were always after them. You could hear the engines shifting in the train yards all night long, and you could hear doors opening and closing all along the hall, and footsteps creaking by as easy as they could, and the rattling of the bed casters in cheap rooms. And everything smelled foul and dark and musty in the room. Your lips got dry, and your heart was pounding in you like a hammer, and every time you heard someone creaking down the hall your guts got numb and you held your breath. You stared at the door knob and waited for the door to open, and you thought it was your time."

"A fine life! A fine life!" she cried bitterly.

"I wanted more than that," he said. "But I was seventeen, away from home, at college. I took what I could get."

"Away from home!" she cried in her bitter tone. "As if that was any excuse!" And then, irrationally and bitterly: "Yes! And a fine home it was, wasn't it? They let you go away like that and never gave you another thought! Oh, a fine lot they were, those relatives of yours, those Christian Baptists! A fine lot! A fine life! And you dare to curse me and my people!"

"You . . . your people," he repeated slowly in his drugged monotone; and then, as the meaning of her words penetrated his consciousness, a black fury of hate and rage surged up in him instantly, and he turned upon her savagely. "Your people!" he shouted. "What about *your* people!"

"Now you're beginning again!" she cried warningly, with a flushed, excited face. "I've told you now——"

"Yes, you've told me, all right! You can say anything you Goddamn please, but if I open my mouth——"

"I didn't say anything! You're the one!"

His anger dropped away as suddenly as it had flared up, and he shrugged his shoulders in a gesture of weary and exasperated consent.

"All right, all right, all right!" he said impatiently. "Let's forget about it! Let's drop the subject!" He made a dismissing gesture and his face smouldered sullenly and morosely.

"It's not me! I didn't start it! You're the one!" she said again in a protesting tone.

"All right, all *right!*" he cried irritably. "It's all over I tell you! For God's sake let it drop!"

Then, almost immediately, in a voice that crooned and lilted gently with a savage and infuriated contempt, he continued:

"*So*—I mustn't say a word about your precious people! They're all too fine and grand for me to talk about! I wouldn't understand them, would I, dear? I'm too low and vile to appreciate the rich Jews who live on Park Avenue! Oh, yes! And as for your own family——"

"You leave my family alone!" she cried in a high, warning voice. "Don't you open your dirty mouth about them!"

"Oh, no. No indeed. I mustn't open my dirty mouth. I suppose it wouldn't do at all for me to say——"

"I'm warning you!" she cried in a sobbing voice. "I'll smash you in your face if you say a word about my family! We're too good for you, that's the trouble! You've never been used to meeting decent people before, you've never known any nice people in your life till you met me, and you think everyone is as vile as your low corner-drug-store mind makes them out to be!"

She was trembling violently, she bit her lips furiously, tears were streaming from her eyes, and for a moment she stood rigid in a kind of shuddering silence while she clenched and unclenched her hands convulsively at her sides in order to control herself. Then she continued more calmly, almost inaudibly at first, in a voice of passionate and trembling indignation:

"Wench! Hussy! Jew! These are some of the vile names you have called me, and I have been decent and faithful all my life! God! What a pure, sweet mind you've got! I suppose those are some more of the lovely and elegant expressions you learned down there in Old Catawba where you came from! You're a wonder, you are! It must have been a fine lot you grew up with! God! What a nerve you've got to open your mouth about *me*! Your family——"

"You shut up about my family!" he shouted. "You know nothing about them! They're a damned sight better than this poisonous, life-hating set of theatrical rats you go with!"

"Oh yes! they must be simply wonderful!" she said, with bitter sarcasm. "They've done a hell of a lot for you, haven't they? Turning you loose upon the world at sixteen, and then washing their hands of you! God! You Christians are a charming lot! You talk about the Jews! Just try to find a Jew that would treat his sister's children in that way! Your mother's people kicked you out when you were sixteen years old, and now you can go to hell as far as any of them are concerned. Do they ever think of you? How often do you hear from one of them? How often does your aunt or uncle write to you? Oh, you needn't speak—I know!" she said bitterly, with a deliberate intent to wound him. "You've told me of this grand family of yours for three years now. You've reviled and hated all my people—and now, I ask you, who's stuck by you, who's been your friend? Be honest, now. Do you think that crowd you came from give a damn about you? Do you think they'd ever understand or value anything you do? Do you think one of them cares if you live or die?" She laughed ironically. "Don't make me laugh!" she said. "Don't make me laugh!"

Her words had bitten deep into his pride, and she felt a fierce joy when she saw that they had rankled deep. His face had grown white with pain and fury, and his lips moved numbly, but she was unable to control herself because her own resentment and her hurt had been so great.

"And what did this wonderful father you're always talking about do for you?" she went on. "What did he ever do for you but let you go to hell?"

"That's a lie!" he said thickly. "It's . . . a . . . dirty . . . lie! Don't you dare open your mouth about him! He was a great man, and everyone who ever knew him said the same!"

"Yes, a great bum!" she jeered. "A great whiskey drinker! A great woman chaser! That's what he was! He gave you a fine home, didn't he? He left you a large fortune, didn't he? You ought to thank him for all he's done for you! Thank him for making you an outcast and a wanderer! Thank him for filling your heart with hate and poison against the people who have loved you! Thank him for your black, twisted soul and all the hate in your mad brain! Thank him for making you hate yourself and your own life! Thank him for making a monster of you who stabs his friends to the heart and then deserts them! And then see if you can't be as much like him as you can! Since that's what you want, follow in his footsteps, and see if you can't be as vile a man as he was!"

She could not stop herself from saying it, her heart was full of hate and bitterness for a moment and she wanted to say the most cruel and wounding thing she could to him. She wanted to hurt him as he had hurt her, and as she looked at him she felt a horrible joy because she saw she had hurt him terribly. His face was the color of chalk, his lips were numb and blue, and his eyes glittered. When he tried to speak he could not, and when he did, his lips moved stiffly and she could scarcely hear at first what he was saying.

"Get out of here!" he said. "Get out of my place and never come back to it!"

She did not move, she could not move, and suddenly he screamed at her:

"Get out, God-damn you, or I'll drag you out into the street by the hair of your head!"

"All right," she said, in a trembling voice, "all right, I'll go. This is the end. But some day I hope to God some power will make you know what I am like. Some day I hope you will be made to suffer as you have made me suffer. Some day I hope you will see what you have done to me."

"Done to you!" he said. "Why, God-damn you, I've given my life to you! That's what I've done to you! You've grown fat and prosperous on my life and energy. You've sapped and gutted me; you've renewed your youth at my expense—yes! and given it back again into that old painted whore-house of a theatre. 'Oh, deary me, now!'" he sneered, with an insane and mincing parody of her complaint. "'What have you done to me, you cruel brute?' What have you done to this nice, sweet, female American maid who hardly knows the difference between sodomy and rape, she is so pure and innocent! What did you mean, you depraved scoundrel, by seducing this pure, sweet girl of forty when you were all of twenty-four at the time, and should have been ashamed to rob this Broadway milkmaid of her fair virginity? Shame on you, you big country slicker, for coming here among these simple, trusting city bastards and wreaking your guilty passion upon this innocent, blushing bride before she had had scarcely twenty-five years' experience in the ways of love! Shame on you, you bloated plutocrat of a two-thousand-dollar-a-year instructor, for enticing her with your glittering gold, and luring her away from the simple joys she had always been accustomed to! When you met her she had scarcely three Pierce Arrows she could call her own—but she was happy in her innocent poverty," he sneered, "and content with the simple pleasures of the Jewish millionaires and the innocent adulteries of their wives!"

"You know I have never been like that," she said, with quivering indignation. "You know I've never gone with any of those people.

George, I know what I am like," she said proudly, "and your vile words and accusations cannot make me any different. I've worked hard, and been a decent person, and I have cared for what is good and beautiful all my life. I am a fine artist and I know my value," she said, in a proud and trembling voice, "and nothing that you say can change it."

"Done to you!" he said again, as though he had not heard her words. "You've wrecked my life and driven me mad, that's what I've done to you! You've sold me out to my enemies, and now they are sniggering at me behind my back!"

The foul words thickened in his throat and poured from his mouth in a flood of obscenity, his voice grew hoarse with violence and hate.

Outside, people were going along the street and he could hear them as they passed below his room. Suddenly someone laughed, the mirthless, harsh, and raucous laughter of the streets. The sound smote savagely upon his ears.

"Listen to them!" he cried insanely. "By God, they're laughing at me now!" He rushed to the window and shouted out: "Laugh! Laugh! Go on and laugh, you dirty swine! To hell with all of you! I'm free from you! No one can hurt me now!"

"No one is trying to hurt you, George," Esther said. "No one is your enemy but yourself. You are destroying yourself. There's something mad and evil in your brain. You must get it out or you are lost."

"Lost? Lost?" he repeated stupidly and numbly for a moment. Then: "Get out of here!" he screamed suddenly. "I know you now for what you are, and I hate you!"

"You don't know me and you have never known me," she said. "You want to hate me, you want to make me out a rotten woman, and you think you can make it so by speaking lying words. But I know what I am like and I am not ashamed of anything but that I should hear such words from you. I have been a good and decent person all my life, I have loved you more dearly than anyone in the world, I have been faithful to you, I have been your dear and loving friend, and now you are throwing away the best thing you have ever had. George, for God's sake, try to get this madness out of you. You have the greatest strength and the greatest beauty in your spirit of anyone I have ever known, and you have this mad and evil thing in you that is destroying you."

She paused, and for a moment he felt within his maddened brain a dim glow of returning reason, a dull, foul, depthless shame, a numb sense of hopeless regret, inexpiable guilt, irrevocable loss.

"What do you think it is?" he muttered.

"I don't know. I did not put it there. You've always had it since I met you. You are dashing yourself to pieces on it."

And suddenly she could control her trembling lips no longer, a cry of wild despair and grief burst from her throat, she smote herself fiercely with her clenched fist and burst into tears.

"O God! This thing has beaten me! I used to be so strong and brave! I was sure I could do anything, I was sure I could get this black thing out of you, but now I know I can't! I used to love life so, I saw glory and richness everywhere, it kept getting better all the time. Now, when I wake up I wonder how I can get through one more day. I hate my life, I have come to the end of things, I want to die."

He looked at her with a dull, lost stare. He passed his hand stupidly across his face, and for a moment it seemed that light and sanity were coming back into his eyes.

"Die?" he said dully. Then the flood of hate and darkness swept across his brain again. "Die! Then, die, die, *die!*" he said savagely.

"George," she said, in a tone of trembling and passionate entreaty, "we must not die. We were made to live. You must get this evil darkness from your soul. You must love life and hate this living death. George!" she cried again, her voice rising in a note of powerful conviction, "I tell you life is good and beautiful. George, believe what I say to you, because I have lived so much, I have known so many things, there is so much beauty and richness in me, and I will give it all to you. George, for God's sake help me, stretch out your hand to help me, and I will help you, and we will both be saved."

"Lies! Lies! Lies!" he muttered. "Everything I hear is lies."

"It is the living truth!" she cried. "So help me God, it's true!"

He paused, staring stupidly and dully for a moment. Then, with a flaring of mad hate again, he screamed at her:

"Why are you standing there? Get out of here! Get out! You have lied to me and cheated me, and you are trying to trick me now with words!"

She did not move.

"Get out! Get out!" he panted hoarsely.

She did not move.

"Get out, I say! Get out!" he whispered. He seized her savagely by the arm and began to pull her towards the door.

"George!" she said, "is this the end? Is all our love going to end like this? Don't you want ever to see me again?"

"Get out! Get out, I tell you! And never come back again!"

A long wailing note of despair and defeat broke from her lips.

"O God! I want to die!" she cried. Then she cast her arm back across her face and wept bitterly, hopelessly.

"Die! Die! Die, then!" he yelled, and, thrusting her brutally through the door, he slammed it after her.

38

The Years That the Locust Hath Eaten

OUTSIDE IN THE HALL IT WAS DARK, AND THERE WAS NOTHING BUT the sound of living silence in the house. Esther went down the old stairs that sagged and creaked, and she heard the sound of silence and of time. It spoke no words that she could hear, but it brooded from old, dark walls and mellow woods and the quiet depth and fullness of an ancient, structural, and liberal space. Its face was dark and imperturbable, and its heart, as the heart of the king, inscrutable, and in it was all the knowledge of countless obscure lives and forty thousand days, and all of the years that the locust hath eaten.

She stopped upon the stairs and waited and looked back at the closed door, and she hoped that it would open. But it did not open, and she went out into the street.

The street was full of young and tender sunlight. It fell like Spring and youth upon the old brick of the dingy buildings, and on all the hard violence of the city's life, and it gave life and joy and tenderness to everything. The streets were filled with their hard, untidy life, so swift, electric, and so angular, and so endless, rich, and various.

Some men with naked tattooed arms were loading boxes on a truck: they dug steel hooks into the clean white wood, and their muscles stood out like whipcord. Some children with dark faces and black Latin hair were playing baseball in the street. They nimbly snatched their game amid the thick flood of the traffic, they dodged among the wheels on strong, hard legs, they called and shouted hoarsely to one another, and the trucks and motors roared past in a single direction. And the people passed along the street in an unbroken stream, each driven to some known end, some prized or wished for consummation. Their flesh was dried and hardened by the city's shocks, their faces were dark and meager, believing in unbelief, and most unwise.

And suddenly Esther wanted to cry out to them, to speak to them, to tell them not to hurry, not to worry, not to care, and not to be afraid, that all their ugly labor, their hard thrust and push and violence, their bitter calculations for mean gains and victories, their petty certitudes and false assurances, were of no profit in the end. The rivers would run forever, and April would come as sweetly and as fairly and with as sharp a cry when all their strident tongues were stopped with dust. Yes! For all their bicker and the fever of their fierce uneasiness, she wanted to tell them that their cries would go unheard, their love would be misprized, their pain unnoticed, that the glory of the Spring would still shine calmly and with joy when all their flesh was rotten, and that other men some day on other pavements would think of them, of all their efforts and endurances, even of all their crimes and boasts of power, with pity and with condescension.

In the living light of April an old woman, a demented hag, poked, muttering, with a skinny finger into the rotting vegetation of a garbage can. Suddenly, she turned her withered face up to the sun, and bared her yellowed fangs of teeth, and shook her scrawny fist at heaven, and returned to her garbage can, and left it once again, holding her wrists together while tears streamed from her rheumy eyes, and she cried, "Misery! O Misery!" Then, the old hag stopped again, she drew her foul skirts up around her buttocks, she bared her flabby yellow thighs, and she danced, mincing and turning in a horrible parody of joy, cackling from the rag-end of an obscene memory. And still nobody noticed her except a slovenly policeman, who idly twirled his club as he surveyed her with hard eyes, above the brutal rumination of his gum-filled jaw, and a few young toughs who mocked at her. They smiled loose, brutal smiles, and smote each other in their merriment, and they cried out, "Jesus!"

And the people passed around her, some with a moment's look of shame and loathing, some with the bitter, puckered mouth of outraged decency, but for the most part with impatient brusqueness, their hard eyes fixed upon their moment's destiny. Then the old woman dropped her skirts, turned back again, returned, and shook her fist at passers-by, and no one noticed her, and she went back to her garbage can. The crone wept weakly, and the soft, living light of April fell upon her.

Esther passed before a hospital where an ambulance was waiting at the curb. The driver, his lean face tallowy, tough, and juiceless, stunned and dried, was bent above his wheel as his hard, drugged stare ate ravenously the contents of a tabloid newspaper:

"Love Pirates Make Whoopee in Love Nest"

" 'Heart-broken, Loved Him!' Helen Cries"

" 'Bigamy,' Sobs Dancer—Asks for Balm"

The brutal and sterile words leaped from the page to smite her as she passed with their foul, leering cheapness, evoking pictures of a life that was black, barren, idiot, and criminal in its empty violence, in which the name of love was mocked by lurid posturings, and in which even the act of murder had no horror.

Over all was the smell of blood and cheap perfumery. Here were the visages of all the human emotions:

Of passion—a vacant doll face and two fat, erotic calves.

Of crime—the flashlit stare of brutal faces and grey hats in the camera, the roadside motor car, the shattered glass.

Of love—"Honest, girlie, if I don't see you soon I'm goin' nuts. I'm mad about you, kid. I just can't get my lovin' baby off my mind. I see that sweet face of yours in my dreams, kid. Those lovin' kisses burn me up. Honest, kid, if I thought some other guy was goin' with you, I'd croak the both of you."

Of grief—a mother weeping for the photographer three hours after her child had burned to death.

She's dead.

"All right, Mrs. Moiphy, we want a shot of you now lookin' at the baby's shoes."

But she's dead.

"That's the stuff, momma. A little more expression, Mrs. Moiphy. Let's have the mother-love look, momma. Hold it!"

But she's dead.

"They'll be readin' about you tonight, momma. They'll be eatin' it up. We'll spread your map all over the front page, momma."

She's dead. She's dead.

Could it be true, then, that under the living and glorious light of these great skies, upon this proud, glittering, sea-flung isle, loaded to its lips with swarming life, the mistress of mighty ships and founded imperially among the flashing tides, among these furious streets and on this crowded rock which she had loved so well, and where she had found as much beauty, joy, and rich magnificence as any spot on earth could offer, that a monstrous race of living dead had grown up, so hateful, sterile, brutal in their senseless inhumanity that a man yet living could view them only with disgust and horror, and hope for their merciful and sudden extinction, with all the hideous life they had created, beneath the clean salt tides that swept around them? Had the city suckled at its iron breast a race of brute automatons, a stony, asphalt compost of inhuman manswarm ciphers, snarling their way to ungrieved deaths with the harsh expletives of sterile words, repeated endlessly, and as rootless of the earth, and all the blood and passion of a living man, as the great beetles of machinery they hurled at insane speed through the furious chaos of the streets?

No. She could not think that it was true. Upon this rock of life, and in these stupendous streets, there was as good earth as any that the foot could find to walk upon, as much passion, beauty, warmth, and living richness as any place on earth could show.

A young interne, jacketed in white, came out of the hospital, threw his bag loosely into the ambulance, spoke briefly to the driver, clambered up and sat down carelessly with his legs stretched out upon the other seat, and the car slid off smoothly through the traffic with a clangor of electric bells. The interne looked back lazily at the crowded street, and she knew that they would return with a dead or wounded man, one mangled atom or one pulsebeat less in the unnumbered desolations of the swarm, and the interne would go in to his interrupted lunch, and the driver would return with hunger to his paper.

Meanwhile and forever the bright tides of the rivers flowed about the isle of life. In the windows of wide-sheeted glass upon the first floor of the hospital, the babies sat up in their sunlit cots, the crisp, starched nurses bent above them, and the children stared into the furious streets with innocence and wonder, with delight and with no memory.

And upon the balconies above the street the men who had been sick and afraid of death now sat in sunlight, knowing they would live. They had recovered life and hope, and on their faces was the proud and foolish look of sick men who have felt the hand of death upon the bridles of their hearts, and who now, with a passive and uncertain faith, renew themselves. Their bodies looked shrunken in their dressing gowns, upon their starved, pale cheeks a furze of beard was growing, the young wind fanned their lank, un-vital hair, their jaws hung open, and with foolish, happy smiles they turned their faces towards the light. One smoked a cheap cigar, his thin hand took it slowly and unsteadily to his lips, he looked about and grinned. Another walked a few steps back and forth uncertainly. They were like children who have been born again, and there was something foolish, puzzled, and full of happiness in their look. They drew the air and light into them with a thin, fond greed, their enfeebled flesh, reft of the coarseness of its work and struggle, soaked in the solar energy. And sometimes the brisk nurses came and went, sometimes their kinsmen stood beside them awkwardly, dressed clumsily in the hard and decent clothes they saved for Sundays, holidays, and hospitals.

And, between the old red brick of two blank walls a slender tree, leaved with the poignant, piercing green of late April, looked over the boarding of a fence, and its loveliness among all the violence of the street, the mortared harshness of its steel and stone, was like a song, a triumph, and a prophecy—proud, lovely, slender, sudden, trembling— and like a cry with its strange music of man's bitter brevity upon the everlasting and immortal earth.

Esther saw these things and people in the street, and everything and all mistaken persons cried exultantly and fiercely for life; and in this she knew from her profoundest heart that they were not mistaken, and the tears were flowing down her face, because she loved life dearly, and because all the triumphant music, the power, the glory, and the singing of proud love grew old and came to dust.

39

Remorse

WHEN ESTHER HAD GONE, WHEN MONK HAD THRUST HER THROUGH the door and slammed it after her, his spirit was torn by a rending pity and a wild regret. And for a moment he stood in the bare center of the room, stunned with shame and hatred for his act and life.

He heard her pause upon the stairs, and he knew that she was waiting for him to come and grasp her by the hand and speak one word of love or friendship to her, and lead her back into the room again. And suddenly he felt an intolerable desire to go and get her, crush her in his embrace, lock her into his heart and life again, to take the glory and the grief together and to tell her, come what might, and be she fifteen, twenty, thirty years beyond his age, and grown grey and wrinkled as the witch of Endor, that she was sealed into his brain and heart so that he could love no one but her forever, and in this faith to live and die with a single and unfaltering affirmation. Then his pride fought stubbornly and wretchedly with regret and shame, he made no move to go to her, and presently he heard the street door close, and he knew that he had driven her into the street again.

And at the moment she had left the house, the aching, silent solitude of loneliness, for so many years before he met her the habit of his life, but now, so had she stolen his fierce secrecy away from him, a hateful and abhorrent enemy, settled upon his soul the palpable and chilling vacancy of isolation. It inhabited the walls, the timbers, and the profound and lonely silence of the ancient house. He knew that she had gone from him and left him in the house alone, and her absence filled his heart and filled the room like a living spirit.

He craned convulsively at his neck like a struggling animal, his mouth contracted in a grimace of twisted pain, and his foot was lifted sharply from the floor as if he had been struck hard upon the kidneys:

the images of wild and wordless pity and regret passed like a thin blade through his heart, a bestial cry was torn from his lips, he flung his arms out in a gesture of bewilderment and agony. Suddenly he began to snarl like a maddened animal, and savagely to smash his fist into the wall.

He could not find a tongue for his bewilderment, but he now felt with unutterable certitude the presence of a demon of perverse denial which was, and was everywhere, abroad throughout the universe, and at work forever in the hearts of men. It was the cunning, subtle cheat, the mocker of life, the scourger of time; and man, with the full glory and the tragic briefness of his days before him in his sight, bowed like a dull slave before the thief that looted him of all his joy, and held him sullen but submissive to its evil wizardry. He had seen and known its dark face everywhere. About him in the streets the legions of the living dead were swarming constantly: they stuffed themselves on straw and looked on glorious food with famished eyes of hunger and desire, and saw it ready to their touch, bursting from the great plantation of the earth the abundance of its golden harvest, and none would stretch forth his hand to take what had been given him, and all were stuffed with straw, and none would eat.

Oh, there would have been a solace for their foul defeat if they had striven fatally with an invincible and fatal destiny which tore life bleeding from their grip, and before whom now they desperately lay lead. But they were dying like a race of dull, stunned slaves, cringing upon a crust of bread before great trestles groaning with the food they wanted, and had not the courage to take. It was incredible, incredible, and it seemed to him as if there really was above these swarming hordes of men a malignant and ironic governor who moved them like the puppets in a ghastly comedy, mocking their impotence with vast illusions of a sterile power.

Did he belong, then, to this damned race of famished half-men who wanted food and had not courage to go beyond the husks, who sought for pleasure constantly and stained the night with the obscene glitter of a thousand·weary amusements, who longed for joy and comradeship and yet, with dull, deliberate intent, fouled their parties with horror, shame, and loathing every time they met? Did he belong to an accursed race which spoke of its defeat, and yet had never fought, which used its wealth to cultivate a jaded boredom, and yet had never had the strength or energy to earn satiety, and had not the courage to die?

Did he belong, then, to this set of meager slaves who feebly snarled their sterile way to death without the consummation of a single moment of hunger, grief, or love? Must he belong, then, to a fearful, fumbling race that twiddled its desire between its pallid fingers and furtively took its love round corners or in uneasy spasms on the distressful edges of a couch or, trembling, upon the rattling casters of a bed in a cheap hotel?

Must he be like them, forever furtive and forever cautious, in all things dull and trembling, and for what, for what? That youth might sicken and go sour, and turn with bitter discontent to grey and flabby middle age, and hate joy and love because it wanted them and was not brave enough to have them, and still be cautious, half-way, and withholding.

And for what? To save themselves for what? To save their wretched lives that they might lose them, to starve their wretched flesh that they might lie dead and rotten in their graves, to cheat, deny, and dupe themselves until the end.

He remembered the bitter and despairing accusation of Esther's cry: "You fool! You poor, mad fool! This is the finest thing that you will ever have, and you are throwing it away!"

And instantly the conviction came to him that she had told the truth. He had walked the streets by night, by day, in hundreds of hours long past and furiously accomplished, searching the faces of a million people to see if there was one who was as jolly, fresh, and fair as she, to see if there was one who had an atom of her loveliness, a glimmer of the glorious richness, joy, and noble beauty that showed in every act and visage of her life, and there was no one he had ever seen who could compare with her: they were all stale and lifeless by comparison.

Now the savage hatred he had felt when he had cursed her in their bitter quarrel was turned tenfold against himself, and against these people in the streets. For he felt that he had betrayed her love, turned on her, sold her out to the dull, timorous slaves, and in so doing, that he had betrayed life and sold it out to barren death.

She had said to him with passionate indignation and entreaty: "What do you think it's been about if I don't love you? Why do you think I've come here day by day, cooked for you, cleaned up after you, listened to your insults and vile abuse, left my work, given up my friends, kept after you and wouldn't let you go when you tried to throw me over, if it wasn't because I love you?"

Oh, she had told the truth, the naked, literal truth. For what purpose, what crafty, deep, and scheming purpose, had this woman poured upon him for three years the lavish bounty of her love and tenderness? Why had she lived ten thousand hours alone with him, leaving the luxury and the beauty of her home for the cyclonic chaos, of his poor dwelling?

He looked about him. Why had she come daily into the mad confusion of this big room in which it always seemed, no matter what patient efforts she made to keep it tidy, that the tumult and fury of his spirit had struck all things like lightning, so that everything— books, shirts, collars, neckties, socks, stained coffee cups half filled with sodden butts, post cards, letters five years old and laundry bills, student themes and tottering piles of his own manuscript, note books, a ragged hat, the leg of a pair of drawers, a pair of shoes with dried, cracked leather, no heels, and two gaping holes upon their bottoms, the Bible, Burton, Coleridge, Donne, Catullus, Heine, Spenser, Joyce, and Swift, a dozen fat anthologies of every kind, plays, poems, essays, stories, and the old, worn, battered face of *Webster's Dictionary*, piled up precariously or strewn in a pell-mell circle round his cot, covered with ashes, hurled face downward on the floor before he slept—was a cyclonic compost of the dust and lumber of the last ten years. Here were scraps, fragments, and mementoes of his wandering in many countries, none of which he could destroy, most of which filled him with weariness when he looked at it, and all of which seemed to have been hurled in this incredible confusion with the force of an explosion.

Why had this elegant and dainty woman come daily into the wild disorder of this mad place? What had she hoped to get from him that she had clung to him, loved him, lavished her inexhaustible tenderness upon him, stuck to him in the face of all the rebuffs, injuries, and insults he had heaped upon her, with all the energy of her indomitable will?

Yes—why, why? With a cold, mounting fury of self-loathing, he asked himself the questions. What was her deep and scheming plot? Where was the cunning treachery that had maddened him with a thousand poisonous suspicions? Where was the subtle trap that she had laid for him? What was the treasure that she coveted, the priceless possession which she planned to steal away from him, and which was the end and purpose of all these snares of love?

What was it now? Was it his great wealth and high position in society? Was it his proud title as instructor in an immense and swarming factory of the brain, the noble honor he shared with eighteen hundred fearful, embittered, and sterile little men? Was it his rare culture, the distinguished ability required to speak to jaded typists and swart, ill-smelling youths with raucous voices of "the larger values," "the liberal outlook," "the saner, deeper, and more comprehensive point of view"? Was it the delicate and sympathetic perception required to see the true beauty of their sullen, stunned, and inert minds, the jewels buried in the dreary illiteracy of their compositions, the thrills and ardors pulsing in "The Most Exciting Moment of My Life," or the simple, rich, and moving truths of "My Last Year at Erasmus High"?

Or was it, now, the elegance of his person, the fastidiousness of his costume, the tender and winning charm of his address, the rare beauty of his form and countenance, that had enchanted her? Was it the graceful and yet nonchalant dignity with which his knees and buttocks dignified these fine old kangaroo bags, through which, 'twas true, his hindward charms gleamed an unearthly white, but which he wore, withal, with what fashionable distinction, with what assured and easy poise? Was it the stylish ease with which he wore his coat, the elegant "three button sack," of which the lower two were missing, and which was dashingly festooned with remnants of last year's steak and gravy? Or was it the ungainly body that urchins gibed at in the streets, the bounding and lunging stride, the heavy, slouching shoulders, the gangling arms, the shock of unkempt hair, the face too small and the legs too short for the barrel-like structure of the body, the out-thrust head, the bulging underlip, the dark and upward-peering scowl? Were these the charms that had caught the lady's fancy?

Or was it something else she prized—something finer, nobler, deeper? Was it for the great beauty of his soul, the power and richness of his "talent"? Was it because he was a "writer"? The word blazed in his consciousness for a moment, making him writhe with a convulsive shame and evoking a cruel picture of futility, despair, and shoddy pretense. And suddenly he saw himself as a member of the whole vast shabby army he despised: the pale, futile yearners of the arts, the obscure and sensitive youths who thought their souls too fine, their feelings too delicate and subtle, their talents too rare and exquisite for the coarse and vulgar apprehension of the earth.

For ten years he had known them, he had heard their words, and seen their puny arrogance, and become familiar with all their feeble attitudes and mimicries, and they had sickened his bowels with hopeless impotence, stunned his heart with a grey horror of unbelief and desolate futility. And now, in a single moment of blinding shame, they returned to mock him with appalling revelation. Pale, sterile, feeble, and embittered, they came—a myriad horde—gnawing the nail of rankling discontent, scowling the venom of their misprized talents, sneering with envious contempt against the abilities and accomplishments of stronger and more gifted men than they, and unconfidently solaced by a vague belief in talents which they did not own, drugged feebly by cloudy designs for a work which they would never consummate. He saw them all—the enervate rhapsodists of jazz, the comic strip, and primitive Apollos, Wastelanders, Humanists, Expressionists, Surrealists, Neo-primitives, and Literary Communists.

The words of fraudulent pretense that he had heard them speak a thousand times came back to him, and suddenly it seemed to him they uttered a final judgment on his own life, too. Had he not scowled and glowered gloomily, whined at the lack of this, the want of that, the intrusion of some shackling obstacle that kept his genius from its full fruition? Had he not bewailed the absence of some earthly heaven in whose unpolluted ethers his rare soul could wing its way triumphantly to great labors? Was not the sun of this base, stinking earth too hot, the wind too cold, the shifting weathers of the seasons too rude and variable for the tender uses of his sweet, fair hide? Were not the bitter world he lived in and the men he knew given to base gain and sordid purposes? Was it not a barren, sordid, ugly world in which the artist's spirit withered and went dead, and if he changed his skies—oh! if he could only change his skies!—would he not change his soul, as well? Would he not flower and blossom in the living light of Italy, grow great in Germany, bloom like the rose in gentle France, find roots and richness in old England, and utterly fulfill his purposes if he, too, like an æsthetic exile from Kansas whom he had met in Paris, could only "go to Spain to do a little writing"?

For months and years had he not fumbled, fiddled, faltered, and pretended, just as they? Had he not cursed at a world that paid no tribute to his unsuspected talents, eaten his flesh in bitterness, sneered and mocked at the work of better men, looked out the window, fumbled, and scowled, and fiddled—and what had he done? Written a book that nobody would publish!

And she, who was the fine, rare artist, the rich, delicate, and certain talent, the person who knew and was sure and had power, the one who worked, created, and produced, had endured it all, cared for him, excused his indolence, and believed in him. During all this time while he had cursed and grumbled at the hardship of his life, coddled his whims, whined that he could do no writing for himself because of his exhausting labors at the school, the woman had done the labor of a titan. She had run her household, governed her family, planned and built a new house in the country, been chief designer for a clothing manufacturer, and constantly improved and strengthened herself in her art, making designs and costumes for thirty plays, doing a day's work in the morning while he slept, and yet having energy and time left over to come to his place and cook, and spend eight hours a day together with him.

This sudden perception of Esther's indomitable courage and energy, her power to work, and her balanced control over all the decisive acts and moments of her life, in contrast to the waste, confusion, and uncertainty of his own, smote him a hammer-blow of shame and self-contempt. And, as if in mute evidence of the contrast, the divided character of the room was suddenly revealed to him. While the part that he inhabited was struck with a cyclonic chaos, the corner by the window where Esther worked and had her table was trim, spare, certain, alert and orderly, and ready instantly for work. Upon the white, clean boards of the table were fastened the crisp sheets of drawing paper covered with the designs that she had made for costumes, each of which was so alive with a brave and jaunty energy, with a delicate and incisive certainty, that they lived instantly, not only with all her own sure talent, but with the lives of all the characters they were designed to clothe. And, right and left, the instruments and materials she loved so well and could use with such sure magic were arranged and ready for her instant touch. There were the tubes and boxes of paint, the fine brushes, the sliding rule, the gleaming compass, and the long, neatly-sharpened pencils, and behind the table, hanging from nails driven in the walls, were the T-square, the yard measure, and the triangle.

And now each thing that she had touched and owned, each vestige of her life within that room, cried out against him with passionate tongue the judgment of an intolerable regret. In their living stillness these things were more inexorable and swift than the black rout of the avenging furies that ever once through dark and fatal skies impended on the driven figure of a man, more eloquent than the trumpet blast of an accusing vengeance. And their mute and scattered presence there evoked a picture of her life more whole and final than the minute chronicle of twenty thousand days, for it ran like a thread of gold back through the furious confusions of time and cities, and bound her to the strange lost world that he had never known.

His mind, now goaded by an intolerable desire to know her, see her, have and own her, to mine her life up bit by bit out of the depthless pit of time and the furious oblivion of the city's life, and to join it, root and branch with all the fibrous tendrils of everything that she had seen and known and touched, to his own, prowled beastwise back across the jungle of the past, scenting the final limits and last implications of every casual word, each story, scene, or moment, each sight or sound or odor he had torn from her in three years with his tireless and insatiate hunger. He wove the web like a terrific spider until two earths, two lives, two destinies as far and separate as any under sun could be, were woven to their jointure by the dark miracle of chance.

Hers, the streets of life, the manswarm passing in its furious weft, the tumult of great cities, the thunder of the hooves and wheels upon the cobbles, and the solid façades of dark, lavish brown.

His, the lives of secret men who lived alone, and who had seen cloud shadows passing in the massed green of the wilderness for two hundred years, and whose buried bones were pointing ninety ways across the continent.

For her, the memory of great names and faces, the flashing stir and thrust of crowds, the shout of noonday in exultant cities, the stamp of the marching men and great parades, the hard cry of the children playing in the streets, and men who leaned at evenings quietly on the sills of old dark brown.

For him, the great winds howling in the hills at night, the creaking of stiff boughs in Winter wind, and the great empurpled hills that faded faint and far into the edges of a limitless desire, the sound of a bell, wind-broken, the whistle cry that wailed away into blue gates and passes of the North and West.

For her, forgotten fume-flaws of bright smoke above Manhattan.

and the proud cleavages of ships, and the sea-flung city masted to its lips with trade and voyages. For her, suave silks and creamy linens, old dark woods, the wink of mellow wines and heavy, ancient silvers, the dainty succulence of rare foods and cookery, the velvet backs and proud-groomed undulance of luxurious beauty, the ornate masks and gestures of the actors' faces, and the lost burial of their eyes.

For him, the lamplight in a close and shuttered Winter room, the smell of camphor and of apples, the flare and crumble of the ash there in the grate, and the ash of time in Aunt Maw's voice, that death-triumphant Joyner voice, drawling of death and sorrow, the sin and shame of his father's life, and phantoms of lost Joyner kinsmen back in the hills a hundred years ago.

Even while all those elements of fire and earth of which he was compacted coursed unresolved in the wild blood from which he sprang, she paced, a child, along the city streets. Even while he stared within his mother's flesh, she was an adolescent girl, orphaned of love, knowledged in grief and loss and bitterness, and strong in hopeful fortitude. Even while he, a boy of twelve, lay on the grass before his uncle's house and dreamed his dreams, she lay, a woman ripe in love and loveliness, in the embraces of a husband. And even while, a youth, he saw afar the glorious towers of the fabled city, and felt along his loins the joy and certitude of all the glory, love, and power that he would win there, she was a woman seated at the heart of power, freed from confusion, and certain of her talent and her strength.

Thus did his memory shuttle back and forth across the skeins of chance until it wove the jointure of their lives together.

And, finally, he saw this brave and faithful spirit which was so certain of its strength, so sure of its power to make its life prevail, faced for the first time by the thing it could not meet or conquer, and fighting wildly, with a desperate and pitiable fury, as if against some intolerable personal injustice, against the common and invincible enemy of mankind—the passing of youth, the loss of love, the coming of old age and weariness and completion. This final, brutal necessity that put the mark of its possession upon the lives of all men living was the thing she would not accept, and that could nowhere be escaped or denied. She was dashing her life against its iron face. Inexorable and wordless, it was present in all the desperate and ugly war that had been waged between them, it stood outside them, waiting while they fought, and it bore the terrible judgment of the clock, the stayless doom of time. It was silent before their words of bitter injury and reproach, silent before love, hatred, faith, and unbelief alike, and its face was grim, immovable, and final.

She would not yield to it, nor admit the justice of the fate it spoke. She shook her fist into the face of iron destiny. And as he saw the desperate and useless struggle, his heart was torn with a wild regret and pity for her, for he knew that she was right, no matter how inexorable or general the fate she shared with all the earth. He knew that she was right, and would be right if she went to her grave with a curse of wild denial on her lips, because such beauty, courage, love, and youth, and strength as she had known should not grow old, and should never die, and that truth was with her, no matter how inevitable the triumph of this all-devouring, all-victorious enemy.

And as he saw the way it was, there came to him an image of man's whole life upon the earth. It seemed to him that all man's life was like a tiny spurt of flame that blazed out briefly in an illimitable and terrifying darkness, and that all man's grandeur, tragic dignity, his heroic glory came from the brevity and smallness of this flame, and that he knew his light was little and would be extinguished, and that only darkness was immense and everlasting, and that he died with defiance on his lips, and that the shout of his hatred and denial rang with the last pulsing of his heart into the maw of all-engulfing night.

And now again the foul, intolerable shame returned to sicken him with hatred of his life, for it seemed to him that he had betrayed the only faithful, strong, and certain thing that he had ever known. And in betraying it, it seemed to him that he had not only dishonored life, spat in the face of love, and sold out the person who had loved him to the hateful legions of rat's alley where the dead men lived, but that he had also betrayed himself and bargained with the dead for his own ruin and defeat. For, if his heart was poisoned at its sources, his brain warped and twisted by its madness, his life polluted and brought to naught, what enemy had worked this evil on him but himself?

Men have their visions from afar and in a lonely place, and the great vision of this earth and all her power and glory has ever had the city at its end. So it had been with him. He had come to the city as young men come, with joy and hope, with certain faith, and with the conviction he had power to make his life prevail. He had possessed the strength, the faith, the talent to do all things if he had played the man and kept the same heart, the same courage and belief, that he had had within him as a child. And had he used his life well and bravely to this purpose? No. Instead, he had spat upon the glory that was given him, betrayed love, and like a whining slave had miserably sold his life into the hands of other slaves, until now, like them, he jeered at his own vision as the day-dream of a yokel, and gave to the passion and belief of youth the fool's mockery of a false, inept, and mirthless laughter.

And for what? For what? He had spoken to her of the "shame" he felt because of her. For what other thing should he feel a second's shame save for the foul insult and injury he had heaped upon the one who loved him, whom he loved? Feel shame! Great God! Before what—or whom? Must he then bow his head and hurry past below the stare of all the grey-faced ciphers in the street?

They say! *They* say! *They! They! They!* And who were *they* that he should strain his ears to hear them in the streets or care the tail-end of a tinker's curse for all their bastardly gentility? *They! They!* Who were *they* that he should sell out the grand woman, the fine artist, and the true aristocrat to any vulgar little slut or snob that aped or swanked its way through the cheap perfumery of a fraudulent society? Feel shame! Apologize! To whom! Good God, must he slink by below the thoroughbred disdain of fine old country-club Princetonians, cringe below the scornful nostrils of high-mettled Junior Leaguers, endure with flaming face the amused, distasteful glances of young princelings of the Harvard Club, cringe and slink it when he faced the noble-blooded heirs of Hayes and Garfield scoundrels who scarcely yet had breathed the sweat and horse-p—s knavery of their fathers from their nostrils? Or squirm, great God, before the amused, ironic glances of a Saturday Reviewer, the fine old culture of the Dekes and Betas, or the snickering whispers and sly nudges of the pale sucks and crawling worms at the School for Utility Cultures?

They! They! And who were *they?* The apes and rats and parrots of the earth without the courage of their own disbelief, the puny pavement cynics who winked and leered with knowing smirk their little hearsay filth. *They!* The feeble little city yokels who sneered and mocked and jingled in their pockets the cheap coin of their stale pick-me-up scurrilities. *They!* The wretched and impotent little in-structors at the School for Utility Cultures, the tenth-rate literary triflers who had no heart or courage for avowal, for any living passion, mercy, love, or strong belief whatever, whose mouths were filled with ugly slanders, and who could be gay and gaudy on a thimble's measure of bad gin, snickering and whispering over some rag of gossip about a lesbic actress, a pederastic poet, or the unclean rumor that hovered about a celebrity they would have swallowed dung to meet.

They! They! Why, how was he any better than any damned dull slave who winked and nodded it with knowing leer and ravenously gulped down the lies and slop a shrewder knave had thrown together for him, saying: "Sure, *I* know! *I* know! You're telling *me*! . . . *I* know! You know how it is, don't you? . . . Nah-h!"—when the poor fool had been blind and ignorant from his birth?

Yes, he had winced and faltered in the stare of men like these, and yet his fathers were great men, and had known the wilderness, and had winced and faltered in the stare of no one. And had their spirit died upon the earth? Suddenly he knew that it had not. He saw that it lived in the very air around him, and he knew it still belonged to the fabric of man's life, as real and living as it ever was.

Had not ten million men before him brought their strength and talents and all the golden legendry of their youth into the city? Had they not heard the accursed clatter of their feet upon the metal stairs, the entrance tilings, and seen the hard, dead eyes and heard the cold and loveless greetings of the men from whom they bought the refuge of their little cells? Had they not with hearts of fire, with the burning hunger of their savage loneliness, hurled themselves out of these little cells into the streets again? Wild-eyed and desperate, mad of brain, had they not coursed the terrible streets in which there was neither curve nor pause nor any place that they might enter, and searched the myriad faces with a desperate hope, and then returned into their little cells, mocked by the city's terrible illusions of abundance and variety, and by the cruel enigma of man's loneliness among eight million, his poverty and desolation at the seat of a stupendous power and wealth?

Had they not cursed in the darkness of their little rooms at night, and ripped the sheets between convulsive fingers, beat their fists against the wall? Had they not seen a thousand insults to the living in the streets of night, and smelled the foul stench of a brutal privilege, seen the leer of a criminal authority, the smirk of a corrupt and indifferent power, and had they not grown mad with shame and horror?

And yet all did not grow grey of heart or dead of eye, or wearily ape the gabble of the dead. All did not madden desperately to defeat. For some had seen the city's stupefying and unnumbered cruelty, and lived upon their hate of it, and not grown cruel. Some had drawn mercy from the cobblestones, found love within a little room, and all the living richness of the earth and April in the furious clamors of a street. And some had struck the city's stony heart and brought forth lucent water, and wrung out of her iron breast the grandest music that the earth has known. They had bloodily learned the secret of her stern soul, and with the power and passion of their lives won from her what they sought in youth.

Were there not still men who strode with confidence the streets of life, knew fortitude and danger and endurance in their daily work, and yet leaned with calm eyes at evening on their window sills? Were there not men who in the rush and glare of furious noon thickened the air with strong, hoarse curses from the seats of trucks, sat with gloved hands of cunning on the throttle, looked with a glint of demon hawk-eyes on the rails, lifted their voices in command to swarthy, sweating laborers, men who drank, fought, whored, and fed stupendously, and yet were brave and gentle in their hearts, filled with the warm blood and the liberal passion of living men?

And as he thought of them, the earth was living with the brave presences of men and women who had torn joy and passion strongly from the earth, just as now the whole of his big room was living with the life of Esther. The memory of her small and bitterly wounded face, stricken with the surprise and grief of a child whose gaiety and affection has been killed suddenly by a blow, returned to twist into his heart its merciless and avenging blade.

But now his life was so caught up and whirled about in this wild dance of madness and despair, of love, hatred, faith, and disbelief, of a savage jealousy and a despairing penitence, that he no longer knew what justice or what falseness rested in his curse or prayer or self-reproach, or whether he was mad or sane, or if his life and sinew had been seduced and rotted by an evil thing, or fed and nourished by a good one. At the end he only knew that, true, false, fair, foul, young, old, good, evil, or anything he thought whatever, she was rooted in the fabric of his life and he must have her.

He struck his fist into his face, a wild and wordless cry was torn from his throat, and he rushed from his room and from the house, out in the street to find her.

40

Pursuit and Capture

ALL AT ONCE SHE SAW HIS APELIKE SHADOW MOVING ON THE PAVEMENT. In firm young sunlight it came bounding after her, the body and the long arms prowling, the legs leaping high in their strange stride, and her heart was twisted suddenly and beat hard with pain and joy. But she did not turn to look at him, she lowered her face stubbornly and went on faster as if she did not see him, and the shadow bounded after her, came up beside her, walked abreast of her, and still she did not look at him, and he did not speak.

At length he seized her by the arm and, in a voice surly with shame and obstinacy, said:

"What's wrong with you now? Where are you going? What the hell's the trouble now?"

"You told me to go," she said with offended dignity, and she tried to pull her arm away. "You told me to leave you and never to come back again. You drove me out. You're the one."

"Come back," he said with sullen shame, and stood still as though to turn her around and head her back down the street.

She jerked her arm away from him and walked on. Her lip was trembling and she did not speak.

He stood a moment looking at her retreating figure, and in his mounting shame and baffled rage the old black fury rose up in him suddenly and he bounded after her, yelling frantically:

"Come back! Come back, God-damn it! Don't disgrace me in the streets!" He seized her arm again and roared: "Don't bawl! I beg and beseech you not to bawl!" he shouted.

"I'm not bawling!" she said. "I'm not disgracing you! You're the one!"

Some people had stopped to stare at them, and when he noticed them, he turned on them savagely and snarled:

580

"It's no business of yours, you leering swine! What are you looking at?"

Then, turning towards her small form menacingly, he said in a hoarse voice and with a contorted face:

"You see, don't you? You see what you've done! They're looking at us! Great God, they're lapping it up—you can see them lick their filthy chops about it! And you enjoy it!" he shouted. "You love it! Anything, by God, so long as you attract attention! Anything to degrade, ruin, and humiliate me!"

He had her by the arm, and he now began to pull her back along the street so fast she had to run to keep up with him.

"Come on!" he said in a frantic and entreating tone. "Come on, for God's sake! You're ruining me! Please come on!"

"I'm coming. I'm coming," she said, and the tears were running down her face. "You said you didn't want me any more."

"That's right"—he said—"cry! Boo-hoo! Weep your glycerine tears!"

"No. They are real tears," she said with dignity.

"Oh, glub-glub! Oh, gul-lup, gul-lup! Woe is me! Oi yoi yoi! Play to the crowd! Get their sympathy!"

Suddenly he burst into a wild, mad laugh, and, turning, shouted into the street loudly, waving his arms meanwhile in beckoning gestures:

"All right, boys! Step right up! We will now witness a very high-class performance by one of our best art-theatre actresses, only a nickel, five cents, the twentieth part of a dollar!"

He paused, glancing at her for a moment, and then he cried out bitterly:

"All right! You win! I'm no match for you!"

"I'm not playing to any crowd," she said. "You're the one!"

"With her nice, damned, delicate little rosy face! Is this another of your tricks? Out here on the street, and letting the tears trickle down your pure, sweet, womanly face!"

"You're the one!" she said. She stopped suddenly and looked at him, her face flushed, her rosy lip curling, and then said in a quiet and scornful voice, as if pronouncing the most insulting judgment she knew: "Do you know what you're acting like? Well, I'll tell you. You're acting like a Christian, that's what you're acting like!"

"And you're acting like a Jew! A damned, crafty Jezebel of a Jew! That's what you're acting like!"

"That's all right about the Jews," she said. "We're too good for you, that's all. You know nothing about us, and you will never be able in your vile, low soul to understand what we are like as long as you live."

"Understand!" he cried. "Oh, I understand enough! You're not so damned wonderful and mysterious as you think! So we're too vile and low to understand how noble and great you are, are we? Tell me, then," he cried in an excited and combative tone, "if we're so low as you say we are, why don't you stick to your own race? Why is it that every damned one of you is out to get a Christian if you can? Will you tell me that? Hey?"

In the excitement of a fresh dispute they had paused again, and now faced each other in the middle of the sidewalk with red, angry faces, oblivious of all the people who passed around them.

"No. No," she said strongly, in a protesting tone. "You can't say that. That's not true, and you know it's not!"

"Not true," he cried, with a wild, exasperated laugh as he struck his forehead with his palm and made a gesture of imploring supplication heavenward. "Not true! My God, woman, how can you stand there and look me in the face when you say it? You know it's true! Why, every God-damned one of you, man or woman, will crawl upon your hands and knees—yes!—creep and crawl and contrive until you have a Gentile in your clutches! . . . Jesus God! That it should come to this!" and he laughed bitterly and madly.

"That it should come to what?" she said, with an angry laugh. "God, but you're crazy! You don't know what you're saying half the time. You open your mouth and it just comes out!"

"Answer me!" he said hoarsely. "Isn't it the truth? You know God-damn well it's the truth!"

"I'm going now!" she cried, in a high, excited voice. "You're beginning again! I told you I wouldn't listen to your vileness any longer!" And she wrenched her arm out of his grasp and began to walk away, with a flaming, angry face.

He followed her instantly, and stopped her, clasping her hand warmly and firmly between his own, and speaking to her in a low, entreating voice.

"Oh, come on!" he said, ashamed of himself and trying to laugh it off. "Come on back with me! I didn't mean it. Don't you see I didn't mean it? Don't you know I was only joking? Don't you see that was all it was?" he said urgently, and again he tried to pass it off with a hearty laugh that rang hollowly in the street.

"Yes! A fine joker you are!" she said scornfully. "Your idea of a joke would be to see somebody break his neck! That's the kind of joke you'd like! . . . I know! I know!" she continued, almost hysterical in her excitement. "You don't need to tell me. You're always reviling us. You couldn't see the truth about us anyway, you hate us so!"

He stared thickly and blindly at her for a moment with bloodshot eyes, in which the fires of love and hate, of conviction and mistrust, of sanity and madness, flared instantly together in one joined flame, and behind which his spirit looked out silently, like something trapped and baffled, desperate, haggard, and bewildered. Suddenly her face shone clearly in his vision, and he saw it, small and flushed and wounded bitterly, at the same instant that he heard her words of resentful indignation.

And then, with a returning sense of his unforgivable injustice, he realized that she had spoken the truth, and that in the furious excess of his exasperation and vituperative bitterness he had said things he had not meant to say, used words the way one uses a murderous weapon, with the sole intent to wound her, words which he could not now unsay or ever atone for. And again a wave of intolerable shame overwhelmed him, and the desperation of defeat now filled his heart. It seemed he was so entirely in the grip of this madness that he could not for five minutes control a sure and certain impulse. The very impulse which had driven him into the streets to find her, the impulse of passionate regret and faith and strong conviction, had been forgotten with the first words that he spoke to her, and again he had fouled himself and her with a vile, choking glut of filthy insult and abuse.

And now, ashamed to look into her face, he looked instead into the street, and saw it plainly as it was—harsh and angular with its chaotic architectures, the raw, prognathous fronts of its new buildings, the grimed dinginess of its old ones, the lumpy copings, the rusty fire escapes, the grimy warehouses, and the occasional glow and richness of old red brick and calmer time. It was simply an American street, he had seen its like a thousand times, and it had no curve nor stay nor pause in it, nor any planned coherence.

They had paused beneath a slender tree, one of the few along the street; it grew up from a lonely scrap of earth wedged in between an old brick house and the grey pavement; and through young boughs, now leaved with the first smoky green of the year, the sun cast a net of dancing spangles on the wide brim of Esther's hat and the rich green of the dress she wore, swarming in moths of golden light upon her straight, small shoulders. Her face, now flaming with her hurt, looked out like a strange and lovely flower below her hat, and it had the mingled looks he had seen in it ten thousand times—the straight, proud, faithful look of children, and their grieved, bewildered innocence; and all the dark opulence of the women of her race.

And as he looked at her, his entrails stirred with tenderness, with the desire to hold her gently and caress her. Slowly he moved his hand until he touched hers with his fingertips, and softly said:

"No, Esther, I don't hate you. I love you better than my life."

Then, arm in arm, they turned and went back to his room again. And everything was with them as it always was.

41

The Weaver at Work Again

MONK LEANED STIFFLY, LEGS APART, AND WITH HIS BACK TO ESTHER. HIS weight was supported on his extended arms and the palms of his hands, which rested on the ledge of sun-warm stone outside the window. With his head out-thrust, half-sunken in his shoulder blades, he glowered right and left along the street. The delicate lights of April passed over his head and shoulders, a breeze fanned past him from the street, and behind him, on the wall, the sheets of tracing paper rattled crisply. It was another day.

Frowning, and slipping her finger rapidly in and out of the old ring she wore—a gesture habitual to her in moments of nervousness, impatience, and serious meditation or decision—Esther looked at him with a faint, bitter smile, a feeling of tenderness and anger and a scornful humor.

"Now," she thought, "I know exactly what he's thinking. There are still a few things in the universe which have not been arranged to suit his pleasure, so he wants to see them changed. And his desires are modest, aren't they? *Very!*" she thought bitterly. "All he wants is to eat his cake and keep on having it forever. He's tired of me and he wishes I would go away and leave him here alone to contemplate his navel. He also wishes I would stay here with him. I am the one he loves, his jolly little Jew that he adores and could devour, and I am also the evil wench who lies in wait for unsuspecting country boys. I am the joy and glory of his life, and I am also the sinister and corrupt harpy who has been employed by the forces of darkness to kill and destroy his life. And why? Why, because he is so innocent and pure— God! Could anyone believe it if they heard it!—and all the rotten people who hate life are staying up at night plotting how to wreck and ruin him. The Jews hate the Christians, and they also love them. The Jewish women seduce the pure young Christian boys because they love

594

them and want to destroy them, and the Jewish men, cynical and re-signed, look on and rub their hands in glee because they hate the Christians and also love them, too, and want to destroy them because they love to see them suffer, but really adore them because they feel such sympathy and pity for them, and yet say nothing because they get an obscene sexual satisfaction from the spectacle, and because their souls are old and patient, and they have known that their women were un-faithful for seven thousand years, and they must suffer and endure it! Weave! Weave! Weave! He weaves it day and night out of his crazy and tormented brain until not even Einstein could make head or tail of it—and yet he thinks it all as plain and clear as day! The Jews are the most generous and liberal people on earth, and have the most wonder-ful food upon their tables, but when they invite you to eat it, they wait until it gets halfway down your throat and you have a look of pleasure on your face, and then they say something cruel and cunning to you in order to make you lose your appetite."

And touched again by the old and worldly humor of her race, she smiled with an ironic expression as she thought: "Lose your appetite! It's just too bad the way you lose *your* appetite! I've been cooking for you three years now, young fellow, and the only time I've ever seen you lose your appetite was when you couldn't lift another forkful to your mouth! Lose his appetite! God! The nerve of that fellow! When I've seen him eat until his eyes were glazed and stuck out of his head, and all he could do for three hours after when I spoke to him was grunt like a pig! Yes! And even when you came to see us all—these horrible people that you say we are—you lost your appetite, didn't you? God, will I ever forget the night he came in when we were at dinner and he said: 'No, not a thing! Not a thing! I just finished a big dinner at the Blue Ribbon and I couldn't touch a bite. . . . Well,' he says, 'I think I will take just a cup of coffee, if you don't mind. I'll drink it while the rest of you are eating.' A cup of *coffee*! It is to laugh! Three heaping plates full of my meat balls, a whole dish of asparagus, a bowl of salad—you cleaned out all that was left in the big salad bowl—you can't deny it—two helpings of Cookie's apple dumplings—and *coffee*! My God, he never thought of coffee till he'd finished! A bottle of Fritz's best St. Julien, that's what you had, my boy, as well you know— 'I don't mind if I do take a glass, Fritz'—and one of his best cigars, and two glasses of his oldest brandy! A cup of *coffee*! That was your cup of coffee! God! We all laughed our heads off at what Alma said when he had gone. 'Mother, if that's his notion of a cup of coffee, I'm glad he didn't feel like having a ham sandwich, too.' And even Fritz said, 'Yes, it's lucky for us that he wasn't hungry. I understand the crops are not so good this year as they were last.' We simply roared about that cup of coffee! Not that any of us begrudged it to you! As cruel and unjust as you have been, you can't say that about us. That kind of smallness and meanness is the thing you Christians do."

She looked at him, the trace of an ironic smile upon her lips.

"Your cup of coffee! Oh, don't worry about that, my lad! You'll get your cup of coffee, sure enough! Just wait till you are married to some anæmic little Christian girl—she'll get your cup of coffee for you. Christian coffee! Two grains of coffee in a bucketful of stale dish water! That's the kind of coffee that you'll get! Yes! Who'll feed you then? Who'll cook for you?"

She pondered with a faint, bitter smile.

"Some little goy with a hank of yellow hair, the hips of a washboard, and the eyes of a drowned cat. . . . I know now what she'll give you. I can see it! Oxtail soup out of a can with all the ox left out of it, picked-up codfish with a gob of that horrible, white, gooey, Christian sauce, a slice of gluten bread, acidophilus milk, and a piece of stale angel cake that the little wench picked up at a bakery on her way home from the movies. 'Come, Georgie, darling! Be a nice boy now. You haven't eaten any of your good boiled spinach, dear. It's good for you, pet, it's full of nice, healthy iron. (Healthy iron, your granny! In three months' time he'll turn green with belly-ache and dyspepsia. . . . You'll think of me every time you take another bite!) No, you bad boy! You can't have any more creamed chipped beef. You've already had meat three times this month, you've had six and three-eighths ounces of meat in the last three weeks dear, and it's very bad for you. You'll be getting uric acid the first thing you know. If you're a good boy, pet, I'll let you have a nice, burned-up lamb chop week after next. I've got the most delicious menu all fixed up for the next two weeks. I read all about it in Molly Messmore's Food Hints in *The Daily Curse*. Oh, yum! yum! yum! Your mouth will water, all right, when you see what I've prepared for you, dear. (Yes, and if I know anything about him, his eyes will water, too!) Next week is going to be Fish Week, darling. We're going to have nothing but fish, pet, won't that be nice? (Oh yes! That will be just too nice for words.) Molly says fish is good for you, lamb, the body needs lots of fish, it's Brain Food, pet, and if my big boy is

going to use that great big wonderful brain of his and think all those
beautiful thoughts, he's got to be a good boy and eat lots of fish like
his momma tells him to. Monday, darling, we are going to have im
ported Hungarian catfish with henhouse noodles, and Tuesday, pet, we
are going to have roast Long Island suckers with gastric juice, and
Wednesday, love, we are going to have stewed, milkfed bloaters à la
Gorgonzola with stinkweed salad, and Thursday, sweet, we are going
to have creamed cod with chitling gravy, and Friday—Friday is really
Fish Day, lamb, Friday we are going— You bad boy! You take that
ugly *fwown* wight off your face! I don't like to see my big boy's beautiful face all *winkled* up by that ugly *fwown*. Open your moufy now,
and swallow down this nice big spoonful of stewed prune juice. There!
Now doesn't he feel better? It's good for my darling's bow-wels. You'll
wake up in the morning feeling wonderful!' "

Proud, somber, darkly flushed, slipping her finger in and out of the
ring, she looked at him with a faint, brooding smile and an exultant
sense of triumph.

"Oh, you'll think of me! You'll think of me, all right! You think you
can forget me, but you can't! If you forget all the rest of it, you'll have
to think of me each time you put a bite of Christian food into your
mouth!"

"Weave, weave, weave!" she thought. "Weave, you crazy and tormented weaver, until you are caught up and tangled hopelessly in
your own web! Use nothing that you have. Go crazy wanting what you
haven't got. And what is it that you want? Do you know? Could you
say? Have you the glimmer of a notion what it is you want? To be
here and not to be here. To be in Vienna, London, Frankfort, and the
Austrian Tyrol at the same moment. To be in your room and out in
the street at the same time. To live in the city and know a million
people, and to live on a mountain top and know only three or four. To
have one woman, one house, one horse, one cow, one little piece of
earth, one place, one country, and one of everything, and to have a thousand women, to live in a dozen countries, to travel on a hundred
ships, to try ten thousand kinds of food and drink, and to live five
hundred different lives—all at one and the same time! To look through
walls of brick into a million rooms and see the lives of all the people,

and to look into my heart, to tear me open, to ask me a million questions, to think about me all the time, to grow mad thinking of me, to imagine a thousand filthy and insane things about me and then to believe them right away, to chew me up and devour me until there's nothing left of me—and then to forget about me. To have a hundred plans and ideas for the work you are going to do, the books and stories you are going to write, to begin a dozen things and to finish nothing. To want to work like a madman and then to sprawl upon your rump and gaze dreamily at the ceiling and wish there was some way that it would all come out of you like ectoplasm, and that the pencil would just walk across the paper by itself and do all that ugly work for you of putting down and working out, of revising, writing, getting stumped, cursing, stamping around and beating its head against the wall, sweating blood and crying, 'Christ! I'm going mad!'—getting tired and desperate, and swearing off forever, and then sitting down to sweat and curse and work like hell again! Oh, wouldn't life be simply glorious if all that part of it could be cut out! Wouldn't it be fine if glory, reputation, love were ready at our beck and call, and if the work we want to do, the satisfaction that we hope to get, would just walk in on us when we wished for it, and go away and leave us when we were tired of it!"

Her eyes flashed with impatience as she looked at him.

"Here he is, lashing about and beating himself to pieces everywhere! Sure of his purpose, and letting himself be taken from it every time the phone rings, every time someone offers him a drink, every time some fool comes knocking at the door! Burning with desire for everything except the thing he has, and tired of anything he has the moment that he has it! Hoping to save himself by getting on a ship and going to another country, to find himself by getting lost, to change himself by changing his address, to get a new life by finding a new sky! Always believing he will find something strange and rich and glorious somewhere else, when all the glory and the richness in the world is here before him, and the only hope he has of finding, doing, saving anything is in himself, and by himself!"

With the hatred which she had for failure, her abhorrence of indecision and confusion, and the almost material value which she set upon success—on a life and talent wisely used, and on a knowledge always guided by a clear design—she clenched and unclenched her fists, trembling in a fury of indomitable determination as she looked at him, thinking:

"God! If I could only give him a part of my power to work and get things done! If I could only set him on the track and keep him there until he does it! If I could only teach him how to collect his strength and use it to some good end, and get the pure gold out of him—yes, the best! the best! for that's the only thing that's good enough!—and not to let it all be wasted, frittered away, and buried below a mass of false and worthless things! If I could only show him how to do it—and, by God!" she thought, doubling her fists together at her sides, "I will!"

42

The Parting

APRIL PASSED, AND MAY CAME ON, AND THERE WAS NEITHER CHANGE NOR hope of change in Monk. In a thousand darts and flicks and fancies of his swarming brain, his life was buffeted in a mad devil's dance like a bird hurled seaward on the wind, and, ever in his sight, always within his touch, forever to be captured and yet never caught, the ever-shifting visages of that mercurial atom, truth, melted from his furious attempt like images of painted smoke and left him baffled and bewildered, a maddened animal that beat its knuckles bloody against the strong wall of the earth.

Sometimes a memory, an evocation of classic purities, swept calmly through his mind and left it for a moment untainted and undistressed. And then he longed no more for rich Cockaigne, for amorous flesh and lips empurpled with ripe grapes, but for even and eternal skies, a parapet of untortured stone, and calm eyes that looked out upon an untumultuous and unchanging sea that feathered with remote and punctual sighings on the rocks. There time went by on unrelenting beat; the even sky hung tragically above the heads of men who thought of living but who calmly knew that they must die. The grief of time, the sorrowful hauntings of brief days, rested upon them, and they never wept. They lived their lives out like the seasons, giving to each its due:

To Spring, all of the leaping and the dancing, the flashing of young forms in silver pools, the hunt, the capture, and the race.

To Summer, battle, the swift thud of mighty flesh, victory without pity or injustice, defeat with resignation.

Then to October they brought all their grain of wisdom, their ripe deliberation. Their calm eyes saw a few things that endured—the sea, the mountain, and the sky—and they walked together, talking with grave gestures of the fate of man. Their feast was truth and beauty, and they lay together on unyielding mats, tasting the wine, the olive, and a crust of bread.

When December came, without lamentings in the room, but by the wall and quietly, they turned their grey heads tranquilly below their robes, and died.

Was this, then, the answer? He shook his head and wiped the image from his eyes. No, no. There was no answer. If such men had lived, they had been touched by all our woes, by all the madness, grief, and fury flesh can know. Torture and maddening of the brain were theirs as well as ours, and through all time, through the brief tickings of all human lives, the river flowed, dark, unceasing, and inscrutable.

And now the worm was feeding at his life again, a knife was driven through his heart and twisted there, and suddenly he went blank and empty and his flesh turned rotten.

So it was that Esther found him when she came that day at noon.

He sat upon his cot in sullen, sodden, leaden apathy and would not rouse to talk to her. And when she saw him so, she thought to draw him out by telling in her bright and jolly way about a play that she had seen the night before. She told him all about it, who the actors were, and how they did, and how the audience responded, and as she brought to instant life the scene there in the theatre, she burst forth in her jaunty way and said how fine, how grand, how swell it was.

These simple-seeming words from her sophisticated mouth now goaded Monk into a sudden fury.

"Oh, *fine!* Oh, *grand!* Oh, *swell!*" he snarled, with savage parody. "God! You people make me sick! The way you talk!" and lapsed again into a moody silence.

Esther had been pacing lightly round the room, but now she spun about and faced him, her rosy cheeks turned crimson with a sudden anger.

"You people! You people!" she cried, in a high, excited voice. "In heaven's name, what is it now? What people are you talking about? I'm no people! I'm no people!" she said with a stammering resentment. "I don't know who you're talking about!"

"Oh, yes you do!" he muttered sullenly and wearily. "The whole damned lot of you! You're all alike! You're one of them!"

"One of whom?" said Esther furiously. "I'm one of nobody—I'm myself, that's who I am! There's no sense to anything you say any more! You hate the whole world and you curse and revile everybody! You don't know what you're saying half the time! You people! You're always calling me 'you people,'" she said bitterly, "when you don't know what people you're talking about!"

"Oh, yes I do!" he said gloomily. "The whole damned lot of you—that's who!"

"Of whom? Of whom?" she cried, with an agonized, exasperated laugh. "God! You just keep muttering the same thing over and over, and it makes no sense!"

"The whole damned crowd of million-dollar Jew and Gentile æsthetes—that's who I mean! With your twaddle about 'Have you seen this?' and 'Have you read that?'—with your bilge about books and plays and pictures, moaning about art and beauty and how it is the thing you all are living for, when none of you care a good God-damn for anything but keeping in the swim! Ah, you make me sick!—the whole damned crowd of you, with your jokes about the fairies and the lesbians, and your books and plays and nigger carvings!" he said with choking incoherence. "Yes. You know a lot about it, don't you? When you've got to read the magazines to see what you should like— and you'll go back on your word, you'll change your mind, you'll betray a thing you said was good in thirty seconds, if you find your dirty crowd's against you! . . . The friends and patrons of the arts!" he said with an infuriated yell of unsure laughter. "Jesus God! That it should come to this!"

"Oh, that it should come to this! That it should come to what? You poor fool, you're raving like a crazy man."

"That the good man—the real artist—the true poet—should be done to death——"

"Oh, done to death, my eye!"

"—by the malice and venom of these million-dollar apes and bastards of the arts and their erotic wives! 'Oh, how we do love art!'" he sneered. "'I'm so much interested in the work you're doing! I know you have so much to offer—and we ne-e-d you so-o,'" he whispered, almost speechlessly, "'and won't you co-o-me to tea on Thursday? I'm all al-o-o-ne—' . . . The bitches! The dirty bitches!" he bellowed suddenly like a maddened bull, and then, reverting to a tone of whining and seductive invitation. "'—and we can have a *nice*. long talk together! I so much want to talk to you! I feel you have so much to gi-i-ve me.' Ah, the filthy swine! And you, you, *you*!" he gasped. "That's *your crowd*! And is that your game, too?" His voice threaded away to a whisper of exhausted hatred, and his breath labored heavily in the silence.

She made no answer for a moment. She looked at him quietly, sorrowfully, shaking her head slightly in a movement of scorn and pity.

"Listen!" she said at length. He turned sullenly away from her, but she seized him by the arm, pulled him back to her, and spoke to him sharply in a commanding tone. "Listen, you poor fool! I'm going to tell you something! I'm going to tell you now what's wrong with you! You curse and revile everybody and you think that everyone is down on you and wants to do you harm. You think that everyone is against you and is staying awake at night thinking how to get the best of you. You think everyone is plotting how to keep you down. Well, let me tell you something," she said quietly. "This thing which you have made up in your mind does not exist. This is a monster of your own creating. George, look at me!" she spoke sharply to him. "I am a truthful person, no matter what you say, and I swear to you that this ugly thing has no existence anywhere except in your own mind. These people that you curse and rail at have never hated you and do not wish to do you any injury."

"Oh," he said with savage sarcasm, "I suppose then that they love me! I suppose they spend their time in planning how they can do me good!"

"No," she said. "They neither love nor hate you. Most of them have never heard of you. They wish to do you neither harm nor good. They never think of you." She paused, looking sadly at him for a moment. Then she said: "But I can tell you this—even if they knew you, it would not be the way you think it is. People are not that way at all. For God's sake," she cried with strong feeling, "don't blacken your mind and warp your life with all these vile and ugly thoughts that are not so! Try to have a little faith and wisdom when you think of people! They are not the way you think they are! No one wants to do you any harm!"

He stared at her stupidly and sullenly for a moment. The madness had flared out of him again and now he looked at her wearily with the old sense of shame and foul disgust.

"I know they're not," he said dully. "I know what they are like. I curse at them because I know I am no good. . . . Oh, I can't tell you!" he said with a sudden, desperate, and baffled movement, "I can't tell you what it is! It's not the way you think it is, either. I don't hate everyone the way you think—in spite of all I say. I hate no one but myself. Esther, in God's name, what's gone wrong with me? What's the matter with my life? I used to have the strength of twenty people. I loved life and had the power and courage to do anything. I worked and read and traveled with the energy of a great dynamo. I wanted to eat the earth, and feed myself with all the books and men and countries in the world. I wanted to know about the lives of all the people, to be everywhere, to see and know everything like a great poet, and I walked and roamed about the streets feeding on everything that the people did or said with a furious hunger that was never satisfied. Everything sang out for me with glory and with triumph, and I was sure I had the power and talent to do everything I wanted. I wanted fame and love and glory, and I was sure that I could get them. And I wanted to do fine work, to make my life prevail, and to grow and come to good and strengthen in my work forever. I wanted to be a great man. Why should I be ashamed to say I wanted to be a great man, and not a little, ugly, sterile fellow? . . . And now all that has gone. I hate my life and everything I see around me. Good God! if I had lived my life—if I were old and worn-out and had never got anything from life I wanted, I could see the reason for it!" he burst out furiously. "But I'm only twenty-seven—and I'm worn-out already! By God! an old and worn-out old man at twenty-seven!" he yelled, and began to beat his fist into the wall.

"Oh, worn-out! Worn-out, my eye!" she said with a short and angry laugh. "You act as if you're worn-out! You've worn me out, you mean. You wear out everybody else the way you lash around. You wear yourself out beating your head against a wall! But—worn-out! You're worn-out about the same way that the Hudson River is."

"Oh—don't—for God's sake—don't!" he said in a choked and furious tone, sticking his arm out in a movement of baffled, exasperated impatience. "Don't give me any more of that soft soap. Listen! I'm telling you the truth! It's not the same with me as it used to be. I've lost the hope and confidence I had. I haven't the same energy and strength I had. God-damn it, woman, don't you understand?" he said furiously. "Haven't you seen it for yourself? Don't you understand I've lost my squeal?" he shouted, beating himself upon the breast and glaring at her with an insane fury. "Don't you know it's been six months since I made my squeal?"

As absurd and comical as these last words were, as incredible as they might have sounded to a hidden listener, neither of them laughed. Instead, they stood, earnest, combative, and passionately serious, opposing hot, excited faces to each other. She understood him.

This "squeal" to which he had referred, and which, curiously, in the midst of all the tortured madness and dark fury of these recent months had seemed a thing of moment to him, was simply a cry of animal exuberance. Since his earliest childhood this tongueless expletive had risen in him in a surge of swelling joy, had collected in his throat and then been torn from his lips in a wild goat-cry of pain and joy and ecstasy.

Sometimes it came in some moment of triumph or achievement, and sometimes it came for no tangible reason, and from inscrutable and nameless sources. He had known it ten thousand times in childhood, and it had come to him upon the lights and hues of a million evanescent things; and the whole intolerable good and glory of the immortal earth, the whole intolerable sense of pain and joy, the whole intolerable knowledge of man's briefness on the earth, had been packed, though in what way he did not know, and in what words he could not say, into each moment that the great cry came.

Sometimes it had come simply in a brief and incommunicable moment—in the sultry and exultant odors of ground coffee, or in the smell of frying steaks across the neighborhood in the first frosty evenings of October. Sometimes it was in the full, thick swells of the rivers after heavy rain, with their alluvial glut; or in the swell of melons bedded in the sweet, ripe hay of country wagons; it was in the odors of hot tar and oil upon the heated pavements of a street in Summer.

Again, it was in all the spicy odors of the old-time grocery stores— and suddenly he remembered a forgotten moment in his childhood when he had stood in such a store and seen a Summer storm collect into black-crested clouds of inky and empurpled light, and then watched for ten minutes the deluge of torrential rain as it had sluiced and spurted on the old, dejected head, the gaunt, grey buttocks, and the steaming flanks of the grocery horse, hitched to the wagon, haltered to a paving block, and waiting at the curb with dolorous patience.

This obscure and forgotten moment returned to him again with all the old and inscrutable exulting the scene had brought to him. And he remembered as well all things and persons in the store—the aproned clerks, with cuffs of straw and armbands catching up their sleeves, with pencils behind their ears and a straight part in the middle of their hair, the ingratiating unction of their tone and manner as they took the orders of reflective housewives, as well as all the rich and spicy odors that rose upward from great bins and barrels in the store. He remembered the smell of pickles brined in Atlantean casks, and the mellow, grainy odors of the floors and counter plankings which seemed to have been seasoned in all the spicy savors of a dozen years.

There were the smells of rich and bitter chocolate and of tea; of new, ground coffee pouring from the mill; of butter, lard, and honey, and sliced bacon; of smoked ham, and yellow cheese, cut in thick wedges from a ponderous chunk; as well as all the earthy smells of fresh garden vegetables and orchard fruits—of crisp, podded peas, tomatoes, and string beans, of fresh corn and new potatoes, and of apples, peaches, plums, and the solid plunk and promise, the strange, sultry thrill of big green watermelons.

And this whole scene that day—sights, sounds, and odors, sultry air and inky light and spurting and torrential rain sweeping in gusty sheets along the gleaming and deserted pavements, as well as the steaming flanks of the old grey grocery horse, and a lovely young woman, newly wed, biting her tender lips with a delicious incertitude as she gave her orders to the clerk who waited prayerfully before her— had awakened in his young boy's heart a powerful sensation of joy, abundance, and proud, welling triumph, a sensation of personal victory and fulfillment that was overwhelming, though in what way, by what coherent and connecting agency, he did not know.

But most often, more obscurely, from more hidden sources of immense and fathomless exulting the great cry had been torn from him as a child in moments when the picture of abundance was not so clearly painted and where the connecting influences, the limitless evocations of triumph and fulfillment, were not apparent or articulate, but in which the full conviction of his joy had been as strong as when the picture was complete and definite.

Sometimes the cry was packed into the passing of a cloud upon the massed green of a hill, and sometimes, with the most intolerable ecstasy that he had ever known, it was in the green light of the woods, the lyric tangle of the wilderness, the cool, bare spaces underneath a canopy of trees, and the gold spangles of the sun that swarmed with a strange, enchanted light in the magic sorcery of cool, depthless green. There would be a dip, a slope, a glade in all this magic, a spring cupped in a cushion of green moss, the great bole of a rotted oak across the path, and over there was the crystal clarity of forest water falling over rock and in the pool a woman with bare legs and swelling thighs and kilted skirts, and all about her the strange lights of magic gold and depthless green, the rock, the fern, the springy carpet of the forest earth, and all the countless voices of high afternoon that, with dart and sudden thrum, or stitch and call or furious drummings in the wood, passed all about her to uncounted deaths and were lost and came again.

And the cry had come upon the faint and broken ringing of a bell in afternoon, over the dusky warmth of meadows, and the strong, hot fragrance of the clove, and upon the raining of the acorns to the earth at night, and on the high and distant roaring of the wind in Autumn. It was in the strong, free shout of children playing in the streets at dusk, and in quiet voices at the Summer's end, and in a woman's voice and laughter in the street at night, and in the tugging of a leaf upon a bough.

In frost and starlight and far-broken sounds at night, in living leaves, in sudden rain, and in the menace of impending snow, and in the soft, numb spitting of the snow against the window glass. In first light, dawn, and circuses, the dance and swing of lanterns in the dark, the green, winking lights of semaphores, and the sounds of shifting engines, the crash and jar of freight cars in the dark, the shouts and oaths of circus men, the rhythm of the driven stake, the smells of canvas, sawdust, and strong boiling coffee, and the lion reek, the black and yellow of the tigers, strong, tawny camel smells, and all strange sounds and sights and odors that they brought to little towns.

And in the solemn joy of quiet fields from which the heat and fury of the day had passed, and in the great body of the earth collecting into coolness and to night, respiring quietly in the last light of the day. In hoof and wheel that broke the silence of a street at dawn, and in the birdsong breaking into light, and in the hard and cloven trot of cattle coming from the fields into the road at dusk, and the late red sun that faded without violence or heat across hill pastures to the wood;

in evening and stillness on the land, and the sharp thought and ache and joy of distant towns.

The wild cry had risen to his lips with all these things and with all movements of arrival and departure, with the thought of new lands, cities, ships, and women; with wheel and flange and rail that bent across the earth like space and a triumphant music, with men and voyages, and the immortal sound of time that murmured constantly about the walls of mighty stations; and with the rush, the glare, the pistoned drive, the might and power of the locomotive, and with great flares and steamings that passed instantly upon the rails at night. It was in the acrid dinginess of enormous station platforms thick with the smoke of forty trains, and it was in the hot green snore of pullman cars at night, in the heart of the youth who listened from his berth exultantly to the slow stir and velvet rustle of a woman as she languorously stretched her thighs in darkness, and as he saw the immense dark structure of the earth wheel calmly past his vision with an even stroke, and heard more strange and more familiar than a dream, in silence and the pauses of the night, the voices of unknown men upon a little platform in Virginia.

The cry had risen from all thoughts that he had had of voyages and distances, of the immense and lonely earth, and of great rivers that from the depths of midnight and lost sources in the hills drew slowly with mined and secret droppings of the earth in darkness their alluvial glut across the continent, and in his thoughts of the lonely, dark, encrusted earth, and of America at night with dark corn steady in the night and the cool rustling of the blades. It was in his thought of all the rivers, mountains, plains, and deserts, and in his thought of all the little sleeping towns across the continent, of great flares flashing on the rails and briefly on great fields of wheat, and of all his dreams and visions of women in the West who stood at evening in the doors and looked with quiet eyes into green, depthless fields of corn or golden wheat or straight into the blazing hues of desert suns.

Thus, in this whole picture of the earth, which, in many years long past and furiously accomplished, and in the constant travail of his mind and heart had been continued, not only out of all that he had seen and known and remembered, but also out of all that his hunger and desire had drawn from the earth which it had never seen, the wild goat-cry of joy and triumph had its life. It had been in his whole design and pattern of the earth which had grown so complete and radiant in his mind that sometimes in the night he thought he saw it all stretched out upon the canvas of his vision—hills, mountains, plains, and deserts, fields printed in the moonlight and great sleeping woods, as well as all its groaning weight of towns and cities. It was in his vision of immense, mysterious rivers flowing in the dark, and in the eighteen thousand miles of coast at which the sea forever was working in the moon's light wink, with glut and coil, with hissing surge, with lapse and reluctation of its breath, feathering eternally at the million pockets of the land.

And the cry was torn from his thoughts of tropic darkness and the jungles of the night, and all things dark and evil and unknown; it rose with demoniac joy out of the sleeping wildness, and from lush, jungle depths where the snake's cold eye lay bedded on a bank of fern; it was torn also from his vision of strange, tropic plants on which the tarantula, the adder, and the asp had fed themselves asleep on their own poisons, and where, green-golden, gloosy blue, and bitter red, the tufted parrakeets awoke the dark with their proud, brainless scream.

And the cry had come, most fiercely and with the wildest joy when it was torn from the heart of darkness and the fields of sleep. In many a silent night, and from the prison of a city room, his spirit had swept out across the fields of sleep and he had heard the heartbeats of ten million men around him, and the wild and wordless cry was torn from him. From those dark tides and waters of men's sleep on which a few stars sparely looked, the cry had called to all great fish that swam in night's dark glades and waters; and to all blind crawls and sucks and grope-things of the brain, to all subtlest, unseen stirs, all half-heard, half-articulated whisperings, all things that swam or stirred or crawled within the fields of sleep, to all the forested and far, it had sent forth its cry of triumph and return.

And finally, in the city streets and at a thousand times, this tongueless expletive of passion and of triumph had been torn from his throat. Sometimes it came with all the warm, hot odors of the pavements in late Spring, and the spermy fragrance of the earth that seemed to burst in waves of rich fecundity through all the steel and stone; and it came with savage joy out of the sorcery of April, the magic of first green in city streets, the pageantry of glorious women who seemed themselves to have burst out of the earth overnight and to be blooming in the streets one day like splendid flowers.

It had come to him when he had smelled the sea-wrack of the harbor, the clean, salt fragrance of the tides, and it was in cool, flowing tides of evening waters and in deserted piers and in the sliding lights of little tugs. And it had risen to his lips when he had heard the great ships blowing in the gulf of night, or heard exultantly the shattering *baugh* of their departure as they slid into line and pointed for the sea at noon on Saturday. And it had come to him each time he saw the proud, white breasts of mighty ships, the racing slant and drive of the departing liners, and watched them dwindle and converge into their shape away from piers, black with crowds of cheering people.

So had it come to him ten thousand times, and in ten thousand places, this wild goat-cry of tongueless triumph, pain, and ecstasy. And in it was the memory of all things far and fleeting and forever lost, which had gone the moment he had seen them, and which, with a heart of fire and an intolerable wild regret, he had wished to hold and fix forever in his life. In other Springs it had risen to the mighty pulsations of energy and joy which swept above all the city's million-footed life, in the winglike sweep and soar of the great bridges, and in all the thousand potent smells of wharves and markets. But now, this cruel Spring, he had ranged the city furiously, had felt as keenly and as piercingly as ever the sorcery and the magic of its vernal tides—and yet no single thing had torn the goat-cry from his lips.

And now that he no longer felt the impulse of this savage and uncontrollable cry, it really seemed to him that he had lost out of his life and spirit something precious and incalculable. For he had always known that it was something more than the animal vitality of a boy.

For the cry had come from no fictitious imagery, no dream or romance of his fancy, no false hallucination of desire. The cry had welled up from the earth with a relentless certitude, and all the gold and glory of the earth was in it. It had been for him a kind of touchstone to reality, for it had never played him false. It had always come as a response to an actual and indubitable glory, and to a reality as tangible as minted gold. Knowledge, power, and truth had been in that wild cry. It had united him to the whole family of the earth, for he had always known that men in every age and history had felt the same wild cry of triumph, pain, and passion on their lips, and that it had come to them from the same movements, seasons, and unchanging certitudes of joy as it had come to him.

This was the true gold of the earth, and now he felt, with a sense of his own ruin and defeat, that he had lost something priceless, irrecoverable, forever.

"And you know it, don't you?" he said bitterly. "You admit it. You know yourself that I have lost it, don't you?"

"Oh, you've lost nothing," she said quietly. "Listen to me! You haven't lost your energy or strength. You'll see you've got it just as much as you ever had. You haven't lost your joy or interest in life. You've only lost something that didn't matter, anyway."

"That's what *you* say," he muttered sullenly. "That's all *you* know about it."

"Listen to me! I know all about it. I know exactly what you've lost. You've lost a way you had of letting off the steam. And that has happened to us all. Good heavens! We can't be twenty-one forever!" she said angrily. "But you'll see that you've lost nothing valuable or essential. You've got all the strength and power you always had. Yes—and more! For you'll learn to use it better. You'll keep getting stronger all the time. George, I swear to you that this is so! That's the way it was with me, and it will be the same with you."

She paused, flushed and frowning for a moment.

"Lost your squeal!" she muttered. "God! How you talk!" Her lip curled slightly and for a moment her voice was touched with the cynical humor of old Jewish scorn. "Don't you worry about losing your squeal," she said quietly. "You worry about getting a little sense into your head—that's what you need, young fellow, a great deal more than any squeal you had. . . . Lost his squeal!" she muttered over again.

For a moment more she surveyed him with a serious and angry frown, snapping the ring on and off her finger with a rapid movement of her hand. Then her expression softened, her warm throat trembled, her jolly face began to bloom with new flowers of red, and suddenly she burst into a rich, choking, woman's laugh:

"Lost your squeal! God, but you're wonderful! Would anyone ever believe the things you say!"

He stared at her sullenly for a moment, and then, wildly and suddenly, he laughed, smiting himself upon the forehead with the heel of his palm and crying, "Haw!"

Then, scowling gloomily, he turned to her and muttered obscurely and incoherently, as if someone else had been guilty of an offense which he would pass over with a kind of disgusted charity:

"I know! I know! Don't say anything about it," and he turned away and began to stare moodily out of the window.

During all this cruel month of May, below pain, below his moods of sodden, dull despair, below the close-spun, thick-wrought fabric of their life together, below all the intense and shifting weathers of their hearts in which at times, for fleeting intervals, their love flared up as warm and tender as it had ever done, an ugly, grim, and desperate struggle was being waged between them.

Day by day, the stubborn, brutal fight went on—the man snarling, raging about among his walls like an infuriated animal, hurling foul curses, taunts, and accusations at her, the woman weeping, sobbing, screaming denials, and finally departing tragically, her face swollen by tears, saying that the end had come, that she was telling him good-bye forever, and that she would never see him again.

And yet, within two hours, she would call him on the telephone again, or a messenger would appear bearing a telegram or a brief, swiftly-worded letter, which he would rip open instantly and read rigidly, with a livid and contorted face and trembling fingers, his features twisted with a sneer of cursing disbelief as he snarled mockery at his own folly, and his heart stabbed fiercely against his will with wild pity and regret by these swift, simple words that cried with truth, honesty, and passion and winged their way straight and sure between his armor.

And then, next day, she would be there at his side once more, her small, sad face serious and resolved, fixed in a solemn look of final renunciation. Sometimes she said she had come for one last word of parting and farewell, in friendship; and sometimes she said she had come to gather materials and belongings which she needed for her work. But she was always there, as certain as a destiny, and he now began to comprehend what he had never been able to understand before, what he could never have believed possible in his earlier youth—that, packed into this delicate figure, behind this flowerlike and rose-lipped face, were stored the energies of an indomitable will, that this exquisite and lovely little creature who could weep bitterly, renounce sorrowfully, and day by day depart tragically and forever, was beyond comparison the most determined, resolute, and formidable antagonist he had ever known.

"All right!" she would say fatally, with an air of somber and tragic consent at the end of one of these brutal scenes of the will. "All right! Leave me if you like. You've thrown me over. You've gone back on me. You've deserted the best friend you ever had." And then, shrugging her shoulders in a little gesture of bitter acquiescence, and speaking in a sing-song voice: "You've done for me! I'm dead! You've killed me!"

"Haw, haw! Whee! Fine! Go on!" He laughed crazily, applauding with his hands. "Give us some more of it! Tomorrow night, *East Lynn!*"

"She's dead! She's done for!" she continued in the same brooding and fatal monotone. "Your darling's dead! She loved you and you killed her! Your Jew's dead! No more! No more!" She smiled a bitter, puckered, turned-down smile and made again the motion of tragic consent. "It's all over. Finished. Done for. . . . You'll be sorry!" she cried, with a sudden change in tone and manner.

He staggered about the room, smiting his forehead savagely with his clenched fist, and reeling with wild, infuriated laughter:

"*Camille,* by God!" he shouted. "That's right! Cry! Weep! Yell out so everyone can hear it! Fine! Great! I love it! It's music to my ears!"

"You'll get no rest!" she cried out in a warning tone. "I'll haunt you. You think you can forget me, but you can't. I'll come back from the grave to haunt you. You'll see! You'll see! I'll bring Azrael and Beelzebub back to haunt you—yes! I'll bring the spirits of great rabbis back who know the cabala! Oh, you'll get no rest! I'll bring the spirits of my people back to haunt you! I'll bring the spirits of my Christian blood back to haunt you, too! . . . God!" she cried suddenly, with a scornful humor, "I'll bet that they're a trashy, lifeless lot of ghosts compared to all the Jews—like these little anæmic Christian wenches that you go with!" She paused, her small face was knotted suddenly with a surge of jealous fury, tears spurted from her eyes, she doubled her fists, drew them up to her sides, and held them tightly clenched for a moment, trembling rigidly with speechless rage.

"Don't you bring any more of them up here!" she said in a small, choked, trembling voice.

"Oh, so that's it, is it?" he said heavily, with an ugly, grating sneer. "That's where the shoe pinches, is it? That's what galls her, eh?" He made a sudden gesture of brutal contempt. "To hell with you!" he said coarsely. "I'll do as I damn well please—and you can't stop me!"

"You'll not bring any more of those girls up here!" she cried, in a high, shaking voice. "This is our place. This place is mine as well as yours. You'll not bring them to my place!" She turned away to hide her tears, biting her trembling lip, and in a moment she said in a tone of bitter reproach, "What would you think if I carried on that way with men? I never have, but if I really did it, how would you feel? God, you couldn't stand it! You'd go crazy!"

Then he cursed and stormed and thought up new accusations to fling at her, bitter, groundless, and unreasoning, and she wept, denied, assailed him as before. And in the end he beat her down till there was no more resistence left in her, and she said with a bitter smile, making a slight gesture of acquiescence with her shoulders:

"All right! Go with your little pick-ups! Do as you please! I'm through!"

And then she left him, saying once more as she had said a dozen times, that he would never see her face again.

He was determined now, by some single and brutal violence, to wrench their lives asunder in a final act of parting, and thus, he hoped, to free himself from the sense of ruin, desolation, and loss unutterable which had possessed and conquered him, and of which he had grown desperately afraid. And the woman was determined that he should not leave her.

But after May slid into June there came a desperate day on which at last Monk forced the issue. He told her he was through with her forever, their life was finished, he wanted to forget her utterly, to tear and strip her very memory from his blood, his brain, his heart, and go away somewhere, away from this accursed city, where he could gather up the shattered fragments of his life and build it back anew to a single integrity of purpose and design. He'd go to Europe—that's what he'd do!—put a wide ocean there between them, and let its raging waters wash away the last remaining vestiges of all their life together. and it would then be just as though the two of them had never met and loved and lived and cursed and fought!

In the white-hot fury of his resolve, he gathered up his books, his clothes, and everything he owned, flung them together, and stormed out of the house, knowing as he stepped upon the pavement that he never would again set foot across that threshold.

43

Esther's Farewell

IT WAS THE END OF THE ACADEMIC YEAR AT THE SCHOOL FOR UTILITY CUL-tures, so there was nothing to keep Monk in New York. He wanted desperately to get away, and, hating the thought of cutting short his trip abroad at the end of the Summer, he obtained a leave of absence for the Fall term. Then, with a lighter heart than he had known in many months, he booked his passage for Southampton.

When he went aboard the boat at midnight, he found a letter from Esther waiting for him. As the purser handed it to him and he saw her handwriting on the envelope, he cursed beneath his breath, and was angry with himself because at sight of it his heart had pounded furi-ously with joy and hope in spite of all his high resolve.

"God-damn it!" he muttered. "Can't she let me go in peace?"—and clutched the letter in his trembling hand as he went to find his room where he could be alone to read it.

He ripped it open nervously, and this is what he read:

My dear,

The boat will not sail until dawn, but I hope you will get this when you go aboard so you can read it before you go to bed.

I thought for a moment of going to the boat to see you off, but then I decided not to. It would have been too much. It's a good thing you're going away now—I don't think I could have stood it another week. This Spring has been the worst time I've ever gone through. It has been worse than hell—I never knew there was any torture like it. My heart feels all sore and bloody as if it had a sword stuck through it. I cried all last night, and I have cried for the last hour and a half—I thought there were no more tears in me, but they keep coming. I never used to

616

cry, and now it seems since I met you I cry all the time. You say I only talk like this to torture you, but I am only telling the truth—I have never wanted to torture you. I have only wanted to love you and do what's good for you.

I am worn-out and heart-broken. Once I thought I was so strong I could do anything—but this thing has beaten me. Last night I did something I haven't done since I was a little child—I got down and prayed to God, if there is a God, to do something to help me. But I know there is no God. You have taken the finest thing you ever had and thrown it away. I have always told you the truth about myself—I have been good and faithful and true to you ever since I first met you, and you haven't got sense enough to see it. Some day you may know what I'm really like, but then it will be too late. There is no wrong or evil in me—it is all in your dark and terrible mind. You think a thing, and then immediately you make it so.

For God's sake, don't let yourself go on like this. Don't throw away the great thing that is in you. Don't let your great mind, your great talent, go to pieces because of these other things inside you that tear you apart. I love you, I believe in your genius, I always shall—no matter what anyone says. ("No matter what anyone says, eh? Oh, the evil-hearted and malignant swine! So that's what they're saying to her! That's it! Their envy and ratlike jealousy squalling with triumph now because they think they have finally done me to death. Meanwhile, what have *you* been doing? Talking up for me, eh? Defending me, eh? Saying how good and fine I am, and that they don't know me. For what? To satisfy your hunger and martyrdom, to appear grand and noble and forgiving, to show how great and good and noble you are, and how mean and low and unworthy I am! I know you!" With livid and contorted face he smoothed out the letter he had crumpled in his trembling fingers, and went on.)

No matter what has happened, no matter what has passed between us, I love you now, with all my heart and soul, and I always shall. No one will ever touch me again. I shall go to my grave with you in my heart. I know you will sneer when you read this, and have evil thoughts about me, but I have told you the truth and nothing else. You have caused me the greatest pain of anyone I have ever known, but you have also given me the greatest joy and happiness. No matter what dark and terrible thoughts are in your mind, you have the rarest and grandest quality of anyone I have ever known. You have made a great music in me. I can't imagine now what life would have been like if I had never known you.

I get so worried thinking about you and wondering what you are doing. Promise me that you won't drink too much. Alcohol seems to have a bad effect on you—instead of making you happy and cheerful it gets you so depressed, and sometimes you get into one of your crazy fits. You simply can't afford to waste the precious thing that is in you.

And please, please, don't go around having trouble with other people. I know I'll get nervous wondering what new scrapes you've got into. For heaven's sake, have a little sense about things. No one's laughing at you—no one's trying to insult you—no one hates you and wants to injure you. These things exist only in your imagination. You have absolutely no idea what effect you have on other people—you do not look like anyone else on earth, and when they stare at you in a restaurant that does not mean they are laughing at you. Please try to be gentle and kind to people—you can do anything you like with them when you are lovely—instead of hating you, they adore you, and will do anything you want them to.

Todd has promised me she'll go around to Waverly Place and put the room in order. I have told her what to do with my paints and drawing materials—I could not bear to go back there if you were not there, and if you do not come back, I shall never go there again.

I wonder if you'll ever miss me, and think about your little Esther. I'm sure of one thing—you'll never again find a cook like her. She knew what her George liked best. Maybe when you've had to eat Christian food again you'll want me back. I can see your sensitive nose now turning up in disgust at the smell of it. When they give you what they call a salad—a leaf of wilted lettuce on a plate with three drops of vinegar on it—just remember the salads I used to make for you. ("By God, and she's right, too," he thought with a tortured grin. "I'll never taste food like that again.")

I hope you are feeling better and are going to bed at night. Don't drink so much coffee—you drank gallons at a time this year. I think that's one reason you got so nervous. You need a rest, too. Getting the book done was a tremendous job and enough to wear anyone out.

Now please, dear, don't get mad at me for what I'm going to say— I know how excited and angry you get when anyone talks to you about the book. But don't lose heart because one publisher has turned it down—you get mad at me when I talk about it, but I am sure someone will take it yet. After all, it is a big piece of work, and some people might be afraid to publish it. Miss Scudder told me it was about five times as long as the average novel, and would have to be cut. Perhaps when you write the next one you can make it shorter. ("I might have expected this!" he muttered, grinding his teeth. "She has given up hope for this one already. I can see that. That's what she means by this talk about the next one! Well, there'll be no next one. No more, no more! Let the rats die now in their own venom!")

Now please be patient with me, dear—I am sure you can do something with this one if you will only make a few concessions. I was talking again to Seamus Malone the other night. He said that parts of the book were "simply magnificent!" ("God, what a lie!" he thought. "What he probably said was 'Not bad,' or 'Rather interesting,' delivered in a tone of impatience or heavy indifference, as if to say, 'Oh, what the hell!'") But he said it was much too long and would have to be cut. ("They can go to hell before I will!") It would have to be published in two big volumes as it stands, and you know, dear, that's not possible. ("It's not, eh? And why? They've been printing Proust for the last five years, book by book. And whether it's two or four volumes, whose business is it but my own? They'll read it, they will, damn them, as I wrote it, if I have to cram it down their lofty throats!")

I keep telling myself it's all over between us. You have thrown me over—left me flat. But when I think of you going with those common women you always pick up anywhere, I go crazy. (He smiled with bitter joy, then with heavy, scowling face read on.)

You would not tell me what you meant to do, and I don't know where to reach you. I'll try American Express in London, and will keep on writing you although I don't know if you will ever answer me. Will you be coming home later this Summer? And if you do come, would you like to see me? If you aren't coming back that soon, and you really cared to see me, I could come to you in August. I think of all the beautiful places we could see together, and my heart aches at the thought of your going to Munich and Vienna without me. ("So! You dare to suggest that! You would come to me, would you? By God, they can wind my guts around a drum before you will!") But I don't suppose you'd want me to, would you?

I don't know what I'm saying. I'm half crazy with this thing. For God's sake, do something to help me. I am sinking, drowning—please,

please put out your hand. Save me. I love you. I am yours till death.
God bless you.

Esther

For several minutes he sat there, silent, tense, and still, the last page of her letter open in his hand. Then slowly, with set jaw, he put the pages all together, folded them with great deliberation, slowly tore them once across, and then again, and slowly rose, walked to the open porthole and thrust his hand through, and let the fragments of the letter slowly sift between his fingers into darkness and the river.

Book VII

OKTOBERFEST

On the boat going over, Monk had time to think his way through the tangled web his heart and head had spun. He thought of Esther constantly. His fury now was spent, his turmoil had subsided, and in the calm of sun and sea, that vacuum 'twixt land and land, he lived again dispassionately the chronicle of their years together. He thought back to the day when he had spoken truly all he felt and knew, the day he had foretold to her the present moment.

"You are the best and truest friend I ever had. You are the noblest, greatest, and most beautiful woman that I ever saw or knew. You are the woman that I love." Those were the words his heart had uttered. And then his head had coldly interposed, with its reasons of which the heart knew nothing: "And no matter where I go, or when I leave you, as I shall—" thus the head; and then the heart again—"down at the bottom of my soul I'll keep on loving you forever."

It was true—all true. The love and now the leaving—all true together. He was going abroad to get away from her, from New York, from the book, from everything that touched their interwoven life—and, with a desperate, childlike hope, he also knew his going was an effort to escape from all the tortures in himself.

But these were not the only reasons for his self-inflicted exile. He went to seek as well as flee. He'd spend a month or two in England and in France, then go to Germany and live there through the Autumn.

He had been to Germany before, but only briefly, and had found the country had an instant, haunting fascination for him. Was it his father's German blood in his own veins that worked this magic? So it seemed to him.

And now he meant to get to know this land, its forests and its cities, which stood already in his heart, not as a foreign country, but as a kind of second homeland of his spirit.

44

Time Is a Fable

HE HAD COME AWAY TO FORGET HER: HE DID NOTHING BUT REMEMBER her. He got sick with the pain and the thought of her, he got physically sick, and there was no medicine for his sickness. His limbs grew numb and weak, his heart was feverish and beat with a smothering thud, his guts were nauseous and queasy, and his throat burned him, his chest was tight with a kind of loathsome dyspepsia. He could not digest the food he ate, and he vomited several times a day.

At night, after prowling about feverishly through the London streets until three or four o'clock in the morning, he would go to bed and fall into a diseased coma in which events and people of his past life were mixed with the present, but during which he was yet conscious that he dreamed and that he could break the pestilential trance at any moment. Finally, in the early morning when people were going to their work along the street, he would fall soundly asleep and lie as if drugged until noon.

When he awoke he grew terribly tired in an hour or two; his mind kept beating with a weary pulse, and she was throbbing like an ache in every pulse of that beat. He drove his mind to focus its attention upon various objects, but he had to force and lift it away from its obsession as an exhausted runner lifts his leaden thighs upon the running track; his eyes were tired, and he squinted constantly in the effort to concentrate.

At last, in a moment of aching desire and total abnegation of the will, he rushed to the office of the American Express and found a letter from her. And then it was as though those months of doubt and hate and bitterness had never been, and he knew he loved her more than he loved life.

He thought about her all the time, and yet he could no longer re-

623

member how she looked. Or, if he remembered how she looked, he could not remember one look but a thousand, and these thousand looks came, passed, shifted, were mingled, mixed, and woven in such bewildering shift and play that no single image of her face remained, and there was no picture of her he could see that was fixed, and certain, and unchanging. And this filled his heart with hideous doubt, perplexity, and confusion, for suddenly he remembered how one could see a face only a few times in his life and yet that face would be fixed there in a single unforgettable image that never changed.

And then he saw that this was true of all the people he had known best and loved the most: when he tried to remember how they looked he could see not one look but a thousand looks, not one face but a swarming web of faces.

In the afternoon he would walk into town to the Oxford post office to see if there were letters for him. As he went down the street towards the post office building his heart would begin to thud feverishly, his legs would tremble, and his bowels would get cold and numb. He would wait there desperately while the man thumbed through a stack of mail to see if there was anything for him. The man took his time deliberately, and Monk felt like tearing the letters from his hand and going through them himself.

If he saw that there were letters, his heart began to beat like a trip hammer, and he was wild with hope and apprehension. But when there were no letters from her, it was just the same as no letters at all. He had no interest in the rest of them; he just thrust them indifferently in his pocket and walked away, and he was sick through heart and soul with misery and despair. The soft, wet skies of humid grey seemed to have fallen on him and broken his back, and his life was drowning in an ocean of sinister and desolate grey from which it could never emerge.

But if there was a letter from her, a feeling of drunken joy and triumph surged up in him the moment that he saw its spidery, forceful, and graceful characters. He would snatch it out of the hands of the man, rip it open and devour it as he stood there, and feel that the greatest poets in the world had never written words of such magic, truth, and love as were in that letter. And he would look up and laugh exultantly at the man who had given him the letter, for now he felt that the man was one of the best friends that he had on earth, just because he had given it to him.

The man came to know him, to expect him, to look for him, and when he saw Monk coming he would reach for a stack of letters and begin to thumb through them even before he got there. Once when Monk had finished reading a letter and looked up at him, the man was looking at him quietly, gravely, and intently. When Monk grinned at him and shook the letter in his fist triumphantly, the man did not smile as he often did. Instead, he shook his head slightly, rapidly, and gravely from side to side, and turned away.

The worst time was at night. For as he sat in his room at night and heard the wind sighing with demented wistfulness in the great trees, the madness would come back to him again, and he would think of home. Over the dark, illimitable seas the fabulous city blazed upward from the evil sorcery of night, and again he thought of the great and obscene avenues of night, the huge street of the living dead, and he would see again the faces on rat's alley where the dead men were— the faces of vultures, rats, foxes, reptiles, swine—and he could not believe that it had ever existed or that he had ever known it.

It blazed upward in some evil sorcery of time, some legend of now or forever, some evil dream of his own dreaming, and intolerably, intolerably, he wanted to go back to see if it was there—and to find and see and know the bitter, strange enigma of that woman's face again.

He saw her face, that thousand-visaged face of joy and love and health and radiance, now fixed forever in that world of evil night, and instantly the shapes of death were moving all around her, the poisonous images of cruelty, faithlessness, and despair had come alive again. He saw her fixed and secure in that infamous world of death-in-life, that poisonous, perverse, and sterile life of vanity, hate, and evil. The madness pierced him like an asp, and the worm was feeding at his life again.

Duped in that legend of enchanted time, he tried to cast a spell across the darkened seas, to catch her life into the net of his despair, to hold her, keep her, guard and prison her with love, to turn on her a light so fierce and merciless, a hunger and desire so limitless, that it could leap through darkness over half the world to find her, and keep her for him against every threatened treachery, moment by moment, as he thought the night away.

But all the time, as he sat there striving to nail down every act and moment of her life, to follow her step by step with these savage watchdogs of desire, he had again been duped by time, and had forgotten that time struck another note for her, and that, false, faithful, evil, good, or bad, she had been living in another land, another time, that she was sleeping while he thought of her, or waking while he slept, alive in all the darkness and desire of evil night when dawn had come for him, and that all acts, ardors, treacheries, or evils that he feared had passed, had long since passed, had passed five hours ago, or were to come.

Time is a fable and a mystery: it has ten thousand visages, it broods on all the images of the earth, and it transmutes them with a strange, unearthly glow. Time is collected in great clocks and hung in towers, the ponderous bells of time throng through the darkened air of sleeping cities, time beats its tiny pulse out in small watches on a woman's wrist, time begins and ends the life of every man, and each man has his own, a different time.

At night, he writes his mistress from a foreign land, he bends his love and hunger over the immense dark vastness of the nighttime seas, he tries to wish his passion and his madness into her, he says, "Where are you now, and in what place?" He hears a footstep in the empty street, the bells of time strike three o'clock for him, he writes: "What are you doing at this time at home? Are you asleep? Alone? Do you hear footfalls in the empty street; and do you think of me? Or have you found new love, and are you stirring at this moment in some other lover's grasp?" Then, as the footfalls die along the street, and the great trembling of the bells upon the air is stilled again, he strikes his flesh in his despair and agony, he thinks of perjured love, but he has forgotten that, whether she be false or faithful to him, time beats another note for her, and in the streets of home the bells are striking ten o'clock.

Thus, even in the memory of love's grief, even at the moment when we hope love's cry will pray a miracle and compass half the earth, time strikes a jagged flash and where we think it fell no love is, the moment of our faith or our betrayal has passed, or is to come, our cry wells out on darkness; and all the earth is peopled by these dupes of time, by these lost cries, by these unmeted, lost, and lonely moments of myriad mocking, and unmindful time.

There is a moment when our prayers are heard, there is a moment when our lives may meet, there is a moment when our wandering might end, and all our hunger be appeased, and we could walk into love's heart and core forever.

But what man knows that moment when it comes? What man can know the door that he may open? What man can find one light out of a million lights, one face out of a billion faces, one meet desire, one mated ecstasy out of the immense and tangled wilderness of love and hunger that covers all the earth? We are small grope-things crying for the light and love by which we might be saved, and which, like us, is dying in the darkness a hand's breadth off from us if we could touch it. We are like blind sucks and sea-valves and the eyeless crawls that grope along the forest of the sea's great floor, and we die alone in the darkness, a second away from hope, a moment from ecstasy and fulfillment, a little half an hour from love.

That is one kind of time; that is one of time's myriad faces. Here is another:

When he opened the door of the little shop in Ambleside and stepped down, the young man with the thin, bright face was waiting for him. Outside, dark was coming and the rain had begun to fall. The day had been wild and grey and beautiful, marked by a spume of flying clouds around the hills and by squalls of driving rain. Now the rain had set in again, it was falling steadily outside along the village street. In the dulling light the young man with the thin, bright face peered at him across the counter and said:

"Good evening, thir." He smiled then, a smile of singular humor, intelligence, and understanding which revealed for a moment the black horror of his toothless gums, the reason for his lisp. "You are late, thir. I wath jutht clothing."

"Is my suit ready yet?"

"Oh yeth, thir. I wath waiting for you."

He pushed the cardboard suit-box, neatly tied, across the counter, and as Monk fumbled in his trousers for some money and looked at him inquiringly, he said quietly:

"That will be two and thix, thir. And I'm thorry that you had to come out in thuch weathah, but—" the tone finely suggested mild and humorous reproof—"you know, thir, you did not leave me yoah ad-dweth. Othahwithe I thould have thent it." He peered into the greying light through the windows of the shop, and then, shaking his head in a movement of sharp disapproval, he said emphatically: "It ith wet-thed weathah! Wet-thed! I am thorry, thir, that yoah vithit thouid be thpoiled by thuch wet-thed weathah."

"Oh, I don't mind at all," replied the customer, as he took his bundle under his arm and prepared to go. "This kind of weather's all right once in a while, and besides, we've had such fine weather here the last two weeks I've got no reason to complain. I had expected some-thing so different from the way it has been. When I saw how fine the weather could be up here I was surprised."

The young man with the thin, bright face turned, and, arching his thin fingers deliberately upon his counter and leaning forward a trifle, he said in a tone of challenging, finely humorous inquiry:

"And why, pway? Why, may I athk, were you thirpwithed? What kind of weathah did you eckthpect?"

"Oh, I expected it to be rotten. That's what they told me, you know. They told me in London that it rained here all the time, and not to expect anything else."

"That, thir," said the young man slowly and emphatically, "ith a *bathe* thlahndah! A *tewwibly* bathe thlahndah! Wain, it ith twue, we do have," he conceded judicially, "but to deny that we have fine dayth, too, ith thimply widiculuth! Why, thir," the young man de-clared with sudden pride, "taking it yeah in and yeah out, there ith no finah weathah in the world than the weathah of the English Laketh—and to deny it ith *theer* thlahndah—the *batheth* thort of thlahndah—*London* thlahndah!"

And suddenly, having delivered himself with great seriousness of these words, the young man with the thin, bright face straightened, and smiled a quick, friendly, and immensely engaging smile.

"Good night, thir," he said quietly, as the other turned to go.

And the customer departed, followed by the young man's smile—a smile that later he could never forget, that would return to stir his heart with warmth and affection as he remembered the character of swift intelligence, quick, kindly understanding, and fine humor that the smile revealed—and that turned his flesh sick with a feeling poign-antly and strangely mixed of pity and of loathing as he remembered the horror of toothless, blackened gums in one so young which that rare and finely-tempered smile had ruthlessly exposed.

Outside, in the village street, there was nothing left but the dull, wet ghost of light, and the steady sound of the rain falling quietly through the leaves, dripping incessantly from the branches to the ground. And he strode onward with cold rain beating in his face, haunted by the poignant revelations of man's brief meeting with his fellows, the thin, bright wonder of a smile.

This is another moment of lost time, another of time's million faces.

Again, the traveler is on a Channel steamer approaching the town of Boulogne, on the French coast, at two o'clock in the morning. It is mid-Summer, the month of July. The steamer moves in swiftly towards the town. The passengers line the rails and watch the breakwater slide past in the darkness, the lights of the town approach. These things, together with the punctual shuttered flash of the lights all up and down the coast of France, combine to touch these travelers with a sense of ecstasy and wonder.

Not only is that *French* earth, not only are the little figures waiting on the brightly-lighted quay *French* people, but these are *French* lights; and it is a part of the sense of wonder and glory that never dies entirely in our hearts that for a few days these passengers will invest every object they see—trees, cats, dogs, chickens—with this same magic of their own weaving: "Frenchness." They will be unable to see even the most familiar and universal thing without feeling that it is somehow "French" and different, and they will examine it curiously with this purpose.

Meanwhile the steamer moves in swiftly towards the town, and the traveler, weary of flesh but gripped again by the excitement of the voyage, by the hope and belief in voyages that never dies, waits nervously for the landing. The little boat churns up beside the stone-grey quays, he sees the people moving quickly along beside the ship, he sees the bright blue and flaming red stripe of a gendarme's baggy trousers, then he touches land again, he passes down the gangway and surrenders his landing card, he is moving swiftly across the quay behind the brawny little blue-jacketed figure of a porter, a vital little

French goat stepping along cockily with his baggage. At the customs counter the man is waiting, he shouts and beckons to the traveler, the fatigued officials mutter the usual formula, to which he replies swiftly, "Je n'ai rien, monsieur," his baggage is swiftly chalked, the examination is over, he is passed.

Suddenly, the traveler is filled with a great regret and hunger for places he has passed unvisited, for mystery he has not fathomed, for doors he has not opened. He knows that life in this little coastal town, which has before this existed for him only as a cluster of lights, a swift, snarled pattern of streets, faces, bridges, the fronts and backs of houses, and the long boat quay where the train halts, which has existed only as a glint of waters, a slap of tides, a confusion of the voices of officials, porters, and travelers, then as a slide of wooden piers, a vision of outer lights, and at length the ship!—he knows that life here in this town will probably repeat itself in the accustomed tones and gestures of all the earth, but he knows also that one of the fateful errors of living is not to obey the impulse which commands us to doubt, to search, and to explore forever, and, turning to the porter, he tells him he will not go to Paris in the train that waits, but will remain in the town.

In another minute, leaving the maritime quay by a new door, he is seated in a rickety victoria, drawn by a rawboned nag. The decrepit vehicle rattles away over the cobbled stones from the surprised porter and the curious group of cab drivers. The quay, the customs, and the train are left behind, he passes new buildings, traverses new streets, the pattern of arrival has been destroyed forever. In a moment more he has called out the proprietor of a small hotel, taken a room, and almost before the hooves of the old horse have clattered away on the cobbles of the empty street, he finds himself and his baggage alone in a big whitewashed chamber. He orders a big bottle of red wine and drinks it just for the joy and jubilation that he feels.

A few minutes later he has undressed and turned out the light. For a moment he stands in the darkness. The old, thick planking of the floor seems for a moment to swing beneath his feet as ships do. He still feels the motion of the sea. He goes to the window and looks out. The sweet air of the night, the sweet air of the Summer earth, stained with the fragrance of leaves and blossoms, with the smell of the sea in a harbor, and with all the old, familiar smells of the earth and towns—of streets, of old buildings, of pavements, and of shops—comes in to him and bathes him with its friendly human odor.

His window looks out on a little street—one of those narrow back streets of a French town, paved with big cobbles and flanked by narrow sidewalks barely wide enough for the passage of one person. The street has the high, utterly silent, closed appearance of a French street at night: the corrugated shutters are drawn down in front of all the little shops, and the secretive people who sleep in the high old houses, which lean steeply into one another with the settled, malleable sculpture of age, have closed their blinds firmly so that no one may look in. Across the street below him he can see the faded letters above the shutters of a little shop—*Pâtisserie*. It is immensely old and immensely familiar. The street sleeps, and yet possesses a strange, living watchfulness—it is as if one great, dark eye was brooding watchfully and sleeplessly over the destiny of the street.

The traveler feels that he has been here before. He stands for a moment longer drenching himself in the fixed and living eternity of the earth, drawing its mighty and potent fragrance into his lungs, a part of the destiny of all its people. Then he gets into the bed, his flesh gropes down into the rich luxury of clean, coarse sheets and deep pillows as into a living substance, and now for a moment he is alive and still with wonder, he becomes a part of that living darkness. The objects of the room—the bed, the chairs, the wardrobe, the washbasin—are grouped like living things in his consciousness, like old, immensely familiar, and essential things, although an hour before he did not know of their existence; and he is conscious as well of the street outside, the old houses, the town, and all the earth.

He is conscious of time, dark time, secret time, forever flowing like a river; he is conscious of the whole family of the earth, all men living seem friendly and familiar to him, and for a moment he seems to be the living heart of darkness, the eye that watches over sleeping towns.

Then, as he waits and listens in the darkness, he hears several of the familiar sounds of all the earth. Suddenly, that living silence is broken by the shrill, sharp whistle—the thin, piping noise—of a French train, and he hears it as it begins its journey somewhere across the country. Somewhere, again, there is that most familiar and evocative of all sounds—the rattle of wheels and the clatter of shod hooves within an empty street. Somewhere there is the faint and broken howling of a dog; and then the traveler hears the sound of footsteps upon the street below his window.

The sounds come closer, making the ringing and somewhat metallic vibration of footsteps on deserted pavements, and now he hears voices— the voices of a man and a woman—and the voice of the man is low and confidential, he cannot hear the words or distinguish the language, but the voices of these two people are like the voices of all the lovers who ever walked through quiet streets at night together: and the rustle of delicate leaves is always over them, they are casual and tender, they are familiar, and their rhythm has all those inimitable shades, pauses, and interjections of people who are unconscious of the world, or of their own words. The feet and the voices advance, grow loud, and pass his window with a moment of overpowering reality.

Suddenly, just as they pass, a low, rich burst of laughter, tender and voluptuous, wells up out of the woman's throat, and at that moment, by the magic of time, a light burns on a moment of his weaving, a shutter is lifted in the dark, a lost moment lives again with all its magic and terrible intensity, and the traveler is a child again, and he hears at night, beneath the leafy rustle of mid-Summer trees, the feet of the lovers passing by along the street of a little town in America when he was nine years old, and the song that they sang was "Love Me and the World is Mine."

Where?

In the town of Libya Hill in Old Catawba twenty years ago, it is about eleven o'clock at night, he hears the soft, cool rustle of the leaves; there has been the broken thrum and ecstasy of music at a dance across the dark, but now this sound has ceased, and the town grows still, save for the barking of a dog, as now; save that, as now, somewhere beside the river in the dark, he hears the thunder of railed wheels, the tolling of the bell, and the long, wailing whistle of an American train at night, a lonely and wonderful sound, as it recedes into a valley in the South.

Now, also, in one of the leafy, sleeping streets of that little town the child hears the sound of a starting motor; he hears, sudden and loud in the night, the roar of one of the early automobiles. He can easily imagine its appearance—it is one of the early Buicks or Hudsons, with roaring engines, a smell of gasoline, and heavy leathers. It is driven by a young town driver, a reckless young tough with a red face and leather leggins who, having completed his day's work, has used his own car, or "borrowed" one from the dim, dreary recesses of some garage, to take his whore or an easy Summer woman on a midnight drive.

The cool, dark air of night, the stir of leaves, the delicate and intoxicating fragrance of flowers and blossoms, the enormous seductiveness of the brooding earth and the dark hills are all spurs and relishes to their potent lust, and the child in bed is alive with the mystery and seduction of the night. The sound dies, and the lovers pass along the quiet street beneath the leafy rustle of the trees: he hears their footsteps and the low intimacy of their voices. Then he hears the woman's low, rich burst of laughter, and that was twenty years ago when the song that they sang was "The Good Old Summer Time."

Thus this scene, drawn from the deep, dark gulf of memory, burns for a moment in the traveler's brain before he sleeps, but whence it came or by what magic who can say? The laughter of a woman in the street of an old French town has made it live again, and with it lives somehow, over the lost image of the child, over the ruin, weariness, and decay of his flesh, all of the enormous wistfulness, the innocence of man's youth that can never die. The memory evokes an unspeakable emotion, an unutterable cry, a meaning that he cannot shape to words in the heart of the traveler, he hears again the sharp, thin whistle of the French train in the night, and a cry of joy, of pain, of twisted grief and ecstasy bursts from his lips in darkness, and he sleeps.

45

Paris

FOR THREE DAYS, NOW, HE HAD LIVED LIKE A MAN WALKING IN A DREAM. The great external world of Paris, with all its monumental architectures its swarming streets, its crowds and movements, its cafés, restaurants, and its flash and play of life, swept by him and around him in the shadowy and muted patterns of a phantasmal world. He thought of Esther all the time, but he thought of her like a man held in the spell of some powerful and evil enchantment. He was full, now, of new doubts and racking fears. Why was there no letter from her?

He was driven about from place to place by a relentless and exhausted restlessness which took no joy in what it saw, which was obsessed only with the notion of change and movement, as if the devils which dwelt in his spirit could be out-distanced and left behind. He would move from café to café, sitting at a table on the terrace, drinking a coffee at one, a picon at another, a beer at another, looking feverishly and unhappily at the hard vitality, the unexhausted and senseless gaiety of the French.

It never changed. It was always the same. First, there were the waiters hurrying back and forth, then there were young men waiting for their mistresses, then young women waiting for their lovers, then family parties waiting for kinsfolk and drawing chairs around in a circle, then young men alone like himself, then two or three stray prostitutes, then Frenchmen talking business together over a bock, then old women at their gossip together.

It was always the same, then? Should he go to the next café and have a bock? Or should it be a *fine*? Always the same forever.

He would leave the hotel as soon as he got up in the morning, unable to endure the place. And he would straightway take a bus or walk with a furious and driving stride along the quays, across the bridge and through the arches of the Louvre, and up the Avenue de l'Opéra, until he arrived at the building of the American Express. There, fuming with excitement and impatience, he would stand in line at the mail-window, sure that today he would certainly find the expected letter from her. Then, when none came, he would fling away out of the place, sick and desperate at heart, hating everything and everyone around him, hating even the soft, grey air he breathed.

Had they forgotten to forward his mail in London? For a moment his hope flared brightly, and he was sure her letter was now waiting for him there. Or had her great, undying love now died? Was he now forgotten and cast out? Was "forever" just six weeks? Was she whispering now "forever" in some other lover's ear?

With each passing day his hope surged up afresh. And he knew with sinking heart exactly who would hand the letter to him at the American Express. By this time he hated the curt, bald-headed little clerk so bitterly that the knowledge of his hate had communicated itself to that disagreeable but harmless little person. For, as Monk was beginning to find out, though men live in a billion different worlds of mind and thought and time, the world of feeling that they live in is very much the same. The dullest slug of brutish earth whose battered flesh and stunned, abortive brain was ever hurtled through the foul and fetid darkness of the tunnel's depths to Brooklyn could comprehend no more of Einstein or of Shakespeare than a dog prowling through a library could know about his master's books. And yet that lump of stunned and brutal consciousness can, in an instant, be stung to fury by the contemptuous look of a cold eye, the sneering disdain of a single word, the arrogant scorn of flaring nostril, twisted lip.

So was it now with this dull and common little man at the American Express. He had come to know the other's strange dislike for him; and now every day they glanced across the counter at each other with hard, cold eyes of hate, their words were harsh and rasping, edged with insult as they spoke, and when he turned back from his mail and rasped out harshly, "Nothing for you, Webber," the look of malignant satisfaction on his face, when he saw the other's anguish and discomfiture, was unmistakable.

On these occasions, when he went stamping out of the place, his grief and bitter disappointment were so great that he hated not only the officials of the place, but all the tourists who went there as well. It seemed to him that the eyes of everyone were old and dead and evil, filled with a filthy jubilation as they looked at his despair. He hated the flat, nasal voices, the dry necks, the meager features and prognathous faces of his own countrymen, men and women alike, the cheap, machine-made, and ungracious quality of their clothes, their crude and arrogant insensitivity which rasped so harshly on the nerves of other races. He hated their whole, stamped-out, and metallic quality, and simply because he had not got a letter, he vented his spleen upon his own people, convincing himself, in an orgy of inverted patriotism, that the whole country had gone sterile, rotten, corrupt, and criminal, that it had created a monstrous, vile, and destructive machine which had stamped out a cheap race of robots, who had betrayed all the ancient joy and life and fruitfulness and honor of "the old America"—of Crockett's, Lincoln's, Whitman's, and Mark Twain's America—and, naturally, of course, his own; and that if the old America was to be restored, the whole world to be saved, this horrible, warped race of perverted robots would have to be destroyed. And all because he had not found a letter from a woman!

He would stride silently by the chattering swarm of tourists in the Express Company offices, and grind his teeth together, as, with a kind of malignant gluttony of hate, an envenomed satisfaction, he seized on every scrap of conversation around him. There seemed to be no joy in it whatever. It was a gathering place of deluded and bewildered people, a vast clatter of excited, complaining, confused, unhappy, hurried, driven, inexperienced people. They were the people from small towns everywhere, the people who had always wanted "to take a trip to Yurup"—the mid-Western schoolteachers, small-town business men and their wives, "club women," college boys and girls—and they were now being herded and driven around like cattle on some horrible tour, jabbered at, confused, and cheated everywhere they went, already sick and tired and frightened and bewildered by the whole business, bitterly disappointed and disillusioned by this great trip to which they had looked forward all their lives, and longing desperately "to get back home again."

On these occasions he could not tell which he disliked more—the tourists, with their nasal, whining, and complaining voices, or the officials, whose manner seemed curt, brusque, hurried, impatient, and unfriendly, and almost openly delighted—even as the little mail clerk was—at the unhappiness, confusion, error, and discomfort of the people they served. The officials were both American and French; all around him as he walked through the offices, they were drumming their fingers impatiently on the counters as they talked, and he could hear them saying with the impatient impregnability of their hard, cold speech:

"I'm sorry, madame. We ordered the tickets for you but we cannot be responsible if you did not like the seats. . . . No. No. If your seats were behind a column and you could not see, I'm sorry, but you took them on your own responsibility. We cannot be responsible. . . . No sir! No! We have absolutely nothing to do with that. . . . No. We cannot be held responsible! . . . We recommended the hotel, it is one of the hotels on our list, we have always considered it a reputable establishment, it has been well recommended by other people we have sent there. . . . If your baggage was stolen, I am sorry. We cannot be held responsible for your baggage." Then sharply—"Who? . . . What's that?"—with cold indifference—"I cannot tell you who to see, sir. You might try the American Consul. . . . You should have appealed to the local authorities while you were there. . . . If the hotel management refuses to settle, I am sorry. But we can do nothing for you here. . . . All right," curtly, coldly, to another patient waiter. "You want, please—? . . . Strasbourg," in a cold, curt tone, rapidly; then wearily, "10:35 in the morning . . . 2:05 in the afternoon . . . and 9:30 every night . . . from the Gare de l'Est"—reaches coldly for railroad folder. rapidly draws a circle round three schedules, pushes it brusquely across counter without looking at inquirer, and, drumming impatiently with hard fingers, turns to next petitioner, saying sharply: "Yes? . . . What do you want? Letter of Credit?"—wearily—"Opposite counter where you see the sign. . . . No, sir. No. Ticket reservations here."

And the poor, driven, confused, bewildered, and bitterly disappointed tourists might be heard on all sides protesting, inquiring, getting rebuffed, wandering around and complaining to each other, uttering words like these:

"But I tell you you've got to change it! What am I going to do? . . . When they sold me the ticket back home they told me ——"

"Sorry, madame, but that's not our affair."

"Oh, there's that man and his wife from St. Paul who came over with us on the boat. . . . Mr. and Mrs. What's-Their-Name—oh, Humperschlagel. . . . Speak to them, Jim! They're the first people we've seen that we know. . . . Oh, how d'ye do, Mrs. Humperschlagel! . . . How are you, Mr. Humperschlagel? . . . Are you going back with us on the *Olympic* next month?"

"Nah-h; I've changed my reservations. . . . We're sailing this month on the fifteenth, on the *Mauretania*. . . . If there was another boat that was goin' sooner, I'd take that one, too."

"Why, what's the matter, Humperschlagel? No trouble at home, is there?"

"Trouble? Hell, no! The only trouble is I can't get back soon enough! The only trouble is I got to stay here until the fifteenth!"

"Why, Mr. Humperschlagel! You sound as if you haven't been aving a good time! Something must have happened to you!"

"Happened! Say, Mrs. Bradshaw, everything has happened but the smallpox! We've had nothing but trouble and hard luck since we left home!"

"Ah-h-h!"—a woman's tremolo of pity—"*What* a shame!"

"The first thing was the wife got sick the minute the ship pulled out of dock. . . . She was sick as a dog the whole way over, I thought she was going to die. . . . They had to take her off on a stretcher when we got to Cherbourg, and she hasn't felt right since."

"O-o-o-oh, Mrs. Humperschlagel! What a shame! I'm so-o-o sorry!" Another tremolo of womanly pity, answered by a whining, nasal, feebly-ailing woman's voice:

"Oh, I tell you, Mrs. Bradshaw, it's just been awful! I've felt terrible every minute of the time since I left home! . . . I haven't got to see a thing. I've spent the whole time laying around in hotels in bed, too sick to move. . . . We did get to take a bus-ride around Par-ris yesterday, but we went to so many places I got all turned round and couldn't remember where we'd been. . . . I tried to get the man to tell me, but if you ask them anything they jabber at you so you don't understand a word they're saying."

"Yeah!" rasped Humperschlagel bitterly. "All you understand is this"—he held out a big paw with a clutching movement of the fingers—"give, give, give—that's the same in any language—only these guys have got it down to a science—they take you both ways, going and coming! Say! They cheat you right and left—if you don't keep your eyes open, they'll steal the gold out of your teeth!"

Meanwhile, the two women's voices could be heard in excited, chattering communion: "Why the *prices* are just aw-w-ful! . . . I'd always heard how cheap it was, but after *this*!—you can't tell me! . . . Why, I *know*! It's *dreadful*! Of course, they think every American is a millionaire and will pay them any price they ask! . . . But the *idea*! To think they had the gall to ask *fifteen hundred francs*! Jim and I figured it up later—it comes to over ninety dollars—for a little rag of a dress you could get in Bloomington for twenty dollars! . . . Why, I *did*! I *did*, my dear! . . . I *told* her! . . . I handed it right back to her. I said, 'You can try to find if someone else is fool enough to pay it, but you'll never get it out of me! . . . Not in a million years!' . . . I said, 'We can get as good as that back home for a fourth the price, without coming over here to be swindled!' "

Meanwhile, Mr. Humperschlagel, with booming finality: "No, sir! Never again! The good old U.S.A. is good enough for me! When I see the Statue of Liberty again I'm going to let out a yell you can hear from here to San Francisco! . . . They say, once a sucker is always a sucker, but not me! One time is enough!"

And Mrs. H: "But how I'm dreading the trip back! I was telling Fred, the other night, if there was only some way they could *shoot* you back . . . *cable* you back . . . I think I'd even be willing to take the chance of flying back in an airplane, I so dread going on that ship! I was deathly sick every moment of the way over, I know it's going to be even worse going back. . . . My stomach has been all upset since we left home. I haven't been able to enjoy anything I ate for over a month. I simply can't eat the food they give you over here."

"Why, hell!" cried Mr. Humperschlagel, "they never give you anything that's fit to eat! A piece of butter and a roll for breakfast, and a little pot of coffee that ——"

"And, oh!" groaned Mrs. Humperschlagel at this point, "such coffee! That awful old, black, bitter stuff they drink! Oh-h! . . . I was saying to Fred the other night, the first thing I'm going to do when I get home is to drink almost a dozen cups of good, strong, fresh, American coffee!"

"And all those little dishes with names no one can read . . . horse's dovers . . . and—why!" he burst out indignantly, "they eat *snails*! . . . Why, it's the truth!" he declared, wagging his head. "The other day at the hotel I saw a feller picking something out of a shell with a pair of tweezers and asked the waiter what it was. 'Ah-h, moun-seer!' " cried Mr. Humperschlagel in an affected voice, " 'eet ees ze snell!' . . . Just let me get home again where I can forget about all them little dishes with fancy sauces and names no one can read and wade into an inch-thick porterhouse—smothered with onions—about a gallon of real coffee!—a hunk of apple pie!—boy, oh boy!" he concluded with a look of lustful rumination on his face as he surveyed the gluttonous future—"Will I murder it, or not!"

"Look here, Humperschlagel," Mr. Bradshaw now interrupted, as if struck by sudden inspiration, "why don't you and Mrs. Humperschlagel come with me and my wife some night to a little place we've discovered here in Paris. Some friends told us about it, and we've been eating there ever since. I can't eat this French grub either, but at this little place I'm telling you about you can get a real, honest-to-God, home-cooked American meal."

"What!" Humperschlagel yelled. "The real thing—and no fooling?"

"No, sir!" said Mr. Bradshaw firmly. "It's the real thing all right—all wool and a yard wide with all the trimmings! Real American coffee, biscuits, corn bread, pork chops, ham and eggs—eggs done the way you like 'em!—toast, real sirloin steak that you can sink your teeth into——"

"And apple pie?" said Humperschlagel anxiously.

"Yes, sir!" said Mr. Bradshaw firmly. "The finest apple pie you ever saw—brown and crusty, baked fresh every day!"

"Boy, oh boy!" roared Humperschlagel jubilantly. "Lead us to it! Tell us where it is! When can we get together—brother, I'm hungry, I can't wait!"

And so it went all up and down the line. A flashily dressed Brooklyn-Broadway Jew, his hands thrust into the pockets of his jaunty, cut-in overcoat, a cigar gripped and wiggled masterfully at the corners of his convulsive mouth, his jaunty grey hat pulled down at a swagger angle over his great, beaked nose, might be observed rocking gently back and forth on the soles of his burnished and be-spatted feet, saying in a rasping and domineering tone to a little circle of impressed acquaintances:

"No, sir! . . . No, sir, mister! . . . I wanted to take a look at what dey had, but one time is enough! After dis, I'm t'roo! . . . I've seen duh whole t'ing now—duh Toweh of London, Buckin'ham Palace, Berlin, Munich, Vienna, Budapest, Rome, Naples, Monte Carlo—*all* dose places," he said, with a tolerant wave of his head. "I took duh whole woiks in while I was about it—an' dey ain't got nothin' here in Par-ris dat I don't know about. F'r Chris' sake!" he snarled suddenly, whipping the cigar from his mouth and looking around him in a menacing fashion. "Dey can't tell me anyt'ing about dis —— town! I been to every —— jernt dey got. I seen duh whole t'ing."

He paused, put the cigar back deliberately in the corner of his mouth, rocked gently back and forth upon his polished toes, and with a little, superior smile, he nodded knowingly, and then said slowly, with telling deliberation:

"No, sir! No, sir, mister! I seen duh whole woiks from top to bottom—an' *believe* me, believe *me*, brother—we got it on 'em comin', goin', an' across duh middle. . . . Yes, sir! *Yes,* sir! Dey ain't got nuthin'—no, sir, not a —— t'ing dat we ain't got ten times betteh. . . . I been hearin' about dis jernt all my life. I t'ought I'd like to take a look at it. Par-ris! W'y f'r Chris' sake!" he snarled suddenly again, whipped the cigar from his mouth, and turned on his audience in such a meaningful fashion that they shrank away. "What are yuh talkin' about, f'r Chris' sake?" he demanded belligerently, although no one had said a word. "W'y I could take yuh to more jernts on Little Ole Broadway dan dis —— town eveh *dreamed of havin'*! Yes, sir! Yes, sir! Jernts dat would make duh best jernts in dis town look like Mulligan's Penny Parlor on Sixt Avenoo! . . . No, sir, mister! Not for me! Not after dis! One time is enough! *I'm* satisfied! I seen what I wanted to see an' now I'm t'roo! Afteh dis, little ole Noo Yawk is good enough for me! Yes, sir! Yes, sir!"

And finally, satisfied by this triumphant assertion of his patriotism, he put his thumbs into his armpits, swayed gently back and forth upon his polished feet, chewed the big cigar around, and let a big coil of fat and fragrant smoke seep from his nostrils.

Such was the office of the American Express in Paris, in the Summer of 1928, where the letter did not come.

He went one night to the Folies Bergère and got there late. The lobby was deserted; the men in the ticket window and the two men behind the high desk by the doors looked at him with cold, Gallic eyes. He read the list of prices; the classifications were bewildering; he did not know what they meant. A man in evening dress came up and spoke to him—a young man of Paris and of the night, in his mid-thirties, with polished, patent-leather hair, dead, reptile's eyes, a large, hooked nose of avarice, a vulpine face.

"Monsieur?" he said inquiringly yet persuasively, "Is zere perhaps somesing I can do for you?"

He turned, startled, awed at the splendid creature's sleek array, and stammered:

"I—what ticket shall I ——?"

"Ah, ze tick-*et!*" the man cried with sudden enlightenment. "Mais, parfaitement! Monsieur," he said smoothly, "permettez moi! . . . I am an attaché—vous comprenez—of ze theatre. I shall buy for you ze tick-*et.*"

"But not—not too dear," he faltered, ashamed to speak of paltry cost before this splendid creature of the night. "Something, something of middle price—you understand?"

"Mais parfaitement!" the sleek, young creature cried again. "C'est entendu. Quelque chose du moyen prix."

He took the hundred-franc note which the youth tendered him, went to the ticket office window, spoke rapidly to the men within, and bought the most expensive ticket in the house. Then, smilingly, with a "S'il vous plaît, monsieur," he took it to the desk, where it was scowled at, scrawled in a book, and torn in two by the two guardians of the door, and then gallantly he returned it to the youth, with a slight bow, and with no change.

"And now," he smoothly said, as Monk, somewhat overwhelmed by the swiftness and costliness of the proceeding, prepared to enter— "and now—you wish to see the danc-*ing* girls, n'est-ce pas?"

"D-d-dancing girls?" he faltered. "No, I came to see the show."

"Oh!" said Night-Eye with a gay laugh and a wave of the hand. "But zere is time! Zere is time! But first we go to see ze danc-*ing* girls, n'est-ce pas?"

"But some other time—not now—I am already late for the show!"

"Mais pas du tout!" said Night-Eye with vociferous dissent. "Du tout, du tout, du tout, du tout, du tout! The representation has not yet commenced. So of time you will have plen-tee."

"And the show has not yet started?" the youth said, with a troubled look at his watch.

"But no! Not yet for half an hour!" said Night-Eye emphatically. "And now—you come wiz me, eh?" he went on cajolingly. "To see ze danc-*ing* girls. I sink you will like—yes!"

"Is that part of the show, too?"

"But yes! Parfaitement!"

"And you are employed here by the theatre?"

"But yes, monsieur! Ze management zey—w'at you say?—zey keep me here to be of sair*vice* to ze strangers," he smiled engagingly and made a graceful, winglike gesture of the hands and shoulders. "So if you like, I show you around a leetle—eh?—before ze show begins."

"What a nice fellow!" thought the grateful young man. "And how thoughtful of the management to keep him here to help foreigners! . . . I suppose, though, that he expects a tip when he gets through." He paused, dubious, not knowing whether so sleek and gentlemanly a creature would take a tip or not.

"And now we go—eh?" smiled Night-Eye. "I sink you will like ze gir-r-ls. Par ici, monsieur!" He held one of the doors courteously open, and, as he left, something swift and instant passed between himself and the two evening-clothed men behind the high twin desk. It was not a smile, and it was not a word, but it was full of jubilation, and hard and cold and loveless, and as old and evil as the night.

When they got out into the street before the theatre, he turned a surprised and troubled eye upon the Frenchman, but, in response to a coaxing pressure on his arm, allowed himself to be led away.

"But—" he protested, "the dancing girls? Are they not here in the theatre also?"

"Mais non, mais non," said Night-Eye smoothly. "Zey 'ave—'ow do you call eet?—a separate établissement."

"But it is all part of the Folies Bergère?"

"Mais parfaitement! . . . Monsieur, I see, is new to Paris, eh?"

"Yes, I have not been here long."

"And 'ow long weel you stay?"

"I don't know—six weeks perhaps—perhaps longer."

"Ah! Zat is good!" said Night-Eye with an approving nod. "Zat weel geev you time to onderstand ze language, eh? . . . Oui! . . . Zat weel be good. . . . Eef you know ze language—" he made an easy, conceding movement of the hands and shoulders, "tout va bien! . . . Eef not!" he shrugged again, and then with a regretful accent, "Ah, monsieur—zere is so many bat pipples 'ere in Paris. Not ze French! Non, non, non, non, non! C'est les Russiens . . . les Allemands . . . les Italiens. Zey are here to take advantage of ze pipples who do not onderstand français. . . . You geeve zem ze dol-*laire* to change!" he cried. "Ah-h! Ze dol-*laire*! You must watch ze dol-*laire*! . . . Do not geev zem ze dol-*laire*! Go to ze bank ven you vish to change ze dol-*laire*! . . . You have ze dol-*laire*?" he anxiously inquired.

"No," the youth answered, "I have only Express checks."

"Ah-h!" cried Night-Eye, and nodded his head approvingly. "Zat ees better! Zen you can go to ze bank americain, n'est-ce pas?"

"Yes," the young man answered him.

"Zat is motch, motch better!" said Night-Eye, and wagged his head with vigorous approval. And they walked on.

Outside the Folies there had been a great, blank glare of light, but now the streets and buildings had the closed, dark, and shuttered look, the monumental barrenness, which is, for the most part, the characteristic visage of nocturnal Paris. Their walk was not a long one. A block or two from the great theatre they turned into another street and paused before a house which had a very closed and secret look, and from whose upper, shuttered windows the light streamed brilliantly in hot, exciting bars.

Night-Eye rang the bell. It sounded loud and sudden with an electric thrill that somehow made the heart beat faster. A girl dressed in the uniform of a maidservant opened the door and smilingly admitted them. They were in a hall or corridor lined with splendid mirrors; the carpet underneath their feet was rich and thick.

From above came sounds of swift, excited movement: the opening and closing of many doors, a scampering of quick feet, a clamor of young, excited voices, laughter, and a voice harsh, tyrannic, and impatient, raised in the strident accents of command. And all the time electric bells were ringing—a sound as urgent, penetrating, full of menace and immediacy as the sudden thrill and violence of a burglar alarm.

As they began to mount the splendid stairs, all sounds stopped. They went up, their feet noiseless in the crimson carpet, in a dead, suspended stillness charged with life. He knew it was all around him, listening behind a dozen doors, peering at him with a hundred secret eyes, waiting, watching, and unseen.

That charged and secret stillness, that closed and sensual light numbed his flesh, gave to his limbs, his heart, his stomach, and his loins, an empty, hollow feeling. He licked his lips with dry excitement, his pulse beat hard and quick like hammer-taps within his blood.

The scene was strange and unfamiliar as a dream, and yet it had a dream's reality. It was like something that he had never seen, but which he had always known, which was congruent to some image buried in his soul, and which, now that he had found it, was unmistakable. And now that he was here, he felt the sense of strangeness and ghastly unreality that comes from the mixture of the familiar and the unknown, which is the essence of all strangeness—as if, suddenly, he found himself in hell or heaven, talking to someone he had known all his life—a town policeman or the village sot.

By pressing a bell and going through a door, he had entered a new world. He had come from the empty, naked, and familiar silence of the streets into the closed and secret world of night. It was a world that was incredible because he had always known it was there behind the plain, untelling façades of familiar houses. And it was a world that was soft, secret, splendid, vicious, and luxurious, a world in which all things—lights, faces, the hue and texture of the living flesh, the beat and pulsing of the blood, and even time and memory, went through the chemistry of a strange and unreal transformation. It was an evil world: it froze his blood, and numbed his flesh, it made the pulse beat in him like hard hammer-taps. But it was, as well, an evilly seductive world; it filled him with its close and languorous perfume, and it stirred his senses with the evil quickenings of rending and insatiable desire.

And he knew it was a world that could be found here only, in the evil secrecy and nocturnal presence of this mysterious and enchanted city—a world strange to an American, and all the naked fear and desolation of his soul. For though shut in, and cut away from the external world of streets and traffic as by a hermetic, tomblike seal, once entered, in its very secrecy it was carnally, unspeakably, with a whole-souled, unquestioning debauchery, free.

It was not a world where that strange and ancient commerce of a woman's flesh was carried on in stealth and fear, and terrified alarm. It was not that poor and twisted world of vice, so brutal, hurried, so necessitous, that one finds down in the wooden shacks and shanties by the tracks, the station shambles of an American town, or in the latticed houses down in Niggertown, or in the cheap and dingy little hotels down on South Main Street. It was not a world where one snatched love and emptied out desire between distressful perturbations of the heart; or where one waited in the darkness of a shabby room half through the night for the expected step upon a creaky board, the stealthy turning of a knob, the whispered admonitions over haste and silence. It was not that world where a knocking on the door smote terror to the heart, and instantly constricted all the hot and lustful ardor or desire, and where people waited, paused, and listened with caught breath for a forbidding step to pass, and where men went and came out quickly with an upturned collar, a pulled hat, and an averted eye.

It was a world where the ancient trade of vice was templed in security, dignified by the authorities of general consent, a profession old, accepted, and confirmed as was the law, or medicine, or the church. It was a world where vice was given the adornment of every sensual and luxurious embellishment, was cultivated by every rare and subtle practice that centuries of experience could acquire; and because of this, the place caught his senses in the spell of a powerful drug, swept his will into acceptance upon the overwhelming tides of a languorous and corrupt surrender.

A woman was waiting for them at the top of the splendid stairs. She was dressed in an evening gown of a glittering, beaded material, her arms were white and dead and naked, powdered, bracelets clanked upon them, and her dead, phthisic hands and fingers were jewel-encrusted; the veins were hard and blue, and as lifeless-looking as a corpse's.

As for her face, it was the most horribly appropriate caricature of a face that he had ever seen. In his greatest moments, Daumier had never drawn its match. It was a face "of an uncertain age" simply because the face was ageless. The woman may have been forty-five, or fifty, or sixty, or even seventy; but really there was no way of telling her age. Her age was ageless with its wickedness. Her face had been steeped and hardened in iniquity, dyed in sinfulness, until it actually had the hard, dried, ageless texture, enseamed and mummified, of one of those terrible trophies of a headhunter's skill. Her eyes might have been dull, hard agates stuck there in her face, so lacking in lustre, life, or humanity they were; her hair was perfectly dead, dyed some ghastly, indefinable texture between tow and straw; and as for her nose, which gave the final and decisive note of avarice, rapacity, and bottomless iniquity to that great caricature of a face, her nose was an incredible, vulturesque beak, as hard and bony as a bird's. Because of that nose, there was no mistaking the final quality of that face: that face was an axe, a human axe, as hard, as sharp, as palpable as an axe, and cold and cruel as hell. It made the faces of Sitting Bull, Powhatan, or the great chief, Rain-in-the-Face, or any of the faces of the Sioux or Apache tribes, look like the faces of sweet, peaceful, benevolent, and Christian old men.

She greeted them with a smile of brilliant cordiality, that had in it all the living and warm-hearted friendliness of a rattler's fangs; and then broke into excited, greedy French with Night-Eye, which immediately established the status and the nationality of her latest victim, and got him instantly ready for the plucking.

They entered a room and took seats in one corner on an elegant gilt-and-satin sofa, old Axe-Face seating herself in a motherly way beside ner youthful client on a gilt-and-satin chair, talking a blue streak all the time.

"And 'ow do you like Paris? . . . Nice, eh? . . . Ven you see vat ve 'ave, you vill like better—yes?" She smiled with crafty insinuation, and at the same moment struck her dead, white hands together, crying sharply the harsh slave-driver's cry.

Immediately, incredibly, with a horrible, comic instancy which he noticed at the moment, music—the music of a large victrola—began to play somewhere, and around him on all sides the walls swung open, and two dozen young and handsome women entered, dancing.

They were completely naked. The walls, which were nothing but mirrors, closed behind them, the ceiling also was a mirror, the floor as well, and now as these naked, young, and lovely girls danced slowly past him, round the room, the blazing refractions of those hundred mirrors multiplied these naked bodies uncountably; everywhere he looked it seemed that he was looking through unending colonnades at the infinite progressions of young, rhythmic, naked flesh.

He sat there, gape-jawed and goggle-eyed upon the gilt-and-satin sofa, throned in a sultan's pride between the solicitous courtiership of old Axe-Face and young Night-Eye, and all the time the lovely girls came dancing by clothed in the maddening allurement of young, naked flesh, inviting him with the soft eyes, the whispered promises, the unheard entreaties of their gay whore's language, smiling at him with all the coaxing cajoleries of light love, the sweet and evil innocence of their young whore's faces.

And then they led him into an enormous room of gilt and mirrors and blue light. They called this place "The Mysteries of Asia." Here there were forty more girls to pick and choose from, and one or two were black, and all of them wore nothing. Some stood on pedestals like statues, and some were posed in niches in the wall, and some were draped across a flight of steps, and one of them was fastened to an enormous crucifix. That was for art. Some were lying on great carpets on the floor—and none could move. But all of them looked at him and tried to speak with their eyes, which said, "Take me!"

When he had chosen one, they went upstairs into a room with shaded lights and gilt and mirrors and a bed, and he tipped the maid, and his girl excused herself to "make her toilette."

She was courteous and good-tempered and polite, and he talked to her. He found there was a lot to talk about. He began by saying:

"It makes hot today."

And she said, "Yes, but it makes less hot, I think, than it did yesterday."

And he said, "Yes, but still the season is quite rainy, isn't it?"

And she said, "Yes, much in retard. It is quite boring."

And he asked her if she was always there.

And she said, "But yes, sir, all the days except the Tuesday, when I make my promenade."

And then he asked her what her name was, and she said it was Yvonne, and he said that she was very amiable and pretty and that he would certainly return and call for her again.

And she said, "Thank you, sir. You are genteel. The name is Yvonne and I am here every day but the Tuesday."

And she tied his tie and helped him with his coat, and thanked him graciously for fifteen francs, and she went downstairs with him.

Now he is walking in a street of small, rich shops, in a street of thronging crowds and traffic, he is walking in the Rue St. Honoré, and the strange, dark faces of the Frenchmen swarm about him, his flesh writhes and is weary with the hard cat nervousness of their movements, the print of a billion men is on his memory, the weight of a million forgotten patterns, and it is all as if it had been forever, his shoulders bow with the immense grey weariness of the unnumbered days, with the idiot repetition of all living.

Then suddenly he sees his face reflected in the mirrored window of a woman's glove-shop, and in a second, as if a lock were shot back in his memory, a door is opened and three years of living drop away from him and he is a youth, amorous of the earth and full of wonder and exultancy, who is in a strange land for the first time and who passed this way once and looked into this window. And the features of that youth stare back at him now, and the moment lives again like magic, and he sees the lost youth staring through the coarsened mask, and he sees what time has done.

The magic dies: he is possessed by the swarm of the crowd again, the coil and weaving of the endless pattern, the tumult, the fever, and the fret that has been and that will be forever; he passes on from one phantasmal ghostliness of time to yet another, but the strange mystery of living is in him, he has had a vision of death and time, and he turns his eyes up for a moment to the timeless skies, which shed their unperturbable light upon the street and all its fashions, and as he looks at the actual faces, the movements, patterns of the men and motors, the mystery and sadness of the human destiny is on him.

He notes the day. It is the thirtieth of July, 1928.

Time! Time! Time!

He passes on.

46

The Pension in Munich

HOW CAN ONE SPEAK OF MUNICH BUT TO SAY IT IS A KIND OF GERMAN heaven? Some people sleep and dream they are in Paradise, but all over Germany people sometimes dream that they have gone to Munich in Bavaria. And really, in an astonishing way, the city is a great Germanic dream translated into life.

It is not easy to find a reason for the city's seductive power. Munich is very solid, very heavy, but not at all dull. The best beer in Germany, in the world, is made there, and there are enormous beer cellars that are renowned throughout the land. The Bavarian is the National Good Fellow—he is supposed to be a witty and eccentric creature, and millions of post cards are printed of him in his national costume blowing the froth away from a foaming stein of beer. In other parts of Germany people will lift their eyes and sigh rapturously when you say you are going to Munich:

"Ach! München . . . ist schön!"

Munich is not, in the same way as many other German towns, a Gothic fairyland. There are many cities, towns, and villages throughout the country that have, in a much greater sense, the enchanted qualities of the Gothic world, the magic of the Gothic architecture, the romance of the Gothic landscape. Nuremberg is such a city, Rothenburg, in a smaller but more perfect sense, is another, the old, central part of Frankfort is another, the ancient town of Hanover has a Gothic wonder of old streets and houses that Munich cannot equal. So, too, with Eisenach, in Thuringia. So, too, with Bremen; so with many towns along the Rhine and on the Mosel, with Coblenz and with Hildesheim, with Strasbourg in Alsace, with countless tiny villages and towns in the Black Forest and in Harz, in Saxony and in Franconia, in the Hanseatic north, and in the Alpine valleys of Bavaria and the Tyrol.

650

There are no ancient castles built upon a sheer romantic rock in Munich, no ancient houses clinging to the rock. There is no sudden elfin loveliness of hills, no mystery of dark forests, no romantic loveliness of landscape. The thing is felt in Munich more than it is seen, and for this reason the seduction and the mystery are greater. Munich itself is built upon a kind of plain, and yet somehow one knows that the enchanted peaks are there. Monk had heard it said that on a radiant day the Alps were visible, but he did not know. He never saw them—not from Munich. He saw them pictured in some panoramic post cards of the city, far off, faintly gleaming in an architecture of enchanted smoke. He thought the picture was a product of the phantasy. The photographer put them there because, like Monk, he felt and knew that they were there.

How to tell about it! It is so certain yet it is a speechless thing.

Each great city Monk had known had had an odor for him. Boston had an odor in its crooked streets of fresh-ground coffee mixed with smoke. Chicago, when the wind from the West set in, had an unmistakable odor of burning pork. New York was so much harder to define, but he thought it was the odor of a dynamo, it was the odor of electricity, it was the odor of the cellar, of an old brick house or of a city building, closed, a little stale and dank, touched with a subtle, fresh, half-rotten smell of harbor. London's odor, too, was mixed of many things and yet was definite. The first and all-prevailing odor was a smell of fog, touched numbly with the faintly acrid smell of soft-coal smoke. Infused in this a malty reek of bitter beer, the faint nostalgia of tea, the faintly sweet aroma of an English cigarette, and all this mixed with morning, fumed with the smoked, slightly acid pungency of grilled sausages, bacon, and a kipper, and filtered through the old-gold bronze of a befogged yet not entirely conquered sun— and you had something like the smell of London.

Paris, too, had its own single, unique, and incomparable stink, a fusion of many smells, a nostalgic blend of many odors, both corrupt and exquisite. To Monk, the first, because it was the most definite of all the smells of Paris—the one that belonged to Paris and to no other city—was the smell of stale and slightly wetted sawdust. It was a smell that came up from the entrances to the underground and up through the pavement gratings. It was a smell of lifeless life, of dead vitality; it was a smell of dead air, used-up, tainted oxygen. It was a smell of millions of weary and unwashed people, who had come and gone and breathed the air and used it up and left it there—dead, stagnant, poisoned, tainted, and corrupted, carrying upon its dead waves the smell of weary and exhausted sweat, the dead, denuded breath of lifeless energy.

Venice had the reek of its canals, that moveless stench, that rank, pestilential, fever-laden smell of suspended sewage floating in old walls. Marseilles as well, a dangerous and diseaseful breath, compact with human filth and fecal matter, the tainted odor of the South, the smell of fish, of the old harbor in the Mediterranean Sea.

And Munich—it was the cleanest smell of all, the subtlest and most haunting, the most exciting, the most undefined. It was an almost odorless odor, touched always with a buoyant lightness of the Alpine energies. In Summer the sun would blaze down bright and hot from a shell-blue brilliance of shining sky. The hotter it became, the better he felt. He breathed in great breaths of the hot air and sunlight. He seemed to be drinking in enormous draughts of the solar energy. He was filled with lightness, exuberance, and vital strength—so different from the sweltering lassitude, the human misery, the heat-glazed skies and steaming blanket, the tainted and miasmic vapor of the New York heat.

He always knew that the Alps were there. He felt them there against the South, an hour away, the shining magic of the ghost-wise Alps. He could not see them but he breathed them in upon the air, he smelled the mountains, the clean, high ethers of the Alpine energy.

August had come and August ended. Something had gone out of the day, something was fading from the sun. There was a sharpness of the Autumn breath at night, a sense of something waning rapidly, just the spirit yet, warm sunlight still by day, but something going, fading, going, a premonitory sadness in the soul. Enchanted Summer was departing, was fading south to Italy.

Early in September the nights were chill, and sometimes he heard a scratching of dry leaves. Sometimes would come a breath of wind and then a leaf would scratch and scamper on the pavement. And someone would hurry past. And he would hear the leaf again, the plash of waters in the fountains, somehow different from the sound of fountains on a Summer's night. He would still go at nights and sit outside in the gardens of the Neue Borse. There were still people at the tables on the terrace. The gardens were almost bare. His feet would crunch sparely on the dry gravel. The doors and windows of the great café were closed. Inside, the place was crowded. The orchestra was playing. The air already was a little thick, thick with the warmth of food and people, thick with music, thick with beer. But he would sit out on the terrace, hearing a leaf that scratched across the gravel, feeling at length the ghost of Autumn in the air.

He was living in the Theresienstrasse, just at the corner where the Luisenstrasse crosses it. The place was called the Pension Burger, but the people who rented it did not have that name. It was a plain, solidly-constructed building of three stories, without much adornment, but with something of that inevitable massiveness, that formidable ponderosity, that gets into almost all German architecture, and that American buildings do not have.

He did not know just how they did it, but it seemed almost to be an architectural ectoplasm of the German soul. There was something so immense and formidable about this kind of building. He supposed you could call it a kind of German Victorianism. It certainly came out of the palmy days of William the Second. It was derivative, no doubt, from what the English call Victorian. But it was Victorian molded by the fist of Wotan. It was Victorian fogged with beer, and heavied with the ponderous mass of an incalculable weight. It was Victorian with the old dark forests in it. It was guttural Victorian. And compared to its crushing mass, its formidable and appalling weight, the choicest examples in the domains of her late majesty the Queen seemed architectures of a fairy lightness. Compared to it, the old New York post office seemed a miracle of grace and soaring buoyancy.

Monk never passed those houses by without a feeling of overwhelming helplessness. It was not that they were so great. It was not that they were really massive. It was just the sense that there was in them a kind of weight that could not be estimated or measured in ordinary dimensional terms. It did not matter that these old buildings were only three or four floors tall; they overwhelmed him in a way that no American building could ever do.

When he would think of home, the whole terrific visage of Manhattan, the cratered landscape of its soaring towers, it seemed to be a kind of great, fantastic toy, constructed by ingenious children, just as children might build little cities out of cardboard shapes, and stamp, neatly and evenly, millions of little window holes in them, and then light candles back behind to give the illusion of a lighted city. Even an old American building, an old warehouse with its scaled and rusted brick, an old tenement with its curiously, pleasantly flat, blank planes (that always made him think somehow of the Riots of 1861 and of the illustrations in ancient numbers of *Harper's Weekly*), seemed to have, compared to buildings such as these, a fragile, almost flimsy, insub-stantiality. He could never come back home and wake at morning on the ship at Quarantine and look out of a porthole to see that so enor-mously moving and hauntingly evocative scene—the first view of American earth, the humid, coarse, and somewhat pallid green, the faded opacity of color, and, most strange, most moving, most imme-diate, recovered instantly with the full impact of recognition and of wonder, the shape of a white frame house, or a building of scaled, rusty brick—without feeling they were all so toylike and so tender that he could punch holes through the flat, blank walls with his toe, reach over to where the spires and ramparts of Manhattan lay sus-tained in mist and morning like something fragile, corklike, floating in the water, and reap the whole thing down with a single movement of his arm, gather them together in a single grip and pull them up as easily as if they had been a handful of quilled onions.

But he never passed one of these buildings in the Theresienstrasse, or one of those tremendous and massive façades in the great Ludwig-strasse, without feeling as helpless as a child in a world of immense objects whose dimensions he could neither master nor comprehend. He felt a little as Gulliver must have felt among the Brobdingnagians. He got the feeling at almost every door he entered that he was having to stand on tiptoe to reach up to the knob. And yet he knew this was not true.

The pension itself was a modest dwelling that occupied the two upper floors of a building. It was run by a young woman whose name was Fräulein Bahr. She had two brothers, both unmarried, both em-ployed in business in the city. The older brother was a man around forty, a pleasant, good-natured man of medium height and rather chunky, with a florid face and a short mustache. Monk didn't know what he did. He worked in an office somewhere. He was perhaps a clerk, a cashier, or a bookkeeper—an office man.

The younger brother, Heinrich, was tall and rather thin. He was past thirty, and had served two years in the war. He worked in a big travel bureau in what was then called the Promenaden Platz. Monk used to go in to see him in the morning. He cashed travelers' checks, made railway and steamship bookings, gave tourists and travelers advice and information of all sorts about travel in Bavaria and throughout Europe, and he couldn't have earned very much. He was neatly dressed but a little threadbare. His face was solemn and bumpy, deeply scored and pitted by old bumpy scars. There was, as with his sister, something very contained and quiet, withdrawn and lonely, and yet likable and true.

They had been, were still, in fact, what is known as "nice people"— not people who had ever been very high up, not people of the university, military, professional, or aristocratic class, but people who had always maintained a certain standard of gentility, and who had probably, before the war, known a condition of greater affluence and security than they knew now. The whole pension, in fact, had that atmosphere if not of shabby, at least of rather threadbare, gentility which one encounters in boarding houses of this type, places of "the better sort," over all the world. One will find it, for example, often in a college town in America. There will be some lady of depleted fortunes who is very firm, however, on the question of her own genteelness and of her family lineage. She is sometimes a little too firm about it. She is likely to inform the college boys from time to time that when she took them "into her home" she had assumed, of course, that they were "gentlemen," that she expects "guests in her home" to behave exactly as if they were guests in any other home, and if and when it becomes apparent to her that she has been mistaken in her judgments and that someone whom she has taken into her home is not a gentleman, then she will be compelled to ask him for his room.

It would not be fair to say that Fräulein Bahr's establishment was wholly of this kind. She was herself much too intelligent and sensible a woman to go in for nonsense of this sort. She was a tall, dark-haired, dark-skinned woman of thirty-five, of the dark Bavarian type, very quiet, very intelligent, and very straight and honest. It is a good kind of woman that one meets in Germany, a kind that seems to be wonderfully lacking in the flirtatious tricks and feminisms which a good many American women have. In her quiet, dark way she was a handsome woman.

Monk never knew anything about her past. He really didn't know much about her present. She had good relations with her boarders. She was friendly, thoughtful, and obliging, but one also felt that she had a life of her own which she kept separate from the direction of her pension. He didn't know whether she had ever been in love, whether she had had any love affairs or not. She certainly could have had them if she wanted to, and he was sure that if she had wanted to she would have had them. She would have had them honestly and simply, with dignity and with passion; and if they turned out badly, she would have felt a deep and quiet hurt and kept it to herself, she would never have indulged herself or her friends in a hysterical neurosis.

Still, the life of that little place did have a kind of self-conscious restraint, the atmosphere of a maintained gentility. It was so wonderfully like a certain kind of boarding house he had seen and known everywhere. It was like a place that he had known in London, in Tavistock Square in the Bloomsbury district. It was like another place that bore the more sumptuous title of "private hotel" in Bath. It was like a pension where he had lived for a short time at St. Germaine-en-Laye, outside of Paris. It belonged, really, to the great company of Genteel Boarding Houses of the Universe, Ltd. One was always afraid to laugh out loud in Fräulein Bahr's establishment, although one often wanted to. One was always a little afraid to talk in his natural tone of voice, openly, frankly, enthusiastically, to engage occasionally in heated argument or debate. Their voices were subdued, their laughter politely restrained, their conversations somewhat delicately limited. They were all a little conscious, he thought, of one another, a little too considerate, he believed, and also a little too critical. It was, in other words, not a very easy atmosphere. One attained gentility at the sacrifice of naturalness, restraint at the expense of enthusiasm, politeness at the cost of warmth.

It was the same way with the food. For the first time in Germany he found himself in a place where there was just barely enough of everything. To his own way of thinking, there was not enough. He never dared to ask for a second helping because no one else ever asked for one. It was embarrassing, this feeling that there was just barely enough to go around, and the painful suspicion that if one had intemperately called for a second portion he would have got it, but that one of the servants, the cook, the waitress, or the maid, would have had to do without. There were eight of them at table, and when the meat was served, whether pork or roast or veal, there were always just eight slices, pretty thinly cut, upon the plate. Each of them took his slice delicately and with refined restraint as it was offered. And the rest of them coyly kept their eyes averted while this process was going on. It was the same way with the bread and vegetables. There was just enough of everything.

Monk used to be ravenously hungry all the time. Whether this was because of insufficient portions in the pension or a kind of enormous hunger of the spirit and of the imagination which reacted on him physically as well, he did not know. It was probably a mixture of both.

But he believed those others, for all their air of refined appeasement and modified restraint, used to feel it too. He knew they would not admit it if they did. It was not the spirit and the temper of that high-toned place. But he often suspected them of having secret sources of refreshment, victuals cunningly cached away in the privacy of their rooms, to which they could gluttonously resort in safe seclusion, faced only by the accusing eye of their own conscience and their God. He used to have his dark suspicions of them all. It seemed to him that sometimes when they got up, said "Mahlzeit," and made their refined and dignified departures, he could detect in their manners traces of unclean eagerness and indecent haste, or observe in the expression of their eyes the awakened fires of a gluttonous and faintly obscene lust. Then he would follow them in his mind's eye as they went from the dining room and down the corridor to their own room. In his mind's eye he could see them, walking deliberately at first with dignified restraint, but quickening their footsteps perceptibly as they went on, until, as they turned the corner and went down the empty hallway towards their own door, they fairly broke into a run, frantically fumbled at the lock, opened the door and closed and bolted it behind them, and then, laughing hysterically, fairly hurled themselves upon a sausage, greedily crammed the dainties of their guilty pleasure in their mouths.

He had, in fact, a grotesque and comic confirmation of this. One afternoon, when he had gone to pay the weekly bill, he caught Fräulein Bahr and her older brother in the act. He had just knocked upon the door of their own sitting room. One of the waitresses was coming out with an empty tray. She opened the door as he arrived, and before they could prepare for him, he was upon them. There was nothing then for her to do, of course, except to ask him in, which she did do very kindly. And he went in, his eyes bulging from his head, fairly glued upon the table, which, it seemed to him, was groaning with a surfeit of Lucullan dainties. Fräulein Bahr flushed a little, then remarked that they were having tea, and invited him to have a cup with them. Tea! Yes, they did have tea all right. But they had many other things as well. They had those fat, spicy, fragrant, delicious little sausages, fairly bursting in their oil-tight skins. They had liverwurst and salami, they had crusty rolls and they had stacks of pumpernickel, they had delicious little pats of butter, little sumptuous jars of jam, preserves, and confitures. They had those luscious, rich, delicious miracles of German pastry, covered with preserved cherries, strawberries, plums, and apples, with an inch-thick roof of firm whipped cream. It was a banquet. He understood now why Fräulein Bahr and her genial and good-natured brother were always so quickly satisfied at table.

Perhaps the other people in the pension did the same. He never knew. He only knew that he was hungry all the time, ravenous as he had never been in his whole life before, and nothing that he did or ate could stop or diminish it. And it was not just the pension. If he had had three times as much to eat, it would have been the same. It was a hunger not only of the belly, but a hunger of the mind and heart and spirit, which got translated in the most astounding and appalling way to all the appetites of sense and flesh. It was a hunger that he had felt from the moment he had entered Germany, a hunger that Munich had intensified, that Munich had concentrated and enlarged. For that was what the place had done to him, that was the kind of place that Munich was.

Munich was not only a kind of German heaven. It was an enchanted land of Cockaigne, where one ate and drank forever and where one was never filled. It was Scharaffenland—it made him think of Peter Breughel's picture of that name, which showed the little roast pigs trotting conveniently to serve your pleasure, with knives and forks stuck juicily in their tender, crackling hides, with pieces cut out of their hind quarters, with plump broiled chickens on their way to feed you, and bottles dropping from the sky, and trees and bushes drooping down with growths of pastry and with fruits of food. It may have been in part the clean vitality of the Alpine air that kept him hungry. It may have been the food he needed but had not been fed. But it was more than this. A raging hunger and a quenchless thirst was gnawing at him, and no matter what he ate or drank he could not get enough.

It cannot be told about, it can never be described, it cannot be called a name. It was appalling, it was revolting, it was loathsome and disgusting. It was a hunger that was no hunger, it was a thirst that was no thirst, it was a hunger and a thirst that grew from everything they fed upon. It consumed him even as he tried to feed it and to conquer it. It was like some enormous consumption of the soul and body for which there is no cure, for which there is no end.

In the morning he would go out while the girl was making up his room and pass along the Theresienstrasse to walk about the English Gardens, and a dozen times along the way he would be halted by the temptations of this agonizing hunger and this thirst. It was as much as he could do to pass a food, a pastry, or a sweet shop without going into it. The whole city seemed fairly to be groaning with these little fat, luxurious shops. He wondered how they lived and how they managed—where, in this stricken land, the people and the money came from to support them. The windows of the "Feinkost" shops were maddening. They were crammed with the most astounding variety of appetizing foods, sausages of every shape and kind that fairly made his mouth water when he looked at them, cheeses, roasts of meat, smoked hams, tall, slender bottles of fine wine, a profusion of luxury, a gourmet's treasure house, that exerted over him an irresistible hypnotic fascination. Whenever he approached one of these places, and they were everywhere, he would turn his eyes away, lower his head, and try to hurry past—but it was no use. If a wizard had drawn a magic line across the pavement and cast a spell upon the place, his effort could have been no greater, his defeat more abject and complete. It was impossible to go by them without stopping. He would stand before the windows and fairly gorge his lustful eyes, and if he got by one, there was always another. If he entered one and made a purchase, he was always haunted by the memory of all the purchases he had not made, the maddening goodies he had missed. If he bought one kind of sausage, there was always the tantalizing memory of a dozen other kinds that might taste better. If he gorged and fed his eyes and spent his money in one shop, inevitably he would see another crammed with good things that made the first one poor by comparison. It was the same way with the pastry shops with their cherry, plum, and peach, and apple cakes, their crusty miracles of bakery, covered with whipped cream. So, too, with all the sweet and candy stores. There were the chocolates and bonbons, the candies and the crystal fruits, the glacéed plums and cherries and the cubes of pineapple, the brandied chocolates and the fragrant gums.

It was the same with everything he saw, with everything he did. He wanted everything. He wanted to eat up everything, to drink up every. thing, to read up everything, to remember and to look up everything, to get his hands upon the palpable and impossible body, the magnificent plenitude, of a whole groaning earth, to devour it, to consume it, to have and hold it for his own forever. It was madness, it was agony, it was a cureless, quenchless, hopeless disease of mind and flesh and spirit. He would surfeit himself with everything that he could buy, with everything he could afford, with everything that he could see or hear or could remember, and still there was no end.

He went to the museums, those crowded and innumerable granaries into which they had collected the enormous treasures of their art. He invaded them, tried to devour them with the gluttony of an impossible and mad desire. He tried to feed upon the very pigments of the canvas. he tried to print each picture in his brain and on his memory with such voracious eagerness that it seemed as if the very color had gone out of them and had sunk through into his eyes. Day after day he walked the crowded galleries of the Old Pinakothek until the guards were fearful of his purpose and followed him from room to room. He almost pulled Mathias Grünewald from the wall; he walked straight out of there carrying those lovely naked girls of Lucas Cranach in his brain. He pulled every ounce of rose-hued flesh, every swirling universe of heaven and of earth, out of the swarming canvases of Rubens, and every canvas in that whole enormous gallery, from Grünewald to Rubens, from Lucas Cranach to Hans Holbein, from Breughel to "The Apostles" of Albrecht Dürer, and from Teniers to the Master of "The Life of Mary." He had them all enlisted in his brain, printed in his heart, painted on the canvas of his soul.

He haunted bookshops with the same insatiate and unreasoning desire. He spent hours before the crowded windows of the book stores, memorizing the names of countless books, written in a language he could scarcely read. He filled notebook after notebook with the titles of these books. He would buy books he could not afford, books he could not read, and carry them with him everywhere he went, together with a dictionary, and so decipher them. That swarming multitude of Gothic print, that staggering superflux of German culture, maddened him with an intolerable and impossible hunger for possession. He informed himself upon the number of books that came out yearly from the German presses. It was horrible, it was appalling. There were over 30,000. He hated them for the same gluttony that was devouring him.

He wondered how they could endure it, how they could ever draw their breath again in peace, in clearness, in repose, under the nightmare superfetation of that flood of print.

He was horribly involved, caught up, entangled, in the Laocoön coils of his own madness. He wanted to satiate himself upon that which was itself unable to be fed, he wanted to assuage himself upon the unassuageable, appease himself upon the unappeasable, come to the end of all Unendlichkeit, unweave the swarming web, unthread to its last filament the texture of a pattern which could have no end. He wanted to possess in its entirety, fathom in its profundity, utter in its finality, that which was in itself unpossessable, unfathomable, and unutterable—the old Germanic and swarm-haunted mind of man.

And it could not be done. He knew it, and because he knew, he hated "them." He loathed the hunger that consumed him. He hated the food of which he ate because he could not eat all that he wanted of it. He hated the family of the earth to which he himself belonged because he himself belonged to it, because its blood was in him, his in it, because twin demons of his soul divided him in unending warfare. He hated the face of the great swine, the creased neck of the unsated beast, because he felt himself the hungers of the beast's never-ending lust, and could find no end of it. There were in him two powers discrete, two forces of the soul and of inheritance, and now they waged contention daily in his life upon a battlefield where there could never be a victor, where he was caught in his own trap, imprisoned by his own forces, held captive by the very powers which were himself. He understood it all so well, because he had himself created it. He understood it all so well, because it had itself created him. He hated it so much because he had such deep and everlasting love for it. He fled from it and knew he never could escape.

At night he walked the streets. He went into the crowded places. He sought the beer-fogged flash and roar, the enormous restaurants. He plunged into roaring tumult of the Hofbrau Haus, swung to the rhythm of that roaring life, breathed the air, felt the warmth, the surge, the powerful communion of those enormous bodies, gulped down from stone mugs liter after liter of the cold and powerful dark beer. He swung and swayed and roared and sang and shouted in the swaying mass, felt a terrible jubilation, a mad lust, the unsated hunger filling him, and still could find no end and seek no rest.

47

A Visit to the Fair

SEPTEMBER WAS ADVANCING TO ITS CLOSE AND THE SEASON OF THE OKTO-berfest was at hand. Everywhere throughout Munich he saw posters announcing the event, and wherever he went people were talking about it. In the pension in the Theresienstrasse the table guests spoke to him about it with that elaborate jocoseness that men use towards a child—or a foreigner who speaks the language badly. His mind was busy with conjectures and images, but he could get no very clear picture of the approaching carnival. But the affair began to take on in his mind a ritualistic significance. He began to feel that at last he was to come close to the heart of this people—as if, after a voyage through the old barbaric forest, he would come suddenly upon them at their altars in a cleared ring.

One Sunday afternoon, early in October, a day or two after the carnival had opened, Monk made his way, accompanied by Heinrich Bahr, to the Theresien Fields, on the eastern edges of the city, where the Fair was now going on. As they walked along past the railway station and towards the carnival grounds, the street, and all the streets that led to it, began to swarm with people. Most of them were native Müncheners, but a great number were also Bavarian country people. These Bavarians were brawny men and women who stained the crowd brilliantly with the rich dyes of their costume—the men in their elabo-rately-embroidered holiday shorts and stockings, the women in their bright dresses and lace bodices, marching briskly along with the springy step of the mountaineer. These peasants had the perfect flesh and the sound teeth of animals. Their smooth, round faces wore only the markings of the sun and the wind: they were unworn by the thought and pain that waste away man's strength. Monk looked at them with a pang of regret and of envy—their lives were so strong and so confident, and, having missed so much, they seemed to have gained so greatly.

Their lives were limited to one or two desires. Most of them had never read a book, a visit to this magic city of Munich was to them a visit to the heart of the universe, and the world that existed beyond their mountains had no real existence for them at all.

As they neared the Theresien Fields, the crowd became so thick that movement was impeded and slowed down. The huge noises of the Fair came to them now, and Monk could see the various buildings. His first feeling as he entered the Fields was one of overwhelming disappointment. What lay before him and around him seemed to be only a smaller and less brilliant Coney Island. There were dozens of booths and sheds filled with cheap dolls, teddy bears, candy wrappers, clay targets, etc., with all the accompanying claptrap of two-headed monsters, crazy houses, fat ladies, dwarfs, palmists, hypnotists, as well as all the elaborate machinery for making one dizzy: whirling carriages and toy automobiles that spun about on an electrified floor, all filled with people who screamed with joy when the crazy vehicles crashed together and were released again by the attendant.

Heinrich Bahr began to laugh and stare like a child. The childlike capacity of all these people for amusement was astonishing. Like children, they seemed never to grow weary of the whole gaudy show. Great fat fellows with shaven heads and creased necks rode on the whirling and whipping machines, or rode round and round, again and again, on the heaving wooden horses of the merry-go-rounds. Heinrich was fascinated. Monk rode with him several times on the breathless dip-and-dive of the great wooden trestlelike railway, and then was whipped and spun dizzy in several of the machines.

Finally Heinrich was content. They moved slowly along down the thronging central passage of the Fair until they came to a more open space at the edge of the Fields. Here, from a little platform, a man was haranguing the crowd in harsh, carnival barker's German. Beside him on the platform stood a young man whose body and arms were imprisoned in a sleeveless canvas jacket and manacled with a chain. Presently the barker stopped talking, the young man thrust his feet through canvas loops, and he was hauled aloft, feet first, until he hung face downward above the staring mob. Monk watched him as he began his desperate efforts to free himself from the chain and jacket that fettered him, until he saw his face turn purple, and the great veins stand out in ropes upon his forehead. Meanwhile a woman passed through the crowd soliciting contributions, and when she had got all the money that the crowd would yield, the young man, whose swollen face was now almost black with blood, freed himself very quickly and was lowered to the earth. The crowd dispersed, almost, it seemed to Monk, with a kind of sullenness as if the thing which they had waited to see had now happened but had somehow disappointed them, and while the barker began his harangue again, the young man sat in a chair recovering himself, with his hand before his eyes. Meanwhile the woman who had collected money stood by him anxiously, looking at him, and in a moment spoke to him. And somehow, just by their nearness to each other and by no other outward sign, there was communicated to Monk a sense of tenderness and love.

His mind was reeling from all the clamorous confusion of the Fair and this last exhibition, coming as a climax of an unceasing program of monsters and animal sensations, touched him with a sense of horror. For a moment it seemed to him that there was something evil and innate in men that blackened and tainted even their most primitive pleasures.

Late afternoon had come; the days were now shortening rapidly, and the air was already that of Autumn—it was crisp and chill, meagerly warmed by a thin red sunshine. Over all the Fair there rose the dense and solid fabric of a hundred thousand voices. Heinrich, whose interest in the shows of the Fair had been for the time appeased, now began to think of beer. Taking Monk by the arm, he joined in the vast oscillation of the crowd that jammed the main avenue of the carnival in an almost solid wedge.

The Germans moved along slowly and patiently, with that tremendous massivity that seems to be an essence of their lives, accepting the movement of the crowd with enormous contentment as they lost themselves and became a part of the great beast around them. Their heavy bodies jostled and bumped against one another awkwardly and roughly, but there was no anger among them. They roared out greetings or witticisms to one another and to everyone; they moved along in groups of six or eight, men and women all together with arms linked.

Heinrich Bahr had become eager and gay; he laughed and chuckled to himself constantly; presently, slipping his hand through Monk's arm with a friendly and persuasive movement, he said:

"Come! Let us go and see the Roasted Ox."

And immediately at these words the enormous hunger woke in Monk again, a hunger for flesh such as he had never known—he wanted not only to see the Roasted Ox, he wanted to devour great pieces of it. He had already noticed one characteristic of this Fair that distinguished it from any other he had ever seen. This was the great number of booths, large and small, given over to the sale of hot and cold meats. Great sausages hung in ropes and festoons from the walls of some of these places, while in others there was a constant exhalation from steaming and roasting viands of all kinds and sizes. The fragrance and the odor were maddening. And it seemed to him that above this dense mass of people that swayed along so slowly, there hovered forever in the thin, cold air an odor of slaughtered flesh.

But now they found themselves before a vast, long shed, gaily colored in front, and bearing above its doors a huge drawing of an ox. This was the Oxen Roastery (Ochsen-Braterei), but so dense was the crowd within that a man stood before the doors with his arms out, keeping back the people who wanted to enter, and telling them they must wait another fifteen minutes. Heinrich and Monk joined the crowd and waited docilely with all the others: to Monk there was communicated some of the enormous patience of this crowd, which waited and which did not try to thrust past barriers. Presently the doors were opened and they all went in.

Monk found himself in a vast, long shed, at the end of which, through the dense cloud of tobacco smoke which thickened the atmosphere almost to the consistency of a London fog, he could see the carcasses of two great animals revolving slowly on iron spits over troughs of red-hot coals.

The place, after the chill bite of the October air, was warm—warm with a single unmistakable warmth: the warmth of thousands of bodies crowded together in an enclosed place. And mingled with this warmth, there was an overpowering odor of food. At hundreds of tables people were sitting together devouring tons of flesh—ox flesh, great platters of sliced cold sausages, huge slabs of veal and pork—together with the great stone mugs that foamed with over a liter of the cold and strong October beer. There was a heavy and incessant rumble of voices full of food, an enormous and excessive clatter of heavy pottery and knives, that rose and fell in brittle waves. Down the central aisles and around the sides moved and jostled constantly another crowd looking restlessly over the densely packed area for a vacant place. And the brawny peasant women who acted as waitresses plunged recklessly through this crowd, bearing platters of food or a half-dozen steins of beer in one hand, and brusquely thrusting human impediments out of their way with the other.

Heinrich and Monk moved with the crowd slowly down the central aisle. The feeders, it seemed to Monk, were for the most part great, heavy people who already had in their faces something of the bloated contentment of swine. Their eyes were dull and bleared with food and beer, and many of them stared at the people around them in a kind of stupefaction, as if they had been drugged. And indeed the air itself, which was so thick and strong it could be cut with a knife, was sufficient to drug one's senses, and he was therefore glad when, having arrived at the end of the aisle and stared for a moment at the great carcass of the ox that was turning brown as it revolved slowly before them, Heinrich suggested that they go elsewhere.

The sharp air lifted him at once from his lethargy, and he began to look about him quickly and eagerly again. The crowd was growing denser as evening approached, and he knew now that the evening was to be dedicated solidly to food and beer.

Distributed among the innumerable smaller buildings of the Fair, like lions couched among a rabble of smaller beasts, there rose about them the great beer halls erected by the famous breweries. And as thick as the crowd had been before the booths and shows, it seemed small compared to the crowd that filled these vast buildings—enormous sheds that each held several thousand people. Before them now, and at a distance, Monk could see the great red façade of the Löwenbrau brewery, with its proud crest of two royal lions, rampant. But when they came near the vast roaring of sound the hall enclosed, they saw that it would be impossible to find a seat there. Thousands of people were roaring over their beer at the tables, and hundreds more milled up and down incessantly, looking for an opening.

They tried several other of the great beer halls of the breweries with no better success, but at length they found one which had a few tables set about on a small graveled space before the hall and screened from the swarming crowd outside by a hedge. A few people were sitting at some of the tables, but most of them were vacant. Darkness was now approaching, the air was sharp and frosty, and there was almost a frantic eagerness to enter the fetid human warmth and the howling tempest of noise and drunkenness that the great hall contained. But both of them were now tired, fatigued by the excitement, by the crowd, by the huge kaleidoscope of noise, of color and sensation they had experienced.

"Let us sit down here," Monk said, indicating one of the vacant tables before the hall.

And Heinrich, after peering restlessly through one of the windows at the smoky chaos within, through which dark figures pushed and jostled like spirits lost in fog, in the vapors of Valhalla, consented and took a seat, but with a disappointment he was unable to conceal. "It is beautiful in there," he said. "You cannot afford to miss it."

Then a peasant woman bore down upon them, swinging in each of her strong hands six foaming steins of the powerful October beer. She smiled at them with ready friendliness and said, "The light or the dark?"

They answered, "Dark."

Almost before they had spoken she had set two foaming mugs before them on the table and was on her way again.

"But beer?" Monk said. "Why beer? Why have they come here to drink beer? Why have all these great sheds been built here by the famous breweries when all Munich is renowned for beer and there are hundreds of beer restaurants in the city?"

"Yes," Heinrich answered, "but—" he smiled and emphasized the word—"this is October beer. It is almost twice as strong as ordinary beer."

Then they seized their great stone mugs, clinked them together with a smiling "Prosit," and in the frosty, sharp exhilaration of that air they drank long and deep the strong, cold liquor that sent tingling through their veins its potent energy. All about them people were eating and drinking. Near by at another table, some peasant people in gay clothes had ordered beer, and now, unwrapping several paper bundles that they were carrying with them, they set out on the table a prodigious quantity of food and began to eat and drink stolidly. The man, a brawny fellow with thick mustaches and white woolen stockings that covered his powerful calves but left his feet and knees bare, pulled from his pocket a large knife and cut the heads from several salt fish, which shone a beautiful golden color in the evening light. The woman produced several rolls, a bunch of radishes, and a big piece of liver sausage from another paper and added them to the general board. Two children, a boy and a girl, the girl with braided hanks of long, blond hair falling before her over the shoulders, both watchful and blue-eyed with the intent and focused hunger of animals, stared silently at the food as their parents cut it and apportioned it. In a moment, with this same silent and voracious attentiveness, all of them were eating and drinking.

Everyone was eating; everyone was drinking. A ravenous hunger—an insane hunger that knew no appeasement, that wished to glut itself on all the roasted ox flesh, all the sausages, all the salt fish in the world, seized Monk and held him in its teeth. In all the world there was nothing but Food—glorious Food. And Beer—October Beer. The world was one enormous Belly—there was no higher heaven than the Paradise of Cram and Gorge. All of the agony of the mind was here forgotten. What did these people know about books? What did they know about pictures? What did they know about the million tumults of the soul, the conflict and the agony of the spirit, the hopes, fears, hatreds, failures, and ambitions, the whole fevered complex of modern life? These people lived for nothing but to eat and drink—and Monk felt at that instant that they were right.

The doors of the great hall kept opening and shutting constantly as the incessant stream of beer drinkers pressed patiently in. And from within Monk heard the shattering blare of a huge brass band and the roar of five thousand beer-drunk voices, rocking together in the rhythms of "Trink, Trink, Brüderlein, Trink!"

Savage hunger was devouring Monk and Heinrich. They called out loudly to the bustling waitress as she passed them and were told that if they wanted hot food they must go within. But in a moment she sent another woman to their table who was carrying an enormous basket loaded with various cold foods. Monk took two sandwiches made most deliciously of onions and small salted fish, and an enormous slice of liver cheese with a crust about its edges. Heinrich also selected two or three sandwiches, and, having ordered another liter of dark beer apiece, they began to devour their food. Darkness had come on. All of the buildings and amusement devices of the Fair were now blazing with lights; from the vast irradiant murk of night there rose and fell in wavelike nodes the huge fused roar and mumble of the crowd.

When they had devoured their sandwiches and finished their beer, Heinrich suggested that they now make a determined effort to find seats within the hall, and Monk, who had heretofore felt a strong repulsion towards the thick air and roaring chaos of the hall, now found to his surprise that he was ready and eager to join the vast crowd of beer-fumed feeders. Obediently now he joined the line of patient Germans who were shuffling slowly through the doors, and in a moment more he found himself enveloped by a cyclone of drunken sound, tramping patiently with a crowd that moved slowly around the great room looking for seats. Presently, peering through the veils and planes of shifting smoke that coiled and rose in the great hall like smoke above a battlefield, Heinrich spied two seats at a table near the center of the room, where, on the square wooden platform, fog-enveloped, forty men dressed in peasant costume were producing a deafening noise upon brass instruments. They plunged directly for the seats, jostling and half-falling over unprotesting bodies that were numb with beer.

And at last, dead center of that roaring tumult, they seated themselves triumphantly, panting victoriously, and immediately ordered two liters of dark beer and two plates of schweinwurstl and sauerkraut. The band was blaring forth the strains of "Ein Prosit! Ein Prosit!" and all over the room people had risen from their tables and were standing with arms linked and mugs upraised while they roared out the great drinking song and swung and rocked rhythmically back and forth.

The effect of these human rings all over that vast and murky hall had in it something that was almost supernatural and ritualistic: something that belonged to the essence of a race was enclosed in those rings, something dark and strange as Asia, something older than the old barbaric forests, something that had swayed around an altar, and had made a human sacrifice, and had devoured burnt flesh.

The hall was roaring with their powerful voices, it shook to their powerful bodies, and as they swung back and forth it seemed to Monk that nothing on earth could resist them—that they must smash whatever they came against. He understood now why other nations feared them so; suddenly he was himself seized with a terrible and deadly fear of them that froze his heart. He felt as if he had dreamed and awakened in a strange, barbaric forest to find a ring of savage, barbaric faces bent down above him: blond-braided, blond-mustached, they leaned upon their mighty spear staves, rested on their shields of toughened hide, as they looked down. And he was surrounded by them, there was no escape. He thought of all that was familiar to him and it seemed far away, not only in another world but in another time, sea-sunken in eternity ages hence from the old, dark forest of barbaric time. And now he thought almost with warm friendliness of the strange, dark faces of the Frenchmen, their cynicism and dishonesty, their rapid and excited voices, their small scale, their little customs; even all their light and trivial adulteries now seemed friendly and familiar, playful, charming, full of grace. And of the dogged English, with their pipes, their pubs, their bitter beer, their fog, their drizzle, their women with neighing voices and long teeth—all these things now seemed immensely warm, friendly, and familiar to him, and he wished that he were with them.

But suddenly a hand was slipped through his arm, and through that roar and fog of sound he realized that someone was speaking to him. He looked down, and there beside him saw the jolly, flushed, and smiling face of a pretty girl. She tugged at his arm good-naturedly and mischievously, spoke to him, nodded her head for him to look. He turned. Beside him was a young man, her companion; he, too, smiling, happy, held his arm for Monk to take. He looked across and saw Heinrich, his sallow, lonely, pitted face smiling and happy as he had never seen it before. He nodded to Monk. In an instant they were all linked together, swinging, swaying, singing in rhythm to the roar of those tremendous voices, swinging and swaying, singing all together as the band played "Ein Prosit!" Ended at length the music, but now all barriers broken through, all flushed and happy, smiling at one an-other, they added their own cheers to the crowd's great roar of approval when the song was ended. Then, laughing, smiling, talking, they all sat down again.

And now there was no strangeness any more. There were no barriers any more. They drank and talked and ate together. Monk drained liter after liter of the cold and heady beer. Its fumes mounted in his brain. He was jubilant and happy. He talked fearlessly in a broken jargon of his little German. Heinrich helped him out from time to time, and yet it did not matter. He felt that he had known all these people forever. The young girl with her jolly, pretty face eagerly tried to find out who he was and what he did. He teased her. He would not tell her. He told her a dozen things—that he was a business man, a Norwegian, an Australian, a carpenter, a sailor, anything that popped into his head, and Heinrich, smiling, aided and abetted him in all his foolishness. But the girl clapped her hands and gleefully cried out "No," that she knew what he was—he was an artist, a painter, a crea-tive man. She and all the others turned to Heinrich, asking him if this was not true. And, smilingly, he half inclined his head and said that

Monk was not a painter but that he was a writer—he called him a poet. And then all of them nodded their heads in satisfied affirmation, the girl gleefully clapped her hands together again and cried that she had known it. And now they drank and linked their arms and swayed and swung together in a ring again. And presently, now that it was growing late and people had begun to leave the hall, they too got up, the six of them, the girl, another girl, their two young men, and Heinrich and Monk, moved out among the singing, happy crowds again, and, arm in arm, linked all together, moved singing through the crowds.

And then Monk and Heinrich left them, finally, four young people from the mass of life and from the heart of Germany, whom Monk would never see again—four people, and the happy, flushed, and smiling face of a young girl. They left them, never having asked each other's names; they left and lost them, with warmth, with friendship, with affection in the hearts of all of them.

Monk and Heinrich went their way, and they went theirs. The great roar and clamor of the Fair suffused and faded far behind them, until it had become a vast and drowsy distant murmur. And presently, walking arm in arm together, they reached again the railway station and the ancient heart of Munich. They crossed the Karlsplatz and presently they had come to their dwelling in the Theresienstrasse.

And yet they found they were not tired, they were not ready to go in. The fumes of the powerful and heady beer, and, more than that, the fumes of fellowship and of affection, of friendship and of human warmth, had mounted to their brains and hearts. They knew it was a rare and precious thing, a moment's spell of wonder and of joy, that it must end, and they were loath to see it go.

It was a glorious night, the air sharp, frosty, and the street deserted, and far away, like time, like the ceaseless and essential murmur of eternity, the distant, drowsy, wavelike hum of the great Fair. The sky was cloudless, radiant, and in the sky there blazed a radiant blank of moon. And so they paused a moment at their dwelling, then as by mutual instinct walked away. They went along the streets, and presently they had arrived before the enormous, silent, and moon-sheeted blankness of the Old Pinakothek. They passed it, they entered on the grounds, they strode back and forth, their feet striking cleanly on clean gravel. Arm in arm they talked, they sang, they laughed together.

"A poet, yes," Heinrich cried, and looked exultantly at the blazing moon. "A poet, ja!" he cried again. "These people did not know you and they said you were a poet. And you are."

And in the moonlight, his lonely, scarred, and pitted face was transfigured by a look of happiness. And they walked the streets, they walked the streets. They felt the sense of something priceless and unutterable, a world invisible that they must see, a world intangible that they must touch, a world of warmth, of joy, of imminent and impending happiness, of impossible delight, that was almost theirs. And so they walked the streets, they walked the streets. The moon blazed blank and cold out of the whited brilliance of the sky. And the streets were silent. All the doors were closed. And from the distance came the last and muted murmurs of the Fair. And they went home.

48

The Hospital

A T NIGHT HE LAY AND TURNED HIS RUINED FACE UP TO THE CEILING, AND listened to the rain out in the garden, making sound. Save for the small and steady rain that beat upon the yellow mat of sodden leaves, there was no sound. It was a dreary and incessant monotone; unwearied, it was the weary reek of time; it was like waiting without hope for nothing, just listening to the rain on sodden leaves as he lay there.

Then there would come a momentary lull, and through the rain would come the distant noises of the Fair. Immense and murmurous, rising in drowsy waves and so subsiding, the broken music and the noises of the carnival would come in upon the rain, rise and subside, recede and vanish; and then there would be the steady reek of rain again. Sometimes, when it was late, outside the garden walls there would be voices and hoarse laughter and sounds of people going home. And he lay there upon his back and waited, listening to rain.

How had it happened? What had he done? Events as he remembered them were vague, confused, like half-lost, half-recalled contortions in a nightmare. He knew he had paid a visit to the Fair again, had drained stein after stein of the heady, cold October beer, its fumes had mounted in his head until the thousand beery faces all about him grew fantastic, ghostlike, in that fetid, smoke-fogged air. Again there had been the roaring tumult of the people rising from their tables, linking arms together with their mugs upraised, the rhythmic swinging, the rocking back and forth to the blaring of "Ein Prosit!" Again the ritualistic spell of all those human rings in swaying, roaring, one-voiced chant there in that vast and murky hall; again the image of the savage faces in the old dark forest of barbaric time; again the sudden fear of them that froze his heart. What happened then he did not know. In that quick instant of his drunken fear, had he swung out and smashed his great stone mug into the swinelike face, the red pig's eyes, of the hulking fellow next to him? He did not know, but there had been a fight—a murderous swinging of great mugs, a flash of knives, the sudden blinding fury of red, beer-drunk rage. And now he lay here in the hospital, his head all swathed in bandages; he lay upon his back and listened, listened to the rain.

The rain dripped down from roof and limb and spout, and as he listened to it he thought of all the glistening buildings of the Fair: within, the gorging, drinking, swaying, singing throngs, their faces gleaming redly in the body-heat of steaming, smoke-filled air; outside, the shambles of the mud and slime that must be there in all those lanes and passages that had been beaten, trampled, battered down beneath so many thousand feet. A clock struck out its measurement of mortal time with a solemn and final sweetness, and the rain drove in between him and that sound and made phantasmal readings of the news it bore. The news it bore to him was that another hour for all men living had gone by, and that all men living now were just that one hour closer to their death; and whether it was the silent presence of the ancient and eternal earth that lay about him—that ancient earth that lay here in the darkness like a beast now drinking steadily, relentlessly, unweariedly into its depth the rain that fell upon it—he did not know, but suddenly it seemed to him that all man's life was like one small tongue of earth that juts into the waters of time, and that incessantly, steadily, in the darkness, in the night, this tongue of earth was crumbling in the tide, was melting evenly in dark waters.

As he lay there looking at the ceiling, the door had opened silently and a nun, in her nurse's uniform and spotless linen and her bonnet with its enormous wings of stiff, starched white, came in to look at him. Her small white face, framed closely in its cowl of holiness, shone from the prison of her garments with a startling and almost indecent nakedness. She came and went so softly in that somber light of the shaded lamp that it was as if he had been visited by a ghost, and somehow he felt afraid of her.

But now he looked at her and saw that her face was pure and delicate; it was a good face, but for men it had neither mercy nor love nor passion in it. Her heart and love were fixed divinely and dwelt among the blessed of heaven. She passed her life upon this earth a shadow and an exile; the blood of the wounded, the pain of the suffering, the cry of sorrow, the terror of the dying, had made her neither hard nor pitying. She could not grieve as he did for the death of men, since what was death to him was life to her; what was the end of hope and joy and blessedness for him, for her was only the beginning.

She laid her cool hand on his forehead, spoke a few words to him which he did not hear, and then she left him.

When he had entered the clinic and Geheimrat Becker had examined the wounds upon his head, he had discovered two on the left side of the skull. They were each about an inch and a half in length and they crossed each other like an X. The Herr Geheimrat ordered his assistant to shave the hair away around the wounds, and this was done. Monk was left, therefore, with a fringe of abundant hair, and a ridiculous bald spot about the size of a saucer askew upon his skull.

At the first, while Geheimrat Becker's brutal fingers probed and pressed and sponged, Monk believed that there was another smaller wound lost in the thick luxuriance of hair at the back of his head which the doctor had not seen. But his fame was so great, his manner so authoritative, and his speech to Monk when he had mentioned it so gruff and so contemptuous, that Monk had said no further word, yielding to the man's authority and to that desire in all of us which leads us to try to escape trouble by ignoring it.

He had at no time been in any danger. His fears were phantoms of his dark imagining, and he knew this now. He had bled copiously and lost much blood, but his wounds were already healing. In time the hair would grow out again and cover the scars on his bald skull, and the only visible results of his injuries in the end might be a crooked set to his broken nose and the small scar of a knife across its fleshy tip.

So now at night there was nothing for him to do but lie and wait and look up at the ceiling.

The room had four white walls, a bed, a night-stand, and a lamp, a dresser, and a chair. The walls were high and square, the ceiling, too, was white, just like a blank of time and memory, and everything was very clean. At night, when just the lamp beside the bed was lighted, the high white walls and ceiling would be muted of their brightness, suffused and mellowed with a shade of somber light. And this, too, was like waiting, and the sound of rain.

Above the door there was a wooden crucifix, nailed with tormented claws, the splayed, nailed feet, the gaunt ribs, and the twisted thighs, the starved face, and the broken agony of Christ. And that image, so cruel in compassion, so starved, so twisted, and so broken in the paradox of its stern mercy, the fatal example of its suffering, was so alien to Pine Rock, to Joyners, and to Baptistry, to all the forms he knew, that it filled him with a sense of strangeness and uneasy awe.

Then there would come an impatient shift in this eternity of dreary waiting. He would hitch around in the hard sheets, and pound the pillow, jerk the covers, curse the hard discomfort of the sloping mattress wedge that always kept the upper body at a tilt. He would run his fingers over the shaved pate of his scarred head, feel the ridges of scabbed scars, and thrust his hand beneath the bandages, cursing where the hair was left, and at the throbbing of the one they *hadn't* got; and, roused to a sudden boil of blind, unreasonable fury, he would swing erect, stride to the door, and down the stillness of the sleeping hall, roar out:

"Johann! . . . Johann! Johann!"

And he would come, hastening along the green oiled matting of the hallway with a heavy limp. His limping, too, infuriated Monk, for Becker limped in the same way; he had been Becker's orderly, both had been wounded in the leg—the same leg, the same limp: "Do they *all* limp?" Monk thought, and the thought would fill him with a bitter rage.

"Johann."

He came up limping. His face, square, brown, and wide, full-nosed, plain, was full of protest, admonition, and bewildered concern:

"Was ist?" he said.

"The *Verbindung.*"

"Ach!" He looked, and then with reproachful accusation, "You moved it!"

"But I'm still verletzt! Look! Tell Becker there's a place he didn't find!" He put his finger on it, pointing.

He felt; then laughed and shook his head:

"Nein, it's only the Verbindung!" Johann said.

"I tell you I'm verletzt!" Monk cried.

Heel-tapping and unsleeping, brisk, along the oiled green hallway of the night, her plain face pleated in her bonnet between enormous wings of starch, the Mother Superior of the night came in:

"Was ist?"

He pointed, mollified a little: "Here."

"It is nothing," Johann said to her. "It is the bandage, but he thinks it is a wound."

"Here! . . . Here!" Monk choked, and pointed.

She put her parsley fingers on the place:

"It is a wound," she said.

"Nein!" said Johann, amazed. "But Herr Geheimrat said——"

"There is a wound," she said.

Oh, sustained now by that reassurance as by the tidings of immediate victory—to know *that* butcher of a doctor was *one time* wrong! That brutal scorner with contemptuous tongue, that hog-necked contemner with the butcher's thumb—was wrong!—was *wrong!* By God! —ah, wounds, scars, and bandages—all was one to him! The limping butcher with the brutal thumb, for one time in his damned butcher's life—was *wrong!*

"Verletzt, ja! . . . And with fever!" gloatingly Monk said.

Between enormous wings of white, she laid her cool and parsley finger on his forehead; and said quietly:

"Kein Fieber!"

"I tell you that I have!"

"Fieber?" Johann turned his square and puzzled face to her.

And she, stern-faced as ever, gentle, grave, implacable:

"Kein Fieber. Nein."

"I tell you that I have!" Monk cried. "And the Geheimrat—yes! the *great* Geheimrat Becker—" chokingly.

And with stern quietude, between enormous wings of starch, with stern reproach, she said:

"The *Herr* Geheimrat!"

"The *Herr* Geheimrat then!—he couldn't find it!"

Sternly, quietly:

"You have not fever. Now, go back to bed!" She went away.

"But the Geheimrat!" Monk now shouted.

Johann looked steadily at him. His plain German face was now severe in a quiet look of outraged decorum and protest.

"Please," he said. "The people are in bed."

"But the Geheimrat——?"

"The *Herr* Geheimrat—" quietly and pointedly—"the Herr Geheimrat also is in bed!"

"Then wake him, Johann! Tell him I have fever! He must come!" And suddenly, shaking with a feeling of outrage and insult, Monk shouted loudly down the hall:

"Geheimrat Becker! . . . Becker! . . . Where is Becker? . . . I want Becker! . . . Geheimrat Becker—O Geheimrat Becker—" jeeringly— *"great* Geheimrat Becker—are you there?"

His face a map of outraged decency, Johann took Monk by the arm and whispered:

"Quiet! . . . Are you mad? . . . The Herr Geheimrat Becker is not here!"

"Not *here?*" Monk stared unbelievingly into the square face. "Not *here?*"

"Nein," implacably. "Not here."

Not *here!*—the limping butcher was not *here!*—in his own slaughter pen! The shaven butcher, with his scarred face, his shaven head, his creased neck—was not *here!*—where he was born to be, to limp along these halls, to probe thick fingers at a wound—in his own slaughter house, the butcher was not *here!*

"Then *where?*" the astounded questioner turned on Johann now. "Then where is he?"

"At home, of course," he answered with a patient accent of reproof. "Where should he be?"

"At *home?*" Monk stared at him. "He has a *home!* You mean to tell me *Becker* has a *home?*"

"But, ja. Natürlich," he said in a tone of patient weariness. "And wife, and kinder."

"A *wife!*" Monk looked blank. "And *children!* You mean to tell me *he* has *children?*"

"But naturally, of course. Four of them!"

The limping butcher with the brutal thumb has——

That the surly Becker with the short, thick fingers and the hairy hands, with his heavy limp, his bullet head, his stiff clipped brush of grey-black mustache, his bald skull with its ugly edge of shaved blue skin, and his coarse, pleated face scarred with old duelling wounds —that this creature had any existence apart from the life of the hospital had never occurred to Monk, and now it seemed fantastic. His presence possessed and dominated the place: he seemed an organism that was constantly buttoned to its thick, strong neck in butcher's robe of starched white, and no more to be imagined without this garment, in the ordinary clothing of citizenship, than one of the nuns in the high heels and trimmed skirts of a worldly woman. He was like the living spirit of these walls, a special creation waiting here to hurl himself upon the maimed and wounded of the earth, to force them roughly back upon a table as he had forced Monk back, and then to take their flesh and bones into his keeping, to press, probe, squeeze with brutal fingers, and if necessary, to chisel upon their skulls, to solder together their broken plates, even to cut down to the living convolutions of man's thought. . . .

Johann looked at Monk and shook his head, and then said quietly: "Go back to bed. The Herr Geheimrat will be in to see you in the morning."

He limped away.

Monk went back and sat down on his bed.

49

Dark October

TO THE SWARMING ROCK OCTOBER HAD COME BACK AGAIN WITH ALL ITS death and eagerness, its life, its lifelessness, its stored harvest and its barren earth, its prophecy of ruin, its hope of joy. It was October, and there had been autumnal sunset, and now brisk stars were winking in the Park.

Esther sat upon a lonely bench and thought of him. Four months ago today he left her. What was he doing now—now that October had come back again?

Was it the one red leaf, the last of its clan, that hung there straining in the wind? The dry leaves scampered down the path before her. In their swift-winged dance of death these dead souls fled along before her, driven with rusty scuffle before the demented wind. October had come back again.

Is it the wind that howls above the earth, is it the wind that drives all things before its lash, is it the wind that drives all men like dead ghosts fleeing?

All things were lost and broken in the wind. She saw the great cliff of the city, immense, incredible, and glittering, rise from the fringes of the Park, a mountain of soaring steel, a diamond dust of lights, a jewel sown against the sky, a boast of princely stone as proud and temporal as a woman's flesh. She had known this place when she was a child, and there were quiet streets and houses here, and one could hear the feet of the people and the sounds of their voices, and the horses coming down the street, and now all this was lost.

The city seemed too great for men to live in now. It was so arrogant and inhuman in its wealth and splendor, it did not seem that little dots of people could have built such buildings. It was like a dwelling place of giants inhabited by pigmies, and it seemed that it must last forever. But she knew it was no more lasting than a dream.

680

She saw how men were all encamped here on the earth in these great tents of stone, and how they wandered in the streets of life. She was not afraid of this immense and swarming camp because she knew that she and all the rest were visitors and strangers on the earth, and that only the earth endured, and that the earth would endure forever. Down below all the pavements and the buildings was the earth. There was nothing down below there but the earth. If all the earth had been completely covered by these pavements, there would still be nothing that endured except the earth.

Suddenly she wanted to get up and go to find him. For a moment she forgot that he had left her, she thought that he was very near her. She wanted to be near him, to talk to him, to tell him what she knew, and to give him some of the strength and faith she had in her. She felt now that she knew so much, that she had known and seen so many things, that there was so much richness, beauty, power, and wisdom in her that all would be well if only he could share it with her.

As she looked at the great cliffs of buildings with their million lights she understood the terror and madness they had caused in him, and she understood how all the country kids who had come here must have been overwhelmed and frightened by them. She wanted to find him then and tell him to take heart. She wanted to tell him how a man can be greater than a crowd and taller than a tower, and because she had lived so much and known so much, because she loved him so much, she wanted to tell him that there are things which will never change, some things which will always be the same, some things which will endure forever.

For a moment it seemed that he was so near to her that she could touch him with her hand. Then she remembered that he had left her, that his lost soul was wandering God knows where upon this earth, driven by what mad hunger, what blind fury, and his letter had said that his lost body now lay battered and broken in a foreign land. She felt she knew so well now what he needed, she felt that she could save him now if she could only speak to him.

She saw him as his talent wasted and lay idle, as his brain grew black with madness, as he used his strength to smash himself to pieces against life. She saw how he was being devoured by his own hunger as the power in him turned tooth and claw, like a wild beast, on itself. and on all the people who had loved him, and she felt that she alone knew how to save and feed him. She was the wall he lacked, the imprisoned warmth he searched through all the world to find. Now that she could not speak to him, she wanted to write it all down for him, all the rich deposits of her life, the harvest of all her seasons to October; but her heart was a tongueless eloquence, she had never tried her skill at putting down such words, although their meaning was inside her.

Why are you absent in the night, my love? Where are you when the bells ring in the night? Now, there are bells again, how strange to hear the bells in this vast, sleeping city! Now, in a million little towns, now in the dark and lonely places of this earth, small bells are ringing out the time! O my dark soul, my child, my darling, my beloved, where are you now, and in what place, and in what time? O ring, sweet bells, above him while he sleeps! I send my love to you upon those bells.

Strange time, forever lost, forever flowing like the river! Lost time, lost people, and lost love—forever lost! There's nothing you can hold there in the river! There's nothing you can keep there in the river! It takes your love, it takes your life, it takes the great ships going out to sea, and it takes time, dark, delicate time, the little ticking moments of strange time that count us into death. Now in the dark I hear the passing of dark time, and all the sad and secret flowing of my life. All of my thoughts are flowing like the river, all of my life is passing like the river, I dream and talk and feel just like the river, as it flows by me, by me, by me, to the sea.

So she sat there thinking of these things until the clocks were striking twelve. The sound of the clocks was lost and broken in the wind, the leaf kept straining in the wind and would not fall, the dry leaves fled along the path before her.

And a policeman came and said: "It's time you were in bed, young lady. Where do you live?"

And she said: "I have no home, for home is where the heart is, and the heart has been taken out of me, the heart has gone out of me entirely, and I am left alone to die here in the dark."

And he asked her if she had been waiting for anyone, and she said yes, and she would wait forever, and he would not come. And he asked her to describe the person she was waiting for, for maybe he had seen him; and she said:

"He has the face of a demented angel, his head is wild and beautiful, and there is madness and darkness and evil in his brain. He is more cruel than death, and more lovely than a flower. His heart was made for love, and it is full of hate and darkness. His soul was made for light and purity, and it is poisoned by evil and vile suspicions. His brain should be a bright and flaming sword, and it is sick and twisted with its nightmares. He flies away from those who love and worship him, he stabs them to the heart and leaves them, he goes away with strangers who will do him harm. He is like a god, all made of light, and he lives alone in chains and darkness."

Then the policeman said he had not seen anyone who looked like that.

And she said: "No, if you had seen him you would remember him, for there is no one like him. 'His face is fair as heaven when singing birds unfold—' " and she could not go on, the tears were flowing down her face so fast she could not see, and they were choking her.

The policeman said she had been drinking, and it was true. She had been drinking all day long and she had had no food, and she had put the enemy into her mouth, and it had done no good. ("And this," she thought, "is what you have brought me to, and we are decent people in my race, and full of pride, and I have been good and faithful all my life.")

Then the man said if she did not go along he would arrest her and run her in; and she did not care, and said:

"I am ready to go. Take me to some other prison."

And he was a good man and kept calling her "young lady," he could not see her grey hair in the dark; and he said he did not want to do that, and he asked her where she lived, and when she said Park Avenue, he thought that she was drunk and joking him. But when she said that it was true and gave him her address, he said, with a suspicious look on his face:

"Is your name in the Social Registeh?"

("God, aren't they wonderful!" she thought. "You walk about and meet them every day, and then when you remember what they said to you, you don't believe they said it, you don't see how it could be

true, it doesn't seem possible, you think that someone made it up.")
So then she said:

"No, my name is not in the Social Register, because I am nothing but a little Jew, and little Jews don't get their names put in. But if there were a Social Register for little Jews, I'd be in that one."

Then the policeman looked at her in a funny way. He took her by the arm and called her "lady," and they walked up the path to the corner and got in a taxi.

The city wheeled before her in a drunken dance—a cliff of lights, a craziness of towers, a spoke of streets, the rags and sudden splinters of chaotic brightness. And in the forepart of her mind she could still see that red leaf tugging at the lowest bough, and the wind blew, and all things were lost and drowned there in the wind.

The light shook and trembled stiffly on the ground, there was a skirl of blown papers at the corner, below the light they chased each other about like winged things in a circle, and they never strayed nor stopped. They were the tattered records of yesterday, and already the immense world they spoke of had died and been forgotten.

She sat beside the policeman in the taxi, and he was quiet, and she listened to her own thoughts in the darkness:

We reach for life with all these traps and nets of words, our frenzy mounts up with our impotence, we try to keep and hold some single thing with all this fecund barrenness of print, and the sum of it all is a few blown papers in the wind. The possession of all things, even the air we breathe, is held from us, and the river of life and time flows through the grasp of our hands, and, for all our hunger and desire, we hold nothing except the trembling moments, one by one. Over the trodden and forgotten words, the rot and dusty burials of yesterday, we are born again into a thousand lives and deaths, and we are left forever with only the substance of our weary flesh, and the hauntings of an accidental memory.

There go two lovers blown by the wind. Their faces are turned towards each other, they are proud and smiling, there is no one like them in the world, and what they know no one has ever known before. They pass. Their feet have made no record on the pavements. They leave the corner to the wind, to emptiness, and to October.

The lights burn green, then red, and cliff by cliff the buildings rise along the avenue, appalling in their insolence, their pride, and their cold beauty. Across the street I see my sister's shop, its eleven slender floors of elegance. The unadorned white flatness of its sides is like the hips of the women it adorns. The building is inspired and perfect, as cold, sensual, and luxurious as the life it feeds upon, for it lives on the insolence of fashion and the death of things. The legend of great wealth and of sterility is written on it, yet there is no sign, no symbol, and no single token in these flat blocks of stone wherein this story is engraved.

Now I see how a snake lies coiled and waiting at the heart of life, and I see how men come to love the adder and the asp. Some of the best and loveliest of us all have been afraid and died, and over all this cruelty of towers is the face of fear.

Oh, I want to cry out to them and tell them they were fools to be afraid! I want to say the things they were afraid to say—that love is rooted in the earth, that love is beautiful and everlasting, and that men must love life and hate the barren waste of death that will not die, and is afraid to die. There is a terrible thing that I have learned and that must be changed in us. These people who have been afraid have hated love. They hate the lover and they mock at love, and their hearts are full of dust and bitterness.

My sister and I were brave and beautiful as children. We were so strong, so faithful, and so full of love. The vexed weave and fabric of our childhood was so rich, but full of pain and joy, and most uncertain. There were my father and my mother, and our lovely Bella. They were so lost and beautiful that it almost seems now we had been the parents of our parents, the mothers of the children that begot us. We were both so young, so clear, so unperplexed, so richly gifted. The gift of structure and of beauty was alive in us, and everything we made was good.

The earth was ours because we loved the earth. We had the touch and gift of nature in us. We saw the life that all things have in them —the life that slowly beats its pulse out of the thickness of an old brick wall, the life that hangs wearily in the set of an old warped door, the life that lives in chairs and tables, and in old knives with worn silver handles, the life of all things that a man has used and dwelt in—a coat, a shoe, the set of your battered hat, my dear one.

And then these streets and motored heights at which your soul shrank, these swarms and movements where your heart grew faint!

"The earth!" you said. "Give us the earth again!"

I tell you that the earth is here, and that we knew it. This is the soil, the harvest, and the earth. I tell you there has never been an earth more potent and more living than these streets and pavements. Perhaps, as you have said, there's something in my rich Jew's blood that loves a crowd. We swarm with honey, we like laughter, richness, movement, food, and the fullness of a crowd. This was my meadow. I knew it and I loved it, I walked about in it, these faces were my blades of grass. I understood the life that dwelt in it—the tired but happy life of streets when crowds have left them in the evening, the brooding calm of buildings breathing after use and labor, the quiet sounds of the day's end, the smell of the sea and shipping that comes forever from the harbor, the last, red, earthless light of the sun that falls remotely, without violence or heat, upon the ancient red of old brick buildings. These, and a million other things, I knew and loved.

Therefore I know this is as good earth as the hills and mountains of your childhood land. What horror did you want to flee? Must you forever be a fool without a faith and eat your flesh?

"The horror of eight million faces!"

Remember eight—know one.

"The horror of two million books!"

Write one that has two thousand words of wisdom in it.

"Each window is a light, each light a room, each room a cell, each cell a person!"

All rooms, all windows, and all persons for your hunger? No. Return to one: fill all that room with light and glory, make it shine as no other room ever shone before, and all life living on this earth will share it with you.

Oh, if I could only cry out to you now and give my wisdom to you, and tell you that you must not fear these monsters of piled stone and brightness! There is no wonder and no mystery here you cannot fathom. If they build a Babel of ten thousand floors, or if a city of ten million men should shrink to a crawling wedge of ants, yet will my heart be whole in me, yet will I remember a leaf, and the coming of young green in April. For I have seen these quiet streets thicken with wheel and fume and clamor, I have seen the merry tide of lives and faces grow dense and wide, I have seen the human house melt down below inhuman towers, and I know no mystery in these signs. I told you once how my sister's shop came from a dress she made for me out of a piece of picked-up bargain cloth: there was a touch of magic in her secret spirit, and out of it this building of proud stone has come. Is not a man, then, taller than a tower? Is not the mystery in an atom of tired flesh greater than all these soaring lights?

And now I think of quiet streets again, and brownstone houses, the old lost city of my childhood, and it seems almost close enough to lay my finger on it. I see the child's face once more, I see the dozen persons I have been and was and am no longer. I hear old sounds, old songs, old laughter. The tide of memory surges across my heart with all its various freight of great and little things—the faces of the men in derby hats as they came towards me over Brooklyn Bridge, the laughter of lovers in dark streets, the tugging of a leaf upon a bough, a pool of sudden moonlight on the sea's dark water on the night I met you, a skirl of blown papers on the street, a gnarled tree that hung across a broken wall in Maine, a voice that cried out and was silent long ago, and a song that my mother sang at dusk as she lay dying.

And I think of you! I think of you!

All things, all times out of my marvelous life come in together, and I think of all the beauty I have made and how it vanished. I see the stages of the theatres I have worked in, the end of the run, and the men taking down the scenes, the actors coming in and saying good-bye to one another: the brief glow and glory of my work and its quick death, the oblivion of the storehouse, the curtains lifted on the rows of empty seats.

And I think of you.

And you, I thought one night, were sitting there in darkness as all my heart cried out, "He has come back to me!" And I said: "Who's there? Who is the man that's sitting there?" But then I saw, I always see, it is not you. It is not you I see. And the ushers keep on turning up the empty seats.

And now I have come home again, home from the park in old October.

The policeman brought her home, and she hoped no one would be there. Katy let them in, and Esther told her to give the man some money and a drink.

And then she went into the darkness of her room, and stood in darkness listening to all the boats there on the river. She thought of him, and everything went whirling in her brain like blown leaves that scurry in the Park in old October.

She thought of him. Long, long into the night she thought of him.

(One!)
Oh now I hear the boats there on the river.
(Two!)
Oh now great boats are going down the river.
(Three!)
As long, long into the night I lay awake.

Time, please, time! What time is it? It's time you were in bed, young lady. It's time that you were dead, young lady. Yes, it's time your darling died.

Time, please, time! I keep thinking of you all the time. Sometimes I cannot see your face, and then I cover my eyes with my hands and you come back, and it is just as if you are there and I am talking to you.

"With thee conversing I forget all time." O God! How beautiful that is, and how true it is! I think of all the time that we have spent together, and all the wonder and the glory we have known. Would anyone ever believe it? Was there ever anything like it?

I take the book, the great anthology you gave me, and I read in it sometimes halfway through the night. God, the lovely things that can be found in it! I see that other hearts were heavy before mine, and that the poets in every time have all written of their grief. It is so beautiful, but what glory was ever greater than our own! Who has written about it? Who has put down my agony? Who ever loved as we did? Who ever knew the glory and the grief and all the lovely times that we have known together?

50

The Looking Glass

IN HIS HOSPITAL ROOM IN MUNICH, MONK SAT ON THE EDGE OF HIS BED. Facing him, on the wall, was a mirror above the dresser, and he stared into it.

"Man's image in a broken looking glass." What of his broken image in a looking glass unbroken?

Out of the dark pool of the looking glass, the Thing hinged forward at the waist, the trunk foreshortened, the thick neck sunken in the hulking shoulders, the barrel contours of the chest, the big paw clasped around the knee. So was he made, so fashioned.

And what nature had invented, human effort had improved. In the dark pool of the mirror the Thing was more grotesque and simian than it had ever been. Denuded of its shock of hair, the rakishly tonsured skull between the big wings of its ears came close upon the corrugated shortness of the forehead into the bushy ridges of the brow; below this, the small, battered features, the short pug nose, up-tilted, flattened towards the right (it had been broken at the center on the other side), the long upper lip, thick mouth, the general look of startled, quick attentiveness—it was a good job. Not since childhood had he looked so much the part the boys had made for him—the "Monk."

He looked at it now, and it at him, with a quizzical, detached objectiveness, not as a child looks in a mirror, at the silent eloquence of his pooled self, unspeaking, saying "I," but outside of it, and opposite, regardant, thinking, "Well, by God, *you* are a pretty sight!"—and meaning, not *Himself,* but *It.*

It looked back at him, breathing thickly through half-parted, swollen lips. (He could smell the odor of stale iodine, the dried, blood-wadded cotton in his nose.) He drew in hoarsely through the battered mouth, and in the looking glass the loosened teeth bared, caked with filaments of blood. Above the mouth, the nose smeared sideways on the face, the

689

blood-injected eyes attentive now; below the eyes, the rainbow purple-green-and-yellow coloration of the face.

"Christ! What a mug!"

It grinned back crookedly through its battered mask; and suddenly—all pride and vanity destroyed—he laughed. The battered mask laughed with him, and at last his soul was free. He was a man.

"Well, Mug?"

"Love's Martyr?" it replied, grinning back.

"Nature's Masterpiece!"

"Art's Exile!"

"Darwin's Pet!"

"Who let *you* out?" his Body said quite pointedly.

"Who let me *out? Out,* hell! Who put me *in,* you mean?"

"Meaning *me?*" his Body said.

"Yes, *you!*"

"I thought the crack was so intended," said his Body. "Well?"

"Well?"

"If you hadn't been put *in,* where *would* you be?"

"In clover, my pug-nosed, thuggish-looking friend. In clover, Ape."

"That's what *you* think," his Body said sardonically.

"That's what I *know!* You gorilla, you! *You* don't belong! You're just an accident!"

"I am, hey? And *you?* I suppose you're something that was all planned out."

"Well——"

"And with pretty little feet," his Body said ironically. "And such fine hands—" it lifted its thick paws and looked at them—"with the long, tapering fingers of the artist—is that it?" his Body sneered.

"Now, Body, don't you sneer!"

"And six feet, two inches of lean American young manhood——"

"Now——"

"—but would compromise on six feet one, bless his little heart! And light blond hair, by nature curly!"

"Your nature, Body, is so coarse and low you can't appreciate——"

"The Finer Things," said Body dryly. "Yes, I know!—But to proceed: blue eyes, a Roman nose, a classic brow, the profile of a young

Greek god—Byron, in short, without the limp or fatness—the ladies' darling, and a genius to boot!"

"Now, Body, damn your soul!"

"I have no soul," said Body dryly. "That's for '*Artists*'—is that the word?" it leered.

"Don't you sneer!"

"The soul is for Great Lovers," Body said. "My soul is suspended down below the waist. True, it has served you in your own more soulful flights—we won't go into that," said Body wryly. "I'm just a millstone round your neck—an accident."

And for a moment more they stared there at each other; then they grinned.

As he sat there staring at the image of his body in the mirror, the memory of their life together came back to pierce him with its poignant mystery. He thought of the millions of steps they had made together, of the millions of times they had drawn upon the air for breath and life, and of the thousands of times they had heard the clocks of time strike out below the timeless light of unknown skies. Yes, they had been long together, this body and he. They had lived alone so much, they had felt and seen and thought so much, and now they knew what they knew, they did not deny and regret each other, they were friends.

There had been a time, a child's time of wish and fable, when he had not seen his body as it was. Then he saw himself clothed in comely flesh. Together they were the hero of a thousand brave and romantic exploits, they were beautiful and brave together.

Then there had come a time when he had cursed and hated his body because he thought it was ugly and absurd and unworthy of him, because he thought it was a cause of all his trouble and grief, because he felt it had betrayed him and shut him away from the life he loved so well and wanted to belong to. He wanted to know all things and persons living, and constantly he wished to say to people:

"This grotesque figure that you see is nothing like me. Pay no attention to it. Forget about it. I am like one of you. I *am* one of you. Please try to see me as I really am. My blood bleeds and is red the same as yours. In every particular I am made from the same elements, born on the same earth, living the same life and hating the same death, as you. I am one of you in every way, and I *will* have my rightful place among you now!"

At that time he had been impatient and angry, and he hated his body because he knew it came between him and his most deep desires. He despised it because its powers of smell, taste, sight, sound, and touch let slip forever, as all flesh must, the final, potent, and completest distillation of life, the matchless ecstasy of living. So he had beaten and smashed at it in his madness, driven and abused it under the terrible lash of his insatiate thirst and hunger, made it the vessel of that mad lust of belly and brain and heart which for four thousand days and nights had never given him a moment's waking peace. He had cursed it because it could not do the inhuman task he set for it, hated it because its hunger could not match his hunger, which was for the earth and all things living in it.

But now he felt none of these things. As he sat there and saw the figure in the mirror, it was like some homely garment which he had worn all his days and which he had for a moment discarded. His naked spirit had stepped out of its rude residence, and this clothing of flesh and bone now stared back at it and awakened in it the emotion of friendship and respect with which we regard any old object—a shoe, a chair, a table, or a hat—which has shared our life and served us loyally.

Now, they had got a little wisdom for themselves. This flesh had not betrayed him. It had been strong, enduring, and enormously sensitive within the limitations of its senses. The arms were too long, the legs too short, the hands and feet a little closer to the simian than most men's are, but they belonged to the family of the earth, they were not deformed. The only deformity had been in the madness and bitterness of his heart. But now he had learned, through a wisdom of the body and the brain, that a spirit which thinks itself too fine for the rough uses of the world is too young and callow, or else too centered on itself, too inward-turning, too enamored of the beauties of its own artistic soul and worth to find itself by losing self in something larger than itself, and thus to find its place and do a man's work in the world—too fine for all of this, and hence defeated, precious, fit for nothing.

They had discovered the earth together, this flesh and he, they had discovered it alone, in secrecy, in exile, and in wandering, and far more than most men living they knew what they knew for themselves. Alone, by their hard labor, they got the cup into their hands and drank it. They learned the things most other men were lucky to have given to them. And now, for all their sweat and agony, what did they know? This: that they loved life and their fellow men and hated the death-in-life, and that it was better to live than die.

Now he looked at his body without falsehood or rancor, and with wonder that he dwelt there in this place. He knew and accepted now its limitations. He knew now that the demon of his mortal hunger would be inches and eternities from his grasp forever. He knew that we who are men are more than men, and less than spirit. What have we but the pinion of a broken wing to soar half-heavenward?

Yes! He knew as he looked at the grotesque figure in the mirror that he had done all with his hunger and his flesh that one man could. And he knew also, although the bleared and battered face might seem to be the visage of a madman, the spirit that dwelt behind this ruined mask now looked calmly and sanely forth upon the earth for the first time in ten years.

"Is it a man," he said, "that waits here so unsleeping in the ventricles of night?"

"Or, so unsleeping, is it not the Body that holds the man?"

"It is not true. Now, Body, let me sleep."

"It is. Now, Man, let me."

"No, Body; it's the brute, compulsive Worm that here, within the ventricles of night, keeps working always, and that will not let me sleep."

"The Worm is yours. There was no Worm when, in the years long past, the Body of your recent wrath and you lay down together."

"But there was the Worm."

"The Worm incipient, Worm progressive, Worm crawling in the blood, first stirring in the leaf."

"Somewhere, somewhere begun—*where? where?* Was that the Worm?"

"Long, long ago—where hatched, God knows, or in what particle of memory—perhaps with sunlight on the porch."

"Which was a good time then, for there were all the things that came and went, the steps, the basket, and the bright nasturtiums——"

"The immediate clackings of the sun-warm hens, the common crack of wake-a-day, and someone's voice in the Immediate, the skreaking halt upon the corner on the hill of street cars coming home for noon, and men and leather in the street, and yard-gates slammed and sudden greetings, the cold invigoration of sawn ice at noon—the hard black stench of funky niggers, and the ice tongs and linoleum—the coarse, sweet coolness of Crane's cow along the alleyway, along the hammocks of the backyard fence——"

"And were *you* there?"

"Aye! To the limits of mortality."

"And to the pits of time and memory?"

"Not so. That was *your* part—here were the first intrusions of the blind, compulsive Worm. But I was there, was *there*—aye, fat-legged in a wicker basket, feeling light."

"Lights going, lights returning—sadness, hope——"

"Yours, *yours*—the sickness of the Worm—not mine! Mine the sun!"

"But sorrow, Body, when it went away?"

"Discomfort sometimes—not regret. Regret's the Worm."

"Would howl?"

"Would howl, yes! When I was filthy and befouled, nasty, wet, sour-bellied, —— upon! Would howl! Would howl!—Yes! Would howl for comfort, warmth, appeasement, a full belly, a warm bottom—sun!"

"And then?"

"No more, no more. The plain Immediate. That was the good time then."

"The time that is good——"

"Is the time when once there was a tiny little boy," the Body said.

"That is the good time because it is the time the sunlight came and went upon the porch, and when there was a sound of people coming home at noon, earth loaming, grass spermatic, a fume of rope-sperm in the nostrils and the dewlaps of the throat, torpid, thick, and undelightful, the humid commonness of housewives turbaned with a dish-clout, the small dreariness of As-They-Are mixed in with humid turnip greens, and houses aired to morning, the turned mattress and the beaten rug, the warm and common mucus of the earth-nasturtium smells, the thought of parlors and the good stale smell, the sudden, brooding stretch of absence of the street car after it had gone, and a feeling touched with desolation hoping noon would come."

"That was your own—the turnings of the Worm," his Body said.

"And then Crane's cow again, and morning, morning in the thickets of the memory, and so many lives-and-deaths of life so long ago, together with the thought of Winter howling in the oak, so many sunlights that had come and gone since morning, morning, and all lost voices—'Son, where are you?'—of lost kinsmen in the mountains long ago. . . . That was a good time then."

"Yes," said Body. "But—you can't go home again."

VOICES OF THE SOUTH

Hamilton Basso
The View from Pompey's Head
Richard Bausch
Take Me Back
Doris Betts
The Astronomer and Other Stories
The Gentle Insurrection
Sheila Bosworth
Almost Innocent
Slow Poison
David Bottoms
Easter Weekend
Erskine Caldwell
Poor Fool
Fred Chappell
The Gaudy Place
The Inkling
It Is Time, Lord
Kelly Cherry
Augusta Played
Vicki Covington
Bird of Paradise
Ellen Douglas
A Family's Affairs
A Lifetime Burning
The Rock Cried Out
Percival Everett
Suder
Peter Feibleman
The Daughters of Necessity
A Place Without Twilight
George Garrett
Do, Lord, Remember Me
An Evening Performance
Marianne Gingher
Bobby Rex's Greatest Hit
Shirley Ann Grau
The House on Coliseum Street
The Keepers of the House
Barry Hannah
The Tennis Handsome

Donald Hays
The Dixie Association
William Humphrey
Home from the Hill
The Ordways
Mac Hyman
No Time For Sergeants
Madison Jones
A Cry of Absence
Nancy Lemann
Lives of the Saints
Willie Morris
The Last of the Southern Girls
Louis D. Rubin, Jr.
The Golden Weather
Evelyn Scott
The Wave
Lee Smith
The Last Day the Dogbushes Bloomed
Elizabeth Spencer
The Salt Line
The Voice at the Back Door
Max Steele
Debby
Allen Tate
The Fathers
Peter Taylor
The Widows of Thornton
Robert Penn Warren
Band of Angels
Brother to Dragons
Walter White
Flight
Joan Williams
The Morning and the Evening
The Wintering
Thomas Wolfe
The Web and the Rock